The Short Stories

of

Alex B. Stone

Books *by* Alex B. Stone

The Short Stories of Alex B. Stone
Sunrise at 7:12
Country Boy
Shades of Benny Roone
Tales from the Prayer House
Benny Roone Detects
Summer
If I Could Sleep
Going Home
A Sabbath Walk

The Short Stories

of

Alex B. Stone

POSTERN PRESS

THE SHORT STORIES OF ALEX B. STONE. Copyright © 2016 by Anne Stone Weaver. All rights reserved. No part of this book may be reproduced, transmitted or stored by any means without written permission except in the case of brief quotations embodied in critical articles or reviews.

Printed in the United States of America.

This book is a work of fiction. The places, events and characters described herein are imaginary and are not intended to refer to actual places, institutions, or persons.

Library of Congress Cataloging–in-Publication Data
Stone, Alex B.
The Short Stories of Alex B. Stone / Alex B. Stone

First Edition: August 2016

Publisher's Note

Alex B. Stone began writing fiction in middle age. He persisted for approximately thirty years, from the 1970s into the early part of this century. This collection brings together all of the shorter works, some of which appeared in publications such as *The Jewish Spectator*. A number of stories were assembled previously in *A Sabbath Walk* (East Hall Press, Augustana College 1990) and in other collections. The settings in almost every instance reflect the Polish-born author's long residence in the Midwest, where he was active in the Jewish community, in cultural institutions, and in business. A reader will notice recurrent names assigned to disparate characters. There are a lot of Harrys and Georges, and Millys and Millies. The social arrangements of Benny Roone, who appears in a number of stories, change from time to time. Sometimes the small Illinois city along the Mississippi River is Rock City, other times Rockville. No attempt has been made to reconcile details in stories written years apart.

Alex conveyed his Midwest honestly, with considerable amusement. The stories are mostly gentle, but the insights frequently are not. Marriages have become claustrophobic, harsh business decisions are "nothing personal," and resentments fester for decades. Like Updike, whom he admired, Alex believed in the generous and unexpected gifts the world bestows. But his world also exacts a price for self-deception, and chance cuts both ways.

The idea for this collection originated in early 2015. The author didn't live to see its realization, passing away on September 13, 2015 at the age of 93.

Cumulatively the stories represent a substantial artistic achievement. Their clearest antecedents include other sometimes bleak examples of Midwestern realism, Edgar Lee Masters's *Spoon River Anthology* and Sherwood Anderson's *Winesburg, Ohio*. These stories are similarly rich in vivid and humane truth.

CONTENTS

That's What Family Is For   1
Sabbath Morning   6
Another Time   12
I Should Have   17
Saturday's Child Works Hard for His Living   22
Options   28
You Are Looking Good, George   35
So the Weeks Go   41
How Are You Going To Keep Them Down on the Farm   46
Falling Falling   52
46 Years Since Graduation   58
Committees Committees   63
Enjoy Enjoy   66
George, Mildred, John and Harriet   74
Only a Half-Step Behind   79
I Like It, Benny   84
Omission   90
How the Mittleberg Book of Hours Came to Rockville   94
The Retirement Party   98
Lightning Struck Once   102
Together   108
In Calhoun County   110
Friends   112
In the Beginning   116
I Came Home To Tell My Folks   118
Nachas fun Kinder   122
A Sabbath Walk   125
Outside Counsel   127
The Klein Amulet   133
With God's Help   139
Cousins   145
Come Out, Come Out Wherever You Are   151
Proud of You, George   159
Fine . . . Just Fine   164
Brother Lenny   171
Who Can I Tell?   176
An Only Son   186
Wait for Me   192
The Best Laid Plans   196
Money, Money, Money   201

The Week Before Thanksgiving   206
So What . . . So Nothing   211
Benny and the James Brothers   216
A Time To Begin Again   221
Water Therapy   226
Such a Beautiful Sunset   230
This from My Daughter   234
Florida Is Where the Sun Shines   237
My Uncle, Melvin, the Conversationalist   241
Each Day a Gift from God   247
Murder Comes to the Leghorns   253
Proof of Ownership   258
Benny Roone and the Catalog Raisonné   264
Apple Pie and Eva Sundine   270
Tales from the Prayer House   283

About the Author

That's What Family Is For

My mother, may she rest in peace, used to say, "Benny, all bad things come in three." My sister, Milly, who lives in California and hasn't been back in twenty-two years to Rockville, where the gray skies envelope us in November and don't depart until the sun appears in May, says, "Benny, you are living under a black cloud."

But what is the only son of an only son to do when aunts and uncles and brothers-in-law, nephews and nieces use me as the family resource because, "now, Benny, that you are retired"—which implies because I have no wife or children, that I do have the hours to convey from one family member to another. "Gertie had a gall bladder attack." "Rosie had her aortic valve replaced." All this telephone time devoted to family health does take time from my delving into the military history of World War II.

Now, back to my interview with a native German speaker who served in the United States Army Intelligence as an interrogator of German POWs. "In the fall and winter, in the months before the Battle of the Ardennes, we got some really significant information from a disaffected, war weary German sergeant who had been busted for insubordination. He was the one who showed us where the Germans had positioned their armor and tanks. We had flyover photos of the German positions to confirm his revelations. We sent all this up to our division G2. Which still leaves the question of why Corps and Army intelligence did not interpret these confirmed reports of a German massive staging of their armor as preparation for a counter offensive." I am just about to start on my next oral history when I get a call from my nephew, Bill.

"Uncle Benny."

"Yes, Bill."

"Lilly is scheduled for a total neck reconstruction next Wednesday." She had no choice, she was losing the use of her right hand. Lilly is Bill's wife. A young woman of forty-nine who, ever so slowly is grasping her way up in the investment world ladder as a "feminist" financial analyst, catering to the not so unhappy widows of Naples, Florida.

"Uncle Benny, you know how important it is for Lilly to be able to use her computer."

"I will pray for Lilly's recovery."

"Thank you, Uncle Benny."

Now that Gertrude, Rose and Lillian are in my medical bank you would think I could return to my military history. I publish an occasional essay in a university monthly which may affect how a senator or congressman thinks about defense spending or the revamping of the CIA, or the reorganization of the Army Intelligence services.

Alas, my life continues to be interwoven with family. My sister-in-law, Janet, calls me from Sanibel, Florida. "The doctors think George had a slight stroke. George's speech is good and his head is good but he is having trouble walking. He doesn't seem know where his left leg is."

My oldest brother, George, and Janet have three grown children who are certainly more qualified than a bachelor brother to render support to their mother and father. I call Janet, tell her, "I will see you tomorrow morning." Naturally, I call my sister Milly in California. "Just so you will know where I will be."

"Benny, you do have a black cloud over you."

"It's not me, Milly. It is George, our brother, George! If you like, you can go to Florida instead of me."

"You go, Benny. George and Janet like you better."

"Why do they like me better than you? A sister is no different than a brother."

"Benny, you are much more generous."

Before I leave for Florida, I call the rabbi, add George to my list for the Meshabaraks, the special prayers to be recited on Monday and Thursday, during the morning prayers which ask for healing of body and soul.

"Four? That is a bit unusual," says Rabbi Shore, "but I can handle it. Benny, you know it is customary to make a donation to the synagogue." I give him my check.

I call my neighbor. "Charlie. I have to fly down to Florida for a few days. It's my brother George."

"Don't worry, Benny. I'll look after your house. It will do you good to get a little sun. Benny, you really don't have to rush back."

"I do have things to do for myself."

"The morning minyan will get along without you."

"I have some research I want to write up."

"You can take that with you." Which of course, is true when you write on a yellow legal pad.

So I load up my dental pic, my yellow legal pads and four unread copies of *The New Yorker*.

At the Southwest Regional Airport Janet, in a white tennis dress, tennis bracelet and one of those white, long billed baseball caps that announces "Sanibel," is all suntanned and smiles. "Thank God George didn't have a stroke at all. The doctors think he had an infection of some sort that affected his brain."

I say, "That is good news," and Janet says, "George still can't walk but he is getting better each and every day. Your prayers must have helped."

My sixty-four-year-old brother, George, is well nourished, well browned and still without the rotund belly of the young-old. George is my brother who did not go into the family business, who did not stay in Rockville, who became a tax attorney in Chicago with two gulfside condos on Sanibel. George couldn't accept running a men's wear store in downtown Rockville. "That wasn't good enough for you." Had I ever said that to him, surely it would have led to George telling me, "So there you are, Benny, running a retail store with a doctorate in modern history. That is not what you should be doing either." Which would lead to, "What could I do in Rockville?"

At Lee County Hospital brother George gives me one of his smiles for clients, lifts one hand off the walker to shake my hand. "Good of you to come, Benny. Janet really shouldn't be alone. Janet hasn't had a free day since I have been in the hospital."

I hug George. "Not to worry. Benny is here." Janet smiles.

"You are a Godsend. I did so want to go to my art lecture. I won't be long. Benny, if you get hungry the food in the cafeteria is really quite good."

George waddles into his hospital bed, falls asleep. I read my *New Yorker*. The Florida sun invades through the dusty venetian blinds, warms my back, and, as Momma always said, "After the clouds comes the sunshine."

George wakes up as Janet lopes in. "I spoke to Dr. Goodman. You can go home. I have a printout of exercises you can do. You may need a little help but now with Benny here . . ."

So I say, "Good news."

Janet says, "You help George, I'll sign the exit forms."

I have the guest room of the two-bedroom, two-bath condo with the view of the sunrise on the Gulf, the beach power walkers and the afternoon joggers and sloggers and always the shell gatherers.

In a week George has completed his course of antibiotics, is able, with the help of a cane, to walk slowly to get his mail, which pleases me, and George and Janet's three children even more, as their father will not require their immediate visitations.

Janet kisses me goodbye. "Benny, it was good of you to come. It was a comfort for me to see how you helped George improve his walking and balancing skills."

So I say, "That's what family is for."

The moment I get out of the cab, Phyllis, neighbor Charlie's wife, is at my side. "Benny, I didn't want to call you in Florida, but Charlie had a heart attack."

"When?"

"Yesterday."

"How is he doing?"

"He is scheduled for a coronary bypass tomorrow morning. I thought you ought to know."

"That's what neighbors are for. Is there anything I can do?"

"You can pray for us."

At the *shacharit* prayer I add Charlie's name to my special prayer list. "Charlie is my next door neighbor. A fine man, Rabbi."

"That is five."

"Five?"

I give Rabbi Shore my check, he looks at it. "Very generous of you, Benny."

"That's what money is for, Rabbi."

"We do thank you."

I call Phyllis in the hospital coronary care unit.

"Charlie is sitting up. He will be coming home in five days."

"Can I help?"

"Charlie has always enjoyed talking to you."

In a week Gertrude is home, Rose is back to walking in the mall. Lillian is home, encumbered by a head-to-chest neck brace, George is walking without a cane, so the evening medical bulletin telephone calls have stopped. I am back into my life. My sister calls every Saturday night as soon as the rates go down in California.

"Benny, George told me all the wonderful things you did for him."

I don't answer.

"I wish I could have been there but you know Harry isn't all that well."

"That I know." And I sigh. "How is Harry?"

"Thank God, a little better. We are going off to Hawaii for a couple of weeks. Benny, would you like to come out and stay in our house? I know how much you like to swim outdoors. You know our pool is heated."

Milly wants me to be there in case of an earthquake so that I can rescue her paintings and pottery and her cat.

"Benny, we could have a few days together."

"I really can't say. There are a few things that I do have to catch up on."

"What do you have to do that is so important?"

"I'll see how much I can get done and I'll let you know."

"I really hate to leave Alex at the vet's."

I answer, "I'll call you on Wednesday."

"Surely what you have to do can wait a few weeks until you get back, Benny. A little rest in the California sun will do you good."

"I was in Florida for a week."

"Now you can come to California."

"I'll call you on Wednesday."

"No later, Benny. I must know by then."

Monday morning I pick up my anti-hypertension drugs, arrange for my annual physical, already six months delayed, for Tuesday afternoon, arrange to see John Thompson, an attorney at law, the third generation of "Thompson and Thompson" who have guarded the Steins of Rockville, Illinois since 1882. John is in his early forties, a taller, leaner replica of his father who has retired to sailing the Florida intracoastal, which makes John the senior working Thompson of Thompson and Thompson. His cousin, Walter, ten years younger, is the junior Thompson. Since "Dad" left the practice John has changed their office decor from something out of a Dickens tale to Al's Fine Experienced Office Furniture. The Thompsons have the earned reputation for being ever more frugal than the Steins.

I am seated across from John at a walnut desk that was new when Grandpa Thompson passed the Illinois bar in 1922. Hanging behind the desk is the black and white photo of the Illinois National Guard in which I served with Judge Kenneth Thompson, the now fishing judge.

"Good to see you, Mr. Stein."

I smile, "Good to see you John."

"Harriet said you wanted to talk about your will." Harriet is Judge Thompson's secretary, whom John acquired with his seniority. John holds the blue-covered last will and testament of Benjamin William Stein, bachelor, in his hands.

"There are changes I would like to make in my will."

"Last time we changed your will was eight and a half years ago." John looks at me. "Everything all right, Mr. Stein? You all right?"

"Fine, John." I grin, being of sound mind and body I thought.

"You do look fit. I heard you were in Florida."

"I was, with George."

"How is George?"

"Better. Much better. Mildred is very well too, thank you."

"I haven't seen them in years."

"They don't come to Rockville very often."

"My dad still talks about your father."

"He was a good man."

"That's what Dad says."

"John, I have been thinking. A man of my age ought to be thinking of what to do with his worldly goods."

"You look pretty fit to me."

"I think it is about that time." John has his legal pad out, his Mt. Blanc pen in his hand. "I would like to cut out all gifts to my family. Every last one. To George, to Mildred, the nieces and nephews."

"You have given these changes serious consideration?"

"I have."

"What are you going to do with all that money?"

"Put it into four trusts. Half to the congregation. Believe we need a senior residence. Something pleasant for those in our congregation who would prefer independent living, for those who do not as yet have the need for a nursing home."

"And the other half?"

"Split half and half again. Half to the congregation's cultural and charitable needs and the other half to the Rockville Charitable Foundation for the support of local charities."

John repeats, half for senior residence, one fourth for B'nai Jacob's cultural programs, one fourth for Rockville community charities.

"Sounds good to me, John." I get up, smile. "Thank you. Say hello to Dad for me."

Wednesday evening Milly calls me before I can call her. "It's eighty degrees here and sunny. You can write your essays on the terrace. I checked the pool temperature—it is eighty-six."

"I'll be there."

"Alex loves when you come."

"Alex is one smart cat."

"Benny, you don't mind taking the limousine from the airport, do you? I have an appointment at the hairdresser." And before I can ask, "Can Harry pick me up?" Milly explains, "Harry is playing golf at the country club. You know how much he looks forward to that."

I don't answer. Milly is peevish. "When will you be here?"

"About two on Friday."

"You got everything done?"

"Got it started in the direction I wanted. I'll finish up when I get back."

"I didn't inconvenience you? Keep you from doing something you wanted to do?"

"No, not at all. That's what family is for, to help each other."

"I am glad."

"So am I."

"Thank you, Benny."

"Not at all, Milly. After all, I am your brother."

Sabbath Morning

This spring has been so wet that on Memorial Day our pink silk tulips drooped their petals onto the grave markers; so dank the prunings from the viburnum and forsythia grew moss; the humidity so high it condensed in the air ducts of our furnace and air conditioner. On Monday we heated to dry out and on Wednesday we air conditioned to get a breath of fresh air. The oil and water puddles refused to dry, clung to the damp concrete floor.

It's this lack of sunshine that I believe has kept my wife, Patty—given name, Pauline—angry. Angry about our toilet that doesn't flush and a lot of other trivial shortcomings in our life.

"Robert, that stool stinks."

"So it does, Patty, so it does."

I open the bathroom window. The wind has stopped, the rain drips from oak leaves onto the lawn that needs cutting, weeding and fertilizing.

It is Saturday morning, the day I trim my full moustache and eyebrows. I have just put down my blunt nose scissor, about to reach for my electric shaver with the quarter inch head to cut my stray gray hairs, when Patty comes up behind me, grabs my shaver, puts it into the pocket of her black apron that proclaims in script, *New York Times*.

"First, Robert, you fix the toilet stool."

"It needs a new part."

"You told me that on Wednesday, on Thursday and Friday!"

"True Value hardware doesn't open until eight, Patty. It is six o'clock, Saturday morning. Go back to bed, read the *Times*, enjoy."

"I have too much to do." Patty throws the shaver on the counter, reaches for the basket of dirty laundry, starts down the basement stairs. When she shuts the gate that keeps Felix, our cat, from coming upstairs, I yell down, "Aren't we lucky to have a toilet in the basement?"

The only sounds that ascend are the whoosh of the water into the washer and Felix meowing for his corn flakes and skim milk. I go down to let Felix up.

Patty is matching socks when she sees me. "Robert, don't you ever finish anything? You know I don't like to roll socks."

From behind, I put my arms around her, kiss her ear. "You are wonderful!" Then I step back, look at her again. Her dark brown hair, cut in front like Janet Reno's, which usually falls on her forehead, is brushed back, held in place with a silver bar pin. Patty looks tired, tense around the eyes. She continues to sort the socks. I pick up a pair of our daughter, Carrie's, gym socks, roll them flat, put them into the carry basket.

"Patty, you look tired. You sleep okay?"

"I was up half the night. The rain got me up."

"The job okay?"

"Another big review coming up, a real biggie. A review of my lending to minorities practices."

"That again."

"It never stops." Patty sighs. "I am tired. I was up half the night."

I kiss Patty's forehead. "You get anything done?" This is a reference to Patty's sleepless hours when she plans, worries and sometimes resolves our life's daily questions.

"We should take two weeks off this July, get to California to see how your folks are getting along."

"Everything in California is fine. The sun is shining, my father is swimming, my mother is doing lunch."

"Robert, that's what I am worried about. Nothing can be as good as your folks make it."

"Okay, we will go to Los Angeles, then we could drive up the coast. I would like to see the new art museum in San Francisco."

"There you are, planning on the things you want to do."

I smile. "You wanted for us to go to California."

"Not to museums, Robert. I want Carrie to spend quality time with her grandparents. Your mother and father."

Patty's emphasis is on "your." I say, "Fine, we will stay in Los Angeles and visit the Los Angeles County Museum, the Getty, the Norton Simon."

"Only three?"

"We could do the Huntington."

Patty smiles, which brings a bit of relaxation to her jaw, then she looks at her wristwatch. "Carrie never sleeps this late."

"So she is sleeping in."

"Robert, go upstairs, see if Carrie is okay."

"Why shouldn't she be?"

"Okay, you finish the socks, I'll go up."

I rush up the central stair of our two-story colonial on a quiet cul-de-sac, turn right to Carrie's bedroom. There is no Carrie. But there is a note on her made bed.

> "Dear Mom,
> Not to worry, have gone with Phil to see the sunrise over Credit Island. Will be back by eight a.m.
> Love, C."

I bring Carrie's note down the basement, hand it over to Patty who reads it. Patty is not pleased. "Carrie should have asked me."

"I would bet they didn't decide to go until after we were asleep."

"Carrie is only fourteen."

I assure Patty, "Fifteen next month. Philip is past sixteen."

"Robert, this is not funny."

I smile. "At least he is Jewish."

"That too, is not funny."

"What do you want me to say?"

"I want you to talk to Carrie. The minute she comes home I want you to talk to her."

"I want to be at the hardware store when it opens."

"Which is more important, our only daughter, or your toilet?"

"Tell me."

"Okay, you will talk to Carrie when she comes back from her cello lesson."

Felix is rubbing against my bare legs. As I reach to free the latch for Felix, Patty pushes me into one of the lawn chairs that have been draped in discarded tablecloths since last November.

"You don't do anything, you don't hear anything, you didn't hear Carrie go out, you don't see anything around this house."

"I told you, I am going to fix the stool."

"It is not the stool I am talking to you about!"

"What are you talking about?"

Felix is in my lap, licking my face.

"Put that damn cat down."

"I didn't pick him up. He jumped up." I look at my wristwatch. "He is hungry."

"Felix can wait for his breakfast until I get upstairs."

"I was going to fix his . . ."

"Robert! You care more about that damn cat than about Carrie."

"Patty, that is stupid." Just then Felix meows and Patty begins to cry. I put my arms around her, she pushes me away, goes back to rolling socks.

"I am going to find out whose idea it was to go joy riding at dawn. If it is Carrie's . . ." Patty sighs, brushes her forehead with the back of her hand. "We are going to have to find something for Carrie to do this summer to keep her very busy, so we know where she is all day long." Then Patty points at me. "Robert, you will have to arrange to be home by the time Carrie comes home."

"No problem."

"For you nothing is a problem because you leave all the problems for me."

I kiss Patty's forehead, whisper, "You want to go to the drive-in movie tonight? We could take Carrie, show her what we did in the back seat."

Patty pushes me away. "Aren't you romantic."

"It beats staying home and watching John Wayne on AMC."

Patty whispers, "We will see," opens the gate for Felix, starts up the stairs with the folded laundry. I follow with the rolled socks.

I feed Felix. Patty goes out to get the Rockville *Dispatch* and *New York Times*. She takes the *Dispatch*, hands me the *Times*. "I thought we would wait breakfast for Carrie."

"Great idea."

"You could clean out the gutters."

"Not on the Sabbath."

"Now you are a religious fanatic."

I smile. "It's too wet to climb on the roof."

"You are right." Patty looks at her watch, then out the window. "At least the kids had a sunrise to watch."

"I am hungry. I am going to make some Grape-Nuts and milk. You want some?"

"You know I can't tolerate milk."

"I will toast a bagel for you."

"I thought you agreed we would wait breakfast for Carrie."

"I'll eat again."

"Go eat your cereal with Felix."

I am at the dining room table slurping cereal on the front page of the *Times*. "Dole will resign Senate seat to run for president," when the phone rings. Patty is right there.

"It's Carrie."

I get up, get the cordless phone from the bedroom.

"Mom."

"Your dad is here too."

"Mom, would you care if I am a little late? Phil has invited me out for breakfast."

"You have to practice."

"Mom, I have the chaconne down pat."

"Ms. Sutton wants you ready for the graduation concert."

"Not to worry, Mom."

Carrie sounds pleased, happy. If not happy, at least cheerful. I ask, "Where are you going for breakfast?"

"Denny's. We are going to pig out on the Grand Slam."

"No meat."

"Dad, you know I don't eat pork." Carrie hangs up.

Patty smiles, "You know she won't eat pork."

I sigh, look at my wristwatch. "I am going."

Patty waves. "Go already." It is then that I take Patty by the hand, lead her out the dining room sliding door into the back yard. The sun glistens from the drying oak leaves. At the bird feeder the swallows wait for the grackles to leave, satiated.

I point to the cloudless sky. "No rain. It's going to be a great day. No gray. Anything special you want to do this weekend?"

"You sure you want to drive thirty-five miles to the drive-in?"

I don't answer.

"We won't be home until midnight. I have the quarterly reports to get out."

"We could neck."

Patty answers, "Huh."

I open the screen door to the gazebo, sit Patty in the one of two chairs I have managed to release from winter storage. I sit holding her hand. With her other hand Patty wipes the oak pollen from the glass top of the round table, looks at her yellowed palm. "Bob, if you want me to sit out here with you, please clean up the pollen." Patty begins to sneeze. I wipe the table with the crumpled tissue I keep in my paint-stained khaki shorts. Patty blows her nose.

"Getting old, Bob. If it isn't one damn thing, it's another. Pollen allergies, food allergies, stay on your diet, Missus Levy. No salt, no fat, plenty of exercise, don't gain any weight, Missus Levy. You'll be fine, Missus Levy. Don't forget to come in for you glaucoma checkup, Missus Levy."

"You haven't got glaucoma."

"My mother does."

Patty looks out at our rusted abstract garden sculpture, "Horse with Head Held High."

"Robert, your horse is peeling."

"That's what steel does as it ages, rusts, peels." I sigh, get up, reach for a worn towel from the waste paper basket, begin to wipe the pollen from the table. Patty gets up. "You had better get to the hardware store. I want you back here when Carrie comes home. I want you to talk to her like a father, not like a pal. I want you . . ."

I interrupt Patty with a kiss on her forehead. "I'll tell her it's not healthy to go out necking with boys. That's what you mother told you when we started dating." I smile, Patty smiles.

"I was a high school graduate."

"You were only sixteen."

"Carrie won't be fifteen until September."

"Not to worry, Patty. I'll talk to her."

"Robert, what are you going to tell her?"

"Like I always tell her. You need advice, speak to your mother."

"Robert, Carrie went out without getting our permission, without telling us with whom and where she was going."

"She left us a note." Then I add, "It's not easy being a mother to a teenager."

I go out the door, turn, come back. "Ask Carrie if she wants to go to the drive-in with us."

"What's playing?"

"*Mission Impossible.*"

"If it isn't sex, it's violence."

As I go out the door Patty is shouting at me. "I am not going to the drive-in."

I come back in. "Fine with me. I'll get a movie at Blockbusters."

On Thirtieth Street the trees are flowering in violet unison. The red buds are blooming pink and white, the forsythia is in full yellow, the red and purple fuchsia hang in baskets from the ceiling of white porches.

At the True Value I get a "Great morning, Bob," from Bill Levander. Then he adds, "Tell Patty we have six more reservations for our class reunion." Bill and Patty are the Homecoming committee for Rockville High School's twenty-fifth class reunion.

Bill takes me to the checkout. "You have any problems, call me."

In the kitchen Carrie is on the telephone talking to Phil. "I can't go out tonight. You won't believe this. My mom asked me to go to the drive-in with them."

I interrupt with, "*Mission Impossible* is on. Ask Phil if he wants to come with us."

Carrie has hung up. "Hi, Pops."

"Hi, kid. Phil coming with us?"

Carrie kisses my forehead. "I didn't ask him to. See you later, Pops. I am going up to practice."

Patty looks at me. "Bob, I think tonight when we are all together in the car, you had best speak to Carrie. Tell her what the rules are."

I say, "Sure."

Patty starts down the stairs humming, "Hey Jude," then she turns.

"Bob, do you think you could get the porch chairs into the gazebo?"

I yell down. "Sure!"

Carrie comes down the stairs, sits me down on one of the porch chairs that I am about to wash. "Pops, do you mind if I don't go to the drive-in with you? I won't be alone, I could have Phil come over. We could study together."

"No way, Carrie. This is family fun. If we go, we all go."

"I just thought maybe you and Mom wanted to be alone."

"No, and don't go asking your mother for permission to have Phil come over."

"Yes, Dad."

SABBATH MORNING

"Carrie, tell your mother we had our talk."
"What about, Dad?"
"About you and Phil going off alone without telling us."
"Dad, you worry too much."
"Tell that to your mother."

Carrie smiles, runs up the stairs to the telephone. "Phil, sorry about tonight. Family fun night at the drive-in. No, you can't come."

Another Time

In the afternoon shade, behind the screen of flowering honeysuckle, Harry Martens dozed on the plastic lounge. His gray head bobbed, his mouth opened, closed; he breathed heavily through his mouth. He opened his eyes, looked at his watch, reached for the Tylenol capsule, sloshed it down with one swallow of Evian.

Harry pulled the crew neck of the sweatshirt from his throat, turned on his back, threw off the coverlet from his legs, folded his hands onto his stomach and dozed into this third day of chills, shakes, and always, the fever. As forever, the fever had been brought on by stress. First the malaise, and then the tired, then the chills accompanied by the rise in temperature, and the night sweats. This, the third morning of shakes and spasms so severe that Harry needed both hands to bring the iced water to his mouth. Tomorrow the fourth day would be better. He would shave, shower, call his daughter, Julia.

On the fifth day, the leg weakness, the exhaustion would bring on the morning nap—and the afternoon nap—the ten hours of fragmented sleep. His daughter would not arrive from New York until Tuesday. By then, Harry Martens would not have to explain, "Been napping, just my fever again."

He had called Julia on the first day, with the first chills. Julia was a precise, correct daughter, more remote than Harry wished, not at all like her mother Hilda had been. Julia would come in, kiss him on his forehead, sit, hands folded, legs together facing him, her back straight like the wedding picture of her grandmother. Blue eyes, curly dark brown hair and reticent good manners. "Do not speak unless spoken to," a child who hoped not to be noticed, now the daughter in New York, connected by AT&T.

At ten o'clock, after *Mystery* went off, Harry readied his king size bed for another alone night of up at twelve, up at one, wine at two a.m., sweats and fitful sleep until six a.m.

Julia called. Julia, always mindful, "Dad, I interrupt anything?"

"Here? No."

"Dad, you okay?"

"Fine."

"You sound sort of distant, Dad. I don't want you to come out to the airport. I'll take the limousine in. I would rather you wouldn't have to wait if I'm delayed. Eleven o'clock is past your bedtime."

Harry nodded. "I'll wait up for you."

That night the fever spiked. On the lounge Harry turned onto his right side, reached for the coverlet, covered himself and began his shaking, spasms that grabbed and let go, gripped and let loose. Forty years in the State Department, the finest hospitals. No diagnosis, no treatment, no disability pay. The pension was adequate, and then there was always the art collection. Harry's breathing sounds rose from his chest, ascended into his throat, once he gargled, "Hilda." The awareness that he was forming sounds aroused him. He turned onto his left side, raised himself onto his elbow, reached for the glass of water.

The morning had been a blue sky, Potthast beachscape, gay with children in bright blues, yellows and reds.

On this late afternoon the beach was bare, freed from the white sun hats, the red and yellow plastic pails and shovels, the hovering mothers and the mothers who sat and read trash novels, who left socks and slippers for Harry to gather.

As always Julia would be in the guest bedroom. She won't hear me pour the four ounces of red Zinfandel into the tumbler. Drink it without tasting it, rinse the glass, replace the bottle. Julia would stay three nights. On the first, she would do her chicken curry. On the second, I make my tuna casserole. On the third night we'll go to Casa Ybel, where as we watch the sun set we choose from the chef's special early menu.

It was then that the surf sound stilled, when the Gulf was the blue of a Luminist seascape.

Harry turned onto his back, swung both feet to the green indoor outdoor carpet. With one hand he held the chaise arm, with the other he pushed up on the lounge frame. He rose, bent down, gathered the coverlet, went to his bathroom, washed his face. Back in the bedroom he turned on the National Public Radio news. Supine on his bed he heard, "The Dow Jones has reached another high," dozed back into the communist "Prague of the 1950's."

Nineteenth and twentieth century American Art History. The perfect background education for an American diplomat in Rumania, Hungary, Czechoslovakia. "Mr. Martens is our cultural attaché, our Eastern European specialist."

In Rumania Harry spoke French. In Hungary he had an interpreter. In Czechoslovakia his German was adequate. The cultural attaché met intellectuals, painters, poets, dissidents, artist, art collectors. The cultural attaché wrote assessments, recommendations, determined who would be invited to visit and enjoy the West, to join the Voice of America.

"I do believe it would be possible for me to arrange your visit with the Czech cultural minister."

"Mr. Martens." Those first times Hilda had called him Mr. Martens. "I have been trying to reach you. I am Hilda Gershon. I was told you could help me."

"I was in Brussels."

"So I was told."

"I would like to have your wisdom."

"No one has asked for that in some time."

My first dinner with Hilda at the Hotel Rex—late nineteenth century gilded, Czech baroque. Dinner was roast duck, for foreigners only.

"My interest is in Holocaust art, Mr. Martens. Could you help me gain access to the Czech archives?"

"I can try. I know someone who knows someone."

"Don't be so modest, Mr. Martens."

"Harry, please."

Red hair, blue eyes and freckled face, about five-eight, spoke English with a trace of accent. Harry had looked through the passport records. Hilda Gershon, twenty-four, born Poland, citizen, USA.

"It's for my doctorate."

"In Art History?"

"No. Holocaust studies."

"I see."

***

Hilda was gone. The obituary cut from *The New York Times*, the proof. Dr. Hilda Gershon Martens, noted Holocaust historian. Sixty-eight, survived by her husband, Harry Charles Martens of Myers Island, Florida and a daughter, Julia Gershon Martens of Manhattan.

The uninvited east wind entered the screened rear porch, then through the open sliding door to Harry's bedroom. The red-eyed clock clicked, glowed 1:00 a.m. Harry turned, mouthed the Tylenol, sloshed the water, added the coverlet to the acrylic knit blanket. Now to Julia.

Julia was Julia. Why didn't matter. Why was not important. On Thursday night Julia had to be told, even if Julia would rather not be told.

"The art collection is yours. Whenever you want it."

Harry had tried it last year, had given Julia a Nolde wood cut for her birthday. "Mann and Frau, 1922." Julia had as yet to hang it.

"It's really too valuable to hang in my apartment. Not where I live."

The polished to copper sun rose at seven-twelve. At eight Harry shaved, showered, made his Colombian coffee. Wrapped in his Reebok sweatsuit he sat on the front porch, elbows on the glass table, watched the pelicans dive, the mullet fisherman throw the red buoys to mark their nets. He would rest, nap, greet Julia with a smile.

"Julia, would you like some Chardonnay before you go to bed?"

I will talk of Julia's career, international law, as befits a daughter educated in Brussels, London and Georgetown University. It is not time yet to talk of Hilda. Hilda we will share silently.

I will tell her how each German Expressionist came into the collection. Talk to Julia so the German Expressionist collection wouldn't become unfinished business interrupted by my death.

"On our honeymoon, Mom and I did every museum in Munich, every museum in Paris. Of course there weren't as many museums then. There was no Picasso in Paris. No Beauborg, just the Louvre and the Jeu de Paume."

Harry Martens drove west to the Casa Ybel restaurant. "Blackened grouper and Buena Vista Chardonnay for two."

"Yes, thank you, Mr. Martens, Miss Martens. We miss Mrs. Martens."

"We do too."

Father and daughter sat at a table for two, the daughter faced west to the sunset over the Gulf, to the pink-purple afterglow sky. The January rocker moon rose. The server poured a second glass of wine for Julia.

"Your mother and I were married six years by the time we were your age."

"Things are different now, Dad." And then his daughter put down her glass, addressed him like a client.

"Dad, a Mr. Hans Reiter came in to see me. He is having a problem with a fake watercolor. An August Macke of the Tunisian Voyage Series that the Hamburg City Museum purchased at auction in the United States."

"If it's false the auction house will refund his bid. All he needs is the proof – the opinion of a known expert will do."

"That's what I told him."

"Did he pay you?"

"Billing is not my responsibility."

The great blue heron waded into the rising gulf tide. Flocks of royal terns flew over Casa Ybel to roost in the Ding Darling bird sanctuary. Harry Martens said, "I want to talk to you about the collection before the tax collector does," and took a sip of the Chardonnay. Julia made no sign of consensus. She sat both elbows on the table. Without makeup she looked younger. Julia could have nodded when I made a joke about death and taxes.

"Mr. Reiter asked me if I was related to you."

"Knowing Hans, I am sure he knew you were my daughter."

"Mr. Reiter mentioned he had met you in Prague, or was it Vienna?"

"It was both."

"Lovely salad, the sourdough bread is very good."

"Not as good as your mama could make. I was going through your mother's things. There is her jewelry."

"I'm not ready for that."

"I have made an inventory of the art collection. I could start the appraisal process. Your base would be the values at the time of my death. You will have sufficient cash to pay the estate taxes."

"A single heir does simplify settling an estate, but you and Mom should have had more children. I really haven't brought you that much joy."

"Julia, I am sorry to burden you. It is as you say, there is no one else."

"There are other choices."

"Don't talk to me about gifting. The collection was my gift to your mother. One painting at a time, one drawing at a time. I gave the Schiele to your mother as a wedding present. We bought the Klimt in London."

"How did you manage to buy paintings on your salary?"

Harry laughed. Julia and he had never reached this level of intimacy. Never talked about money, never talked about anything really. It was Hilda who had been the reteller to Harry of Julia's words and world.

"Your mother was a very good manager."

"Not that good."

"We paid for each acquisition. There is a receipt for each purchase."

The blackened grouper finished. "Two espressos."

"Dad, you shouldn't drink coffee. You won't sleep."

"I don't sleep anyway."

Julia waited for her coffee to cool. The afterglow had left the sky. In the cool clear night two boats trawled their nets, their lighted arms extended. On the horizon the lights from Vanderbilt Beach winked and twinkled; the headlights on the beach road.

"Mr. Reiter said you had a business relationship for some years."

"Not for long. He did well enough with it. It was a long time ago."

"He said you gave him his start, his first sales."

"Hans knows German Expressionist art. There were areas your mother knew better. Hans knew people. Although I must say, he was not my choice as a partner."

"Why?"

"Hans was a braggart."

"He still is." Julia smiled. "Reiter told me how well he had done for you."

"He did well for himself."

"He told me about your acquisitions. Such a simple idea. You arranged for the exit visa, Reiter called on the beneficiary, suggested 'just a token of your appreciation, a small gift for Mr. Martens. I have a Beckman self-portrait that Mr. Martens has admired, that I can let you have at a good price.' Very innovative."

"Everyone benefited."

"You represented the United States of America. People looked up to you."

"The gifts were made after I had approved the travel grants or the visa, not as a condition of my issuing them."

"You took bribes!"

"No, Julia. No. It wasn't like that. The people who made the gifts were grateful that I had made it possible for them to leave war-torn Europe. The owners of the prints were grateful that Reiter bought them, because with the dollars they could get a bit more to eat. Everyone was happy to show their appreciation. Most of the beneficiaries would have sent a small gift instead of cash or flowers. I chose German Expressionist prints. Gifts were the custom. That was . . ."

Harry didn't finish, Julia did. "It was a foolproof idea to exploit the beholden."

"I didn't make those conditions. Hitler did."

"Reiter said you came to him. Whose idea was it? Tell me! Dad, tell me!" Julia had raised her voice.

"Your mother's! She thought it was the way to bring German Expressionist art to the United States."

On the drive home Harry Martens said, "I hadn't wanted to tell you, Julia, I should be getting my affairs in order."

"Your fever?"

"It's been more frequent. More stress, more complications."

"You miss Mama."

"I have been very busy with the things your mother usually did."

"I'm sorry I couldn't help more with settling Mom's estate."

"You did what you could."

"Give me time, Dad. I need more time."

"That Julia, is something I may not be able to manage."

Julia said, "I understand," took her father's hand. "I know it was another time. Don't forget, Dad, I read all of Mama's books, but . . ." Julia did not complete her sentence. Hand in hand, father and daughter drove home in silence.

I Should Have

I am five—five and a half that first summer of memory. My father, tall, thin, squats among his roses. The roses are red, yellow and pink, each labeled with names I do not remember. I sit in the shade of the pin oak, guarded by Suzy, the family Boston terrier.

It must be a Sunday because my mother is not with me. She has taken my brother, five years older than I, to Sunday school. It is warm or my father would not have allowed me to sit in the pea gravel of his rose garden. It cannot be summer; it must be late spring in western Illinois, before school has been let out. Days that I recall as hot. Warmer than the summers in northern California where I now live.

My dad plants the roses in a single straight line, to receive the all-day sunshine, to climb the salmon red cement block wall of the garage. The grass of the backyard is fertilized to deep green. The redwood fence is freshly stained.

My mother had stopped on her way out. "Honey, don't get the stain on your clothes."

I am a chubby child who has dressed herself in a white T-shirt, blue jeans, blue Keds tied with red laces, a two-gun belt around my middle, a tan sombrero held in place with a chin strap. My mother, born in America, calls me "Honey." My father calls me "Chane." It is difficult for Mama to evoke the "ch" sounds of my Hebrew name that my immigrant father produces so easily. My father wears his green Army overalls. Arms around my dog I watch my father dig, plant, water, clean his trowel.

Dad picks me up, hugs me. He smells of sweat and dirt. "I dirtied your shirt." He wipes at me with his handkerchief. The imprint of his hands under my arms remains to annoy my mother.

"Honey, don't forget to change your shirt before we go out."

It is Sunday. We will have a late lunch at Bishop's Cafeteria, across the Mississippi River in Davenport, Iowa. We will meet my parents' friends, the Goulds, and their son who is my brother's age. My father will select coleslaw in vinegar, chicken and dumplings, corn muffins, black coffee and apple pie, no ice cream, thank you. My father's choices at restaurants are the American home cooking he first met in the Army. Chicken fried steak, fried chicken, buckwheat pancakes, meat loaf. At home, Mama decides what is for dinner, rib roasts, lamb roasts, fish, hamburgers. Dad finishes each meal with, "Great dinner, Jenny. Great dinner." Father clears, Mama stacks.

For the past three months, at seven in the morning, California time, I call my father and mother in Rockville, Illinois.

"I am doing better, really. I am doing more. I drove to the store."

"How is the walking?"

"Tough, Dad. Still tough."

"Doing your exercises?"

"Doing fine, Dad."

"I made a special prayer for your recovery."

On Monday and Thursday when the Torah is read in the Rockville prayer house my father makes mi sheberach. "May Chane Malke, daughter of Shane Rachel, daughter of Isaac, be blessed. May she be healed in mind and body."

***

"Dad, I have been cleaning drawers. You won't guess what I found."

My father does not guess.

"Dad, you remember you took pictures of me and Mom on the way to my first day of school. I have an entire album. I was wearing the red-checkered dress with the white piping around the pockets. The one Mom made for me."

Dad is there on the extension phone.

"Would you like that Mom and I come out?"

I answer his question with a question. 'How is your ankle? Mom says . . .'"

My father answers. "No problems with my new shoe inserts. I no longer use my cane. Mom and I could come out."

"Really, Dad, I am doing fine. George has been wonderful. I am getting better. Believe me."

My dad doesn't answer.

"This morning I took a shower all by myself."

"When are you seeing the neurologist?"

"Thursday afternoon. Dad, don't worry. George will take me. Dad, we will manage, believe me."

Right beside the photos was the little gold heart locket, the one with my initials on it.

My dad doesn't answer.

My father, in red bathing trunks, sandals, is drying in the afternoon sun. I am in my Nike nylon warmup suit. We sit beside the heated community pool. My mother, afloat in her blue aquajogger, is in the deep end doing knee bends, leg lifts. I admire my mother's determination to rebuild her right leg which has yet to fully recover from her hip replacement surgery.

Dad looks a Mom, then at me. "Your exercises help?"

"Some." I add, "It takes time. I wish I could do more. I wouldn't be getting so fat." I point to my belly.

"You don't look all that fat to me."

I grin. "That's because you are my father."

My father smiles slowly, gets up from the plastic lawn chair, kisses me on my forehead, wraps my mother in her beach towel. My mother sits in the sun patting herself dry. She covers her varicosed legs with the beach towel. Her brown hair is untinted, cut short because she swims every day, has only a few gray "highlights." Mom wraps the free end of the towel around her back, shoulders, upper arms. In the last four years she has had two skin cancers removed surgically. One from her face, the other from her leg. "When I met your father I was a red-haired, freckle-faced teenager. On those summer weekends we went to Rockaway Beach, we got burned to blisters. Who knew from sun block, from skin cancer?" After fifty years of living in western Illinois Mom's vowels and speech rhythms pronounce Brooklyn, New York.

My mother looks at the sun, looks at the weather report in my newspaper. "At home it is cold and drizzling." Mama thinks of Rockville as home. Is it because my brother is buried there?

The black marble marker has our family name engraved on its polished face. Below that in gray script is inscribed, "Seek justice, love mercy, walk humbly with thy God. Micah."

I SHOULD HAVE

Tonight we will have dinner with my Aunt Ellie, my father's sister. We will talk of American art. She is a lecturer docent at two Los Angeles museums. We will get her review of what is showing and what will be coming. My aunt is also, as I am, a recent immigrant to northern California.

My father is back to reading *The New Yorker*.

My mother gets up. "I am going to take a shower. Steven, don't get cold. Move into the sun." She looks at her watch. "We have to be at Ellie's in an hour."

"Plenty of time, Mom."

"Is George coming with us?"

"He will meet us."

I pick up the newspaper, start on the crossword, Dad looks at the sky. "Such a lovely day. None of your neighbors swim? We have been the only ones in the pool."

"Papa, it's winter. Or what passes for winter in L.A."

"Chane, you like living in L.A.?"

"George likes his job."

"You have made friends?"

"Not yet, Pop. At first we were too busy just getting settled. And then when I got . . ."

My father interrupts me before I can say stroked out. "You should join a synagogue. I don't mean just join, I mean to go, too."

This time it is I who doesn't answer. What can I say? Dad, George and I don't find religion and prayer as necessary as you do.

"At the synagogue you would meet other young people."

"Dad, we are not so young. We are getting close to fifty."

"That is young. Until I was fifty-eight I jogged three miles a day." He says no more, goes back to his short story.

My dad is sun-tanned, still thin, flat bellied, bald and gray, yet he is so arthritic he must use both hands to lift himself out of a chair. He walks bent over until he remembers, when he shakes himself, pulls his shoulders back, pulls his chin up. But too soon the back pain again pushes his face down towards the ground.

Dad looks at the cloudless sky, at my watch, moves his chair into the sun, returns to reading. I ask him, "Good story?"

"Another fourteen-year-old girl exploring sex." Then, "Chane, did you have a happy childhood?"

I wait a moment. "I would say I did. Compared to what I heard from my college roommates, my life in Rockville was better than most."

"Do you remember your confirmation party?"

I nod a yes.

My father sighs. "When you get to be my age you start thinking. Not that I have that much to complain about."

I look at my dad who has had reparative surgery of both of his hands, a hip replaced, a toe corrected, his lower back injected with steroids, who can't use his right shoulder.

"There are things I could have done differently," he says.

I don't answer.

"Chane, you had a happy childhood?"

After a moment for review I answer, "I would say so."

Dad smiles. "Good, I am pleased. I was always worried about that. I was afraid

Mom and I had neglected you. Once Billy took sick all we did was run to Mayo with him."

"I don't think of myself as neglected."

"There are things I could have done differently that would have made it easier for you, for us." Dad stops, sighs, adds, "For our old age."

"You are not old."

Dad sighs, smiles. "Okay, Mom and I are not old."

"Tell me what you would have changed."

He doesn't answer. I begin to gather up my newspaper, sun block, place my cane at ready between my knees.

"If I didn't have all those business obligations we could spend our winters with you in California. We could have come out when you needed us, not just for two weeks."

"Dad, we are getting along fine. George is here. Ellie calls."

"Think of it, Chane. If I would have stayed in the Army I would have been retired with an inflation-proof pension."

"So why didn't you."

Dad doesn't answer. I stand over my father, he looks up at me. With both arms he pushes himself up from the chair. We walk. He is just a step behind me. I let us out of the gate, we walk through the parking lot, by the townhouses to my condo. He looks at the sky. "November and we can swim."

"So why didn't you stay in the Army?"

"At that time I thought I couldn't. Now of course, I think maybe I should have."

Dad lets me lead up the two steps to the rear door. Up goes my good leg, then the cane follows with my right leg, the bad leg. My dad is watching. He assures me, "Your leg will get stronger."

It is the end of November, a week before I will go back to work at the bank, three months since my stroke.

My mother has come downstairs in her two-piece, tan cotton dress accentuated by an orange T-shirt and broad black belt with a handmade-in-Morocco silver buckle, the only memento of my father's service in North Africa that my mother wears. The French military badges, the raised silver sword of the paratroopers, the crossed, bronzed field pieces of the artillery rest in the top drawer of her dresser.

"Steven, go upstairs, get dressed."

"Honey, are you changing?"

"No need for me to."

I follow my mother out the dining room door to the leaf-covered trellis of the front patio. It is a refuge of quiet and cool. The only sound is the score-keeping from the tennis court. "Love-love forty."

"Honey, I could stay on. Dad has to be back for a board meeting but I could stay on, help you."

"Mom, I am doing good, better each day."

"If this is good I don't know how you managed three months ago."

"I told you. George stayed home mornings."

"I forgot," was Mother's explanation. It was not an apology.

Now was the time to talk about my dad, not about me. "Dad and I were talking. I have never heard Dad say it before."

My mother is impatient. "Say what?"

"He said he should have stayed in the Army."

It's a minute or two before my mother says, "Before we got married the Army was like his mother and father. His family." Then, very quietly, "The first year out of the Army Dad couldn't work. He could hardly eat. It was like he was in mourning. Your father had lost both his parents by the time he was nineteen. The rest of his family was in Poland. You know what happened to them."

"I know." My uncles, aunts, cousins are sepia photographs in a cardboard box in Dad's desk. "So, why did Dad leave the Army?"

Mama sighs. "It had to do with atomic warfare. Your dad was against atomic warfare." Then Mom smiles. "He wasn't against killing. It was mass killing. Killing of civilians that he was so against. That's how we ended up in western Illinois. Your dad resigned his active duty commission and we stayed in Rockville. We had a little four-room house to live in, two wonderful children and now we wouldn't have to move anymore. Your dad didn't see Billy until he was three months old. You know what he said when he saw him? He said, 'He is so little.'"

"I remember that house."

To herself I hear Mom say. "We were happy there."

My father, in khaki trousers, gray golf shirt, is at the patio door. My mother looks at Dad. "Steven, you look nice." My dad looks at me. "Chane, I can drive."

I get up, Mom and Dad follow me to the garage. I get into the passenger seat, my mother sits in the back, Dad in the driver's seat. My father backs out, turns right onto Colfax. My mother says, "Honey, if you are tired we don't have to go. Ellie will understand."

"It's okay, Mom. She made a standing rib roast just for you and Dad."

At the red light Dad takes a long look at me. "You didn't nap today."

"I haven't napped since you have been here.'"

"How is your leg today? Getting any stronger?"

"Dad, I told you, I'll tell you when . . ."

My mother is there with, "Steven, you know Honey doesn't like when you ask questions."

Dad drives silently.

"Turn right here." He turns. "Turn left at the second block." He parks in front of my aunt's duplex townhouse, watches me lift myself out of the car with the help of my cane. I put the cane back into the car, start down the walk. My father is at my side. "Some things you have to do for yourself, can't anybody help you. Not even your father or mother. The physio-therapy will help you Chane. It will."

Mom calls out to me. "Honey, you sure you can make all those steps?"

"No problem."

My dad says, "Good," stays beside me on the stairs. Up with the left leg, then with my right hand on the railing I pull myself up. Left leg and pull, left leg and pull up another step, another step. My dad is watching.

"Proud of you, Chane. You done good!"

"Thanks, Dad. That's what every kid wants to hear from their parents." I hear Dad, more to himself than to me. "I should have done better for my children."

Saturday's Child Works Hard for His Living

On the second day of spring, the clouds, massive and organized to keep the sunshine from the upper Mississippi River valley, departed. The tulips and crocus broke through the earth.

Charles Karp raked the wet russet oak leaves from his lawn onto the burn pile, sang, "Welcome sweet springtime, we greet thee with joy," to the tune of Mendelsohn's spring song, as taught sixty years ago at Franklin school by Mary Sullivan, his sixth grade music teacher.

The leaf fire burned to smudgey dense acrid smoke, seared his throat, made him cough. He turned to his kitchen drawer of anti-asthmatic sprays and pills to hear his wife, Milly's, admonition. "I told you to wear a mask."

"I should have."

"You want to kill yourself, go ahead, have an asthma attack. I'll call 911. You will be dead before the medics get here."

Charlie sang, "Ah, sweet mystery of life at last I've found you," to Milly. Milly sighed, shut the window to the smoke.

Charlie swallowed his pill, kissed Milly's forehead. "Milly, you are right. I shouldn't be around a leaf fire."

"You are a stupid old man." Milly stirred the gurgling blueberry jam boiling on the stove.

Charlie said, "I was stirred by spring to do yard work."

"Charlie, where are you going?"

"I have to put the rake away."

"Shut the garage door. Don't let the smoke into the house."

"Don't I always?"

Charlie, with a pleased-with-himself smile, came into the kitchen. "I sprayed for the roaches."

"About time."

"I killed one big enough to carry off a cat."

"That big?"

Charlie smiled. "I did it for you."

"Did what?"

"I raked the leaves from around the house so I could spray to kill the roaches."

"My hero." Milly stirred the jam.

Charlie Karp massaged his right shoulder.

"How is your shoulder?"

"My shoulder is fine. My hands hurt."

"I didn't ask you about your hands."

"I was sharing with you. If I don't share my pains with my wife, who else can I share them with?"

"Charlie, do me a favor. Don't share with me. Tell Dr. Rosen."

"You are my love."

"I can't help you."

"Doctor Rosen doesn't help either."

The leaf fire died to wisps thin and blue, to rise through the bare branches, becoming invisible in the gray twilight sky. Charlie freed the fire with his rake. The flame flared and then died. It began to rain. Charlie opened his mouth, let the drops into his mouth, coughed, hung the rake onto the garage wall, came into the kitchen, put his arms around Milly.

"It gets cold when the sun goes down."

"It's only the second day of spring." Milly wiped her hands dry on the embroidered sunflowers of her apron. "Your famous, wealthy, charming brother called."

"How are things in beautiful California?"

"He wants to talk to you."

"He wants my advice on whether he should take a job."

That brought a smile to Milly. "Danny boy isn't going to work. Not as long as the fair Ellen has interior design contracts."

"Milly, you are jealous."

"Not of those two. Only of their winter weather. We could have stayed longer in Florida."

"I had work to do."

"You had better call Danny before Ellen sits down for her afternoon 'high tea'. You wouldn't want to disturb America's most distinguished interior designer while she is eating her lettuce on toast sandwiches and drinking imported British tea." Milly mimicked, "I just love this Earl Grey special blend. We have it sent over from London." Milly turned to Charlie. "You want some reheated Lipton's for supper?"

"Sure. Let's live a little."

"Throw your clothes in the washer. You stink from smoke. And take your shoes off. Don't come into the kitchen with your gardening clothes."

Clad only in underwear and his Nike swim sandals, Charles Karp, supine on the daybed in the small bedroom that Milly used for her afternoon nap, dialed his brother Dan in California.

"Charlie, so good of you to call. Milly good?"

"As good as ever. You know Milly. Busy. Busy."

"How are you, Charlie?"

"Good enough."

"Your hands hurting?"

"They always hurt when I do yard work."

Dan was enthusiastic. "I want you and Milly to come out, stay with us for a week of sunshine, swim in our heated pool. You can visit the new Getty. How about you and Milly come out next week?"

Charlie sighed. "Can't for a couple of weeks."

He heard Dan clear this throat, cough, pause. "Charlie, I need ten thousand. Twelve would be better."

"Until you sell a story to a producer?"

"I have two being read."

"Dan, have you considered borrowing from a bank?"

"Charlie, it's not like the money isn't mine. All I want you to do is send it to me six months ahead of time. I am not asking for a loan, just an advance from Papa."

"Can't you wait three months until the next distribution?"

"I need the money, like yesterday. Charlie, please don't tell me to ask Ellen, I can't. You know how she feels about my gambling."

"Slow horses?"

"I was in Vegas on a business trip."

Charlie sighed. "Call me tomorrow. I'll see how much cash is available."

"Can't you sell some of Dad's stocks? You have had a great run on the stock market."

Milly was calling from the kitchen. "Dinner Charlie."

"Dan, I'll call you tomorrow evening."

Charlie set the table, poured the Heineken dark beer, a half glass for Milly, half for himself. Milly was at the microwave. Charlie took the tray she had prepared, set out the plates, the cutlery, the cornbread, the melon cut into exquisite squares, sat himself at the foot of the table opposite the TV. Milly, at Charlie's right, served the chili, turned the weather station to mute. Warm days and cool nights will continue for the rest of the week.

"Great chili, Milly. Better than ever. A new recipe?"

"Same as always." Milly munched in silence. Charlie tasted and swallowed the cornbread. "Cornbread and chili. Great supper."

Milly shut the TV, turned to face her husband of fifty years. "What did your genius of a brother want?"

"He wants us to come out, spend a couple of weeks. Wants us to greet spring in California, swim in their heated pool."

"I am not going unless Ellen invites me. You know how I feel about that."

Charlie drank his beer. Milly left her melon uneaten. "How is the great writer's life going?"

"He is on a roll. He has two stories being read by producers."

"It has been eight years since he has sold a story."

"You heard Dan's explanations. 'There is no place on TV for thoughtful, sensitive drama.'"

Milly's answer was almost a sneer. "That's what Dan says whenever."

"Milly, please, not that again. Dan does the best he can."

"He could get a regular job like you and me." Milly got up, started off with the tray of dirty dishes, turned to Charlie. "How much did Dan ask for? I heard you talking about money."

"He is calling back tomorrow."

"How much does he want?"

"He needs ten thousand."

"You are not going to give him an advance from our share."

"I'll straighten it all out in July when."

"You are not going to give him from our share! That's not fair to yourself. Dan is taking advantage of you!"

"If he sells a story he will pay back the advance."

"Like never, like last year. He can ask Ellen. Why does he come to you?"

Charlie coughed, went to shut the kitchen window. "I am his brother."

"Who stayed home and worked and took care of his parents."
"Please Milly. I didn't have the talent for writing that Dan does."
"Okay. So that gives him the right to live off of you?"
Charlie put his arms around Milly, kissed her cheek. "Dan can't ask Ellen for money."
"But he can ask his brother."
Charlie smiled, "You shouldn't get so angry."
"He lost money gambling, didn't he?"
"Milly, you know how gamblers are. They always think they are going to win."
"I don't know any gamblers except your brother Dan, who takes advantage of you like he took advantage of your mother and father."
Charlie coughed. "Nothing has changed. Nothing to get excited about. I am Charlie and he is Dan."
"What are you going to do, give him the money?"
"I am his brother. If he asks, I give."
"You are like your father. You spoiled the genius. You are not doing him a bit of good sending him money. He could work. He could get a day to day job."
"Milly, please let it be. I am not Dan's keeper. All I am is the administrator of Dad's estate."
"Dan sweet talked your dad, now he sweet talks you with promises he can't keep."
"He has scripts out. If he sells only one he will earn more money than we make in four years."
"That's what he tells you."
"Now why would he lie about that?"
"A liar is a liar."
Charlie coughed, wheezed.
"Go take your asthma pill."
"It makes me stupid."
"You are not going out tonight."
"I wanted to read."

In the living room Charlie sat in his arm chair, a mystery novel on his lap. He looked up, saw Milly doing her crossword. He shut his eyes, dozed.

Dan was back from Vietnam. Tall, thin, almost gaunt, Lt. Daniel Karp was home, talking, talking, telling, planning his future. *You know what I am going to do? I am going to go to the University of Iowa, going to learn to write children's books so that kids learn about Nam, about death and destruction and the waste of war.*

Dan had written his children's book, *An American in Vietnam*, the story of an American advisor to a South Vietnamese infantry battalion. The slim volume was illustrated with action photos taken by combat photographers. It had sold well, caught the attention of a producer of true life dramas for Public Broadcasting. Dan went to California to be the technical advisor.

The producers failed to find a sponsor to continue the series, although the video sold surprisingly well in Europe, especially well in Sweden and Finland. So rewarded, Dan stayed in California to write scripts for children's television. *That's where the money is, Charlie.*

Dan was a good son. When Mama and Papa were alive he returned to Rockville twice a year; in the spring for Passover and in the fall for Chanukah, and Ellen came with him.

I want you to meet Ellen Shaw. We are going to get married.

Tall, thin, poised and elegant. "Self-made" is what Milly called her. Thirty-two-year-old Dan was marrying an older woman. A woman of a certain age, who was beyond her child bearing years, who was a successful business woman.

Ellen is a very well known set designer.

Charlie coughed and wheezed again.

"You okay?"

"My throat is dry, that's all it is. The pills dry my throat."

"You are mumbling."

"I was dozing, dreaming. I saw Ellen. That is, the Ellen of twenty years ago."

Milly smiled. "Before her first face lift?"

"I can't remember." Charlie coughed. "It was stupid of me to burn the leaves."

Milly, irritated, said, "You didn't have to be out there poking around in the smoke. Breathing smoke is what brings on your asthma. You did it to yourself."

Charlie looked at his wrist watch. "It's only eight o'clock in California. Mr. and Mrs. Karp have just sat down to their Pritikin dinner. I should call Dan to tell him that I will wire the money tomorrow."

The phone rang, Milly looked at Charlie. "It's your brother, you answer it."

"Hello? Ellen?"

"Charlie, may I speak to Milly?"

Charlie grinned, "For you, my dear." He bowed, handed the phone to his wife.

"Milly, could you and Charlie come out, spend next week with us? I am between jobs. Next week would be just ideal for us. We could go to the Getty, do some of the galleries. I could get theater tickets."

"Charlie, could we get away, like a week Thursday?"

Charlie nodded a yes.

"Milly, have Charlie get on the bedroom extension. Dan has something he wants to tell you."

Dan was exuberant, gleeful. "I just got a call from Australia Broadcasting. I had forgotten all about them. It took them eighteen months to reach a decision. I got a contract to write a series and they paid in dollars!"

"Great! That's great, Dan."

"Charlie, what I called you about? You can forget what we discussed."

"All forgotten, Dan."

"Charlie, I didn't keep you up, did I?"

"You know we don't go to bed before ten o'clock."

"Good night, Charlie."

Charlie turned down the bed, Milly turned down the thermostat. Supine, side by side, paperbacks in hand, Charlie read his mystery novel, Milly read her mystery novel.

"Good night, Charlie." Milly shut her reading light, turned to Charlie. "Sometimes I think I am too hard on Ellen."

Charlie consoled, "She can't help what she is."

"A Hungarian immigrant girl who speaks English with a British accent." Milly mimicked, "Shall I brew the Earl Grey, or would you prefer Lipton's?"

"She was annoyed when you chose the Lipton's."

"She shouldn't have asked if she didn't want me to choose. Lipton's is what I buy, Lipton's is good enough for me."

SATURDAY'S CHILD WORKS HARD FOR HIS LIVING

Charlie shut his light, groaned, coughed.

"Charlie, you okay?"

"Fine, just fine."

"What's the matter, Charlie?"

"Nothing."

Charlie turned, dozed, shivered, slept, dreamt of when he and Dan had gone camping in the Minnesota wilderness. A sudden rainstorm had come up on the lake as they were returning to their island camp. It was Dan in the bow who had kept the canoe into the waves, kept the canoe from being swamped. It was Dan who saved their lives.

Charlie awoke, coughed, reached for the extra blanket he kept on his side of the bed, spread it over himself, took a sip of his water.

Milly had heard. "You okay?"

"Fine, Milly, fine."

"You were thrashing."

"I was cold. It was the asthma pills. I have the strangest dreams when I take them."

"Good night, Charlie. Try to get some rest."

"Good night, Milly."

"Charlie, you all right?"

"Fine, Milly. Just fine."

Options

In our office, there is a "Don."

Atherton. Donald C. Atherton III, in Corporate Trusts; who, on the same salary as mine, drives a Mercedes while I struggle to pay off my Saturn; who dresses better, looks better, younger and lives in a better part of town and certainly goes more places and does more than I who have the office next to his and must each Monday morning share his weekend triumphs. "We drove up to Galena, up to the Eagle Ridge Golf Course. Hear this, Charlie. I was hot, Charlie boy, only four over par on the front nine and only six over on the eighteen. You know the course, Charlie. I one-putted the eighteenth. It's a shame you had to give up golf, Charlie. You were good!"

"I didn't give it up. It gave me up." I point to my back. Don, slim, trim and fit, all five feet eight inches of him, rises to his toes, walks over, slaps me on the back. "Charlie, I feel for you," and is out the door for his coffee and bran muffin. I mutter, "I am sure you do." I adjust the bolster that supports my lower back, call home, greet my wife, Ellen.

"What is new and wonderful?"

"Your son needed a new swim suit. While I was at the athletic shop I bought Katie a pair of soccer shoes."

"Ellen, soccer camp is not for two weeks."

Ellen clucks. "Not to worry Charlie, we are on budget."

"That's good news."

"You okay, Charlie? You sound down."

"I just had a wonderful, fabulous weekend of golf with Don Atherton."

"Charlie, don't pay him any attention. I would bet he makes up his 'wonderful weekend' stories."

"The money he spends is real."

"Goodbye green eyes, and Charlie, see if Don will give you a lift home. I have a swim team meeting at 4:30 p.m."

I hang up because Don has returned with a smile. "Brought you a chocolate cookie to take with your Aleve. You look like you hurt."

I munch the cookie, a bank freebie left over from our Friday offering to the elderly when they withdraw their weekend mad money from their savings accounts, earning three percent in interest.

As predicted on the Weather Channel, it has begun to rain. It is on these gray, dank days that I am best able to wipe out the thoughts of what I used to do; a two-mile jog along the river, then into the Y hot tub, a shower, an apple and yogurt. It is on these dark, dreary days that I get the most done, when I make my calls with a hearty, "Good morning, Mrs. Gates. Charles Crown, your trust officer calling."

"Mr. Crown, are you sure I can give away ten thousand dollars a year to whomever I wish?"

"Yes, Mrs. Gates." "Yes, Mrs. Sorenson." I sing, "It is better to give than to receive."

The rain drops explode, glitter and slide down my one window to the downtown as I buy two thousand shares of PBT Corp, this on the recommendation of our research department. After I distribute the stock into my accounts I read annual reports, stretch, lift myself up—left hand on my chair, right on the desk, do five deep knee bends, five finger tips to toes. Make ready for my break with Don Atherton, the third.

Don, feet up on the desk, is reading a prospectus for an initial public offering. Donald points me into his side chair.

"Interesting reading?"

"Usual crap, usual disclaimers. I don't know who would buy this issue. But then every IPO looks good in a rising market." Don asks me, "Charlie, what's good in equities?"

"Research says PBT."

"What do you think, Charlie?"

"I only work here. Don, are you going right home?"

Don smiles. "You want a ride? Ellen can't pick you up?"

"Something like that."

"You got it."

In my office I open the window. It has stopped raining, it is muggy, humid but not quite so hot. The traffic on the one-way west has eased off. The gray hangs over the green wooded bluff.

Don, blazer over his arm, has come in. "Counting your blessings, Charlie?"

I give him, "The rain makes the grass grow."

"No grass to cut when you live in a condo."

I nod an agreement which I quickly modify with, "I don't know as we would have enough room for two growing kids, an old lame dog and a scared cat."

Don scores with, "We have a two-and-a-half-car garage."

The leather seats of the Mercedes are cool. We drive home in air-conditioned splendor with the total sound immersion of the business news, assuring, comforting, "Dow Jones hits a new high of 7600."

Don swings into our drive. I grab my briefcase from the back seat, run for the side door. Kathy, our twelve-year-old talking on the telephone, gives me a wave. Our nine-year-old, Keith, looks up from his computer game, delivers his message. "Mom won't be home before 6:30."

"You kids hungry?" I get two nods. I give each a Fuji apple, advise them, "We will wait supper until Mom comes home."

As I go upstairs to change into my yard clothes, Kathy—mouth full of apple—is still into conversation. Keith is polishing the Fuji on the sleeve of his gray Reebok T-shirt, contemplating the best place to bite.

I put the briefcase by my side of our queen bed, look out the bedroom window at all the signs that read, "Charlie Crown, you are not keeping up with you yard work." Branches of viburnum have grown up and beyond the flat top I like to keep on my high bush cranberries. I am pruning the wandering limbs when Ellen parks the gray Saturn in the garage.

Ellen, tall, tan, thin, five feet ten, red hair turning to brown cut swimmer short, is concerned. "Charlie, you sure you should be doing all that reaching and bending?"

"Who is going to do it?"

"You could hire Brad." Brad Packer is the sixteen-year-old who lounges his summers away at the second house to the east, the red brick colonial with the lawn that needs cutting, weeding and spraying.

"He did a good job cutting the lawn."

"I had to draw a diagram for him so he would not mow down the hawthorn."

"He is only fifteen."

"Sixteen next month."

"How about your back?"

"It hurts." Then I add, "No worse than before I did the pruning." I point proudly to the four shorn tops of the bushes that camouflage the six-foot Ozark wood fence, guaranteed for twenty-five years against rot, vermin and the corruption and degeneration of aging.

"You hungry?"

I smile. "Don brought me a chocolate cookie left over from Friday."

"Charlie, you should speak more kindly of Don. He also brought you home."

"I paid for that. I agreed there were advantages to living in a condo."

"Tell me."

I hug Ellen. "No grass to cut."

"What would you do on the weekends?"

I don't answer Ellen. I put my left arm—my right I can't raise—around her shoulder, kiss her ear. "What's for supper?"

"Last Monday's cheese and mushroom pizza, salad, and for dessert, fruit and graham crackers."

"My favorite dinner."

Dinner was a quiet affair, almost serene. Perhaps it was because it was late and we were hungry or because we all adhered to the house rules—no talking with a mouth full of food, not at our dinner table.

I crunched a Thompson green grape silently. . . . I was four over on the eighteenth when I hit my six iron to the right and below the pin. I read the green, stroked through smoothly for an easy eleven-foot putt for a two. I had beaten Don Atherton III by two strokes.

"Great supper, Ellen. You sit, I'll clear."

"The kids can do it."

"Okay, kids do it." And they did.

When we went up to bed Gene Kelly was dancing on the skylight to the tune of "Singing in the Rain."

"Charlie, shut the light, come to bed."

I kissed Ellen on her bare left shoulder, the only possible site as she was flat on her back reading *Great American Short Stories by Women Writers*.

"Hot stuff?"

"It was in 1912. Charlie, you were a long time in dressing room. What were you looking at?"

"The patterns the raindrops make as they splatter and slide down the skylight."

"You okay, Charlie?"

"Fine."

"I thought you had work to do."

"I do." I reached for the briefcase.

"Don't rattle your pages. I am reading."

OPTIONS

"Ellen, would I do that?"

"You always do."

Instead of the printout of last quarter's gains and losses for the equities that I manage, I had in my hand a clasp envelope addressed to Box 201, Davenport, Iowa, which is just across the Mississippi. This was not my briefcase, but Don's. Both briefcases were last year's Christmas present from our economics research chief in Chicago. Both look alike except for our initials in gold. Haste, the rain, Ellen's meeting, had brought me Atherton's case.

I placed the envelope beside me, leaned over, began my prowl. In the first packet were offerings for government instruments, bonds, forwarded from research in Chicago. In the second packet, in a slit business envelope, was last month's statement of transactions in Donald and Ann C. Atherton's money market account. Checking account deposits listed as purchases, withdrawals listed as sales.

In the left column interest paid daily: 5.4%. The Athertons did not do all their personal banking at Rockville National where Donald was VP for Corporate Trusts.

Two salaries in, five hundred to a thousand dollars withdrawn once, twice or three times a month, transferred to personal checking at Rockville National to pay for utilities, subscriptions, petty cash and for our employees flower fund.

"Charlie, what are you doing?"

I had my head into the briefcase. "I took home Don's briefcase."

"Big deal."

"I was peeking into the Athertons' money market accounts."

"How much is Don spending for his single malt Scotch?"

"I can't tell."

"You are a regular Sherlock Holmes." Ellen shut her reading light, turned onto her right side.

"You don't mind if I keep the light on for a few minutes?"

"Charlie, it's late."

I shut the light, took the envelope into the bathroom. Should I or shouldn't I? I'll have a look. Why not? The envelope isn't sealed, all I have to do is replace whatever it is in the same order. Tomorrow morning I'll call Don. Please stop by for me. By the way, Don, I took your briefcase by mistake. I am sorry. . . .

Another bundle controlled by a green rubber band. DAME Ltd. The receipts made out to DAME Ltd. from the Lombard Bank, Jersey in Guernsey, were stapled to note paper on which amounts from the receipts in British pound sterling, had been recalculated to show the equivalent value in dollars based on that day's exchange rate. On the first receipt $1.593 was necessary to pay for one pound sterling, on the second it was $1.602, then $1.633, $1.64, $1.65. It was evident that with each purchase Don was spending more dollars to replace his pounds for whatever he was accumulating.

The second receipts were the explanation for what DAME was buying daily. It was thousands of options giving DAME the right to buy within the next six months the shares of Round Table Foods of Chicago at a fixed price. Rumors about Round Table had been in, out and around Wall Street for months: a sure takeover candidate, likely to be acquired and, or, merged. It could be reorganized to profitability. The shares listed on the New York Stock Exchange had not moved significantly up or down—that in an equity market that had gained 23% in six months.

Some months ago research had issued a "For your eyes only" on Round Table, now at

$4-$5, a likely takeover candidate. Mason and Coventry of Manchester, the United Kingdom's largest grocery chain, is anxious to make an acquisition, to enter the American market. It is most likely that M&C's offer for the Round Table stock will be somewhere between $10 and $11. M&C would introduce its upscale product line, revitalize management. M&C has the money and skills, a combination that had made Mason and Coventry "where most Britons shop for their meats, vegetables, fruits, groceries, wines, flowers and personal products."

In the dim of the night light I sat on the stool, bent forward, my belly folds on my thighs, my head in my hands; the position in which I did my best deductive thinking.

"DAME" was Don's drop-box company in whose name Lombard Bank on the island of Guernsey bought the thousands of Round Table options. In comparison to monies spent to own the stock, buying the stock options cost less and controlled more. Should the Round Table stock go up, which is the only value of an option, the profits would be very much greater and the risk lesser.

DAME had paid Lombard Bank almost $400,000 in dollars drawn from its account at The Royal Bank, Liechtenstein, a member of L.B. Global Syndicate. Where had Donald A. Atherton III gotten $400,000 to deposit in Liechtenstein, the land of bank secrecy, numbered accounts and no income tax for foreign investors? If the acquisition of Round Table by Mason and Coventry was inside information, Don Atherton would be free to trade on it if he obtained his information innocently. If he received a tip from an insider he would still be liable to prosecution by the Federal government, but the government would have to show that Don Atherton knew this insider information was violating a confidence. If, in the next months M&C bought Round Table, DAME would profit more than handsomely and Donald A. Atherton III's risk would be minimal at best. However, if there was no buyout, the cost of the options would be lost forever and $400,000 was more dollars than the salary of a senior VP trust officer at Rockville National Bank and his school teacher wife could save. That I was sure of.

"Charlie, shut the bathroom light and come to bed!"

I shut the light, walked down the hall, listened to Keith and Kathy breathe, opened the door to the deck. The rain had stopped, the breeze from the west was blowing the wet from the oak leaves onto the glistening redwood.

In bed beside Ellen I reached the decision not to mention Round Table or Mason and Coventry to Donald Atherton, to Ellen, or to anyone at research or our trust department.

Donald Atherton called as I was on the floor halfway into my stretches and back strengthening exercises.

"Charlie, Don will pick you up?" I heard Ellen. "Thank you, that will save me a trip downtown."

The Mercedes appeared with a da-te-da, sun roof open to the hot and humid morning and Don smiling. I set the briefcase onto the back seat beside its look alike with my initials, "CCC" on the latch, folded my suit coat over it. From all appearances my case had not left Don's car unless Don had positioned my case as carefully as I had replaced his.

The 9:00 a.m. public radio segment reported the stock market as opening higher. Don switched the station to "The Morning Blues." Mike Howard sang, "Tain't nobody's bizness if I do." I sat slumped, opened my collar, fanned myself with the *Daily Express*. Don shut the roof, put on the air conditioning.

"Charlie, you look awful."
"I didn't sleep well last night."
"Kids okay?"
"Fine."
"Ellen sounded good."
"Ellen is fine."

Don parked in slot #4; one to six are reserved for the trust department. "I know why you don't look so good, Charlie. Your back hurts."

"It always hurts."

"Charlie, how about coming down to the Y with me over the noon hour. You can swim, take a nap, rest your back and come back a new man."

"Let's see how the day goes. I haven't finished reading the research reports." I put on my jacket, grabbed my case, smiled my way through customer service to my air-conditioned office. Tuesday morning. Our monthly reports to our clients had been mailed yesterday. The queries would not start until tomorrow.

The sun shone through the blinds, reflected off the glass top of my walnut banker's desk. I redirected the Venetians to block the sun. In the still, dull blue sky, God had shelved layer upon layer of gray puff clouds. It was going to be another hot and muggy day in the Mississippi River Valley.

There was a knock. Marian, our receptionist, was there, fax in hand. "From research—just came in for you."

Feet on the side chair to ease my back, I read, "Round Table Markets is a buy at 5, or even 6." I punched in RTMC. The quote was $5.75, a gain of seventy-five cents—or 15%—since closing on Friday. DAME Ltd. was on the rise to profitability.

I bought five thousand shares at $5.75, five thousand at $6. The stock was 6.25 when a jovial, happy Don Atherton appeared.

"Lunch, Charlie? All work is bad for the body. Exercise time."

At the Y, Don parked under the shade of the one maple, presented to me, "Two free passes for you for the Business Men's Club. You can use my locker."

What could I say but thank you.

On the way out, Don gave me an application for membership with, "You can always ride with me. I work out every noon but Thursday." Thursday is our staff lunch and meeting in the executive dining room.

"Good idea."
"Charlie, do it."

I didn't answer. Don drove with the windows closed, the air conditioning on high.

"You need a ride home I would be glad to. Really, no problem for me."

I chuckled, "Ellen would like that."

"You are feeling better."

"Thank you for the pass. I needed that swim."

"Anytime, Charlie. Anything you can recommend for my personal account?"

"Research is hot on Round Table. I bought 10,000 shares for my trust accounts."

Don smiled. "That Charlie, is a promise fulfilled. A recommendation from our research department pushed up the price for our clients."

I agreed. "I only work here."

Don smiled. "Somebody from research knows somebody at Round Table."

"How do you know?"

"The smart money is buying Round Table options."

"How do you know?"

Don sighed. "I only work here."

Don parked in #4. I stopped him when he went to open the door of the Mercedes. "Don, I took your briefcase. It was by mistake, of course, but I read through the DAME transactions. I shouldn't have. I am sorry."

"It's not that big a secret, Charlie."

"Don, do you realize that you could be the one that would get hung for insider trading?"

Don smiled. "Not to worry, Charlie. Not me. I only work for DAME. There is no way anyone could prove that it was my money in DAME Ltd. We Athertons don't have that kind of money."

"I thought, with the way you live . . ." I pointed to the car.

"Credit cards, Charlie, and Christmas gifts from Ann's folks."

I said, "Really. Whatever you say is okay by me. If that is what you want me to believe, I will." I had my hand on the door latch of the Mercedes. Don took my hand, held it.

"Charlie, let's say you never saw the DAME file. I think that would be better yet."

I smiled. "What file?"

"I knew you would understand. Take you home tonight?"

"Sure."

Don freed my hand. I opened the door of the Mercedes to the heat from baked-in-the-sun concrete, stepped out. Don was beside me. "Charlie, have you bought any RT for your personal account? For early retirement?"

"With what?"

"How would you like to have a couple thousand until."

"Until when?"

"Until you sell out for a large, long-term gain."

"I don't think Ellen would like that."

"You don't have to tell her. Charlie, what are friends for but to help each other? Charlie, you and Ellen are our friends."

I nodded and said, "Thank you."

Don was whistling our advertising jingle. "Now, not tomorrow. Now is the time to invest."

You Are Looking Good, George

As it was Saturday, George Harris stood at his shaving mirror that accentuated the creases that descended from each nostril to the corner of his mouth. Dr. Harris realized that he had to trim his eyebrows and scissor the hair from his nostrils. George Harris, a man so ritualized that every morning he weighed himself, had the same breakfast: a quartered orange, a half bowl of Grapenuts with skim milk; the same lunch: a green salad, half of a hard-boiled egg with the yolk removed and two packets of Rye Krisp, with honey if he weighed less than one hundred and seventy seven and without the honey if he weighed a half pound more. George Harris stared at his face.

On this pre-dawn Saturday, the red electronic numbers on the scale had presented 179, not a happy number with which to begin his weekend of cultural and dining activity.

At the mirror, George pulled at his wattle, contemplated his green eyes. No sense in getting a face lift. No sense getting Freda angry. Every day Freda's gray hair was more visible. Her arthritic hands and the stress of planning their forty-fifth wedding anniversary were all Freda could bear. To nurse George after his face lift was more than Freda would tolerate. She would say, if the subject came up, "George, I'm not going to take care of you. I do more than enough in this family."

George Harris, his face shaved, the aberrant gray hairs of his moustache trimmed to above his full lips, applied the after-shave lotion followed with the natural-tone face powder sprinkled on his left hand and then spread onto his nose and forehead. George Harris rinsed his double-edge Gillette razor clean, placed it horizontally on the second shelf of the medicine cabinet, took a last look at his still smooth face in the mirror.

There they were again as in his dream. Hereford steers, lean with thin rumps standing at the feed lot troughs eating their grain mixture, their tails stained with blood-tinged mucoid diarrhea. The owner is quite desperate. "Dr. Harris, I can't afford the weight loss. You are the third veterinarian I have called. There has been no response to any of the drugs that have been prescribed. Do you realize how much weight these steers have lost?"

"I'll get my microscope. Give me a moment to do a fecal examination. . . . Coccidia. Just as I thought. Add this powder to the drinking water for two weeks. By the end of the week the steers will all be back on feed, gaining weight again."

Why the dream? Why not? Dreams don't mean anything. Just garbage in the head.

"George. George!" It was Freda. "I heard you walking around. What time was that?"
"About three."
"What was the matter?"
"Nothing."
"You don't usually get up."
"I went right back to bed."
"No, you didn't."
It was pain in his groin that had aroused George Harris from his dream just as he was

rinsing the manure off his seamless rubber boots. After the self examination, George had reached a decision, "only a muscle spasm." That was after he had excised and discarded the sweat-producing fear of enlarged lymph nodes, "acute lymphoma; dead in six weeks."

George had felt the lump at three a.m. It wasn't until four a.m. that George was asleep again. At six-twenty, the lump was gone, lost, mixed among all names and ages and ailments of the animals that he had treated in his forty years as a veterinarian.

"George, Missy is coming in Sunday. I promised her you would take her to the zoo. George, your granddaughter is coming to see you."

"I'll take her out to the farm."

"George, you promised to take Missy to the zoo."

Animals in cages. What right do we have to put God's creatures on display? So that the children will recognize and understand. Understand? How can children understand the pain in the cow's eyes, the bellow of pain, the grunts and moans of birthing. That was what Dr. Harris remembered without effort. The dead and dying pigs of the last cholera epidemic, the spring calves with ringworm on their necks.

"I haven't forgotten."

"Why didn't you answer?"

"I'm coming, Freda! I'm coming."

Freda had prepared breakfast. "George, don't do too much today, watch your back. Take a day off. Enjoy. You can do the yard work on Monday."

What Freda means is, "George, you are getting old. No accidents now . . . Be careful, George."

"George, don't go out to the tree farm. Not unless David goes with you. Use your cane, George, don't go sliding down the hills. It rained yesterday, the road to the creek is slippery."

"When it's muddy I walk along the fence line."

"Not without David. You are not going to the farm on your own. Remember!"

Freda had stopped at remember—"remember what happened to Chuck Herring."

That was a bizarre accident. Chuck was using his post-mortem knife to cut out dandelions, like we did every spring at Kansas State. Much safer than spraying with pre-emergents. Dandelion Day was fifty years ago, before chemicals came into farming. Chuck Herring was digging dandelions. His back hurt, so he sits down, starts cutting out the broadleafs that are between his legs. How should I know how it happened. Chuck cuts into his femoral blood vessel, bleeds to death right there out on his lawn. That was as good a way to go as any of my other classmates had. Twenty-two of our class of seventy-one already dead. Chris Larson died the best. All alone in the sun, in his boat fishing off the coast of Fort Myers on a warm, pleasant, bright winter day in Florida.

"George, do you want some coffee? I made coffee. George, I made half decaf, half Colombian like you like."

"Thanks, Freda. That would be nice."

Through the sliding door of the dining room, George Harris saw the old white and red oaks.

"I should have gathered the acorns. The forester is looking for acorns for the southern Illinois reforestation project."

George sat at the head of the rosewood table, Freda beside him. Four times a year when the children come, Freda sat at the other end. Then David sat opposite Doris and Missy.

George Harris peeled the quartered orange with both hands, sucked up the pulp and the juice, spit the pits into his hand, returned the pits to the plate.

"George, why can't you drink orange juice like the rest of the world?"

George grinned. "I am utilizing fiber that would otherwise go to waste. Like a cow." He grinned again, reached for Freda's hand, kissed the top of her hand.

"George."

"Yes?"

"Nothing."

"With you it's never nothing. What is it?"

"I wasn't going to tell you until Tuesday."

"What?"

"Betty Hansen died. The funeral is Wednesday. Doris called, told me while you were shaving."

"Good coffee, Freda. I'll be there. I'll be at Hudson's on time. Just let me know what time. How old was Betty?"

"Seventy-four."

"That's pretty good for a diabetic."

"George, you shouldn't talk that way about the dead."

"You are right, Freda. I won't."

"Sure, until the next time. That's all you talk about, who died and how old they are."

"You know that's not all I talk about."

"No, you tell everyone how bad the price of timber is."

"Ten cents a board foot for oak is not very good."

"George, no one likes to hear about death and low timber prices."

"What would you I rather talk about? The weather?" George placed the bowls, plates, coffee pot on the plastic tray and walked off into the kitchen.

"George, please don't talk to me as you leave the room. I can't hear what you are saying."

Freda won't admit to her hearing loss. She can't hear a thing unless they are face to face.

"George, should I call Ethel, tell her Betty died?"

"If you like, Freda. Whatever you like."

"Betty was your friend too."

"Poor planning."

"What did you say?"

"I said, poor planning. Every death is poor planning; so much left undone."

"What can we do about that?"

"I'm trying, Freda."

George sat in his green velour Lazyboy, easy in-easy out, the ideal chair for a seventy-year-old with an arthritic back, read the Saturday morning *Blaze*. The early spring sun rose, angled onto the leg rest, warmed George Harris. Harris had discarded without ever opening the classified section and the spring automotive special. He glanced at the religious page; tourists had returned to Jerusalem. He read the obituaries to Freda who sat in the dining room doing the crossword.

"Betty Hansen was only seventy-two. She looked awful the last time we saw her."

"It's the diabetes, George."

"Their youngest, James, is in Burlington."

"What is he doing there?"

"Doesn't say. Last I heard he was working on a newspaper."

"In Burlington what kind of paper would that be?"

"The funeral is Wednesday at eleven at the Congregational Church. Reverend Winston preaches a good eulogy."

"George, I want to go to the cemetery."

"Whatever you like, Freda."

"Do you want to go?"

"I didn't say I didn't."

"You didn't say you did."

George rose slowly, went into the garage, sat down to put on his faded green air force coveralls. The coveralls were exactly three inches too long, the three inches that spinal stenosis and scoliosis had taken from him.

The grass was greening. The forsythia presented its yellow blossoms. The oaks were in leaf. The viburnum was old, dry, broken, should be cut out, replaced. David would help.

David was busy teaching literature to last chancers at the Junior College, and then he had to help Doris with Missy. Doris should give up her job at the bank, at least cut back. Spend more time with Missy. Missy had called on Friday. "Grandpa? You won't forget, I'm coming for Sunday dinner with you and Grandma."

Missy was going to be twelve. She no longer asked, "Grandpa can we go to your office." Missy understood the veterinary office had been sold. Grandpa no longer practiced. Grandpa was no longer Missy's "best veterinarian in the county."

"Where is your mother, Missy?"

"Mama is playing tennis."

"Who is with you?"

Friday afternoon was David's in-office counseling hours. Missy says, "Papa, I'm old enough to be alone."

"What are you doing?"

"Watching television, Grandpa."

When I was Missy's age, George remembers, I read Jack London's *White Fang, Dog of the North*.

George shoveled the ash and compost from his burn pit into the wheelbarrow, added the handfuls of shady mix grass seed. The mole runs signaled spring. Moles have to dig to get at the white grubs. That's what moles eat, grubs.

"George, you work so hard in that yard. Why don't you poison the moles? Feed them poison pellets, save your back."

"I will Freda, I will."

"You said that last year!"

George Harris trod on each mole run, covered the runs with the grass soil mixture. Each year the moles advanced their trenches, conquered more western yard. Two years ago, George Harris had spread "Microbial," a soil doctor's genetically engineered grub killer, guaranteed to control moles without soil contamination like pesticides did.

He'd tried, and the moles conquered more yard. "Moles have their rights too," he'd told Freda.

"Yes, George, they have a right to eat white grubs, but you have the right to kill them with poison peanuts."

With just a flick of the wrist, so skillfully, George Harris reseeded the wasteland of the trench warfare.

"So that the moles will have more to eat!" Freda said.

"Freda, if I do the yard work, if I am willing to do my annual lawn reconstruction, it's not anyone's affair! Not yours, not Doris's."

Three wheelbarrow loads, twelve pounds of shady lawn mix dispersed, George walked bent, waddled. Both of his hips pained in spite of the three coated aspirin swallowed at dawn. George rinsed the dirt from the spade, the wheelbarrow, removed his coveralls. All returned to their pegs in the garage. George came into the kitchen through the side door. Freda had the cinnamon apple cake she made when Missy came to dinner out of the oven.

"Freda, I am going to the Y."

"Why don't you shower at home?"

"I thought I would get into the Jacuzzi."

"I told you not to overdo."

"How about a little taste?"

Freda cut only the smallest square from the corner for George.

"Can I have another piece?"

"Wait till Sunday. Everything takes me so long. Takes me forever to make a cake."

Freda was at the sink counter, her back to George.

"We are getting older, Freda." This, so quietly Freda could not hear.

Freda had wrapped the cake in foil. She turned. "George, I want to go to the cemetery. Don't go making any other plans for Wednesday afternoon."

George drove east through the Highland shopping district. The fading, faded, miracle mile. Thirty years since Sears came in. Eleven years since Sears left for the mall. The Sears store was empty. For sale. The automotive department was still there. "Buy two get your third tire free. Save thirty-three percent." There had been an apple orchard where Sears had decided to build a mega store.

Not a tree remained on the miracle mile, no trees on the one-way that feeds into Highland. All gone thirty years ago, all victims of Dutch elm disease. Why didn't the mayor set aside funds for replanting? Why? Nothing is forever, George. You built your clinic forty-one years ago, you practiced there for forty years. Everything is finite, you know that. Dr. Harris, we are all a biological clock waiting to run out. The only question is when.

Dr. Harris parked his Lincoln in the handicapped, placed the wheelchair emblem on the dashboard. He swung out slowly, walked even more slowly, waved at the secretary.

"Dr. Harris, you are looking good."

George heard but did not answer. At the locker control, a new black kid working his way through junior college said, "Your card, please."

"George Harris, my card is hanging there."

George pointed to the nail above the key slots. His key in hand, George opened the door to the Fitness Club. MTV video was on. All that sex, a blond, bare-chested, long-haired bisexual or homosexual was singing, "I Want it All, I Want it Now!" It wasn't singing, it was more a chant, a prayer. Just the two lines. "I want it all, I want it now," repeated, "I want it all, I want it all." The video faded into a commercial for lace bras.

"He'll be lucky to get average earnings," George told Dr. Ralph Chester, one of the younger members, who sat in the club lounge reading the Chicago *Tribune*.

"Showing your age, George. That's your generation gap showing. Saying unkind things about today's children."

"How do you know so much about that generation?" George pointed to the MTV. Another barefoot, black leather, bare-chested shaker, microphone in hand, had appeared.

"Learned it all at the prison. Twenty-two years a physician at the county jail."

"How do you stand it?"

"Somebody has to do it."

George sat to undress, made it into the steam room, pulled himself into the Jacuzzi. When he headed to the shower, Ralph was there.

"Going swimming?"

"I swam twenty-two minutes on Monday, Thursday and Friday."

"Best thing for your back."

"You convinced me. I'll give it twenty minutes. Freda is waiting lunch."

They swam in adjoining lanes, side by side. Crawl, breast stroke, back stroke, crawl, breast stroke, back stroke. The water parted, became swirls around George's head and shoulder and then reformed into the still waters to reflect gray-green from the ceramic tile of the pool floor.

George and Ralph showered, George stood to put on his trousers.

"You are looking good, George. You looked real good in the pool."

"Feeling good, Ralph. Feeling real good."

So the Weeks Go

By four-thirty the news boy, or his mother, had ridden their bicycle east on Oak Street and put the Rockville *Sentinel* through the mail slot of the Metz house. At four forty-five, "old Doc Metz," newspaper under his arm, unfolded the plastic and aluminum rocker, placed it in the shade of the oak that guarded the two-story frame home that in 1962 Annie Metz had painted earth-tone brown. George Metz sat and muttered, "Perot is a quitter!" When the going got tough, Perot quit. He made a bundle doing it, but he quit. GM went back to Texas.

Jason Lovell, nine, corrugated box in hand, his brother, Ron, six, beside him, walked up the drive. "Grandpa says you would look at the bird for me."

"He did, did he? How is Grandpa?"

"Grandpa is fine. He said you would look at the bird."

Dr. Metz opened the lid; the black fledgling fluttered.

Jason pointed. "See, he can't fly."

"True . . ." Dr. Metz held the blackbird, this spring's hatch, in his left hand, spread the right wing, transferred the bird into his right hand, spread the left wing. "Nothing broken, Jason, just a muscle pulled from his chest wall. You take him home, Jason, give him some of your dog's food and he should get better and just fly away."

"Grandpa said you would know what to do."

George Metz grinned. "What else does Grandpa tell you about me?"

"He says you and he were in the Army together."

"Only in the reserve after the war."

"My mama says you are the best white neighbors on the street."

George muttered, "Pretty soon I'll be the only one. You come back, come back tomorrow about four. We'll shoot some baskets."

"Thanks!"

"See you kids tomorrow."

Anne Metz, in blue jeans and a yellow sweatshirt, "Iowa" in black across her chest, opened the door as the two boys left. She had heard George's invitation through her open kitchen window. "Don't you go breaking your back bending down to pick up the basketball," she said. "Bud Lovell could put up a backboard. Jason doesn't have to come down here—bounce, bounce, it drives me crazy!"

Anne unfolded the straight back lawn chair, picked out the Local and Entertainment sections of the *Sentinel*.

"The fireworks are scheduled for Friday night. Whoever heard of celebrating July Fourth on July third?"

"There will be fireworks at the ball park after the game."

"Who told you?"

"Read it yesterday."

"What did Jason want?"

"He found a fledgling blackbird that couldn't fly. Bud sent him over."

"Sure, for free Bud sends Jason. When you were running the veterinary clinic, Bud never brought their dog to you!"

"It's a long drive to our clinic."

"What are old friends for?"

"Not friends, Anne. Neighbors."

Anne put down the newspaper, looked across the street at the empty Myers house, a two-story colonial with the most perfectly tended lawn. Rick Myers had sat for hours, feet spread, butcher knife in hand, excising the broadleafs by their roots. To mark the entrance to his drive, Rick had planted the knee-high ceramic planters with variegated red and rose impatiens. Pots of ferns hung from the ceiling of the front porch.

"Rick Myers left the new owners a beautiful lawn," Anne said. "Look at yours, browning out at the curb."

"I'm not going to water. I put in fifty-four pounds of shady lawn mix. Let God provide the rain."

"I am not going to tell your son that you are not using the sprinkler system he bought for you. Fred went to a lot of trouble to put all those easy-on and -off plastic gadgets on the faucets."

"It's a wonderful idea."

"Why don't you use it? Look at your lawn; look at Rick's. Yours is getting browned out. . . . You met Jason's new dad yet?"

"No—I see him in the mornings. He's getting into his Mercedes when I walk to services."

"He ever speak to you?"

"No. Why should he?"

"You speak to everyone."

George rose and folded the rocker. "Come. I'll help you set the table."

"Supper won't be ready for a half hour."

Anne folded the lawn chair, stacked it beside the rocker, under the overhang, beside the front door.

The Metzes sat at the rosewood dining table. George sat the far head of the table, Anne to his right. They could watch television as they ate. The portable phone was at Anne's right. The sound zapper to mute the TV was at Dr. Metz's left.

"When are the new folks moving into the Myers house?"

"Over the weekend, no doubt. Rick didn't say."

"Say anything about them?"

"Only that they had three children."

"What does he do? He has to do something to afford that house."

"She is a teacher."

"Rick say anything before he left?"

"Said he got every penny he asked for."

"That's not too bad. Not in this economy. I haven't heard of anyone getting their asking price for their home."

For the Metzes, Wednesday was like Tuesday. That is, until 7:30 when they walked two blocks west and turned right to the Jewish Center to join the Rabbi's adult education class. In the upholstered arm chair in the hum of the air-conditioned library, George dozed in the dreamless after-dinner sleep of the young-old. Anne poked George once. He opened his eyes.

"I heard what the Rabbi said. 'Deeds of loving kindness,' that's where it's at."

"You slept through most of the lecture!"

"I heard every word."

Thursday was like the other Thursdays. The Metzes heard *Mystery* and read at the same time: George, *The New York Times*, Anne, Nadine Gardiner short stories that would be discussed at her Tuesday morning book club.

At five on Friday afternoon, Jason appeared without Ron, stood in front of Dr. Metz. Dr. Metz rocked once, twice, propelled himself up. "One game of 'horse,' that's all."

Jason said nothing. Dr. Metz opened the garage door, returned with the basketball. "First shot is yours, Jason."

They played, George Metz careful to bend his knees as he reached for the bouncing ball, aware of the back pain of his spinal stenosis.

"Beat you again, Jason. Come back next Friday, we'll try it again."

Anne came out, sat down, began to read the *Sentinel*. "You didn't play that much with Fred."

"Too busy, always too busy. Country calls in the morning. Office hours. I took an afternoon off now and then. Now that I have the time, Fred is too busy." George sighed, muttered, "From generation to generation, nothing changes."

In River Park Friday evening, the Metzes strolled with the families of Rockville, listened to the cowboy's lament come from the Hitching Post Bar as they ate their funnel cakes, waited for the fireworks. At dusk, bouquets of red, yellow and green rose from the barge to fall into the Mississippi where the sparks frightened the white-bread mallards.

Saturday afternoon on the levee, in the shade of the maples, they rocked in their lawn chairs as they listened to "whites" play and sing "black man's blues."

Sunday was bright, clear, cloudless. The Metzes slept later, were not up until 7:00 a.m. Anne did the laundry, George put up the flag, raised the clearance on the Lawn Boy mower to four, mowed the front yard only, raked the oak leaves from the pea gravel border that girdled the oaks, swept this week's oak twigs from the drive.

Anne stuck her head out the door as George, aluminum bushel basket full of debris in his hands, came into the garage to replace the bamboo rake. "You are not going to burn today!"

"Why not?"

"First of all, it's too dry. Then it's Sunday. Folks are home today, I don't want you stinking up the neighborhood."

"Oak limbs and leaves don't stink!"

"No burning!"

"No burning."

"Sit down, rest, read your paper."

George sat. Read, "With decline in industrial jobs, Rockville suffers ten percent loss of population," "average incomes in Rockville reduced by fourteen percent," "more black children to live in poverty."

The moving truck, followed by a Ford van, a four-door Toyota, a Chevrolet station wagon, parked on the street. From the entourage came a white man, twenty, twenty-two, in a T-shirt that permitted him to present his pectorals; two middle-aged black men, a bit stooped in blue coveralls; a man in his forties, tall, curly-headed, lighter colored than mulatto tan; a woman of the same age and hue, three children of similar color; a boy about eighteen or so, a girl a bit older, and four youngsters about the age of Jason, perhaps a year older. A smaller moving van with two shirtless whites drove up, parked. All carried from the van into the Myers house chairs, rugs, end tables, bookcases, furniture. Anne, who had witnessed from the kitchen window, came out.

"Must be the new folks moving in."

"Must be," said George.

"There are whites going in and out. Which are the new owners?"

George laughed, "I say the blacks. Bad times make for economic opportunities."

Anne returned to her laundry. George to his newspaper. The trucks drove off as Anne announced, "Lunch is ready. I made a coffee cake. I think I'll take a piece across the street."

"Let them get settled in."

"The man is outside now. Is he busy?"

"Putting a lawn mower into the garage. It's a John Deere."

"Much newer than yours, George."

"Cost twice what our Lawn Boy did."

"George, that was fifteen years ago. You coming with me, George?"

Anne led, the coffee cake in extended hand, George well behind her. Anne offered the cake and a hand shake. "I'm Anne Metz, my husband George."

The man did not accept the cake and did not meet her proffered hand. "I'll get my wife."

The woman came forward with a smile and a hand shake. "1 am Jane DuBois, my husband Charles. I'll never get our kids out here. They are all over the house."

"I thought you might like this."

"It's very thoughtful of you, Mrs. Metz."

"Call me Anne."

George turned to Charles. "You have a beautiful lawn there. I don't know how Rick Myers found all that time to devote to growing grass."

"I don't do yard work."

"What Charles means is with Junior home this year, Junior just graduated from St. Joseph's High School, Junior has to do the yard work."

Anne smiled "So nice to meet you, if we can help in any way—please."

The Metzes turned to go. Jane DuBois called out, "Thank you for the cake."

In the house George stood at the kitchen window, sighed, "There goes Rick Myers's lawn."

"Your lawn isn't so hot, my friend."

Monday was the third day of the July Fourth holiday. The hour for morning prayers at B'nai Jacob, western Illinois' only Jewish congregation, had been adjusted accordingly, moved from 6:50 to 8:00 a.m.

On his walk home after services, George Metz stopped at the Lovell split-level. Bud Lovell was astride the only riding mower on Oak Street. George waved, Bud smiled, waved back. George did not go on. Bud pulled up, put the motor on idle. "How's it going, George? Playing any golf?"

"Not with my hip. How did Jason's bird do?"

"Must have gotten better. The bird flew away."

"Jason didn't come by on Friday."

"Helen took him and Ron swimming."

"Nice lawn you got there, Bud. Better than mine."

"Can't anyone grow grass under oak trees. Not even you, George. You do pretty good for an old man."

"Thanks, Bud. Say Bud, you know the DuBois family that moved into the Myers house?"

"Met them once at a King Center doing."

"In this town, I thought you would know them."

"I know most all the Afro-Americans in Rockville, but they are not black like us. They are Catholic Creoles from Louisiana."

The moment George came in the door he transmitted. "The DuBoises are not black—they are Creole."

"They look black to me. George, sit down have your breakfast. The coffee is getting cold."

George went off to wash his hands, muttered, "*Es is nisht ameleke zeiten.*" Things aren't as they were.

"George, don't talk to me from the bathroom. I can't hear you. What did you say?"

"I said, times are changing on Oak Street!"

"What else is new, George?" And without waiting for George to answer, "George, pour the coffee. George, I am hungry!"

How Are You Going To Keep Them Down on the Farm

We were nine at our Sanibel condo for our class reunion dinner of Milly's apricot chicken, squash and Chenin Blanc. We were to have been ten but Rosemary Ingram had been down and up and down, with cough and fever. She was recovering slowly, very slowly, so Ralph Ingram came alone. With Rosemary it's been last year she fell and broke her ankle, with that she got arthritis, with the arthritis came the rehab exercises. It has been two years since Rosemary has been able to walk the beach, which is why the Ingrams came to Sanibel in the first place.

Ralph left early. "I don't like to leave Mary all alone. She forgets to take her antibiotics. Thanks for getting me the pills."

Mary had run out of antibiotics to complete her ten days on Ampicillin. All I did was call Eckerd Drugs. "This Dr. Benjamin Klein. Please prepare twelve Ampicillin, 500 mg., for Rosemary Ingram."

The dinner was on the Thursday before the Saturday on which we started home to Rockville via our annual visit to the cousins and aunts on the East Coast of Florida. We then drive west to Natchez, Mississippi to view the antebellum homes and to Vicksburg to visit the battlefield. That diversion to family and Civil War history made it ten days before we were back in western Illinois.

Our first week home is the usual frustrating review of business during the ten weeks of our vacation. All I heard was, "Sorry, Ben, nothing will be resolved until May."

It was about the middle of March that Ralph Ingram called my office. "Ben, what are you doing on Thursday?"

"Thursday I'm taking my blood pressure to the doctor."

"How about Friday?"

"What about Friday?"

"Drive down to see me. I need you."

"On Friday . . . lunch."

Ralph and Rosemary live about sixty miles south of us. The Ingrams drive north or we drive south . . . or we meet at Jumer's in Galesburg for a before-sunset dinner, before the jazz trio comes on because, "Ben, I want to talk, not listen to music."

I tell Milly, "I'm going to drive down Friday to have lunch with Ralph."

"Ralph say what he wanted?"

"No doubt he wants to show me a new sow that he bought in Texas."

"Don't go breathing that hog dander."

It was this allergy to swine that gave me asthma and early retirement. Ralph is still working mornings. His son Chris is doing more and more of the hands-on veterinary work, but when it comes to blood lines and nutrition I hope that Chris is letting Ralph do it. Ralph has a proven record of success. For forty years Ingram farms are supplying prize-winning hybrid boars to America's finest hog farms. Most of our classmates have done well. It's just that Ralph has done it better.

The drive south to Ralph's office is down 67, a two-lane that goes over the Mississippi bluff through the Edwards River Valley bottom and on to the flat Muscatine loam prairie that on a good year makes 160 bushels of corn to the acre and surplus for the Department of Agriculture to dispose of with export credits.

Last week's winter rains have melted the gray grimy snow that filled the roadside ditches since November. This morning the road is kept wet by the snow fluffs that melt as they hit the pavement. The audio system of the Lincoln wraps me in Vivaldi.

The first time Milly and I went south on 67 through Missouri to Mississippi was the Christmas week of 1948. The Klein family in a new blue two-door Ford, off for their first winter vacation. Two years out of veterinary school, an employee of the State of Illinois eradicating tuberculosis from western Illinois cattle, with a per diem and mileage sufficient to support a week at the Grand Hotel Biloxi and a new car.

George was three, a blond kid in short pants running across the terrazzo of the Grand Hotel's silent public rooms—"Mommie, Mommie!"

George in California—redundant, fired, laid off, an attorney who wanted to do big deals producing movies. "Dad, you work too hard. Seven days a week, nights. Veterinary medicine is not for me." George—running, running. His made-in-Poland documentary still without a distributor. George's last movie got rave reviews. "George Klein shows the Afro-American middle class as it is." First movie without stereotypes. George Klein. A big man on the black TV talk shows.

The Japanese bought the film company; told George's boss, "Cut back." His boss said, "George, your films made no profits. Sorry, George, no job."

The only improvement in forty years on 67 is that the shoulders are wider. South on 67 to test the beef and dairy cattle for tuberculosis; inject the tuberculin in the tail fold on Monday morning; back on Thursday to palpate the injection site. No swelling, no TB. Swell, a large "T," branded on the left jaw. "The state will give you a fair price for your tubercular cow, but she most go to market in ten days."

Just passed the county line road. That was the end of my district. Farming has all changed. No plowing, no disking, no harrowing. No topsoil loss. Now it's all minimum tillage.

On the early spring days when the farmers were in the fields, it wasn't easy to get them to stop their tractors, bring their cattle into the barns for the testing program.

The wind was from the west. The sky was the total gray that sent Midwesterners to the Florida and Arizona sun.

Eleven fifteen. Milly would be leaving to do lunch with Billy Simpson. "Benny, why do we have dinner with the Simpsons and you just sit there not saying a word? It's because they're my friends, that's why. You just sit there not paying any attention to what George Simpson was saying."

"All George Simpson wants to talk about is his brilliant son, William. 'William was made partner in his law firm.' 'William is making a speech in Berlin.'"

Three hundred feet down the lane to the Ingram home, Ralph and Mary's home, a red roman brick three-bedroom, two-bath built in 1958 on six hundred forty acres of the best corn ground in western Illinois. Ralph's office was added to the farrowing house at the time he erected the "Harvestore." The farm buildings are painted Midwest barn red. The white sign, large enough to be read from the highway: "Ingram Farms – Champion Boars."

Mary heard my car, came to the door. Mary is a blonde, every hair like she just came out of her eleven o'clock on Thursdays from Raymond, the best haircut in town. Mary is standing, leaning on a tripod cane. Her hand that holds the cane is protected by a bicycle rider's glove.

"Okay, tell me what happened to your hand."

"Nothing. Just my arthritis."

I must have been staring at the cane, the glove.

"Don't say it, Ben. I look like an old lady. I saw myself this morning when I was sitting down to put on my old lady shoes."

"We aren't any of us getting younger."

"You and Milly look good. Come in. I'm sure Ralph saw your car. He'll be in for lunch."

"You don't have to cook. We could go out."

"No trouble at all. That's about all I can do anymore."

Ralph came in. Took off his coveralls.

"How's Milly?"

"Good."

"Anything new?"

"Same old thing. Started a split-level spec house. We are going to undersell the market."

"How are things at the clinic?"

"Young vets. New ideas. Last week they ran an ad offering ten percent off on dog food. I don't know how we made a living before we learned about marketing."

"You forget, Benny, if we had done all that well, you wouldn't be building single-family homes and I wouldn't be raising hog."

"You are right, Ralph."

Lunch on the farm is dinner or supper in Rockville. Broiled chicken, a cucumber salad, homemade brown bread, cherry jam and tea.

"Look at us, Ben. You don't eat pork. We don't eat pork. Pork consumption is down and it's never been a more profitable time to raise pork. The price of feed is low. Slaughter prices are good."

I try comfort. "In farming, if it's not the weather, it's the prices."

"We do well enough." And Ralph grinned.

After lunch, Mary is in the kitchen stacking the dishwasher. I ask Ralph, "How is Mary doing?"

"Mary is just not trying hard enough to get herself to go out. Stays in, watches television, reads, naps. She should get out more. I talk to Mary about making improvements, making changes in the farm set-up. All I get is, 'Ralph, we don't need it. It's good enough.' Ben, it's not good enough if I am ever going to quit. We have to make changes. Let's face it, I need someone to come in and take over running the hog operation."

"What about Chris?"

"He has enough to do with the country practice."

"Are you sure?"

"Every Sunday, when he comes to dinner, I ask him. Chris is just not interested in raising hogs. That is, raising hogs and running the large animal practice, too."

"Mary and you did it."

"We had no choice."

Mary comes back into the living room, tucks her red sweatsuit trouser, places her ankle on the foot stool. "Ralph tell you what he wants to do?"

"Not yet."

"That's why you called Ben."

"We have a neighbor girl . . ."

"She is not a girl anymore, Ralph."

"How old is Fran?"

"Thirty-four, thirty-five."

"Fran went to vet school, got married, has two children."

". . . and no husband," adds Mary.

"She wants a job close to home so that her mother can help her with the children. Mary, how old are Fran's girls?"

"About ten and six."

"Fran was raised on a hog farm."

"You don't know anything about her veterinary capabilities?"

"We know her family. Fran would be willing to join our practice. Maybe help Chris develop the small animal work. And best of all, she's willing to take over the breeding operation if we build her a place to live."

"I don't like it, Ralph. Why did Fran walk out on her husband? If she walks away from obligations, that's not for us."

"Do you know that?"

"Her mother told me."

"Maybe he was no good. Ben, you know how long we have been looking."

"Don't say it, Ralph. Don't say we are running out of time. We're lucky we have Chris to take over the practice. We can always sell the hog operation with the farm."

"That's not what we worked for."

"We will get paid for it."

That's when Ralph gets up, looks at his watch. "Come on, Ben. Let's go out to the office. I have the house plans there. Dr. Erickson will be coming by at one. I wanted you to meet her."

"Don't be inviting Fran Erickson over for coffee. I'm not entertaining this afternoon."

"Dr. Francine Erickson . . . Dr. Ben Klein. Ben and I went to school together."

Francine was Rosemary in 1946 on the steps of the TriDelt house. Not exactly, but close enough to bring comparisons. Francine was taller, broader in the shoulders. Her blond hair was straight. Rosemary had a smile and bangs like Mamie Eisenhower.

Francine Erickson extended her hand. "Heard so much about you, Dr. Klein."

The blueprints spread over the top of the office desk. Ralph sat at the end of the desk, away from the computer. I sat beside him. Dr. Francine Erickson took off her raincoat. She was wearing a denim dress, thirty-six-inch pearls, a gold Victorian bracelet, about a two-carat diamond and gold wedding band . . . on her right hand. She sat down opposite us.

Ralph pointed to the blueprints. "Simplest design the lumber yard had. Two bedroom, two bath, living room, kitchen."

Francine rose. Her perfume was noticeable.

"The house can be pre-cut in Cambridge, put up in two or three weeks," Ralph said. "That is after the basement is dug."

Francine continued her examination without a smile, said nothing.

I asked, "Are you living with your folks?"

"We came back September so that the girls could go to school. It would really be better if we had a place of our own."

"Have you been practicing?"

There was the first smile. "No . . . living on my divorce settlement."

To turn the blueprint to page two, Francine leaned forward toward Ralph. Ralph looked at her cleavage and a brassiere that was a vain effort at containment. Her face was out of a Lovis Corinth print of a satyr standing behind a maiden, with both his hands on her bared breasts. That was the etching Milly made me sell.

"What have you been doing since you graduated?" I asked.

"Mostly small animal work."

"Where?"

"In the north Chicago suburbs. . . . Another bedroom would be nice."

Francine was positive about that.

Ralph didn't agree or disagree, so I said, "So good to have met you." With that I reached for Francine's coat, held it while she fixed her silk scarf around her neck. Francine drove off in a white Volvo.

"Well, Ben. What do you make of Francine Erickson?"

"She has been to the big city, Ralph. Do you think she will stay on the farm?"

"I never thought of that, Ben."

"I didn't either, until I had an associate like Francine. That was when I began the building company. I thought I needed someone to take over the clinic."

"What happened?"

"She fell in love with a man . . . went off with him to Alaska."

Ralph and I went back to the house. Mary had made coffee, laid out cookies on the kitchen table. She said, "So what's your decision, Dr. Ingram?"

"What do you think, Ben?"

"You want me to answer?"

"I asked you down."

"I wouldn't want to be dependent on Francine Erickson."

"Okay, I'll tell her no. I wasn't so crazy about her either. It's just that she came to me and asked for a job."

Ralph walked out to the car with me. The wind had died, the highway was dry.

"I forgot to thank Mary for lunch," I said. "Please thank her for me. I enjoyed getting back to the farm."

Ralph grinned. "That Francine looks like a lot of woman."

"More woman than you or I need."

"Not more than we want." And Ralph grinned again.

"Before you buy, you have to consider the cost-benefit ratio." With that and a wave, I drove home to the music of Aaron Copeland. I called Milly from my office.

HOW ARE YOU GOING TO KEEP THEM DOWN ON THE FARM

"What did Ralph want?"
"Wanted to build a pre-cut, two bedroom, two bath."
"What did you tell him?"
"I told him to decide for himself."

Falling Falling

Fully aware of the medical injunction *He who treats himself has a fool for a doctor*, Bernard Sturman, Chief of Neurology at the University Clinic, was concerned about his failure to successfully treat his own "falling syndrome." He kept his deficiencies in the diagnostic process secreted from himself, untold to his colleagues and overly simplified for his wife, Janet.

"I tripped, that's all. My falling was an accident."

For himself, Dr. Sturman had considered his falling syndrome as a progressive loss of nerve conduction to both legs. He had set aside his winter vacation on Sanibel from December 15th to January 13th to deal with his disease, to write a letter to the editor of *Lancet*, the British medical journal, in the hope that other clinicians who may have seen a similar condition would report their findings and observations to him.

"Dear Editor: December 27, 1991

This past year at a reunion of prisoners of war held in Germany in Stalag 1014, three of us in casual conversation reported falling. As the only neurologist there, I was particularly intrigued. I quote: 'As I look back, I believe the first symptoms appeared some six or eight years ago with pain and spasm in my legs. It is only recently, the past two to four years, the pain is severe enough to wake me.' Two other ex-prisoners also complained of leg weakness, inability to rise from the sitting position without the help of arms, and falling. 'My legs went soft, there I was on my side.' No fractures due to falling were reported to me.

I do recall that in 1944 there was a large British contingent in Stalag 1014. If the 'Falling Syndrome' has been seen in your practice would you please write to me.

Sincerely, B. Sturman M.D.
University Clinic, Rockville, IL
Department of Neurology."

Finished with the letter, Bernard Sturman returned to his year-end report to the Valley Medical Association. As chairman of the Impaired Physicians Committee, he reported six licenses to practice were revoked: three for drug abuse, one for Medicare fraud, one for kissing vulva—which description Dr. Sturman deleted and replaced with "unprofessional relationship with a patient"—and one for child molestation. This description he also deleted and put a "2" in front of "unprofessional relationship with a patient."

Janet Sturman came onto the porch where Bernard sat. "What time did you get up?"
"As usual."
"You were up during the night."
"I had to wire myself. I had to put on the TENS unit."
"Your legs again."

"Still."

"Why don't you take the pills Jack Curran prescribed for you?"

"They make me stupid."

"Bernie, we are here on vacation. You don't have to get up at 5:30 and start working. You should be resting more."

"There will be plenty of resting when I retire."

"That's what this vacation is for. It's to get us ready for retirement."

"Time enough for that in sixteen months."

Bernard pushed himself up from the chair, put his arms around Janet. "I still have sixteen months of work. I don't want Jack Curran to come into the lunch room . . . you know Jack . . . and announce 'Bernie hasn't been holding up his share, not since he's been going down to his Florida cottage.'"

"You're right, Bernie. It's only sixteen more months."

"It's tomorrow, Janet."

The rose red sun penetrated the morning haze, dried the dew from the porch screen, reflected from the white sand of the low-tide beach, shimmered on the still gray Gulf. The first walkers were now visible silhouetted against the hanging haze. The sun rose through the thinned clouds to backlight the walkers.

Janet in a gray sweatsuit drank her morning coffee, poured Wheat Chex into two bowls, added skim milk. "Bernie, you could stay in bed, try to fall asleep again. You don't have to get up."

"Six hours' sleep is enough."

"Everybody we know naps in the afternoon."

"Reversion to infantile sleeping rhythms. That's what that is."

"Bernie, do you have to be so damned scientific?"

Bernie laughed. "Our speech is determined by our education."

"Bernie, when are you going to quit lecturing?"

"In sixteen months, Janet. That should please you." With that, Bernie Sturman rose, shut his writing tablet into his briefcase.

"Wheat Chex and skim milk okay?"

"Fine."

"Don't forget to take your pills."

"One for my hypertension, and one for my arthritis. Poison, that's all they are. Don't do a damn bit of good."

"You know better than that. Don't talk like that when Jack Curran comes."

"I know Jack cares about me."

"He insisted you start treating your high blood pressure."

"The pill makes me cough."

"If I am willing to listen to you cough, you take it."

"Sacrifices . . . that's all marriage is. A series of sacrifices."

"What did you give up, Dr. Sturman. Living in a back one-bedroom by yourself?"

"Eating sandwiches. I loved eating my own cooking."

"You looked it, too."

"We were all thinner then." Bernie looked at Janet. He thought: We are the same age, but Janet looks ten years younger than "old Dr. Sturman." But then all of Janet's sisters looked younger than the Sturmans. The prison camp didn't help your good looks, Bernie. The prison camp didn't help anything. It *did*, Bernie. It taught you patience and prayer and death. That's what turned you to medicine, Dr. Sturman. War and death. Medicine is the antidote. Preventive medicine, adequate nutrition, client information. No more tuberculosis, no more syphilis. You want to know about old times, go talk to Dr. Sturman. As him a question, he will give you a lecture.

"Bernie, the tide is out."

Dr. Sturman, in khaki shorts and a university shirt, sat to put on his Illinis jacket and baseball cap and beach slippers. Noted that his left ankle was swollen.

"You coming?" Janet was down the walk, down the four steps to the beach trail to the low-tide sandbar.

They walked, Janet as tall as he. Bernie inches shorter than when they married. Next year was their anniversary year, his compulsory retirement at seventy after forty years at the university; their fortieth wedding anniversary.

The sun reflected off the beach sand. The Sturmans walked east, Janet flinging her arms, flipping her wrists. He keeping in step with her. She stopped, picked up a shell.

"An olive shell."

"Very perfect."

The first green beach marker: one and a half miles to the lighthouse. The sand smooth, hard, darker where the incoming tide had already covered, soaked in, invaded to erode furrows, into which rivulets flowed back with the tide to rejoin the gulf waters. The Sturmans sloshed east through the tidal pool onto a still-dry sandbar. The sanderlings fled. The short-nose dowitchers rose, circled, settled behind them to poke for coquinas at the water line. The one white heron walked in the surf. At mile one, Bernie took off his Fighting Illini cap, sweats jacket, secured the arms over his belly.

"You tired, Bernie? Want to go back?"

"We've only done a half mile."

"It's another mile to the lighthouse."

In the last years both the Sturmans had gained weight. Not enough to impair their health, their weight well within the acceptable guidelines for the old-young in their sixty-four-and-over profile.

Jack Curran would tell him, "Bernie, try exercising more."

"Can't, Jack. The more I do, the worse my night leg pains."

"Try swimming."

Swimming kept the heart rate up, but it couldn't keep the weight down, as jogging had at first. Swimming made the nights almost tolerable. The pain was less severe than after jogging.

Bernie and Janet walked east past the white three-story, million-dollar "cottages" with purple Victorian moldings and too-small swimming pools. On the left, in front of the condos, were a field of sea oats and a neck-high cluster of sea grapes. To the right, the white lighthouse with Australian pines behind it hid San Marcos Bay and the causeway. As the Sturmans turned back, the tide gained the beach. To keep dry they now walked on the looser sand, roughened where sea shells lay buried. The morning sun had risen above the Sturmans. Bernie donned his baseball cap and pulled it down to shield his eyes.

"Janet, you should wear a cap to protect your eyes."

"My sunglasses do fine."
"The less light, the fewer cataracts."
"Lecture to the first-year medical students."
On the soft sand Janet walked ahead, Bernie a step or two behind. Bernie caught up as Janet picked up a turkey wing shell.
"Fine example."
"Thank you, Dr. Sturman."
"Bernard will do."
The cottage came into view. Janet cut across the beach grasses and vines toward the worn wooden steps. Bernie, behind her, snagged his left toe on a vine and his right knee gave way. As he fell, his body turned. He landed on his right shoulder, on his right hip. Nothing broken.
Janet had turned. "You want me to help you up?"
"I can make it." Dr. Sturman turned onto his chest, onto his knees, rose to his left leg and slowly onto his right. With the final heave he stood erect. Not fully erect, a bit bent forward but no more bent than before he had fallen.
"You all right, Bernie?"
"Fine. I tripped on a vine."
"You tell Jack what happened."

My night pains begin as tingles, then intensify to hot stabs to my thighs, to my calves. I went to bed at 10.30, awoke at 2:07 to distress so severe that the TENS Unit could not contain it. At 3:00 a.m., I took two Tylenol and four ounces of wine. I do believe white is better, not so much next-morning dead mouth. I fell asleep a little before four, slept until 6:20.
"That, Dr. Curran, is old age. Wake up tired, go to sleep tired."
"Bernie, I'm quite sure that if you had a good night's sleep you would have better days."
"Jack, I can't work and take those pills."
"Have you thought of early retirement, Bernie?"
"Sure, Jack." So Jack Curran can become head of the department.

Janet says, "You had best take a nap after lunch, Bernie."
"I know Jack is coming over about two to see me."
"That's what he said."
"He's in Naples visiting his mother-in-law."
"Don't be so cynical, Bernie."
"Why should Curran take an afternoon away from his tennis game to visit us?"
"Just to see you, Bernie."
"I know, he cares about me."
"You are his patient."
"I should have gone to the Mayo."
"Jack is a very competent physician. You have said so yourself."

The cottage, built eighteen years ago to face the Gulf, was by Florida standards if not aged, old. The two bedrooms were in the back. The entry path began at the sand parking lot behind the house, went up two steps, turned at right angles in front of the cottage and then turned back to the front door that opened into the living room, dining room, kitchen. "It's a two-bedroom, two-bath motel," is how Janet Sturman described the cottage to her book club in Rockville.

"Right on the beach," added Beth Curran. "Jack and I drove over from Naples last year. Imagine having the only cottage on four hundred feet of Gulf beach. Anytime Bernie decides to sell, there will be four condo developers bidding to buy the cottage."

"We would never sell. That's where Bernie and I are going to spend our winters. Bernie is planning to write a medical history of psychosomatic illness."

When Janet left to make the tea, Beth whispered to the faculty wives, "Jack says Bernie hasn't written more than a letter in two years." All nodded. "We know . . . we know."

Jack Curran, jogger-thin, tennis-tanned, drove up in a leased LeBaron convertible with the top down. Kissed Janet on her cheek.

"Bernie is sleeping. I'll get him up. We thought you would be a bit later."

"Bernie's asleep? I'm glad. It will give us a chance to talk."

Janet, agitated. "We have talked enough."

"I couldn't, Janet. Not to Bernie."

"You should have when I first told you a year ago. When I found the syringes in the garbage."

"We had to have proof."

"You wanted me to break the bathroom door when Bernie is injecting himself. Take the vials from his medical bag. I couldn't do that. What did you do, Jack, when I told you Bernie needs your help?"

"Bernie is a friend."

"Say it, Jack. Bernie is a member of the club, honored ex-president of the medical society."

"Don't get bitter, Janet. I came here on my vacation day."

"For this I will always be thankful. I'll get Bernie, get this over with. I'm sure you don't want me around. Just you two old boys."

"Janet, please, as I have been telling you . . ."

"On the phone . . . you couldn't even face me."

"We have to be careful."

"For what? For Bernie's career? Bernie is sixty-nine years old. His career was finished four years ago. I called you four years ago."

"We had hoped . . . Bernie was functioning fairly well."

"You had hoped. Not me, I had no hope. I kept telling you."

"Janet, please, we are friends."

"Friends, it's easy. You don't have to live with Bernie. See him fall, watch him take two weeks to write a letter."

The door from the bedroom opened. "Good to see you, Jack." Bernie shook Jack's hand, then sank into the rattan rocker, began to rock. Jack Curran took the arm chair, pulled it forward to face Bernard Sturman. The sliding doors from the living room to the porch were open, the Gulf sounds faintly audible. A mullet boat headed to Fort Myers Beach.

"How are your folks, Jack? Still playing tennis?"

"Doubles only."

"How old are they?"

"Seventy. Older than you."

"The way I feel, that's old. Though Janet and I did walk to the lighthouse this morning."

"Janet told me you fell again."

"Only the second time this week."

Janet came in from the kitchen. "I made coffee. I'm going to the store."

"Janet, why don't you stay?"

"It's best Janet not be here."

"What's all this about?"

"It's about you, Bernie. About you and Janet and the department."

"And you, Jack. Why don't you say that?"

"I came out to talk about you. How are you feeling, Bernie?"

"I wish I could sleep at night. I have no trouble sleeping in the afternoon. I begin to read . . . I am asleep. No leg pain to wake me."

"You are awake every night?"

"Usually between one and two."

"To inject yourself full of Demerol."

"Who told you that, Jack?"

"Who is not important. I have known for more than three years."

"It's the pain at night, Jack. I couldn't stand it. I spoke to a couple of friends of mine at the POW reunion. Same pains."

"They managed."

"We are not all the same."

"No, they didn't have access to Demerol."

"That's a very scientific observation, Dr. Curran."

"No rationalizations, Bernie. No excuses. I have made all the arrangements, all legal, all approved by the dean. You go into a drug abuse residency program right here in Fort Myers. You apply for immediate retirement, stay here with Janet. Put your life together."

"Janet knows this?"

"Janet has insisted."

"Jack, the pain in my legs is because of my falling syndrome. My legs get hot. After the Demerol, I can sleep."

"Bernie, there is no 'falling syndrome.'"

"You shouldn't have said that, Jack. You'll see. Wait until the letters come from England. Look . . ." Bernie opened his briefcase, gave Curran a copy of the letter to *Lancet*. "Jack, read the letter."

"Don't worry, Bernie, I'll forward the answers to you. I promise I'll send all your mail to Florida."

The late evening walkers have appeared on the beach, the thin browned older woman with the too fat collie, the obese German in her black bikini and gold sandals who walks east and then turns west into the sunset. In an hour only the sanderlings will be left on the beach. The lights are on in the Sturman cottage. Janet prepares supper. Bernard Sturman, M.D. sets the table.

Forty-Six Years Since Graduation

The call from Ralph Miller came on Thursday evening while Joel Diamond was watching *Mystery*, the only television program the Diamonds watched between Sunday's *Masterpiece Theatre* and Friday's *Washington Week in Review*. Joel immediately recognized Ralph's pure southern "Do you want to meet us for Sunday dinner in Galesburg at Jumer's?"

"Anytime you say, Ralph."

"Five-thirty."

"How is Jean?"

"Recovering. Two weeks in Europe—Jean came back exhausted."

"How did you manage all alone?"

"I had the dog. I took the dog fishing. Caught enough bass for me and the dog both!"

"How are you feeling?"

"Pretty good!"

"We should meet for golf at least once before we lose out on this summer, too. Okay, Ralph, see you on Sunday."

Gertrude Diamond had heard the conversation. "It's nice of Ralph to call."

Joel counted on his fingers. "It's been six months since we have seen the Millers." He thought: Haven't seen Ralph and Jean since Florida. December, January in Florida; back to Rockville in the middle of February. This is July—no, it's June 25. Forty-six years since Ralph and I graduated. Still four from our class alive and well in western Illinois. Fred died in April. That's eighty percent still present and accounted for.

"Ralph say anything?"

"No."

"If Ralph calls, there is something he wants to tell us. Ralph say how Jean is?"

"Recovering from Europe."

There is a north-to-south interstate between Rockville and Galesburg. The two lane is still there as a feeder to the interstate, to the regional shopping mall, to the airport. It's the interstate that carries the truck traffic . . . Galesburg, Peoria, Champaign, Paducah, Nashville, Atlanta, Tampa, Sanibel, Florida. We will leave the day after Thanksgiving for Sanibel. By the time we get to our condo, we will be exhausted. Take us a week to recover. Our lives are divided into three-month segments. December, January, February—Florida; March, April, May—catching up and business; June, July, August—family and business; September, October, November—getting ready for December, January, February in Florida.

"Did you find out what Ralph wanted?"

"We only spoke about dinner."

"You didn't ask Ralph about his blood pressure?"

"I don't like to pry."

***

Ralph Miller, second lieutenant infantry, joined our reserve unit in May of 1943. That is almost fifty years ago. Ralph could shoot the head off a dove. He still can. . . .

By the time the Diamonds passed the airport, the air conditioning had conquered the heat and humidity in the Lincoln. Joel turned left. The road followed the Rock River bottom where the flood plain was diminished by the third year of drought. The four-lane ran beside the old Highway 6, curved by the foot of the bluffs, the zoo, the golf course, then mounted the bluff, turned south: Galesburg-Peoria-East is what the green highway sign proclaimed.

At the junction Joel muttered, "Galesburg is south. If you weren't local . . . look at that damn sign, 'Galesburg East.'"

"Tourists use maps, Joel, Triptiks from the AAA."

"Stupid—Peoria is south! Poor signs causes accidents."

Gertrude shut off the radio symphony, looked out the window. Joel made conversation. "The corn is stunted. It's not going to be knee high by the fourth of July. It's lucky we decided to put in beans this year. In these drought conditions the beans are going to do better."

"That's what you said last year, Joel."

Joel answered, "Trucks out on a Sunday. No one respects the Sabbath."

"Joel, you are going too fast."

"Have to pass, I can't stay behind a truck—can't see around them. It's safer to pass."

BISHOP HILL EXIT - HALF A MILE

"We should go out to Bishop Hill."

"Anytime you say."

"We never have time to do anything."

"All you have to do Gertie, is say, 'I want to go.' You name the day, I'll be there."

"You are doing too much, Joel. Breakfast meetings, lunch meetings."

"That's what I need to do. You wanted me to get rid of the real estate. That's what it takes, Gertie, meetings with surveyors, appraisers, real estate agents."

"We should have started years ago."

"We did!"

In a "set-aside" field the sign written in gold gothic script read, *Jumer's - Exit 48 A&B*. Joel slowed at Exit 48. "No A, no B. How the hell would anyone know whether to turn east or west?" Joel turned east.

"See the Jumer's sign?"

"Sign is too damn small."

"Don't drive so fast!"

The Millers were in the lobby in the soft, violet stuffed arm chairs. Jean in crisp white; blond hair, pink lipstick, white sweater. Ralph was also carrying a white sweater.

"We get cold in these air conditioned dining rooms."

That's what Jean Miller always says. Thank God Gertie doesn't carry sweaters. Old folks dine early—get up early, sleep poorly. The hostess, green menu in hand, offered, "Booth?"

"It's too close to the door. We would like some place quieter."

Gertie wants to be able to hear all about Paris and Rome. She will seat herself next to Jean so that no one will notice her hearing loss.

Too late for the Sunday Champagne Brunch. So early that all the tables are available. Gertie chooses a table for four to the right against the wall with a planter divider between us and the adjoining table. The waitress presented the triptych dinner menu.

Ralph: "I'll have the chicken."

Jean: "The chicken looks good . . . the chicken."

Gert: "The veal for me."

Joel ordered, "The swiss steak with red potatoes and a Heineken."

Joel placed two capsules on the place mat, which Ralph noticed. "New pills?"

"Same damn arthritis, just changed from one anti-arthritic drug to another. Every time I get a flare I get a new anti-inflammatory pill."

"Do we have to talk about pills?" Gertie hears when it's me complaining.

"That's what old folks do, Gertie. Talk about pills and ills."

Ralph laughs. Jean puts down the menu. "There are no early bird specials."

"Not on Sunday."

Joel leaned over to Ralph. "How are things at the bank?"

"The merger has helped, our stock has doubled."

Gert heard that. "Joel, tell Ralph about the construction business."

"We're building a spec house."

"Joel is going to lose another six months out of his life and . . . tell Ralph."

"All right. The house should have been pre-sold. We have it priced at no profit just to move the land."

"Tell Ralph!"

"I told him!"

Jean told of Europe in June. "I was so tired when I came home. We walked and walked. When I needed to rest, we stopped for coffee. Six dollars for coffee and a cheese sandwich."

"Did you get to Louvre?"

"That's too big for me, all those stairs. I remember that from our last trip. We didn't buy a thing. It took me a week to rest up."

"When did you get home?"

"A week ago Friday. We are going to California next month."

"We just came back from visiting Joel's sister in Los Angeles."

The waitress extended the dessert tray over the table. "Cheesecake, chocolate mousse, black forest cake, strudel." Ralph and Jean said, "No." Joel chose, "The chocolate mousse."

He handed the cup to Gertie, who tasted and rejected. "Not very good."

Joel scraped the last of the mousse, ordered coffee when the waitress came back.

"You still drinking coffee? It's six-thirty!"

"It will keep me awake for our drive home."

"I couldn't sleep if I drank coffee." That from Jean.

"I don't sleep anyway. Might just as well enjoy. So I'll have three months less in the nursing home."

That's when Ralph leaned over to Joel and said, "Gary Knowlton died last week. My sister wrote to me."

"I haven't seen Gary since we graduated. That's forty-six years ago. He must have been . . ."

FORTY-SIX YEARS SINCE GRADUATION

"He was seventy-four, just my age," says Ralph.

"He was from Mount Carroll. Last time I was in Mount Carroll . . . you remember, Gert? I asked about him."

"Joel, that was in 1960 when you were trying out your MG."

"So it was."

Joel put both hands on the arm of his chair, pushed up to rise. "Call us when you get back from California. Maybe we could do nine holes of golf and then have dinner. Have you made any plans for Florida?"

"Not yet."

"Gertie has us at Sanibel from December second to February eighth."

They hugged, Joel kissed Jean's cheek.

As Joel pulled out of the parking lot, Gert pointed to the Shell sign. "Do you have enough gas? That is four cents less than in Rockville."

"Can't stop if we are going to watch *Masterpiece Theatre*."

"How much was dinner?"

"Twenty-six dollars for two beers, one dessert and one coffee, including the fifteen percent tip."

"You are getting extravagant, Joel."

"Nothing to save for. Not at our age."

The traffic north was from light to none. It was no heavier on the interstate west into Rockville. The Diamonds drove into their garage at eight-fifty, put on their night clothes, their bathrobes. "You know—Gary never came to a class reunion, not once since 1946. It would have been nice if we had stopped off to see him."

"He could have stopped in Rockville to see us. That's no further out of the way for him."

Joel turned on the TV. Gert turned up the sound. Joel pulled out two dining room chairs, sat on one, put his left leg up on the other chair. "To ease my hip."

Gert placed her briefcase on the rosewood dining room table, spread the bills, time cards. Monday was payday at Diamond Construction. Gertrude Diamond was the signatory on the checks.

"Joel, promise me when you sell the spec house, no more building."

"I promise." Joel got up, kissed Gertrude on her forehead. "You want anything?"

"No. Where are you going? Stand up straight—straighten your shoulders before you start walking."

Gertrude heard the toilet flush. Joel was back in his chair, his leg up.

"Hurt?"

"No more than usual. Now I know why Ralph wanted to meet with us. You know, the last two years when we came back after the war, Ralph and Gary lived in the same house."

"Do you think Ralph has seen Gary since graduation?"

"I didn't ask him. He didn't say."

At ten o'clock Joel set the thermostat on the air conditioning at seventy-one, pushed the switch that activated the house fire and burglar alarm. At ten-o-five he was beside Gertrude under the Pima cotton blankets in the king-size bed with the twin mattresses. Gertrude picked up her novel. Joel reached for the Sunday *New York Times*.

"Don't rattle the paper. You know I can't stand that."

"I'll only read the front page. Why do you think Gary never came to a reunion?"

"Maybe he didn't want to hear you and Ralph talk about banks, sports cars, fancy vacations and money. Always, money."

Joel put down the paper very quietly, turned onto his left side, pulled the blanket over his shoulders, shut the fluorescent that was over his half of the bed.

"Chances are you are right about Gary. Women do have more insight."

Gertie shut the light, turned onto her right side.

"Good night."

Committees Committees

The first Tuesday of the month is when the constitution of the B'nai Jacob congregation ordained, "that a meeting of the four-person religious committee be held. Three shall constitute a quorum. In case of a tie, the chairman's decision will prevail. The Rabbi will be an *ex-officio* member without voting rights."

The four committee members sat in the library at the oblong walnut table for ten: Herman, the chairman who leaned on the north wall of the prayer house when he recited his morning prayers; William, who during the silent devotion, stood, swayed from right to left as the congregants swayed forward and backward; Mort, the honor giver, who flitted from one congregant to the other, who whispered on Monday and Thursday and Saturdays, on the first of the month, on the festivals, on the Holy Days, on the Torah readings days "You may lift the Torah" "You may tie the Torah" "Please take the Torah from the Ark" "Today you will be the third or the fourth called to read from the Torah"; and almost at the corner of the table, apart, Art Gordon, ex-president of the B'nai Jacob, the last of the three generations of Gordons buried in the Hebrew cemetery.

Art dozed, dreamt of lower interest rates, refinancing and how that would save his shopping center development, on which he feared the bank would surely foreclose. Art dreamt for a miracle, without hope or conviction. Herman sat across from Mort and Bill.

The Rabbi sat at the head of the table. The Rabbi was reading *Vanity Fair* magazine: "The Kennedys: These Are Our Heros?"

Herman had come in early, sorted the mail. "First on the agenda," he began, almost annoyed. "It's Paul Kramer. This is his second petition. He wants to be buried from the synagogue. You remember last year, we refused him because of our tradition. Now Paul writes it's time to change tradition."

"What is your pleasure, gentlemen?"

"I vote no."

Art, roused by Herman's positive strident tone, stirred. "The Kramers are pious, observant members of our congregation, almost big givers. I think Paul would become a bigger giver if we gave him an okay."

"Everything you say is true, Art, but why isn't it good enough for Paul, like for everyone else? We'll stop the hearse, open the door to the synagogue, hold it open for a minute and then go on to the cemetery." Herman, anxious to go on to item two, permission for Sunday night bingo, was again interrupted by Art.

"Paul wants the eulogy—the prayers—before the burial to be in the sanctuary. They do it in Des Moines."

"This is Rock City, Art. What they do in Des Moines is not an issue here."

The Rabbi listened to the debate. "Don't expect me to tell Dr. Kramer no. I told him the last time. Let somebody from the committee tell him."

"Okay, Rabbi, I'll tell him," Herman said.

"In this community, it has always been no."

"We are not concerned with anything but our congregation."

Herman, hearing Mort's support, called, "Vote. For?"

Art raised his hand.

"Against? Mort."

"I'll tell Dr. Kramer myself. I'll do it nicely after morning prayers."

"I'll bet the Kramers become Temple members and we lose their total support."

"It's a chance we have to take, Art. No choice. Burial from the synagogue has never been permitted in Rock City, and it's not going to change."

"So."

"So it stays."

Art mumbled . . . mumbled very quietly.

"What did you say, Art?"

"I said, so what if we say yes. Those who want to be buried from a funeral parlor can be buried from a funeral parlor. The ones who use the synagogue, we charge them a heavy fee. We get the money instead of the funeral director."

"It has been decided."

"Sure, Herman. But remember we can't afford to lose the Kramers."

The next morning, after the service, Herman stood beside Paul Kramer as he was folding his tallith.

"Paul, last night the religious committee considered your request to be buried from the synagogue."

"Not for me alone, Herman. There are others."

"The committee voted no."

"About what I expected."

"When you are dead, what difference does it make?"

"The funeral is for the living."

"Paul, you are a young man. Bother yourself with something. Why bother us with your dying."

Paul laughed.

"First of all, I am not so young. I'll be seventy next spring, and second of all, everyone dies, so everyone is affected by your decision." Paul looked at his wrist watch. "You have a minute, Herman. I'll tell you a story. A simple story."

The two sat, sunk in the soft chairs of the lounge that divided the prayer house from the gift shop. Herman, short, thin with quick hand movements. Paul, heavier, slower, almost six feet tall, bent forward to ease his back pain.

"I'll tell you a story. Thirty, forty years ago when I first started practicing, I had a client who raised hybrid hogs. 'The master's eye fatteneth the calf,' Herman."

"From hogs and calves, I don't know."

"It's a saying, Herman."

"From retailing, I know."

"Anyway, my client, Russell was his name, was a fine stockman. I worked for him for fourteen years vaccinating his hogs, treating his beef cows. Never did I hear an unkind word from him. When we finished, I was always invited to lunch with the family. Six months ago, he died. He was eighty-three. I went to the funeral at the United Methodist Church. A little country church of forty families. The pastor gave the eulogy. He looked like Dr. Hoop with his aggressive chin whiskers. You know what he said? He said, 'Russell was the first into church. He put on the heat, wound the clock. The last to leave, to lock the door.' The casket was in front of the minister. The congregation sat in rows like in our sanctuary. Afterwards everyone walked behind the casket to the cemetery, no farther than from our sanctuary to our cemetery. Afterwards we all returned to the church for the meal consolation, same as we do. I spoke to Russ's wife, to his children in the church dining room."

"I am sorry, Paul. Not at B'nai Jacob."

"The family gathered in a church they had been members of all their lives. It was a comforting experience, Herman."

Herman rose.

"Give me a hand up."

Herman extended his hand. Paul grabbed his elbow.

"Such is life."

"What?"

"Forty years a member of a congregation."

"I am sorry."

"Nothing to be sorry about. Doris and I will join the reformed Temple."

"I am sorry."

"If you were all so sorry, you could change."

"I am sorry you are going to the Temple."

"Don't worry, I'll keep my membership here."

"We need you for the morning minyan."

"Don't get started, Herman. Let it be. You need me for this and you need us for that. We need each other, but if I want the use of the sanctuary for a funeral, you don't care enough for our needs to permit it."

"There is a committee."

"Don't worry, Herman. I won't bother you again. We'll join the Temple. That will solve the problem."

"Paul, why do you bother yourself with this dying? These funerals. This is your second petition. What's so important? The sanctuary or the funeral parlor?"

"Herman, I am not a member of a funeral parlor. I am a member of a congregation."

"We could hold a memorial in the sanctuary, after the funeral."

"I am talking about a funeral, before the burial."

"What is so important about dying? Judaism is about living."

"Dying is part of living. I heard the committee approved bingo."

"Only on Sunday evening. We need the income."

"Charge a fee for the funeral."

"It's not in our tradition."

"With bingo, you made a new tradition."

"That's different, Paul."

Enjoy Enjoy

On his Wednesday afternoon at home, B.J. Roone, Lt. Col. United States Army, retired six years and three months, sat at his desk leafing through this month's accumulation of "American" painting, "Modern British," and "German" paintings, catalogs for the fall art auction.

With each slit of the white mailing envelope from Christie's, King Street, London, Benny Roone recalled his uncle Al's weekly letters that had brought the Roones back to Rockville, Illinois.

> "Benny you and Milly come home to your family. You'll take over for me just a few hours a week. You'll have time for yourself, for your art collecting, for your golf. You want to write? Write at your desk at our downtown office. What kind of life is it for you living among strangers? You have had more than thirty years away from home. Rockville has changed. Milly will love the Mozart concerts. Last November in one month we had performances of *Tosca* and the Chicago Symphony. You want a big city? Chicago is only three and a half hours. Why would you want to live in Washington? London is too far from your family, too expensive. So you collect British moderns and German painting—you'll collect from Rockville."

The Roones' move from Washington to Rockville had achieved one tangible improvement in their life. They didn't have to read Uncle Al's weekly, "Life in Rockville is getting better and better" letters.

Milly had quickly integrated her days into swimming at the YW, fund-raising lunches with the girls from the congregation B'nai Jacob sisterhood, and always, the concerts.

Benny Roone looked out the window at the dull gray sky, heard the roll of thunder that would bring the showers to cleanse the humidity from the Mississippi River Valley. It had been the second coolest summer ever recorded in Rockville. A few more sunny days, if it stayed warm, the soybeans would fill out nicely into another record crop. Increased yields in the Midwest depressed world markets.

The oaks were still in green full leaf. Another month the oak leaves will cover the lawn.

Sunlight had pierced the northern sky. The showers were over. Benny heard Milly's '84 Olds enter the garage. Milly would need help with her packages as Wednesday was ten percent off for seniors at Venture.

The trunk of Milly's car was open. Benny reached into the trunk for the case of toilet tissue. "Leave that, I have no more storage space."

"What are you going to do with a case of Angel Soft?"

"I got a three dollars and fifty cent rebate."

"Minus twenty-nine cents for the stamp."

"I thought you would be on the golf course."

"I wanted to go through the art catalogs."

"No more buying, Benny! Not until you sell some paintings. There is no more wall space."

"The British contemporaries . . ."

Milly didn't allow Benny to finish. "I know John Hoyland's abstractions are a bargain, Colonel Roone. Where are you going to hang a five-by-three-foot canvas?"

Benny Roone gathered the paper sacks, followed Milly into the kitchen. He said, "Sit down, I'll get you some water."

"Shopping is hot work."

"I have the air conditioning on."

"I know you, Benny. Not for me, for the paintings!"

Benny grinned. "Not like London."

"I can't remember."

"Six years last May since we are at home in Rockville. Where were you this morning when I called?"

"Emergency sisterhood meeting."

"Another after-funeral lunch to serve?"

"Not quite. Almost. The Lieberman house and contents are going on sale. The sisterhood will be serving lunch for the entire week. The nephew hired an antiques dealer to value the household things. I don't know of anyone from the congregation who has been in that house since old Max died. You remember? Al wrote to tell us. If Maggie Lieberman was alive today, the Knights of Columbus would be doing the lunch."

"Uncle Al liked Maggie."

"I'll bet your uncle Al was the only friend from B'nai Jacob that Max had left."

"When Max Lieberman married Margaret Culligan, the Catholic girl from below the hill, his parents said prayers for the dead for him."

"They must have loved each other. Max and Maggie stayed married—too bad there were no children."

"I think they had a son. There was an accident of some sort. It was a long time ago when Uncle Al had just opened his veterinary practice."

"All that money going to nephews. I'll bet not one gave a damn about Max or Maggie."

"Max was certainly different. I remember I was riding with Uncle Al—it was Al's day for horse practice."

"Horses in Rockville?"

"Lots of horses in Rockville then. All the peddlers had horses and Max Lieberman had a pony . . . a little white pony with founder. I'll never forget, the pony was walking on his heels. The toes were all turned up, grown real long."

"So?"

"Uncle Al is clipping the toes short. Max is standing on that bluff hillside watching. To me, Max looked ten feet tall. Al is directing while he clips, 'Less feed, more exercise . . . pony needs exercise, Max, or you'll be calling me again.' Max, he just stands there and nods until my uncle says, 'Waste of money to treat problems that can be prevented.' 'Not your problem, Dr. Roone.' Max gives Uncle Al twenty dollars, says, 'Put the change in the charity box for me.' Al says, 'I'll tell the Rabbi . . .' but Max doesn't let him finish. I never forgot what he said. He said, 'If I wanted the Rabbi to know, I would tell him.' So Uncle Al says, 'I won't tell,' and Max says, 'I know you won't.' That was the last time I saw Max Lieberman."

"You remember that? That was more than forty years ago."

"I remember. When is the sale?"

"A week Friday. I don't know if the sisterhood will serve the Saturday lunch. That's usually a big sale day."

"Speak to the Rabbi, Milly."

"Not me. I just serve—and smile. 'Thank you, thank you. Another cup of coffee?'"

"Milly, do you know if there are paintings in the house?"

"You want to know, ask your Uncle Al. He was the last friend old Max had."

On Thursday, every Thursday at nine, Uncle Al appeared at the Roone Company offices. "What's new and exciting, Benny?"

That had been Uncle Al's salutation to his nephew from the day he had been assigned the undefined duties of manager to the Roone Properties Companies.

"Same old thing, Al. A roof leak—I just called the roofer."

"I hope you haven't paid him."

"The work was done. Don't worry, the check hasn't been mailed."

"Roofers don't come back unless you owe them money."

"Al Hansen always comes when you call."

Still standing, Al leafed through his mail. "Garbage, nothing but garbage."

Knowing that the only way to get his Uncle Al to sit was with a cup in his hand, Benny offered, "I'll get you a cup of tea."

"Not the decaffeinated you drink."

"For you I bought Lipton's Brisk."

Al sat, sipped his tea from a disposable cup. "Fancy tea, Benny. Not like you to spend money promiscuously. Thanks for the tea, Benny. I have to go. We are going to West Branch. There is a new exhibition at the Hoover Center." Al put his hands on the arms of the char to begin his efforts to get up.

Benny asked, "You knew Max Lieberman?"

"I knew him."

"Max have any paintings at the house?"

"Lots of paintings."

"What did they look like?"

"Little pale nudes, thin little green-assed girls without boobs. There were some still lifes of fruit. Lots of red pears."

"Sounds good to me. I'll go out, have a look on Friday afternoon."

"You had better be careful, Benny. I have heard Milly. You buy another painting, she'll . . ."

"I promised to sell a couple."

"When?"

"I am planning on it."

When Max Lieberman purchased the Ely Estate, he acquired a one-hundred-sixty-acre bluff farm, mostly pasture and timber, a three-stall garage with servant quarters above, a thirty-room Italianate villa with spreadwing cherubs painted on the ceilings and walnut wainscoting in the downstairs library. Max neglected the farm, rented the villa to a restauranteur, erected a privacy fence between the villa and the garage.

The walls of the servant quarters came down. Skylights and picture windows went in, 1950s teal wool carpets covered the pine floor, an elevator rose. Above the three-stall garage the Libermans lived in isolated splendor guarded by an iron gate, opened only with the approval of Max or Maggie.

Visitors waked up carpeted steps into an office, sitting room, living room. The south windows overlooked the blacktopped Rock River Road that divided the flood plain from the bluff. To the west, the brown gray Rock River flowed into the Mississippi.

On this Friday afternoon the late sunlight highlighted faded wall-to-wall carpet in the Lieberman home. The diligence of the six-person pricing crew was evident. From the paintings and furniture white tags signaled to prospective buyers "bargain . . . bargain, buy . . . buy."

To celebrate the successful completion of tag day, the crew sat around the white, porcelain-topped kitchen table drinking coffee from Styrofoam cups.

"I am Benny Roone. I had called."

No one answered.

"Mrs. Roone's husband . . . the lunch lady. I was to ask for Viola."

A woman of a certain age, protected by a brown smock, rose from a kitchen chair. "You understand, Mr. Roone? Cash only."

"I understand, Viola."

"The paintings are in the master bedroom. Follow me."

To the left, through a bathroom that was certainly 1909, was a bedroom sufficiently large for a chest of drawers, an arm chair on casters, a television on rollers. On one side of a double bed stood a walnut valet.

Benny asked, "Mr. Lieberman's room?"

"Looks like it to me. Mr. Greenhill didn't say."

"Mr. Greenhill?"

"He's the nephew who ordered the sale."

"Has he been through the house?"

"May have, but if he did, he didn't take much. Haven't seen so much stuff in years."

Viola opened the closet. "Suits, slacks, shirts, shoes, all size forty-two or forty-three regular . . . three dollars each."

Benny Roone was not diverted by Violas's sales efforts. His collector's eye had seen the paintings. Classic female nude standing figure, still lifes, the largest a red peach against an olive green background, pears in bowls, pears half-cut, flat nudes with expressionless faces, painted front view, rear view, three-quarters view. One, two, three, four, five, six, seven, eight canvases in simple narrow wooden frames painted to match the dull greens oranges, yellows of the nudes and fruit.

"I'll take all eight."

"The smaller ones are forty dollars, the bigger ones sixty."

Viola took a receipt pad from her pocket. "That's three hundred and eighty."

Benny separated six fifty-dollar bills. "Three hundred."

"Three hundred and eighty . . ."

"Three fifty . . ."

"Three eighty."

"You are a hard woman, Viola."

"It's a hard life, Mr. Roone."

"Okay, three eighty."

Viola placed the five twelve by fifteen paintings in one plastic sack, the three fourteen by eighteens in another, gave Benny Roone a receipt. "If anyone in the parking lot stops you, show them the receipt."

"Thank you. You ever met Mr. Greenhill?"

"Just a voice on the telephone."

"I thought he might be here for the sale."

"He won't be here till next week to pick up his check. Have a look at the suits, the beautiful suits. I think they would fit you. You take a forty-two?"

"I'll stop by tomorrow."

"You're better off before the crowds get here. By tomorrow afternoon it will all be gone. We have a grandmother clock in the missus's bedroom. Only four hundred and fifty dollars."

"Any more paintings?"

"No, all the paintings were in this bedroom. You want to buy a crucifix? Beautiful crucifix in the lady's bedroom."

Benny went past the pedestal tub through the bathroom into the missus's bedroom. A chaise longue covered in Provencal chintz faced the television set. A gold crucifix protected the four-poster bed.

Viola opened the closet. Evening dresses, day dresses, woolen suits, all size twelve, from the fancy Chicago stores. "Not a thing less than fifteen years old."

"I'll tell my wife."

Benny Roone started down the steps. Viola's voice followed him. "Don't forget to stop in the garage. Got two 1953 black Cadillac sedans, hardly used."

Benny stopped in the garage, called up to Viola, "Thank you."

Viola answered, "Enjoy!"

Benny whistled a joyous non-tune as he drove home. He came into the kitchen with a broad grin and an ebullient greeting for Milly. "Roone triumphs again! Bought eight Hans Kufers for three hundred and eighty dollars!"

"I am sure they were a bargain. Where are you going to hang eight paintings?"

"See if you like them." Benny placed the eight on the kitchen counter.

"They are small enough." Milly held each painting to the light.

"Max had these paintings in his bedroom."

"Not very sexy nudes . . ."

Benny nodded. "Better than what was in Maggie's room. The only decoration she had on her bedroom wall was a crucifix."

"These are very dead, dull still lifes."

Benny grinned. "My dear Milly, the painting in your hand, those six pears in a ceramic bowl, will bring forty-one thousand Deutschmarks, twenty-five thousand dollars in the Karl & Faber auction. Any time I want to sell, all I have to do is mail it off to Munich."

"Sure . . . sure . . ."

"I'll show you the May sale catalog. A similar canvas signed with the Kufer monogram and the date inside it did a thousand better."

"'I'll believe that when I see the Deutschemarks in my hand. You had better set the table. Al and Clara are coming for dinner. I hope you are not going to tell your uncle about your triumphal purchases."

"He knows I went to the sale. There are no secrets in this town."

"Do me a favor, Benny. Don't do your value assessments. Like eight paintings times twenty thousand dollars each is one hundred sixty thousand dollars, more or less. It sounds very greedy."

"Milly, I know what I am talking about."

"Benny, pour the wine."

After supper, Benny skillfully led the conversation to Max Lieberman. "Al, you knew Max?"

"I knew him. We got acquainted because I took care of his old white pony. After the Liebermans lost their son, they just wouldn't get rid of the pony. You buy anything, Benny?"

"All the paintings that were in Max's bedroom."

Al laughed. "After Max died, Maggie must have got religion. Last I remember, the paintings were in the living room."

"Al, did Max ever say how he got eight Hans Kufers, all dated 1943, 1944, 1945?"

Al sipped his tea. "There used to be a black and white photo on the big desk, the one in front of the window, of Max in his World War II uniform, medals and all. Max was a colonel in the Transportation Corps. He ran the U.S. Army truck line that went into Berlin. That's why he bought the Ely estate. He wanted to build a truck terminal on the River Road."

After more than fifty years of Alan Roone's stories, repeated and repeated, amplified and embroidered, his wife Clara interrupted. "Al, Benny asked a simple question. The paintings were all dated 1943, 1944, 1945. Do you or don't you know the answer?"

"Not exactly . . ."

"Tell Benny what you know and let's go home." Clara gathered her purse.

"Milly, thank you for the dinner. Great dill sauce on the salmon."

Benny filled Al's tea cup. Al began again. "Hans Kufer was living in Berlin. As I remember Max's story, Kufer was bombed out, had lost all his paintings. Things were bad in Germany after the war. Somehow Max met Kufer or heard about him. Max feeds Kufer. Kufer gives him the eight paintings." Al laughed. "Max must have gotten a bargain. Max liked bargains. If he could get a better price on two, he bought two. He had two Cadillacs and three refrigerators in the garage. He kept the refrigerators full of Jewish rye. Every week his trucks that ran up to Chicago brought him back bagels and bialys."

"This you remember?" The question from Clara. "Max is dead, must be close to eighteen years, and this you remember?"

"I remember."

"What happened to you? Yesterday you forget!"

"This I remember! I remember when Max's truck line went bankrupt. That was before Max died. I remember when Maggie died. Remember, Clara, we didn't go to the funeral. I wanted to, but . . ."

Clara finished the sentence for her husband. "I can't stand it when Al starts recalling the good old days in Rockville. They weren't all that good. Al, you do remember that?"

Al rose. "Benny, what are you going to do with the money when you sell the paintings?"

"Keep half to buy more paintings. Half I would give to the charities."

"Half is too much, Benny. Ten percent is sufficient. If you give more, then there is the danger that you will become self-righteous."

"That's no danger for my Benny," Milly said.

"Okay, Milly, tell me why?"

"I'll tell you. Benny can't sell a painting! Benny can only buy!"

Benny defended himself. "I am going to send photographs of the Kufers to Munich for a sale estimate."

"You'll find an excuse not to sell. 'The economy is off in Germany.' 'We should wait for a better price.' You always do. Have you ever sold a painting?"

"No, not really. But I have given some away."

"Sure, for a tax deduction!"

Benny Roone did not tell Milly, but neither did he tarry. On Thursday morning, eight Polaroid photos of eight Kufers left Rockville for Karl & Faber Art Auction in Munich.

On Monday afternoon, Benny called his home. "Milly, any mail from Karl & Faber?"

"No, Benny."

The answer did not arrive until the following Friday.

> "Dear Mr. Roone:
>
> Thank you for considering our house as the seller of your eight Kufers. As you noted in your letter, the monogram and dates are in the right upper corner of the canvas. We have had many opportunities to offer similar Kufer paintings to our clientele, but we cannot do so as our expert, Manfred Huber, considers these Kufers as copies, copies of earlier works that Hans Kufer had stored in shelters because of the bombings. After the war Mr. Kufer retrieved the earlier works and sold them quite successfully. Mu Huber respectfully conveys his regrets for this news that we send to you. Should you acquire Kufer paintings of the 1942-1945 era on which the monogram signature is in the left hand corner, please do write to me again.
>
> Sincerely,
> Eva Daum Gras
>
> P.S. The original Kufer works dated 1936-1942 were in frames that Hans Kufer carved by hand and then covered in gild leaf."

Benny sighed, put the letter down, turned to Milly who was scraping carrots in the sink. "Not good news from Munich."

"Read the letter to me."

Benny did.

"Not good news, Milly," Benny repeated.

Milly said, "Not bad news. Now you won't have to worry whether to sell or not to sell eight paintings worth a quarter of a million dollars."

"What do you think I ought to do with the paintings? Tell me."

"You like them?"

"They are quite lovely. Huber didn't really say Kufer didn't paint them."

"He didn't say he did."

"Maybe he had studio assistants like Rubens."

"Those Kufer nudes are ten percent of the Rubens women." Milly dried her hands, chuckled. "Those were hard times in Berlin. Kufer had to eat, so he dashes off a painting, trades them to Max Lieberman. What's the sin of it. Max gets a bargain and Kufer stays alive and well. Huber classifies them as copies. You like them. I like them."

"What should I do with them?"

"Hang them in the stairwell."

"Eight?"

"Hang four in the stairwell and put four in your storeroom with your other treasures."

"What if someone asks, 'Benny, are those Kufers?' What am I going to answer?"

"That's another advantage of living in Rockville, Illinois, Colonel Roone. No one is ever going to ask you for the painting's provenance."

George, Mildred, John and Harriet

This morning George and I were sitting on the porch of our condo facing the Gulf. I was watching our neighbor feed the gulls. It was about eleven or eleven-twelve. I am very precise with numbers. My husband George said to me, "Mildred, I have just called Rockville. We should be starting for home as we planned."

I don't get to plan anything beyond breakfast. Bran cereal and skim milk at seven-fifteen. Lunch, salad and bread, at twelve-fifteen. Dinner is always at six o'clock p.m. with the *McNeal-Lehrer* news report. George doesn't really like for us to have dinner guests for they would interfere with his routine. This George justifies with, "Mildred, we don't want you to be entertaining. This is your vacation too."

"George, I really don't mind having the neighbors over."

"You really shouldn't strain yourself, Mildred."

All our friends say we are a happy couple, to which I just nod and say we have had our problems but then who hasn't. Things were worse when Harriet lived with us. Now that Harriet is at the Congregate Home, George and I have finally quit quarreling over bringing up Harriet.

Quarreling is perhaps a bit harsh. George so permissive, too permissive. "Mildred, you can't be on Harriet every minute."

"George, how will Harriet learn?"

"She will learn slowly, very slowly."

Harriet did—but it took longer than the doctors said. It took years, but Harriet makes her own bed, slowly. Harriet does dress herself, takes a shower, does her own hair. Since our daughter has left our home I am afraid she will not get her pills. George is more confident. "Mildred, that's what extended care homes do, watch, make sure the residents get their medications. Harriet is very well taken care of. Mildred please . . . Mildred, don't *you* forget to take your pills. You know what happens when you forget to take your pills."

In some ways George is more considerate than I am. He never really screams "Milly, take your pills!" but so many times I think I see it in his eyes. Sometimes he says things like "Girls are different, it's how they are brought up" . . . "Girls Mildred's generation never played games. All they did was play with dolls. Now if they had played games . . . in games, one wins, another loses. That is an early start to experience loss and rejection. Then when rejections come, then perhaps it wouldn't create such a breakdown."

It pleased George when I agreed to the home in Des Moines for Harriet. "It's the best thing for Harriet." George actually said that. I never answered him, "George, it's a three-hour drive to Des Moines and in the winter we are away for two months."

George kept his promise, we do visit Harriet once a week. George tries to make that day pleasant for me. We leave Rockville after breakfast. George always stops at the discount mall in Iowa City so I can shop. George always takes Harriet and me to lunch. Harriet loves to go to Bishop's Cafeteria. She does take more than she should eat. Getting fat is the worst thing that can happen to Harriet. There is so little she can do to control her body. There is a pool at Congregate House; Harriet does do some water exercises. I don't think the aides are going to watch Harriet as I did. Watch her portions, watch her salt intake, count her calories, keep her on skim milk, NutraSweet and dietetic cookies. Harriet loves ginger snaps. Before we left for Florida, George explained to Harriet, "Mom and I will call you every week and you call us whenever you like."

"There are rules, George. Harriet has to get permission from the dorm mother to call."

George is no help when he promises Harriet things that the rules don't permit, leaves her with a whole box of Archway ginger snaps. Maybe George doesn't realize how much harm he is doing. How can Harriet learn to be on her own, without constant supervision? What does George say? "Harriet has to have the opportunity to succeed or fail. If she fails she will try again."

I told George when we first started looking for a home for Harriet, "Harriet can learn to live on her own." I never said, "All those years it was you who was for keeping Harriet at home."

George finally agreed we can't go burdening John, our oldest who lives in Florida, with having to take care of Harriet.

Thank God, it's not a financial burden. Harriet has the trust fund my father set up for her, but trust officers, what do they know about buying little bits of jewelry and pretty night gowns. There is no reason that Harriet shouldn't wear my grandmother's gold bracelets. George was very reluctant to permit that. George is so "things" oriented. Harriet will forget where she puts the bracelets, or she will lose them altogether. He says, "Your Victorian bracelets are museum pieces."

"The bracelets are mine to do with as I wish!" If I scream, George hears me.

"As you like, Mildred."

I gave Harriet Mama's bracelet; the one with the best clasp and the gold chain guard. I gave it to Harriet the day we left her in Des Moines. The next week, the bracelet was gone. I am sure it was stolen. They have "those" kind of people working at the home. For her fortieth birthday I am going to give Harriet a gold chain necklace; the one George bought for me when we went to Florence on the museum tour. George won't like that, but I am not going to tell him. George never looks in my jewel box. When he sees Harriet wearing the necklace, I'll face that then.

This morning I was sorting my shells. I have this very beautiful deep brown Florida crown conch, the prize of my this-year's collection, in my right hand. In my left hand I am holding my new copy of Peterson's *First Guide to Shells*. George comes, picks up my handbook, takes the conch out of my hand, looks at the shell, looks at page twelve, puts the book face down and says, "Your shell is too small."

George knows how I hate when he breaks the back of my hooks. I don't understand why George can't use a bookmark as I do. George didn't have to say, "What are you going to do with all those shells? You still have last year's shells and the year's before." George absolutely sneered at my shells.

I had the shells on paper, the glass top of the table perfectly protected. The shells were all in a circle, the whelks on the outside, then the murex, around them the augers. I was just adding the olive shells when George said it again. "You making more picture frames?" That was a sneer, George. I recognize your condescending sneer. But I didn't answer. I didn't say Harriet uses my shell frames. They look very nice on her dresser.

Yesterday George told me, "Mildred, we are going home on the first." George never asked, "Mildred, when would you like to go home?" or "Mildred, would you like to go home on the first so that way we can get to Des Moines by the twelfth? We can drive home through Louisiana, come up Interstate 35 to Des Moines." George knows how much I enjoy our car trips. Just George and I alone, me watching the Triptik. George tells me when and where we will stop and if there is no hotel with a heated indoor pool, George is very good about it. George will drive an extra hour so that I can swim. It's my arthritis.

We are very comfortable in the Lincoln. My seat goes down or up. I can change the position to ease my back. I like the quiet of the road. George stops every two hours; we get out, walk around. When the weather is good we picnic. George likes King Oscar sardines and an apple for lunch. If it's raining we stop at a restaurant. George is into southern cooking, corn muffins and mush, biscuits and gravy. George ate southern when he was in the army. George was in the army when we were married. My mother said a lot of things like, "George is marrying you for the Goodman money. George will never earn a proper living for you. Sure he is the first Taylor to ever go to State but what did it do for him? He ended up in the army."

George believed in the army, in equality of opportunity and no prejudice. Just judge a man by how he does his job.

John was born when George was in Europe. I was back in Rockville living with my folks. When Harriet was born, George was back in the army. George would have stayed in the army. That was my first "crisis" as George calls them, when Harriet was born, when I learned about Harriet. George got forty-two days compassionate home leave over Christmas and New Year's. George saw things I didn't realize until much later. "Mildred, we are neglecting John."

John was a very quiet, almost withdrawn child. Played by himself, learned to read very early and then spent days alone in his room reading or making models. George resigned his commission in 1954; John was nine then. We never had any problem between John and Harriet. John loves Harriet. It's just that Harriet required so much care.

When we are driving down the interstate, I get drowsy, George notices that. "Mildred, go to sleep. I'll wake you if I need you."

I close my eyes and then the wheels start in my head. I see John, a thirteen-year-old John, tall and thin and blue-eyed with a butch haircut. Then I lose the picture. It's all lost, gone until his forty-fifth birthday. It's all blank. I told that to George once. "I am afraid, George. I have lost so many years." George nodded and said nothing. So I said again, "George, I can't recall all those years—lost, all lost."

"Maybe it's the pills, Mildred. I read that your sleeping pills could do that."

"George, you know I can't sleep without those pills." I told him again, "You don't know anything about the pills I take."

"Mildred, I read it in *The New York Times*."

Everything George knows he read in *The New York Times*. That's all he does on our vacation; sit on the porch, read *The New York Times*. The only time we go out is two times a week to early dinners. Tuesday and Friday. That's because George hates restaurant cooking. We usually go to nice places where there is a cloth table cloth, cloth napkins, a good salad and good bread. The main dish, George doesn't care about. Maybe that's why George stays so thin. He can fit into trousers that were part of his 1950 dress uniform. Pink trousers, olive green jacket, trench coat. George is still a very good looking man.

I look at myself, getting fat in all the wrong places. That's what happens to a woman's body. My belly bulges, the fat rolls on my back, my breasts surely aren't what they were!

"Mildred, did you do your exercises?"
"I don't have to do my stretches and sit-ups if I go swimming."
"You haven't been swimming in four days."
"It has been too cold."

This has been our coldest January in Florida in fourteen, fifteen years. Our condo faces the Gulf, only two steps down to the beach and two steps to the parking lot. Each year we see more just sitters in the sun. Neither George nor I sunbathe. We have both had skin cancers removed; George from his head. Mine was on my right leg.

George reads *The New York Times*, I write letters to Harriet, block print the sentences: "Dear Harriet, Do write to tell us what you are doing."

Harriet has yet to write. George did leave pre-addressed envelopes with the dorm mother. Harriet should be encouraged to write. She can write and if she doesn't, she will lose her skills, like I lost my typing, shorthand. No one uses shorthand anymore.

I read Jane Smiley, Tobias Wolff. He is the next author for our Rockville Visiting Author Week.

When we are driving, George likes to listen to story tapes, mostly novels. George says it keeps him alert. After an hour or two of John le Carré, he shuts the tape.

George takes my left hand, kisses it, holds my hand until we get to the rest stop.

George says that if you recognize a problem, it doesn't have to become a crisis. That may work for George in the construction business, but what about problems like Harriet's. God given they are and nothing and no one can help her.

"Who is going to take care of Harriet when we are gone?"

"We can only do so much, Mildred. We have done all we can."

George is right, at our age how much more can we do.

George should retire. It's not a matter of money with us. George says if he quits, there go six or eight jobs, so George builds a house or two, puts down sewer, water, puts streets in, and then he is stuck with a subdivision he must sell out. George is superstitious. He will not name a street or a road after anyone in the family. There is not a "Taylor" name on anything George has developed. George says my dad took care of that. "Goodman" Lectures at the Y and the "Goodman" Wing at the Art Museum.

I, Mildred Goodman Taylor, am the last Goodman. Maybe that was why my father put Goodman on every donor plaque in Rockville.

In the afternoon, after four, George and I walk on the beach. The pelicans are no longer on one low-tide sandbar. The gulls sit, shoulders hunched, face into the wind. You have heard about "birds of a feather." That's how it is on our beach: sanderlings with sanderlings and dowitchers with dowitchers, but the royal and common terns do fly together. The herons are the ones that are always alone: one at a time, wading in and out of the surf.

Mostly I sit on the porch, listen to the surf winds. George could have asked me, "Mildred, would you like to go home in time for Harriet's birthday?" or "Mildred, I'd like to be home in time for Harriet's fortieth birthday," or "If we start home on the first we can easily get to Des Moines on the twelfth." I don't know why George can't admit he is anxious about Harriet, that he wants to go home to see if she is all right. Why does George have to tell me, "I just called Rockville. Ed tells he needs me to come home."

"That suits me fine. George. I think it's time to go home."

That's when George grins. "Now Milly, you won't have to do any more shopping. We'll just eat what is left in the freezer."

I know what it will be like, our last two weeks or the island. George won't go anywhere, won't do anything. George just sits on the porch and reads *The New York Times*. Sometimes he reads a line or two to me. "Milly, do you know that geese mate forever?"

There is no sense answering George. *That* I learned. George won't hear me unless I scream.

Only a Half-Step Behind

Dressed in khaki shorts, black Nike sweatshirt, my father sits in full December, Florida sun. He writes a letter to my sister, Helene, the banker. I, Leonard, his eldest son, sit beside him on the screened porch that faces the Gulf.

"I am cold, Lenny."

I don't answer. I read *The New York Times*. The Lannan Literary Awards and Fellowships are announced in large print; the publishers of these now anointed works congratulate the recipients of the Lannan Fiction Fellowship. That same publisher held my novel for fourteen months before he rejected it.

> "Dear Leonard Shapiro:
> After two careful readings . . . too regionalist, too many details . . . of course others may find . . . I wish you well in placing your work.
> James Carr, Senior Editor"

On page four of the "Living Arts," the *Times* B section, there are holiday gift suggestions.

"Papa, do you think Mom would like a cook book?"

My mother cuts recipes from the *Times*, files them between the pages of Shapiro Companies ledgers and forgets them.

My father hasn't answered. On his legal pad are numbers, evidently projections of earnings for the next seven years. A father at seventy, almost seventy-one, projects the future values of his present-day decisions. Last week, Dad was ready to sell for a note due in nineteen years.

I put page four before Dad. Dad looks at the illustration of the *Native Indian, Wild Game, Fish and Wild Foods Cookbook*.

"Go ask your mother. You had better not wake her up."

"Papa, if I ask Mama, it won't be a surprise."

"Lenny, at our age we don't need surprises. Our best surprise is that you are here. That's good enough for us."

"I'd like to get Mama something special."

"Your mother doesn't need anything."

"Nobody needs, Papa. It's a gift, a special surprise. A joyful thing it is to give."

"What great writer said that?"

"I said that. Papa, did Mama read my short stories?"

"Lenny, you ask her when she gets up from her nap."

"Dad, you read them?"

"Of course I read them."

"What do you think of my stories?"

"You are not an upbeat person." Papa laughs. "I know better, but if I read your stories, the industrial economy is in decline and getting worse and things on the farm are no better."

"Papa, we are in a depression, an economic downturn. Look at yourself. How much have you lost?"

"Took a little from my winnings, Lenny. Fewer death taxes for you to pay. Diversify, Lenny. To survive you have to diversify. If commercial real estate goes bad, you have the farm. "Lenny, I am thinking of buying a grain farm."

"Papa, don't let Mama hear you. She'll scream!"

"Your mama is a screamer, a good woman, but she has no vision of tomorrow."

Dad moves his chair to follow the sun. "I am cold, Lenny."

I nod. The wind is from the east. The clouds gray and mist this narrow barrier island. This will be an evening without the red, copper, gold flare of sunset.

My father, a bent old man with green eyes, in a black Reebok sweat jacket of white shoulders and teal arms, adds and divides six-digit numbers. My mother is like my father. Fifty years together. She too dresses in tan shorts, black sweatshirts. They walk hand in hand into the sunset. When they reach the hotel they will turn back, arrive home in time for *The McNeal-Lehrer Report* and tonight, Wednesday, for the fish supper that I have prepared.

Thursday is pasta and *Mystery*. Friday, the Sabbath, it's Mama's baked chicken and fruit compote topped by *Washington Week in Review*.

Mr. and Mrs. George Shapiro of Rockville, Illinois, supporters of three congregations, the Salvation Army, the YMCA, the arts, and their alma mater, Rockville College, western Illinois's only small liberal arts college, founded in 1860 on the shores of the Mississippi.

In the *Alumni News:* "Class of 1943, George and Milly Shapiro will be in residence at their Florida Gulf shore condo from the week before Thanksgiving until January 30, when the Shapiros return to their busy lives in Rockville."

On the first day of their drive back to Illinois, Dad will drive to Perry, Georgia. They will have their supper in the dining room at the New Perry Hotel. On the second day Dad will reach the Holiday Inn in Mattoon, Illinois. "An inside room, please, close to the swimming pool. The senior discount, thank you. Mr. and Mrs. George Shapiro, General Partners and Managers of the Shapiro Companies."

I hear from my sister Helene. "Lenny, I'm sorry I can't make it down for Thanksgiving. Becky is in a school play. Bill has to be in Washington the day after Thanksgiving, and I have the budget to get out."

"Helene, the folks were counting on you and Bill. You know how much Mama looks forward to seeing Becky."

"Tell the folks we'll be down in January."

Why didn't you say it, Helene? ". . . after Lenny goes back to teaching English composition to the poor deprived 'last chancers' of Rockville Community College." Say it, Helene. "I don't want to hear anything more about poor Lenny! But then, Lenny has always had health problems."

I can hear my sister: "You, a Stanford graduate with a Masters in English Literature from the University of Chicago, staying in Rockville."

Rockville gives me a chance to write.

"You live in a one-bedroom in Papa's apartment complex, you drive a Shapiro company car, you . . . Lenny, you are pissing your life away in Rockville, Illinois. Papa doesn't need your help. Has Papa ever asked you for advice? If Papa needs counsel he has two accountants and three lawyers!"

Say it Helene! *And his daughter, Helene!*

Mom and Dad are back from the beach. Dad is starting up the four steps from the beach. Right hand on the rail, Dad winches himself up. Left leg, right leg; left leg, then slowly, very carefully, the right. At the landing, Mom waits with her instructions. "George, up with the good."

Dad nods, strides down the concrete walk, with his left foot forward and a sway to the left to ease his right hip.

"You should use your cane."

Mom holds the screen door open. Dad enters.

"Any messages, Lenny?"

I know his head. Business before vacation.

"No one called."

"What's for supper, Lenny?"

"Broiled grouper. I told you that this morning when I came back from Fort Myers Beach, from the fish pier."

"So you did, so you did."

Dad is first for supper. His is the seat with the straight ahead view of the television.

"Mom, I can do that. Mom, sit down, I'll get the salad."

"Thank you, Lenny, great supper."

My father watches *McNeal-Lehrer* and reads the financial pages of *The New York Times*. "Time is money, Lenny. A penny saved is a penny earned."

Mom is into the refrigerator. Everything is wrapped, ziplocked to survive in its most pristine state. I hear Mother start the dish washer; she comes to sit beside me on the couch. "I read your stories, Lenny. You are getting better."

"Thanks, Mom."

"You are gaining insight."

"I am forty-six years old."

"So you are." Mom laughs. "Your father say anything to you?"

"About what?"

"About his hip. Your dad needs a hip replacement."

"He didn't say. All he said was that he was cold."

"That's his arthritis. All old arthritics are cold."

"It was in the mid seventies today."

Dad sits in full shade, writes letters of direction to his managers, wisdom to his diary, financial advice to my niece, Becky. This is Becky's first year at the U. of I. Introduction to Economics, macro and micro with exegesis by her grandfather, George Alan Shapiro, B.A., Rockville College.

"That's what it takes, Lenny, to be in business. You need to learn to integrate information. This is the age of surplus information. More information than anyone can use in the decision process. In the last twelve years, Lenny, I have had years where the Shapiro Companies spent more on accountants and lawyers than we had as profit."

"You are lucky, Dad. You knew you wanted to go into business with Grandpa."

"There is nothing wrong with teaching in a community college. Unions for college teachers, I don't know, Lenny. I didn't know you joined the union."

"I am the fortunate one, Papa. I have you to help and no one to support. For a man with a family—most of the teachers have little children—they need a union."

"No, that is not very much, Lenny, not for a full year's work. It may be enough if your wife is working. From pensions I don't know, Lenny. Mom and I never had a pension plan. We put everything back in the business. Thank God, it all worked out."

"Papa, would you like to go for a walk? You have been sitting long enough."

"Leave a note for your mother."

"Do you want your cane?"

"I'll take it, I'll take it."

We walk east to the lighthouse. The highrises on north Fort Myers Beach are sunlit. I hum, "The sun shines bright on my old Kentucky home."

Dad walks very slowly, drags, limps, each step a determination to move forward. Dad played Class A tennis until he was thirty-eight; until he was sixty, he jogged three miles a day on the banked, green, padded YMCA track, Monday, Wednesday and Friday, clockwise. On Tuesday, Thursday, Saturday, counter-clockwise.

When I was four, the year Dad came home from Korea, we lived in a bungalow in the east end of Rockville. Dad drop-kicked a football over the house. I had a sandbox in the back yard. Dad planted a wall of viburnum to keep me out of the alley. Helene was born five years later, after we had moved up on the hill, after Dad had begun building rental housing. When Mama tells of those days, "Lenny, your dad is a man of vision. He built the first integrated housing in western Illinois."

I sit beside my dad. He writes a letter. I read the *Times*.

"Tell me, Lenny, what did the doctor say?"

"I'll know when I get home."

"I heard you talking to him. You called from your bedroom when Mama was sleeping. I heard you."

"I'll have to have more chemo."

My dad puts his left arm around me. "When?"

"When I get back. I should have a very good response. There have been lots of improvement in therapy."

"I'll tell Mama. She won't mind. So what if we come home a couple of weeks sooner. When do you start teaching?"

"I have taken a leave for this quarter."

"Lenny, are you going to tell Helene?"

"I'll tell her soon enough. I'll get that done before I start my therapy."

"I am sorry, Lenny."

"'The best laid plans of mice and men do often go astray.'"

"Who said that?"

"Robert Burns, after he turned over a mouse's nest with his plow."

"Is that what you teach, Lenny? Poetry?"

"No, Papa, I teach writing."

On the south horizon, a fishing boat speeds home to Fort Myers Beach. Nearby a big white heron places a foot into the low-tide surf, withdraws his foot, shakes the water free, web-prints the wet sand.

"I like your last stories, Lenny. They are more full of description. I like your descriptions of the room with the paintings in the story about the house auction."

"Papa, I'm not going to tell Helene. I can't tell her that I am going for more treatment."

"Helene is a big girl."

"You tell her, Papa."

"Mama will tell Helene."

A pelican dives for supper, swallows, dives, swallows, dives.

"You'll move back in with us, Lenny."

"I'll have to."

My father stops, kisses me on the forehead. I begin to cry. "Cry, Lenny. Cry if you want to. I won't tell you not to cry."

"I wasn't crying because of my relapse, Papa. I was crying that you and Mama are still taking care of me. I should be taking care of you."

"You do enough for us, Lenny. Just being with us is enough."

On our evening walk on the beach, Dad turns back at the three-quarter-mile marker. The sun breaks through the clouds. Dad takes off his Reebok jacket. We walk, Dad in front of me, cane in his left hand. He places little weight on his right leg. He leans left. At his right, I am only a half-step behind.

I Like It, Benny

The full moon lights the beach so that an old man with macular degeneration could have found the body on the sandbar. The body lies with the face down, half buried in the wet, soft sand. I pull the head up by the hair into the moonlight. What was a face is a fluorescent green tomato with a moustache.

I look to the shore. I am opposite the Hotel Sanibel. Of that I am sure, because there are the For Rent catboats and windsurfers whose yellow and red sails reflect the moonlight.

This is like a John MacDonald Florida mystery, except that there is no wad of fifty-dollar bills in this dead man's mouth. He is only a very dead, forty-, forty-five-year-old in a black Speedo bathing suit.

I let the head go. The head sinks back into the sand. I walk back through the tidal pool to tell of my "head" to my brother, Benny, who adds direction to my life.

"Billy, what are you going to do with the rest of your life? You going to spend all winter sitting in the noonday sun, ogling Angela Lowry, hoping to catch a glimpse of her bare boobs? Billy, she is a fifty-year-old trying for thirty-eight. Billy, she is not for you."

I see Angela, the cigarette in her left hand, then both hands in motion, talking, talking with gestures through puffs of cigarette smoke.

I woke up my brother Benny, told him "The Mystery of the Body in the Sandbar."

"Dead?"

"Yes."

"Billy Boy, as they say in the detective novel, 'What do we know?' You went for a walk in the surf." Benny points at my wet khakis. "Opposite the hotel you step on a dead man with a big moustache dressed only in a Speedo swimsuit. You leave his head wedged into the sandbar, and now no doubt his body is covered by the incoming tide."

Benny gets up, looks out the porch screen. "Incoming tide," he confirms. "The problem, Brother Billy, is to tell, or not to tell. To call, or not call the police. Okay, you call the police from the corner telephone on East Gulf Drive."

"Why not from the kitchen?"

"So you can remain in the background, like any good writer. Then what?"

"Tell me."

"The police can't ignore you, but if you don't give your name . . . they probably won't send out boats to drag the shoreline. Maybe a couple of men with flashlights come out. If they find something, fine. If they don't, they tell themselves it was a prank."

Based on Benny's positive advice, just before midnight, I call 911 from the roadside phone. ". . . yes, on a sandbar opposite the hotel . . . that's where I stepped on a head of a dead man. . . ."

"Billy, what did the police say?"

"Asked for my telephone number. I hung up."

"You done good, Billy."

I LIKE IT, BENNY

At dawn, there is no sign of police or medical examiners down by the hotel. Benny and I are in the surf, opposite the stacked red and yellow sails. We slide and shuffle in the hip high, 72-degree water. Right foot, left foot: one hundred feet west on the sandbar, then one hundred feet east on the sandbar.

On the beach the power walkers race their heart. The shell pickers stoop and pick and choose. In the surf, Benny and I find nothing. Not even a star fish or sea urchin. On our way back, Benny says, "Billy, you sure about last night?"

"Benny, please."

"You were drinking."

"At seven o'clock."

"You took a Valium."

"At eleven."

"Billy, we could study the tide tables, see if the coastal patrol would drag the shoreline. That is police work Billy. Just be patient. Let's see how the newspapers play it."

On Thursday in the second section of the weekly *Island Reporter*, the "From the Police File" headlines: four missing cats, one alligator wandering from the sanctuary across the Sanibel-Captiva road, one Peeping Tom and sneak thieves, numbers unknown, who have been breaking into unattended cars.

"Benny, not a word about my dead man—"

This statement I cut short because an enlargement of Angela's breasts has appeared in my binoculars. Benny looks up from his *New York Times* crossword.

"Billy Boy, you started your mystery novel?"

"I am thinking. I am developing a plot line."

"You are thinking about Angela's boobs is what you're doing. Go over there and introduce yourself. 'I am William Roone, your neighbor. Please Mrs.—' What is her last name?"

"Lowry."

"'Please Mrs. Lowry, may I ask you not to sunbathe between the hours of ten and two. Those are the hours that I write.'"

"Benny, that is stupid!"

"You'll get a close up, and that may finish your boob fetish."

"What?"

"Get it over with, visit Angela. That's better than wasting hours watching Angela smoke and play mezzo, mezzo with her hands."

Benny demonstrates Angela's mezzo, mezzo movements. He has his left palm up, wiggles his hand at the wrist.

"I was over to the Lowrys' once. I got some of Angela's mail. That was when she and her mother moved in."

"Are you sure it's her mother?" Benny laughs. "You have no evidence that the older woman who sits and listens and nods is Angela's mother. I don't think it's her mother, I think it's a servant of some sort. A mother would talk back. Who picks up the patio when Angela goes in?"

"The older woman."

"That proves it. Billy Boy, I'll bet you one hundred dollars that nice older lady is not Angela Lowry's mother."

"You wouldn't be betting if you weren't sure."

"Take a chance, Billy. You win a hundred if I am wrong."

"How are we going to find out?"

"Elementary, my boy, elementary. Do as I tell you." Benny takes my binoculars. "You are off to meet sweet Angela. She will stink from Gauloises blue. Her teeth are tobacco-stained. Look around her eyes, note the wrinkles at the corners. Look for the tuck scars behind her ears."

Then Benny is up shouting and pointing. "Dolphins! There, just to the left of the palms."

Angela has heard Benny's roar. She is standing up. Regretfully, her bikini stays with her boobs.

I point, mouth, "Over there."

Angela shakes her head, forms her mouth into, "Where?"

Binoculars in hand, Benny is down the beach to Angela's house. Angela up close is not that different from Angela through my binoculars. Angela glistens and glows with sunblock from the top of her head, protected by a baseball cap bill, to the red nails of her toes. Her breasts heave, her belly and bottom are almost too full, her legs a trifle too short to be ideal, but, all together, still an admirably packaged product, not often bettered on this barrier island inhabited by wintering senior citizens.

Our dolphins have reached the causeway bridge. Pelicans are on their way to their roosts in the mangroves. On the Lowrys' deck, it's Angela and Benny and Billy. Angela of the Gauloises breath is charm and lilt. Benny of urbane wit has shared reminiscences with Angela. Now Angela is telling, "I was born in northern Italy. I went to Paris to study art history. Then I was at Sotheby's in England. I came to New York when Christie's needed an expert in European paintings. That is how I became Mrs. Lowry. At that time, Herbert, Mr. Lowry, was buying the contemporary Germans, Kiefer and Baselitz, and I said to Herbert, 'Saatchi is selling the most beautiful late Gustons.' So Herbert bought the Gustons. Saatchi needed the money."

"Angela, have you seen the price of Saatchi stock?" is what Benny asks. To which Angela answers, "Saatchi stock is up from its all-time low, but I do believe he is still selling paintings from his collection."

Benny and Angela are sharing tea and milk and a catalog from the Contemporary Art Fair in Chicago. On the beach sanderlings hunt their coquinas supper. When the sun's rays point to Captiva, Benny picks up the tea tray.

"Bill, would you please open the door for me?"

Angela says, "You mustn't. Rosa will get it when she comes back from shopping."

Benny says, "Not at all." Benny is the butler in a Noel Coward farce. I open the sliding door. Benny is into the living room, dining room, into the kitchen. Angela is beside him taking the tray. I close the doors to the deck. The cottage is dark, cool, air-conditioned.

Paintings, water colors, prints, not in clusters, but each in its own discrete space, are on every antique white wall. Benny is beside me in the living room. He stops, calls to Angela. "How wonderful, so many beautiful Georgio Morandis. Never have I seen such wonderful still lifes." The Morandi paintings are of gray, umber, tan bottles, jars and jugs. In one small canvas, the jars are in front of the bottles. In the next, the bottles are beside the jugs. The water colors are of a single jar or jug or bottle. The prints are more jugs, bottles, cross hatched into a background of grays and blacks. Under the bay window is a glass-topped gray metal desk. Three drawers on the left, three drawers on the right.

I LIKE IT, BENNY

On the desk, in an 8-by-11 art deco sterling silver frame, is a photograph of my dead man with the untidy moustache. The photograph is by "Karsh of Ottawa" and is inscribed, "For my dearest Angela. H."

Benny has completed his rounds, his "Ooh-Ahh" of the "greatest collection of Morandis I have ever had the pleasure to view. So nice to have met you, Angela." This salutation with a hesitant hint of a bow. I am waiting for the hand kiss and the heels together click. At the door, Benny shakes Angela's nicotine-stained hands. "Don't forget to come by. We are so looking forward to meeting Mr. Lowry."

Angela mouths, "Ciao."

It's a very pleased-with-himself Benny who pours four ounces of the red Zinfandel from the bottle in our kitchen, the brand that Aunt Clara uses only for her Thursday Beef Bourguignon.

Benny makes a toast. "To your mystery novel, Billy Boy. You can quit thinking, quit worrying. All you have to do is write. Take out your legal pads and commence." Benny is ever the exuberant, optimistic Roone.

"Not yet, Benny. I can't, start a mystery novel with only a dead head and no resolution. I need to know who, when, why."

Benny doesn't answer my question. He overflows: "Billy Boy Billy Boy, your fortune is made. You have a million dollar bestseller."

I get a glass of iced water, add lemon. "Tell me!"

"Angela has a husband—had a husband, Herbert. A man of wealth, taste and distinction like in the Hart Shaffner ads in the Sunday *Times Magazine*. This, my boy, is husband number three. Husband number one was French. He supported Angela through her advanced degree at the Sorbonne. There is when she learns to smoke Gauloises blue, the trade mark of the contemporary French cultural heroes. Husband number two was British. Is he alive, or is he dead? Only of historical interest because you are only concerned with husband number three. Herbert Lowry, who is a very well known collector, is on the board of 'this' Museum of Contemporary Art and 'that' Foundation for the support of young—that is, under forty—emerging artists. That, Billy, you can substantiate in *Who's Who in American Art* or in the Vanity Press where important collections are displayed monthly. You can begin with when Angela meets Herbert.

"Herbert, a recent widower in despair, sells his home in Connecticut, his contemporary art collection at a huge profit, moves into Trump Towers or the Hotel Pierre. Herbert meets Angela DuPre-Powers in the health club. He is enchanted, delighted to discover that he and Angela share an interest in art, body rebuilding and safe sex. Chapter two or three or four, that is up to you, Billy.

"Angela gets Herbert to buy ten, twelve Georgio Morandis. You saw them on the wall. A Morandi painting, let's say, is five or six hundred thousand, maybe a million. Let's presume that Angela arranges for herself from the grateful sellers a small commission; ten percent would be usual. For Angela it's cash for a rainy day, as they say on the North Shore. Diamonds and gold go with everything. Then it's art, love and marriage.

"Now is the time for your flashbacks. Could the Morandis have been stolen from some old friends of Georgio. Call the IFAR office in New York or Geneva; they collect all the data on who lost what painting, when. Herbert, unknowingly or knowingly, buys the stolen Morandis. He takes possession in Switzerland where—how shall I put it?—the sale laws are less demanding of proof of ownership.

"Add a couple of chapters of experts, provenance makers, clandestine meetings, intrigue in Paris, Geneva, Milan. Jean Le Mairie—he used to be a curator at the Louvre—is an expert on Morandi water colors. You now have a tale 'based on tomorrow's headlines.' An assured bestseller."

I am beginning to understand why Benny never made colonel; he can't be questioned, can't be interrupted. Without time out for a sip of wine, Benny is off in full force.

"We could presume that the Morandis are legit with perfect provenances?"

I nod, once only.

"Not to worry, Billy. Angela is building her nest egg. She arranges for a Morandi or two to be stolen. The Morandis will end up on the wall of a Colombian drug lord. Picture scenes with drug trafficker types, heavy gold jewelry, white Mercedes and thin Scandinavian bimbos.

"The heist is successful: the Lowrys get the insurance, Angela adds a couple of hundred thousand in laundered hundreds to her lock box. How do you like that, Billy?

"Or try, Lowry Industries has had one bad year, two bad years. Herb needs dollars. If he sells Morandis at auction or by private treaty, the word gets out. The next time Lowry goes to sell, he gets less. Angela is the killer, because you and I know Herbert is in the surf. Or, if you like, Herbert can be alive. Why not? Angela and Herbert quarrel. 'Angela, no! Never will I allow you to sell my Morandis.' '*Your* Morandis! *Our* Morandis! If I hadn't introduced you to Italian paintings . . .' Confrontation, yelling, cursing. Herbert sulks, swims out by himself, never to be seen again. Or Angela in a moment of passionate Italian temper grabs a conch shell, hits poor Herbert on his head, drags him into the surf. Herbert is of sainted memory."

Benny is unstoppable.

"Billy, let's go back to Herbert and Angela. Herb suspects Angela of setting up the caper to defraud the insurance company. How he finds out is your problem, Billy, because Angela has been very discreet. She meets her Mafia contact, Big Joe Pisano, at the Island Marina. Big Joe arrives in his 34-foot yacht from wherever you like. Angela and Big Joe sit next to each other at the bar in Grandpa's, the marina's very busy luncheon spot. Just two strangers who meet over a fried grouper sandwich and a Miller's Lite to plan a two million dollar robbery.

"Herb finds out, accuses Angela. She screams, 'Never! Never! That is stupid, Herb.' Herb says, 'As you wish, Angela. But I intend to put a couple of my best security people on this!' That very evening while the sun sets in the west and the moon rises in the east, under the light of the twinkling stars, Angela dissolves a little chloral hydrate or a couple of Valium in Herbert's Scotch. You like Valium, don't you, Billy? Okay, Valium. Then, the Lowrys go for their togetherness swim into the sunset. Only Angela comes home."

Benny is up into the kitchen for the Sutter Home Zinfandel. I follow for my iced water. While Benny sips, I interrogate. "Okay, Benny, the body. What about the body on the sandbar?"

"Definitely foul play. Big Joe Pisano, Mafia hit man, takes out Herb so that he can move in with Angela. Big Joe is crazy to own those Morandis."

"Benny, is the dead Herbert Lowry ever seen again?"

"Herb has to appear. A body found on the beach waiting to be identified. If Herb isn't found murdered, there is no story."

"I found him—"

I LIKE IT, BENNY

"And lost him." Benny finishes my sentences; that's why Benny was passed over for promotion. "That's it, Billy. A dead man is found on the beach."

"Why hasn't Angela reported Herb missing?"

"Good, Billy. This will make a great mystery novel for you. All you have to do is write it."

Between Benny's sips of wine, I try, "Benny, what if the body is not Herb Lowry? Just another man with a moustache."

"Billy, you saw the head. You saw the photos. Trust your judgment: the head is Herbert Lowry."

"Still."

"Play it for certain, Billy. Play it your own way. Tomorrow you go over, call on Angela very casually like and question her. 'Who is that man in the photo? Where is that man in the photo?'"

"Huh. Just like that?"

"Don't 'huh' me Billy. You have the plot for a love story or a mystery. You are the narrator. Widow Angela is the husband killer. Angela seduces the narrator into silence. How can he squeal on his lover. Or, better yet, she seduces him into the silence of marriage!"

I scream, "I like it I like it!"

Benny is silent.

Omission

On Friday morning after the *shacharit* service, Robert Hart asked David Lowe, "How is it going?" David Lowe answered that cursory question with, "Rabbi, my right ankle is turning out which flattens my arch. I am getting a molded plastic shoe insert, which I hope will support my ankle. Then perhaps I will be able to do without my cane."

The Rabbi, his back to David Lowe, said, "Huh," continued to fold his prayer shawl into its sack. Sack in hand he darted out the back door of the prayer house, down the hall of the school house wing and out the emergency door to his car, his breakfast, his yesterday's *New York Times*.

David Lowe limped into his Lincoln, opened the roof to the white and purple of the blossoming trees, to the sun glistening off the rain soaked lawns, to another warm to hot, muggy May morning in Rockville, Illinois, where the Mississippi flowed from the east to west, where the gambling boat with the lowest take in the state cruised between the highway 280 bridge to Iowa and the Hampton lock and dam.

David Lowe, infused with the glory of God's earth, drove slowly by the blossoming trees of Thirtieth Street. With this morning's prayers he had praised the Lord for all the goodness He had bestowed on him, for his very life, for his awakening from sleep.

At the traffic light, David turned right through Rockville College. He stopped to permit a young woman, eighteen or nineteen, so young, so thinly dressed in gray sweatshirt and white shorts, to cross Seventh Avenue. She smiled a thank you. David gave her a half wave as he pulled the bill of his baseball cap down to keep the rising sun from his eyes. He continued east on the one-way into the downtown. Yes, gasoline prices were at an all-time high. The price of gasoline was not of any significance to the Lowes, not as few miles as he and his wife Annie drove. The only place Annie drove was to her aquatic exercising class which did help to keep her blood sugar down.

David parked on the street. He again blessed God for his and Annie's lives which were in His hands. Cane in advance he rode up to the fifth floor of the Reliance Building. In the outer office the message light winked red.

"Mr. Lowe. This is Bob Wall. Please call me. I would like to talk to you about your land in Rockville."

David heated water, threw a Lipton tea bag into the white plastic cup, dialed Chicago.

"Robert Wall, please." David spoke slowly, careful to subdue the eastern vowels he had brought with him more than forty years ago when he and Annie had come to Rockville. The aroma of the tea brought him back to his dream of Thursday night, in which he had soiled, fouled himself with yellow splotches of feces. He saw his droppings, flattened like cow manure, on the white wool of the bedroom rug. Not really like cow manure, because in the spring, when the cows were first turned out on pasture, their manure was almost dark green in color, not like the yellow droppings in his dream. And the odors were different. His stool had smelled of disease and death, while the cows' . . . the cows' smelled of new grass and spring.

The phone rang, once, twice, three times.

"This is Bob Wall." Then a long pause. "Mr. Lowe, our acquisitions committee has just completed a review of the profiles you sent out."

Another pause. David Lowe said, "Yes."

"I am sorry. I thought we could use the acreage, but the grades and the layout of the road are quite wrong. Just too much dirt to be moved to make it work for us."

Another pause, which David answered. "I could adjust the price to offset any land moving costs that you would have."

"I am sorry, Mr. Lowe. The drainage is also a problem and the utilities are in the wrong location."

David Lowe murmured, "I understand. Please do send the prints back."

"It is a shame, Mr. Lowe. A wonderful location, a fine piece of land. Shame it was ruined by such bad engineering. Sorry we can't use your land. It would have been good for both of us." With that, Bob Wall hung up.

David Lowe walked down the hall to Doyle and Associates Engineering. Archie Doyle, forty-five, tall, thin and dour, was on the phone. He motioned to David. David spread his drawings across the 1950s glass-topped desk. Archie took the high stool beside the drafting table, looked down at David Lowe. David Lowe looked out the window beyond the desk at the half-leafed-out oaks on the bluff, turned to Archie, pointed to the blueprints, handed him the list of deficiencies that Robert Wall had so carefully noted. Archie read the list, said nothing. David pointed to the drawings on the desk.

"True?"

"Could be. You know this layout was designed for exposed basements on the south side of the road. That way the extra dirt that came off the north hillside could be used as fill on the south."

"I left all the design responsibilities to you. You know I have no engineering background."

Archie grinned. "You didn't make all that money in the building business without learning something about drainage and layouts and the cost of moving dirt."

"Archie, that's why I am here. That's what I thought. You ought assume the cost of moving the dirt across the road. After all, it is your faulty design that makes the acreage unsalable."

Archie didn't answer. David went on, smiled. "I thought just to keep up the reputation and the integrity of Doyle Engineering."

Archie got up, rolled the drawings, reached into the desk drawer for two rubber bands, snapped one onto either end of the roll.

David Lowe stood up. Archie gave him the blueprints, threw the list of design deficiencies into the waste.

"Archie, are you going to take up my case with your insurance company?"

"I don't know that you have a case."

"Why not talk to your insurers, let them decide?"

When Archie Doyle didn't answer, David Lowe tried, "Archie, tell me how is business?"

"We pay our rent on time."

"That I know, I am your landlord."

"The downtown is finished. This is no longer a good location for me. No offense, Mr.

Lowe. I'll tell you, when my lease is up I am moving out on the beltway. The only way I am going to make it is by upgrading the image of this office. I need new modern equipment in an up-to-date, centrally located, air conditioned office."

David Lowe said, "Thank you. I understand you have to do what is best for yourself."

In his office David stacked the drawings with others of Lowe land holdings, dialed Annie at home. There was no answer. He hit the automatic dial for Jess Palmer, attorney at law.

"Mr. Palmer will call you right back."

David Lowe leaned back into his Herman Miller office chair, looked out the window at the chimney that needed tuck pointing, the copper roof that should have the flashing replaced, the vacant suites on the second and fourth floors.

The phone rang.

"David, I am returning your call."

"Jess, remember the topographical drawings I went over with you for those twelve acres I own in the southwest corner of town?"

"Yes."

"I think it's time we file the suit against Doyle Engineering."

"One moment, David. I have that one in my pending file. Here it is. You are asking a lot of money for moving dirt."

"Jess, double that amount. The more we ask for the more we will get."

"I don't know . . ."

"The insurance company will settle. According to my information this is the fourth or fifth claim against Doyle Engineering. There is no reason they won't settle this one as they have all the others."

"We can try. As I said before, it will be difficult to prove."

"Remember, Jess, nothing ventured, nothing gained. The more I get, the greater your share."

David Lowe dialed his home. Annie answered. "I'll be about a half hour late," he said.

"Anything the matter?"

"I have to stop by Palmer's, sign some papers for a lawsuit I had on hold."

"David, you don't need the stress. Remember what the doctor told you."

"No stress, Annie. I waited like I promised you. I waited until I got Bob Wall's list of deficiencies."

"David, we don't need this."

David hung up the phone, sighed, redialed his home. "Annie, I forgot to tell you. Archie Doyle will be moving out in October."

"You expected that."

"You are right, Annie."

"David, you don't need this lawsuit."

"We will see. Let's wait and see."

David Lowe hung up the phone, reached behind him for the key to the men's room, pulled up his right leg from behind his desk, started left foot forward, right leg, left leg, right left, his right twisted. Tomorrow there should be a call from the orthotics fitter.

OMISSION

In the washroom Archie Doyle was combing his hair. He turned, noticed that David was limping. "Hurt?"

"It's my right ankle."

Archie Doyle reached and opened the door

"Archie, hold on a minute, I am coming." They rode up the elevator together. "Archie, you have a minute?"

"For you? Anytime."

"Come in to my office, sit down." David Lowe pulled a side chair closer to his desk.

"Archie, nothing personal, I wanted to tell you before you received the summons. I have asked Jess Palmer to file an error and omission suit on your design."

"About what I expected when Bob Wall called me from Chicago. From my conversation with Wall I got the impression you offered to pay for moving the dirt." Then Archie added, "That is if Wall bought the land and you got the money from the insurance company."

"So what is wrong with that?"

"Nothing, David. Nothing." Archie got up to leave. David shook his hand.

"I am sorry. Nothing personal Archie, you know that."

"Nothing personal, David. As you say."

How the Mittleberg Book of Hours Came to Rockville

I was raised in a God-fearing, God-worshipping family, attending morning and evening services seven days a week. We practiced the virtues: humility, charity, diligence, patience. "David, if you work hard this will be your America. You will succeed." My father worked hard and died at the age of forty-six of tuberculosis.

I do tell a roundabout story. You asked how I acquired a Book of Hours, illuminated by Robert Testard in about 1480, and how and why I donated it to my alma mater Rockville College instead of selling it at auction. I also donated at the same time a Gaugin wood cut of the crèche series. That was when Gaugin was in Brittany. You have the press release from the Rockville College Art Museum. You came from *Art News* to interview me. Art is now reported like a commodity, like soy beans and corn. Today everyone knows how much the Gans Collection sold for at Christie's Auction. More than two hundred million dollars! Of course my collection is nothing like that.

My father died, my mother was a widow, my sister was still in high school. What is a poor boy to do but work his way through college and help support his mother at the same time. The YMCA ran a student employment office. The office was in Old Main. That is where the English department now has its copy machine.

I had jobs no one else would take . . . working half the night unloading trucks, and I had good jobs, delivering the campus mail. But my best job was stacking books in the Art Library. That is when I saw my first great art as illustrations in books I was returning to the shelves. I learned from pictures. At first I couldn't read French or German.

I learned my foreign languages and my art by reading. Later, when the Army sent me to Europe, I had the vocabulary from the book learning and the ear. I spoke decent French and adequate German, that is for an American.

You graduated in 1942 . . . ?

I didn't get to Europe until right after the war.

Rockville College also received your record collection, which the music department described as a significant addition to their archives.

It's mostly Satie piano music. Satie and the French Impressionists works not frequently performed. Do you know Honegger's piano music? I never had a course in art in my life. Never had the opportunity. Not at Rockville. I never had enough time for electives. What few hours I had for myself, working and going to school, I had to study and chase a girl or two until Sarah caught me. That was many years later. I was a lot handsomer then, four inches taller. I was getting bald by the time Sarah came into my life. No, Sarah and I didn't get married till after I came home from the Korean War.

You were telling me about The Book of Hours illuminated manuscript.

Oh yes, the Book of Hours. I was in Paris for a public health conference. The conference ended on a Thursday afternoon, so I stayed on. It started to rain, so I ducked into a burlesque show. There was a comic who made eyes at a bare-breasted nurse. I was trying to learn French argot, the street language slang, which I never did learn. My French was school French, florid.

There were very few in the audience. The French didn't have the time or the money to spend on coarse comedy. There was an intermission. I got up, went outside for a breath of air. It was still raining. Under the marquee was another American smoking—you could tell Americans in Paris by their shoes and clothes and by the way their hair was cut. He asked me, "You understand what they are saying?"

"Not all of it."

"For me it's not any of it. I am doing Medieval French. My name is Harry Applebaum."

"I see you are in the Veterinary Corps. I did intelligence in Germany."

His English had a very faint German accent. "I took my discharge in Europe so I could go to the Sorbonne."

It had stopped raining. I didn't have my raincoat with me. My Army raincoat was heavier than the rain. If I wore it I sweated on the inside and was dry on the outside. If I didn't, I was wet on the outside and dry on the inside. Army officers were not allowed to carry an umbrella.

Harry asked, "You hungry?"

I was twenty-six. At twenty-six I was always hungry. Today it's just a bagel and coffee for breakfast. For lunch all I eat is a small salad of romaine lettuce, a half an egg, a half a tomato and matzah. Have you ever eaten matzah? Very good food, high fiber, low fat. Really no fat, no salt. An ideal diet for the elderly.

You're not that old.

I am old enough to be careful of what I eat.

Harry took us to a kosher restaurant. Not a delicatessen but a two-star French restaurant where one dines on four to six courses with the appropriate wines and after-dinner espresso. For dessert I had my first strawberry flan. . . . The only dessert I eat now is a graham cracker. Sarah bakes a bread now and then for the Sabbath, but she hasn't baked a cake in years. She is slightly diabetic and I am always dieting, trying to get some of my belly fat off . . .

We were walking back to the Metro. I was staying in a small family-owned hotel near the National Library. The library had a print room. That's where I saw my first Villon prints. The things we remember. It must have been about 9:30, the late papers had just been dropped at the news vendors. We each bought a paper, stopped to read the headlines. The vendor looked up at us, smiled, actually he laughed at us. "American soldier, reading a newspaper is not the way to learn French. Find a nice young woman, she will teach you—in bed when you make love."

The Book of Hours?

I was coming to that.

Harry Applebaum was studying middle French. That's the fourteenth-fifteenth century, a very church-ridden time is how Harry explained it to me. He was considering giving up Medieval French and going to medical school in Chicago. He was from Evanston. That is what he did in June; gave up his French studies and took up medicine. He became a pediatrician.

Harry has been dead for more than twenty years. He died at fifty-one or fifty-two of lung cancer. No. I never smoked cigarettes. Never had the time to spend smoking. Smells bad, tastes bad, is bad for you.

Whenever I had a free weekend I headed to Paris. Brussels to Paris by train is only three hours. I liked Brussels well enough but Paris had the great museums. Harry and I were museum goers. Young men who went to museums. Stupid, now that I look back. When you are young it should be wine, women and song. We went to the opera, all to improve ourselves. We were feasting on the Impressionists, on the Fauves. The exhibitions of contemporary art at the galleries was also very exciting. We saw Alberto Giacometti's sculpture, Diego's furniture. Yes, I saw Picasso and Matisse and Cezanne. I should have bought Picasso, but I didn't have the money. Even then Picasso was expensive. I was saving for getting married, for starting a practice. That took years of savings.

I got a GI loan. I worked for the State of Illinois as a public health officer. I got a car, a supervisor a hundred miles away, an adequate salary and a pension plan . . . and annual transfers to the other parts of the state. When Sarah and I decided to get married is when I decided to try private practice.

The Book of Hours . . . I was helping Harry pack for his trip home, crating his books. Harry hauls out his foot locker, unfolds from tissue paper the Book of Hours, hands it to me.

"Here David, a present for you from the citizens of Mittleberg, Germany. Not a one knew about the death camps or about the furnaces. Everyone in Mittleberg told the same story. 'The Jews left before the war. My father's tailor was a Jew. We had a Jewish doctor in Mittleberg.'"

I asked Harry, "Don't you want the Book of Prayers?"

"No, not anymore." Then Harry asked me, "You believe in prayer?"

I said, "Yes."

"You keep it. You now have prayers for every hour of the day."

I too kept the Book of Hours in my foot locker. I leafed through it once or twice. The calendar illustrations are very beautiful.

The trunk and I came home to Rockville. The trunk to be stored in the basement of the clinic that I built with the help of a GI loan. Sarah had a few precious mementos of her own she kept in the trunk. It was like our safe. Our children's first shoes, a couple of aprons her mother had embroidered for her trousseau. All those thirty years I knew where the Book of Hours was.

But we had lost the key. I had to get a locksmith to open it. You know how life is always too busy. First it's work, then it's getting ready to retire. That's when I started cleaning out. When in doubt, throw it out.

I gave some of my veterinary library to Rockville College, but most of the books, mostly old texts, only had historical value, if that. If you want to see my old Army uniforms you have to go to the County Museum.

I didn't know the exhibition of the Book of Hours in the library of a small college in western Illinois would cause such a ruckus. The FBI came with a representative from the City of Mittleberg. The city of Mittleberg wanted their Book of Hours returned. I don't even know where Mittleberg is.

You asked me what do I think. What do I think. I look at the prayer book as the words to help medieval man deal with sin and corruption. This I understand—that prayers are important. They do sustain and support. This I know from personal experience.

What I meant, Dr. Keller, was do you think that the Book should be returned to Mittleberg?

Whatever is decided is quite all right with me. There is a very good possibility that the college will be rewarded if they agree to return the Book to Germany.

What did you say, Dr. Keller?

What I said was, the Germans stole magnificent nineteenth century, twentieth century and contemporary paintings from the Jews of Germany, France and Hungary. Then the Russians, the victors, took the paintings home as war booty. Last year there was an exhibition of these liberated paintings. You know what I think? Give the Book back to Mittleberg. Let it be returned to their church, to city hall, to be put on exhibition with a note, "Returned by the United States of America."

I should be going. I have a five-thirty flight.

I can drive you to the airport. You have never been in western Illinois before.

I was admiring your art library, Dr. Keller. How did you acquire a French, German—I saw some Italian too—how did you acquire those books living in Rockville?

From book dealers, and auction sales. Some I bid. Most I bought.

You have some rarities.

Some. I did quite well considering I have lived along the Mississippi all my life. When I was a boy we lived where the poor do, in the bottom. Our clinic is only two blocks from where the river flows from east to west. Our home is on the bluff. After the war, the new construction had to begin on the bluff. This was a woodland pasture when I started practicing.

Is it always this gray?

Don't look at the sky, Mr. Bowen, look at the oaks. Magnificent native red and white oaks on this bluff.

I wanted to thank you and Mrs. Keller for you hospitality.

I will tell Sarah. Would you like to cross the Mississippi? I can take you to the airport the long way, via Iowa. Perhaps the next time you will have more time.

I want to be quite sure you said that the Book of Hours was in a trunk for more than thirty years.

Thirty-three years exactly. As long as I practiced veterinary medicine in that clinic.

You didn't look at the Book of Hours for thirty-three years.

Praying to combat sin and evil is not the Jewish concern. Ours is a more active approach. We try to do good and leave the rest to God. Sometimes he helps us, and sometimes we have to wait.

I didn't think about this medieval illustrated book until Sarah asked me to get her mother's aprons. She wanted them for our granddaughter. Perhaps someone in Mittleberg was praying for the return of their Book of Hours.

You believe that Dr. Keller?

The rabbis assure us that sooner or later our prayers are answered. Sometimes not in our time but they are answered.

You believe that a German's prayers would be answered?

They would be if he or she were righteous.

The Retirement Party

The autumn days were warm, the nights had turned cool but without the threat of frost. Weather this pleasant kept the combines working in the soybean fields until they had to put their lights on to find their way back to the farm yards.

On the bluff above the Mississippi, in the oak wooded cul-de-sac where the Sauk Indians had hunted wild turkey and deer, Steven and Gertrude Berg had built their dream home.

The acorns had fallen. The curled, dried-to-russet leaves lay on the parched, unmown lawn. Early this Saturday morning Steven Berg, in khaki trousers, black cotton knit long sleeved shirt, came out of the garage to water the pots of red, white and pink impatiens that ring the oak that shaded the front door and the window walls of their living room. The impatiens watered, he cut the wilted stalks of the daylilies that this year had produced so few flowers. The lilies, planted to camouflage the splash block, were getting on . . . aging, tired . . . tired of blooming and performing.

On the back fence line, the lilac, the oldest of the flowering bushes, transplanted from the home the Bergs had lived in for thirteen years before they could move up to Oak Hills, had died in the winter freeze. The hawthorn that Gertie had insisted Steve plant to block her front door from the drive-by gawkers who had appeared every Sunday afternoon, when Oak Hills addresses had been the most desirable in Rockville, had succumbed to the July drought. Its browned branches and thorny limbs lay on the back yard burn pile waiting for the oak leaves falling, blowing, waiting for the Bergs' yard man to come for the day when burning was permitted.

"Steven." Gertie was at the side door. "Get dressed. I don't want to miss the Rabbi's sermon."

Steven parked in the mostly empty lot. Gertie had dressed for services: lightweight gray woolen suit, Hermes scarf knotted to display the prancing horses. Gertrude Berg waited for her husband to lock the car. "I am glad you wore your blue suit."

"Only suit that fits decently."

"You could buy another."

Steven Berg shrugged an "I could" but did not answer.

The usher greeted the Bergs, they made their way to the sixth row, right front of the upholstered seats. There were no assigned seats in Congregation Beth El, but neither were there any challenges by visitors or newcomers to the places chosen by the twenty to thirty regular Sabbath worshipers.

On this first week after Simchat Torah, the Torah portion to be read was Genesis. "In the beginning."

Steven Berg read the fifth portion, pledged his traditional eighteen dollars, Chai, that signified life, shook the Rabbi's hand, returned to his seat, nodded off during the reading from Prophets, awoke to Gertrude's nudge as the Rabbi began his sermon.

"Today I wish to tell you of a man who was always there whenever I needed him. Who

THE RETIREMENT PARTY

never failed to support our community needs, who tonight will be honored by his business associates. Congratulations for your many years of leadership, Steven Berg, for a job well done. We are proud of you."

The Bergs drove home in silence. As Steven came through the garage into the kitchen, Gertie warned, "You had better take a long nap this afternoon. I don't want you falling asleep at the party."

Steven smiled. "Would I do that?"

"You have."

Dressed again in his khakis and knit shirt, Steven reclined in his arm chair, feet up on the foot stool. The morning mail sorted, he turned to yesterday's stock market quotes. His RexCo stock was up another twenty-five cents.

Gertie had shed her Sabbath suit for stretch jeans and gray sweatshirt. She drew up the rocker to be closer to her husband.

"You okay, Steven?"

"I am okay."

"You look tired."

"It has been a tough couple of weeks."

"You disappointed?"

"RexCo's offer was more than fair."

"You look down."

"I know. It's no one's fault, Gertie. I was just thinking of years ago, of what could have been."

"You can't blame Scot . . . or Betty. Children have their own lives."

Steven Berg chuckled. "Their generation has it the best yet. They do what pleases them and then they inherit from their parents. No one has ever had it that good before."

"Don't get cynical, Steven. You really didn't expect Scot or Betty to spend their lives running Three Hills Pharmacies, 'that serve you best because they know you best'."

"Advice and service is what built our stores."

Gertie took the mail from Steven, patted his shoulder. "Take your nap."

The lights on the Victorian porches of the Country Club dining rooms came on as the Bergs drove up. Steven stopped at the side steps to let Gertrude get out, parked in a handicapped slot, watched his wife go up the three steps. Gertie was gaining weight, although her long sleeved silk aqua suit hid most of the spread. She held and pulled on the railing to go up the three steps. Hand firmly on the railing, Steven Berg slowly followed.

At the door to the dining rooms Gertie turned, straightened her husband's blue rep tie. "You do look good in your blue suit."

"Suitable for funerals."

"This is not a funeral, Steven."

"You are right."

The bulletin board directed, "RexCo Company — River Room" The entire top management team of RexCo was there in their blue blazers, red logo ties, their wives in little black dresses accented by genuine pearl necklaces.

Ross Harding, the district sales manager, was first with hand shake and smile. Jim Peal, the VP for finance, followed with, "So good to see you Mr. and Mrs. Berg."

A young man, twenty-six or twenty-eight, came up to the Bergs, introduced himself. "I am George Lang." There was no recognition from either Steven or Gertrude. "My dad is the CEO."

Gertrude extended her hand. "Of course, you must be Roger's youngest son. He told us so much about you. You do look like your father."

"Mrs. Berg, you should see my brother, Andy. He is a real look-alike of my dad."

Gertrude Berg smiled.

"My dad would have come but Mom has him fully scheduled on the weekends. You know, she is on the symphony board."

"Steven was on the Arts Board for twenty years."

"We know that, Mrs. Berg. That is what made Rockville so attractive for us," and with a smile, "That and Mr. Berg's reputation as a merchant."

They were ten for dinner, toasts and applause. Ross Harding spoke as the host. "We welcome Mr. and Mrs. Berg to the RexCo family." His speech was followed by toasts of Korbel champagne and applause. "Mr. Berg, would you like to say something?"

Gertrude opened her slim handbag, took out a folded sheet, passed it down the table to her husband. Steven stood up, held the table with his left hand. "Mrs. Berg and I thank you for honoring us at this dinner." Steven sat down.

Gertrude leaned over, whispered, "Steven, your speech."

Steven got up, spoke softly, as if to himself. "Once, many years ago Three Hills Pharmacies was a first class operation. But that was years ago and the times have changed. The too few changes that I did make failed. So we became second rate owners of three seedy stores in changing neighborhoods." A pause, then, loudly so he could be heard, "Your offer to buy us out was . . ." Here, Steven stopped, picked up the printed sheet, read loudly. "Mrs. Berg and I are very pleased for Three Hills Pharmacies to be merged into RexCo. We thank you for honoring us with this dinner."

There was applause, Steven sat down. George Lang was the first to rise. "Don't get up, Mr. Berg. I just wanted to tell you how much I enjoyed meeting you and Mrs. Berg." George Lang turned to Gertrude who had now stood behind her seated husband.

He whispered, "Mr. Berg all right?"

"He has been under a great deal of stress with the sale and all."

"I understand."

The Hardings accompanied the Bergs to their car. "Good night."

"So nice to meet you, Mrs. Harding."

The harvest moon lit the river. The swing bridge from Arsenal Island to Rockville was open. Steven Berg closed the sliding roof half way, shut the motor of the Lincoln, pushed the seat control back so that he could see the moon through the steel frame of the railroad bridge. Gertrude Berg looked up.

"Lovely night."

"It's late. Eleven-twenty. We haven't been out this late in twenty years."

The barge, loaded with grain for New Orleans, passed through the lock. The gate went up. The Rockville industrial riverfront was dark, shut except for the liquor convenience store.

In the cul-de-sac the west wind had accumulated the fallen russet oak leaves in front of the double garage doors.

THE RETIREMENT PARTY

***

Gertrude followed Steven into their walk-through closet. Steven sat taking off his shoes. Steven sighed, smiled. "By me, it hurts all over."

"You are beginning to sound like your mother when she was an old lady."

"I have lived twenty-six years longer than my mother."

"We are all living longer."

"Steven, you do know that we were fortunate to sell out to the Langs."

"It saved me from closing down two of the stores and I don't know how long the Fourteenth Avenue store would have remained profitable if RexCo would have opened up down the street."

"Steven, you should be very proud of what you achieved."

Steven Berg stood up, took out the printed page from the inside pocket of his jacket, read loudly. "I am honored to have joined the RexCo family."

Steven sat down, put on his slippers. Gertrude put her arms around him. "You all right, Steven?"

"Fine, Gertrude. Just fine."

"Have you taken your pills?"

"I will, Gertie. You know I always do."

Lightning Struck Once

I had seen the house on my morning jogs through the Oak Hills neighborhood, recognized it as the Appleton house from the photo accompanied by the brief history, presented to the city of Rockville by Anne Appleton, in the loving memory of her mother, Ruth Fuhr Appleton, etc., a landmark to be returned to its former splendor with Federal funds. Appleton house, a two-story colonial with a central stair, two white-painted brick columns, was built by Philip Appleton, a manufacturer of bread-slicing machines. It was lived in by his widow, who willed it to their only child, Anne Appleton, now a resident of the Lutheran Home, who divided the upstairs and downstairs into apartments in her failed effort to maintain the property with the rental income.

Appleton House stands on its own half-acre in a grove of mature native oaks that provide cooling shade in the he summer and a protective wall against the west wind in winter.

On my next visit to the Rockville Library, the first in western Illinois, I asked the reference librarian, "The Appleton Home?"

She smiled back. "I have Mrs. Appleton's obituary. She was on our board of directors from 1922 to 1928. The children's reading room in our southwest branch was named in her memory."

In the cool of the business reading room, between the gleeful retirees punching numbers into their electronic calculators, I read the Rockville *Journal*, dated October 11, 1948. Ruth Fuhr Appleton died at home on October 10, 1948. Widow of Philip Appleton, she was preceded in death by a sister, a brother and a son. She is survived by an only daughter, Anne Wilma Appleton, of this city. Mrs. Appleton was born on May 24, 1881 to John and Mildred Goodwin Fuhr of Prairie Township. She attended local schools, Oberlin College. Married Philip Appleton (no date). Ruth Appleton was well known as a public benefactor, exhibiting her collection of contemporary American paintings at the Rockville Library for the benefit of the Fight Tuberculosis Fund. Ruth Appleton was the author of *Rockville Tales*, a collection of short stories that were highly praised by Thompson Bell, literary critic of *The New York Times*: "Ruth Fuhr's *Rockville Tales* may be as significant an addition to regional American writing as Sherwood Anderson's *Winesburg, Ohio* and Edgar Lee Masters' *Spoon River Anthology*." Which brought me back to what I was doing this summer of 1989.

My summer of 1989 in the heat and humidity of the upper Mississippi River, after twenty-five years in the cool and calm of Malaysia, Senegal, Gambia and Israel, where I had presented the best of American culture, films, books and visiting authors for the State Department; here I was, fifty years old, single, retired with a handsome pension; a devoted son who had come home to live with my recently widowed mother until she had her life together and going forward. Six months later my mother's progress was impressive. Within the last weeks she had made plans for an Elderhostel trip to London and Paris, had reserved a condominium in Sarasota to be shared with an old college roommate during January and February, while I went without any particular direction through my day to day; to morning services to recite the Kaddish memorial prayer for my father, who each day became more remote and more saintly. Not at all like the tennis-playing, cigar-puffing father that I had spent my home leaves with for twenty-five years.

Rockville was very much the same as when I had left for six years at the University of Chicago, where I had accumulated an M.A. in Art History, B.A. in American Literature and the realization, with my father's insightful guidance, "Buddy, with your credentials, it's a government job for you. Good salary, early retirement, travel, adventure." As my mom said to me this morning at breakfast, "Buddy, you done good, but you should get on with your second career." A career that so far had consisted of reading the *Times* in the morning, leafing through back copies of the Rockville *Journal* in the afternoon, searching for that scandal, or a murder, or a grand theft, that would intrigue a publisher to give me a contract to retell this lurid tale into a national bestseller.

Six months later I was still looking, still using my search as a dinner conversation with my mother who had spent a full, productive day either at the Botanical Center or the Art Museum or sorting rummage at B'nai Jacob. After dinner, the time my mother reserved for my counseling, she told me, "Buddy, another misspent afternoon at the library."

I got up, put my arms around her shoulders, kissed her unfurrowed brow. "Doing research, Mom, picking up local color like Tom Wolfe." My mother looks up at me. "Write about where you lived. Most Americans can't even pronounce, let alone find the countries on a map."

"Shall I write of the stench of garbage burning in the Embassy compound in Monrovia, Liberia?"

"Liberia is in the news."

"The world is tired of reading of African tribal feuds, of dictators killing each other for the winner to take all to a numbered account in Swiss banks."

My mother sighs. "You may be right. The Swiss banks are not what they used to be. Not since they admitted to stealing funds from dead Jews."

I try to explain to my mother. "That's because the Swiss bankers had the opportunity. They had other people's money." But Mom is off with the last tray of her dirty dinner dishes. She returns to continue her advice.

"Rockville isn't that dull that you cannot find something worth telling."

"So far I haven't met a villainous character. Only do-gooders. I spent the afternoon with Ruth Fuhr Appleton. Her obituary tells only of her virtues as a civic benefactor and club woman. Not much of interest there for me."

Mama offers, "There were all sorts of rumors about her and Cyrus Larson being an item."

"Mama, you know from this?"

"I heard it from the secretary of the YW."

I count on my fingers. "You couldn't have been more than . . ."

"I was seventeen, working as a lifeguard. Mrs. Appleton was on the board of directors. Whenever she came in for the monthly meeting, the rumors started. Someone had seen her in Chicago at the horse show with old Cyrus." It is Mama who now counts on her fingers and laughs. "Mrs. Appleton couldn't have been more than about forty-five then and old Cyrus was no more than fifty-some. Cyrus had the only Packard convertible in town. Ruth Fuhr Appleton—'Missus A' to the Y staff—was into show horses. She dressed like a horse woman in the Sunday society pages, in British hunting jackets and jodhpurs she filled out so fully that whenever she walked through the Y doors, everybody could notice her bottom jiggle." Mama giggled. "That, Buddy, was a time when even young girls like me without asses wore girdles."

"Not much of a story, Mama. No violence, no conflict."

"I don't know about that, Buddy. There were rumors all over town about her and her husband, Philip, having words. He had chased her to the airport where she and Cyrus were going off in his private plane to the Kentucky horse sales. In those days things like that never got into the papers. Not in Rockville when Cyrus owned the *Journal*."

The next morning the low hanging, gray-bearded clouds descended into the Mississippi River valley to push the humidity up so that my jogging became slogging and I was pleased to stop for a moment to have another look at the Appleton house.

I sit on the warm brick steps admiring the peeling columns, the oaks that shade the lawn. A white, Rockville Department of Public Works sedan comes up the drive, parks. The driver opens the door for a thin, bent woman of surely seventy, possibly eighty, pale faced with accented red cheeks. She wears a floral Sunday "go to church and lunch at the country club" dress, complete with a white plastic clutch bag and a natural color straw cloche with a pink ribbon. She moves forward on the arm of the driver, comes to the steps, waits, appraises the obstacle, holds on to the column with her left hand. The driver asks, "You all right, Ms. Appleton?" She smiles down at me.

"Right as rain, Mr. Anderson."

"Ms. Appleton, can you stand right there? I forgot the photographs. I'll be right back." Anne Appleton doesn't answer.

She extends her hand to me, I steady her as she pulls her left foot onto the first step, waits for her right foot to follow. Left foot, right foot, she is up the two steps, leans over me. "Thank you, young man."

I introduce myself. "Ms. Appleton, I am William Miller, Sarah Miller's son." Ms. Appleton comes so close I can see that her eyes are hazel.

"You look like your father. What was his name? Marvin Miller?"

I offer, "Morris."

Ms. Appleton says, "Of course. Morris. We bought our wine from him."

Mr. Anderson is back with the photos. He leans forward to present a grainy black and white 8x10 of the Appleton mansion for Anne Appleton to view. She puts the photo as close to her eyes as her nose will permit. Mr. Anderson gives me an *on your way* stare, which sends me jogging into the cooling summer drizzle

My mother is on the way out as I arrive with the revelation of, "I just met Anne Appleton." Mom snickers, adds, "The heiress."

I ask, "Heiress to what?"

"She still owns what is left of the Rock Hill Horse Farm."

"She live up there on the Ridge Road?"

"Last I heard, she moved into the Lutheran Home." Hearing is the advantage of living in Rockville, because sooner or later, my mother, locally born and bred, who swims with the Catholics, volunteers at the museum and botanical garden with the Presbyterians and Lutherans, and prays with the Jews, knows about most everyone.

I begin my search for evil and skulduggery in Rockville by calling the Lutheran Home for the Aged. I learn, "Ms. Appleton will be out until four. Would you like her voice mail?"

At four-thirty Anne Appleton has returned my call. "Bill Miller, of course. You are Sarah's son. I should have known. You look just like her."

I mumble, "Thank you for calling back, Ms. Appleton. I was reading about your family." This brings a long silence. "I wanted to talk to you about your mother. Do you remember I met you this morning?"

"Were you with that nice Mr. Anderson?"

"No, I am doing research for . . ."

I don't have the opportunity for further explanation, for now Ms. Appleton is questioning me. "Do you know the Village Pancake House on the Ridge Road?"

I say, "Yes."

She whispers, "You can pick me up at my condo tomorrow at eleven-fifteen for an early lunch."

"No problem."

"I will have to be back by two-thirty. It's my nap time."

I say, "Thank you."

Ms. Appleton responds, "Thank you for calling."

At eleven-fifteen I am parked under the porte-cochere at the Lutheran Home, admiring a cubist ascending Christ carved into the mahogany door, which opens into an entry lit by cheering pink fluorescence. On a bench for two Anne Appleton waits in khaki shirt, khaki trousers, gleaming boots. She carries a riding crop.

"Good morning, Ms. Appleton."

"Good morning, Morris."

I do not correct that I am Bill, Morris's son, because Anne Appleton, seated in the passenger seat, has begun a reminiscence of my Miller and Stein families. My aunt, Lilly, had married David Stein, who practiced veterinary medicine in Rockville and owned the Ridge Farm which he inherited from his father. The farm was the first on the east (if you were driving south) after you passed the Appletons' Rock Hill Horse Farm.

"Your Uncle David still living?"

"Living in Florida."

"Your Aunt Lilly doing well?" I nod a yes. "I heard she had a bit of breast cancer. That was three years ago. You were in the Army. No, in the Foreign Service. Your Uncle David was very good with lameness. Best vet we ever had to diagnose lameness. A bit conservative with his treatment, but very good. Only Jewish veterinarian I ever met who knew his way around horses."

"My uncle grew up with horses."

I begin my family legend about my great grandfather, Abe, who ran a livery stable, bred dray horses on the Ridge Farm and wouldn't ride in an automobile until he retired at the age of eighty-two with all of his mental faculties, but unfortunately, no longer able to walk without a cane.

Anne Appleton sighs. "Before my time, but I remember Dr. Stein." She looks out at the green, suburban lawns, says, "You do know your way through southwest Rockville."

"I rode with my uncle."

"Your uncle was the only vet we could trust with our horses."

I say, "He'll be glad to hear that. I'll tell him."

"Please do give him my best regards." She looks at her large-face wrist watch with

Roman numerals. "Morris, I am getting hungry." I murmur, "Bill," but receive no acknowledgment.

"We are here. Right on time." I point to the orange roof of the Village Pancake House, receive an approving, "Good, good." Anne Appleton has the car door open before I am around to help her out. She leaves her cane in the car. "Don't need it until I go to the Rock Hill stables. You know the way to my stables?"

Which is the first that I am told of another destination. I say, "Yes, ma'am."

Seated at a table for two with a view of the potholed parking lot, Anne Appleton confides, "The coffee at the Lutheran Home is dishwater," then orders, "Three dollar pancakes, two basted eggs, and a pot of coffee." I order the same.

Three cups of coffee later, Anne Appleton pushes her shoulders back, looks up at me. "Now we will go to the Rock Hill Farm."

I follow the highway west, turn south over the abandoned railroad tracks, onto the upper Ridge Road. I receive another nod of approval which I justify with, "Thirty years since I was on your farm and I still know the way."

Ms. Appleton smiles. "I made some changes on the farm after my mother died."

The Ridge Road mounts the Mississippi bluff in an S curve which straightens when it reaches the loop road to the interstate. Thirty years has brought a fire station, a library, an under-used city park, a county golf course with driving range and a subdivision that offers incentive loans by the Rockville Bank to first-time home buyers.

The traffic going south is sparse to none. Only a school bus, a mail truck and my Lincoln. Anne Appleton nods off to the quotations of the noon soybean meal prices from the Chicago Board of Trade. She awakens as I drive into the farmyard, park beside a metal sign of a white Arabian stallion in profile against a verdant green background that years ago faded to an indescribable shade of umber. I help her from my car. Cane in advance, she is following a lane overgrown with native grasses. I follow a step or two behind.

At the end of the lane, Ms. Appleton stops, sits down on an oak log, turns to face me. "You remember what was here?" Before I could answer, she points to my left. "There was a house and horse barns. My dear mother built a riding hall right there. A beautiful riding hall where she could show off her Arabian horses."

"Did you have a horse of your own?"

"Me? No. Horses were my mother's and Cyrus Larson's thing."

I ask, "Did you ride?"

Anne Appleton smiles, takes off her sun hat, wipes her forehead with a white handkerchief, hits at her boots with her crop. She does not answer my apparently foolish question. She looks up at the sky. "It was on a hot and humid day just like this that I burned the buildings down."

My puzzlement must have been obvious as she explained. "Mr. Miller, I had inherited the farm. It was mine to do with as I wished. I wished to burn down all I could. Every last stick of it." She pulls herself up with the help of her cane, starts back to my car, opens the door. "Bill, will you please turn on the air conditioning. I am very warm."

On our half-hour return trip to the Lutheran Home, Ms. Appleton made no further explanations. I asked no more questions. As I opened the door, Mrs. Appleton murmured, "Thank you. I had a lovely day." I answered, "Thank you. You have been very helpful with my research project."

LIGHTNING STRUCK ONCE

From the shade of the Lutheran Home turn-around to the sun-sweated downtown is down the hill and two blocks west. Seated in the cool of the microfiche corner, I located the appropriate headline in the *Journal*. "Lightning Destroys Stables," accompanied by a gray photo of smoldering embers.

> "Last night's lightning storm killed fourteen horses at Rock Hill Farms. Rural township volunteer firefighters tried in vain to control the spread of flames from the barn, where the fire apparently started by lightning, to the adjacent riding hall and historic farmhouse. Anne Appleton, owner of Rock Hill Farms, is spending the summer at her Michigan cottage and couldn't be reached.

I made a copy of the headlines and story, returned to the Lutheran Home.

Ms. Appleton's room is fourth on the left, down the hall of teal, paste-on, nylon carpeting. I knocked on the closed metal fire door.

"Come in."

Anne Appleton was seated, feet up, to view the television. She pointed me to an upholstered arm chair. I sat in the air conditioned gloom, watched a muted *Jeopardy* accompanied by closed captions. The program ended, the screen blank, Ms. Appleton sat upright.

I presented and read, "Lightning destroys."

Anne Appleton interrupts. "I thought you would be back."

I point to the last sentence. "You were in Michigan at the time of the fire."

She chuckles. "That's what Cyrus Larson's newspaper says." Anne Appleton giggles, whispers to me, "The reporter printed what I told him, William. The truth is that I had driven back that day to see my dentist. I am sorry about one thing though. I hadn't planned for the horses to die. That was an accident. But then, they had to die."

I can think of nothing to say.

Anne Appleton is out of the recliner to be sure I had closed the door. Pleased that I had, she pulls up the other arm chair beside mine, confides, "If I had cut the horses loose, well, you didn't have to be Sherlock Holmes to realize that the fire had been set. It was God's wish that I take revenge against a whoring sinner."

Together

He had slept quite well. It was every second night when he slept well. The good nights were the nights the dreams didn't disturb, and the pain didn't penetrate his sleeping-pilled mind. He had become nearsighted at 12; at 64 he could make out the red two inch numbers on the bureau beyond his bed: 6:33, February 1, or was it January 31? He and his wife had been sleeping together for forty-two years in the double bed, with bed boards. She got up earlier each day and went to bed later each night. She was dieting—maybe she was hungry. She was anxious. The doctor said she was anxious. The heavy breathing, the sudden bursts of temper, not that she had ever been tranquil.

His neighbor had told him one time, "She was the best looking woman in town." Tall, straight, small breasts, red hair, not too thin, not too fat, never did respond to his sense of humor. "How can I have a sense of humor when all the jokes are at my expense?" He had been very careful with what he said. This week it had been difficult to avoid confrontation.

The doctor told him, "Have her call me, maybe I can get her to see someone."

"I'll try to have her call you."

Growing old together, so soon.

Her girlfriend has Parkinson's; she calls her friends in Florida on their birthdays, on Sundays. One talks about nothing but her children. She wants to talk about literature, movies, art.

Take my arthritis pill, shave, breakfast: half grapefruit, two bran muffins and skim milk. Retired means I can get downtown anytime: Best time is the right time.

Are you spending too much time together? No Doctor, I have an office downtown. I'm out by 8 a.m., not home until 4 p.m.

Please try to get her to call me.

Go swimming. I'll meet you for lunch. Lunch: we split a sandwich, talk about the changes Parkinson's brings. I tell her about our daughter, our granddaughter, I called that morning to see how they are getting on.

"Why don't you and Mom go somewhere?"

"Now is not the time to talk to her."

We did talk about going somewhere, maybe some place with more light. Two hours in the light stops depression, anxiety.

"I'm not telling you where to go, I'm just saying we can go anywhere."

"I'm not going to Brussels, and Israel, Paris, and London."

"I didn't tell you where to go. I said we can go anywhere you like." It did not go badly. It never goes too badly in restaurants, it's at home that discussions lead to challenge, opposition . . . peace in our time.

. . . pick up three red roses before I go home, Friday afternoon. First it's Monday, then it's Friday. Sabbath candles, wine, chicken, Sabbath peace—"Shabbot Shalom." Blessed be our God who brings forth bread from the earth.

. . . we'll go to services. Tomorrow maybe we'll drive out to Iowa City, go to the art museum, look at the Hannah Hoch oil—$80,000 for a second level German painting to be

TOGETHER

hung in a Midwest university museum. The symphony tomorrow night. The fiftieth anniversary reception Sunday afternoon. Busy is better.

"Her anxiety is not your fault. You have always been the same, nothing much has changed." It's not how things are, it's how you respond to them, it's how you perceive them.

I kiss her goodbye on the throat, on the ear. I hold her in my arms. I go out to sweep the powdered snow off the drive. It's 7:30 a.m. Get to the office, see what God hath wrought to our boiler, our elevator, on this gray day.

In Calhoun County

The winter of '46 was warm without snow cover. By 10 a.m. the February sun came over the Illinois River bluffs to soften the dirt country roads. In two hours the roads would become impassable. The veterinarian learned about Calhoun county roads in the first few days of bouncing and jouncing the 1941 yellow Ford coupe, with the State of Illinois shield on the doors, off the soft shoulders into the ditches. He made the acquaintance of the road repair crews and learned to wait for their yellow truck to hook onto the coupe, pull him back onto the road, wave him on his way with "Drive slow, Doc—it may be a State car, but it's your neck."

The sun's rise, his schedule, the distance between the farms, the few cattle, the narrow dirt roads on both sides of the bluff, the absence of connecting roads, made him drive too fast.

In Hardin, the county seat, the state road ended and the country road began. In the square, a two-story Grecian Romanesque Court House squatted. Stores hugged the square on the north, east, south and west. General dry goods, five-and-dime, bank on the corner. The "Eats Cafe" opened at 5:30 a.m., special breakfast with grits, seventy-five cents. In the summertime, flat-bed apple harvest trucks drove around the square. In the winter, the State of Illinois sent its Division of Livestock Industry veterinarians to test the cattle for tuberculosis.

The Herefords have been on the bluff pasture since the spring grass came. By winter they are still there, with no grass and less shelter. The Jerseys and Guernseys stand tied in the lean-to barns under the bluff. The Rhode Island Reds lay the occasional egg in the wooden feed-boxes of abandoned horse stalls.

He arrived at the Graves farm house with the first light, parked beside a warm manure pile, noticed the smell, the steam rising and hoped that George Graves has cleaned out the gutters of the cow stalls.

He banged the coupe door shut to make as much noise as he decently could. That ought to get George away from his coffee.

Opening the coupe's trunk, he put on seamless rubber boots, his left leather glove, felt for the record book in his hip pocket, adjusted his duck hunting hat, and touched the tuberculin syringe to be sure it was securely positioned in the left breast pocket of the green army coveralls.

He waited; no one came from the house. He knocked on the wooden screen porch door. No dog harked. Calhoun County apple farmers spent more time drinking coffee than caring for their stock.

Finally . . .

"Good morning. I'm the State vet."

"I know—I got the postcard. Just didn't think you'd get here on time. The other one never did. Just finished milking. I left the milk cows in the barn for you."

The vet walked into the barn, put his left hand under the Jersey's tailfold, wiped it clean with cotton, and injected the tuberculin, thankful that there was enough light to read the ear tag numbers. He entered these carefully in his record book. "Thank you, Mr. Graves, that really wasn't too bad. You know, I'll be back Thursday same time to read them. Is this all the cattle?"

"No, there're some Herefords on the bluff—couldn't bring 'em down—got no way. The other vet never tested 'em. You'd have to walk up the hill, Doc. I can get them in a pen—there's no barn up there."

"How many are there?"

"Twelve cows and calves and the old bull. I'm planning to ship him this spring, Doc; need to test him?"

Getting the quick release lasso and the bull nose-lead from the car he followed Graves up the hill.

"There they are, Doc. You stay here—head them off. I'll throw some corn in the pen and chase them up." . . . First stop for the day and fifteen minutes behind schedule.

The Herefords came over the crest, Graves well behind. The cows came slowly with heavy udders, looking back for the trailing calves, the bull behind them, and Graves last. The cattle, entering the pen, snorted, turned their backs to the west and began to crunch the corn kernels. The vet walked among them, mostly silent. As he injected the 0.1cc of tuberculin, he marked each tail-head with the yellow crayon. So far, so good.

"Best throw in some more feed. We'll tag them today—make it easier, quicker on Thursday." He leaned over one cow to reach the neighboring cow's right ear with the ear tag pliers. He was well away by the time the Hereford raised her head to look for the intruder on her grain feast.

"What are you going to do about the bull, Doc?"

"Let's see if we can tie him behind the gate—shouldn't take but a second."

Graves let the cattle out; the bull stayed in the pen eating. The vet quickly threw the rope around the bull's neck. "Help me tie him behind the gate." As he mounted the gate, reaching for the tail, the bull leapt up taking the gate off the hinges. The bull lunged forward, dragging the gate, followed by the vet on his bottom, all held securely by the wrapped manila lasso. Together they started across the pen for the barbed wire fence.

The gate began to splinter. The bull turned to the noise, stopped for a moment; the vet managed to undo the first rope loop from his left thigh. The bull resumed his surge toward the fence, stopping again to look at the gate that slowed his pace. The vet unwrapped the rope from his calf. The bull stopped again, this time to measure the height of the wire fence. The vet freed the lasso loop from his ankle seconds before the bull cleared the fence. The gate crashed into the fence.

The vet raised himself onto limp legs, wet with the sweat of fear.

George Graves came quietly towards him. "Gee, Doc, I thought you were gone. I'll take him to the sale barn Wednesday. He's a bad actor—had him loaned out last year to my uncle, almost got him, too." He followed Graves, protecting his left leg by digging his right heel into the now muddied path. He eased into the coupe, glad he had winter underwear under his worn coveralls—he was only fifteen minutes behind schedule.

Friends

Everyone knows in real estate it's location, location. There are locations that start out 100 percent, and in thirty years they are zero, nothing, a liability. You can't give the building away. That's the way it is in deindustrialized Rock City. You would think this is unfortunate. It may be, but it's not as bad as what happened to Harry and Sybil Baum, friends of mine, who, thirty years ago, started a little veterinary practice, a cat and dog hospital in a square cement block building of no great architectural merit or distinction, along the main highway between Washington and Richmond.

Veterinary hospitals can be noisy: barking dogs in outside exercise runs. So my friend Harry buys two lots, one on either side of his clinic. Then he buys the six stall motel that's next door. He renovates the motel into a pet store and a place for Charlie, his black kennel "boy" to live in. This is the south after World War II; who wants a black man in the white part of town?

Business is good; the suburbs are moving out.

Harry and Sybil have two boys, beautiful children, bright, intelligent, good in school. Charles, the older one, is a doctor in Cincinnati. But it's the younger one who makes Harry proud. "Papa, I want to be a veterinarian like you, heal the animals, comfort the sick."

No one could have been prouder than Harry and Sybil when Phil—that's the younger boy—graduated from the University of Pennsylvania College of Veterinary Medicine in the top ten percent.

"Al, Phil is going to do a residency in neurology and then he is coming back to join me in practice." So it is. Phil is with Harry for ten years.

Every year I see Harry in Florida; it's the same thing. "Our gross is increasing. Sybil has to have another girl to help her in the office." Sybil has been the office manager from the day Harry started the practice.

"Phil *this* . . . Phil *that* . . . Phil is specializing in neurology . . . the practice is growing, growing."

I don't know anything about the Baums' arrangements, but, based on their gross, it's a very substantial income for Harry and Sybil. What it is for Phil, I don't know. The practice is so big that about four years ago, Harry adds another veterinarian to the staff, Conover, whom I have only heard about and never met.

Two years ago, the day after Christmas, Harry calls me. "Al, Sybil and I need to talk to you."

I tell this to Mamie. "Fine. Thank God they called after Christmas. Last year I had to invite them to dinner."

It's not easy for Mamie in Florida. That year we had sixteen cousins for Christmas dinner, one brought a Key Lime pie and another a bottle of California Sauvignon Blanc. Still it's not easy even if I do help.

Harry and Sybil are our age. Through the years I wouldn't say they look as well as we do because Mamie has always looked younger than Sybil.

Harry and Sybil walk in empty-handed. They look awful, if not awful, not great. I would

FRIENDS

say *appreciably aged* since we have seen them a year ago. We sit on the screened porch. It's warm. Sybil answers Mamie's "How have you been?" with "It's not been a good year, Mamie. I have a little heart trouble." She points to her chest. "And Harry gave us a scare. We thought he had stomach cancer. He was so bad he couldn't eat a bite. Thank God it turned out to be an ulcer.

"Al, that's what we came to see you and Mamie about. You and Mamie are business people, in real estate, in developing. You and Mamie have always worked together. Harry and I value your friendship and your judgment."

With an introduction like that, I warn myself: *Al, don't say too much. Listen.* About Mamie's good judgment, I don't have to worry. It's my mouth that gets us into trouble.

"Harry and I want to retire." Which Mamie seconds with, "Forty years of practice is enough. It's time for you to do what you want to."

"Naturally, we want Phil to have the practice. After all he has worked with us for ten years, so we speak to Phil. 'Phil, Dad and I will put a fair price on the real estate, the exact market price. We'll keep the real estate; you'll pay us rent. We'll give you fifty percent of the practice; fifty percent you'll buy. From what we get from the practice and from the real estate, we'll have more than enough.'"

"Sounds fair to me," is Mamie's comment as she pours a second round of iced tea and lemon.

"We thought so, too. And when we go, the boys will each get half of our estate."

"So, what's the problem?"

"It's Phil. He gets a lawyer. He starts negotiations. He doesn't want to pay so much rent. But I told him, the rent is based on the value of the property."

I try to moderate. "But sometimes, Sybil, a veterinary practice may not be able to pay that much rent, regardless of the value of the property."

Harry answers me. "Al, I can sell the property for $2,500,000."

I try to explain. "Harry, you have two things: a practice and property. Phil is buying the practice. He may not feel secure paying rent without controlling the property. God forbid, Phil is still a young man, but when you are gone, the property could get sold. Phil is out—where can he take his practice?"

"I can sell the property for two and a half million," Harry repeats.

"But that doesn't solve Phil's problem, does it? So, talk to Phil, see what you can work out. Try to reassure him. After all, Phil is a son. You have been together for ten years. Hasn't he helped build up the practice?"

"Yes, he has."

Harry and Sybil drink some more tea. Their faces relax. At sunset we go for a walk on the beach; then we all go out to dinner at Casa Ybel. That night Mamie is pleased with me. "Al, you gave Harry good advice. There is nothing more important than peace in the family. Business is important, but peace is more important."

You would think that, in an intelligent family, some sort of solution could be reached after a year of negotiations. Not true. A year of negotiations and the only thing that is settled is Phil has accepted fifty percent of the practice. And Sybil is no longer the office manager. She is completely out of the practice.

"I don't think Phil likes me anymore. He told me," is what she tells us the day after Christmas.

"Told you what?" Mamie insists.

Sybil starts to cry.

"My son, my Phil, told me on my birthday. I thought he had come over to wish me a happy birthday. Phil comes in, says, 'Mom, you don't understand me. You never did. All you know is work.' And he walks out. I had baked a cake."

So it goes, until one night last spring. Sybil calls us.

"Al?"

"Yes."

"Phil has left us."

"What do you mean, 'left' you?"

"He left us. Went off, got married and bought a practice in Connecticut. Harry is back in the office and so am I."

Mamie is concerned. "Can you and Harry take care of the practice?"

"We got Dr. Conover to come back."

It seems that, when Phil was running things, while Harry and Sybil were in Florida, Dr. Conover had left because he no longer saw any prospects for himself.

"Why?"

"I guess it's the price of the property. I told Phil he would get his half when Hany and I are gone."

"All I can say is I guess Phil didn't want to wait," to which Mamie tells me when I hang up, "That wasn't so smart, Al."

Christmas, we are in Florida again. Harry and Sybil's place is just west of ours, about twenty miles. On the 27th, that's two days after Christmas—I remember because our cousins from the east coast had left and Mamie said, "It feels good to be alone"—after we have changed the two beds in our guest room, the Baums call.

"Harry and Sybil want us to go out with them. They want us to meet them at the Mucky Duck."

At 4:45 we are seated on the bench, waiting for the restaurant doors to open ("No Reservations Accepted"). Harry is almost his old self again, and Sybil is smiling and kissing us.

"Al, I owe it all to you. It's your wisdom."

I hadn't known I had imparted any wisdom to Sybil.

"You remember what you told me last year, after we had been negotiating a whole year with Phil and his lawyer. I think we could have reached an agreement with Phil, but his lawyer was something else."

"What did I tell you?"

"You said, 'You have to be satisfied with yourself for whatever decision you reach, or you'll always be guilt-ridden.'"

Harry and Sybil don't look furrowed or guilt-ridden. They are back to their intense, smiling ways. It turns out that, when Dr. Conover came back, he offered to buy the practice. His father gave him the money, and Phil gave back his fifty percent of the stock—it's a corporate practice.

So, Harry and Sybil got everything they had asked for. But, as Mamie says, "They lost a son." Phil doesn't call them, and when the baby was born, Phil didn't invite his own parents to the *brith*.

I change the subject. "Mamie, do you know how it's going with their older boy, Charles?"

FRIENDS

"They are going to have a baby in the spring. Sybil is planning to go to Cincinnati when the baby is born. Al, now you know why I didn't want our children in the business with us."

Mamie goes in to brush her teeth. I don't answer.

It would have been nice to have our son with us.

In the Beginning

Veterinary clinics are open on Saturday. Last June Woody changed our hours: closed Saturday, open Monday night until 8:00 p.m. In June I gave up management and full practice responsibilities for Diseases of the Eye only.

"Forty years. You could tell lots of stories."

"Write it down . . . you have been writing haven't you?"

I have been keeping a journal for sixteen years. The journal took the place of the letters to my son, the musings: the business, the vet clinic, the daily rhythms.

It's snowing, the driving conditions are hazardous. First came knobby snow tires, seat belts, and then steel coverings for the pan to fortify the underside of the 1949 Dodge. To protect the oil plug. The chains are a curiosity in my garage, replaced by all-weather belted tires.

The four room rental bungalow, without garage, on 50th street, from which I started my first practice in Rock City, was off the main highways. We partitioned the basement into an office: the old porcelain-top kitchen table an examining table, water bath glass syringe sterilizer, two green painted steel cages behind the plaster board walls. The spring rains brought water in the basement. We spread tons of dirt around the foundation to change the drainage direction.

Our first new house. The smell of cleanliness, new paint, green shutters. The sign in front read: A. Roane D.V.M.—Veterinarian —>, arrow around to downstairs. Garden and sand box for our son in the backyard. I listened to the winter weather reports of 1948, '49, '50. I prayed and hoped the Dodge would start when I got that call. The garage on the main street corner was helpful. Dr. Reynolds in Port Byron was supportive.

"Alan, I'll recommend you for all the calvings. I can't really go out these winter nights, gettin' too old."

Old Dr. Coleman in Albany was gentle and kind.

"Alan, if you run out of hog cholera serum or vaccine come up to the house, take mine. It's closer for you than driving all the way back to Rock City."

The old timers gone thirty years. Horse and buggy doctors, they were good with horses. Dr. Smith could lasso, cast and castrate a colt while I was getting the anesthetic ready.

"Anesthetic is fine Alan. But it's how you make the incision that determines how it heals. Cut out the raphe, you'll get perfect drainage. Quick in and out—that's what counts."

A "starting in practice" vet takes all calls, at all hours of the day or night.

"Do you descent skunks?"

"We descent skunks."

I had a classmate living across the river. He was between advanced degrees. He and his wife had just returned from Mexico where he had worked with the U.S. Department of Agriculture, eradicating foot and mouth disease. Karl was the Community Public Health Officer until he could go to the University of Wisconsin to begin his pathology studies. He had absolutely no practice experience.

"Karl, how would you and May like to come by for supper tonight? There's a little something I want you to help me with."

Karl and May came willingly; we ate supper together. Put our son to bed. Karl and I went down into the basement surgery.

"Karl, I think we have to learn to dissect this skunk's scent gland."

"Alan, we never did that in school."

We never did any surgery in school. We never did pregnancy exams on cattle. We never delivered calves. Couldn't even drive a car in school. We read books in school.

We dissected the first skunk gland very carefully. Karl dripped the ether on the cone modified for skunks. My first incision avoided the rectum. The gland dissected out completely, intact. Cut the rectum and the stools will leak out forever.

The second gland—there's one on each side of the rectum—I broke the second gland. The odor—uniquely skunk—went up through the heat ducts, into the dining room, kitchen, living room, the two bedrooms. Tomato juice doesn't destroy skunk odor. Only time does.

"Alan, no more skunks in my house."

Karl and I descented the next skunk on a park bench in Hampton, in the open air overlooking the Mississippi.

Karl and May laugh when they recall Rock City and starting out. Those were good times. May tells us she had forgotten the skunks. Kitty and I don't forget starting out in Rock City.

On Sundays Karl and May came by. We picnicked on the bluff. Played with our son in the sand box, threw a football up and back. "Daddy, you kicked the ball over the house."

All we wanted was to earn a living.

May calls on Sunday.

"How are you, we haven't heard from you?"

All right May, just a little arthritis. Nothing life threatening. I fell on the ice. I'm healing, it just takes longer.

Reynolds, Coleman, they must have been at least sixty when I came to Rock City. March 14 I'll be 64.

How many years since we were at school in Kansas? Forty, forty-one? In Manhattan, Kansas, at six o'clock in the summer afternoons, the breeze stopped. It was in the nineties—hot, dry and partly cloudy in Kansas.

The warm weather is expected to continue. Kitty and I sit on the screened-in front porch, rocking; I fan her.

"This time of the day I think I'm going to faint."

"It will be cooler when the sun goes down."

The house on 50th has been replaced by an air conditioned sixplex.

I Came Home To Tell My Folks

It is the first time I have slept in the bed of my childhood. The bed, my mother has covered with purple flowers for my seven-year-old daughter, is in the same position as when I left home, my head to the east window. The unshaded early sun wakes me through the bare oak limbs.

The neighbor on the east has opened his door. He is walking his Afghan hound.

I was seventeen when I left home, went down to State, graduated, married Norm. Then I started at the bank in Chicago. Then we moved to the suburbs. Then Amy was born.

It's not that I don't keep in touch with Mom and Dad—I do. I call Saturday afternoon when Norm and Amy are at Indian Princesses or Amy is following Norm around the basement as he repairs this or fixes that in our fifty-year-old, three-bedroom, one and one-half baths bungalow in a better suburb on a busy through street.

The south window looks onto the white colonial that is across the street. The owners are new. Mom says, "I was hoping for young people. But they have been very good to us, helpful. Very thoughtful. They are people our age. I think she may be a little younger. Both retired."

Amy knows all the neighbors. They make over her when she visits. She helps walk the Afghan hound. She makes cookies in the colonial across the street. This weekend Amy and Norm are away, on a camp-out at the Y camp at Lake Geneva. I spoke to Amy last night, Friday night.

"Mom, we went snow sliding on tubes."

Mom and Dad had taken my brother and me up to George Williams. We had a toboggan. Mom wore a long camel's hair coat over her pants. That was . . . it must be thirty years ago. Before middle-aged women wore jeans. I was nine, my brother fourteen. Ours has always been a Y family, swimming, jogging. My brother taught swimming, swam free style on the Y teams.

Dad has his medals in the jewelry box that is on the bureau of my parents' downstairs bedroom.

"Smartest thing we ever did, Clara, a bedroom downstairs."

My parents' house in Rock City is thirty years old. It has two stories, gray siding and an orange door. The downstairs is a two-story living room, kitchen, dining room, and a bedroom that opens onto a library with bookcases full of my dad's art books.

"I gave up my dressing room so your dad could have a den."

It's not a den; there's no place to sit. No place to rest, hardly a place to sit and talk to my dad. There is only his Herman Miller arm chair and a chair opposite it.

I don't talk much to my dad. That is, I do on the telephone when he calls me at the bank.

"Hello, daughter."

"How's it going, Dad?"

He usually calls when he has good news. As Dad says, "The bad you'll get soon enough."

"*Benny Roone* came back again. That after Pocket Books had it a year. It would have made a great mystery series. That's what Barbara said."

Barbara is Dad's agent. She has always liked Dad's writing. I can't really say that either Mom or I have been encouraging. I'm the publications editor at the bank; I know how difficult it is to get fiction published. Mom and I were really trying to protect Dad. At Dad's age, what does he need all that rejection for?

Dad began writing four years ago, when he retired. A profusion of words, thousands every month. Six novels, eighteen short stories. And letters. Dad writes to me every week. And to Amy, too, in block print so Amy can read for herself. Amy is in first grade. We do keep in touch. It's just that we are so busy. Amy's school schedule, work, and, last year, we started looking for a larger house.

We were looking for a house with a bath and bedroom downstairs for Mom and Dad when they drive up. They come up about once a month. That is, when they are not in Sanibel, which is usually in December and January. We go down to Sanibel for Christmas, so it isn't as if we don't see Mom and Dad. Norm's folks are both dead, so Mom and Dad are the only grandparents Amy has. Amy is just crazy about Papa and Grandma. She insists on calling Papa. "I want to talk to Papa."

"I love you, Papa. I want to talk to Grandma . . . Grandma, can you come for four days?'

We looked a year for a larger house, but you know the North Shore. $500,000 and we would have to add the air conditioning and re-landscape. Norm is a landscape engineer. He can't abide a yard that he hasn't designed for continuous and harmonious color and balance using native shrubs and bushes. None of the houses we saw had a bedroom and bath downstairs. Mom had a new hip two years ago, one that wasn't cemented in, so it was healing slowly and she was using crutches.

Two years ago we decided to put an addition on our house. Just what we needed, nothing more. Air-conditioning, bedroom and bath downstairs, a loft above where Dad could write or Amy could play. While we were designing, we added a breakfast room with two sky lights and a deck. Norm got the plantings in immediately, so they would be there when the addition was completed.

The next year, because of the construction, we couldn't leave the house; it was all open. Anyone could have walked in. We had a burglary a couple of years ago. We are going to install an alarm system in our home, that is, if we can work out a way that a cat won't set off the system.

Amy is our only child, and surely, it looked like she was going to remain one. I had a terrible, frightening pregnancy, and no doctor knows or will tell me what will happen the next time.

"Mrs. Warren, we have had no experience with your syndrome. That is, we haven't had any patients who have had a second pregnancy." That is a nice way to tell me, "Be satisfied you survived your first."

So I remember. I try to forget, but I remember. That's when I smoke, when I remember. My brother . . . my pregnancy . . . and Amy in the hospital, so tiny. Amy was premature.

She was in the North Shore Hospital for six weeks before we brought her home. That's the advantage of living in the Chicago suburbs: the medical services.

"I don't think you and Amy would have done as well anywhere else. That's when having

Northwestern University Medical School staff makes a difference," is what my internist told me.

I have tried.

"Mom, Dad, move up here. I'll buy the house next door."

Either Mom doesn't answer or she says, "I'm not ready yet."

I drove in last night in my old Volvo. I don't mind the shaking as long as it's safe on the highway.

Sabbath dinner was set. Mom had the St. Louis crystal out; the candles were lit.

I have candlesticks. I don't light mine on Friday nights. Maybe when Amy stalls Hebrew school and I'm not working on Fridays. I'll make chicken soup and matzah balls and set out the Kiddush cup.

Norm will make Kiddush. Norm's Hebrew is "limited." He studied with the rabbi at State, but it still is not easy for him to read the blessings.

When Amy goes to Hebrew school, Norm can take an evening adult education course, "Hebrew for Beginners."

I wish Norm wouldn't order bacon when he takes Amy out for breakfast. He is getting better about that. I think it's more that he is concerned about his high cholesterol count than when I whisper to him, "Norm, no pork, not in front of Amy."

Dad reads the Kiddush; he really doesn't have a singing voice, not at all. Mom is the only one in the family with a voice. My brother played the guitar. He and his wife, Jane, sang folk songs. He did most of the playing. It was Jane who sang.

Jane remarried. She and her husband, Jim, and her two girls come down to Sanibel. Mom invites them every couple of years. They were there for this Christmas.

"It's not Jane's fault that our son died."

Jane doesn't sing anymore and complains about how little she and Jim have after ten years of working day and night.

They have a half million dollar house in the New York suburbs. And debts. I know that Mom and Dad still have her in their will.

That may be the only way they'll ever get out of debt, with my parents' hard earned money.

Dad made it developing real estate. Jane and Jim . . . well, if they would manage better and do without a little bit, and quit borrowing. The interest on their loans is eating them up. Management or frugality, you have to practice it.

Norm and I paid cash for the addition. I'm a saver, not equal to my mother, who takes a year to buy a washing machine. I wait for sales, and Norm and I save—more than any of our friends do. And we invest.

If Mom and Dad hadn't helped us, we wouldn't have as much but we would have enough for anything we wanted to do. Anyway, we wouldn't be in debt like Jane and Jim.

I came home to tell my folks: "I'm pregnant. Don't be frightened. I have been to the doctors, and, this time, everything will be ready, the blood transfusions—my own blood this time. No, I didn't plan it, but it happened and it will be for the best."

The addition is ready for Mom and Dad's visit. The downstairs shower has a place to sit down. Dad is getting awfully arthritic. He is walking more slowly, more bent.

The new family room has the largest pull out bed we could find. My folks should be very comfortable. Amy will love having Mom and Dad with her. The baby is due at the end of August, if all goes well. And if it doesn't, Mom and Dad will be there to help

Norm and Amy. It's the thought of Mom and Dad . . . losing a son nineteen years ago. And if I died . . . ?

I light a cigarette before breakfast. I blow the smoke out the east window.

My dad is very slowly raking the lawn. I hear Mom making coffee. She buys half and half for me alone. Mom and Dad drink their coffee black and sugarless.

I shouldn't smoke.

I flush the cigarette down the toilet.

I'm thirty-nine years old. I'm frightened. My hands are sweating. I'll tell Mom this morning at breakfast. She'll tell Dad. I can't tell him. He hasn't spoken to me about my brother since that gray snowy February day when we buried him on the scrub Iowa hillside.

Nachas fun Kinder (Joy from Children)

"Nachas fun Kinder." I was going to have that inscribed on a button, sell the button through the mail with little personal ads in the *Hadassah* magazine as a perfect gift for all family occasions: birthdays, anniversaries . . .

My wife, Mamie, says I'm too cynical, there are families that are getting at least a little joy from the children.

"No one will buy your button—who would want to advertise that their children are giving them heartaches? Isn't it bad enough that their neighbors and family know it? You want to advertise it?"

Our neighbors in Rock City are in no better position than we are when it comes to joy from their children—and in our family I can't think of anyone who has had better than average "earnings." Five children, and two are still calling Mamie and me, one is still writing twice a year. The other two . . . well that's a long story. Except for Harry—Harry is our brightest, our first horn son. Maybe because Harry is such an idealist—"Papa, I want to help the poor, the unfortunate."

"Harry, we help the poor and unfortunate by building apartments for them."

"Not like that, Papa: face to face counseling—helping hands on. . . ."

So Harry goes downstate to the University. First a B.A. in Sociology, and then it's social work, and then it's the retarded and birth defects. Thank God the construction business is good and Harry gets a HEW scholarship. I'm not complaining to you about parents' financial sacrifices to get a boy a Ph.D. There is really no better way to spend money than to educate a child. The education is forever, the money . . .

Harry is in Tennessee, his first job after school. Assistant director of a state school. He met Betty there. "So she isn't Jewish. Her family is one of the oldest in the state. Her grandfather was a judge, you should see the antiques in their home. Her father is a lawyer, her brother is a professor, she is a fine counselor—really cares about her clients. She is very good with the children."

Mamie, of course, had her reservations. "You have to look at the mother to know the daughter."

"Her mother is dead, Mama."

"What did she die from?"

"Mama, you don't ask questions like that."

"Why not?"

"They are not Jewish—" to which Mamie only answers, "Her lips are too thin."

"This is the seventies, Mama, we are not living in a Polish shtetl. Times are changing, even in Rock City in western Illinois. Children are moving, taking their educations and careers from coast to coast."

I don't have to tell you that our Hany and Betty get married. Harry is a beautiful boy, our first son, blue eyes. He plays the guitar. He sings.

Betty is one of those thin, sharp-boned little women with quick actions. To us she is always more than polite. She calls us Papa and Mama Kramer, thank God, not Al and

Mamie. "You'll come out to our cottage in the mountains. I want you to meet more of the family."

At the cottage Betty and Mamie are getting along very well. "Mama, I want your recipe for matzo ball soup." Betty's effort to preserve our Jewish heritage, at least in her kitchen. Never do I hear that they go to a synagogue. Parents learn to be satisfied with very little. We are satisfied our son and Betty are not going to church. This is how it is.

The first week in July we spend in Tennessee with Hany, Betty and the children. Alex is eleven, Mary four.

The children call at least once a month, always on Mamie's birthday and Father's Day. On the Fourth of July, Hany and I play one round of golf. Mamie and Betty cook together.

"This trip, Al, is to be with grandchildren."

We play: swimming together in the pool, watching sunset over the valley, eating pizza on the porch, giving Mary a bath. It's a routine—on Saturday Betty's father, the counselor, comes out from town for dinner. That's when Betty uses the cloth napkins and matching tablecloth.

On Sunday morning Harry makes pancakes and biscuits. We begin our return drive north to Illinois. Mamie never says anything until we cross the Paducah bridge.

"Al, did you know that Betty had been married before? She told me. Only for a year, while she was in college. It didn't last."

"Why?"

"That's what Betty wants to find out. That's what she told me: 'I'm a counselor and if I don't know myself, well . . . it's really important for me and for my career to go through analysis.' That was two years ago."

The next year, again on Sunday on our way home:

"Al, did Harry tell you he is going to a counselor?"

"What kind of a counselor—?"

"A marriage counselor."

"Is anything wrong?"

"I don't know, Al—you know how it is once you start looking—" *Pfun vanent de fis vaxen* (from where the feet grow). Where do you stop. This is Mamie's Jewish wisdom: that sometimes it's best not to know, or, as we say in the western Illinois building trade, "If it's not broken, don't fix it."

That year son Harry is made the director of the school—that gives him more care than money. "That's how working for the state is, Papa. There is so much that should have been done for the children—should be done."

"Rome wasn't built in a day, Harry."

That July when we see Harry, he looks awful, thin—like an older man.

Alex is the one who told us the first night we are in Tennessee when he came in to kiss us goodnight: "Mom and Dad are going to get a divorce but Dad is still going to live in the house with us."

Mamie doesn't say anything, neither do I. This is not the first divorce in our family; my nephew was divorced—my sister didn't tell me for a year. We are not so modern yet that we send out divorce notices.

"Al, you find out. Speak to Harry. You're playing golf with him tomorrow."

***

"Harry, you know what Alex told me last night?"

"What?"—this while I'm putting on my golf shoes, my head in the trunk of my car. I can't face Harry.

"He said you and Betty were getting a divorce."

"That's what Betty wants. The last couple of years we haven't had . . . we haven't been living as man and wife."

Harry puts it very delicately. That's how Harry, the counselor, is with parents and children. How can Harry know what I heard in the streets when I was growing up in Brooklyn?

We tee off. It's cool in the mountains. The morning dew lingers in the valley, the fairways are green, the green slow.

"Dad, I'm going to stay on in town to be with the children, so they can have a father while they are growing up. Betty has been in analysis—I guess it sort of freed her up—I didn't think anything about it, until she moved out of our bedroom. I didn't tell you and Mom—what was there to tell?"

Harry's details do not affect his golf game. Harry has a beautiful swing—from boyhood lessons at the Country Club. Harry comes in at four over. My score? I don't keep score. I enjoy the game too much to keep score.

"I didn't think anything about Betty moving out, women go through phases like that. Until Betty brings her friend, Nora, into the house as a 'housekeeper.' How shall I put this, Dad? Nora is more than a housekeeper to Betty."

We drink our 19th hole beer. The sun shines in the green valley; the yellow triangular flags on the greens wave and die and wave again in the western breeze.

"Dad, Nora is a lesbian. I'm getting used to it. Last week, Nora, Betty and I went to the movies together, like a family. Betty told the children—you tell Mom."

Sunday morning on the way home I tell Mamie.

"Poor Harry, my first born," she cries.

I try to comfort Mamie. "It's not the end. Harry is young yet. He'll remarry."

"It's the children, Al, the poor children."

Mamie is always right. But for me it's not only the children—it's the grandparents, too. We no longer see the children of our first born. Harry moved out; Betty remains the chief counselor at the state school. Harry has Alex and Mary every second weekend and on the Jewish holidays.

It has been two years since that last week in Tennessee. Last year Harry and the children flew up for Passover. This spring Harry was too busy; he has promised to come for Rosh Hashana, the New Year. Mamie has decorated a room for Mary in Laura Ashley; Alex will sleep in Harry's old room; Harry we'll put in the guest room.

A Sabbath Walk

We both wore black billed caps with CAT DIESEL POWER embroidered on the crown; we stopped to talk. We stood like long-haired, hard-wintered horses, our backs to the wind off the Mississippi River. The river was open. The ice remained on the backwater pools. The ice fishermen wore insulated boots. The barricades barred the riverfront road. The Boy Scouts, with their scoutmasters, were leaving the quarter mile spit of land that forms the entry to the marina where they had been looking for the American bald eagle.

He was black, medium height, medium length beard, smiling and brown-eyed. I was taller and stooped, white and green-eyed. I carried a walking stick handmade in Haiti.

I asked, "You like to walk alone?"

I had noticed him, alone, during my after-Sabbath walks along the river. We had passed, we had smiled, we had greeted once in passing.

We passed the Caterpillar equipment left out for the weekend, at rest from its daily tree removal tasks.

"Do you think the walk will look better without the trees?" I asked as we passed.

"It will open the view," he answered and we did not stop.

I walked north and he went south.

It had been a mild winter without the accumulation of the 27 inches of snow and ice layers that are our allocation in western Illinois. My wife, Marsha, lets me walk along the river when there is no ice.

It had been the finest Saturday for walking since '82.

He wore blue jeans, an insulated jacket, and tennis shoes. I was wearing Tartan plaid woolen trousers, insulated jacket, and Rockport walkers.

'You like to walk alone?"

"I like to walk alone. It gives me a chance to speak to Him."

I could agree with that.

"This morning I went to services, but I have to get outdoors by myself just to look up."

I agreed. "Do you work for Cat?"

"Seventeen years."

"What do you do?"

"I'm on the D-7 assembly line. I have to get outdoors on the weekend. I have two boys, 14 and 11. I married a girl from Rock City but I was born in Mississippi. When I get laid off, I'm going back. To Mississippi. But first I'm going to finish high school. No one hires high school dropouts anymore. I would like to go back to Mississippi."

That was revealing. I try not to comment.

My daughter always says, "Daddy, you're giving advice again!"

But what is a man to do with all the accumulated wisdom and experience?

I answered, "When I came home from the war, I was only gone a year the first time, I got off at the railroad station; nothing was the same. You know Mississippi has changed while you've been in Rock City."

This is not a very profound observation, yet I owe it to our conversation.

'You're right, you know. I was down to see my father. I spent a week down there. It wasn't the same. My wife has a job here, the boys are in school. I could possibly work with my father-in-law. He has an air-conditioning and heating business. Walking out here gives me a chance to think. I should have gotten more education."

I am an enthusiast about education, for how else could a Jewish boy from a poor working-class family become a veterinarian?

"I don't think you'll find it too difficult to finish high school. You know, there is as much danger in too much education as too little. Too much limits career choice."

He doesn't answer that.

It is our first "talk." I try to remember my daughter's warnings. He looks up at me—I am still facing north. The west wind reddens my face. He looks at my CAT cap.

"Where did you get your hat?"

"A friend of mine is an engineer at CAT; he bought it for me."

My answer doesn't seem to have separated us. A UAW member, earning $16.00 an hour, plus $8.00 in fringe benefits an hour.

He walks south. I walk north, back to my car, drive to my home on the bluff.

The bluff is where the retired Farm Machinery Company executives live. It's where our combination branch library and fire station are. The bluff is where the churches named after saints cover our corners. St. Pius protects his Catholic congregants behind modernist stained-glass windows. The Greek Orthodox church, St. Michaels, looks across the street at the Baptists, who make do with an ascending cross. The Jews, in the next block, have only a marble sign: "Jewish Center."

He walks south to his home by the river, by the project housing, by the warehouses. He earns at least $30,000 a year; his wife works. They should have some savings. CAT won't close until next summer. He lives in the low rent, low tax district by the river. It's a little far from the schools, and not too convenient for shopping. That's where the black churches are, the black barber shops, and their pool halls.

"Did you meet anybody you know?"

"No, Marsha, not too many walkers out today. It's still a little too cold."

"I was getting worried about you."

"Stopped off to chat for a few minutes."

"See any eagles?"

"No. Just some gulls and Boy Scouts."

Outside Counsel

"Benny, come, fly down to Sanibel. I need your advice," invited my Uncle Al. So my wife Milly and I did. Southwest Florida, away from the ice, sleet, sunless days of Rockville, Illinois, to this semitropical island of Australian pines and sea shells for a Christmas week of copper dawns and sunsets that flare reds and salmons into San Carlos Bay.

New Year's Friday was half sun and half gray with only a few minutes of afternoon showers from the folded gray-blue clouds. Saturday was showers in the morning and half sun in the afternoon. At dawn Sunday, the fog rolled in from Captiva. At first it was only a drizzle contained by the porch screen, to drip and dribble into the Cape Hyacinth. Then the wind shifted to the east, the rain became a windstorm that forced the four Roones from the screened porch into the dining room-living room.

My Uncle Al is in his rattan rocker, the *New York Times* a hazard of litter at his feet. Al reads and ruminates, "Benny, Clinton isn't going to have it easy. In order to create new jobs, our GNP will have to grow three percent a year. In Rockville, that is impossible unless Clinton creates a miracle recovery. Based on what? More taxes for the rich. There aren't enough rich to tax. The best bet would be to get the housing industry going by liberalizing the depreciation schedule. That would start employment."

My uncle is a dedicated believer in free enterprise. An entrepreneur who votes Democratic, who affirms, "There can be no recovery unless it is aided by federal tax incentives."

After fifty years Aunt Clara knows that once my uncle starts on the condition of the American economy he will not quit until she announces, "Lunch."

Clara is in the kitchen. Milly, ever the cooperative niece, the ideal guest, sets the table.

Uncle Al looks at me. "Benny, after lunch I want to go for a walk on the beach, just the two of us."

Which means that Al is in the midst of another "business situation."

"No problem" is my answer.

I follow my uncle down the four steps to the low tide beach; the sun reflects and shimmers off the breakers. To the east, there is only the silhouette of the high rise on Fort Myers Beach. To the west, the clouds in their blue and black shrouds cling to each other.

"Benny, it's a better day than the forecaster promised."

Which I answer with, "It's better on Sanibel than in Chicago."

"Benny, I have troubles in Chicago."

I sing an atonal "trouble in River City" like from *The Music Man*.

"Worse, Benny. Death and taxes."

"Tell me."

"You won't mention it to Clara? Anyway, this story goes back almost thirty years ago." Al sighs, "We were all younger then. Benny, what do you remember from Vietnam? You were in Vietnam in 1968. Me, I remember every detail of my business deals. From World War II, I remember only the dead."

With my Uncle, it's not conversation, it's philosophical, ethical, religious musings, then as always, back to business.

"In 1967 I was beginning my first multi-family project. I built it and found out that I had more depreciation than Milly and I could use. Lots more. You understand, Benny. That excess depreciation can be sold, not for much but there was a market. So my banker recommended a broker in Chicago who finds me a buyer, a law firm, DRW, Dick, Richards and Wolf. Dick and Richards are the movers in this deal. They repackage the deal and sell it to others, investors whom I have never met. They had to be people of some means or why would they buy depreciation?"

My uncle, of course, is well informed on the answers to his own questions. All I have to do is provide an approving silence or a nod whenever my uncle provides an interlude.

"I built a limited income project to provide rental housing for families of moderate income or below moderate incomes."

I nod yes.

"I run the project eighteen years, I get no fee. The partners get no cash distributions. Everyone is pleased, at least I never get a visitor, never get a word of complaint, that is from the investors.

"Dick or Richards call me once a year, usually when they receive the yearend audit. Six-seven years ago, Dick and Richards—they are a team—like 'good cop, bad cop, white hat, black hat', arrive in Rockville, put legal documents on my desk. I had to sign. What can a minority partner do? I only owned a third, we had sold two thirds for what for us was found money. I am sure what Dick and Richards got from the investors was a lot more than they paid me. It had to be. I was just starting out. What did I know about the value of tax shelters?"

Coming from the south are huff and puff clouds carrying the rain in their bellies that has already chased the late lunchers from the terrace of the Naples Ritz-Carlton.

During a pause I try, "Al, it's raining in the south. You want to go back?"

"Let's go on to the lighthouse. If it starts to rain, there is a shelter there.

"I sign the documents which takes the management from me. Now D&R are the partners in charge. A year later, I am invited—invited is not a good word—more like 'told' to appear in the offices of Dick Richards and Wolf. Again I am asked to sign a document. 'Mr. Roone, please sign. We are gifting The Bluffs,' that was the name of the project, 'to a not for profit. You will get your necessary IRS forms with your yearend audit.'

"By this time I know from tax shelters and gifts to reduce taxes, so I ask Herbert Dick, who is playing white hat, 'Herb, did you run the gifting by Abner Cook?' Cook is the outside counsel for our partnership. Cook has been with us since I was acquired by DR&W. You met Cook, a very decent sort who knows more about housing law than any attorney in Chicago.

"So Herbert Dick says, 'Al, you worry too much. Jim and I' (that's James B. Richards, his team mate) 'are both attorneys. We drew these papers. All you have to do is sign them. That's what minority partners do, Al. Sign!'"

I nod again. The sanderlings have fled the beach. There isn't a walker or shell seeker in sight.

When the rain blows through us, we look like two contestants in a wet T-shirt contest. My uncle looks up at the sky.

"Benny, even the pelicans were smart enough to see the rain coming. We might just as well go back, get into some dry clothes before we chill out."

The rains came, the rains went. My uncle goes on.

"I told Dick, the IRS is hell on gift valuations. He says, 'Not to worry, Al. I chose a most competent appraiser.' All appraisers are competent until the IRS reviews. So it turns out exactly as I hoped it wouldn't. Two years and eleven months afterward the IRS picks up the returns. That was six years ago. The IRS is very clever or Dick and Richards are very stupid because what started as a simple valuation case has become a major fraud inquiry, and now the IRS claims that Dick and Richards received a fee for preparing the documents for the 'gift' and also a fee from Charles Fish who promptly bought the property that Dick and Richards gifted to the not for profit."

The east wind blows the clouds into weathered turrets and spirals from which gargoyles and dragons hiss into the blue sky. At the condo, Clara is up and at the ready for Al.

"I never seen a man like you. You saw the rain coming, that's not bad enough, you take Benny out and get him drenched."

"It's only a summer shower."

"It's winter! Go change your clothes."

"I needed a shower, so now I'll take a hot one."

My uncle departs for the master bath. Clara is still a roaring wife.

"Your uncle reaches one bad decision after another. I have never met a man with such consistently poor judgment."

"He chose you for a wife, Clara."

"Benny, I chose him."

Milly, who is into the crossword, laughs. "Family fun at the Roones."

Clara finishes, "As if Al doesn't have enough stress with the business. Your uncle has to go out, get himself chilled."

"We turned right around."

"Sure, when you were wet."

"We didn't finish our walk."

"Talk, is what you should say, Benny. I know why you are here, because Al is going to send you on a mission. You never say no to your uncle, do you?"

To that accusation I don't reply, because as Milly said when I retired from the Army, "That's what you wanted, Benny. Adventure, romance, intrigue. Twenty-two years in the Army counterintelligence wasn't enough for you."

Monday afternoon Milly and Clara leave for their shopping. "Benny, time for our walk on the beach."

With the wind behind us we head west into the sun. Al has pulled the bill of his Cubs baseball cap over his green eyes. The gulls laugh, the common and royal terns squat disdainfully beyond the surf's reach. A lone heron is in and out the surf. My uncle walks on the high ground, on the flat compact sand. I am a step behind when I reach him. He begins.

"Benny, there is a meeting next Thursday in Chicago. The IRS vs. the Bluffs Partners. That's me, Dick and Richards. If Dick and Richards can't get some sort of settlement with the IRS attorney . . . the amount involved is a fortune, hundreds of thousands, that's because of all the interest and penalties that have accumulated in the six years since this case has been unresolved."

"So."

"Why don't you run up to Chicago on Wednesday or Tuesday, look around, speak to Herb Dick, to Jim Richards, then go to the meeting. You would be back by Friday."

Before I answer Uncle Al says, "Tuesday would be best, in case the weather gets ugly on Wednesday."

We come back, Milly greets me with "You going to Chicago on Tuesday?"

"Who told you?"

"Clara."

Wednesday morning, after a businessman's breakfast at McDonald's, I am in the waiting room of Dick, Richards and Wolf counselors at law. Four red leather arm chairs with copper tacks, British hunting prints, a gentleman's club without the ashtrays and the decanters of sherry and port.

"Yes?" The teeth-on-display smile is from Amanda, the name on the desk plate next to the discreet *Please Refrain from Smoking*.

"I am B.A. Roone. I called. I am to see Mr. Dick and Mr. Richards at 10:00 a.m."

More of Amanda's teeth. Amanda interrupts her word processing, looks at her Swatch watch, runs her finger down the appointment ledger, points to an arm chair.

"May I get you some coffee?"

"No, thank you."

I leaf through *Fortune* magazine, read the *Wall Street Journal*, admire the Oxfordshire landscape and the rump of the hunter as he clears the stile, until a middle-sized, middle-aged, all-business type in navy blue three-piece suit enters from the hall, smiles, extends a hand.

"You must be Mr. Roone. I am James Richards."

Richards' hand is wet, and this most carefully put together counselor has neglected to get his hair trimmed to blend into his well-fitted hair piece.

"Sorry to keep you waiting. I was waiting for Herb Dick."

Amanda has overheard.

"Mr. Dick went to the washroom."

"I just came from the washroom. Mr. Dick is not in the washroom."

We visit for a moment and then a Chicago traffic cop carrying an open wallet in his hand enters. He goes to Amanda, shows her a driver's license. "Herbert Dick?" pointing to the photo.

Amanda says, "Yes."

The police officer says, "He is dead, out on the sidewalk. I called an ambulance."

I follow Richards and the police officer down to the street.

The ambulance is there. What was Herb Dick is a bloodied pile of macerated brains over a bankers gray three-piece suit. Dead is dead. Richards is with the police. I head for the washroom to wash away death. The door to the men's is locked. Amanda, now without the teeth, provides the key. The one window is up two, three inches, which is sufficient to allow the Lake Michigan breeze to chill the room.

I rinse face, hands, go to place the disposal towels into the waste. Clinging to the plastic can liner is a hand-lettered "Out of Order - Use 10th Floor Mens." The lettering is square in black ink on a gray 8x11 cardboard that has two staple holes at the 8-inch margin.

Jim Richards, without comment, comes in, begins to wash his hands. Dries, balls the toweling, washes again, balls the toweling.

He throws one ball of wet towel in the waste, the second misses. Richards picks up the balled towel, opens it, places it very carefully to cover the gray cardboard. Only then does he speak to me.

"Business is business, Mr. Roone. You came a long way. Dead is done."

Richards leads me back to the corner office. Three walls of Richards' adorable children and spouse climb a cliff face, reel in a brown-speckled trout. A vital American family in L.L. Bean outdoor wear.

Richards sits me down across his desk, clean except for two side-by-side legal pads, a fountain pen in a desk holder, coughs . . . hums.

"You look like Al Roone."

"I am his nephew."

"Fine man, Al Roone. Did a lot for Rockville."

"I am here about the problems the Bluffs Partners are to settle with the IRS."

"Been settled, Mr. Roone."

"When?"

"Yesterday, Tuesday at 10:00 a.m. Herb Dick met with the IRS attorney."

"I thought Herbert Dick told my uncle the meeting was on Thursday, tomorrow. I was to be there. Those were the arrangements as I understood them."

"That's what Herbert Dick told your uncle?"

"That's what I understand. That's why I came to Chicago."

Big smile from Jim Richards. "That's like Herb, tells you Thursday, does you on Tuesday." Then an extended grin, "Herbert A. Dick won't be doing you or me anymore, will he now?"

To that self-evident truth I nod and murmur, "I am sure he will be missed."

"Not me, I won't miss that S.O.B. He went to the IRS without me, made the settlement to favor himself."

Richards doodles with his fountain pen on his legal pad.

"You know what Herbert A. tells me? Jim boy, you have always had a second rate mind. Partners pay the IRS according to the percent of the property that they own. That's why it's 'Dick and Richards.' Herbert A. tells me that while we are in the washroom standing side by side. He didn't even have the courage to tell me that face to face. Herb made the most profit. He should have paid the greatest part of the settlement."

I don't answer. I reach across the desk, turn both legal pads over. Neither has a cardboard backing. Richards puts his left hand down into his waste basket, begins to feel, places the gray cardboard that has been torn into two pieces, on his desk. I turn the cardboard over, there is black ink splatter and blotch over most of it.

Richards has watched silently. "I was filling my fountain pen."

"Mr. Richards, the color of the ink on the blotch and the ink on the 'out of order' sign are the same! Not too many fountain pen users in RDW, are there?"

I take the pen from the holder, squeeze three, four drops beside the blotch.

"Same ink, Mr. Richards."

"So it is, Mr. Roone."

Richards retrieves his pen, inserts it back into the holder, sits back. Now for my two hand, sure shot from the foul line. "Herbert Dick only smoked in the men's washroom."

"How do you know that?"

"There were cigarettes on the sidewalk, all around Herbert Dick."

"He jumped."

"You pushed him. He opened the window to blow the smoke out. He stood there with his back to you, smoking, ignoring you. You were ready for your private talk. You had put the 'out of order' sign in the washroom door. You didn't want anyone to overhear you in case there was an argument. Wasn't there an argument?"

"I didn't push him. I just wanted Herb to agree to a fairer settlement. For him to pay his fair share."

"You pushed him and then pulled down the window."

"He jumped and then I pulled down the window." And then Richards begins to laugh. "It doesn't matter whether I pushed him or Herb jumped. He's better off. He didn't have to think about dying."

With that, Richards takes off his toupee, points to a scar on his head. "Just been operated on for brain cancer. I may be dead in six months or I may not. I may even recover." Then he laughs again. "Sorry your trip was wasted."

Richards gets up, I get up. Richards doesn't shake my hand.

I catch the afternoon flight to Southwest Regional. Uncle Al is at the airport. He drives very carefully as I tell all.

"Nothing ventured, nothing gained, huh Benny?"

I nod.

"You think Richards killed Dick?"

"Why should he jump?"

"You can't tell about people. Thirty years we are partners and I never knew a thing about either Dick or Richards' personal lives. Nothing. Maybe he had family business troubles."

"All God's children got troubles, Uncle Al. I got troubles, you got troubles."

My uncle sighs. "I hope Mrs. Dick has enough money to pay the IRS. Maybe that's why Herb jumped, to leave the insurance to his wife."

"While he was smoking his after-coffee morning cigarette."

"At least the case is settled with the IRS." Then my uncle laughs, "Strange world. Dick does, I pay."

That is when I answer, "Dick paid."

The moon shines on San Carlos Bay. The Christmas lights in Periwinkle twinkle "business, business."

My uncle says, "There will be a bit of fog tomorrow but it should clear in the afternoon."

I nod, listen for the surf.

The Klein Amulet

Sunday, at bedtime, Charles Klein in preparation for the fourth Monday of negotiations with John Martens readied his Carnelian amulet ring. He touched the engraved acrostic of Hebrew letters, admired the grace of the Arabic calligraphy, read, "May the good Lord watch over you and preserve you."

The ring had "protected" three generations of Kleins since Abe Klein had purchased the Carnelian mounted in gold amulet in a Dakar Souk. Charles Klein placed the ring in his teakwood tray beside the folded twenties, tens and ones in their Tiffany money clip. The ring brought Charles to—

If Bill had the amulet, he wouldn't have been blown up by a mortar. The telephone call: "Your son, William B. Klein . . . missing in action." The confirming telegram: "Your son, Lt. W. B. Klein . . . dead . . . body recovered." The letter from the Corps Commander, twenty-two years ago this summer: "Your son . . . in the defense of a forward position, . . . during a night attack. I wish I could have gotten to know William better. All who served with Lt. Klein will miss him."

Bill had come home after graduation before he reported to Vietnam. That was the time he could have given Billy the amulet. Billy had his class ring. University of Illinois, 1967. He was so proud of that ring.

"Billy, this is more than a ring. It's a family amulet. May the Lord watch over you and preserve you."

"Dad, do you really believe in amulets?"

"Grandpa wore it in World War I. I had it in World War II."

"Dad, this is ridiculous in this day and age."

When May and I are gone, who will remember Billy? It's Billy who should be negotiating with Martens. Face to face. That's young people's work.

Billy would be forty-four. Martens is in his thirties; aggressive, arrogant. He wants Klein Industries. It's only a little company that makes wire, in a small town in western Illinois—Rockville, on the Mississippi. The management is old, tired, like the plant.

"So you don't sell to us Mr. Klein, What are your alternatives?" Martens chuckled, not quite a laugh. Martens could wait. What's a week, a month to a thirty-year-old?

May and I no longer talk about Billy. We go to the cemetery, we come home. What is there to say?

The new secretary was the last one to ask about Billy.

What is her name? Gutierrez, Rodriquez, Gonzalez. It's Rita Gonzalez, like the-movie star. No, that was Dolores Del Rio . . .

"We have to make sure you won't move the wire plant out of Rockville."

"I'll guarantee that for you, Mr. Klein."

"For how long, Martens?"

"Would two years please you?"

"Five years would be better. The young can move to where the jobs are, the old can get on Social Security, the wives can get jobs."

"Mr. Klein, it's not your responsibility. That's what the union is there for."

Martens had begun with, "Mr. Klein." In four weeks it was arms around me. "How is the old man today, Charlie?" "How is your back, Charlie?" "You are looking good, Charlie!"

"Miss Gonzalez, that's a picture of my son, Bill, taken in 1967 when he graduated from the University of Illinois."

"Very handsome young man."

Rita was forty, forty-one. Another divorced single mother back to work to support her children.

"Where is he now?"

"He died in Vietnam twenty-two years ago last February."

"I'm sorry."

"So am I. So am I."

"You must miss him."

May had shut the television, come into the bedroom. "Charlie, are you worried about tomorrow?"

"What's to worry about? We have to sell, Martens knows that. The only thing we are talking about is what will be left for us and for the employees."

"Charlie, try to sleep later tomorrow. You can miss services. You need all the rest you can get."

"My legs hurt."

"Go to bed."

"I had better take my pain pills."

"Don't broadcast to me what you are going to do." Charlie swallowed two pills. Charles Klein laughed.

"I thought you wanted to know about my good health?"

"I know enough after living with you for fifty years. I know. You don't have to tell me."

Charles Klein turned onto his left side to relieve the pressure to his right hip.

"Blessed be our God who guards our life. Please dear God, give me the insight, the wisdom to deal with the day-to-day."

He slept the fragmented sleep of the young-old, up once, twice, another pill, another three hours of sleep; up at five.

Charles Klein parked his Lincoln in the reserved space, between handicapped and Rita Gonzalez' red Escort. Charlie got out, looked up. The lights were on in the conference room. *Klein Industries—Wire Makers to the World* painted in 1951 on the three-story, red-brick factory would become visible when the sun highlighted the faded green cursive trademark.

Charlie opened the metal fire door, strode through under the Employees Only sign into the receptionist's office. Rita stood up. Rita tried. Rita was on time. The last secretary was worse. The next would be no better.

"Any messages?"

"No, Mr. Klein. Yes, Mr. Klein."

THE KLEIN AMULET

"Rita, please, write the messages down." What can I expect? Rita has too many personal telephone calls. Her kids keep calling her, too much on her head. Her daughter can't be eleven yet, the boy is about eight. Rita is lucky her mother lives in Rockville.

"You may not remember me, Mr. Klein, but my grandpa, Joe Ramirez, worked for your dad."

No one said Mexican anymore. Hispanic was the word.

"We need a Hispanic in the office, Mr. Klein. The men in the shop, the union, it would be . . ."

Rita tried and if she forgot, well, Charles Klein could still remember. But then Charlie Klein kept a gray 3x2 note pad in the breast pocket of his white short sleeved shirt. An old habit, picked up when he did his inspection-walks through the shop.

"Billy, you can't run a wire mill from the office. You have to go among the men."

The mill was closed on the day of Billy's funeral. The men in the shop had sent flowers. The Rabbi had told May and Charlie: "There were hundreds of people standing outside. The Mexicans from your shop were there."

The funeral director had presented the Kleins with the white register. May and Charlie had yet to open it. Charlie didn't know where May had put the Memorial Book. "Son" was embossed on it, Charlie remembered.

"Mr. Klein, Mr. Martens is here. I told him I expected you any minute."

Charlie Klein looked at his wrist watch. "I stopped for morning prayers on the way in. You didn't apologize for my being late?"

"No, Mr. Klein. I gave Mr. Martens a cup of coffee, put him in the conference room. Mr. Peterson is with him."

"Thank you, Rita."

"You want your tea?"

"No, thank you, Rita."

Charlie Klein took off his chambray sport coat, straightened his stoop, walked through his office into the conference room. Martens had hung his blue pin stripe; summer-weight suit jacket across the back of the adjoining arm chair. His starched, white-cotton shirt collar held the purple-flowered tie firmly.

May described the decor of the conference room: "Tables, chairs, photographs of the deceased Kleins, like something out of late Dickens." The sepia photo of Ben Klein, Charlie's dad, had been added when Charlie took over Klein Industries. That was 1951.

The sun that could not penetrate the etched glass walls diffused on the glass top of the walnut conference table. In the only window the air conditioner hummed. Of the eight matched walnut arm chairs, three on each side of the table and one at each end, two were occupied. Martens in the near center chair, Harry Peterson, treasurer of Klein Industries, at the head of the table to his right. Harry had it just right. Not too close, not too far.

Martens rose when Charles Klein entered, extended his hand.

"How are you, Mr. Klein?"

Back to Mr. Klein. Mister good guy. Charm school graduate. Charlie shook Martens's hand, seated himself across the table, face to face, eye to eye.

"Fine, just fine. Waiting long?"

"Only a few minutes."

Harry Peterson looked pale. Harry should get more exercise. For a fifty-year-old he looked sixty. All accountants did was sit. Sit and produce printouts, spread sheets.

"Charlie, I was telling Mr. Martens of our prospects in Europe. The dollar being down, I project a twelve percent increase in export sales for next year."

"That could be, and that could maybe not be." Martens again.

"Mr. Martens, my projections ate very conservative."

"I am sure they are, Harry."

Don't get irritated, don't say anything to Martens. Let Harry handle Martens.

Martens opened his collar. A gold medal on a gold link chain. A Catholic Saint to help those who help themselves. Charlie fingered his amulet ring.

Martens again. "Last week we had left off . . ." Martens reached to the seat of the empty chair between him and Harry Peterson, produced his leather-covered legal pad, opened it. "We are ready, Mr. Klein, to determine the value of your stock. The amount was satisfactory wasn't it?"

Martens looked at Harry Peterson, who paled, flushed and paled, then turned to Charles Klein who said nothing.

Peterson answered. "The price depends on how the payments are structured. There are tax implications and of course we must consider Mr. and Mrs. Klein's age. You understand, Mr. Martens, that our cash requirements are not negotiable?"

Harry speaks without rancor, in normal tones in the manner of a trusted employee who has guarded the future value of Klein Industries for their owners, May and Charles Klein.

"Mr. and Mrs. Klein will have to have final approval."

Harry is protecting us again. May must have called him. "Don't let Charlie get angry. Martens is not stupid. He'll offer Harry a sweetheart contract. Consultant to John Martens, CEO of Klein Industries."

"Okay, let's get down to work." Martens had the annual certified audit of Klein Industries on the table. "Four dollars for the common stock. That's sixty cents more than you'll get from anyone else, Mr. Klein."

Harry counter attacked. "That's twenty percent under our book value."

"Mr. Peterson, if I didn't need you and Mr. and Mrs. Klein's shares, I would not give you a penny more than three dollars."

Charles Klein looked at the photos on the wall, Grandpa in black and white, Papa in sepia, me in black and white forty years ago. You still look good, Charlie. Bill's picture should have been there right beside mine.

Billy could have gone to graduate school. Not a one of Bill's friends was killed while studying in a college library. The kids who went to high school with Billy, what can they say when they see me? "How are you Mr. Klein? How is Mrs. Klein?" Billy is all part of our shut-away past. Last Memorial Day, the rabbi forgot to have a service for those members of congregation B'nai Jacob who died in the defense of their county.

"Mr. Klein?" John Martens in his want-something voice.

His father worked on the railroad. Local Mexican boy makes good, goes to college, gets a law degree, becomes a labor lawyer. The union leaders trust their own. They speak Spanish to each other. Martens gets concessions from the unions that I couldn't get. That will make Martens a successful steel mill operator.

"Mr. Klein, we are all making concessions."

"If the unions had made concessions when I asked, when I needed them . . ." Charlie

THE KLEIN AMULET

stopped, looked up. Harry was sucking his wet lips. The little blue vein on his left forehead was popping, vibrating.

That didn't help your case, Charlie.

"Sorry, what were you saying?"

"Mr. Klein, I was saying that the price for your common stock was negotiated last week."

Charlie Klein turned to Harry Peterson. Harry gave half a nod.

"Okay, what's next?"

"The amount of interest the fifteen-year bonds will bear will determine what you and Mrs. Klein and Mr. Peterson will get quarterly."

Harry hasn't told me. I'll bet Harry has been talking to John Martens. They have had meetings or telephone conversations. That's a necessary part of negotiations. Charlie, don't start on Harry. Harry has to think of himself. We sell, no more stock options for Harry Peterson and family.

Still, Harry should tell me if he has been talking to Martens.

Charlie Klein looked at his watch. "You'll excuse me, Harry. I have to go into the shop. Would you like to go with me?"

Harry, surprised by the request, rose, followed Charlie through the door into Charlie's office. Charlie shut the door, pointed Harry into the Scandinavian side chair. Harry seated himself. Charlie turned the window air conditioner on high.

"What's the best bond interest we can get from Martens?"

"Thirteen, maybe fourteen percent."

"Can Martens pay it?"

"He has the wage concessions from the union."

"He gets concessions, we get junk bonds."

"Don't get bitter, Charlie."

"I know, Harry. We did the best we could. If I had gotten the wage concession Martens got, when I asked for them three, four years ago . . ."

"He is giving the union part ownership."

"We have profit sharing."

"Charlie." Harry was coughing; sweating.

"You okay, Harry? I'll get you some water."

"I'll be fine, Charlie. Just my anxiety acting up."

"Okay, sit here. I'll go into the shop. We'll finish up with Martens when I come back."

Charlie opened the door into the shop, reached to the rack on his left for his hard hat, strode between the yellow safety lines to the furnace, into the heat and roar of wire making.

Len Montgomery, *Foreman* printed in safety orange on his hard hat and across the tight chest of his shop coat, got up from behind his gray steel desk as Charlie approached.

"Any new problems?"

"No, Charlie. Got the breakdowns fixed during the night shift."

"You better go home. You had a long night."

"I'll leave when Gomez comes back!"

"Thanks, Len."

"How are the negotiations going?"

"I got a promise for the jobs."

"When you go Charlie, I go. The old lady and I are going to move down to Arkansas. Only thing I am going to do is fish and drink beer."

"What do you hear from Peter?"

"He'll be on sabbatical this quarter. Going to France." Len and Elsie Montgomery's son, a college professor. "Peter couldn't have gone to college without you, Mr. Klein."

"The William Klein Memorial Scholarships were Mrs. Klein's idea."

"Anything I can do, Charlie, tell me!"

"You've done enough, Len. You made the best wire we could."

"I am sorry about you being pushed out."

"Tell Gomez I'll stop by to see him after the shift change."

Harry Peterson had regained his "Treasurer of Klein Industries" calm, relaxed into his meditating position, his head hung onto his chest, his hands in his lap. Charlie Klein stood above him. Harry opened his eyes.

"You feeling better?"

"I'll make it."

"You'll have to. You have a brilliant career ahead of you with John Martens."

"Not me, Charlie. I am quitting, I am not hanging around here. I saw what this business did to you. I am getting out."

Charlie sat down, reached for a pill, waited for a mouthful of saliva, swallowed.

"Billy would have done better."

Harry didn't answer. He asked, "Thirteen or fourteen percent: What do we hold out for?"

"The hell with it, Harry. Let's settle for thirteen and a half. Let's get out of here."

"Let's think it through before we go back in. I have some questions for Martens."

"About?"

"What if Martens doesn't make it? The bonds aren't worth wallpaper."

Charles Klein fingered the gold scroll work of his amulet ring.

"Harry, you believe in amulets? You know, protection from the good Lord?"

"I never thought about it."

"Come on, Harry. Let's give Klein Industries to John Martens, with a smile."

As Charles Klein opened the door to the conference room he said, "Old, old."

Harry, a step behind Charlie, had heard only a mumble. "What did you say, Charlie?"

"I said, if I had given Billy the amulet he would be here today."

"Not that again, Charlie."

Charlie entered, smiled at John Martens. "Harry will work out the details with you."

"Won't you stay? I had hoped to have your input."

"Harry does the numbers. I make wire. See you next Monday."

"Sure."

"Harry, I am going to talk to Billy. Tell him about our deal." Charlie smiled at Harry Peterson. Harry breathed, slowly. "I'll be back about one-thirty.'

Charlie extended his hand to John Martens. "You look like my son Billy. Same can-do look he had." He turned, walked out to Rita.

"Going to see my boy, Mrs. Gonzalez. Be back at one-thirty."

"Yes, Mr. Klein."

"Rita, please write the messages down."

With God's Help

It was at the insistence of Harry Charney, our president, that we invested our congregational funds in the stock market and that came very close to destroying B'nai Jacob, organized in 1883, the oldest synagogue in western Illinois.

You ask, how could we choose such a man as our president, our leader? Small communities, such as ours (ninety-nine families and one hundred and twenty-four singles) to these few we may with God's help, add six new members a year. But remember, each year we are diminished by death and departures to Florida, California and Arizona. The weather in Rockville, Illinois, in the upper Mississippi River Valley, where the great river flows from east to west, may be character building, but it is not exactly healthy for the elderly, and thanks to God, most of our congregants are well beyond three score and ten. The November to April ice and snow and sunless skies frighten us. The July, August and September heat and humidity keep those of us who have a little heart trouble in the air-conditioning. So you understand why the exodus from Rockville.

I must admit, May and June are lovely, warm, sunny days, with cool, pleasant evenings, and sunsets in colors that cannot be described. October and November are joyous color changing months; when the corn and soybeans are ready to be picked, when by noon I can take off my jacket, sit in the sun under our aged red oaks, watch the folded clouds ride east in the hazy blue sky.

Back to B'nai Jacob, our congregation had the usual problems, only more so, because what two hundred and fifty of us could do easily thirty years ago—maintain a synagogue with a prayer house, classrooms, an all-purpose room, an auditorium, a kosher dairy and meat kitchen, a gym, a mikvah, a library, a lecture series—became in the last twenty years from difficult to very difficult to impossible.

The gym we rented to the church basketball league, the community room we rented to Weight Watchers, the prayer house was not used from Sunday to Friday. So Harry Charney, our president, cut our maintenance staff in half—to one, our office staff by fifty percent and still, our deficit lingered and grew.

It was about ten years ago that our religious committee approved Sunday night bingo and that did balance our budget for the next eight years. But even paid for buildings need new roofs, and the cost of heating and air conditioning is the same whether there are twelve or twenty for the evening service, twenty-six or forty-six at Saturday services.

Harry is not an aggressive business type. He is more in the scholar tradition, who ran a business. Call it a business? He sold lighting fixtures wholesale and retail. What kept him from the threshold of bankruptcy was his good fortune. As my mother, may she rest in peace, said, "Better to be lucky than unlucky." That is what happened to Harry. He got lucky.

The City of Rockville needed to expand its bus garage. Harry's "wholesale to everyone" lighting emporium is next door. Harry gets $400,000 for his building which was more a warehouse than a retail space. You ask how I know how much the city paid? The price was in the Rockville *Journal*. But when I asked Harry how much, he told me $200,000, which is not exactly a lie. $200,000 he received up front and the rest he received when he gave possession. Harry is not stupid. He sold his inventory at a going out of business sale, applied and received a Federal moving grant because he was displaced. That is how Harry retired early, a young, vigorous, man of fifty-eight, who, in one spring, went from being a member of the executive committee of the Chamber of Commerce to president of B'nai Jacob, which gave him time to study both Talmud and our future needs.

I thought that for Harry, retirement was a very clever move, as that year Wal-Mart, Lowe's and Menard's all opened stores on the loop road. As it says in Ecclesiastics, bingo too was not forever. The gambling boats arrived in Illinois and Iowa and the gamblers who come to our Sunday night bingo, kosher hot dogs, only one dollar, moved up-market to free appetizers to desserts for seniors aboard the paddle wheeler gaming boats.

We were sitting in the library which no longer has a librarian, which is why we now hold our monthly meetings there; me, Max Stein, head of the House Finance committee, Harry Charney, president of the congregation and chairman of our religious committee, our secretary, Lily Green, the charitable widow of Abe Green, the Matzo King, who made his fortune by creating multi-flavored Matzos, chocolate, strawberry and cherry.

Lily is sitting taking notes, nodding a little. I can't tell whether she is approving Harry's investment ideas or just nodding. Harry, of course, presumes that Lily has just voted yes to investing in the stock market because if we can double the income of our Trust Fund from five to ten percent, that would offset the demise of our bingo income.

Harry looks at me. "Max, we are in an up market in equities."

Harry is giving out statistics like on the money station on television. Stories about eighty-year-old grandmothers becoming millionaires. "Max, we have a computer. We can trade for pennies on the Internet."

I asked, "What shall we buy?"

"Buy the gambling stocks. The boats took our business; we will participate in theirs. And look at Tama. The Indians are making a fortune, and if Indians can do that, we can too."

I warned, "What goes up comes down. There are no guarantees. What do we know from gambling stocks?"

Harry has the answer. "I listen to Philip Gross, the TV stock maven."

At that moment Lily wakes up. "My Abe invested in drug stocks. He made a fortune in drug stocks."

I tried again. "What do we know from stocks?"

The vote was two against one, and Harry Charney moved the B'nai Jacob monies from savings to the trading floor.

Each month Harry gives me the purchase receipts. Each month he buys more. Each month I ask, "What is this CRC?" "It's a casino in Las Vegas recommended by Philip Gross, the Channel 99 specialist in gambling stocks."

The next month it is GEA. "Tell me, Harry, what means GEA?"

For my question I receive, "It was highly recommended by Philip Gross."

By the end of that year we are fully invested, which Harry explains to me, "That, Max, is cost averaging."

"Harry, where is the income?"

"Income? We did not invest for income, we invested for growth."

Lily nods, repeats, "Max, we invested for growth. That's what my Abe did. He invested for growth."

'How am I going to pay bills? I am short. I need."

Lily leans over, taps my elbow. "Max, you worry too much."

"I know, Lily, but our income from these investments is half of what we received from our savings account."

Lily checks my figures. "So it is, so it is. Not to worry, Max. My foundation will send you a check."

Lily's check pays the bills, but with us it's always the same thing. Harry comes to me. "Max, I know what we need to restore our congregation. A dynamic rabbi. And with the money from the stock . . ."

I interrupt, showing my books, "Harry, we can't afford a rabbi. We can't pay his salary. And with the salary there is a retirement program and health insurance for his family."

"Max, you don't understand. We will hire a retired rabbi who has all his benefits from his previous congregation."

"Sounds good to me, Harry. Let me try."

I try the Rabbinical Association. I get from the director, William Teller, "Quite impossible, Mister Stein. We have forty congregations waiting for rabbis."

I said, "We will take a lady."

"Mister Stein, all our ladies are of child bearing age. They will not take a pulpit that does not have a Hebrew day school in which to educate their children."

I said, "If they will come we will build a day school."

"That, Mr. Stein, is baseball. That, Mr. Stein, is a field of dreams in Dyersville, Iowa. You are in Rockville, Illinois."

I tried to explain. "Dyersville is only ninety miles from Rockville." But Mr. Teller, the placement officer, has already hung up.

I report my failure at the next meeting. Harry assures me, "Max, all is not lost. I will advertise in the *Wall Street Journal*."

Harry is now a daily—except for Saturday and Sunday—reader of this leading journal of finance.

The next month I receive from Harry a big bill and a copy of our ad. "Rabbis. Come to Rockville, Illinois on the Mississippi. Great fishing, great boating. Come join B'nai Jacob, the oldest congregation in western Illinois. Box 0007, Rockville, IL. Salary open."

"Harry, what is this salary open?"

"It means open to discussion. The rabbi asks 'How much,' we say 'Not so much to begin with. Next year when our investments come in we will see.' By that time he is loving Rockville."

Then, a strange and wonderful thing happened. Like the miracle when Queen Esther saved the Jewish people from Haman. We received a letter from a Rabbi Marsha "call me Malke" Apple, from Iowa City, Iowa, which is only sixty-five miles on the interstate to the west. One hour and ten minutes away. Malke is not only an ordained rabbi, but also has a doctorate in English literature. Of course, she is not a conservative, orthodox, graybeard rabbi like our Rabbi Levine of sacred memory, may he rest in peace, but even a female reformed rabbi is a rabbi.

Lily is concerned, says, "A young woman without a husband, she may be a lesbian, which is not a good example for our congregation, which has two girls of high school age."

I say, "She may be an African-American for all I care. We need a rabbi. She was the only rabbi to answer our ad. If she will have us, she gets the position."

Our president agrees with enthusiasm. "First, let's interview Rabbi Apple."

Rabbi Apple is, to say the least, gorgeous. A tall, thin, athletic forty-four or forty-five year old with a great figure, blue eyes, red hair. She comes in wearing a mini skirt. To tell the truth, the skirt was up to her knees when she stood and became a mini when she sat down at the library table across from me.

Harry takes one look, he smiles at me, whispers, "Max, Malke is a gift from the Almighty sent to revive our community." Which implies that we are dying, which is not far from the truth. Of course, we don't tell that to Malke. We show her our up-to-date building, show her our up-to-date office with a computer and printer and copy machine, and then the negotiations begin. Malke smiles, lights a cigarette. Lily, God bless her, coughs, but Harry saves the day; he goes into what was Rabbi Levine's private office, comes back with a glass cut tray that twelve years ago held Rabbi Levine's half smoked Primo Havana cigars. When our rabbi was eighty he cut his smoking in half, but sad to tell, he only lived another six years.

Rabbi Apple "call me Malke" talks first to me. "I understand the congregation provided a home for the rabbi." That incentive has not existed since the untimely departure of Mrs. Levine some ten years ago, when the finance committee rented the house most advantageously and used the rent to offset our deficits. To her question about a home, I do not answer. Harry, who cannot keep his eyes off Rabbi Apple's beautiful bosom, turns to me. "Max?"

I say, "It is possible."

Rabbi Apple takes a notebook from her red Coach shoulder bag, opens the notebook, looks at me as if I should have worn a name tag. "You are Max Stein, the finance officer?"

I smile. "I pay the bills."

"You are an accountant?"

I smile. "Not by profession. I am a volunteer." Which seems to satisfy, at least for now, the candidate for the position of Rabbi at B'nai Jacob.

Rabbi Apple takes out our ad from the *Wall Street Journal*, reads, "Great boating, great fishing. That I know. Salary open?"

As my rich Uncle Al taught, "Don't make the first offer." Harry smiles, I smile, Lily grins and nods. I see Lily's chin descend to her chest, her eyes close. Rabbi Apple writes a number on her notebook, passes it to me. I say nothing. I pinch Lily awake as I pass the notebook to her. She nods a yes. Lily never says no to anything I ask of her. I pass the notebook to Harry, who silently passes it back to me.

I say, "Rabbi Apple, am I correct that starting next September you will be teaching the Victorian Novel at Rockville College?"

Rabbi Apple is disturbed. "That is what I wrote you."

"You could assume your position at B'nai Jacob by the time of the High Holy Days?"

She says, "Of course."

I say, "That is settled." Rabbi Apple gives me a vigorous hand shake.

Just then, Harry passes a note to me. "Benefits?"

I continue. "Rabbi Apple, I presume that you will receive a full benefit package from Rockville College? Health insurance, retirement, etc., etc.?"

Malke smiles. "And free tuition for my daughter." Out comes a photograph of seventeen-year-old Gloria Apple, as gorgeous as her mother. And that was when our brilliant president asks, "Rabbi Apple, why did you leave your last congregation?"

As I said, Harry is not exactly stupid, but a question like that you don't ask a single mother. You write or call the congregation and ask there. Which I had already done, but for me sexual preference is a private matter. What matters to me is, will Rabbi Apple give an intelligent sermon? Can she read from the Torah? Can she teach a page of Talmud and would she reinstate the morning prayer service? To all these questions she had answered yes, yes, yes. Now Malke looks at Harry Charney, looks at me, smiles. "I left my last position to return to the University of Iowa to complete my Ph.D. in Victorian Literature."

I say, "Rabbi Apple, welcome to Rockville." She says, "I have been here before." I say, "Really?" She says, "I was the assistant women's basketball coach at Rockville College the year before I went off to the Seminary to become a rabbi."

Harry says, "Max, prepare the contract for Rabbi."

She says, "The house, Mr. Stein, we were talking about the house?"

"The house will be ready by September 1st."

Malke smiles, "August first, Mr. Stein." She gathers up her notebook, gets up, pulls down her skirt. "I will keep in touch." Handbag on her shoulder, she leaves us. Harry looks at me. I look at Harry. "Max, did you see what I saw? Did you see her beautiful boobs? Who did she remind you of?" It is Lily who answers.

"Monica Lewinsky. She has a bosom like Monica Lewinsky." Then she adds, "Malke Apple is God's gift to Rockville. I only wish my Abe was alive to see our new Rabbi."

Harry turns to me. "Now we must sell some of our stock. But remember, Max, only enough to pay one year's salary."

I take my stock certificates to Mike Cohen's brokerage office. Mike is no longer a member of our congregation; he joined Temple Israel, the reformed congregation. But, for the memory of his father who was a member, I am seated in his private office while Mike is punching CRC-GEA into his computer, adding, subtracting, smiling, frowning.

"Max, CRC is not an investment quality stock. It is a gamble."

"Yes, I know it is a gambling company stock."

"CRC has not done well, which is an under-estimation of our situation. The stock is worth about a fourth of what I paid."

"Mike, that was only two years ago."

Mike sighs. "The market today is risk aversive. The Dow may be up, but . . ." Then he clucks in admiration, "Your GEA, Gene Experimental Associates, has tripled. My advice . . ."

I am hearing genes. "I thought Harry bought gambling stock?"

Mike grins. "Two years ago Gene Experimental was a gamble. That turned out very well for you. Tell me, who recommended GEA to you?"

"Philip Gross, the maven on gambling stocks."

Mike Cohen laughs and laughs. "Philip Gross went to jail for touting stocks, for taking money to push stocks on his TV program. Of all the hundreds of stocks he ever recommended GEA was the only one that was a winner."

I smile, a hand shake and a thank you and do my arithmetic. "If I sell twenty percent of my GEA I will have enough for this year."

"Good move, Max. By next year CRC may be bought out. There are rumors. just rumors, about either a sale or merger so that you could recover a little."

At the June board meeting, a beautiful cool night, so lovely a night that I move the meeting outdoors into our atrium. I announce, "Rabbi Apple's salary is in our savings account."

Lily says, "Max, we have to plan for the future, think ahead. That's what my Abe used to say. Business is thinking about tomorrow."

Harry adds his wisdom. "Lily, I am confident that with God's help we will be able to meet our future budgets." Harry is bragging again about his investment insights. "You see the benefits of investing in stock."

I don't say anything. I remember what my mother said. "Remember Max, God answers all prayers. If not in this generation, in the next."

Cousins

My father, David Baron, has spent sixteen months simmering in his faulty decision, upset. How could he have allowed Alfred Belinski to leave Cosmopolitan Compounds, his pharmaceutical company, taking his now famous and successful udder balm formula with him? And now Dad needed Belinski shaving gel, and Belinski was offering his gel formula to other pharmaceutical chemists than "poor" Dad who was quite convinced that with Belinski shaving gel and his sun block, he would produce a most astonishing product that with one application and one stroke of the razor would forever eliminate the need for both pre-shave and aftershave, a product so unique that it would not only be used for shaving but for summer and winter skin care.

These were the revelations I had listened to every Saturday afternoon for sixteen months over father-son golf, at the Pleasant View Golf Club nestled in the verdant hills above the Pacific where, in every season, pleasant California breezes prevail.

My father, a pharmaceutical chemist, couldn't accept that Alfred Belinski, a country veterinarian, had compounded products that major generic drug manufacturers vied to buy, and now worst of all, Belinski, who had created the most superior udder balm, a protectant of the milking cows' mammary glands against cold, heat, abrasions and contact dermatitis, had again stumbled onto something as revolutionary, as wonderful, as profit-producing, as his shaving gel.

Under the cloudless southern California sky, Dad and I, iced tea in hand, sat in the shade of our purple blossoming Jacaranda tree. My father plotted how to acquire Belinski's shaving gel formula for Cosmopolitan Compounds. My father is not a compounder of drugs to cure dread diseases but of formulations mostly ancient that he revives and modifies to improve skin tone and retard aging by adding a U.V. sun blocker. When Dad hisses U.V. between sips of tea it sounds as ominous and threatening and dreadful as a social disease.

My father leans toward me, "Gary, I must have Alfred Belinski's gel formula and I need you to get it for me. Belinski likes you. He has always liked you. So talk to him."

"Dad."

"Don't Dad me, Gary. One day Cosmopolitan Compounds will be yours."

Which is undeniably true as I am an only son, an only child, and that I am now in my third year of Art School at UCLA is of no importance to my father, who hears only David Baron and not his son Gary when I tell him, "Dad, I want to do art."

I looked up at the cloudless sky, looked at my watch. I had eighteen minutes before my tennis lesson with gorgeous Gloria Goodman, the tennis pro at my Studio City Tennis Club. My father, who notices everything, smirks. "You think you are going to get into Gloria's pants by taking tennis lessons from her? Not with that Beverly Hills beauty."

I smile. "It's worth trying and my tennis game is improving."

"Gary," my dad sighs, "we will talk when you get back."

As I come in the door, Dad waves and points me to join him poolside where he reveals how "we" will get the gel.

"At exactly 7:45 a.m. Belinski eats his breakfast at George's. He will be seated in the second alcove on the right; we casual like will join him. Of course, I will have a contract ready. You pat Dr. Belinski on the back, 'Alfred, let me buy your breakfast.' You ask him to sign; he says, 'Yes, of course.' You continue, 'You have your formula?' Something like that." My dad twirls his mustache as the villains did in the silent movies. "Gary, whatever it takes, the formula has to be ours." Which is as close to humor as my dad gets when he is talking business.

Just then my mom calls "supper." Sunday evening it is hamburgers, beer and the CBS broadcast of the Oak Hills Golf Classic from the Coal Valley Country Club on the bluff above the Mississippi in beautiful western Illinois where the heat, humidity and haze have reduced the gallery to the sponsors.

My mother, the Angelino, who swims daily and speaks of golf as a waste of time, asks, "David, did you ever play at the Coal Valley club?"

"Me? Not me. I was a public golf course kid."

I can't let that go by. "Dad, tell me how a poor boy from Illinois worked his way through Stanford."

My mom, who has heard, kisses my dad on the head, "He married a school teacher."

Dinner done, Dad shuts the TV off. I follow him to his poolside arm chair with the view of the million dollar homes clinging to the brown and green hillsides of the valley lit by the motor cars on the interstate. Dad leans back, master of all he surveys, puts his legal pad on his expanding belly that once a week golf will not keep tight and flat. Dad is forceful. "Gary, it took me twenty years at Cosmopolitan Compounds, thirty years if you count my going to school and working for others to get this house on a hill for you and your mother."

I am a supportive son. "You done good, Dad."

"Thirty years is a long time. I wouldn't want to lose all this because of Belinski."

I smile, "Not to worry, Dad, the house is paid for." Dad doesn't notice my quip. He is back to Belinski.

"Gary, you know how important the gel formula is and don't tell me I shouldn't have quarreled with Dr. Belinski." After a pause, "We were together for almost twenty years. We were good together as long as I agreed with Alfred." Dad has raised his voice, "The minute I disagreed with what Belinski did . . . All I said was 'Dr. Belinski, the base of your balm is too heavy, there will be more ointment left on the fingers than will stick to that udder.' I was watching Alfred's demonstration, and all I did was describe what I saw. The ointment was too heavy. Alfred says, 'You know nothing about cows.' Which I admit but I do know from ointments."

My mom comes in with our iced teas and lemon, joins us at the patio table. Mom holds the iced tea glass to her permanently tanned cheek. My father picks out the lemon slice, sucks it dry and swallows it.

Mom says, "What a lovely cool evening." Which Dad confirms. "Not like summer in the Mississippi River Valley." Mom sips and then faces Dad. "David, don't get Gary to do what you should be doing."

I smile, "All I have to do tomorrow morning is eat breakfast, and bring Belinski and his formula back to Cosmopolitan Compounds."

"All your father has to do is apologize to Dr. Belinski and make him an honest offer." Her statement completed, my mother looks at the sky. A jet has started to descend into Burbank airport.

My dad looks up, "Not a cloud in the sky. Okay, Betty." Betty is Mom's name spoken by my dad in anger. Then Dad turns to me. "Gary, you heard your mother. Make Dr. Belinski an offer he can't refuse." My dad is very pleased with his witticism.

My mother, the voice of conscience, returns. "David, you have to apologize to Dr. Belinski. Gary can't do that for you!"

"Who says that?"

"You know that."

Dad then turns to me. "Gary, you can tell Dr. Belinski that whatever I said that offended him I apologize for saying it." That said, Dad looks at Mom for approval.

My mother sips her tea. "Good beginning, David. All you have to do now is tell that to Alfred."

"Betty! I know Alfred. He will want a royalty deal. You know how greedy he is."

My mother puts down her tea, looks at my dad and gives him instruction. "David, give Alfred a chance to talk. Ask him what he wants. If you had listened to Alfred . . ."

My dad interrupts. "Betty, he would want too much."

"Would it be fair?"

"Who knows what is fair in business?"

"David, you know." With that my mother gathers up her iced tea glass and leaves us for the enchanted England of *Masterpiece Theatre*. I smile an understanding, caring smile at my dad.

My dad smiles at me, "Tomorrow morning, you and I go to George's for breakfast with Dr. Alfred Belinski."

"That's 7:45 a.m."

"That's up at 7:00 o'clock, Gary boy."

I point to the moon rise, put my arm around my dad. "Pops you do business every day of the week, even on Saturday afternoon at the golf club, and here we are at the after Sunday dinner planning session for Monday; now do you know why I want to do art?"

"Gary, you can have your art and business if you own the business."

"But Papa, what if the business owns you?"

Monday morning, the moon roof of Dad's Lincoln Continental open to the gentle California sun and breeze, Dad and I are riding down Ventura Boulevard for breakfast at George's with Belinski. George's on Ventura Boulevard is where the big movie deals were made. Along the right wall are the alcoves, so designed that in order to see who is raping whom it is necessary to walk up the main floor of the restaurant and look very deliberately at the contestants. To reassure privacy, each alcove has a wall telephone hanging at arm's reach from the round table and four cane chairs.

As a twelve-year-old sitting beside my father eating my breakfast bagel special, I thought the seat closest to the phone was occupied by the dominant deal-maker male because that was where my dad sat and lectured to me of the benefits that could be derived by being in business for yourself.

Now of course, with cellular phones, pagers and voice messages, the ringing telephone is not as frequently heard in the alcoves and so access to the unlisted number of the phones is not the symbol it was; but then George's isn't what it used to be when Hollywood was where movies were made. The regulars still order without looking at the menu. After their second cup of coffee they nod a yes to the waitresses, who are all tall, thin, ass wiggling, pony-tailed blondes who are sweating it out at George's because that is where the producers eat kosher style and a friendly producer is a friend in deed.

At George's, on Ventura Boulevard, breakfast is served all day, from bagels to blintzes to pastrami and eggs, Eastern European cuisine brought to the United States and then on to California by the pioneers of the movie industry (comfort food, nostalgia food) who disdained the low salt, low cholesterol diet as dangerous to your health.

Alfred Belinski, his white short sleeve shirt open at the neck, was seated with his back to us. Dad had dressed in his go to the bank for a loan Brooks Brothers navy blue pinstripe, accompanied by a white oxford cloth long sleeved button down shirt, which this morning he accented with his red and blue rep silk power tie.

Dr. Alfred Belinski, twenty years older than my dad, has seen us. Slowly he pushes up from his chair, reaches for my hand. "Gary, so nice to see you," to which he adds a welcome-to-my-table smile.

My father sat himself to be closest to the red phone, which put him beside Dr. Belinski and facing me.

The waitress appeared. Her name tag announced Peggy W. She smiled at Dad. "The usual?"

He nodded.

Belinski ordered, "The bagel special."

The waitress asked, "Sesame, pumpernickel or plain?"

"Sesame, please."

"I will have the same," I said.

"Three coffees?" to which Peggy W. received three yes's. From my father, "One bill, please."

Alfred Belinski murmured a just audible, "Thank you," then added, "David, you do look well."

To which Dad responded with, "How are you feeling, Alfred?"

"Good, good as an old arthritic can be."

Each year Dr. Belinski walks a bit more slowly and is a bit more bent.

My dad takes out his pocket notebook, opens it, and places his Mt. Blanc pen beside it. My dad is ready to negotiate for the Belinski shaving gel formula. Knowing Dad he wants Dr. Belinski, the millionaire, to make the first proposal.

Dr. Belinski turns a little to the left to face me. "Gary, I saw your prints at the UCLA student exhibition. Very good. I particularly liked the woodcut landscapes of your California Coast series."

I say, "Thank you."

My father defends, "Elizabeth and I are going over to the UCLA Gallery tomorrow afternoon."

Belinski sips his coffee and says nothing.

I sip my coffee. My father reaches into his inside pocket, pulls out two folded typewritten pages, presents them to Dr. Belinski. "This is where we were with our contract."

Dr. Belinski finishes, "When I walked out." Dr. Belinski reaches into a black vinyl portfolio that is on the seat of the empty chair beside him, presents my dad with two double spaced sheets that look very much like my dad's.

The waitress is there with the bagels for Belinski and me, and the four slices of French toast made with challah bread for Dad.

Dad puts the Belinski offer to his left, reads, as he cuts the fried bread with his right hand, forks with his left hand. Reads, cuts and forks mouthfuls of thick saturated, overflowing in egg batter, fried bread. Without looking at Belinski my dad mutters, "That is where we were."

Belinski swallows his toasted sesame bagel. "David, I can't hear you when you talk with your mouth full."

Dad wipes his gray mustache, his lips, and raises his voice. "Alfred, I said this is where you walked out."

Belinski grins. "Because you said, take it or leave it."

My dad continues to chew his toast and says, "Alfred, I am listening. Tell me what you want."

"Just the usual residuals like the ones I received from Smith Brothers for my udder ointment, nothing more, the same deal."

I give Dad my "Go for it, this is your chance" smile. Either top the offer or at least meet it.

Dad signals to the waitress, "One bran muffin for" and points to Dr. Belinski.

For this deed of loving kindness my dad receives a cheerful, "Thank you, David, you remembered."

Dad is pleased, "Alfred, I want the right of first refusal of any of your future formulations."

Dr. Belinski sips his coffee. "David, if I agree to that, you will have to decide in thirty days whether you acquire or not. David, I am going to be seventy-eight next spring, I don't have as much time."

My dad nods, understands and murmurs, "May you live to be a hundred and twenty."

Which Alfred confirms with, "From your mouth into God's ear."

At that moment Alfred Belinski waves a friendly good morning to a short, stocky, middle-aged, full-bearded, full-mustached man wearing a white shirt, black tie, black suit topped with a black knitted skull cap firmly pinned to the back of his head.

I ask Dad, "Who is that?"

My dad looks up, doesn't answer. He wipes the sugar into the last bite of his French toast.

Alfred reveals, "That is Dr. Hershel Smith. He and his brother, Simon, own Smith Brothers Chemicals. They headquarter in Tel Aviv."

"Israelis?"

"No MIT grads, they are Boston Boys." Dr. Belinski cuts the muffin into quarters, offers me a quarter.

I accept, "Very good. Thank you."

Belinski confides, "Gary, your grandmother, may she rest in peace, made wonderful bran muffins."

"I never knew her."

Dr. Belinski takes out his Dr. Grip pen designed to ease the pain of writing with arthritic fingers, fills in a series of numbers under Royalty agreement, and places the paper in front of my dad.

Dad reads, sips his third cup of regular, nods an okay, swallows, manages a "You got it." Dad copies the Royalty numbers onto his two sheets, signs both at the bottom, then Alfred Belinski signs.

Dad says, "Excuse me," leaves for the distant washrooms identified in red neon cursive.

Dr. Belinski asks me, "When does your dad begin his radiation therapy?"

"Radiation therapy?"

"Yes, for his prostate cancer."

"I didn't know."

"I am sorry, I thought."

My dad is back. He extends his hand to Alfred which Dr. Belinski accepts. Then my dad says, "Welcome back, Alfred."

Dr. Belinski says in Yiddish, "Be well." Which is about all the Yiddish I understand.

Dad is up to pay at the cashier. I linger to be with Alfred for whom getting up is to push up slowly with both hands. As Dr. Belinski gathers his portfolio I ask, "Dr. Belinski, why did you walk out on the negotiations and then come back?"

Belinski pulls back his shoulders in a vain effort to straighten up, reaches for his cane with the red, yellow and green serpentine engravings. "Your dad said, 'Al, take it or leave it,' and went off to the bathroom, so I thought I would teach him a little something about negotiations, but then I didn't know he had prostate cancer and that you were going into the business with your dad."

In the shade of the parking lot Dad reviews Alfred's black Lexus, "How much?"

Alfred says, "I love the seat."

Dad says, "See you tomorrow morning at the shop." Alfred waves a yes and backs out slowly.

It is a gentle, sun filled, most pleasant southern California summer morning, the weather my father left western Illinois for. Dad drives north on Ventura Boulevard to our home on an Encino hill in silence, without his usual exuberant cheerfulness. When Dad pulls into the drive I ask, "Do you have any idea why Dr. Belinski walked out of your original negotiations?"

"Sure, he wanted a royalty agreement."

"Would you have given it to him then?"

Dad grins. "Not if I didn't have to."

I put my hand on my father's. "Pop, do you know why Alfred . . . ?"

Dad completes my sentence. "Alfred signed this morning because he is a tired old man who doesn't trust Hershel Smith." Then he chuckles, "I knew Alfred would come back when I told him you were coming into the business."

"Why did you tell him that? I haven't."

Dad finishes another of my sentences. "He likes keeping his business dealings within the family."

"I didn't know that Dr. Belinski was family."

Dad puts his head back, looks up at the cloudless sky through the moon roof, "Alfred is my cousin, three times removed. Somewhere back in Poland his grandparents and my grandparents were brothers and sisters. 9:15. Gary, I have to go."

"Go where?"

"To the hospital. Six weeks of radiation and my prostate cancer is gone."

"Dad, I haven't said I was joining Cosmopolitan Compounds."

My father, David Baron, hasn't heard me. Dad backs the Lincoln out of the drive, gives me an exuberant hand wave. When he turns I see his smile has been replaced by a grimace of pain.

Come Out, Come Out Wherever You Are

Parental abuse, that's where it's at for the '90s, is the memo George Talbot, our producer sent around with the admonition, *Meeting to do pilot, 29 December, 3:00 p.m. Billy, please be there.*

I sang, "Going to Mama's house for Christmas" into George's voice mail, added while still in tune, "See you January 3, Happy New Year. Don't call me, I'll call you. We'll do lunch. Billy."

At the Southwest Florida Regional Airport, my mother, Arlene, gives me a hug, a peck and "so nice to see you, Billy . . . if we hurry I can save seventy-five cents on the parking."

"Mom, I have to wait for my luggage." For which I get, "What did you bring me?"

"What do you need?"

Mama laughs, then answers a question with a question, "What do I need?"

In pink T-shirt with a red grazing flamingo that proclaims "Sanibel Island" across her bosom, white, almost to the knee, shorts, white thong sandals, black-lensed sunglasses shoved onto her untinted brown hair, a three-emerald ring on her left pinky, two gold wedding bands on the third finger of her right hand, Mama appears as an independent Florida widow with no need for worldly goods in this season for giving.

"Okay, Mom, so you don't need. What would you like to have? Tell your son, Billy, the magician."

Mama puts her arms around me, hugs me again. "Billy, tell me confidentially—now you are a magician? I thought you were in TV production."

"It's the same thing, Mama. We take a good story, good ideas and we turn it into dreck. For this I get a big bonus so I can come to see you."

"It's your life, Billy, but as my papa used to say, 'You play with dreck, you get covered with dreck.'"

I cannot answer my dear mom—she is on the down escalator and I am four steps behind, wedged in place among the young-old in their white trousers, red golf shirts and golf caps with "Beach Club," "Hunt Ridge," "Bay's End," pronouncing their affiliation and loyalties.

Mama is at the luggage carousel. "Your golf clubs just went around."

"I'll be right there."

Mom looks at her watch. "Don't run. We still have twenty minutes on the meter."

As I pull off my non-crush, thirty-two-inch case Mama is there. "With your back you shouldn't carry anything so heavy. I told you, to go to Crate and Barrel, buy yourself a couple of nylon sacks. Billy, go get a luggage cart."

"Yes, Mama."

"How is your back, Billy?"

"Fine, Mama, fine."

The moon roof open and the speedometer at exactly six miles over the speed limit, Mama drives the Continental down Daniels Road.

"You are driving too fast."

"What policeman would give a nice old lady like me a ticket?"

Now Mama is the innocent, mature, responsible senior citizen for whom speeding is a one-time momentary distraction, not a continuum that the tweets of her speed warning beeper impede.

"How is Harry, Mama?"

"Harry is back in his own condo!"

"Because I was coming?"

"You had nothing to do with it."

"What happened?"

Mama is out of the toll plaza and stopped by the red lights of "Bridge Open," before she answers.

"Billy, I married your father because he had a beautiful body and I was lucky he had a good head, a fine sense of humor. Now Harry is the exact opposite. A fat, flabby old man who sits around, eats only low salt, low fat and does nothing but read the *New York Times* and pontificate. I don't need it!"

"Harry is very good company."

The bridge down, Mama is off. I hear another "I don't need it.'

"It's your life, Mama."

"Right on, Billy Boy-Billy Boy. Tell me now, Billy, how is your love life? To me, Billy, you look tired."

"Mama, I am doing push-ups at two in the morning. Where am I going to meet girls?"

"Go to the laundromat—look, you'll find. It's not healthy for you to be alone."

"That's what I told you, Mama."

"For an old lady, it's different."

"You are not an old lady. Why do you call yourself an old lady?"

Mama answers in disparate phrases.

"Every time I drive the causeway I think of how lucky I am, Arlene Keller from Rockville, Illinois, an owner of two gulfside condos on a semi-tropical island. Look at that pelican, Billy. There will be a full moon tonight. We'll go out, walk on the beach. I want you to see the moon shadows."

I support Mama with, "That's what money is for. You enjoy, that's all the better."

Mama sighing, "If only your father had lived."

"Mama, Dad died fourteen years ago."

"I can't help it, Billy. When I see you and Ralph, all I can think of is that my boys needed a father."

"Ralph did fine, I did fine, Mama. I had a very happy childhood."

"Yes, you did. It's not every son that produces TV plays."

The tide is low, the Gulf sounds are soft. The immature ibis, brown backs and wings turning to white, peck for worms on the lawn; only a hand rail separates the beach grass, the beach sand, the beach sounds from Mama's screened porch.

Next morning Mama is sitting on my single bed, "Billy, you should have told me you needed a new mattress. With your back you shouldn't have to sleep in a hole."

"It is fine."

"It is awful, Billy."

"Mama, okay, it is awful."

"Now you tell me."

"Mama, it wasn't important."

On the bed beside mine Mama has laid out my T-shirts, my khaki shorts, my two swim suits and a new yellow terry robe. "It's been cold. For after your swim."

"Thank you, dear Mother."

"Now tell me, what do you have for me?"

"Well, wait until—until I get your undivided attention."

"For what?"

"My market study . . . after you take part in my market study."

"How long can you stay?"

"I'm not going to tell you."

"I'm your mother. You have to tell me."

So I tell Mama.

".Billy, can't you stay longer? Your brother and Gloria and Josh, cousin Etta and Uncle George and Aunt Rosa will be coming on Wednesday, just to see you and Ralph and on Friday night we can all go to services. On Saturday . . ."

"Mom I just want to be with you."

"Family is very important. Aunt Lilly called, she wants you to call her."

I see Mama's New Year's Day calling list. Cousin Lilly and her mother, Blanche. My cousin John, his wife. Mama's Aunt Bertha, who lives with her sister Gertie, who last year gave up smoking and has been talking about it ever since.

"Mama, how has the weather been?"

"Good, Billy, good."

"How have you been?"

"For an old lady, I'm good."

"Tell me, what have you been doing?"

"Running the business on the telephone."

"I mean for yourself."

"I made a basket." Mama presents me with a hand-woven ash market basket. "You can put your *New Yorkers* in it."

"I didn't know you knew how to make baskets."

"Fifty dollars and six hours of instruction—I am a basket maker. Billy, have you seen *Remains of the* Day?"

"A beautiful flick, Mama."

"Lost opportunities, Billy. Remember lost opportunities."

"Mama, I'll start looking for girls as soon as I finish this next pilot."

"That's what you said last year."

"I have been busy."

For emphasis Mama tells me, "I was twenty when I was married."

"There was a war on, Mama. You told me."

"I didn't have to get married. Your father and I wanted to."

"Mama, I promise." I hug Mama, dance her around between the twin beds of her guest room.

"You'll have to marry a younger woman."

"I'll marry an older woman with both kids in college."

"You'll have to pay their tuition."

"You know from everything."

"I know what happened to your cousin, Alan."

"Alan is a tight wad. I am a man of means."

"Sure, because you don't spend."

"I have been too busy!"

"Too busy to fall in love."

"Mama, I am only forty-three years old."

"You'll be forty-four in March. You'll be an old man without children. No one to say Kaddish for you."

"The Rabbi will do it."

"You are right, Billy, nowadays you can buy a Kaddish sayer. In the old days, when I was a girl, we had children. Ralph and Gloria and Josh are coming tomorrow night."

"They going to be here for New Year's?"

"They are going to Gloria's folks for Christmas week."

"To deck the halls with ivy and drink the Christmas cheer?"

"Don't get nasty. Gloria is a very nice girl."

"Gloria is a user. Ralph takes a lot of dreck from Gloria."

"You know everything."

"I have heard her."

"From this I don't know. Like my Dad used to say. Marriage is a private contract between two people."

"Is that what you said when Ralph brought Gloria home to you?"

"Ralph was of age."

"You were so anxious to have a married son, you."

"What was I supposed to say?"

"Gloria is a tramp."

"How do you know."

"Everyone knows. Ralph knows."

"So why doesn't Ralph leave her? Take Josh and leave her."

"He is afraid of losing Josh."

Mama is crying. "Why did you have to."

"Quit it, Mama. You and I know. Don't make like an offended mama."

"I'm crying because you thought I should have stopped Ralph from marrying Gloria."

"Mama, all Gloria wanted was a house in Oak Hills, with a convertible of her own, so she got knocked up."

"I tried to get her to go for an abortion."

"What did she tell you? It was against her religion? How much did you offer the virgin, Mama? Ten thousand? Twenty?"

"Billy, why are you so angry with me?"

"You were a lousy negotiator, Mama. You could have saved Ralph. All you had to do is say 'How much, Gloria?'"

"I thought maybe . . . I thought Ralph loved her. He told me he did."

"Ralph is an idiot."

"He is a good father."

"He is an idiot! He is still doing everything you tell him."

"Ralph is running the business."

"Ralph is your ventriloquist's dummy. Your voice in his body."

Ralph wanted to please Mama, a widowed mama with an older son—so he went into the business. "Billy, I'll write in my spare time." Ralph has never completed a short story. Every Christmas he began the same story; a rich boy without a mother . . . a loving war hero father who taught him to play tennis, to swim, to shoot. On his last spring vacation from college he and his father go skiing in Austria. The father dies in an avalanche. Miraculously, the boy survives, left alone, despondent. That very year on his way to Grandma's house for family Christmas, he parks beside the causeway to Sanibel, takes the pistol his father carried in the Korean War, blows away his head.

So, Ralph pleased Mama and went into the business where Gloria found Ralph. Gloria cooed. "Ralph, you are wonderful." Ralph followed Gloria into bed.

Ralph loves Josh; Gloria loves Josh. Although their marriage may not be the marriage made in heaven, they are still together.

With the door open to the surf sounds, mother and I sit in the rattan arm chairs of the living room. When the phone rings, Mama answers. "It's Ralph."

"How is Ralph, Mama?"

"You talk to him?"

"Not with Gloria on the line."

Mama says, "Good—good," hangs up. Pulls me from my arm chair. "I am getting stiff from sitting, Billy. Time for my evening walk."

Step in step, we walk the moonlit beach, our beach shoes crunching and cracking the barnacled pen shells, to reveal their opalescent lining to the moon glow. Offshore the day trip gambling boat, its three decks defined by yellow incandescent bulbs, flees the incoming fog to its North Fort Myers Beach harbor.

"It's been cooler than usual." Mama zips up her leather jacket. "You warm enough, Billy?"

"Yes, Mama." I open my jacket, point to the insulation.

"Fine dinner, Mama."

"Hamburgers and a salad and dark beer. I know you like dark beer. Big deal."

"Mama, how is the business going?"

"Ask Ralph."

"I am talking to you, Mama."

"We are refinancing. Reducing our debt, hunkering down."

"You expect bad times in River City?"

"We got bad times in River City."

"Things will change."

"We'll be ready. Ralph is working on a new marketing plan."

"How is Josh?"

"Josh is a clever kid. Twelve years old, he plays Ralph against Gloria. Gloria against Ralph. Josh is the Itzak Perlman of family conflict."

"I thought Josh played drums?"

Mama doesn't laugh—or even smile or answer. I try, "I made a funny. Mama."

Mama stops, faces me, "Billy, Ralph is not a lucky man."

I say nothing—what can I say?

Mama is at the dining room table sipping her after-walk tea. I sit beside her.

"Billy, what did you get me?"

"Mama, George Talbot wants me to do a series. Three, four units on violence."

"Like *NYPD*. I don't watch it."

"No, Mama, like the violence adult children do to their aged parents."

"I have read about that."

"The point is, would anyone watch three episodes of public service TV on abusive children."

"Parents are used to abuse from children."

"I am talking about starving your parents, not giving them medical attention, taking their social security payments for their own use, letting their old mama sit alone, isolated, tied into her chair, dirty, just mama and a black and white TV in a back bedroom."

"You expect a big audience? I wouldn't watch it."

"On his grant application George Talbot wrote, 'Let's take violence out of the closet and into America's living room.' You know what . . . he got the money to make the pilot."

"Billy, TV is your world, Billy. You want some ice cream? No sugar, no fat, tastes good."

"We got the money to make a pilot. You make a pilot. Be a good boy, Billy. Make it look real gritty. You know how, Billy."

"George, I quit."

"Don't be stupid, Billy."

"I quit!"

"The next shop will be worse. Be careful, Billy, you'll end up doing bare boobs and butts for MTV!"

The 2 o'clock United from Chicago emptied pale, booted, sweatered, insulated, isolated faces. Gloria, blond for winter, the first off of the Kellers, in white stretch pants, her mink lined jacket, short and open to reveal her tight little ass that body sculpturing created and massage maintains.

Her upright tits are into my chest, she kisses my ear and whispers, "Faggot. You told your mama yet?"

Ralph, who is almost six feet tall, comes off bent by a carry-on over each shoulder and Gloria's sack of magazines in his right hand. By the time Ralph hugs me twelve-year-old Josh has arrived with three tennis rackets held to his chest. Josh stands behind Ralph. I pull his Cub cap over his eyes and ask, "Tennis anyone?"

The only response I get is Ralph's, "How are you, Billy? Mama said you aren't feeling well."

"It was only a cold. A couple of days in the Florida sun—I'll beat you all at tennis."

I drive a silent Keller family to Sanibel. I did try.

"Doing good in school, Josh?"

"Fine, Uncle Bill."

"Playing a lot of tennis, Gloria?"

"Some."

Which brings us to the condo Mom keeps for the family across the walk from hers, and that's when Gloria says, "I hope you let Mom do the cooking. I won't eat yours."

To which I answer, "You know I don't cook until tomorrow. Mom always cooks the first day." Gloria is about to say something—she doesn't—instead Gloria starts after Ralph and Josh who are at the door. I shout, "Dinner at six. Mama doesn't like to be kept waiting." Gloria turns to me, "Billy boy, tell your mama I am going to finish up my Christmas shopping, not to wait dinner for me."

Which I duly convey to Mama.

"Billy, I saw you talking to Gloria. What more did she say?"

"She said she would like the car to finish her Christmas shopping."

"She has to go shopping on one of the two days she'll spend with us?"

Mom has cut the stems of the pink gladioli, divided the bunch in two, half are on her coffee table in a green glass vase, the other half she has put into a cut glass vase.

"Billy, be a good boy, take the flowers over to next door."

I knock—no answer. Flowers first, I enter. "Delivery!" Josh is on the couch, his head into his Walkman. I put the flowers on the dining room table. "Josh, why don't you go out in the sun?"

"We are going shopping as soon as those two quit yelling at each other." He points to the master bedroom.

Gloria comes out, screams at me. "Faggot! Tell your brother! Admit it, tell him you are a faggot!"

Now Ralph is there. "Gloria called you a faggot!"

I smile at Gloria. "Gloria is angry. What are you angry about, Gloria?"

"Faggot!" Gloria screams—I slap her once across the face. Not too hard, just hard enough to stop her screaming. Then I throw her narrow hips across my lap, slap her hard little ass, just easy, three-four times; let her up. Gloria runs out the door. Ralph starts to laugh.

"I should have done that."

"What set Gloria off?"

"Oh that." Ralph is grinning. "Gloria told me she wasn't going to eat your special meatloaf, not when your infected, HIV positive, bare hands did the mixing. She wasn't ever going to be anywhere near you, so I said you weren't a faggot, Gloria said you were, then she heard you talking to Josh."

Josh is out of his Walkman. "How Are you, Uncle Billy?"

I hand the car keys to Josh. "Your mom is waiting for you. Go shopping with your mom!" I scream like Gloria. Josh is out the door, Ralph is grinning.

"I wish I could manage those two like you did. Wait a second. I'll change. I'd like to go for a walk."

Ralph and I walk east on the low tide beach, past the lighthouse to the fishing pier. The pelicans perch on the guard rail, the gulls fly off, return, hover on the beach. The terns sit—their heads to the wind. The sandpipers dart into the surf, retreat and advance, retreat and advance from the rising tide. The winter afternoon sky is the faded blue of washed denim.

"Ralph, this faggot business with Gloria is my fault," and I laugh, chuckle. "Gloria has been calling me faggot ever since . . . since a couple of years ago when she came to New York to shop. She called, 'Billy, I love your cooking.' I invited Gloria over for my meatloaf special."

Ralph repeats, "'Billy, I love your cooking.'" I laugh. "What's so funny?"

"I remember I had both hands in the meatloaf. Out comes Gloria from the bathroom. 'I'll just go in and freshen up.' All she is wearing is her black bra and red bikini pants. No hose, no shoes. She puts her arms around me, kisses my ear and whispers, 'You can cook later.' I whisper back, 'Get dressed, you'll catch cold.' Gloria screams, 'Faggot! I knew you were a faggot!' Maybe I should have told you."

Ralph doesn't answer; that way he is like Mama.

Then he says, "I don't think I'll go to Gloria's folks for Christmas."

"That will please Mama."

"Please tell me more," is what Ralph answers.

By the time we walk up the four slatted wooden steps onto the concrete walk that unites the gulfside condos, the sunset sky is layers of copper with a topping of deep blue. Mama is on the porch looking at her watch. Through the open door I see the table is set for five.

"Ralph, you want to wait for Gloria?"

"I don't think so, Mama."

Ralph turns to Josh. "Shut the TV off, go wash your hands for dinner. You know Grandma doesn't like to be kept waiting."

Proud of You, George

I had delayed and rationalized through June, July and August, the hottest summer for western Illinois in sixty-two years. I'll go next week when it gets cooler. By the last week in August it wasn't cooler and my mother had become very insistent. "George, you have to get to Rockville before the holidays. There are those things you promised to help your Uncle Al and Aunt Carol with. You know how much they look forward to seeing you."

On Thursday before Labor Day, I drive west from Chicago on Interstate 88, through tightly planted fields of tall corn in tassel and soil-hugging green rows of soybeans interrupted only now and then by set aside acres sprouting weeds. The road is a straight, four lanes of divided concrete that has had little traffic since I passed DeKalb. Add the heat haze to the monotony of driving, it takes my every effort to keep awake.

I get off in Rock Falls, drink two cups of coffee in the dark and cool of the Ramada Inn. Awakened, in one hour I am in Rockville from where my mother fled more than thirty years ago.

"George, I just couldn't see myself staying in Rockville. What for? Golf and swimming at the Country Club. The big social events in my life, the Hadassah style show and the Federation dinner where I would be with the same people I grew up with. I knew what they were going to say before they said it. Good people, George, but what a dull life it would have been." The first time I heard Mama's "Why I left Rockville," was when I had just turned sixteen, the first time I drove Mama the one hundred eighty-three miles to visit the family in her hometown. My mother spoke without regrets, without guilt for leaving her aging, ailing parents to go into banking in Chicago because her brother Al and sister-in-law Carol were there. So, if Al and Carol hadn't stayed in Rockville would Edith Hess have become the first woman vice president of Illinois Trust?

I park under the shade of the oaks. My uncle, more stooped each year, has heard me, has the door open. He hugs me. "George, you look good."

"You do too, Al."

Al grins, hands me over to Carol, a diminutive, thin woman, hardly five feet tall with full size hips she calls her "family curse." Carol grins, "So nice to see you, George."

"You too, Carol. Been hot?"

"We haven't had the air conditioning off in three months. Your room is ready."

My uncle carries the paper sack with the four dozen bagels he asked me to buy for him from New York Bagel and Bialys on Dempster. I carry my hanging bag in. The house is cool, quiet. The radio plays Mozart. My aunt says, "You don't have to look in the refrigerator. I made the kugel."

I smile, hug my Aunt Carol. "You shouldn't have bothered as hot as it's been."

"You don't come that often, George."

My bedroom in the four-bedroom, three-bath house, that Grandpa and Grandma had built and that Al and Carol had moved into to take care of them, is upstairs and to the right of the bath. It is a small, square room with a sloping ceiling. Two vertical windows offer a view of the trunks of the burr oaks. My uncle has drawn the shades and opened the registers. As always it is cool and dim. There is a thriller on the bed with a note from Uncle Al.

> "Dear George,
> Just some junk food to get you away from your too serious thoughts.
> Love, A"

Neither my uncle nor my aunt eats lunch at home; at noon he swims at the Y and then eats his salad at the Village Pancake House. My aunt is scheduled to take Sadie Brill, her elderly widow friend, to whichever restaurant Sadie wants.

My uncle calls up, "George, I am going. Do you want to meet me for lunch?"

"One o'clock?" I ask.

"About one-fifteen. I am getting a massage today."

"See you, Al." I come down the spiral staircase, give my aunt the best seller novels my mother reads before she goes to bed.

My aunt takes the books, places them on the coffee table, points me into Al's arm chair, pulls up the rocker to be closer to me. "So, George, how is your life?"

I grin. "My love life?" Because, each year Carol explores and disapproves of my "celibacy," "being alone." Carol nods a yes, I don't answer, she says, "So don't tell me."

I laugh, "There is nothing to tell."

"All right, don't tell your only aunt."

"When the time comes you will be the first to know."

I see her disappointment, so I say, "I am waiting for a Jewish heiress."

This brings a smile to Carol. "At least when you talk about money you aren't serious like your mother."

"I have just been too busy to date. What girl wants to date a resident? I promise next year at this time I will be looking for a nice Jewish girl," and then after a pause, ". . . unless I decide to go to the seminary."

"You going to be a rabbi?"

"I haven't decided yet."

"Have you told your mother and father?"

"Only hinted."

"Can I tell Al?"

"Nothing to tell. The seminary is only a maybe after my residency is finished."

"It is good of you to come out to see your old aunt and uncle as busy as you are."

"There is no place I would rather spend the Labor Day weekend than with you and Uncle Al."

My aunt finishes with, "In Rockville?"

"Rockville isn't all that bad—for a rest." On my way out to lunch with Al I kiss Carol on her forehead.

My car thermometer registers outside temperature as ninety-six degrees. The only green on the brown lawn are the oak leaves that the squirrels have chewed free and the broad leaf weeds.

From the hostess at the Pancake House I get an uplifted arm pointing. "Your uncle said you were coming." My uncle, as always in short sleeve oxford shirt, sun tan trousers and cross training shoes, points to a seat.

I ask, "Who else is coming?"

"Carl, and maybe Bill Evans."

The usual, the same middle-aged, upper middle class, white American males that my uncle has lunched with for thirty years. It is like the Rotary Club without the compulsory singing and hearty fellowship. I sit next to my uncle, pour a cup of coffee from the never empty coffee jug. The waitress brings another jug of coffee, places it in front of me. "You boys all right? You want to order?"

"Patty, Carl and Bill are coming." Al turns to me. "George, you haven't met Carl. He is new to the Y. He started coming after his son died." My uncle sips his coffee. "Carl is not in too good a shape." I sip my coffee. "That is why I asked you to come. Sometimes he opens up, then afterward, he feels a little better. I told him you were a doctor."

I say, "I'm used to listening."

"I told Carl you were a great listener." Al smiles slyly at me, "You didn't get that from your mother."

"Mom is okay."

"There are times, George, your mother tells me more than I want to hear."

"Mom means well."

"That I know, but it doesn't make it any easier to be told—like she always knows what is best."

"Don't let her tell you, Uncle Al. I don't."

Al sighs, "I only have one sister."

A tall, thin man, about seventy but could be younger, stands to the left of my uncle. "George, I would like you to meet Carl Remtz. Carl, George is my nephew, the doctor."

I extend my hand. "How do you do?"

Carl smiles, says nothing. His hand shake is vigorous. He sits himself to my left. I offer, "Coffee?"

"I had better not." Carl points to his belly. "Hurts when I drink coffee."

The waitress brings a jug of hot water, two tea bags, two slices of lemon, places them in front of Carl Remtz. "You want to order?"

Carl answers, "Bill will be late. He decided he had time for a massage."

Patty looks at my uncle. "The usual salad?" My uncle nods. The waitress points her pencil at me. "Salad is fine." She turns to Carl. He asks, "Which soups?" She answers, "Vegetable beef, split pea, Wisconsin cheese."

Carl turns to me. "I am a vegetarian." I nod with understanding. To the waitress—"The split pea has pork in it?"

"Yes."

Carl orders, "Wisconsin cheese."

I offer, "I don't eat pork either." Carl smiles, his face made longer by sideburns that reach to the bottom of his earlobes, asks, "You a vegetarian?"

"No, I am Jewish. Jews don't eat pork."

Carl smiles in recognition of my revelation. The salad and soup served, uncle eats with fork into the lettuce into his mouth. Carl blows on his soup before he sips it very slowly. Carl, noticing that I am watching him, explains, "I am now very sensitive to hot. I think it is because of some drug the doctor gave me when I had my chemotherapy."

I nod in understanding, sip my coffee.

Carl pours his tea, stirs, turns to me. "What kind of doctor are you?"

"I am doing internal medicine and infectious diseases. I have another year of residency."

"The doctors couldn't keep my boy alive." Tears are in his eyes. I say nothing. I pick up my cup, Carl continues. "They didn't try very hard."

I drink my coffee.

"They could have tried harder. It was the pneumonia that killed him. Pneumonia is curable, isn't it doctor?"

The emphasis is on doctor, so I answer. "Mostly . . . ," and sip my coffee.

Carl finishes his tea, looks at the clock, turns to me. "Glad I met you," picks up his bill, leaves, comes back, places two quarters on the table. "Al, you going to come in tomorrow?"

"The good Lord willing."

Carl says, "I'll try to come in tomorrow," leaves.

I turn to Al. "You believe in the good Lord, Al?"

Al waits a moment, sips his coffee. "Sometimes more than others."

"You still going to morning services?"

"Yes. That is when I thank God for our lives, our world, for what we have." Al doesn't wait for my comment or question. "Carl tell you what his son died of?"

"No."

"He died of AIDS."

"That is tough."

"It is more than two years and he is still . . ." My uncle doesn't finish immediately. "He is still feeling guilty about not having done more to save his son's life."

"Does he really think his son could have lived?"

My uncle puts down his coffee. "George, you don't understand. You may not until you have children. Every father who loses a son feels he should have done more."

In my doctor's voice I say, "There is no way to survive AIDS. Not today. Maybe soon, but not today."

"Carl knows that but he thinks if he had done more, taken Roy to Mayo, he would have survived this pneumonia."

I finish Uncle Al's sentence, which now I know I shouldn't have, "So he would have died from his next pneumonia."

It is then that my uncle looks at me. "George, that is harsh to say to a father."

Then I remember, that before I was born, Uncle Al and Aunt Carol had lost their only son at age four. My uncle looks at me. "It's all right, George. I know you didn't mean to hurt. It's just how it turns out."

Al stands up, takes my tab, places a dollar on the table. "Thank you for coming out to lunch."

We walk into the full sun. The heat haze rises from the blacktop of the parking lot, from the hood of my car. We stand together beside my uncle's car. He puts his arm around me. "It's all right, George. I understand. You weren't thinking about my son, Frank. How could you? You weren't even born yet and your mother and I never talk about death—not in front of you."

It is then that I say, "I am sorry."

"I know you are, George." Al explains. "That is when I began to pray. I started by saying Kaddish for Frank. Thirty-two years later I am still praying."

Al opens the door to his car. Turns to me. "George, don't ask me why I continue to go to service beyond the required eleven months."

"Al. Why?"

Al gets into this car, turns on the air conditioner, takes the windows down. I stand beside the car, the door open. "You want to know?"

I nod.

"Because I am afraid to quit. I can't start the day without saying thanks for what we are, for what gifts God has given, for our lives."

"Al. Al, after my residency I am going to apply to the seminary."

I start to walk off to my car, my uncle calls out. "I am proud of you George," and then he grins and yells as he backs his car out. "Your mother will be proud of you, too."

Fine . . . Just Fine

Last Wednesday, my mother, seventy-six and only a little arthritic, said to me, "Gerry, it would be nice if I could find someone to help me with the heavier work around the house—especially now since my shoulder is hurting again." On Saturday Mother called to tell me of her good fortune.

"Gerry, you wouldn't believe it. I had my ad in for only one day and—she used to be Caroline Conroy—showed up. You remember Helen and Bert Conroy's girl. She says she remembers you from high school."

The Caroline Conroy I dredge up was a placid blond with a "Botero" body that made her head seem small. I remember her as very quiet and to herself like most of the girls who made it out of the east end into Rockville High School.

My parents knew the Conroys because they had lived neighbors to them when my dad came home from World War II into the housing shortage. They had rented Max Langman's four-room bungalow on an unpaved street, with a fuming coal furnace that produced more ashes then heat, a yard without a tree or grass to cut. Max Langman paid no attention to the house as he had bought it for his son, Maury, to come home to after the war. Morris Langman crashed his bomber and became a Gold Star on the lawn of the county courthouse. All this I knew only from stories my mom and dad had told me as I was only five when we lived on this dead end street in the east end, across the ravine from the Conroys.

When my sister, Lily, was born, Dad built a two-story, four-bedroom, three-bath house on the hill in the Oak Hills addition. Two of the bedrooms and two of the baths are downstairs. That is where my mother still lives, alone, two years and eight months after Dad died.

Mother sounds very pleased with Caroline. "Caroline will come in every morning, make the beds, clean up, do the laundry, sweep the gazebo."

"What are you going to do on the weekends? That is, if you need a bit of help."

"I haven't really thought of that, Gerry," and Mother is back to, "Caroline is such a cheerful girl."

"Mom, Caroline is no girl. She has to be more than fifty."

"I still think of her as the little neighbor girl."

"Okay, she is a girl."

"Gerry, I tell you I was lucky to find someone I know. That is, I knew her father and mother. Good, hard working people. Her brother is a college professor in Chicago."

"Charlie, a professor?"

"That is what Caroline said."

"Mom, don't go out in this heat and humidity."

"Don't worry, Gerry. The house is air conditioned; my car is air conditioned."

Every Saturday morning Mom calls, asks the same question, "Gerry, when are you coming home?"

"Mom, I wrote to you. I will be in Rockville on the tenth."

"How long are you staying?"

"I told you, Mom. I will have a week with you, then I have to pick up Julie in Michigan."

"I would like to see Julie."

"Mom, I told you. Julie will fly out to see her folks while I drive up to see you; then I'll pick up Julie and we will drive back to Kansas so we can stop in Minnesota."

"Gerry, you and Julie could stop here on your way back, just for overnight like you used to."

"Mom, I explained it to you. We haven't seen Mary and the children in six months and we thought we would take the ferry from Ludington and drive up to Minnesota along the Mississippi. It really is our only chance for a mini vacation."

"You could all meet here. That way I would see my grandchildren. Gerry, I would love to see the boys."

"Mom, it is much too difficult for you to play hostess to six of us."

"I promise not to cook. Caroline would help. She tells me she is a fine cook."

For a moment my mom sounded sad, so I say cheerfully, "Mom, I'll be home on the tenth and we'll have a whole week together."

I watch the weather in Rockville, in western Illinois; this is the hottest summer since 1936. Temperatures in the high 90s and once or twice last week it reached 101 degrees, high humidity, intermittent heavy rain. Funnel clouds and storms are reasons enough for me to call my mom every two or three days just to say, Mom, how are you.

"Gerry, you should have seen it. The winds blew down four limbs from the oak in the front yard. One rotted branch was eight feet long, six inches around. It came down with such force that one end was buried in the lawn. Caroline had everything cleaned up in just minutes—as soon as the rain stopped she was out there, took the limbs to the bum pile. Gerry, you eating right?"

"Yes, Mama. Julie left more than enough frozen dinners."

"Julie is a very good cook. You are a lucky boy to have Julie for a wife."

"Yes, Mama. Mama, be careful driving in the rain."

"Gerry, you worry too much." Then, with a giggle, Mom whispers, "I have a surprise for you. I bought a new car. Caroline was so helpful. She arranged everything for me."

I know I should have said "how nice," but I don't say anything. What can I say. Mom is pleased with Caroline Conroy, Mom is pleased with her new car, good help is hard to find and I am in Manhattan, Kansas, four hundred forty miles to the west, tied to a research project.

I call Mom the night before I am to leave Manhattan and Mom is neither pert nor cheerful. "I tore a ligament in my right shoulder. Don't worry, nothing serious."

"That is very painful, Mother."

"Caroline took care of everything. I was home all alone and she came right over. It was lucky you gave me that automatic dialer, although I could have dialed the doctor left-handed if I had to."

"Mother, go see a doctor."

"I will tomorrow, Gerry. Don't worry about me."

"I'll see you tomorrow evening. Don't wait supper for me."

I drive north through the Flint Hills into Nebraska. The farther north I drive the better the grass grows. In Iowa the corn is tall, green, erect, in tassel with no sign of storm damage. The soybeans glow with green good health.

I cross the Mississippi into Illinois on the I-280 bridge as the *Lady Luck*, the Rockville gambling boat, turns and lets off its blasting whistle. Ten minutes later I kiss my mom on her forehead. She stands five feet, eight inches tall; her right arm is held to her chest by a four-inch Ace band.

I smile and cheerily say, "You look like a mummy." With that, I give my mother a careful hug and another kiss.

"Caroline has just been wonderful to me. She cuts up my food and she even signed my checks for me."

My first evening with mother it's "Caroline, Caroline." At 9:30 in the evening Mom turns to me—"Gerry, help me take my bandages off and don't worry, I can get undressed by myself. Caroline says I can sleep with just a sling and tomorrow morning Caroline will help me get dressed."

"Mom, I can help."

"No need, Gerry. That is what Caroline is for."

At 8:00 a.m., Caroline is in the side door with her key and a toothsome smile.

"Good morning, Mrs. Gross."

I am pleased that she hasn't taken to calling my mother by her given name—Pauline, or Peppy, as her oldest friends call her. "Good morning, Caroline."

"I'll get your tea and then I can help you dress."

"Gerald has made the tea." My mother proudly introduces me, "My son, Gerald," and with a grin, "the doctor, but he is not a people doctor."

I extend my hand. "Mother has told me how helpful you have been."

In a half an hour Mom is back into the dining room, dressed in khaki trousers, white top and her immobilizing elastic bandages that leaves only her right hand free. Mom joins me at the table where I am reading the Rockville *Morning Press*.

"The heat wave is going to continue into next week," says Caroline, who has seated herself beside my mother and across the teak table from me. Mom adds, "It is going to be hot and humid in Michigan, too." And Caroline adds, "I won't let your mother go out in this weather, not even for shopping. It is much too dangerous."

I say nothing.

"Mrs. Gross, if you don't mind, I'll just run over to Eagles right now, get the groceries before it gets too hot."

"Don't forget the fish. Be sure Marsha gives you the fresh fish. Tell her it's for me."

Caroline is back with mother's Coach bag. She opens the zipper, reaches in for mother's wallet. "I think fifty or sixty dollars will be about what I need."

Mother takes three twenties from her wallet, replaces the wallet in her purse, hands it back to Caroline. Mom's purse in her right hand, money in her left hand, Caroline, on her way out, passes closely to me. So close that she brushes my shoulder. I smell mother's Deneuve, or is it Nina Ricci. Whichever scent it is, it is certainly the perfume mother uses.

With Caroline off shopping it is my opportunity to check up, review what has happened since my last visit.

"Mom, are you still swimming?"

"Every morning until this happened." She points to her shoulder. "I'll be able to go back to water jogging by Monday. Caroline can drive me down to the Y. She said she would come a bit earlier."

"She seems very willing."

Mother answers, "Let me show you my new car."

The double garage is attached to the freezer, furnace, laundry room, which opens into the kitchen. Mother is up, leading the way. She opens the door to the garage, throws the light switch to reveal a sky blue Lincoln Continental.

"You like it?"

"Beautiful color."

"Come, I'll show you something."

Mother leads me to the driver side door with the electronic code door opener, touches 0 and four other numbers. The car's inside lights go on, mother opens the door, shuts the door, touches the two last numbers. "That locks the car. There is no way I can lock myself out. So if I leave the keys in, I can just open the door with the code." Mother laughs. "I won't forget the code. I chose the house numbers."

"Does Caroline know the code?"

"Of course. She has to drive me. That is, she has to drive me until my shoulder heals. Gerald, don't look so worried."

Mother shuts the garage light off, leads me back to the dining room table. "I'll be all well in a week or two at the most."

"Have you had the doctor look at your shoulder?"

"No sense running to the doctor. I spoke to him on the phone, he said we were doing everything right."

"Maybe therapy could help." Mother doesn't answer, so I continue. "I am going to call Dr. Kaplan, speak to him."

"Gerald, you worry too much. All I am is a little arthritic."

Which leads me to ask her, "How are you sleeping?"

Mother sighs before she answers. "I wish I could sleep better. Maybe I wouldn't be so tired."

That is all the health information I can gain from my mother because, again, we are talking of her new Continental.

"Caroline said I shouldn't be driving a ten-year-old car that didn't have air bags and anti-lock brakes."

"Caroline is a car maven."

"Her husband raced cars. That is how he died . . . in an auto crash. He was only forty-three. Caroline raised three children all by herself."

"That is an achievement. What did you do with your '84 Oldsmobile?"

"I sold it to Caroline for the exact amount that her brother-in-law said it was worth as a trade-in. That is why I bought the Lincoln. Walt, that's her brother-in-law, assured me that Rockville Lincoln-Mercury still had the best service in town."

"Mother, you should have called Fred Seitz at the bank. He would have told you the exact value of your Olds."

"All right, so maybe I sold the Olds for a few hundred less than I should have. Caroline had to have a reliable car to get here."

"Has Caroline paid you for the car?"

"She is paying a little each week."

My mother, who is usually slow to anger, is upset by my inquiries into her affairs, but I continue. "How much did you get for the Olds?"

"If you must know, two thousand dollars."

I make a note of that for my conversation with Fred as to the value of an '84 Olds in quite perfect condition with only 84,000, carefully driven miles on the odometer.

"Is Caroline keeping up her payments?"

"You sound exactly like your father used to. He didn't trust my business judgment either."

It is evident by mother's tone not to pursue Caroline and the '84 Olds. So went my first morning with mother, until, "Gerald, come on. Let's go for a drive. You drive. I want to show you what's happening in town."

This is what we do. I drive down Deere Road and my mother is the prideful voice of Rockville Chamber of Commerce. "The Wal-Mart store will be open by next May; the Farm and Fleet should be open just a bit sooner. Now Gerald, drive back to Seventh Street."

I drive west. "Drive in as if you are going to Menards." My mother points out, "That is the largest parking lot in Rockville. That's where the new Target store is going and Kohl's is going to be just next to it, and across the road will be the hospital's new emergency center."

"Lots of changes in three months."

"Drive me downtown, Gerald."

When mother says, "Gerald," that signals that we are to have a conversation—either about her estate or my sister, Lily, whose lifestyle she can't approve of. "I do try to understand Lily—I just can't." Our downtown office building is Mom's topic for this morning. Thank God she is not going to talk about Lily. "Park here."

I park in front of the bank.

"Look."

I look. Two, black-on-white signs, four feet by six feet, proclaim "Available." One from the vacant retail space and the other from the long unrented, street level, office suites. Mom is telling me, "I am not going to wait for an increase in the value of downtown property," a pause, "At my age, with all this business activity, the time to sell Papa's office building is . . ." she laughs, ". . . whenever I get the first offer."

I nod approval.

"I am glad you approve, Gerald."

"Why would you think I wouldn't?"

My mom laughs. "I wouldn't want to do anything that wouldn't please you. After all, you are my only heir." Which implies that the disinherited Lily and her family are going to be my responsibility.

I look at my watch. "How about a bite of lunch?"

Mom grins. "How about the Pancake House?"

"Fine."

It is a bit early for lunch, which gives us our choice of seating. Mother is received with, "Booth or table? Smoking or non?"

"Nonsmoking and a table please." To me she explains, "Since the booths have been raised they are just too difficult for me to get into. Belle tripped on the step down. That is how she broke her wrist." I nod. Mom orders decaf. I ask, "You off coffee?"

"I think I do better on decaf." That is all the explanation I get until mother takes the last bite of her omelet and then cups two little white pills into her hand which she quickly swallows with a sip of water and, "Just something to help my digestion. Gerald, do you mind if we go home?"

"Why should I mind?"

"Well, I know you like to go to the cemetery."

"We can go tomorrow."

"I think I'll lie down for a few minutes."

"Do you want me to help you?" I point to her wrappings.

"Gerry, you could do me a favor and help me off with my shoes."

I take off her "go to town," Easy Spirit shoes. Shoes in her left hand she goes into her day room. A half hour later I look in on her. She is supine on the bed, the light on, the *Best American Short Stories* face down on her chest. I shut the doors, go into the kitchen to use the telephone at mother's desk.

"Fred Seitz, please."

"Gerry Gross! What brings you home?"

"It is my week with mother."

"How is Peppy?"

"She looks good to me."

"The value of her '84 Olds was about $2600, give or take. I no longer see her come into the bank. I understand Caroline Reed—she used to be Caroline Conroy—is . . . you remember her . . ." and Fred Seitz doesn't finish.

"Is what?"

"Sort of taking over your mom's personal banking."

I say, "Thank you."

Fred says, "Come by to see me, Gerry."

I answer, "I'll try" and hang up.

An hour later Mom is still resting so I go upstairs to my bedroom to use the telephone there.

"Mr. Gross, can you hold? Dr. Kaplan said he would talk to you in just a few minutes." I hold for Dan Kaplan with whom I went to high school.

"Gerry, how are you? You want to play golf?"

"Maybe on Wednesday or Thursday if the heat breaks. I was calling about mother."

"Anything the matter?"

"She seems more frail. A little slower, more bent."

"You ought to see some of my other patients. You are lucky you are a veterinarian, Gerry. You don't have to watch your patients deteriorate."

I sigh. "What worries me more is her dependency on Caroline."

"It happens all the time, Gerry. Your mother wants to trust her care giver like she was family, so she does."

"Dan, I think Caroline has taken advantage of mother. Mother sold her, her '84 Olds and I doubt if she is even making the payments."

"Happens all the time, Gerry. Wills in favor of care givers are even worse."

"Dan, my mother may have lost almost three thousand dollars."

"Thank God your mother can afford it," and then, after a pause, "And that she is well enough not to be abused physically."

"Mother's shoulder is what I should be talking to you about. She says she tore a ligament. She seems to be in a great deal of pain."

"Chances are she did tear the ligament. That is what I told her. That happens with advanced arthritics. Have your mother come in, I'll have a look. Tell her it is just to be sure there is no nerve damage."

I sigh.

"What's the matter, Gerry?"

"I wish there was a better answer for providing care for Mom."

"What shall I tell you, Gerry? You can't, your sister won't. Every adult child with aging parents is in the same situation."

So I say, "Thanks, Dan, I'll bring Mom in to see you."

"Gerry, call me anytime."

"Thanks, Dan. Family okay?"

"Real good, Gerry. Real, good. Yours, Gerry?"

"Fine. Just fine."

Brother Lenny

My brother, Lenny, wouldn't let me do for him, not even when his wife Hilde died. I tried. "Lenny, I'll come home. I'll help."

"You'll come after the funeral, Emma."

After the funeral I called again. "It's no trouble, Lenny."

"I won't have the time to be with you."

"I could see you in the evenings."

"It's a bad time of the year, tax season, you know."

My brother is the VP for accounting, taxes, and planning for International Byproducts.

"Maybe next month, Emma, when I'll be back from Florida. I have to look at a warehouse complex we bought."

"Hilde died in February from an accident," is all Lenny said. It wasn't until May that I got to see Lenny. Lenny met me at the airport. I tried to hug him. He kissed my forehead. Lenny, in his dark blue pinstripe suit, black wingtip Church shoes, and soft blue black felt hat with a medium wide brim, not too wide and not too narrow.

After supper, after Lenny had stacked the dishes in the washer, Lenny unbuttoned his white, spread-collar, starched shirt, turned up his sleeves one roll. We sat in the kitchen. I drank coffee, Lenny crossed his legs, uncrossed them, rubbed his eyes, stretched back. "How is your life in England, Emma?"

"Fine."

I hadn't seen my "baby" brother in ten months. I was expecting he would talk about Hilde, about how it was to be alone after eighteen years of marriage, how Hilde died. I drank coffee and Lenny said nothing until I had complimented him. "You make a mean salad."

"Not bad for an accountant."

"Not bad for a cook, either."

"A cook I'll never be—sandwiches, salads, bread and coffee, that's all I do, that's all." But then Lenny was never into food; for that matter, neither was Mama.

My first overseas assignment was to Brussels. I invited Lenny to come over, a combination "going into the Army" and a college graduation present. "Might just as well, Emma. I have a couple of weeks before I have to report for basic training."

We went to the three-star fish restaurants around the old harbor. Lenny ate what I ate, drank what I drank, only once did he comment and then it wasn't about food. "Can't we find a restaurant where we don't come out stinking from cigarette smoke?"

Last two days of Lenny's visit, we went to Bruges, rode on the canals, visited the museums, drank coffee in the outdoor cafes. On the train back to Brussels Lenny said, "Good of you to invite me, Emma. Thank you. I'll write."

I got air letters from Vietnam with weather reports: "It has been raining for weeks. This makes our missions somewhat uncomfortable. All is well. Lenny."

After Lenny came home, he lived with Mom until she died. All that time he was an auditor at McGorvey Flint, and went to Loyola at night. That's where he met Hilde. When

Lenny received his master's in taxations he and Hilde were married, very quietly. Lenny had called me. I was in London then. "I'm going to get married next Saturday, a girl I met at Loyola. We love each other."

"I could come to the wedding."

"It's just Hilde's family and a few friends from the office. If you don't mind, we would like to come to London for our honeymoon. I want Hilde to meet you. I have told her so much about my big sister who works for the State Department."

I inscribed the wedding date, December 27, in Mama's family bible and sent an invitation to Hilde and Lenny with my telegram of congratulations. In five days I had an answer. "Dear Emma, thank you so much. Hilde and I will arrive Heathrow TWA FI 270, 18 April."

Which is *after the tax season* —

Hilde wasn't as I had pictured her, not the brown mouse I thought Lenny would be comfortable with. Hilde was as tall and thin as Lenny, her light brown hair permed fashionably short. Her eyes, gray, and deeply set behind high cheek bones, adored Lenny. Hilde smiled quietly, spoke rapidly in a flat tone that spelled northern Minnesota.

Lenny was in love. Lenny hovered over Hilde, smoothed her hair, touched her shoulders, held her hand under the dinner table and let go when I entered the room. Lenny and Hilde were no trouble. During the week they spent with me, they went to the museums and the matinees. Evenings we were together.

"We came to London to visit with you," Hilde said. This after I had urged them to go to the opera. "We came home early. I wanted to make dinner for Lenny. Lenny doesn't like to go to restaurants." Hilde did make a great stew.

About a year after Lenny took the job at International Byproducts, Hilde left McGorvey Flint and went to work at the county auditor's office. Her monthly letter had explained the change. "The hours are regular, the vacations are longer, and best of all, I can pretty well come and go as I please. Lenny is doing very well at International. Last Sunday we saw a house on the Thirtieth Street bluff that we are seriously considering buying."

Lenny and Hilde bought the house, described by Hilde as four bedrooms upstairs, your bedroom is next door to ours, you will have to share our bathroom. I do hope you won't mind. We are expecting you home for Christmas. For the next few years I took my annual leave over Christmas and New Year to be with Lenny and Hilde.

On Christmas afternoon Lenny and Hilde had created a tradition, cake and presents for the neighbors' children. It was when I was helping Hilde clean up after the last two-year-old had been called for, Lenny was napping in his Eames chair, I remember like it was yesterday, not twelve years ago. I asked, "Hilde, why don't you have children of your own. You would make wonderful parents."

"We tried, Emma. We have tried for years; it's Lenny, something that happened in Vietnam. Lenny had a fever, he was hospitalized several times, now he is sterile."

"Lenny never told me."

"You know Lenny."

Mama had always warned me with Lenny, "Emma, leave things alone. I know you mean well, but you can't go around giving Lenny advice. He really doesn't take kindly to it. Even if you are the older sister, Emma, don't tell him."

I thought about children. Here I was unmarried and Lenny and Hilde without children.

BROTHER LENNY

I thought I should talk to Lenny, carefully, of course. I waited until Lenny was in the basement laundry. He was folding towels. Hilde was babysitting at the neighbors across the street.

"Can I help you?" I picked up a towel.

"No, Emma, thanks."

"You hiding out in the basement?"

"I like to be alone." I should have stopped. I reached into the dryer, for the towels, for Lenny to fold.

"Lenny, you never told me about not being able to have children."

"What's to tell?"

"How it happened."

"I was in a fever hospital, twice. I got home. I was luckier than some."

I consoled Lenny, "I never got married—once I thought about adopting but what sort of a life would it be for a child without a father and a career mother."

"You could still get married. You are not that ugly, you know."

"Thanks."

I had mentioned adoption, but Lenny hadn't picked it up. I tried again.

"Our economic councilor adopted Korean twins, two little girls, cute, bright."

Lenny quit folding. "I know you mean well, Emma, but, it's a risk, with unknown gene pools. It's a risk I can't take." He didn't say we, he said I, so I never spoke to Hilde about adoption.

I came home to Lenny all alone in four bedrooms, two full baths, half bath in basement. Hilde everywhere, not a thing of Hilde's had been removed, not her Volvo, not her underwear in her half of the his-and-her chest of drawers, not a dress from the full length closet on Hilde's side of the bed. In the bathroom Hilde's winter robe, red quilted satin, hung on her hook.

Lenny rinsed the dishes, stacked the washer, I made the Kenya coffee strong, black.

"Coffee, Lenny?"

"Thanks, Emma. I can't sleep if I drink coffee after 6."

"How are you sleeping?"

"You'll hear me, walking around. Don't worry, I'm OK."

We sat in the kitchen, I, like our Mama, drinking coffee, Lenny the father we never had known. Lenny sat, his legs crossed, drying his hands on a kitchen towel.

"Is there anything I can do, while you are at the office?"

"No. You can drive Hilde's car if you want to go anywhere."

"I would like to go to the cemetery."

Lenny didn't answer for a moment. "I'm going to have a double footstone put up, for Hilde and me, to match Mama's and Dad's."

"You going to stay in the house?"

"I haven't thought about it."

"Seems awfully big."

"Does, doesn't it. When you stop to think, Mama, you and I lived in a two-bedroom, one-bath third-floor apartment."

Lenny got up and turned to me. "Emma, sometimes I think it's good Mama didn't live to see how we turned out."

I try to be cheerful. "You should be pleased, Lenny, with what you have achieved at International Byproducts."

"I wasn't talking about that, Emma, I was thinking about Mama and children, how she used to say, 'If your father hadn't died, we would have had more children, a whole house full; my grandmother had nine, you know, and six lived.'"

"Times were different then, Lenny. That was a long time ago, women didn't have careers then."

"Hilde would have given anything for children. It was my fault."

"It's too long ago, Lenny."

"You are right, Emma. Sit, I'll get your coffee."

Lenny poured a second cup of coffee for me, looked at his watch—"Early enough"—poured a half a cup for himself, sat down, sipped. "Strong like you like it, Emma. I missed you when you went to Washington."

"I missed you, too." I reached my hand across the table towards Lenny, we touched, and Lenny picked up his coffee cup. "Aren't you going to ask me how Hilde died?"

"I wanted to, but —"

"I'll tell you." Lenny's voice, quiet, calm. "Stupid, a wasteful death. Hilde was driving home, on the new one-way, the road south of Blackhawk. You haven't been on it. Hilde got a flat, it was just at dusk, she got out, she was hit by a kid in a truck. Two days after he received his driver's license. No pain, no suffering, Hilde died instantly, broken back, ruptured spleen, what difference does it make what the coroner finds once you are dead."

I repeated, "Senseless stupid death." Emphasized, "So many unnecessary deaths."

"I have known that for a very long time, Emma, since Vietnam."

So I changed the conversation to "Would you like to come to London for Christmas?"

"No, I have the party to give, the party for the neighborhood kids—they look forward to it." Lenny stopped, went on, "Emma, have you ever thought of what you are going to do when you retire?"

"I could come back, keep house for you."

Lenny didn't answer. He put our coffee cups in the sink, shut the light off, went upstairs. I heard the television until past midnight.

The next day I went to the cemetery. After that, there was nothing more I wanted to do. I tried a girlfriend I had gone to high school with.

"Sorry, Emma, I can't go to lunch—Emily is sick. I couldn't trust her to a sitter."

"Wednesday, then."

"Wednesday I have a P.T.A. meeting."

On Wednesday I went to the matinee at the cinemas. We were four young women and two senior citizen couples who watched the dead pile up to achieve eternal "Glory" but fail to take the fort that guarded the Savannah harbor.

After supper Lenny and I sat in the kitchen like when we were home with Mama. "Emma, where did you go this afternoon. I called."

"Saw *Glory*, I doubt if all those dead even influenced the outcome of the Civil War one bit."

"Dying well is important, Emma. You have to be lucky to die well, quickly, without suffering. That's a good death."

That was when I told Lenny, "I have to go to Washington before I return to London."

Lenny didn't complain, or insist that I stay. In Washington I went to the National Gallery and the Phillips, had dinner with a training officer from our department who was polite but not overly pleased to be taken away from his poker night in town. I was back in

BROTHER LENNY

London a day before I had signed out to return, so I went to the opera, caught up on my diary, wrote under October 1: "Explore Christmas—package tour to Vienna."

In September I tried again. I wrote to Lenny: "I could take early retirement. I could come home."

The answer came in five days via air letter. "Thanks, Emma, but no thanks; it took me too long to learn to live alone."

Who Can I Tell?

Friday afternoon after a non-strenuous swim in the smaller, warmer, pool of the Y, the one favored by the arthritics and the young-old, Tom Miller and Mel Gordon, the only diners, sat at the round table for six in the Pancake Palace. The four waitresses were behind the service wall counting their luncheon tip dollars, readying for the two o'clock shift change. Sally Archer, the first woman manager since the Pancake Palace had arrived in Rockville fourteen years ago from somewhere out west, stood, her back to Tom Miller and Mel Gordon.

Sally, on toes, in profile, had her fingers pointed at Phil, the bus boy, who had his head in the air conditioning duct and his feet on the top step of the aluminum ladder.

"Phil, put these napkins in the corners, take the old napkins, wipe the grill dry."

"Miss Archer, the napkins are only half wet."

"Change them anyway."

Mel Gordon ran his eyes up Sally's legs, over her breasts, followed her bare arm to the dinner napkins folded into the corner of the grill.

Tom Miller noticed Mel's full body review. "You want a piece of that?"

Mel laughed, "Does lusting in your heart count?"

"Doesn't count if your wife doesn't catch you."

"Getting too old. Price is too high."

"Can't tell till you look at the price tag."

Tom Miller looked out the window at the parking lot, at the pools of water in the hollows of the cracked black top.

"The rain is going to ruin the golf tournament."

"I used to play in the rain."

"Once the lightening starts the committee will stop the play." The rain began again. As Sally walked by the table, Mel Gordon called out, "Great dress!"

Sally stopped, leaned over the table. "I need a new fall wardrobe, Mel. How about a weekend shopping spree to Paris?"

"I would need more than a weekend." Mel laughed. "At my age everything takes longer."

"Don't worry, Mel. We'll take all the time you need."

With that reassurance for Mel, Sally left for the cash register.

"Better be careful, Mel. You're getting into sexual harassment."

"That was only a mild flirtatious remark between an old man and a young woman."

Tom sipped his coffee. "I went back to Nebraska for my fortieth class reunion."

"Don't tell me everyone looked old but you."

"This December and May thing, like you and Sally, it went beyond that with Fred Cullen, a classmate of mine. Fred got hold of me during the cocktail party at the Country Club before the class dinner. Fred walks me out onto the golf course—why he told me, I don't know. I was only medium friendly with him at school. I saw Fred at the thirtieth, thirty-fifth reunions. I hardly know his wife, Alice. I only met her once, I really don't know either Fred or Alice that well."

WHO CAN I TELL?

"Fred told you what?"

"I was coming to that. It's raining again."

"Fred is teaching some sort of English literature, or maybe it was Elizabethan drama. I don't remember."

"Where?"

"I think it's Kansas State at Manhattan, Kansas. He has put in for retirement. The chairman says 'Fine, but who is going to take your Christmas Theater tour to England.' Seems Fred has been running this trip for the last five or six years. So, Fred says if there is no one else, he'll go and Alice says, she is going to Florida to be with their grandchildren. Fred takes the student tour group to London. The way Fred told it to me, he was seduced, raped, by a twenty-year-old English major from Wichita."

"Just like that."

"Just like that. His study trip became a week of sexual orgy with a twenty-year-old. That, my boy Mel, could happen to you too. See how that Sally girl looks at you? Notice the way she leaned her boobs at you. Very nice boobs too, and you—you drink coffee and make jokes."

"Tilly would kill me."

"Tilly doesn't have to know. I'll bet Alice never found out about Fred and the coed."

"Coeds graduate. Sally is here every day but Wednesday."

"Sally knows you go to Paris two, three times a year."

"Tilly would kill me!"

"Not if she doesn't find out. No reason for Sally to tell her."

"Why wouldn't she? I can hear Sally when we get back. 'Mel, I need a new dress, something nice like Tilly wears.'"

"So you buy her a dress. What's a couple of hundred to you?"

"So I buy her a new dress. What's to stop her from asking for a new car?"

"So you buy her a car. She'll pay you back."

"Sounds too complex."

"Not for you, Mel. Not a deal maker like you."

"That's business."

"Suit yourself. Take my word for it. Sally is ready, willing and able. You are wasting the best years of her life."

"Too young for me. I would bet she is not a day over thirty."

"That's because you look at her body. Look at her eye lids. The lids and the hands don't lie. Sally is pushing thirty-five to forty!"

"She looks good."

"That, Mel, is aerobics three times a week. Look at yourself. You look good too. Flat belly, look what swimming does for you. You don't look sixty-three either."

Tom left. Mel dawdled, eyed the 'chocolate silk' pies in the counter, looked at Sally behind the register, paid Sally. Sally put the coins into Mel's hand, pinched his fingers shut. Mel smiled. "You really want to go to Paris?"

"I'll carry your suitcase."

"You'll have to do more than that."

Sally didn't answer. She came from behind the counter, brushed against Mel on the way to the kitchen, turned.

"I'll see you tomorrow."

From the cellular phone in his Cadillac, Mel called his travel agent in Chicago.

"Call Sally Archer at the Pancake Palace—she'll answer. Give her the dates of my trip. She flies alone to Chicago; she picks up her ticket to Paris in Chicago. Give her the name of the hotel in Paris with a couple of hundred francs for a cab."

"Anything else, Mr. Gordon?"

"Don't bill Miss Archer's ticket on our office account. I'll pay you in cash when I come to Chicago. If you need anything, call me on my car phone, not at the office."

In Paris, at the Hotel Ile Saint-Louis, Mel Gordon waited for Sally. He sat in the lobby reading the Paris *Herald,* watching for Sally to arrive from the airport.

Sally bounced out of the taxi, threw her duffel bag on the sidewalk. Mel paid the driver, made the effort to pick up the bag . . . too slow. Sally had picked up her luggage, taken Mel's hand in hers. She followed him through the etched glass doors into the foyer lobby only large enough for the registry desk, two arm chairs covered in a Provence print and the three person elevator. The desk clerk grinned at Mel, spoke rapidly in French.

"What did she say, Mel?"

"Madame du Bois said it was better for me not to be alone."

"For me, too."

"Tired?"

"I slept on the plane."

"I used to be able to do that."

"None of that, Mel. None of that 'used to be' stuff. This is a week of todays! Beautiful room, Mel."

"It's a bit small. This is an eighteenth or seventeenth century townhouse converted to a hotel."

"Just as I thought it would be."

"The back rooms are quieter, but they have no view of the street."

"Don't apologize. It's just as I thought it would be."

"Hungry?"

"No."

"I have business appointments this morning. Get some sleep, I'll be back about one."

Sally put her arms around Mel, kissed him lightly on the lips. "Thanks, Mel."

"Thank me when I get back."

"Just as I thought. You would be a romantic lover."

"Just slow and old."

"None of that now. I don't want to hear that again." Sally placed her fingers against Mel's mouth, drew him into her.

In the afternoons they visited the museums. The Picasso, the Pompidou, the Musée D'Orsay, returned to the hotel to shower together, to sleep together and afterwards, dinner at one of the family restaurants that crowded the narrow cobbled streets of this island in the Seine.

On the sixth day, at their last night dinner, Mel and Sally sat face to face. Sally aglow, Mel still bewildered by this joy she had brought with her.

"More wine, Sally?"

"No, I don't want to get stupid. I'll try to remember things as they are. The lace curtains, that French couple feeding their dogs from their plate."

"Would you like dessert?"

"No. I would like to walk along the river."

They walked slowly, her arm in his. She held him to her. He was gray and bald, wore his tan cotton slacks loosely, his leather jacket open. She was as tall, almost five feet ten, slim in her jeans, white silk blouse and bulky knit sweater. He made efforts to keep his shoulders back, to walk upright and straight backed. He did not succeed. With every third or fourth stride, he leaned to the left which eased the pain in his arthritic hip. She spoke more than he.

"Just as I imagined it would be, the lights on the river, the lovers along the Seine."

"Would you like to take the boat ride? The landing is just across the bridge."

"No, I just want to stand here and look."

"You haven't gone shopping. You haven't bought your Paris wardrobe. I could take tomorrow morning off. We could go to the stores."

"That was only an excuse to get you to spend a week with me. I knew you went to Paris on business."

Sally put her arms around Mel. "Look at the moon, Mel. Make a wish."

"Too old for that. Wishing doesn't make it so."

"My wish may come true. If it doesn't, I'll try again."

Mel laughed, "Okay, tell me what you wished for."

"My first wish came true. I wished for a week in Paris with you."

"That didn't take a lot of doing."

"It took me a year. You weren't quick on the pickup. My second wish, I have to wait and see. It's too soon to tell."

"You'll tell me what that is?"

"You may not want to know."

"It can't be that bad."

"I'll tell you when the time comes. Some things we don't know in advance."

"That's about life and death. We are not talking about life and death."

"We are too, Mel. I am talking of life, Mel. A new life for me."

Mel did not answer. They had reached the Cathedral of Notre Dame.

"It's getting cold, Sally. Time to go home."

The restaurants were closing. Mel zipped up his jacket; Sally clung to him more closely.

"The ice cream store is still open."

"No, thanks."

They walked in silence.

"Don't pout, Mel. So I don't tell what I wished for, so what? My second wish is yet to come. Right now it's only a wish, sort of a hope. You may not like the truth of it."

"I don't think you would lie to me."

"I wouldn't do that, Mel. This has been the best week in years. In thirty-eight years."

"It's up to you, Sally, but I can't think of anything that you would tell me that would hurt me."

"You are too kind. That's why I picked you. You were my first choice."

"For what?"

"For a shopping trip to Paris."

"*Chacun a son gout.*"

"What did you say?"

"Just a French saying. 'Each to his own taste.'"

"Mr. Gordon, I am very pleased with my choice."

"Why me?"

"Well, I saw how you had turned out. You learn a lot about people in a restaurant. You never get angry, you are patient, you are generous. You have lots of friends." Sally put her head on Mel's shoulder, kissed him on his ear. "So, I figured you have good genes."

"So?"

"Now you know."

"Know what?"

Sally stopped. "I wanted you to be the father of my child."

"My God, you are a schemer!"

"No, Mel, only a planner. That's what I learned in college. You aren't angry with me for telling, are you Mel?"

"No, just somewhere between flattered and amazed. What would you have done if I hadn't succumbed to your charms?"

"I would have tried harder. You know, a girl my age doesn't have forever. Don't pout, Mel. It's been good for you too."

Mel didn't answer, "I am the lucky one?"

"You didn't get angry when I told you."

"No sense getting angry after the fact, is there?"

As they walked, Sally held Mel's hand once, and then again she brought his hand to her mouth, kissed it playfully.

"Enjoy, it's later than you think."

Again, Mel didn't answer.

"I meant for the both of us, Mel."

By Monday, Mel Gordon was back into his Rockville life: the noon day swim, the spare frugal lunch with Tom Miller.

The first russet red oak leaves littered the parking lot of the Pancake Palace.

At the same table, at the same time, Tom Miller complained to Mel Gordon.

"The bumper corn crop is going to put prices down."

Mel smiled. "I am glad we planted beans this year. That is the smartest thing I have done this year, chose to grow beans instead of corn."

"It wasn't so stupid for you to take Sally to Paris."

"You said that, not me."

"Sally was gone—you were gone."

"Maybe she went home to Omaha."

Tom grinned, "Maybe she did." Tom put down his coffee cup. "Turn around, Mel. Sally is up on her toes again, putting up her hanging pumpkins. That's for you, my friend. You get the side view of her swelling breasts and tight little butt. Have a look."

Mel looked up from his salad plate. "Good looking body."

"More enthusiasm please. She couldn't have been that bad in bed."

"Sally was in Omaha with her mother."

Mel put down his fork to add a rye cracker to his mouthful of lettuce.

"Tom, you keep eating strawberry sauce, you'll get a pot belly."

"I don't have anyone to save myself for."

"You can't tell when someone will come along."

"Three divorces, three strikes. I am not out looking."

"At least you tried."

"I can't understand you—you and Tilly. Forty years with the same woman."

Mel chuckled. "That's because I am a pessimist. I never thought that the next wife would be any better."

"I guess that makes me an optimist. I tried three times."

"You succeeded."

"Not with marriage."

"No, but you have three daughters. Tilly and I are living in a big empty house on the bluff. The neighbor's grandchildren come for Christmas, come for holidays, birthdays. We let them use our upstairs bedroom."

His salad consumed, Mel drank his tea, squirted the lemon's juice into the cup each time he poured from the pot.

"We were always too busy. First, I was in the army, then I was building the business. Tilly wanted to adopt . . ." Mel left the sentence unended and said, "At least you have daughters."

"Three wives, three daughters, and living alone."

"At least you have daughters, Tom. I shouldn't have said that. Tilly and I have each other."

"You should have had kids."

"We should have had at least three, but I didn't understand that until it was too late." Mel poured another cup of tea.

"My sister adopted two boys. One turned out okay, the other . . ."

"We thought about adopting. By then I was forty. I thought we were too old, and the kind of children you can adopt . . . I didn't want to take a chance they wouldn't be all that Tilly expected, or that I wished for."

"That's the same with your own children."

"We should have taken the chance. No risk, no chance to succeed." Mel sighed. "Time to go."

Tom made no move to pick up his check. Tom licked, cherished the last of the strawberry sauce from his spoon.

"You are close to your nephews."

"Nephews are somebody else's children."

Tom gave up on children, asked, "How is the economy in France?"

"No better than ours. Same dumb quarrels going on as here, fighting about the same damn things. Agriculture subsidies, European Union. As long as the dollar stays weak we can export beans. That won't last long; the dollar is undervalued. Paris is still very expensive."

Tom smiled, picked up his check. "Can two live as cheaply as one?"

He didn't wait for Mel to answer, walked to the counter, turned. "Sally is smiling more."

"Looks about the same to me," Mel answered.

At the cash register Sally asked Mel, "Have a good trip to Paris?"

"Excellent, thank you, Sally."

Sally turned to her cash register where the waitresses waited to exchange their coins for dollar bills.

Outside, Tom waited for Mel. "That's one manager that is going far. I didn't tell you, but I hear that Sally is going to be district manager in Omaha."

Tom grinned broadly and Mel answered, "That's not all bad."

Sally left for Omaha without a goodbye for Mel. A month later he received at his office a Hebrew New Year's greeting. "May you be inscribed for a Healthy, Happy, Prosperous New Year." Signed, Sally M. Archer. The return address was Pancake Palace, District Headquarters, Box 109, Omaha, Nebraska.

In Rockville, where the Mississippi flows from east to west, where the east-west Interstate 80 crosses the north-south Interstate 74, where de-industrialization is more a topic of conversation than jobs, the new manager of the Pancake Palace was a young man engaged to be married, too busy to notice Mel Gordon and Tom Miller.

Tom and Mel sat at their round table. The oak leaves dropped to fill the hollows of the north parking lot. It was a rare fall day, an Indian summer afternoon, sufficiently warm that the tops were down on the convertibles.

A wind-blown, full-bodied blonde got out of her white sports car. Tom more than noticed.

"From the side, she looked like Sally."

Mel looked up from his salad, "Compared to Sally, that is one ugly blonde."

"Nice car. You ever hear anything from Sally?"

"Not for a year. Not until I got this Jewish New Year card. It's just a greeting card. Nothing more."

Mel took the card from his inside wallet, gave it to Tom to read.

"Who is Micah, Mel?"

"A prophet."

"No, Mel, on the back the card is signed, 'Sally and Micah,' and something is written in Hebrew."

Mel took the card, read the Hebrew aloud: "Sarah and Micah, son of Mordechai."

"I didn't know Sally was Jewish, did you?"

Mel didn't answer.

The waitress brought the French toast to Tom, the salad for Mel. Tom showed the waitress the card. "Mel got a New Year's card from Sally and Micah."

"Isn't that a beautiful name for a boy? Micah. I wish I had thought of Biblical names for my kids. I wrote that to Sally when I got the announcement."

Mel asked, "When was that?"

"Must be four, five months."

"When did Sally get married?"

"No one said she got married, Mr. Gordon."

"Must be difficult for Sally, alone with a child."

"She has her mother in Omaha, and a couple of sisters." Then, Mel spoke to Tom of the World Series. On the way out, Mel tore the card into fourths, and then eighths, dropped it into the waste basket.

All he could think of was, Why didn't Sally tell me? Tell me she was Jewish? Tell me we had a son? Only once during Sally's first spring in Rockville when Sally had seen me eat the Passover matzos with my salad, watched me when I left the matzo with her. "Six more days of Passover, Sally. You save on the rye crisp. I brought my own matzo." It was then that Sally had asked me, "What is your Hebrew name?" That is how she knew. "Mordechai ben Abraham. Mordechai, son of Abraham."

"Melvin is nice too."

"My mother named me Monroe."
"I like Melvin better."
"So do I."

Call Sally? Tell Tilly? We have a son. No, I have a son. We have a son. We three have a son. Sally M. Archer, Matilda Newman Gordon and Monroe Abraham Gordon have a son. Micah is Sally's son. Only Sally's son.

Sally waited until her second year in Rockville before she made her move on me. All that time, she never said a thing about being Jewish. Maybe she went home to Omaha for the High Holy days. In Paris, Sally had said, "My mother is from Rockville." If Sally is Jewish, her mother is Jewish. If her mother is from Rockville, Tilly would know her and that's what Sally had said. "My mother knows your wife. She was Matilda Newman, wasn't she?" What did I say then? I joked! "I married the last Newman. The heiress to the Newman fortune." Sally couldn't have understood that by the time I married Tilly, the Newman fortune was long gone. I married Tilly because we cared for each other and we still do! I still love Tilly. There was no way that Sally could have understand all that.

Stupid how things come back. Things that were lost in my head, lost in Paris, set aside to be thought of only in Paris.

Try to get to Omaha—to Omaha, with Tilly or without her. Invite Sally to Paris again. Better not. What went well once may not be that good as an encore. Better to keep a memory. If the community finds out—the Newman name still counts—my God, what will that do to Tilly? It was bad enough that Matilda Newman married Monroe Gordon, a west end boy from an immigrant family who by marrying Matilda Newman made it up into the Outing Club, and the Bluffs Country Club.

At the congregation, the whispers when Tilly and I will come in.

"Monroe Gordon fathered a son, at his age! Went off to Paris. A week in Paris with a bimbo! So she is a Jewish bimbo."

I can hear Tilly. "Explain it to me, explain it to me, Mel! At your age, sixty-four years old you have a six-month-old son. You going to stand beside Sally at Micah's bar mitzvah?"

"I want you to meet the seventy-seven-year-old father of my son. This is his wife, Matilda Newman Gordon!"

During his swim, during his sleep-deprived nights, Mel continued to review the implications of fatherhood.

Matilda is the last Newman as I am the last Gordon. An only son of an only son. But now, we, you have a son. Micah Archer Gordon. Micah, son of Mordechai. Micah could carry on for Tilly and me. That means telling Tilly.

Assuming that Tilly would welcome Micah as a Newman, Mel tried "Micah Newman Archer Gordon." Mel, you don't know if Micah is your son. If Sally says he is—is he? You are just assuming he is because of a greeting card. If Sally didn't want you to know that Micah was the son of (Melvin) (Monroe) (Mordechai), why would Sally send the card to you?

Perplexed, in need of a resolution to unite his fragmented days and nights, Mel Gordon swam breast strokes and planned.

Tell Tilly, "You like car trips. I have some grain bins I want to look at in Omaha. If you like, we can stop in the University Museum in Iowa City, or the shops at the Williamsburg Discount Mall. We'll stop for lunch in Des Moines, spend the night in Omaha, be back on Friday morning in time for your hair appointment."

Mel, pleased with the possibilities of being alone in the car with Tilly—if Tilly screamed, got angry when he confessed his one and only lapse in forty years of marriage, there would be only he to hear her pain and agony.

I'll not tell Tilly. I'll just lead into the Sally story, see how it plays. It may be better, wiser to do nothing.

Mel drove west on Interstate 80, by the Iowa fields of stubble, all that remained of this year's hybrid corn and soybeans.

On the hillsides, cross-bred feeder cattle grazed, their backs to the prevailing west wind.

Mel shut off the University radio station. Tilly reclined beside him. Now and then, she shut her eyes.

"Not as many cattle in Iowa as there used to be."

Tilly smiled, "Nothing as it used to be. Look at me, a size sixteen. No wonder I can't find clothes that I like. I was a twelve when we were married."

Mel reached for Tilly's hand, held it, drove with one hand until he had to pass one truck and another.

"You look good to me."

"You say that to all the girls."

Afraid to answer, Mel said, "We should have spent six hundred dollars for the Morandi still life we saw on our honeymoon in Bologna. It would be worth three, four hundred thousand."

"That was forty years ago, Mel."

Tilly shut her eyes, stretched her legs, looked at her legs. "My legs still look good. Not bad." Then suddenly, "Don't talk 'should have' to me. Don't look back, Mel. I can't stand that. You know that. We should have had children when I wanted them. By the time you got around to wanting children, it was too late for me."

Again, Mel took Tilly's hand in his.

Tilly shut her eyes, opened her eyes as Mel went by another truck. "I shouldn't have listened to you. That was our generation, a generation of obedient, servile woman."

Again, Mel didn't answer.

He said, "Who would think a discount mall in Williamsburg, Iowa, would be a success?"

In Des Moines, they ate a quick lunch in a back booth at the McDonald's closest to Drake University. Mel and Tilly sat face to face sipping coffee, watching the students at the order counter. "They look so young."

"They are young."

Back on the interstate, the noon traffic was now heavier, required more of Mel's attention. Tilly looked out the window, sighed, "Another year."

Mel passed another truck, nodded.

Tilly continued, "It was nice to see the kids that came home for the holidays. I'll have to answer the New Year's cards we got."

That's the opening.

"You'll never believe who sent me a New Year's card. Sally Archer, the girl who managed the Pancake Palace."

"She's Elinore Morris's daughter. You don't know her. She was Elinore Davis."

Surprised and pleased with the way the conversation with Tilly had turned, Mel asked, "How do you know Sally?"

"I really don't know her. I saw her once when I was in the restaurant."

"I mean, how do you know who she is?"

"Elinore told me. I saw Elinore at our high school reunion. It was when you were off in Europe. Sort of a sad story about Sally."

Afraid not to find out, Mel asked, "What about Sally Archer?"

"She was married to this Archer. Elinore said he was a very decent sort. Sally got into drugs, the court gave the father custody of their children."

"How many children were there?"

"I don't know. Elinore never said."

Then Mel asked, "Would you like to go swimming when we get to the hotel?"

Tilly didn't answer. Her eyes were shut. She slept in the seat beside Mel. Mel took her hand. Tilly stirred, awake again. "We can swim after I look at the bins."

"Whatever you like, Mel. Whatever you like."

An Only Son

I finish my lunch of yogurt and cottage cheese, bock beer and the *Bluff City Dispatch*, announce to my wife, Agnes, "I'm going out to start the lawn mower."

"Not until you get rid of that cat. The cat is back."

"What cat?"

"The kitten from the cemetery. While you were playing golf, he crawled up the screen. I put him back across the fence. He's back. Look —"

I turn around; there is this spring's orange kitten climbing the dining room screen door so discretely I had not heard him. "I can put the cat in the garbage pail, keep him in the dark for a few hours. He'll never come back. That will teach him."

"George," my name is George, "it's a cat, not a child. I didn't let you put Perry in the dark closet to discipline him. I am not going to let you put a cat." Then Agnes raises her voice to me, "We should have done something. Good Lord knows I don't know what we did wrong. Perry called while you were playing golf. He wants us to come to St. Louis, to meet a girl. To meet her family."

Perry usually calls on Sunday morning. Monday to Saturday Perry works at the Houston emergency veterinary clinic. A most kind, good and caring son. A son who has never given us sorrow and very little disappointment. Although I must admit that I was somewhat disturbed when Perry quit going to St. James Lutheran with us.

It's what all teenagers go through. They come back to the church when they get married, have children of their own. Now, of course, Agnes is afraid that Perry will go over to the Catholics. Agnes is at the age when women become anxious. Perry is our only son. I always thought that Agnes was overly concerned about Perry. Perry was a quiet kid who preferred to stay in his own room and play his saxophone to going out for the high school baseball team. He would have been a great short stop, good arm and quick. Once or twice I talked to Perry about trying out for the high school team, but nothing came of it. Perry isn't the sort of a son that talks back. He just doesn't answer. All the years Perry was at Kansas State Veterinary College he came home every summer to help on the farm. That is, until his last two years, when he had clinic assignments.

After Perry graduated, he returned to Bluff City. "Just thinking, Dad, wanted to come home before I decided."

Agnes became overly concerned. "You would think after eight years of college Perry would know what he wants to do with his life."

"I'm thinking of grad school, Dad. Marine biology."

Perry has always been interested in fish, is what I explain to Agnes. That summer at home Perry played his saxophone and sang with the phonograph, "Pretty women, here's to pretty women . . . all the pretty women," or he would put Judy Collins on and listen to "Running for My Life," and Agnes would come into the gazebo where I was reading my way through the nineteenth century.

"I wish Perry would go out, go downtown, take some girl to the movies."

"Who? Any particular girl you want to pick out for him?"

"Men are supposed to know." With that, Agnes went back to cooking the blueberry jam.

Perry is a good son. Before he went to Texas he helped me spread the three tons of gravel around the oaks. I wheeled the barrow; Perry raked and spread.

"Dad, you always knew what you wanted to be?"

"Yes, but those were different times. We didn't have as many choices then, not many specialties in veterinary medicine in my day."

Over the Fourth of July weekend, Perry flew down to Texas. "Tom Cook is working at a small animal hospital in north Houston. He called me, wants to know if I would like to join him."

Tom Cook lived in the same house as Perry did in Manhattan, Kansas. Two or three times Tom came home with Perry. Agnes never cared much for Tom. "Tom doesn't know who he is, and he smokes too much. Tom's from Kansas City, and his mother is Jewish and his father is divorced. I think he is on his third wife."

"That's not Tom's fault," didn't appease Agnes.

"Tom is a bad influence on Perry."

"Perry is over twenty-one."

Agnes was pleased with what Perry reported from Houston: "I don't think working with Tom would have worked out. Tom just hasn't put it together yet."

Bluff City, Nebraska, is a pleasant enough place, good schools, not far from Omaha, but not attractive enough to keep our children at home, not unless they want to teach or go back to the farm.

It was in August that Perry drove across Iowa to Rock City, Illinois, to visit Bill Kentor. Bill is a classmate of mine. The only time I see Bill and Ruth is the Kansas State reunions. I had noticed his ad in the *Journal of the American Veterinary Association*. "Associate wanted for small animal clinics in western Illinois." Perry must have noticed the ad too, because he asked me about Bill. I had assured him, "I always heard good things about Bill. He runs a real up-to-date practice, and he is a good manager, and you'll like his wife." When Agnes heard that Perry had signed a year's contract with Bill Kentor, she said, "I don't know why he wants to work with a Jew."

To which I laughed. "Bill and Ruth aren't going to convert Perry. You have nothing to be afraid of." There are many times that Agnes doesn't think much of my sense of humor. That was one of those times.

"You don't understand, George. Bill and Ruth have different ways."

I don't like to aggravate Agnes because she will tell me, "George, your life could be better directed." Like when I told Agnes I was going to take early retirement. "What are you going to do with yourself?" That was after I had rented my veterinary office to young Lucas. I had assured Agnes that Perry didn't want to be a country practitioner in Bluff City, Nebraska, and that the rent from the farm and from Dr. Lucas was more than enough for us. So far, it has been. The free time has given me *choice,* and that's something I hadn't had during my thirty-five years of practice, when I was answering, "Yes," to each client's telephone call: "Doctor, can you come right out?"

It was after the year with Bill Kentor that Perry took the job in Houston at the emergency clinic where he really is his own boss. When Perry got settled, we went down to Houston to visit the clinic. As Perry explained, it's not in the best part of town, a "transitional" neighborhood. Middle class black and middle management whites who are raising kids, cats and dogs in little white bungalows with green yards; that is what makes the location so good.

Agnes is back from the kitchen. "George, I want to talk to you."

I had put the kitten across the cemetery fence onto a windrow of last fall's oak leaves, was changing into my yard shoes, about to start the mower.

I sit in the corner of the garage; Agnes wipes her hands on her apron, stands over me. "Perry wants us to meet him in St. Louis on the Fourth of July weekend. He has made all the arrangements. He wants us to meet the young woman he has been seeing in Houston."

"No problem, Agnes. Call Bonnie." Bonnie is Bluff City's one travel agent.

"I did."

"So?"

Agnes is still standing. "George, I'm so glad that Perry has someone he wants us to meet. Do you realize that Perry will be twenty-nine next March? You know, for a while I was afraid that Perry wasn't interested in women!" Which is about as much conversation as Agnes and I have ever had about Perry's sexual preference.

The Saturday before July 4, a Monday, Agnes and I are in St. Louis, checked into the Marriott. Perry has reserved a room with a view of the plaza and the Arch. On the table there is a note and one pink rose for Agnes. "Esther and I will meet you for dinner in the Mississippi Room at six. We are off to see Esther's folks. Love, Perry."

Agnes and I are touched by the note.

We go swimming in the indoor pool with the skylight, walk around the Arch, visit the Museum of Western Expansion. At five-thirty p.m., Agnes is dressed in her best, a red and white striped cotton knit two piece that she ordered from the Neiman Marcus catalog.

Agnes is like all the Nelsons, tall, straight, thin. Brown hair without a gray hair in it, cut fashionably short by Sally of Omaha. Her youthfulness I attribute to the Nelson family genes, as Agnes's Aunt Margaret is eighty-six and doesn't look a day over sixty.

Agnes is evidently in an approving mood as she doesn't criticize my shirt and tie combination. "George, you look good." Which must be true, as my tan poplin suit is the one Agnes chose for me. "Makes you look thin and distinguished, George." In the Mississippi Room we are shown to a table for four, reserved in the name of Dr. and Mrs. George Church. Agnes and I are seated. "It was so thoughtful for Perry to get us a table by the window. He knows how much I love to people watch."

We are not seated a minute when Perry comes in with a tall black woman. Perry is six feet four; she must be almost six feet tall. In the window light she is more brown than black, with hair cut into a round halo, wearing a straight line black dress, long double strand pearls. It's her very large brown eyes that I see when Perry introduces her. "Esther Johnson, my parents, George and Agnes Church."

After the introductions and hand shakes, the conversation is a little forced, full of pauses that I try to fill.

"Miss Johnson, do you enjoy living in Houston?"

"Please, call me Esther. Or Essie."

Agnes can be very charming; she smiled at Perry. "Perry, you didn't tell me how you met Esther."

"I answered an ad in the supermarket bulletin. You know single woman interested in art, music, film, conversation, country walks."

Essie smiles. "It pays to advertise."

Agnes changes to, "Esther, how long have you been in Houston?"

"Just a little over two years."

"How do you like it?"

"NASA was a wonderful job opportunity for me."

"Esther is going to school at night. She has begun her M.B.A."

"You are both so busy." I made my remark sound very positive.

"Esther and I have Sundays together, and sometimes an evening or two during the week. We saw a wonderful exhibition of paintings at the art museum. Amazing amount of talent. And we have been to the Houston Symphony twice."

Then the conversation turns to food and beer. "How can anyone drink a twenty ounce glass of beer?" That from Agnes.

"Practice, Mom. It takes practice." And Perry drinks six ounces with one swallow. Agnes does not comment about the sins of excessive alcohol consumption.

Things are going well. Agnes asks, "Essie, have your folks announced your engagement yet?"

"There is only my father. Dad left the social things to my mom. And since my mom died . . ."

It is then that I step in with, "We had hoped to meet your family. Perry has told us so much about them."

To which Perry answers. "There will be other times after our engagement is announced. Mom, I was hoping you would announce it in the *Bluff City Dispatch*."

Agnes is very gracious. "Is there a special photo you would like for me to use?"

"Esther and I have made an appointment to have a studio picture taken."

"That's next Wednesday afternoon, at two p.m. Perry, don't forget. I'll pick you up."

"You be sure to send us two photos. I want one for Grandma Nelson."

"Agnes' mother," I explain to Esther.

Then I add, "When will you come to Bluff City?"

And Agnes says, "Perry, are you and Esther planning to come to Bluff City?"

Perry looks at Esther, then at Agnes, "Not unless you insist we do. I doubt if we would have more than one or two free days before the wedding."

Agnes does not insist. She returns to the security of, "The duck is very good." I support with, "My lamb and rice is beautifully spiced." The dinner went well enough, better than if Agnes had gotten into the church and abortion or the church and contraception. How Agnes became a feminist liberal is the story of Populist Nebraska farmers who educated their daughters at Grinnell.

Once Perry did touch on religion. "My dad was a Quaker until he married my mom." Which he follows immediately with, "I can get a post-doctorate fellowship in Aquatic Medicine at Scripps in California. Esther can get a transfer. In three years, I could get a Ph.D. Then I could teach, or do research. I don't think practice is for me."

I try to stay on veterinary medicine, but Agnes always returns to the Johnson family.

"Esther, what does your dad do?"

"Dad owns his own cab."

"Perry told me about your sister, Norma. I'm sorry she had to work tomorrow."

"The V.A. is short of nurses, especially on the holidays."

I offer, "Perhaps we can meet your family the next time we come to St. Louis."

"I would like that." Agnes confirms our willingness. "Now, about tomorrow. Is it possible we could meet your dad or Norma for lunch?" Agnes is persistent.

Perry looks at Esther, who says nothing. He turns to us, "I am afraid not tomorrow. I did try, Mom. I know how important family is to you."

I give a cheerful, "There is always next time." Agnes responds to my optimism about the future as an effort to lead the conversation away from the Johnsons with a direct question to Perry. When he doesn't answer she repeats, "Are you planning to get married in St. Louis?"

Neither Perry nor Esther answers. Agnes won't leave it alone. "Church weddings are a family tradition. George and I were married at St. James, like my mother and Grandma Nelson."

Perry changes the conversation from weddings to art. "Don't forget. Dad, Mom, tomorrow I'll pick up Essie and then we'll go to lunch. We'll have all afternoon together. Tomorrow is the last day of the Guston exhibition at the art museum."

"Dr. Church, I do hope you like modern art." Esther is talking to me.

It's Agnes who answers. "We don't get too many contemporary exhibits at the Joslyn."

"That's the museum in Omaha," Perry explains. He is attentive, quick to fill in the pauses.

I assure, "I like to see what is new, contemporary. I'm looking forward to tomorrow."

After dinner, that is about half an hour after dessert, Esther and Perry get up. Agnes extends her hand; Esther comes forward and hugs Agnes and says, "So glad that we finally met. You are just as I imagined." Then Esther extends her hand to me, and I embrace her, and I see that Perry is pleased when I say, "Thank you for asking us to St. Louis."

"I'll take Esther home. I'll be back in half an hour."

Agnes and I sit in the lobby. People watch. Agnes, by my side on the love seat.

"George, did Perry tell you when they are getting married?"

"No."

"George, do you think we have to invite Esther to Bluff City—that is, for a shower, to meet our friends?"

"Not unless you wish to, Agnes. I think Perry would like it."

"I don't know whether I'm ready for that."

"Well, maybe after the wedding."

"George —" Agnes begins to cry.

"She seems like a very nice girl."

"I'm sure she is. I wasn't crying about that."

I take Agnes's hand, give her my handkerchief. "Now quit crying. We don't want Perry to see you crying."

"Perry won't be back for an hour. He told me that."

"Do you think it's because the Johnsons didn't want us to see where they lived that they didn't invite us."

"I'm sure Perry would have been pleased if they came to the hotel. George, do you know what Perry is getting into?" And, before I could answer: "Where can a couple like that live? What kind of friends will they have?"

"They aren't coming back to Bluff City."

Agnes begins to cry again. I put my arm around her.

"I'll stop crying so people don't think we are quarreling."

"You have a good cry, Agnes. But I don't know what there is to cry about."

"George, you don't understand. You never did. You just let things go by. When Perry quit St. James you didn't say a word. You didn't say anything when he talked about getting a Ph.D. in Aquatic Medicine. Now I know you won't say anything to him about marrying Esther Johnson. Fathers are supposed to talk to their sons, give them advice."

"Perry didn't ask me for advice."

"George, you don't understand. You never did."

"Agnes, Essie and Perry are not a tragedy yet. Just something that happens when two people fall in love."

"Perry should have known better, ruining his whole life. Think of the children. Inheritance is very important — you know about that."

"Esther seems like a very bright young woman. Ambitious, too. Going for her M.B.A. She wants us to like her. Why shouldn't we? It isn't her fault, you know. It's always possible it will all work out fine."

"George, how can you?"

I hold Agnes and she quits crying. She goes off to wash her face, and, by the time Perry comes back, we are again a hand-holding couple watching the Marriott's guests.

Perry has pulled up an arm chair to face us. "I was hoping we could all meet for Sunday breakfast, you and Johnsons. Norma excused herself. She said she had to work at the hospital."

"What about Mr. Johnson?"

"I'm sorry, Mom. He didn't accept. I asked him twice, and Esther has asked him, too. She told me she had."

I offer, "We'll meet him at the wedding."

"We haven't picked a date yet, Dad."

As we are going to bed, Agnes turns to me. "Perry tried to do the proper thing."

Our Sunday afternoon with Perry and Essie was most pleasant. We went to the zoo and to the art museum. Esther and Perry evidently share an interest in art and music. They walked hand in hand. He tells Agnes and me, "We opened a joint savings account for the move to California. We are not living together—too inconvenient with my working nights and Esther working days."

Monday morning we all went to the airport. I kiss Esther goodbye, and Agnes does too which makes Perry happy, smiling.

It was after we left St. Louis, over Kansas City, that Agnes turns to me. "Esther seems like a very nice girl."

"I am sure she is, or Perry wouldn't have . . ."

"George, you know what you are?"

"What?"

Agnes doesn't answer that. She says, "George, I have made up my mind. I'm not going to give Esther's picture to the *Dispatch* when I put in the engagement announcement."

Wait for Me

Max Frish, conquered by a bronchial cough, a full body ache, a fever, a loss of appetite, lay isolated and lonesome; the door to his downstairs bedroom closed by his wife, Eva, who had removed herself to the upstairs guest room.

"I am not going to catch your fever. You use the downstairs bathroom. Don't you dare come out until you get well."

Supine, Max read Shirer's *History of the Rise and Fall of the Third Reich*, a tragedy he pursued during his days of enforced bed rest.

To Max's left, his telephone, the link to his business life, Max Enterprises. "The Company That Cares for You."

Max read, shivered, dozed, awoke, shouted, "Eva, Eva." Eva, in blue jeans, Aztec geometric design T-shirt, appeared at the foot of Max's bed.

"Eva, I just had a wonderful idea for next year's spring line. An underarm deodorant for our living doll series."

"What?"

"For our line of dolls that sigh and urinate. Remember?"

"Now I do."

"Neat idea, huh Eva?"

"Great idea, Max. Now you rest, drink your iced water. Anything else you want?"

"I got so warm, maybe you could open the window." Eva hesitated. "Just a crack."

The last knobs of ice that had been protected from the winter sun by layers of last fall's oak leaves had finally bared their cold bald domes to the spring wind.

"'Just a crack, Max. You get cold, ring your bell. The bell is easier for me to hear than your shouting at me. You know that, Max."

"Sorry, I forgot that, Eva. Sorry."

Max pulled the cotton cover over his right shoulder, turned on his side, left his ear and moustache uncovered, heard the winter leaves rattling, crackling on the lawn. Max dozed, awoke, drank his iced water, took his temperature. 102° F. He dialed. "Max Enterprises."

"George around?"

The receptionist answered, "Mr. Frish, you don't sound so good. You feeling any better?"

"Not yet."

"It's only your second day. Mrs. Frish says you have been coughing and coughing. She says you are having trouble breathing."

"It's easier after the crud comes out of my lungs. George around?"

"It's Thursday, Mr. Frish. George is at the design meeting."

"Please have him call me. Tell him I have a couple of great ideas I want to talk to him about."

"You want him to call you today?"

"Today, tomorrow, whenever George has a chance. It doesn't look like I am leaving home for a little while."

"You do as the doctor says."

"I do what Mrs. Frish says. She speaks to Dr. Gordon," Max laughed, "and then she tells me what to do."

"You take care of yourself, Mr. Frish."

"Don't forget to tell George to call."

"I will, Mr. Frish."

In the rise of the Third Reich, Hitler schemes to annex the Czech Sudetenland to his new greater German fatherland. The Sudeten was never German but had been a part of the Austro-Hungarian Empire. That is of no legal significance to Hitler. Not in his new world where threats—aggressive arrogant threats, are successful. The Sudeten to Germany or war in Europe.

Hitler triumphs, Czechoslovakia is desecrated, divided, abandoned. War is delayed. Czech refugees flood Europe. Slovakia becomes a German puppet and Hitler begins to plan his takeover of Danzig, Memel and Poland.

Max slept deeply, awakened only to cough, spit into the tissue that he balled into the paper bag pinned to his bed sheet. At five-thirty, Max turned the PBS *National Business Report* on mute, watched the dollar fall, the Dow Jones drop and bond prices decline. Max shut the TV when Eva placed the yellow plastic tray on the bedside table. Applesauce, grape nuts and skim milk, a glass of water and his four evening pills. The orange for hypertension, the two white for arthritis, the yellow and black capsule, the antibiotic of Dr. Gordon's choice. Eva turned to the door, turned back.

"Amy wants to come by this evening. I told her she shouldn't, but she insisted. She wants to see her best grandpa—that is what she told me. Don't let her get close to you. I'll ask Amy to sit in the chair. I don't want her mother blaming me if Amy gets sick."

Max nodded, added to Eva's injunction, "If Amy wasn't here all the time, Vickie wouldn't be running here and there."

Eva sighed, "Vickie would be going even if she didn't have us down the street."

Max swung his feet off the bed, sat, ate, swallowed his pills with the water, began to cough. The bronchial mucous plug ascended the bronchus, gained the trachea, entered Max's mouth. Max coughed again, choked. Light headed, he sat up in bed, coughed again, gasped and expelled an "ugh" which freed another mucous plug from his bronchial tree. Max spat into his tissue, breathed deeply, began to cough again. The phone rang—it was George.

"George, I have a great idea that I want to present at next Thursday's design conference."

"Dad, you are sick. You get well first."

"George, put me down for Thursday!"

"Dad, next Thursday, the Thursday after, what difference does it make? First you get well."

"This is one great idea for our next Home Aid catalog. This will be our greatest seller since the medical bracelet."

"Your fever is no better?"

"It's only a little fever."

"Dad, a hundred and two is not a little fever for a man over seventy. Mom told me."

Max coughed, spit.

"Tomorrow, I'll be better tomorrow."

"You don't sound so good, Dad."

"It's only a cough. Don't forget, George. I'm down for Thursday, next."

"Dad, what do you have that is so important? That won't wait?"

"My boy, an idea that will revolutionize the home care industry."

"Okay, Papa, tell me."

Max coughed, spit, coughed, sat up.

"George, I want to make extra large placemats. Large print, drool proof, soft washable placemats. Each placemat will have a different non-denominational prayer printed on it. Think of the market, George. Every nursing home in America will want a Max Enterprises prayer mat that can also be used as a feeding bib."

Max slept, his mouth open to breathe more easily. He turned from his back to his left side, opened the top two buttons of his pajama top.

From the heights, the German 88's were shooting into the valley at the two columns of advancing Americans who clung to the valley wall. Since dawn the infantry had pulled and pushed from Italian farm house to barnyard, from farmyard to the churchyard where the road from the valley ended.

In the basement of the priest's house, under two GI blankets, Sergeant Max Frish slept, coughed and shivered, waited for the pack mules to bring up the ammunition for his 30 caliber light machine gun. The battery of American 105 howitzers that had come up the valley road after dark stood in the church yard ready to commence firing.

Before first light the howitzers started. Boom! Whoosh. Boom! Whoosh. Short, short, still short of the dug-in German 88's at the crest.

Max Frish slept, groaned, shivered, sweated, pulled the blankets over his ears. The boom and whoosh of cannon reverberated through his head.

"Papa! Papa, you okay? You were groaning." Amy was at his bed.

Max felt his forehead, wet and cold. His pajamas were soaked from his sweat. In the light from the bathroom, Max saw the fear in eleven-year-old Amy's face.

"You okay, Papa?"

Max opened his mouth, mouthed, "Grandma." Amy ran from the room. Max reached for the thermometer on the side table. He could see its long thin mercury nose beside the telephone cord. The thermometer was there, his left hand was there. His left hand would not rise from his side. He heard Eva scream.

"You okay, Max?"

Why was she screaming? Max could hear Eva.

"You okay, Max?"

Max nodded.

"Say something, Max!"

Max lifted his right hand, pointed to his throat, then shook his head to "no." Eva was at the phone. Max saw her dial 911. Max smiled at Amy, beckoned for Amy to come towards him. Max sat up. With his right hand he reached for Amy's hand, took her hand in his, held her hand to his lips, fell back, freed Amy's hand. Amy cried.

The paramedics held the oxygen mask to Max's nose and face. Max heard, *"He is still breathing. I don't know if he knows you, Mrs. Frish. Try talking to Mr. Frish."* Max opened his right eye. George was there, his arm around Eva. Eva had her arm around Amy. It was Amy who noticed.

"Papa has his eye open." Max shut his eye.

"Grandma, Papa winked at me!"

"Sure he did, Amy."

"Grandma, he did!"

The boom, whoosh of the howitzers had resumed. The lieutenant pulled the blankets from Sergeant Frish's ear as he kicked him lightly on his stocking feet. Rise and shine, Sergeant. Time to load up.

Max rose, began to fold his blanket, turned to Lieutenant Cullen. "What's it like out there?"

"Cold and wet, Sergeant, cold and wet."

"I don't think he can hear you, Mrs. Frish."

Between the booms, Max heard Eva.

"Grandpa is going to be just fine, Amy. Just fine."

The howitzers had quit firing. Lieutenant Cullen was at the door again, on his face that silly grin.

"Dress warmly, Sergeant. It's cold out there. I wouldn't want you to catch pneumonia."

The Best Laid Plans

That Victor Gaines had after his World War II service returned to Rock City, Illinois, should not be interpreted that he lacked entrepreneurial spirit. It was more that his wife Sandy's folks owned Nelson's Insurance, one of our leading agencies. Victor, while flying night fighters off the carriers in the South Pacific had envisioned it all. Buy a house on the bluff, raise a family, Sunday dinner with the Nelsons, Thanksgiving with the Gaineses, Christmas with the Nelsons.

It was roots, anchors into the stability of our Rock City social structure that returned Victor and Sandy to their hometown, where the Mississippi river flows from east to west, a city which in the fifties had all the qualities that Lewis Mumford wished for, a manageable size, under a hundred thousand, a viable industrial base, farm machinery manufacturing, surrounded by a green belt of bluff and river bottom farms.

What I most admired about Victor Gaines was his infallible decision-making process, his foresight, his willingness to act, his unwavering faith that the future would reward. This ability, this skill, this grace was not only visible in Victor Gaines's business affairs but also in the way he and Sandy planned their lives. When most of us veterans were content to live in four-room wooden bungalows in the east end of town, the older part of town along the bus route, Victor bought a 160-acre farm just over the bluff from Rock City. I should have listened to Victor. "Tom, there is no other place for Rock City to grow—can't go north, the factories are in the way. It won't go south for years—not up and down those hills. It's too expensive to bring sewer and water that way. "Why don't you and Judy come out one Saturday to the farm, I'll show you around?"

We didn't visit with the Gaineses until the following summer when we heard that Victor and Sandy were building a new house on the farm site, a brick with "a basement we can finish off when the girls get bigger and want a place away from us."

We visited the Gaineses as a change from our Sunday drive through the new subdivisions that now marked the bluff. Brick veneer or wood frame two bedrooms, one bath, unfinished basement, one story or split level, the homes appeared each May and were sold by July—before Judy and I could decide to go down to the Rock City Bank with my G.I. Veterans loan guarantee and see if we too could live in a home with oil heat.

It was after our visit to Victor and Sandy, after I joined the Rock City Bank Trust Department, that we bought in the east end of town, a prewar three-bedroom, one bath, brick veneer with half an unfinished basement and oil heat. Judy is not a nag, but when she saw me waterproofing the basement, putting up the wooden storm windows, she said, "Tom, if you had gone into business with my father we could be living in a new home in the Harris bluff addition. All your years in law school. It wouldn't hurt if our life was a little easier."

Then our boys came along—and with us and the Nelsons going to different churches I would run into Vic only occasionally. Until one day Vic came into the Y over the noon hour. That is the old Y when it was downtown. He joined the business men's club. We began to jog together, that's how I again kept up with Vic, Sandy and the Nelson Companies.

THE BEST LAID PLANS

I reported to Judy, "Vic and Sandy joined the Country Club."

"Tom, why doesn't the bank sponsor your membership?" And I had to explain, "Those kind of perks are for the bank's president not for new attorneys in the trust department."

Vic played "expense account golf" with clients on Thursday, tournament golf on Saturday. On Sunday Vic played with Sandy, and their girls as soon as they were old enough to swing a junior set. For the next fifteen years or so—the golfing Nelsons were pictured either on the sports or society page of the Sunday Rock City *Journal* "Life" section.

On those Sunday mornings I had to answer Judy's "How can they afford all that?" with "Vic sold a piece of the farm off to developers—with that money he bought a cottage on the river. He wants the girls to learn to canoe. Vic needs a weekend place he can take clients to." Judy would add, "We could have a life like that if you would go into business with Dad." Judy's dad had just gotten a contract to build housing for the elderly.

Each year before the pro golf tournament the Gaineses invited the "Y boys" and their wives out for brunch at the farm. Eight or ten of us who had lockers in the same aisle jogged over the dirt roads, returned to coffee, scrambled eggs, bacon, sausage, pancakes, and Sandy's homemade pineapple cheese cake.

It was the year that we had to park on the Gaineses' front lawn because the asphalt drive to the triple garage had been taken out to make way for a covered pool and guest house that Vic confided, "We had a chance to sell the cottage on the river at a profit—so I said to myself, 'We could use a heated pool.'"

On the way home, Judy turned to me, "I don't know how Vic and Sandy do it." After eleven years in the trust department I had the answer. "It's timing, all in the timing: buy a 160-acre farm for $300 an acre, sell off 20 acres to a developer at $14,000 an acre."

"Don't you learn anything at the bank?"

I didn't answer because what is the use of my understanding economic trends, long term and short term, regional and international if I had no belly for risk.

During these good times Vic Gaines kept the Nelson Agency growing and when Pa Nelson died he left half to Sandy and half to her brother George. George is an oncologist in Louisville, so he left the management to Victor, who was now president and chief executive officer of the Nelson Companies Inc. as they were now known since Vic had bought up five or six of the smaller, older Rock City agencies. Vic hadn't overpaid; he paid with Nelson Companies Class B non-voting stock, a round of golf once a year, and an invitation to the Gaineses' Christmas party.

The Nelson Companies were running out of space. This was about ten years ago when the Rock City downtown retailers were moving south into the Rock River Mall with its surrounding specialty strip shops and urban office space: wallboard cubes with two juniper bushes at the front entrance and an undulating blacktop parking lot that collected water in the spring and ice in the winter.

Vic Gaines bought the Brady building on the main downtown street, on the anchor block, next door to the Rock City Bank. Vic bought the building by bidding $10,000 more than our realty manager had been authorized to bid. Vic rents one third of the building to the Nelson Companies. That the rest of the building is more or less empty is of no consequence, as it is Vic who sets the rents for the Nelson Companies. Not exactly arm's length but not illegal even if your wife is the majority stockholder of the tenant company.

The president of our bank is so upset by our failure to outbid Vic that he maneuvers the realty manager off our bank board. Now he doesn't have to be reminded that it was his instructions, his limit to the bid that the realty manager followed unsuccessfully. All our president knows is that he has to buy a storefront one hundred and fifty feet from the bank and transport our paperwork there by cart. So that's how it is that Vic is headquartered next door which is about the time that we began to eat lunch together, usually on our Y jogging days, Monday, Wednesday, and Friday. That's how I heard, "Nelson Companies are going public." This was in the late seventies—the farm machinery factories paid UAW wages, operated at capacity. So I'm not surprised. Naturally I tell all to Judy, who asked, "Do you think we ought to buy some of the stock?"

"Not with two kids at Northwestern." That's one thing about Judy. She does not say "I told you so"; not even after the stock goes up—and up and up does Judy say a word. The shares were issued at 12 and in two years they are at 26—that's when Vic makes an appointment to see me in the trust department.

Vic came in, shut the door before he sat down. Vic is a tall, thin calm man, a three-piece Brooks Brothers gray pinstripes type who slumps in his chair, smiles, never saying much, a listener who then reaches a decision alone—not one to appoint management committees, not Victor B. Gaines at age fifty-five, chairman of the board of the Nelson Companies Inc. who drives a black Cadillac, is a member of two country clubs and has an unlimited undisclosed expense account. That day Vic sat very straight in the red leather chair that he had drawn as close to my desk as possible. "Tom, are you sure we will not be disturbed?"

"I left word, Vic."

"Tom, the Rotterdam group wants to buy us out at 36—I hope you have shares in the Nelson Companies."

"Never got around to buying any—you know how it is with two in college at the same time."

"It's not too late, Tom—not too late yet—"

I said, "Thank you," gave Vic our pamphlets, *Estate Planning* and *Trust Services*.

The Rotterdam group bought out the Nelson Companies. I didn't see Vic as frequently because the Gaineses had bought a home in Captiva, Florida, a home that according to rumor, brought back by Sandy's cousin, cost almost a million dollars.

Vic and Sandy are spending two months, December and January in Florida, coming home brown and thin. "You are looking good, Vic" is what greets him at the Y.

It was about a month before we had lunch together. "Catching up is hell on me, Tom—all that stress," Vic tells me. I didn't ask him.

"We have the two trusts set up—the one for Sandy and me—I know I should get to the others."

Nine years ago last spring, was when our Midwest economy began to disappear—ten percent of our population left when the shops started firing and offering early retirement bonuses. The loan demand went down at the bank as the interest rates went up. The Rock City downtown had so few stores left, the free parking lots couldn't find patrons. After the deindustrialization comes downtown redevelopment. Which is a boon for Victor Gaines's office building, sixty thousand square feet on the Keystone block—across the street from the now to be built parking garage civic center and hotel complex next to our bank. The president of our bank sits me down. "Tom, we want to rent more space in the Gaines building. We could build a skyway—it would be very convenient. Renting from Gaines would be cheaper than remodeling the trust department."

To which I nod in agreement.

"You are a friend of Vic Gaines, aren't you?"

"We jog together—"

Then I get the suggestion: "See if we can get some trust business from Gaines's pension plan, retirement fund, anything." Our president didn't rent from Vic—I continued to try to get Vic's trust business. I sent our brochures that described remainder trusts, GRITS charitable trusts, memos to Vic Gaines marked confidential—the mailings finally brought a response. Last November Vic invited me to lunch at the Country Club to tell me, "One more year, Tom, I'm going to take early retirement. I'm going to quit, go fishing."

Then early the next year it happened, the Rotterdam Group stock went into a decline, a meltdown from the years' too high of thirty-six. In four months it's three and three quarters and that's when Vic comes in to see me.

Calm as ever, he explained, "Tom, it was nothing I did in the Nelson Companies; it was somebody in Europe at headquarters."

I add an, "I understand." We shake hands.

In December Rotterdam stock went down to two. In January, in response to our Christmas card we got a note from Vic, "I'll be in to see you to finish our estate planning."

It was on February 5 after lunch that Vic comes in; on a day when an eight-inch snowfall had covered Rock City. I remember because Vic was our only client that day. My surprise showed. "Vic, what are you doing here?"

"You really want to know? I'm going to finish my estate planning."

"Why aren't you in Florida?"

"We rented our place, for the rest of the season."

He sits down, reaches into his inside pocket, "I made an inventory of our holdings."

"That's a good first step."

I looked at the value of the house on Captiva—it seems modest to me—less than a million dollars.

"Did you get an appraisal to determine the fair market value of the Florida house?"

"Yes."

"Seems a bit low."

"The Florida market for expensive homes is down," he informs me.

"With the value of your Rotterdam Group stock at two there is no need for estate planning—the existent Victor B. Gaines and Susan M. Gaines Trusts are all that are necessary."

Vic gets up. "Thanks, Tom."

"Glad I could help."

"I'll see you at the Y."

As I opened the door, the Gaines financial statement still in my hand, "Tell me, Vic, didn't you have any other reserves, any holdings other than your stock in Rotterdam Group?"

"No, didn't seem necessary."

I offer, "The stock may come back?"

Vic opens the door, leaves.

I told the story to Judy. "Vic did get some carry-over benefits from his losses."

"Tell me counselor, what benefit can there be in the loss of a family's life savings, something Vic worked and planned for forty years?"

I put my arms around Judy, "They saved the cost of probate, estate planning, trust fees, estate taxes."

Judy freed herself from my arms, turned, walked into the kitchen. I knew what she was thinking: "If Tom had joined my Dad, we would be spending our retirement winters in Florida in a house that we owned free and clear on Captiva."

Money, Money, Money

My daughter, Margie, is a woman of the electronic age, of wire transfers, a sophisticated investor, a careful shopper who uses coupons and discounts, a manager more frugal than she need be. Margie's husband, Harry, appreciated her accounting skills so fully that Margie did all the family bookkeeping, bill paying, tax forms, just everything that required the handling of money. That, since the day they were married.

Margie, of course, is very methodical. She checks the receipts to make sure that her electronic transfers are credited to her account; she checks to assure that only the amounts that she has directed are automatically deducted; she keeps records of ATM withdrawals; she keeps records of personal checks and deposits. Margie is a stay with it, stay on top of it, accountant. Unpaid bills do not accumulate in her pending file.

Neither does she pay interest on her Visa charge card as she banks airline mileage for each dollar paid by credit card.

Year after year, Margie's records are reviewed by Bill McMurry, CPA, tax specialist, and found to be perfect. "Fine, Mrs. Schwartz. Just fine."

My daughter had provided her husband, Harry, twenty-four years of peace, harmony and perfection in managing a household, so that he could pursue the contemplative life.

Harry is a good enough man, a caring husband, a good provider, but Harry Schwartz, professor of Polish History and Literature at Rockville College, does not do accounting. He teaches one graduate seminar, edits *Reading in Contemporary Eastern European Short Stories*. Once every three or four years he translates a Polish novel which sells four hundred copies. He plays golf three times a week at his country club, and after dinner walks Tom, the greyhound that Margie adopted to save from being put down. Once a month, as he smokes his evening professorial pipe, Harry leafs through his bank book so he is aware of the Schwartz family's bank balance.

Me, Margie's mother, I thought, well, if Margie and Harry are still together after twenty-four years, something must be right. Although, let me tell you, Gertie, as my dear, departed mother Sophie always said, what goes on behind closed bedroom doors, it's better not to know.

No, Gertie, I didn't notice signs of family friction between my Margie and her Harry. Certainly not about money. Harry's salary was generous, his pension more so, his teaching obligations minimal which gave him the time to write and edit, which gave him additional income. So all seemed idyllic. Every couple of years Harry enjoyed long vacations at the Chopin Foundation's expense. "Looking for lost manuscripts" is how Harry explained his prolonged visits to Paris and Stockholm; the historic refuge of generations of exiled Polish intellectuals, all of whom had written memorable novels or short stories that were worthy of being translated into English or, at least, noted and archived by Harry Schwartz.

Last fall, on the Thursday evening after the High Holidays that Margie and Harry spent with me in Chicago, Margie called me. Usually she calls on Saturday afternoon.

"Mom, did you or Dad wire $20,000 into my account?"

I giggled, "Not your mother. You know we don't get our gifting done until December."

"That's what I told Harry."

Margie sounded puzzled. "I have $20,000 in my money market account in Boston that I don't know where it came from."

I said, "That's unusual."

"Mom, I called the bank."

"So?"

"They can't tell me who the $20,000 came from. They say they don't know. That all they know is it was wired through our Rockville bank."

I sighed. "Maybe it's a mistake? Wait for your monthly statement. If it's a mistake you will get a correction slip."

About the tenth of the next month, it was a warm October morning, that I remember. I was watering the pots of fuchsia and impatiens that sit on the railing of our deck. The phone rang and it was a very disturbed Harry. I knew he was disturbed because he called me Cora.

"Cora, there is another $10,000 in our money market account. Did you or Dad . . . ?"

"Harry, sit down, enjoy the day. The mystery of who is sending you $10,000 a month will certainly be solved. Harry, let me speak to Margie."

Margie said, "I told Harry that you and Dad had not wired the money."

"We haven't, and tell Harry that your father and I are fully competent and when we gift I will inform you by letter so that you are aware of our generosity."

"That's exactly what I said to Harry." And Margie tells me, "Mama, you know what Harry called me? He called me an incompetent and worse yet."

I told her, "Margie, don't go crying over money." Wouldn't you tell your daughter that?

I forgot all about Harry and the money until the second Saturday in November when Ben and I drove the one hundred eighty-three miles west to Rockville. I made the excuse we wanted to see the Rockville-Wesleyan football game. Rockville was last year's co-champion. My Ben had played quarterback on the 1951 team. So that was a credible excuse. Truthfully, I was worried about Margie. She had called again the Thursday before.

"Mom, there is another $10,000 in our account. And then she began to cry. "Harry thinks it's all my fault. Something I did or didn't do."

I interrupted. "It's not as if you are going to spend the $40,000. Sooner or later you will find out, the mystery will be solved."

"That's what we are fighting about. Harry wants to buy a Mercedes sports utility vehicle. I insisted the money is not ours to spend."

I chuckled, "Ask Rabbi Kalinski," who is not only the rabbi of the Rockville Jewish congregation but also an attorney.

Margie said, "Good, I'll call you with his opinion.

Harry did not wait for Margie's consultation with Rabbi Kalinski. He bought his Mercedes the very next day, for which he traded a perfectly good Taurus with only 50,000 miles on it.

Spending the $40,000 made Harry happier and Margie more miserable. "Mom, we will certainly have to give the $40,000 back," she cried to me.

"You can sell the Mercedes."

She tells me, "Thanks, Mom." And I thought I had resolved another Margie-Harry crisis.

We drove west to Rockville under a blue November sky, a sky without haze, without the gray stacked clouds that so commonly hang over western Illinois in the fall. In the fields along the tollway the corn and soybeans stood brown and strong, ready, waiting for picking.

Ben had the sliding roof open. The radio was playing tango, to which he tapped along on the steering wheel. It was a tranquil, lovely day all the way to our daughter's home. A lovely day until our early lunch in the gazebo.

Margie had set the table. I had my picnic basket heavy with fried chicken that Harry adored, vinegar coleslaw for Margie, cornbread and honey for Ben. The gazebo, all screens under a shed roof, is shaded by two one hundred and forty year old oaks. I remember the jays were feeding on the safflower seeds; a rabbit was into the seed that had fallen from the bird feeder onto the gravel below. Along the fence the sunshine was glistening off the wet euonymus ground cover. Evidently, there had been a pre-dawn sprinkle on the Mississippi bluffs.

At the lunch table, Ben offered, "I'll get the coffee." I looked at my watch. It was 11:30 a.m. Harry looked at his watch, said, "Let's wait lunch. There is no hurry. I have to make a telephone call."

I knew Harry to be a man of habit; breakfast at 8:00, lunch at noon. I learned that twenty years ago the first time Harry and Margie had spent Christmas with us at our Florida gulfside condo.

Ben, Margie and I were sitting around the set table visiting, making small talk, waiting for Harry. Margie said, "Mom, I made sugar free brownies for you." We have a little diabetes on my mother's side of the family. I said that was lovely, thank you. Ben read the Rockville *Journal* sports page. I was in the swivel arm chair from which it is easier for me to get up and out. Margie sat beside me. She moved closer, whispered, "Mom, another $10,000 was deposited to our account on Thursday."

I smiled. "Somebody loves you."

Margie began to cry really big tears like she was thirteen years old, when I had insisted go take a shower before you go to bed.

"Somebody hates me, Mama. That money that isn't mine is turning Harry against me. All we do is quarrel. We quarreled over the Mercedes, and now we quarrel what to do with the money. I want to put the money aside in its own account. Harry insists it is ours to spend. I know the monies are not mine, not mine to spend."

I didn't say a word, because just then, Harry came in and sat down across from me and ate my chicken without even a thank you, Cora. It was Ben who told me, "Lovely fried chicken, Cora. Best you have made in years. It will be even better cold." To make it worse, Harry ate the brownies that Margie had made especially for me. He sat there drinking his coffee, eating my brownies, not saying a word. So I said to him, "Margie does have a point about not spending the money."

Harry gets up, looks at me, "Too late, Cora. All spent." Gertie, you wouldn't believe what my son-in-law said to me! He said, "Cora, I will beg you not to interfere in our life."

Ben and I cleared the dishes, then we went off to the stadium. Rockville beat Wesleyan by two goals. After the game I called Margie from the parking lot on our car phone. "I think we had best head for home. It looks like there are rain clouds in the west."

"Mom, I was planning for you to come for a light supper."

"We will see you in Florida."

That was the last Christmas that Margie and Harry came to our condo as husband and wife. The minute they came down the escalator at the Fort Myers International Airport, I saw they were not the happy couple of yesteryears. On the drive to Sanibel, Harry sat beside Ben. I was in the back with Margie, telling her of all the plans we had made.

"I have tickets for Saturday evening for the Gershwin Musical Review and Sunday evening there is a lecture at the Congregational Church that you and Harry may be interested in."

Margie took my hand. "Mama, you will be the first to know what Harry told me on the airplane while we were having our dinner. Just like that he poured my Chardonnay, lifted his glass, 'To twenty-four years of marriage. I want a divorce.'"

I asked, "Just like that?"

Margie said, "Just like that."

Harry had heard us. I am sure Ben had too. Ben never said a word. Harry turned, looked right at me. "Cora, we can't go on quarreling our lives away. I have to have a bit of peace. I can't work, I can't sleep and I can't go on like that!"

What went on that Christmas week between Harry and Margie in our guest bedroom, which has two beds, I don't know. In front of us they were civil and courteous. We went to the theater; we went to the lecture on the archeology of Jerusalem. New Year's Eve we were at Santini's, a family tradition for our early dinner. As ever, Harry sat on the porch, wrote and wrote. Margie walked alone to the lighthouse and swam and read Danielle Steele.

It seemed like the only time I was with Margie was when I was preparing supper and she came in to help, and even then, she did not talk about her divorce.

Margie and I talked about the weather; that year in that one week we had two bad storms that came up very quickly from the Gulf. We talked about the neighbors and their children and grandchildren. The one thing Marge did say, was, "Mama, maybe it was ordained, *bashert*, that Harry and I didn't have children," and then she added, "or adopt children."

Just then, Ben came into the kitchen to get the dishes to set the table for dinner. I waited until he had returned to the porch before I asked Margie if the divorce was for sure.

"For sure, Mama."

"Maybe Harry will change his mind." And then I asked, "Would you take him back?"

Margie laughed at me. "Mama, you are naïve. If it hadn't been the $50,000 in transfers Harry would have created another reason to get a divorce."

"You sure?"

That's when Margie sighed, "Mom, I am sure."

I put my arms around my forty-six-year-old daughter, who has a beautiful figure, great hair and gorgeous blue eyes and doesn't look a day over forty and I cried, and she comforted me.

"That's life, Mama."

"Margie, you will be all alone."

"I know, Mama. And I also know where the fifty thousand came from." She laughed. "I had to open Harry's mail to find out, but I resealed the letter very carefully."

"Tell me."

"From his publisher. He had his publisher wire the money directly into our money market account. All these years Harry has been getting his royalties in check form. I would deposit them in the Rockville Bank."

"Why, Margie, why?"

"Please, Mama, I'll tell you after the divorce." Margie went out the kitchen with the salad bowl.

Margie got the house. Yes, she is coming to spend her Christmas with us. You were right about there being another woman. I couldn't believe it, Harry giving up my Margie.

Ben is the one who suspected that Harry had a younger woman in Poland. He got suspicious when right after the divorce, Harry took his sabbatical in Cracow.

Me, I don't understand divorce for money. Gertie, you may be right. This divorce wasn't about money.

Yes, Margie is putting her life together. She took a job as the office manager for McMurry and Poole Accountants.

Gertie, I am lucky that I have you to talk to, to write to. There is nothing like having an old friend to confide in. You know what I can't understand? Harry and Margie were married for twenty-four years. During that time he must have translated ten books from the Polish. Not a one sold more than a few thousand copies. Harry had to give them away. Who in America reads Polish literary novels? You read mysteries, romances, you read for enjoyment, for a little relaxation. And this last novel Harry translated, makes him fifty thousand dollars in royalties. I never read the book. Why should I? It's something about spies and murders.

You are right, Gertie. Money does give one a choice. Got to go, Gertie. Time for my swim.

The Week Before Thanksgiving

The week before Thanksgiving: The acorns and oak leaves heaped into a pinnacle of compost, the flower pots in the garage, the porch furniture in the garage. Max Kramer sat at his Rolodex viewing the year passed. He peeled from his file *Nancy Crayton*, director of the Rockville Museum. Thirty-six or -seven. Dead. Cancer. Left an inept husband with a year-old girl.

Sandy Dreger, cancer again, bone cancer. Sandy who brought the Arts Council to national attention. Introduced visiting authors, dancers, fiddle players to the school children of Rockville, Illinois. Sandy Dreger's card went into the waste.

Bernard Gordon. The word was out all over town. Bernie will be gone in a month. That would be number twenty-three or twenty-four for the Rabbi to bury this year. It was Bernie's heart. A surgical intervention could not save Bernie, or he would have flown to the Cleveland Clinic in his own jet, had surgery, been home in two weeks doing acquisitions. Max left Gordon's number in the Rolodex.

The next discard, *Greg Horath,* had been the presenter at the Rockville Civic Center. Greg had given up presenting basketball and craft shows to join his wife who was pursuing an acting career in New York City. New York City where it wasn't safe to walk the streets, let alone the subways. In April the Rabbi had been mugged right in front of the Whitney Museum in broad daylight at 11:15 in the morning.

Max Kramer at age seventy and eight months removed his memory like he peeled an apple or a pear that had begun to soften to show decay. Max cleared his no longer necessary to call telephone numbers as he had helped his mother peel onions, quickly without crying.

Mama gone forty-eight years. Everything of hers gone, not even a keepsake for me. By the time I came home from the army nothing left, all gone. Mama was only a name on the Memorial wall. A name, Chana Gittel Kramer, read by the Rabbi after the Torah reading.

Where were Mama's etched glass plates, little angels with wings spread on which Mama served the quartered and peeled apples? The fish plate with the fins, gills and scales so clearly carved in the glass. Where do you see such plates today? Not even in museums. All gone.

My sister, Molly, knows. She never told me, never will tell me where Mama's household went to. Distributed to Molly's children with the warning, "Don't use until Uncle Max is dead. Don't use when your Uncle Max visits."

Don't forget—forgive, but don't forget. Memories were all that was left of Mama; of Jadja (Grandpa). My sitting beside Jadja in the sleigh, on the way to the post office. "Best behaved team in town. Max, have a *shmech laboc* [take a bit of snuff up your nostril]." Then to the blacksmith to shoe the matched grays. The bellows, the hiss of the hot forged shoes when dipped in the cold water.

On the summer days we went to the farms to sit under the willows beside the drainage ditches. Grandpa whittled a fife for me. He peeled the bark and then slid the bark back. Then Jadja played a tune on the fife.

My daughter, May, was a planner.

"Max, you always wanted to learn to carve. Now that you are retired you'll need a hobby."

"Retired? I'm still working."

Max stopped at the "I" on the index cards, looked at his Accutron watch, a gift from May. "So you won't have to remember to wind your watch."

It was 9:12; the pharmacist would answer at Walgreen's. "Yes, Mr. Kramer. Two months' supply of your arthritis pills and two months of your high blood pressure pills?"

"Dave, I'll pick them up this afternoon about four."

"You going to Florida?"

"The day after Thanksgiving."

Helen had come into the office next door to Max's. Helen, his executive assistant, came into Max's office by invitation only.

"Come in, Helen. Sit down."

"Mr. Kramer, are you getting ready to go to Florida?"

"Not yet. I have a week yet. Sit down, Helen."

Helen, stenography pad in hand, waited for the second "sit down" before she sat in the Breuer chair across from Max.

"Helen, please call the roofer. There is a leak where he fixed the flashing. Water is leaking into suite 506. Helen, don't sign the leases with the township until you receive the addendum. If Bailey wants to pay you, don't take the money. Have him pay the attorneys."

"You have been busy this morning, Mr. Kramer."

"Just another beautiful morning in downtown Rockville."

"You'll feel better when you get to Florida."

"I don't feel bad now."

"Mrs. Kramer called. She said you had a bad night with your back."

"My wife is a blabber mouth. Helen, if the White case comes up for trial, don't get a delay. You can testify. Just tell it how it was, we asked him to sign a lease, he wouldn't. No more, no less."

"How can White say he doesn't owe you? It's all in the lease."

"The Whites say they didn't renew the lease, so are under no obligation to pay."

"Nothing was changed, Mr. Kramer."

"We'll see. We tell it how it was; the judge will tell us what it is."

Max rose. On this signal Helen rose.

"You were in early this morning."

"Went to services this morning. Today is the anniversary of my mother's death. Special memorial. We remember those days with prayer."

"I know, Mr. Kramer."

Helen, same age as my youngest. She managed to put her life together again. A divorce, now two families. His and hers integrated for Thanksgiving and Christmas. Helen was too thin but what can you expect, jogging before work, tennis after work and low salt, no fat, no protein for supper. Helen will give me five pounds of assorted health-filled nuts for a Christmas present. "To munch on your drive down to Florida. The nuts will keep your energy up."

"I'm going down to the Ford garage."

"Don't forget, Mr. Kramer. Mr. Sawyer at 3:00 p.m."

"I know. The new man from the Downtown Development Association."

Max drove across the Mississippi on the double-span Interstate bridge, turned left on Kimberly. To the right was Eastern Avenue. Up Eastern through Green Peace Cemetery to Mt. Nebo, a bare knoll on the Iowa bluff until Max had planted a pin oak on the family plot. There were four graves remaining, waiting for the Kramers. Max and May beside Mama and Papa. That would leave two. Let the kids fight over the burial plots. At least they are paid for. Judy will get the condo in Florida and Harold the house in Rockville.

At the Lincoln garage the manager was there waiting. "I'm sorry your new car didn't come."

"Mrs. Kramer wouldn't have wanted to drive to Florida in a new car."

"Would you like some coffee, Mr. Kramer?"

"Thank you, Bob."

In the service area waiting room, Max read this week's *Newsweek*. The top five percent had incomes of more than $94,000 per annum. The top five percent was good enough from where the immigrant Kramers began. It was all an economic miracle. A truly golden country, America.

"I'll keep your new car inside until you come back from Florida, Mr. Kramer."

"I know you will, Bob. Have a fine holiday."

"You too, Mr. Kramer."

On the return trip to his office, Max opened the sliding roof of the Lincoln, put on his Italian driving gloves, a gift from Judy. "Dad, you should buy yourself nice things. You can afford it. You buy for us. You buy for Mom."

There was one advantage to owning vacant downtown property. A reserved parking space in front of the freight elevator where the enamel sign read, "NO PARKING."

The stores had been empty for six years—eight years, who could remember. The elevator was used once a week, Monday morning to take out the trash that John, the Kramers' one maintenance employee, collected daily. Max walked through the alley that separated the stores from the bank. The bank had a new sign, had replaced all its 1920 wood windows with 1991 aluminum sash. The bank was prospering.

Max Kramer was a planner. Next year he would finish the painting, clear the limestone frieze.

The elevator to the fifth floor was slow. Slow, but safe. Helen was waiting, notebook in hand, smile ready. Max grinned. "What's new and exciting?"

Helen looked at her watch.

"I'm always on time, you know that."

"Except when you forget."

Max grinned. "When I forget, you can blame it on old age."

"You are not old."

"I'm not young."

Helen never asked, "Have you had lunch? How are you feeling?" For this Max was grateful.

"Promise me, Mr. Kramer, you won't lose your temper with Mr. Sawyer. He's new in Rockville."

"When Sawyer comes, you come in with him and if I'm rude, you can interrupt."

The door between his and Helen's office was open. Max returned to his Rolodex, to eliminating the year that was. J, K, L, M—Sawyer appeared as Max was on Newman and Doby Architects.

THE WEEK BEFORE THANKSGIVING

Sawyer was young—very young, about thirty-eight. Max knew all about his last job; how he had chosen to leave Naples, Florida, for the reawakening opportunities in downtown Rockville. Opportunities the Chamber of Commerce and Downtown Development attributed to a Civic Center that would open next year and riverboat gambling that had brought tourists.

For one third of what Sawyer had sold a home for in Naples, he had bought another of greater quality in Rockville. Three bedrooms, two baths, double garage, colonial brick, center hall, in an older bluff neighborhood. A fitting home for the new executive director of the Downtown Development Corporation.

Sawyer had dressed carefully, in gray pinstripe suit, blue cotton shirt, red rep tie; red was this year's power color!

Max could not see if Sawyer wore suspenders. He did wear twenty capped teeth that presented themselves as he extended his hand to Max Kramer.

"I have heard so much about you, Mr. Kramer. You and your family."

"All good, I am sure."

Sawyer sat in the Breuer chair facing Max and Helen.

"Helen, I want you to meet Mr. Sawyer."

Helen smiled, clutched her steno pad to her flowered silk blouse, pulled her chair exactly half way between Kenneth Sawyer and Max Kramer.

Max leaned forward, placed his left hand with his University of Iowa class of 1941 ring on the legal pad. In his right hand, at ready, was his Mt. Blanc ballpoint.

Sawyer began, "Has Mrs. Wells told you why I called?"

Max grinned, "Helen?"

"It was about the downtown holiday decorations."

Sawyer began again. "Your building is right in the center of our 'super block' project," a pause and then . . .

Max then saw himself. An older replica of Kenneth Sawyer—pinstripe suit, blue rep tie and black wing tips. It paid to buy better clothes. My Brooks Brothers suit was fourteen years old, still fit. So the vest didn't fit, but if the jacket wasn't buttoned, who would notice. Elbows on his desk. Max waited.

"We are going to string Christmas tree lights the day after Thanksgiving."

"I told Mr. Sawyer that was the day you were leaving for Florida."

Max nodded.

"There will be a Christmas tree, a thirty-foot Norwegian pine, in the Plaza across the street at the Heritage Building. The Chamber of Commerce will pay for a tree, if we could put a small tree, decorated with little gifts for children, that tree would be lovely in the lobby of your building."

Max nodded that he understood.

Helen answered, "The Kramer Building has never had a Christmas tree in the lobby."

To which Max added, "It isn't going to either—not in the lobby. On the outside. Whatever you like. The city has always strung white lights on the trees in front of our building. They are quite lovely. Mrs. Kramer and I do enjoy seeing them."

"I thought perhaps this year . . . I had seen your ad in the *Tree of Lights* book that the Arts Council published last year."

"That was a charity."

"Mr. Kramer is on the Arts Board," Helen was explaining.

"This year our holiday donation was to the Arts Building Fund, not as sponsors of a Christmas tree display."

Max looked at his watch.

Kenneth Sawyer turned to Max. "In Florida we had many downtown merchants that decorated their windows for Christmas."

"Downtown *merchant*. That's the 1990 word to replace the *Jewish* shopkeeper!"

Max got up. Helen sat, her notebook at her mouth. Max stood over Sawyer. It was coming, the historical review, the Kramer history. Nothing would stop Max now.

"Mr. Sawyer! The Kramers are not merchants. We are land owners, farmers, property owners-developers. In the three generations of Kramers that I knew, we have never had a retail merchant in the family. My uncle was the Imperial Architect for the Czar, for all of Poland. The first Jew to be appointed to that position in Russian history. Kramer's *don't do Christmas trees.*"

Sawyer rose, extended his hand without presenting his toothsome smile. "So nice to have met you."

Sawyer left—Helen sat. Max turned to her. "All right, Mrs. Wells. I should have been gentler with Mr. Sawyer."

"I didn't say anything, Mr. Kramer."

"You should have!"

So What . . . So Nothing

The Oak Hollow addition to the City of Rockville is a pocket of tranquility and domesticity. A cul-de-sac shaded by hundred and fifty year old red and white oaks; without sidewalks to attract the "walk for health" fanatics who stride north and south on the main through street only two blocks away.

The homes in Oak Hollow were all built some thirty years ago which is when we moved up on this bluff from below the hill by the banks of the Mississippi River. The smaller homes—three bedrooms, two baths, on a split level, with one garage, are closest to the main street but by the time you get to our street, the homes are larger and set back among the oaks.

The lots are laid out as you would cut a pie, so that neighbors are closest to conversation when we are wheeling our waste to the street. Oak Hollow is not a chummy enclave with block parties and Fourth of July picnics. None of this "I baked a cake, come on over for dessert." It is more a wave hello, a wave goodbye neighborhood.

Waste recycling has yet to come to Rockville, and garbage pickup is only once a week on Thursday morning which means that on Wednesday afternoon the trash, the empty beer cans or bottles, the yard debris in special sacks are at the curb.

The split level to the west of us was built by the Gordons, about a year before we built our two-story with vaulted ceilings, three bathrooms, gazebo and double garage. The ranch house to the east, with only the front door visible from the street, is now on its third owners, Mr. and Mrs. Chadwick Brown, formerly of Marietta, Georgia. Usually the third owners are a young couple, both working to maintain their Oak Hollow lifestyle with two or three school age children taken care of by a widowed grandmother who comes home from bridge club minutes before the children do, or the children are on self care instructed by a note tacked on the refrigerator door.

The Chadwick Browns are a two-car, one-motorcycle family in their late sixties, with three discreet Boston terriers as dependents. Chad is a tall, thin man with a beautiful golf swing, which is what he told me some four years ago when we met while I was taking out the garbage and he was chipping golf balls on his lawn.

Monday, Wednesday and Friday mornings, Chad drives his Cadillac to one of the municipal golf courses of which there are six or eight if I count the two courses that the county maintains.

No more than fifteen minutes later, Barbara Brown, just as thin and only a bit shorter—she must be five foot eight—has backed her Mercedes out the drive and has gone "shopping." This I learned from my wife, Lilly, who once a year joins Barbara for lunch to celebrate the birthday of a mutual friend.

The Gordons, on the other side, were a one-car family, so when Mike went off to walk the mall Sheila waited at the curb to be picked up to play tennis. That is also on Monday, Wednesday and Friday. Tuesday and Thursday and Saturdays the Gordons did "easy does it" aquasize at the Rockville recreational center, heated pool, until Michael died some four months ago. Coronary disease, diabetes and obesity, they do add up.

Last Wednesday afternoon Chad Brown and I, wheeling our trash, met at the curbside. Chad walked over to help me unload my garbage trolley.

"Harry."

"Yes, Chad."

"Have you noticed, Doris Gordon is getting ready to sell her home." Chad points to a painter unloading his ladders from a pickup parked in the Gordon driveway.

I answer, "Could be. I'll ask Lilly. She is in the same book study group as Doris's sister-in-law, Enid."

Chad Brown puts his arm loosely around me, whispers, "Those kind of people are trying to buy in Oak Hollow."

I say, "What kind of people?"

Chad looks around. "Undesirables who won't keep up their property."

Lilly is at the sink, above which is a window to the street, converting mealy pears to edible compote. I stand behind her. "Chad thinks Doris is getting ready to sell her house." After a pause I add, "To undesirables, so she can get top dollar."

Lilly says, "So?"

"I told Chad you would ask Enid if that is so."

"I could."

Next Wednesday I have an answer for Chad, so when he is dragging out the last of his plastic sacks of yard waste I wheel my cans out. "Enid said she knows of no immediate plans for Doris to sell."

Chad grins. "I know women. Doris wouldn't have her back garden replanted and re-rocked if she wasn't preparing to sell. She isn't one for spending."

I nod. "Could be, but . . ."

Chad answers, "That Doris is a tight mouthed one. I have a sister-in-law like that. Never said a word, one day she packed her car, drove off to California, left my brother without." Chadwick doesn't explain without what. He turns to go, then turns back. "Harry, I'll bet you a hundred dollars that in one year, Doris is out of here and we have black neighbors."

I say, "Could be," but I don't take up his bet.

Evidently Lilly has been watching us. "What are you and Chad so chummy about?"

"I asked him if he wanted to save his acorns for the state forester." Then I grin, give Lilly a hug. "Chad is worried that Doris will sell to blacks."

Lilly corrects me, "Afro-Americans."

I smile. "I told him what Enid said, but he is worried about his property value."

Lilly stops stacking the dishes, says, "What would we do if an Afro-American family with three basketball playing kids moves in next door?"

"I wouldn't let them use our basketball hoop."

"Racist!"

"No, just too old to tolerate that bounce-bounce-bounce."

"And you, an old basketball great who was out there playing one on one with the kids."

"That Lilly, was thirty-five years ago when our boys were home."

Lilly finishes stacking the dishes, puts on the classical music station. We sit in the living room; the warming afternoon sun comes through the window walls onto the couch. Lilly reads her book club novel for the week. I turn my Eames chair just a little to the left so that my head is in the shade, my legs on the foot stool. Neither the Gordon nor the Brown house is visible. I read *The New York Times* business page.

The sun reflects off the reds and yellows of the floral border of our antique Chinese rug. I doze. The phone rings. It is Enid, for Lilly.

"Harry, go next door to Doris's. The police called Enid, Doris has had some sort of an accident."

Doris is a tennis playing, swimming, thin, spry, without an arthritic joint, young-old. A most unlikely accident victim. But there she is, unconscious, wrapped in blankets, oxygen to her nose, drip in her arm, being transported to Rockville Memorial Hospital.

Lilly is still on the phone to Enid when I report. "Looks like Doris may have had a severe stroke."

Lilly conveys my opinion to Enid. "You sure that is what the paramedics thought?"

Lilly sighs. "Not a one of Doris's three daughters is in town."

I offer, "They left home twenty-five years ago. At least Doris has a brother in town." Which is my reference that not one of our family has chosen to stay in Rockville where the Mississippi flows from east to west and the gambling boat does leave the dock to cruise.

It isn't twenty minutes later that Barbara Brown is at our front door, the second time this year. Two months ago she was here for the cancer drive. Lilly asks her in. She sits on the edge of the couch, feet close together.

"I don't want to be a bearer of bad news, but I know how close you are to Doris." She stops, Lilly pulls up the rocker, sits down across the coffee table from Barbara. Barbara continues. "I was doing my volunteer work at the hospital when poor Doris came in. Dr. McCully did all he could. Dr. McCully is a very fine emergency room physician, but . . ."

After Doris's funeral the three daughters came by to tell us that they wouldn't sell the house right now. First off they had to decide who wanted what and as all three were working and real estate taxes were so reasonable in Rockville, would we sort of just look over when we were passing by and if anything seemed wrong call Enid and if Enid wasn't home . . . We received their names, addresses and telephone numbers in Arizona, Nevada and California.

The next Wednesday afternoon Chad Brown joins me at the curb. "I saw that the Gordon girls visited with you before they left."

At fifty-one, forty-eight and forty-six, they are hardly girls but I say nothing. I just nod a "yes."

"Harry, they are going to sell the house just as I said."

"It will take some time. They think they will have it ready to sell by next June."

Chad says, "Thank you, Harry. Nice talking to you."

In Sunday's Rockville *Journal*, under Houses for Sale, there is a picture of the Browns' exquisite ranch home in Oak Hollow. Three bedrooms, three baths, double garage. The for sale signs go up on Monday. Three weeks Thursday morning, as I am taking in my empty garbage cans Chadwick Brown is up the drive, into my garage.

"Harry, we will be leaving for Georgia on Saturday. I thought you would like . . ." and he gives me his leaf rake.

I say, "Thank you. Have a good trip. You were a good neighbor to us."

Chad gives me a hearty goodbye hand shake. "You will like your new neighbors."

I agree, with, "I am sure we will if you say so."

"Lilly, the Browns sold their house. They are going back to Georgia."

"I heard they got top dollar. Every penny they asked for."

I murmur, "Very fortunate," because Rockville has been a non to down market for twenty or so years since the farm machinery factories departed.

"How do you know?"

"One of the girls in the book club told me; she knew we lived next door. Her husband was the agent."

"She sound pleased."

Lilly says, "Very. She said getting the asking price was a very welcome surprise."

On the next Thursday morning, I am driving Sally, our African-American household helper, home. To make conversation I say, "The Brown house has been sold." Sally smiles. "I know. Laura told me. It's all over the bank." Sally's daughter, Laura, has worked for the Rockville State Bank, where she is the VP for human relations, since she graduated Rockville College more than twenty years ago.

Saturday morning the Browns wave us a goodbye. That Monday there are three pickup trucks in the next door turnaround; six painters are inside, outside; two carpenters are installing a European kitchen. "Made in Germany" is what is printed on the cartons. Lilly says, "Expensive! You seen anyone that looks like an owner?"

"Not me. They all look black to me."

"Racist."

"Afro-American. Is that better, Lilly?"

Two weeks ago Thursday, I know it was a Thursday because Sally was upstairs changing the linens in the bedrooms, and it was she who noticed the two moving vans with the Louisiana license plates, followed by a white convertible, a green sports car with two exhausts and a red Taurus . . . a model I can recognize.

Sally called down, "Mrs. Silver, your new neighbors are here."

Lilly goes to the window. A tall, thin, dark brown man, dressed in a gray, double breasted business suit, the kind advertised in the Sunday *Times* menswear magazine, has stepped out of the driver's seat of the Taurus. A woman, a shade lighter, in blue jeans and brown leather jacket, joins him. Two jean-clad boys, one about seventeen, the other about eleven, are out of the sports car. A girl about twenty with a white silk scarf over her tan head unwinds herself from the convertible.

"Them are the Thomases, Ms. Silver. Their daddy just bought them the Rockville Bank."

Lilly gasps. "You know them?"

"No, Ms. Silver. My daughter, Laura, knows them. Mr. Thomas gave a fancy dinner party at the hotel to introduce himself to the staff. That's when Laura heard he would be your next door neighbor."

"How come you didn't tell us?" asks Lilly.

"Ain't for me to say, Ms. Silver."

Lilly starts out the door, turns to Sally. "You want to come with me to meet the Thomases?"

"No, Ma'am. Not me." Lilly goes off all smiles.

I ask Sally, "Tell me how come you don't want to meet the Thomases."

Sally gives me a smile that rewards my twelve years of driving her home. "Dr. Silver, the Thomases are not black like me. Me, I am a Baptist country girl from Alabama. The Thomases are Catholics from Louisiana. And Dr. Silver, please tell Missus Silver not to recommend me to the Thomases. Ain't no way I am going to work for them. Laura has to; I don't."

So what do I do but offer, "Sally, I bet the music is better at your church."

"I know it is, Dr. Silver. You coming to our Thanksgiving concert?"

"I'll buy two tickets right now."

"Ms. Silver has already bought them."

Oh yes, the Gordon house was sold last month to a young couple. Jim Warren works at the newspaper, his wife, Beth, at the hospital lab. It is her mother who helps out with the children; a boy of twelve and a girl of nine. Beth told me she thought the Gordon house was an absolute bargain, that they had looked at it some six months ago but couldn't afford it. But they liked it so well when they saw it re-advertised by another agency they went out to the open house. Jim Warren told me that six months later they saved twenty percent over last year's price. I convey all this to Lilly.

Lilly listens.

"So Harry, so what?"

"So nothing."

Benny and the James Brothers

My uncle calls as I take the first bite of my low cholesterol dinner. That's before the rates change at 5:00 p.m. so I know it's important.

"Benny, Sadie got a ransom note. It's signed by Rover. The kidnappers want $424.00. Benny, Rover's paw print was on the note."

My uncle has forty years' experience as a veterinarian; from large animals to small animals, my Uncle Al has a reputation as a man who relates to his patients. There is no doubt when he says paw print, it's Rover's paw print. But $424.00 is hardly a ransom to call Washington for advice.

"Uncle Al, pay the ransom. Get Rover home to Sadie. And let . . . ." I was going to say, ". . . and let me eat my supper," but of course I didn't, not to my uncle.

"Benny, you don't understand. Sadie is a big shot in the No Deals for Hostages Committee. She sees Rover as a hostage. If we pay ransom, what stops the kidnappers from taking more hostages. She told me, 'Get your nephew; find Rover. I'd rather pay your nephew a thousand dollars than give a penny to kidnappers.' You have to understand Sadie. Her sense of logic is irrefutable."

"Uncle Al, her logic may be great, but I don't understand her economics. For $424.00 she gets Rover. For $1000, all she gets is my best efforts."

"I told Sadie you would be here tomorrow."

I can't say no to the patriarch of the Roone family: my mother's older brother, the founder of the Roone family fortune, the endower of scholarships and the supporter of the arts in Rockville.

"Benny." My uncle is not his usual calm self when he meets me at the Rockville Airport. "Benny, Sadie got a clump of Rover's hair, with another ransom note. Sadie is waiting for us." Bizarre, is all that runs through my mind. Benny and the Case of the Poodle. My only hope is that none of my CIC classmates hears about my adventures with Rover

". . . The problem to be solved in each case, gentlemen, is much the same. Why? Who?"

"Uncle Al, tell me, why Rover?"

"Didn't I tell you? Rover is the richest dog in Illinois. He is the heir to the Marcus millions. He is the sole beneficiary of the Rover Living Trust. Moe Marcus was crazy about dogs. One time he had four dogs, a Russian wolfhound, a boxer, a Boston terrier and a standard poodle."

"What does Sadie think about all this?"

"Sadie is the third Mrs. Marcus. Old Moe was no fool. Sadie signed a pre-nuptial agreement in which she agreed not to challenge Rover's trust."

This only adds to my perplexities. "Tell me, Uncle Al, does Sadie like Rover?"

"I don't know if Sadie is crazy about Rover. I'm sure Rover can be a pest at times. He sleeps on the couch, he doesn't wash his feet when he comes in the house, and I don't think he showers before he swims in the pool, but Sadie knows when she has a good thing. Rover's foundation pays for her BMW and the house. And her trips to Florida.

Rover has a little arthritis of the spine. I've advised that Rover spend the winter in a warmer climate."

I am still in a state of wonderment when Uncle Al pulls up behind this five thousand square foot, 1930 red brick, two story. The drive circles the house. The back of the house has a view of the Rock River Valley, and the front has two white pillars, like in *Gone With the Wind*.

My uncle starts on through the back door. I follow, past a chain link enclosure with a twenty-four-inch by twenty-four-inch painting of a cocoa-colored standard poodle. I stop, take a good look. Yes, the picture is signed, "To Rover, J. Wyeth."

"Benny, I want you to meet Sadie."

Sadie is a round, smiling woman of a certain age, not too tall, not too short, who doesn't seem unhappy to be the victim of a vicious kidnapper's plot.

"Sadie, this is my nephew, Benny, the one I told you was . . ." My uncle stops right there, begins another sentence, "Sadie, I told Benny everything."

When I recall the Moe Marcus of thirty years ago; he was then sixty-five if he was a day. That would make him ninety-five today but he died ten years ago. So, a man of eighty marries a woman of thirty-five. In the movies it's always a conniving nurse or housekeeper. Sadie is a nice Jewish girl with dyed brown hair, for whom getting into size eighteen would be difficult. Her slacks are a little tight and her sweater could be looser which makes her equally attractive from the back.

Sadie greets me with a sigh and a smile, "Benny, I'm so glad you were willing to help me. Your uncle and I are about out of ideas of what to do." That's what must have appealed to old Moe, the dependent female gambit. Did she flutter her eyebrows at Moe as she clung to him?

My response is in an official tone. "Mrs. Marcus, I want to see the ransom notes."

"Call me Sadie. Everyone does. Sit down. I'll be right back."

Sadie comes back wrapped in Coco perfume, $150.00 an ounce. (Coco I would know anywhere as I file all the scent samples that come in *Connoisseur* magazine); carrying an ostrich attaché case with the initials M.M. engraved below the brass latch. Sadie takes out an envelope, hands it to me.

The ransom note is right out of Wednesday night's *Mike Hammer*. Cut out letters, pasted on ruled notebook paper, two Polaroid pictures of Rover, one lapping water and smiling, and the second, full face with one hairy ear and one bald ear. I don't have to ask which came first.

"How were these delivered?"

Sadie gives me two envelopes. The address is hand printed in square blocks. There is no stamp and no postmark.

"How did the notes get to you, Mrs. Marcus?"

"I'll tell you all I know. I get up to get my *Wall Street Journal*. It comes through the front door slot. And there is the note."

We sit and talk about Moe of sacred memory and what a wonderful man he was to set up a foundation for Rover. Sadie loves Rover but cannot compromise her principles to pay the ransom. To all of which I nod while my Uncle Al assures and reassures.

"Don't worry, Sadie, Benny will know what to do."

As my uncle is talking, there is very little I am sure of, but certain possibilities must be assumed. ". . . Gentlemen, develop a premise. Think like the perpetrator."

One: The kidnappers are no doubt local, and fully aware of Rover's habits and wealth, and:

Two: We need help to find Rover.

As in the classic textbook case, I must interview the friends of the victim.

"Uncle Al, did Rover have any enemies?"

"Not Rover. I can honestly say there isn't a finer dog in town."

"Uncle Al, did Rover have any close friends?"

"Only Billy the bloodhound. Billy sang in the bars; Rover would just listen and applaud. But that was years ago, when they were both pups."

It came to me like a flash. It takes one to know one. We'll get Billy the bloodhound to sniff out Rover.

"Uncle Al, where is Billy?"

"I think Boyd has him down at the Muscatine County Fair. He is doing a two-a-day."

"Doing what?"

"Billy is the Miraculous Singing Bloodhound."

"Uncle Al, can Billy follow a trail, sniff around for Rover?"

"I don't know why not; I'll run you over to Muscatine."

We drive west on Andalusia Road, through Loud Thunder Forest Preserve where the deer cross the roads at sunset to drink in the Mississippi, into the bottom land and then across the toll bridge to Muscatine County Fair Grounds. The fastest growing city in Iowa, three percent increase in population in ten years. Home of the Hon Industries and Bandag and Max Allan Collins, the voice of Dick Tracy.

The canvas sign flapping between two posts reads, "Billy the Singing Bloodhound, appearing at 4:00 p.m. and 8:00 p.m. Free entry."

We are in time to catch the 4:00 p.m. show. My Uncle Al buys popcorn. We sit on a backless, twenty foot long bench with a couple dozen of four- and six-year-olds sucking raspberry juice from shaved ice.

Billy comes on with the roll of drums coming through the speakers tacked on each sign post. Then Boyd Bradford. Yes, it's Boyd, talking down home Southern, cowboy boots, straw hat and blue checked gingham shirt. "Presenting! For the fifth year, Billy, the Miraculous Singing Dog!"

Boyd Bradford recognizes us, comes down off the truck-bed stage. "My god, Benny, a sight for sore eyes! You've come back to live in Rockville? Your Uncle Al has finally talked some sense into you?"

Boyd and I go back to when I was riding with my Uncle Al out to Bradford Farms, six hundred forty acres of the best corn and soybean ground between Taylor Ridge and Edgington. My uncle vaccinated the hogs and I hung on the fence, breathing hog dander and listening to the pig squeals.

"Good to see you, Boyd. How long you and Billy been doing fairs?"

"Fifth year, Benny. You ought to try it. Take early retirement, do what you want to do. Catch our eight o'clock show. I play the guitar; Billy and I sing a duet together. 'Pony Boy' or 'Home on the Range.' Stick around, we'll do both for you."

My uncle is evidently not interested in Boyd's performance. "Boyd, you remember Rover, the standard poodle Billy used to do the town with years ago? He has been kidnapped. We need Billy to find him, trail him."

"Can't this afternoon, Dr. Roone. You understand, Billy has to rest between shows. Tomorrow morning, I'll meet you wherever you like. Be there at 6:00 a.m., before the dew goes off. Best time for trailing. Just get Billy something to start the scent with; he'll show you." He pats Billy, and Billy licks his hand in appreciation.

"Rover hasn't been home in five days."

"No problem, Dr. Roone. Not for Billy. Nice to see you, Benny."

On the way back, Uncle Al is very talkative, a sign of his returned good humor. He brings me up to date on the Bradford brothers and how they made all that money raising hogs. "The last few years, what with low grain prices and high pork prices and subsidies and payments, Boyd and Bartlett had so much money they quit and cash rented the farm. Boyd went into show business and his older brother, Bartlett, has been hunting and fishing all over the world. Brought your uncle back a turkey from Idaho." By the end of the story, we are back to Sadie, whom we reassure with, "See you at 6:00 a.m. tomorrow morning. We'll surely find Rover."

Next morning my Uncle Al gets me up at 5:00. "Benny, I'll buy your breakfast at Dunkin' Donuts." We each down three chocolate donuts and coffee. My Uncle Al has a coupon which makes every third donut free. It is most fortunate that our family tree does not carry the recessive diabetic gene.

When we arrive at Sadie's, Boyd and Billy are sitting on the back steps. More of Sadie's bosom is showing through her Pierre Cardin jump suit than yesterday.

"Tell me what you need, Dr. Roone. Anything to get Rover back."

Boyd is the perfect gentleman. He keeps his eyes off Sadie's revealed breasts, which is more than I can do. My Uncle Al is all business.

"Sadie, I need the pillow that Rover sleeps on."

Sadie brings out a red and black, hand appliqued *mola*, a twelve-by-twelve-inch example of the San Blas Indian handicraft.

"Sadie, we'll be back with Rover." My uncle is very positive. He places the pillow in front of Billy's nose. Boyd puts on his cowhide gloves, grips Billy's leather lead. Off we go, my uncle, with the pillow, Billy and Boyd, and then me.

We go up and down, west across Thirty-eighth Street, up and down behind the Methodist Church, and then down into the ravine by the Swim Club. Billy is singing something out of "Home, Home on the Range." My uncle is following Boyd. I'm on the street above. Billy and Boyd are in the creek bottom, sniffing around. Billy is going north, up the creek, pulling Boyd. My uncle has scrambled down the hillside, wading ankle high in the creek, when Billy starts barking and Boyd starts yelling, "We got him! We got him!"

I scramble down through the creek bed, wet up to my knees. There, in a clearing beside a plywood lean-to, sits Rover, eating popcorn, chewing on beef bones. Two blue-eyed, yellow-haired, jeans-clad boys, one about eleven and the other about eight, are throwing beef bones up and back between themselves. My uncle is aghast.

"Rover, don't eat those bones! Not with your kidney problems!"

Rover comes over and kisses my uncle. Billy licks one boy and then the other. Boyd stands there, holding Billy. I take the oldest boy, sit him down on an overturned plastic pail. "Why did you send the ransom note?"

He begins to cry. He points to his brother. "It was his idea."

I walk the accused brother up on the ridge, sit him down on the street curb. (During an interrogation of two prisoners, separate them, rough one up. Gain the other's confidence.)

I sit down beside the eight-year-old, give him a half piece of Dentyne. I put the other half in my mouth. "What's your name?"

"Harry. Harry James."

"What's your brother's name?"

"Jesse. Jesse James."

"Why did you send the ransom note?"

It all comes out in a hurry. "Rover followed us home. We deliver the *Wall Street Journal* in the morning to Mrs. Marcus. Rover came home with us." He begins to cry.

"Why the ransom note?"

"We need two bikes for our paper route. Two bikes at Cal's Bike Shop—the Schwinn Road Special —costs four hundred and twenty-four dollars. With tax."

We retrieve Rover. We arrive at Sadie's with the James brothers. "Found the kidnappers, Sadie."

Sadie is so pleased to see Rover that she lets him slobber over her purple velour legs. My uncle, who is ready for all emergencies, takes Rover's temperature, examines him from nose to tail and pronounces him, "Fit as a fiddle!"

Boyd sits down on the back steps and reads the *Wall Street Journal*. Billy is licking himself to take off the grass burrs. And I'm sitting beside Sadie, telling her why the James boys sent the ransom note.

Sadie makes out a check for $424.00 to the James brothers. "I don't want to lose such good newsboys. Best newsboys I have had in years."

I go back to Washington with a thousand dollar check from Rover's Trust, six ears of Sweet Sue corn and my uncle's praises. "Benny, I knew you could find Rover."

A Time To Begin Again

It was on a day late in May that Robert Leman took the driftwood that surrounded the base of the oaks at his front door to the backyard pond, where he carefully arranged the logs among his stone statuary frogs. It was then he realized, Fran was dead, gone, buried.

The Lemans had certainly been considered as one of Rockville's fun couples. The Lemans had taste and wit and the means to show it and share it. Although there were some in town that thought Bob's quips were a bit cutting, a bit superior, like he was looking down at those he thought stodgy or intellectually slow.

Fran was the one with the friends for she was into doing for others. She served on the art museum board, on the symphony auxiliary and was a director of the YWCA—quite daring for a Jewish woman of her age. Bob, who had retired early when he sold Leman Insurance, played golf at the country club, gardened, read the *Wall Street Journal* and served on no boards, joined no volunteer committees. "I leave all that for Fran."

All in Rockville understood that Fran's most generous support of the arts, of the synagogue, of the community could not have been without Bob's approval.

After Bob retired, Fran bought a condo as a refuge from Illinois winters on Sanibel Island, on the southwest sun coast of Florida. They walked the beach, gathered shells for the Rockville kindergarten. Each March they returned to the gray spring of western Illinois, brought with them driftwood as souvenirs of the sun and beach of the Gulf coast.

On their fourth winter in Florida Fran was elected a director of their condo association; three meetings a year in Sanibel—April, October and November; air fare and car rental paid for.

"Bob, you don't have to go with me. It's only for two days. You want to play in the golf tournament. Drive up to Cedar Rapids," is what Fran said when she left to attend the October board meeting.

Because of high winds, heavy rains and flooding her flight was diverted, delayed for almost three hours to Atlanta. Fran did not arrive at the Fort Myers Regional Airport until after dark. It was 9:10 p.m. when Fran drove her red LeBaron convertible rental car off the highway into a ditch full of water and drowned.

There was much to be explained how Fran, who swam laps for an hour three times a week, could drown in four and half feet of water, and why had Fran, who had never lost control of a car, left a divided two-lane highway, to end up in a ditch that only held water because of that afternoon's heavy rains. Fran was dead and the why and how didn't matter as much as for the first time in thirty-six years Bob Leman was alone.

The girls from Fran's bridge club whispered, "He will be married in a year to a blond Florida divorcee," but Bob continued to play in his foursome, ate his dinners at the Golf Club. After three years there was still no one else in Robert Leman's life. Not one furtive, nighttime visitor had been reported as entering or leaving the Leman two story in the Oak Hills cul-de-sac.

Fran's dresses, blouses, slacks, shoes, hung in her walk-in closet, her underwear lay washed and still in her bureau. Fran's sweaters peeked at Bob from their plastic covers; her coats hung beside his in the entry closet. Both their daughters had pleaded, "Dad, let me help you sort things out."

"You have your lives; go on home to your children. I'll get around to the closets, I promise."

And when the daughters asked, "When?" he answered, "Everything in its time."

His first year of mourning had passed slowly, fitfully, with long nights of fragmented sleep. The second year was better. Bob continued to attend the morning service at B'nai Jacob, spoke to Fran during the meditation, dedicated a stained glass window in the sanctuary to her memory, played golf and remained alone in spite of the whispered advice he received.

"Life must go on you know," said the Rabbi. "I know that," answered Bob.

In December he drove to Florida, walked the beach alone, cooked Lean Cuisine, gathered sea shells, played golf at the Dunes Country Club, returned to Rockville in the first week in March to begin his yard cleanup, re-seed, fertilize, blow the oak leaves from the vinca, plant the impatiens in the pots, arrange the driftwood around the oaks.

It was in the third spring, a wet, cold, rainy spring; not as memorable as the spring of '93 with its floods but biting enough so that Bob Leman would rather do yard work than play golf, that he burnt the prunings. It was that evening when he had finished his cheese sandwich and coffee that he realized that this was the first time since Fran had died that he had disturbed, destroyed, her handiwork. For it was she who had draped the foot of the oak with the driftwood. "The driftwood reminds me of Florida." Best thing you ever did, Fran, was buy the condo in Florida. We would never have had the months when we awoke to the sunrise, spent our days together, walked the beach into the sunset if you hadn't insisted we go to Florida for the winter.

So, when the Rabbi made the announcement, "The sisterhood rummage sale will be on June 10. Please call Ella Markowitz," Robert Leman called Ella.

"Bob, there isn't anything we can't sell. Bring all of Fran's things over to my place. You know where I live."

Ella Markowitz lived in the District, alone in a faded to yellow, wooden two-story workingman's cottage with a single, detached garage, a home so common that even with the cash incentives from city hall the gentrifiers hadn't come to rehab this street, where day-old bakeries and antiques shops occupied what had been corner groceries when the District housed the railroad workers.

Bob Leman parked his Town Car in the alley, rang the back door bell. Ella, in green coveralls, round, smiling, came to the door.

"I'll help you."

"Ella, just tell me where. I have the shoes in plastic sacks, I separated the sportswear from the dresses."

"We'll have to put it all in the living room. My house is such a mess. It will look better after the rummage sale. We couldn't get the store until next Wednesday. That doesn't give me enough time to sort and price before the sale, so here I am living with rummage."

Bob Leman smiled, made one, two, three, four trips from the car, up the four steps into the back porch, through the kitchen into the dining room and into the front parlor where he stacked all on the green velour couch, chairs. Ella pointed to clothing on the dining room table. "It's my hobby."

"You took early retirement for this?"

Ella sighed. "Teaching high school English is not what it used to be. By the time I quit I couldn't have read another essay."

"Ella, I have at least a couple more car loads all ready to go."

"Bring it down."

All afternoon Bob drove from the bluff above the Mississippi down to Ella's below the hill. It was five-thirty when Bob Leman unloaded the last of Fran's golf shorts onto the coffee table.

Ella took off her coveralls, led Bob into the kitchen.

"Sit down. You might just as well stay for supper, courtesy of the sisterhood chairwoman for the rummage. You earned it."

"Ella, you look tired. I don't want you to fuss. How about just making a hamburger and beer?"

"Bob, you chose my kind of supper. The working girl's choice; thirty minutes from freezer to wash up."

"Ella, do you have onions?"

"Sure."

Bob sat on the back porch, watched Ella put the hamburger on the gas grill. Ella added the buns.

"Not like my mother used to make. Mama fried her hamburgers and then served canned, stewed plums as dessert. She thought that cut the grease but then—everybody ate prime beef."

Bob and Ella sat in the kitchen with the view of the four tomato vines garden, of the one galvanized garbage can, of the garage that needed a window pane replaced. Bob Leman finished his dark Augsberg beer. Ella noticed that Bob had reviewed her back yard.

"The old neighborhood has changed."

Bob nodded, sipped his beer.

"Big changes since the synagogue moved up on the hill."

"Ella, that was more than twenty years."

"That I know."

"So why do you still live down here?"

"That is what everyone in the congregation asks me."

"So tell me."

"You know how old maid school teachers are set in their ways, taking the easy way out."

"That is no excuse, Ella."

"Do you want me to tell you the truth?"

"You could."

"Until Mama died this was Mama's home, so I lived with Mama. Now it is two years and four months later. I keep saying to myself, Ella, you should move into a condo up on the bluff. That way I could travel, get away for the winter. I guess it has been easier for me not to make changes."

"That I know, but then a time comes." And Bob Leman pointed to the racks of Fran's shoes stacked in the corner of the kitchen. "Ella, what do you do? That is, now that you have retired."

"About the same as I did before. I read, mostly the contemporary novels. You know that is what I taught," and then brightly, "I made a couple of day trips into Chicago with the Museum Guild."

"You still into art?"

"You remembered."

"In this town everybody knows everything about everybody."

"You are still playing golf three times a week."

"It keeps me busy."

"I hear you have been attending the morning minyan."

"Since Fran died."

"It is a good thing you are doing. The Rabbi told me, told me how difficult it has become to get ten."

"I am up anyway, so I go help out."

They sat and talked—the widower and the old maid—about Ella's sister Shirley, who was in Los Angeles, about Bob's two daughters and only granddaughter who lived in the north Chicago suburbs. Bob turned, looked into the dining room, living room, all stacked with clothing.

"How are you going to get all this downtown?"

"We have a committee. Fewer each year but we will manage."

"Could I help?"

"That would be nice. I'll call you when the store is available."

Bob helped and Ella paid him with lean hamburgers, onions, bread and butter pickles and Heineken's dark beer.

"We could use one or two for the morning's minyan, Ella." Ella Markowitz came to the *shacharit* service, sat, prayer book in hand, in the center section to the right of the left aisle where Bob sat in the security of the east wall. None of the congregants, no one, said or even whispered about Bob and Ella until they were seen after services having coffee and toast at the HyVee on 18th Avenue. Then the country club set noted that Ella had joined Bob for Sunday dinner with his foursome, and the ladies of the Art Gallery Guild told that Bob Leman had sat beside Ella Markowitz on the day trip to the Chicago Art Institute to view the Monet exhibition.

So it went until one Friday evening in November when Ella had invited Bob for Sabbath dinner. The apple pie finished they sat at the round oak dining room table, the curtains drawn over the windows against the western Illinois wind.

"Ella, I should get your storm windows put up."

"That's not your job."

"Don't be so damn independent."

"I am perfectly capable of putting up my own storm windows." Ella laughed. "I just haven't gotten around to it. I have been cleaning up, throwing out. This is going to be my last rummage sale for the sisterhood. Twenty-two years of fixing and cleaning someone else's castoffs is enough."

"Good for you! And then what?"

"I am thinking of spending the winter in Florida. You made it all sound so wonderful. The beach, the birds in the sanctuary."

"The pool at our condo is heated."

"You inviting me?"

"Yes, Ella."

"You sure?"

"I am sure. Ella, I want for us to get married."

Ella grinned. "I want a premarital agreement."

Bob leaned across the table, took Ella's hand. "I couldn't have gone off to Florida without you."

"I would have followed you. I'll put my house up for sale. I promise I'll take the first offer I get."

"Ella, just leave it. Leave it for the realtor to take care of." Bob sighed, "I guess we were lucky, fortunate. You know, for me, for us to have the rest of our lives together."

Ella didn't answer.

"Ella, don't you believe in luck?"

Ella smiled before she answered. "My mama taught me, Ella, you make your own luck. You are right, Bob. Lucky is good!"

Water Therapy

In August, when the heat descends into the Mississippi River Valley, when the leaves of the dogwood yellow and curl and fall on the browned lawn, I float on my back, in the swimming pool, my body supported by an Aquabelt, my eyes protected by sunglasses. I stare at the sky, play cloud geography. There . . . the coast of Norway . . . the boot of Italy . . . Ireland . . . Britain and just beyond, the coast of Normandy.

The clouds have drifted to shield the sun, the west breeze cools.

The loudspeakers announce, Adult swim. All children under eighteen out of the pool.

The children scamper out, their mothers begin their head out of the water breast stroke, their aquatic exercise walk, backwards, walk sideways, jog in place. I float, my head in the water, my ears shuttered with conforming wax. I frog kick, I back stroke.

The children are back into the water. Then the shriek of the whistle and again the loudspeakers. All out of the pool. The whistle, harsh and raucous, penetrates my tranquility. The children climb up the sides, I stroke to the ladder, wait behind two eight-year-old girls. Children under seven must be accompanied by a parent.

Again, the whistle. The emergency is over. You may return to the pool.

The first aid guard, red First Aid fanny pack wound around his white T-shirt, stands above me, I hear his report to the pool director, a muscular twenty-two-year-old, "Kid jumped in, hurt his back. He's okay."

"Fill out the accident report."

The director looks at his watch. The first aid guard is off with the director. I see them enter the pool office.

I walk backward in the waist-high water until I float up, kick, float on my back. The yellow sun outlines the fjords of Norway.

I float on my back. I am sixteen, six feet tall and 160 pounds thin. It is 1938, I am a qualified lifeguard, tested and approved by the Red Cross, hired by the pool director James Dalton, my swim coach at Rockville High.

"David, your duty as a lifeguard is to prevent accidents, maintain order and cleanliness. Youngsters must shower before entering into the pool."

My weapon, a whistle; my uniform, a white sun helmet and a white T-shirt. On my chest, Bluffs Swim Club, Rockville, Illinois in red cursive. On my back, Life Guard.

I am wearing khaki shorts and sandals. I sit at station number four at the shallow end of the pool, five steps up that lead to a platform with a chair.

Mr. Dalton's orders are posted in the lifeguards' locker room. Change stations every fifteen minutes. Do not come down from your observation post until your relief has assumed the ready position beside the ladder. "*Do not descend the ladder until your relief is in position. You will stand beside your relief guard while you will both observe the area assigned to your station. You will stay in observe position until your relief is seated in the chair. Only then will you proceed to your next station. You may not leave your chair unless you have been relieved. Four short whistles will bring the roving guard to either replace you, or help you with whatever your problem. My hours are the same as yours, so call me if you need me or better yet, come in to see me in the swim office. James Dalton, Director.*"

"This is your first job, David?"

"Last Christmas I was a guard at the Y pool."

"Bluffs is a private club with members who pay your salary with children who may be a bit rambunctious. But kids are kids." Jim Dalton put his hand on my shoulder. "You are a bright young man." I said nothing. "I know how much this job means to you. I heard you have a full scholarship at State?"

I nodded in agreement. "I am saving for books, clothes."

"I know it hasn't been easy for you. Your mother is a widow, your sister is still in school."

"She will be a sophomore."

"You will be meeting members at Bluffs who could be very helpful."

Again, I nod.

"David, I know you want to do well. I know how seriously you take your responsibilities."

I said, "Thank you."

"And David, the pool opens at ten a.m., so if you want to come in before then and swim or give private lessons, you may."

"Thank you, sir."

"Don't forget, David, you have any problems, that is what I am here for." Mr. Dalton looked at his clipboard. "You will teach the five- and six-year-old learn to swim class on Tuesday morning at ten a.m."

Jim Dalton's worksheet read six sessions, below that a list students telephone numbers, parents' names, some of which I recognized. There was a star beside Florence Gibson. I pointed to it; Jim Dalton explained.

"The Gibsons are in Europe. Either Mr. or Mrs. Dover, that is the couple who work for the Gibsons, will be with Florence. The star means Florence will need special attention."

I said nothing. Jim Dalton offered, "She throws temper tantrums. If she acts up just motion to the Dovers. They will take her home." Then, in a whisper, "Mr. Gibson's family owns Interstate Power."

Florence, in her green and red flowered one piece swimsuit, was the only girl in the class. A sullen, non-smiling, round faced child with permed red hair and deeply set, dark brown eyes that gave her the look of a frightened rag doll. She clung with both hands to the corner of the pool where the water was only to her waist. The five boys stood back to the pool wall, arm's length apart.

"We will begin our learning to swim class by floating like a jelly fish, arms down, face in the water. But before we do that, we will put our face in the water and blow air through our nose." I demonstrated, bubbles blowing. The boys put their heads in the water, exhaled through their noses, coughed, choked. Only Flip Anderson, the number five boy, gave a successful demonstration. "My dad taught me!"

Florence did not put her head into the water.

"Would you like to hold my hands?"

I received both her hands. Florence gripped my wrists, put her head into the water, blew bubbles.

"Fun?"

I received a smileless yes.

I went to the number two boy, to number three, to number four. Number five, Flip, was the model for achievement. Florence gripped her pool corner, let loose of the gutters only to grab my hands.

Mrs. Dover, Florence's minder, sitting in the shade of an umbrella looked up from her *Movie Magic* magazine at us. Loudly, so Mrs. Dover could hear me, "Good! Now I will show you how we float like jelly fish. We reach for the pool bottom. Watch what I do. As I reach for the pool bottom, I will float up on my chest." I floated, blew bubbles, raised my head, returned my head to the water, floated on my chest, blew glorious, vibrant bubbles.

"Florence, would you like to try?"

"No."

I pointed to number two. "Your turn." He put his head in the water, went forward, his hands down. "Reach for the bottom. Good! Good!"

Again Flip excelled. I called a ten minute break.

Mrs. Dover, middle-aged and dumpy with breasts and belly protruding from her white uniform, wrapped Florence in a bath towel, dried her, rubbed her bare shoulders with some sort of oily skin lotion. The boys chased each other into the toilets.

I sat under the umbrella of the pool side table, did my progress reports. Mrs. Dover, with Florence in tow, sat down beside me.

"Florence, you sit with Mr. Cohen."

I corrected, "Kahn. David Kahn."

"Florence, you sit with David. I'll be right back with your medicine."

Florence sat on her wet towel, feet dangling.

"You did very well."

She answered without a smile. "Thank you, Mr. Kahn."

"Are you Jewish?"

"Yes."

"My Grandma Bessie is Jewish."

Mrs. Dover was back with a Dixie Cup of water and a white capsule. "Florence, swallow your pill." Florence swallowed. "You know what happens if you don't take your pills." And then to me, "Florence gets fits. Real bad, dangerous fits."

By week six Flip Anderson was doing the Australian crawl in the slow lane. Boys two, three, four and five could float on their chest, float on their back and propel themselves slowly with a modified crawl and frog kick. Florence Gibson stood, her back anchored to the pool wall and smiled only when she held my hands to blow bubbles. Both times she had let go of my wrists to reach for the pool bottom, her effort to float had ended disastrously with Florence choking, coughing, spewing water and bits of vomit over me. Her head had gone back, her neck tightened, her eyes closed in what I thought was the beginning of a seizure each time. I sat Florence up on the pool deck and motioned to Mrs. Dover, who promptly wrapped her in the terry robe and took off with her to the parked Packard.

I reported to Mr. Dalton. "Florence Gibson had some sort of seizure. She didn't go unconscious but . . ."

"That's what Mrs. Dover is there for. Calling on her was the right thing to do." I received a well done pat on my back.

I didn't see Florence Gibson again until the night of the Labor Day party. Sort of the last fling of summer, when Chinese lanterns hung at each poolside table and lit the outdoor bar patio where the Russ Paul Trio was playing slow and easy dance music.

WATER THERAPY

Florence came into the pool area holding on to a tall, suntanned man, dressed in a tan Palm Beach suit, and a woman as tall, as thin, with short blond hair, wearing a white sundress with an open back. Florence held their hands, led them both toward me. I was seated in the chair of the number four station, guarding no one as it was an adults only evening and the club members were not swimming. They were drinking and dancing to the tunes of "Harvest Moon" and "Moonlight Becomes You." Jim Dalton had warned me. David, they could get drunk enough someone will fall in or be pushed in or take off their clothes and jump in. You stay cool.

I was cool in my Illinois State red sweatshirt.

"Daddy, I told you about David."

I leaned down extended my hand. "So nice to meet you, Mr. Gibson." Mr. Gibson smiled a how-do-you-do. Mrs. Gibson smiled, said nothing, went off to the bar. Hand in hand, father and daughter followed mother.

Mr. Gibson was the attentive father. He came back to a poolside table with two tall drinks, sat there with Florence sipping, listening to the music. Maybe he was waiting for Mrs. Gibson. In a few minutes Mrs. Gibson was back, standing talking to Mr. Gibson, her back to me, pulling him to the dance floor. He finally got up, they danced, her head on his shoulder, her arms held him lightly. Florence sat, sipped her drink and then she began to undress. First her white shoes, then her socks, then her white dress. She stood in her undershirt and panties for a moment, looked up at me, started down the pool ladder, waved at me. She put her hands down to reach for the pool bottom, floated like a jelly fish, blew gurgling bubbles, put her head out, breathed, floated and bubbled, floated and bubbled. I encouraged, "Very good, Florence, the best you have ever done." The Gibsons came back, holding hands and smiling at each other. They saw the pile of Florence's clothes, screamed at her. "Get out of there! Look what you've done to your clothes! You naughty child. You will catch your death of cold."

Florence climbed up the ladder. I gave her a pool towel; she smiled at me. "See David?"

"I saw! You did beautifully."

Mr. Gibson glared at me. "You shouldn't have let Florence into the pool!"

I did not answer.

"I'll make sure you don't ever get a job at this club again!"

I said nothing.

The next year I guarded at the Y pool. Jim Dalton did not recommend me for a swim scholarship. I went down to State on the Army ROTC program; then the war started and four years later, when I came home, the Gibsons and Florence had left Rockville. I didn't think of Florence again until forty-five years later, when I was standing in the corner, clinging to the pool wall to stay upright while doing my rehab exercises. Not as afraid as Florence Gibson was, not of drowning for I wore an Aquabelt, but of failure. Would my muscles ever again be strong enough for me to discard the canes? Could I walk the few yards to the showers and then to my car, to the restaurant, the library?

I remember Florence's smile as she gurgled and floated on her chest. I turned on my back. The sun came out to warm me.

Such a Beautiful Sunset

Mildred Levine was an angry lady. There are those in Rockville who attribute her constant irritability to an inherited personality defect, dismissing her with "all the Marcus women are like that." Her mother, Rachel, may she rest in peace, if she wasn't angry with Rabbi Kahn she was angry with Rabbi Gross. And Mildred's younger sister, Sophie, is just like Mildred. Instead of helping her father (after all, she is a partner in their law practice) so that he can get away for a few weeks to Florida, Sophie takes up causes. First, it's battered women, then it's abused children, and her dear father, Ira, never complains. That is another way all the Marcus girls were lucky. They married men as placid as their father.

The Marcus girls' husbands smiled, stayed silent. How they learned that I don't know, but they did know better than to express an adverse or alternative opinion to those of their aggressive, assertive wives.

Mildred, the eldest, God bless her, has to be past sixty. She doesn't look a day over fifty—fifty-two at the most. Sophie too could look younger but then the way she dresses—no style at all—black pants that are too long in the back which certainly doesn't go with her high heeled pumps. Why Sophie doesn't trip and hurt herself fatally like her mother did is beyond me.

I really don't know how Sophie even sees. Most of the time she forgets to wear her contacts, and if she wears her glasses they rest on her forehead. And even if she could see, how could she see over the stack of files she carries into the courthouse. God watches over her. God should have watched over her dear, departed mother, Rachel, who fell down the basement stairs and ten days later, on the first day of Passover, she is an obituary with a twenty-year-old photo on page one of the Rockville *Dispatch*. "Rachel Levine, 72." If I hadn't been in her high school graduating class I wouldn't have believed she was that old, she looked that good.

Rachel was going down to the basement to get another jar of horseradish that she had ground for Passover. It shouldn't be a total loss, when she was going to get the *chrane* she has an armload of her everyday dishes. How she fell she never said. All she said was, "Now I will have to buy a whole new set of dishes." Would you believe that in this day and age you could die from a fractured hip. An embolism is what it was that killed Rachel. An embolism to the brain.

Mildred and Sophie are just like their mother. They want a more perfect world, not like my mother who only wants a bit of tranquility, peace and to be left alone.

Mildred is a very talented lady. An accountant, a money manager, a pillar of the community and a doer of deeds of loving kindness. You need a ride to the post office? Call Mildred Levine. You need a ride to the doctor? Call Mildred Levine. All right, so Mildred drives her Lincoln a little too fast and once or twice a year Sophie has to arrange for old Judge Stevens to put her on court supervision for three months so that her speeding tickets don't get recorded on her driver's license. Deeds of loving kindness are what makes our world a little better. (That is what Rabbi Kahn said last Saturday.)

So here is Mildred Levine, a caring woman, married to Phil, who not only understands her but is a good provider. They have cleaning help once a week, a condo in Florida. Phil never says an unkind word to Mildred, never asks, "Where were you, I have been calling you for hours. I needed a little help at the office." Phil comes home with a smile, kisses Mildred, sits down and listens to Mildred's morning on the telephone with the insurance company and "my Federation lunch, to which the Rabbi should have come but didn't"; "tonight is hamburgers because all the fish was gone when I got to Jewel's."

It doesn't take all that much for Mildred to become angry and involved with another crusade. "I'll show the insurance company sending me bills a week before the payment is due, threatening to cancel my insurance. I am going to stop that."

I can hear temperate Phil. "'Insurance companies want to get interest on your money so they ask for it ahead of time. All you have to do is not send it to them."

"I didn't, but what if."

"So the insurance company invests that money for a couple of weeks—that increases earnings for its stockholders. You want to get even, buy stock in International Assurance. Share in their ill-gotten gains."

Sad to say, when it comes to causes Mildred has absolutely no sense of humor. "Phil, you don't understand," and she is back to calling the State Department of Insurance. When Mildred starts calling the 800 numbers and writing letters and calling her girlfriends to write letters, or when she calls her sister, Sophie, "We will sue them!", that is when Phil takes their dog out for a walk.

When he comes back Phil sits himself in his easy chair, puts on his earphones, his Dave Brubeck tapes, shuts his eyes and eats an apple because tonight, supper will be late.

When Milly finishes her campaign against insurance companies that send threatening, past-due will-cancel letters to extract premium payments weeks before they are due from the unwary, the elderly, the gullible consumer, it is time for our Illinois primaries.

So she and Sophie back Charlie Palmer for State Representative because Charlie is going to provide increased state monies for our local schools. They do the whole thing. Knocking on doors, personal letters of endorsement to everyone in our B'nai Jacob congregation, signs on Thirtieth Street, neighborhood coffees. Thank God she didn't put signs on the synagogue lawn.

All day Mildred is rushing from one end of the district to the other arranging for Charlie Palmer to speak to PTA, volunteer firemen, senior citizens clubs. Rushing rushing. I can tell her car a mile away. She has "Win with Palmer" signs on both back doors and standing upright on the trunk lid.

Sophie solicits votes for Charlie Palmer from all who owe Sophie because she did for them and from some who simply want to be there when Charlie Palmer goes to Springfield.

As my husband, David—he does only estate law—says, "The road contractors, the health providers with state contracts, the ghost workers on the state payroll, they have to kick in.'"

I run into Mildred in front of City Hall. I am going in to pay my water bill and she is coming out with a handful of envelopes addressed to friends of Charles Palmer. When I see the envelopes I smile at Mildred. "Money is a politician's best friend."

Mildred answers, "We are taking pictures of the Palmer family with Charlie's golden retriever on his lap."

"That should lock up the campaign for you."

As David says, Charlie Palmer may be a smart lawyer—he is the junior partner of

Levine, Levine and Palmer—but he is one stupid politician. He goes on a TV forum with Herb Duncan, the incumbent. Herb asks Mr. Palmer, "How are you going to provide more state funds for local schools?"

Charlie answers, "Increase the income tax and cut back on the real estate taxes."

When this segment airs on the six o'clock news, which forty-three percent of Rockville's families view, when Charlie says "tax increase," the camera leaves Charlie, swings to the grinning Herb Duncan in his "I told you so" smile. That assures that Charlie Palmer will be back to doing real estate and divorce.

The only one in all of Rockville who is disturbed by Palmer's defeat is my mother. The day after election day she called me at six-thirty in the morning.

"Such a nice family man. You saw Charlie Palmer's picture in the paper." I am too sleepy to answer.

"Mildred and Sophie worked so hard on his campaign. Mildred brought Mr. Palmer to speak to our garden club."

"What did he say?"

"Say? He wanted real estate taxes reduced. That would benefit widows like me."

So I say, "For politicians there is always the next time."

Mom says, "Mildred's such a nice lady, always doing for others."

I answer Mom with, "You need anything?"

"No, thank you, Gloria. Thank you for asking."

Next, Mildred is off to the charities office to organize a daily calling system to monitor that half of her congregation that are shut-ins and widows living alone. The charities office is in downtown Rockville which, since the farm machinery companies have either downsized, departed or died, is not exactly a frequently visited part of town. Truthfully, even the three-hour free parking spots are mostly vacant. This is not exactly correct, because around the post office and the library there are still meters and meter maids.

That is where Mildred leaves her car parked for twenty-two minutes in a twenty minutes parking slot. As I come down the stairs of the post office, she is glaring at a parking ticket. I smile. "The ticket comes with an envelope. You can put the three dollars in and throw it into the collection box." Which Mildred does, then she asks me.

"So tell me, Gloria, how is your mother?"

I answer, "Deaf and ornery."

"We are organizing a calling system to check up on the live-alones."

"Don't bother to call my mother, she won't answer."

"How come?"

"She won't wear her hearing aid and without it . . ."

Mildred says, "I never thought of that." Gives me a wave. "Good to see you, Gloria. I have to go, got a Y board meeting," and she is off.

Mildred must have chosen to drive west on the two-lane River Road where there are few lights and the traffic does move faster than along Railroad Avenue. Anyway, it is on the River Road that she had a head-on crash with an oncoming truck. I heard the driver of the truck on the six o'clock news.

"I had no place to go. This car pulls out from behind a truck that it was following—hits me."

At the next morning's *shacharit* service, the Rabbi begins a special prayer because

SUCH A BEAUTIFUL SUNSET

Mildred Levine is not doing so well. That afternoon I go up to City Hospital. "Mrs. Levine has been transferred by helicopter to the University of Iowa hospital."

When a patient goes from Rockville to Iowa City to visit the professor, the specialist that our physicians refer to, that is never good news. At least hardly ever.

Three days later there are more at the B'nai Jacob for Mildred's funeral than come for Yom Kippur. There are more flowers than I have ever seen. Flowers from the "YW" board, from the Museum docents, from the Arts Association. Even my ninety-four-year-old mother insisted she come to the funeral. "Such a shame a young woman should die like that."

The Rabbi said, "A true woman of valor. Why did she have to leave us in the vigor of her life? A woman who had done so much for both our congregation and our community."

Sophie cried. Her father Old Ira just sat there. Phil, his arms around his two sons, looked like he was a hundred years old. Gray, bent. Can you blame him? One minute Mildred is a young, active woman. Four days later she is a corpse.

I am driving east on the River Road to take Mama home, and when I realize that, I say to Mama, "Right here is where Mildred had her accident." Mama says nothing. I turn and see she has her hearing aid in her handkerchief.

As Mama goes into her bedroom to take off her go-to-funeral, gray suit, she shouts at me. "Gloria, go make a glass of tea. The lemon is in the refrigerator. I left the sponge cake in the cupboard."

I make the tea, cut the cake. Mama comes out in her pink chenille robe, sits across the dining room table from me, looks out the sliding door at her hundred-sixty-year-old red and white oaks, at the birds at the feeders. We sit, sip tea. I say, "I will miss Mildred. She was a very good woman."

Mama says, "What did you say?"

I say, "Put in your hearing aid," and point to her ear. Mama puts in her hearing aid, pours me a second cup of tea. "Gloria, it was such a lovely day. Beautiful funeral, so many people. Phil and the boys and Ira should be proud of Mildred."

I can't understand my mother's reasoning. I am angry. What's to be proud of when Phil loses a wife, when Ira loses a daughter, Sophie a sister. So I ask, "Mama, why did Mildred have to die in a stupid automobile accident?"

Mama takes my hand. "Who knows why? But if you want my opinion, Mildred was like her mother. Everything she did, she did like Rachel. I remember for ten years I stood beside Rachel frying latkas for the sisterhood smorgasbord. For ten years I don't get a spot of oil on the stove, not a splatter on me. I don't even need an apron. I don't get a drop on me or on the stove. Poor Rachel has oil burns on her arms, on her hands." There is no sense talking with my mother, especially since she has taken out her hearing aid. I don't know why, but I shout in her ear, "It was an accident! A stupid accident! Why did Mildred have to die?"

My mother turns to me. "Look, Gloria. Such a beautiful sunset."

This from My Daughter

Our family had always united at bar mitzvahs, weddings and funerals. We were cousins, nieces and nephews, bound by birthdays and anniversaries. Now, since Aunt Sophie's death three years ago next October—may she rest in peace—to put it as nicely as I can, for me things between us are not as they were. I had seen other families split apart by inheritance: my son-in-law, Harry, hasn't spoken to his sister, Lilly, since their dear father passed away nine years ago next month. Harry's anger and disappointment I can almost understand. Still, Lilly *was* taking care of her dear father when he passed on. "I am sure Dad wanted me to have his CDs or he wouldn't have put my name on as joint owner," Lilly assured me. Harry of course, remembers, "Half for you, Harry, half for Lilly."

It isn't as if Harry needed the money, not that there was so much to divide after Lilly wheedled out her dad's power of attorney and began paying herself for "just the little extras" that her dad needed. Lilly didn't leave enough in that bank account to talk about. So their real quarrel was about what their poor departed father intended.

When my mother-in-law died, now I am going back almost fifty years, my dear husband Phil was in the Army. So his sister Bella got everything. I remember the letter she wrote to me.

> "Dearest Faye,
> I have put aside a couple of the embroidered table cloths for you."

The rest she took or threw out or sold. When Phil came home, even his school books were gone. From this Bella claimed to know nothing. That too I can almost forgive. A mother dies suddenly; Bella was only a girl of nineteen. No doubt she thought a daughter should have all of her family's silver and dishes. We got nothing but the two tablecloths and Bella's permission to copy, at our expense, their parents' and grandparents' wedding photos.

Sophie was my mother-in-law's youngest sister, my husband Phil's aunt. A lovely lady, a cultured lady. All her life she read novels: Galsworthy, Kipling and Pearl Buck, and short stories, too. On her bedside table she had a complete set of Maupassant in a pocket book edition.

Sophie lived all alone in Santa Monica on a street—where the only view was parked cars—in a 1930s, wooden, California bungalow, four rooms, one bath, a front porch, a back yard so small there was only room for a one-car garage and her four tomato plants.

My nephew, Arthur, the big shot attorney who lives in Studio City "so I can be close to my movie industry clients," sold Sophie's property for just a bit more than four hundred thousand; that after his fee. Imagine, an heir who takes an up-front fee from an aunt's estate. Then I didn't complain. Really, who was there to complain to? The self-serving executor, Arthur.

Where did Sophie get those millions? For thirty-eight years she was the private secretary to J.G. Torrance. Now she would be called an executive assistant. You may not remember, but once J.G. Torrance was a biggie distributor in the black and white art movie industry, scratchy French movies with illegible subtitles. From Jean Gabin's profile, J.G. made millions. My mother always said that J.G. and Sophie had a thing going. Me, I think J.G. was queer, a closet gay.

That Sophie spoke Italian helped when they imported Fellini's films, and her French with a Spanish accent was more than adequate. And speaking Yiddish didn't hurt her either because J.G. Torrance was just a fancy show biz name that Hershel Fein created for himself. Hershel may have given himself a wasp name but he still looked Jewish to me. I'll show you that fancy photo of him he gave Sophie when she retired. That was when Torrance Distributing was bought out by a Japanese company who lost their ass on that deal. Sophie got a very nice cash retirement package from J.G. J.G. moved to San Francisco, bought himself a condo penthouse with a view of the Bay Bridge.

Sophie invested in the stock of companies that had a significant market share, and in an up market she is a millionaire twice over. This money she leaves to Jewish museums in Israel, in New York City and here in Los Angeles. What Sophie does with her money I don't quarrel. Still, it would have been nice if maybe half had gone to the cousins and nephews and nieces, not that we are not comfortable, but spending inherited money is a wonderful way to remember a loved one. Every time I spend what Sophie did leave me I think of her.

There wasn't a *Simcha* that Phil and I did not invite Sophie, and after Phil died I continued to invite her to my grandchildren's bar mitzvahs and weddings. She always sat with me, between me and my daughters. I tell you she enjoyed. What did she send as gifts? Books, always books. Sophie was the last of the self-taught immigrant Jewish intellectuals, but mention Edith Wharton or Henry James or even John Dos Passos and Ernest Hemingway. "Nothing!"

She would give me her little smile. "But you, Faye, had the advantage of a university education," implying "I, Sophie, had to go to work when I was eighteen and when your folks needed money to pay for your tuition it was I who lent it to them." You can say this for Sophie, she never showed her money but if you know clothes and drawings it was there.

I remember the little Chanel suits that she wore with the Hermes scarfs. She looked good in her clothes but then the tall, thin ones who wear a size ten or twelve always do. Me? I have been fighting to stay in sixteens since I graduated college, and you know how long ago that is.

There wasn't a week that I didn't visit Sophie. For this I have no big thanks coming. Sophie was always very pleasant company and very generous too. She never let me leave without a little package. "Just a little something for you, Faye." French silver ice cream spoons, a Delft trivet, a Limoges demitasse.

We sat in her dark front room, she in her red velvet chair with the hand carved frame, me on the loveseat opposite her. The only light in the room was from the Art Deco torchier that stood behind her. Sophie only turned on the lamp when she read, although in her last years my aunt was more of a napper than a reader. When I said "Tanta Sophie, it is so dark I can hardly see you," she smiled. "Faye, it is cooler with the lights off."

"We could turn on the air conditioning."

She would answer, "Faye, I am getting forgetful," but didn't turn on the air conditioning.

I sat, looked at the drawings on the walls behind her: a Modigliani head, a couple of Morandi still lifes, a Villon head. Me, I think Sophie kept it so dim so as not to fade her drawings. Strange, but Sophie never did talk about art. Sophie wasn't a big collector, not like Edward G. Robinson or Paulette Goddard. Sophie knew all those old time movie stars.

She bought her drawings from the same dealer as they did, Louis Levine. He had his gallery in the Ambassador Hotel. Sophie paid so little for her drawings she didn't even insure them. So Arthur, the executor, figures no insurance records, no inventory, I'll keep them for myself. First off, he sold the cubist Villon. He doesn't tell a soul but I saw it in the Sotheby's sale catalog. I wait. After all, it's only a couple of thousand dollars. Maybe when he gets the proceeds he will share with the family. Or it could be Arthur was busy and he is waiting until he sells another couple of drawings and then he will call us together and make the distribution. He didn't.

Next he sells the Modigliani. So now he has almost twenty thousand dollars. I don't say anything; I just watch the sales. A year goes by, and he sells the two Morandis for a very good price. I know because I am the under-bidder on one, and so now he has more than fifty thousand dollars from Sophie's estate.

I see Arthur at my granddaughter's bat mitzvah. I take him aside, sit him down. When the band gets up for a drink I say to him, "Arthur, when are you going to distribute the proceeds from the sale of Sophie's drawings?" He smiles. "Aunt Faye, Sophie gave those to me. The drawings were a personal gift to me."

I smile. "Because you are an art lover?"

"No, for services rendered. After all, I drew Sophie's trusts and wills." To which I add, "For which you were amply compensated."

Arthur smiles his capped tooth smile. "But think of all the estate taxes I saved for the heirs."

"You say the drawings were yours?"

Arthur smiles again, takes another sip of his Evian water. "All mine, Auntie Faye."

"Sophie never told me that."

Arthur picks himself up, get himself another slice of the bat mitzvah cake and walks off.

The next day I call my sister, Yette, tell her, "I am going to call all the cousins, tell them what our dear nephew Arthur did. I am not going to let that shyster get away with not sharing. I could swear Sophie didn't know what she signed."

Yette says, "You got the energy, you fight with Arthur."

I speak to the cousins, to the nieces and nephews. What do I accomplish? Nothing. Because what happened is that now they won't talk to me. It's me they blame for starting the quarrel, not Arthur, who wouldn't share from the sale of the drawings. My own daughter, Harriet, won't help me get a little justice for our family. I asked her yesterday, "Come with me. We will go downtown, talk to your cousin, Arthur."

"I can't, Mama. You know I can't. You know Arthur sends me clients." Then she smile a little smile. "Mama, it's that kind of a world. Why don't you just forget, forgive?" And then my own daughter turns her back on me and walks off. Just like that.to me, her mother.

Florida Is Where the Sun Shines

After more than twenty years of tranquility at Aarons and Miller, not the most prestigious law firm in Rockville, but certainly well respected, perhaps a bit stodgy and slow in handling their estates, about what you would expect from a couple of old bachelors, Lew Miller had dissolved his partnership with Herman Aarons.

No one in Rockville ever thought of Lew Miller as contentious. Lew Miller, who attended Saturday services at B'nai Jacob more regularly than not, who took pro bono cases to the Court of Appeals with a shrug and a smile, who wore suspenders and a belt.

For me, Lew Miller was a cautious, concerned, middle-aged bachelor, who, while I swam away an hour at the Y fitness center, fought against his expanding belly on the body machines for exactly forty minutes, then walked one block to eat the same daily lunch, a salad, at the Horizon Pancake House.

A couple of weeks had gone by since I had read the two lines in the Rockville *Journal* that Lew Miller had asked for a review and accounting of all Aaron and Miller's joint assets. In that time I had seen Lew three, four times, mostly in the whirlpool where we had been visiting for years without achieving any level of confidence or intimacy. Lew spoke sports, the Chicago Bulls, and golf, and I gave him the morning report from the *shacharit* minyan at B'nai Jacob, who had died and who was sick and for whom we had said special prayers.

I am sitting beside Lew in the whirlpool doing my leg lifts. The gurgling water is warm; the jets are massaging my back. Miller has his eyes shut in what I take to be deep meditation, no doubt enjoying visions of Florida sunshine, because here in western Illinois in April it is raining sleet and hail, it is gray and thirty-three, a day to enjoy the indoors.

Lew opens his eyes, looks at the clock that guards us whirlpool addicts from reaching that stage of euphoria that requires an afternoon nap before going back to the office. Lew says to me, "Four more minutes, Al, then it's back to work."

So, I ask Lew, "What is with you and Herman?"

"Al, it is always the same thing. That *chazar* is into the good life at my expense."

Herman Aarons is even less of a big liver than Lew Miller. Ask at the charities office and they would describe Aarons's lifestyle as somewhere between cautious and frugal, very far from profligate. The only extravagance I could ascribe to Herman is the number and quality of his designer tennis outfits. Herman is a tall, thin, sixty-four-year-old, the most elegantly outfitted player of senior doubles at the Rockville Tennis Club.

For Lew Miller to call Herman Aarons a *chazar*, which in Yiddish is an unsavory, greedy person, is also out of character with Lew Miller's sedate manners and speech pattern.

So, I ask Lew, "What did Hermie do?"

"Do?" Lew looks around, and sure enough George Simmons, the dentist, is sitting in deep reverie beside me.

"Al, you want to know, I'll tell you but not here," and Lew sort of motions in George's direction. Given that opening I pursue.

"People ask me and maybe if I knew."

So Lew says, "Do you have to go back to your office?"

"Not quite yet."

"Come over to the Pancake House," and then he smiles, "and I'll tell you."

The restaurant is a two minute stroll up the street just beyond the south parking lot of the Y. In this freeze and drizzle I drive over.

Lew is seated at the table between the kitchen and the "Men's," a most undesirable corner. The only other lunchers are a youngish long-haired, jean-clad couple in a booth, playing footsie right there where we can see and not really caring either. He has his left hand above her knee to which she is paying no attention as she has not missed a forkful of her three berry pie. Lew pours vinegar and then oil, and then vinegar and oil again onto his romaine lettuce, looks up at me. "The way I eat you would think I would lose weight. Look at you, Al. French toast, strawberry sauce and you stay thin and you are as old as I am."

This requires an explanation. "It is the damn arthritis, Lew, all that constant inflammation just burns up the calories." I show him my swollen hands.

"I didn't know. Hurts?"

I nod.

"Al, life is a surprise and a disappointment. Lots I didn't know about Herman. I work in the same office with him for more than twenty years and I didn't know."

"Didn't know what?"

"I should have watched him. Watched the bills he was paying. Hermie was using our travel account for entertaining himself and Sarah Hirsh."

Sarah Hirsh is one of the more desirable, younger widows in our congregation. Sarah is of the country club, golf- and tennis-playing widows, with enough dollars to get her hair done at Chez Charles at a hundred dollars a cut and buy her clothes in Chicago at Neiman Marcus. My wife, Anne, has assured me, "Al, each one of her little black St. Johns suits is a thousand dollars." That I learned when I admired Sarah Hirsh's outfit at last month's Israel Bonds dinner. Anne's implication being that I should be delighted that *she* is a wife who shops in Rockville and saves the difference for the grandchildren. All this means that Sarah Hirsh could very well go Dutch treat or pay for Herman's company. With Herman's reputation for reluctance to part with a dollar that is what I would expect. To quote Anne again, "It's not that Herman doesn't like the girls; he is just too tight to support a wife."

So I ask Lew, "You say that Herman is spending your money to pursue Sarah Hirsh?"

"I say my money; Herman says our money. He treats our money as seed money because he tells me, 'Lew, once I marry Sarah and get the Hirsh family legal work, the money I spend is going to come back to us with interest.' I tried to explain to Herman. 'You can't use our money to take Sarah Hirsh to Palm Beach.' Al, Herman has an answer to everything. 'Believe me, Lew, I was developing Sarah as a future client. After tennis one day Sarah makes a point of telling me that John McCloud is so old that whenever she goes up to see him, he nods off while they are talking. Sarah told me, "Right there in front of me John dozes off and I never did find out if I had to file a gift tax or not."'"

Lew puts down his tea cup, turns to me. "Al, would you believe a story like that?"

I nod a "yes" again and cut my last slice of doused-in-strawberry-sauce French toast into bite-size segments. This gesture Lew Miller is watching with great intent.

I ask him, "You want some toast? Four slices is really more than I can eat."

Lew sighs in resignation. "You don't know how tired I get eating salads every day."

I transfer the toast onto the plate that had held the strawberry sauce and pass it over to Lew.

"Thank you, Al."

I wave my hand nonchalantly. "Enjoy."

The toast consumed, Lew confides, "I don't allow myself luxuries. I have to save for my old age. You know how much it costs in a nursing home?" And Lew answers his own question. "It's a hundred dollars a day right here in Rockville. I have no one to take care of me, not since my sister Ethel died."

I nod knowingly.

"Al, you are lucky. You have Anne, you have your children, your grandchildren."

Then the revelation. "Herman and I were going to retire, live together in Florida. A two-bedroom, two-bath, right on the Gulf. Herman could play tennis. I was going to take up fishing, and then Herman starts this running around with Sarah Hirsh and she, not a month after she finishes saying Kaddish"

"Is he seriously involved?"

"They flew to Atlanta to visit her son, the economist."

I say, "If Herman is spending, it sounds serious to me."

"There is nothing Herman can't afford as long as it is our partnership monies and not his money."

I try to lighten the accusations.

"I don't understand why Herman didn't use his own money. He could get frequent flyer miles if he used his own credit card."

That is my oblique reference to Herman's reputation for careful planning before spending anything more than twenty dollars.

"That's what I said to Herman. And he says to me, 'I was getting us a very important client. You have to spend money to make money.' Imagine Herman spending. This from Herman who made his fortune by not spending."

Lew has waved to the waitress, points to my empty coffee cup.

"I wish I could drink coffee. I love coffee." Lew pours himself his second cup of decaffeinated tea, sips. "Herman is going to retire, leave the firm, leave me. Tell me, Al, you really don't believe that Hermie intended to pay back what he took from our joint account?"

That one I don't answer. I drink my coffee, shrug my shoulders into a maybe.

"Herman is going to move into Sarah's gulf-view condo on Sanibel Island."

"Are they going to get married?"

"Not only married. Herman has told Sarah that they would become Florida citizens. Tell me, Al, you are an accountant. How is Sarah going to become a valued client if she and Herman are going to live in Florida?"

To that, I answer, "Thanks for lunch."

Herman retired, left Rockville. Lew dropped his lawsuit, not that he ever told me. I heard that from Margie Lesser, my wife Anne's cousin who just took early retirement from Rockville Junior College. Anne told me that for the past two months Margie and Lew have been going together very seriously and are even planning a trip to visit Sarah and Herman on Sanibel, which explains why now, in the whirlpool, Lew talks of the Chicago Bulls and retirement to Florida.

"Al, you know how much it costs to live in a gulfside Sanibel condo?"

I don't answer.

"Herman has it all figured."

When Lew tells me how much I do agree. "That is a lot of money, Lew."

I shut my eyes, lower myself into the whirlpool so that only my head is out of the warm, gurgling water. Lew pokes me, whispers in my ear. "Al, it's less than a nursing home."

I sigh, "That is true, Lew. That is true."

My Uncle, Melvin, the Conversationalist

My uncle, Melvin Stern, my mother's oldest brother, lived alone in what had been Grandpa and Grandma's home, a two-bedroom, one-bath, wooden bungalow in the west end, which is the least desirable address in Rockville. This northwest crescent of Rockville is sequestered, surrounded by the beltline going north and south. The west end is the oldest part of town, settled years before zoning so that even on days of full sunshine the shadows of a truck terminal and a plumbing warehouse wrap the Stern bungalow in shades of gray.

When there were other homes on Seventh Avenue, there was a pocket playground: a bit of greenery, a tree and a bench for the older residents, a basketball hoop for the teens. When the residents left, so did the park. Today the street department has on deposit a brown hill of de-icer waiting for when the arctic snow storms descend into the Mississippi River Valley.

My sister, Amy, who is a weather person, more accurately a Ph.D. in Astrophysics, told me that the first freeze in western Illinois, statistically speaking, is about the 25th of October, which was the very day the ice and snow descended on Rockville, when Melvin, on his way to get his *New York Times*, slipped down his front steps, broke his hip. The next day my uncle had his hip replaced and one week later was incarcerated by my mother into Rockville Manor for his rehab and convalescence, because, "Melvin, I can't run up and back and anyway, you shouldn't be home all alone. You know how busy Ellen is with her studies."

"Manor" is a euphemism for this nursing home destined to become a motel when it loses its license. Sunday morning my Uncle Mel is in the day room, the room at the end of the hall with a view of the parking lot, with four plastic arm chairs and a muted television tuned to black and white American Movie Classics. Melvin is reading *The New York Times* while Tarzan and Jane cavort in darkest Africa.

Melvin is dressed in khaki trousers and an only a little too tight University of Illinois sweatshirt. A very old one from when the Indian chief in full feather headdress was a permissible symbol of alumni loyalty. Melvin looks good; his brown hair is combed, his face ruddy. My uncle focuses his china blue eyes, the Stern eyes like Mama's, Grandma's and mine, on me, smiles, points me to sit down beside him.

"Ellen, don't you have anything better to do." This was not a question.

"It's the end of the quarter."

"Already?" I nod a yes. "This is your time to study. So how does it feel to be a senior? Still doing art history?"

All that a one-breath sentence. My uncle, retired for almost twenty years, is still busy-busy, occupied, hurrying, afraid to waste a moment. When our uncle visits us and Mom's television program is on, he will read a novel. He is still reading the novelists of the 50s, Wright Morris, Steinbeck, Bellows. When he is about to leave, which is as soon as *Biography* comes on, he kisses my mother's forehead, says, "Becky, you are wonderful," starts for the door. "I have things to do."

"Melvin, relax, stay. I'll make a cup of tea. I made some mandelbrot."

"Got to go."

When Melvin has driven off in his Volvo, Mom sighs, "My poor brother. He doesn't know how to enjoy. All that money, he never spends a penny on himself. He hasn't bought a new suit in twenty years."

I would describe Melvin Stern's wardrobe as classic 70s, like early Ralph Lauren. Khaki or gray trousers, blue oxford cloth shirts so soft as only home washing and no starching and loving, caring ironing can produce. Uncle Mel whistles while he irons, tunes from the fifties, forties and thirties, non-recognizable to me but they do sound cheery. "Ellen, we danced to those songs. Me and my shadow, my sweet adorable you, you made me love you, I didn't want to do it. Ask your mother. I took her dancing."

"Uncle Mel took you dancing?"

"Once, when I went out to visit him at Ft. Riley. We danced at the officer's club."

"Becky, it wasn't the officer's club. It was a special Purim party at Hotel Warren in downtown Manhattan."

"Ellen, your Uncle Mel never forgets. Me, I have other things on my head. I had a family to raise, my parents to look after."

Then my mother, who is not a smiler or a laugher, chuckles. "And I had to sort of keep an eye on Melvin so he wouldn't get into bad company."

My uncle Mel emphasized, "I was never a problem."

"In high school you and Sarah Freid were a hot item."

My uncle grins. "On Saturday night we went to the movies. I bought Sarah a chocolate ice cream cone, walked her home; we sat in the front room, the room the Freids never used, on a green velour couch until her father, Izzy, yelled down, 'Mel, go home. Sarah, go to bed.'"

"You are lucky Izzy Freid liked you."

"He would have liked for me and Sarah to get married and go into his business. Imagine me in Freid's Cleaning and Alterations. Suits made to measure."

"Rose Fried sewed beautifully."

"So what happened, Uncle Mel. Tell me."

"I went to college, joined the ROTC, the war came and I was in Italy, then France."

My mother finishes, "After all those sophisticated, educated Italian and French women, American girls, down home Jewish Rockville girls, weren't good enough for him."

Those were the Saturday night dialogues I recall from when I was seven or eight. When Mom and Melvin drank tea and lemon and dipped mandelbrot into the tea before they crunched and swallowed and returned to old times in Rockville, before the war when children respected their parents, when Grandpa was just starting out in the scrap yard. "Only in America. You start as a junkman, you end up a steel pipe distributor, and Melvin, you could have gone into the business with us." That's my dad and mom. "You have to work for the government, fly all over Europe." My uncle would smile, put his finger over his mouth. "Becky, what you said . . ." My uncle joked about his trips to Europe. "I went over to see my tailor." "What did you bring me?" "For you, Ellen, you like chocolate." I still remember the brand, dark, Cote D'Or, made-in-Belgium chocolate.

When Uncle Melvin came home from his trips, he was usually gone just about a month, my mother would survey him. "You have lost weight." Uncle Mel would smile and never explain beyond, "There are still places on God's earth where there is not enough to eat."

The only clue to where Uncle Melvin went on his trips was the paintings that would appear on his bedroom walls, went on to cover the living room, the dining room and even the kitchen. Mom and I usually spent our Friday afternoons at Melvin's, whether he was at home or away, cleaning up, making beds. There are two bedrooms; Melvin's with the view of his tomato patch, the pots of petunias on the back stairs and under the pin oak, the bench Melvin made in high school shop for Grandma to sit on while she read *The Forward*, the Yiddish daily newspaper that came by mail. The second bedroom, the guest room, dark in the morning sunlight and no brighter at noon with only the view of the back of the truck terminal, was used by Melvin's "friends" to whom we were never introduced, whom we cleaned up after, when they left.

Those were the days when smoking was still tolerated, when cigarettes were cheap and plentiful, so that it took days of open windows and bottles of Air Wick to restore the guest room to a faint odor of exotic foreign tobaccos.

When I was about thirteen, Uncle Mel quit traveling, his friends no longer came to Rockville, and the paintings marked "Fragile" no longer arrived from Europe. That was when my Uncle Melvin took a job with the Department of Defense as a contract specialist. The furthest he traveled was across the Mississippi River to his desk on Arsenal Island, his lunch at the Officer's Club or the golf club if he was playing his twice-a-week eighteen holes.

As ever, Melvin continued to eat his Friday night Sabbath dinner with us. He came with a bouquet of flowers for Mom which she always described as she cut their stems, spread the flowers artfully into her ceramic bowl, the gray one with the Japanese motif she had made at the community center. "The flowers you get from Grace are always half dead."

Uncle Mel put his arms around Mom. "Grace is a single mother." Mother would sigh. "So how is Grace making it?"

"It takes time, Becky. It's not easy for her."

My uncle reached for the crutches at his left foot. I am up to help him. He leans on the aluminum arm of the chair, puts one crutch under his right arm, the other under his left. Right foot held up, we are off, Melvin on his crutches, I behind him, down the hall back to his room.

"It should be clean by now. I don't like sitting out there in full view." He smiles. "Too many questions after you leave. 'Your daughter? She looks like you.'"

I offer, "It's the Stern eyes."

"Ellen, if you are going to become a curator you will need 'a good eye.'" I nod agreement.

We are seated in Uncle Mel's private room. One bed, two straight back, tan plastic side chairs. Uncle Mel has shut the door, not fully, but sufficiently to keep out the vagrant looks of his wandering neighbors. "The nurse knocks before she comes in."

My uncle sits in the chair closest to the newly made hospital bed where he can reach the call cords, the TV controls, the lifeline of nursing care. I sit with my back to the window that looks out on the visitor's parking lot.

"Your mom told me you were applying for positions on the east coast." Then I get avuncular advice. "There are lots of opportunities in Iowa."

I nod, but don't explain.

"You haven't told me where you want to go."

"I was going to tell you." I pause. "Uncle Melvin, it's because of you that I became interested in art history."

Uncle Mel is quick to answer. "That I know. You were the only one in the family who ever asked me, 'What is that painting about?' 'Who did that water color?' You were a very perceptive child."

I smile. "I was lucky to have you to talk to."

"I only gave you books and catalogs to read. You learned by yourself."

I smile broadly. "You were my role model."

My uncle is embarrassed. "I was glad I had you to talk art with."

"Weren't there others?"

My uncle stops. "In Rockville, after the war, only Grace, but she got married. That didn't work out for me or Grace. She ended up arranging flowers instead of painting. She was a very talented painter. She should have gone to art school in New York or Chicago."

"Why didn't you and Grace . . . ?"

My uncle smiles. "I was a travelling man who was off to make a better world. By the time I wanted to settle down all the girls I knew were grandmothers." He stops. I say nothing. He continues.

"Later on maybe it was like your mama said. It happened so fast I found myself without a wife. I accepted that. I could see that life alone could be simpler and it was more tranquil, less of a challenge. When I broke my hip I realized that even old bachelors have to get their lives in order for . . ."

I interrupt, "For when, Uncle Melvin?"

"For when we must all dispose of our worldly goods. You want my old Volvo?"

I smile, "If you insist."

"I'll drive it until next spring. I get a new car every eleven years." My uncle is triumphant. "We solved that, Ellen, just the two of us."

I get up, look at my wrist watch.

"Not so fast, Ellen. I want to talk to you about my art collection and the art library."

"You know how much your library is worth?"

"I am not selling it at auction unless you don't want it."

"I'll take it, but not until I have a home of my own."

"Ellen, don't wait too long to get married, settle down, acquire my art library."

"You are the one to give advice."

"Early marriage is better. Look at your mama and papa, and my dad and mother, your grandparents." My uncle chuckles, "I had to go to college. I had to become an officer and a gentleman. I had to learn languages. One thing just led to another and here I am."

"Your French is still good."

"Not as good as it was. My Yiddish is very good. When you have the time I will tell you some stories about Paris and Munich and Bucharest after the war."

"Were you ever in Amsterdam?"

My uncle sighs. "Yes, after the war, before Anne Frank became a Broadway play. Imagine, a play about Jews being killed. And not one word is said against the Germans who organized their murder." As always, when my uncle speaks of the evil of the Holocaust he hesitates, flushes, searches for words and repeats himself. "Imagine a government organized to kill its own citizens. Imagine that." My uncle has used "imagine" three times. He shakes his head in disbelief.

I ask him, "What made you think of collecting paintings?"

My uncle sighs. "I knew the Germans had looted from the museums and from the

MY UNCLE, MELVIN, THE CONVERSATIONALIST

Jewish families. The Russians and the Americans then took the Matisses, Picassos, Monets and Degas . . . other important works from the Germans. This I understood." My uncle shut his Stern blue eyes, opened them, looked at me. "Ellen, what started me collecting was what I saw after the war. Paintings, prints that families had held on to, clung to. I thought of these pieces of colored canvas and paper as an antidote to death and destruction. A bit of joy, a bit of beauty, like an amulet against the angels of death. These household treasures were being sold for just a few dollars. Sometimes to buy food, sometimes to buy American cigarettes." My uncle chuckled, "With American cigarettes you became a merchant, a trader. You could buy anything. In a way I became a trader. I didn't smoke, so I traded cigarettes for paintings. That is how I got the Tryon 'Spaniels' and the Puvis De Chavannes 'A Wooded Glen'."

I ask, "Fantin Latour 'Flowers' and the Carrière 'Landscape'?"

"The only thing I paid dollars for was Steinlen drawings of cats. I missed my cat, Winky. When I brought Winky into my room, the minute I left your grandmother would open the window and put Winky outside. Mama fed Winky, but never in the house."

"I didn't know you had a cat."

"Had him for sixteen years. From the time I was four until my first summer camp at Ft. Riley. When I was a junior in college I came home and Mama told me Winky died in his sleep. We buried him in the back yard. That is where the tomato plants are now. Mama always protected her only son. 'Moishe,' my mother called me Moishe. That's Yiddish for Moses, like in the Bible."

"That I know."

My uncle, now silent, is back into his youth, playing tackle for Rockville High School, unloading Grandpa's junk wagons. Freezing or sweating as he sorts scrap.

"Uncle Melvin?"

"Yes, Ellen?"

"Why did you start collecting nineteenth century French art?"

"I have thought of that once or twice." My uncle grins. "As always there are several reasons. Never just one. With one reason you can never know the truth. I learned that from a Russian philosopher that I escorted across . . ."

To keep my uncle directed, I ask, "Why Carrière? Why a French Symbolist who painted landscape and portraits as soft gray or brown shadows?"

"It was the serenity, the tranquility. That's what I wanted on my walls in Rockville."

"Melvin, you had a good eye."

"I had a larcenous heart. I knew for what I paid I would make a handsome profit."

"You weren't that clever. If you had bought Picasso and Matisse you would have been a millionaire many times over."

My uncle sighs, "The more property, the more thievery."

I get up, look at my wrist watch.

"Thank you for coming, Ellen; we had nice talk. When are you coming back?"

"For Mom's birthday in January. I promised her."

"Ellen." I stand above my sitting uncle. He beckons and whispers, "You will help me with the collection?"

"You know I will."

"Good, it's all yours."

"You can't; it's too valuable."

"You will know what to do with it." I begin to cry. "Why are you crying?"

"You enjoy your paintings so much."

My uncle smiles. "You don't get the collection until I die or become incompetent, whichever comes first." I kiss his forehead. My uncle whispers, "Thank you, Ellen. You have taken . . ." He doesn't complete his thought. He has returned to wherever he goes when he shuts his eyes and a tear appears.

Each Day a Gift from God

The internist, Gerald Silver's boy Donald, had been assuring without being authoritarian. "Mr. Kahn, from insomnia you don't die. You don't sleep one night, you'll sleep better the next night. Mr. Kahn, many of my patients your age have trouble sleeping. We'll talk again in three months."

On the second visit, Fred Kahn again introduced the subject of sleep. "I have too many bad nights. I am so tired the next day. Could I have a little something to get me through the night?"

"Mr. Kahn, the pills are worse than not sleeping. Count sheep, read, enjoy, sleep later in the morning. I'll see you in six months."

"But I am still working."

Dr. Silver was out the door.

Fred Kahn counted sheep, but quickly shifted to counting dollars invested in mortgage bonds. Fred Kahn fell asleep, awoke an hour later. One thirty-two on the digital clock whose numbers lit his way to the bathroom. Up and urinate, up and urinate, that's what Dr. Silver called fragmented sleep problems. One sleepless hour, another counting and recounting, that's two hours of useless "head work." Up to three hours of wakefulness brought a marginal loss of function for Fred Kahn. More than three hours of sleep deprivation and Fred was totally dysfunctional. Tired, stupid, irritable. Once or twice he even lost his appetite, the rarest of events for Fred Kahn. Up to three hours of insomnia was manageable if Fred could have a twenty-minute nap around four. Then he could stay up to watch the ten o'clock weather and news.

This week, Fred's days and nights had become more difficult, more disturbed, less tolerable. This Fred Kahn attributed to his wife Fern, "Feigele," "Little Bird," a name he spoke with endearment in Yiddish. In California, visiting their oldest daughter Harriet, Fern called every evening.

"You doing okay, Fred?"

"Doing fine!"

Alone in Rockville was better than being with Charlie, Harriet's husband, in Studio City. Harriet married Charlie, let Harriet talk to him. My oldest daughter didn't take my advice, that's her problem. The only way I can get along with my son-in-law is by avoidance. For me Charlie doesn't exist. How Fern tolerates Charlie is beyond me.

"Believe me, Fred," she says. "I spend very little time with Charlie. Harriet and I do girl things. We had a wonderful time just shopping. I bought three pairs of shoes at Nordstrom's. Wait until you see them. California styles are years ahead of what we see in western Illinois."

That night for Fred was like the night before and the night before that. Fred awoke at one, into the bathroom, a drink of water, and he was awake. Fern's and his wedding picture on the bureau caught his mind. He replayed their honeymoon. New York during World War II, crowded with soldiers, sailors on leave. Fifty years ago . . . no, forty-nine. Next year would be fifty years. Fred fell sleep in the joyous sweat of sexual discovery, awoke in an hour, turned over and slept and slept until five-thirty.

On his way downtown to Kahn Investments, Fred stopped, picked up a *Wall Street Journal*. In his car he read the market report. *Embezzler pleads guilty in exchange for three years of community service. Market drifting in spite of decline in interest rates. Low consumer confidence blamed for slow retail sales.*

Fred edged his Cadillac ever so carefully into "reserved," waved at the parking attendant.

"Nice day, Mr. Kahn."

"Lovely, Emmie, just lovely."

Kahn Investments, two rooms in a 1912 office building, an answering machine, a copier and stark Scandinavian furniture, softened by McGarrell and Lester Johnson water colors: there was none of the elegance that Fred's earnings could provide. Suite 501 was furnished only with sufficient quality to sustain the confidence of Kahn Investments' clients, mostly middle-aged dentists. Subdued décor was designed not to evoke the thought that "Fred gets his fees up front—market goes up, market goes down, Fred gets his with no risk—it's our retirements at risk while Fred buys fancy furniture."

The recorded messages were routine: a bond dealer with a dubious issue that was difficult to sell . . . a client, Martin Brook, who wished to be called as soon as possible.

Fred hung up his chambray sport coat, turned to the obituaries. Robert Muldoon was dead at seventy. New Zealand Prime Minister Muldoon had been an accountant who had become finance minister, prime minister. Fred Kahn was an accountant who had become an investment counselor, had made more money than anyone in Rockville could imagine. Made it all by himself by saving and investing. An up market in real estate had helped, as had an extra fee here and there from an obliging broker. Setting up retirement plans for dentists was not like being prime minister of New Zealand. For me, Fred Kahn, Polish immigrant boy who had worked his way through the University of Illinois selling Fuller Brushes . . . for me, I did very well. I'll bet everyone in Rockville will be surprised by what Fern and the kids inherit when I go. The thoughts of Muldoon, dead in New Zealand, returned Fred to Poland.

The month before we left Sczuczyn, my mother visited the cemetery every day. There I was, a five-year-old, holding onto my mother, she crying at my grandmother's grave. We entered the cemetery through a door within a door. Just inside was a green caretaker's cottage. It must have been ivy-covered. I remember. Go back and see what has become of your birthplace. Go back and see the Jewish cemetery that is now a potato field?

Four of the offices on the fifth floor were occupied by the middle-aged and "young-old" who had not made it up and out to suburban office space. Of the four, one was an attorney to whom Fred only said "good morning." The second was an insurance agent who had long ago given up on selling Fred on annuities. The third was a writer who wrote advertising for sustenance and short stories (as yet unpublished) as penance for having sold out to the market demands of cereals and automobiles. The fourth was Don Heller, retiree and nine years younger than Fred, also a member of B'nai Jacob, western Illinois' only conservative Jewish congregation, who between morning prayers and his eleven-o'clock golf foursome at the Bluffs Country Club, read the *Wall Street Journal*, sipped the coffee he ground and brewed, while he listened to a radio symphony hour in the office next door to Fred's.

As Fred picked up the phone, Don, tall, thin, rosy-faced by sun and Finlandia vodka, came through the office door that Fred had left open to the hall.

"Busy?"

"Not too bad."

Look at Don. Plaid golf trousers, violet golf shirt, early retirement is where it's at.

"Fred, at morning services . . . Harry Stern and Bill Marcus were on the sick list. We prayed for their speedy recovery. Imagine, both of your neighbors, one on either side of you, sick!"

"Thanks for telling me. I'll look in on them when I go home."

"I think Bill is in the hospital. Take a little time off. Enjoy." Don grinned. "Try to come to morning services on Tisha B'Av. We need a minyan."

"What's the matter with the regulars?"

"Sick and dead. You come to services you get one free round at the Bluffs, courtesy of Don Heller."

"I'll see."

"Try."

"I will. I am not retired yet."

"I know clients come first."

Don left without a goodbye.

Martin Brook picked up the phone on the first ring. "Dr. Brook."

"Fred Kahn."

"Fred, everybody in town will know soon enough, I may as well tell you. Marge and I are getting a divorce. Marge wants a home of her own and," a pause, "a cash settlement. Can you free up two hundred thousand for me?"

"Do-able. How soon before you need the money?"

"Two, three months."

"No problem."

"Fred, thank you."

There were no more problems. Fred charted the stock that would be required to free Margaret Brook from her upper middle class struggle, ate the lunch he had been eating for twenty-three years: a green salad, two Rye Krisp, two cups of tea and lemon.

At two, Fred typed his letter to Dr. Martin Brook.

> "6 August
> Per your telephone instructions I have made the necessary arrangements to meet your demands.
> Sincerely, Fred Kahn"

At three, Fred was at home: a two-story board and batten painted earth-tone gray, a color Fern had chosen to keep their home in touch with the hundred-year-old red and white oaks that surrounded it.

Harry Stern's was the Roman brick ranch on the left. Bill Marcus's the white Colonial on the right. All had been built to order thirty years ago when lots on Oak Street in

Rockville's first naturally wooded subdivision had been marketed. After a mild heart attack, Harry Stern had sold his scrap yard to the first bidder. As Harry described himself, "I am not a man who needs to work. I have enough to do." Harry read science fiction and the morning Rockville *Republican*, walked in the mall or along the Mississippi, traveled to visit his children.

When Fred came to see him at the hospital, cheerful Harry said, "Thank God it was only an angina attack. For a moment I thought I had a heart attack." He chuckled. "The food is getting better at Union Hospital. I had two desserts on Sunday. A rice pudding and an apricot Jello."

Fred listened, offered, "More competition makes for better service, even in hospitals."

"Thanks for coming over, Fred."

"Call me if you need me."

Fred drove home, took his one plastic garbage pail to the street, went to see Bill Marcus. Bill sat in a green velour swivel arm chair. Both hands rested on a cane. Fred sat closest to the ear in which Bill wore his invisible electronic hearing aid.

"Don tells me you were hospitalized over the weekend. Why didn't you call me?"

"I wasn't really in the hospital. I was in the rehab center. I was in for my sciatica. Just couldn't stand the pain anymore. Dora was going to Chicago for her sister, so I said, 'Dora, drive me to the rehab center.' Look at me! Can't walk without a cane."

"You are looking good, Bill."

"Not so good, Fred. No more golf. The next time I get a sciatica flare it's two weeks flat on my back."

"Did you know Harry was in the hospital?"

"The Rabbi told me. He came to visit."

Fred said, "Two with one blow. You and Harry, that's getting close to old Fred."

"After seventy, you praise God for each day. Every day . . ."

"You need anything?"

"Dora is home."

"Where is she? I'll say hello."

"She went to her exercise class. I'm all comfy." Bill pointed to his portable telephone, his remote television control, his Rockville afternoon *Dispatch*. "When is Fern coming home?"

"Monday next."

"How about coming over Friday night? Dora won't mind. You shouldn't be alone for Shabbas dinner. How come you don't go to California?"

"Clients' needs, Bill. Clients come first."

"See you Friday?"

Fred ate his 1,000-calorie dinner, a Lean Cuisine cannoli, a low-fat blueberry yogurt with two slices of three-grain bread, finished his *New York Times*. He fell asleep with *Institutional Investor*.

At twelve-o-six he awoke with a start. He was back into his Polish childhood. He and his mother were going through the door within a door to stand beside a fresh grave. From that image, Fred retreated to the visions of his grandmother's last illness. He saw the succulent blood-filled leeches on his grandmother's shaven head. Fred got up, poured four ounces of chilled chardonnay down his throat and returned to more pleasant, rural Poland. In this segment he sat beside his square-bearded grandfather as he drove his matched gray mares to the post office, to the butcher. Fred awoke to the hiss that the red-forged horseshoe made when dropped into a bucket of water. It was five-twenty.

Fred shaved, dressed, read *Barron's Financial Weekly*, made notes of which stocks to watch, arrived at the prayer house at ten to seven. He was number ten. The tenth man necessary to make the minyan so that the Bible lessons could be read.

On this fast day of mourning, the Rabbi sat in the darkened room, read from Isaiah 22: "Thus said the Lord, *Let not the wise man glory in his wisdom. Let not the strong man glory in his strength. Let not the rich man glory in his riches.*"

As the tradition demanded, the ten left the service in silence. Fred drove to his office without turning on the morning news, forgot to stop for his *Wall Street Journal* and *Times*. Fred sat at his desk, began his weekly letter to his children, Mildred and Jonah and Harriet.

> "Dear Children,
> Today for the first time in too many years I went to services to recall the destruction of the Temple in 586 B.C.E. by the Babylonians and in 70 C.E. by the Romans. . . ."

Don Heller was knocking on the door. Fred rose and opened the door. Don shook his hand. "Thank you for coming. We needed you."

"So I saw, only ten."

"Ten is all we need. Come again, Fred. We need you."

Fred finished the letter with, "Through a friendly dealer in Chicago, I have been able to secure some very well-rated muni bonds at a good price." Fred made three copies, mailed them on the way to his noon swim.

That night, as Poirot faded into Art Deco London, the phone rang. It was Fern. "You getting along all right?"

"Fine, just fine."

"You don't sound so good."

"It's not me, it's Harry. He spent the weekend at Union Hospital. His angina . . ." Fred paused.

"So is he better?"

"Much better."

"So?"

"Bill had a sciatica attack."

"That's not life-threatening."

"You are right."

"So why do you sound so down?"

"Who is down?"

"I'll be home on the two thirty-five. You won't forget?"

"Not me, Feigele. I'll be there."

In bed, looking for sleep, Fred read the *Times* financial section. "As reward for cooperating with the U.S. attorney for the Southern District, the sentence of convicted embezzler I.P. Willis has been reduced to thirty months of community service."

Fred turned to his bedside notebook, wrote, "Form Kahn Foundation." "Time to review wills."

Fred, asleep, again with his grandfather. "Fred, you have not been sleeping well."
"No, Grandpa, not too well."
"You have much to worry you."
"Enough, Papa. It's a down market."
"Fred, you don't have to finish everything you started. Enjoy. Take Feigele for a trip. You haven't seen your son Jonah in almost a year. It's time to rest, Fred."
"Grandpa . . ."

Fred awoke, turned on the reading light, read, "Proposed tax changes will benefit only the very rich, says Senator Bradley."
Fred began to add his real estate assets to his stocks to his bonds to his savings . . . fell back into his fragmented sleep patterns.

Murder Comes to the Leghorns

Phil Gruber, police chief of Sanibel, Florida, called as my wife, Millie, and I were finishing breakfast. Phil and I go back twenty years to our C.I.C. days in Brussels.

"Benny, I want to talk."

"Anything special?"

"See you at Beachview at two p.m."

Beachview at two p.m. was between deserted and abandoned. The only ones on the golf course were Phil and me and a pileated woodpecker. Ten years after our retirement from the C.I.C., Phil is thinner and looks taller. I, with my arthritis, am now three inches shorter and look squatter. Every time I see Phil, I admire his military created square shoulders. Although we are both the same age and height, about five foot ten inches, Phil certainly seems the younger, in his ironed tan cotton trousers, white golf shirt with the yellow Brooks Brothers sheep embroidered on his left pocket. What we share in appearance is our hair, too short to be stylish, and our shoes, too polished to be anything but retired military types.

At the first tee Phil puts his beeper in the pull cart, drives two hundred yards down the center. I drive ten yards further but to the right. We score a couple of fives on the par four. The sky has no haze, the fairways are mowed and our talk is about restaurants, on Sanibel and beyond.

"Benny, where have you taken Millie for dinner? I found a great fish place on Fort Myers Beach, but you have to get there before five-thirty. No reservations."

I attribute Phil's current and recurrent food knowledge—"The Hilton has a great prime rib dinner on the early bird"—to his never having married, never having acquired hypertension or high cholesterol. At sixty-two, Phil is still jogging and eating French fries while I am swimming and dieting. At the fifth hole, Phil sits me down on the bench beside the water tank, hands me a paper cup half full of water.

"Benny, I need your help. You are the only one I can turn to. I was hoping I wouldn't have to ask you, but. . ." Phil's brown eyes look over my shoulders. I turn. Not a soul. "You are the only one I can trust not to laugh at me."

"Tell me."

"Marina Fattini, the Italian fashion designer, has a cottage on the Gulf Road, just a little four bedroom with guest house, pool and double garage. Benny, if you spend more than a million and a half for a little island retreat, well, you are entitled to your privacy and adequate police protection. Fattini is here every year sketching her next year's collection; from October to January. She comes with a cook, a butler and a gardener. This year she has her mother too. Fattini keeps white Leghorns, egg-laying chickens, twenty-thirty white hens. She lets the chickens run free. There are no close neighbors, so the chickens are no problem."

"So?"

"The chickens have been dying."

"Oh?"

"Murdered, one a week, usually on a Friday. Yes, four dead. The veterinary college at University of Florida at Gainesville has confirmed it. Murdered. Each chicken had its neck wrung the same way, from right to left, and then was laid out at the back door entry to the kitchen. Four dead chickens this month, and Marina Fattini is not taking it at all well."

All I can ask is, "What the hell is she doing raising chickens on a million-dollar Gulf front lot?"

"Fattini is half-way vegetarian. She will only eat eggs from happy, free-range hens that deposit their eggs in nest boxes lined by virgin sea oats. At night, the Mercedes stands outside to rust in the fog and the hens roost in the rafters of the garage, listening to classical music. Fattini wants the murderer caught, the deaths stopped, or she will speak to the mayor."

"So stake out the barnyard. Send out one of your detectives on Friday with a pair of binoculars to catch the culprit."

"I tried, Benny. Both detectives laughed at me, told me to call Dr. Crow, the veterinarian at the endangered animal rehab clinic. I was desperate, Benny, so I did. You know what he told me?"

"Tell me."

"Well, Leghorns are not endangered. But if I can stop the murderer before he kills the Leghorn, if the bird is injured, Dr. Crow will try to save her life."

I didn't answer. It surely was no laughing matter to Fattini to be without eggs from her happy hens. What were old friends for? If Phil didn't need me, he wouldn't have asked me.

"Okay," I said.

"I knew I could count on you, Benny." Phil shook my hand. "Solve this case, I'll take you and Millie to dinner at Truffles."

"When?"

"Anytime you say."

I went home, repeated the story to Millie.

"Get your binoculars, Benny. I'll iron your safari jacket. You'll look real good with it, guarding the Fattini chicken coop."

"Millie, this is no laughing matter. You are talking of the protein supply of one of the world's leading fashion designers. Fattini of Milan is a household name among the European cognoscenti."

"Only if they are size fourteen or larger. Marina Fattini designs for the mature figure." With that dismissal, Millie went back to cooking cranberry compote.

"Phil is going to call Marina, tell her I'm coming."

"I can just hear him. . . . 'I'm sending my best investigator. Lieutenant Colonel Benjamin Roone, Retired, has an outstanding record of successful apprehensions of chicken murderers.' You know what, Benny? I'm going to give the story to the *Island Reporter*. 'Lieutenant Colonel Benjamin Roone to investigate Leghorn murders.'"

"You can't do that, Millie. It's a secret mission."

"You have twenty-four hours, Colonel Roone. After that . . ."

I put my arms around Millie, kissed her neck and ear, whispered, "Jealous?"

"Just don't let Marina put her hands on your beautiful body."

At four-thirty p.m. the next Friday afternoon, I parked in the shade of Australian pines at the turnaround of the Fattini cottage: four thousand two hundred square feet of Victorian contemporary, above two two-car garages that were separated by a work room. Two outside stairs, trimmed in sky blue, rose from beyond the garages to the porch that faced the road.

I stood at the back door, tried to peer through the red and gold of the cubist, geometric stained glass. Nothing. I rang. The door was opened by a woman forty . . . or thirty . . . or fifty. Taller than I, jeans and gray sweatshirt, sleeves cut to above the elbows. Dark curly hair, close to her head, a boy cut or scissor cut by Sassoon. Millie would know. A gray hair, singular, on the sculptured forelock. Her orthodontically correct teeth smiled, antiseptically white. They couldn't distract from the deep lines that accented the corners of her blue-green eyes. The eyes lit up, then went out, lit again.

I told her, "I'm Benny Roone. Chief Gruber's friend."

"Thank you for coming. Do come in. I'm Marina. Please sit down."

The English without distinctive accent, certainly not Italian. We sat in a room of rattan furniture, I in a rocker, Marina on a loveseat upholstered in Liberty chintz; between us a square, glass-topped coffee table of rattan. In the corner behind me, between a west and north window, was a drafting table and chair, lit by a four-tube industrial fluorescent fixture. To the left a dining room and beyond a tiled floor of what surely had to be the kitchen.

"It was good of Chief Gruber to send you."

"Phil is concerned about your losses." My sympathy was restrained to show we cared, but if we couldn't stop this heinous crime wave, the serial murders of Marina Fattini's Leghorns—well, at least we had tried.

"Mr. Roone, Phil tells me you were in the C.I.C."

I noticed the "Phil."

"It was some years ago."

"Phil told me you were in Brussels together. Our company has a boutique on Avenue Louise."

"My wife told me."

"I would love to meet your wife. Phil has told me so much about her. Millie, isn't it?"

"Miriam, actually. Millie is her 'in the family' name."

"Mine, too."

From the dining room a clatter of glasses. Then the door fully filled by a silhouette, wide and square, of a woman's figure no more than five foot two or three. With the light behind her, I couldn't see her face.

"Mama, come in. I want you to meet Colonel Gruber's friend."

The barefoot figure moved quickly toward me, reached down to shake my hand. She had the same blue-green eyes, the same short hair, but it was entirely gray and her teeth were nicotine-browned. She wore a square sack dress of black silk whose two pleats began above her bosom, fell loosely to hide her waist and disappear down the skirt. It was the buttons that I noticed as she came nearer. Buttons from the Peter Pan collar to the hem, black with a red-combed rooster, his yellow tail feathers over his back, etched into each one-inch button. Her eyes reviewed me like a white-gloved Army inspector. I must have been found at least acceptable, for she asked, "Would you like a glass of tea? I have some made."

"Yes, thank you."

The rising inflection, a glass and not a cup; middle European usage. Her accent was not Italian, perhaps Czech-Polish. Marina rose.

I followed Marina into the dining room. Her mother, already in the kitchen, returned with a Japanese tea service; pot, cups, saucers and lemon quarters. We sat around a glass-topped, tan-enameled wrought-aluminum table, the standard dining room set developers provided in furnished Gulf condominiums. Behind me was a sideboard painted to match the table. On the sideboard, two crystal candlesticks. To my right, a screened front porch. The sliding door opened to the Gulf surf, the gulls, the skimmers taking off, circling, returning to the low-tide sand beach. All could be seen if not heard from the dining room. The house had been set back, well behind the sea oats, and another row of ornamental Australian pines had been planted to provide a great shaded front lawn on which twenty Leghorns fed in galvanized waterers and feeders. The Leghorns' white feathers, red combs, yellow beaks moved with determined precision, eating to make eggs from happy hens for Marina Fattini.

"Mrs. Fattini?"

The mother turned towards me. She had been pouring a second cup of tea for Marina.

"Mrs. Schneider—the family name is Schneider. My name is Anna."

"You found the dead chickens?"

"Yes . . ."

"Always on Friday, wasn't it?"

"Yes . . ."

I turned to Marina. "It was you who called the police?"

"I didn't know what to do with the dead chickens."

"I told Miriam I could make chicken soup. Why waste a chicken? Boiled chicken makes a fine chicken salad with my vinaigrette dressing."

The enthusiasm for food no doubt contributed to Mrs. Schneider's bulk. Marina was annoyed; a chicken soup on Friday, chicken salad on Saturday, a subject her mother had no doubt introduced before.

"Mama, I don't eat chicken. I don't eat meat. You know how I feel about that."

Anna turned to me. "Phil Gruber is married?"

A question that direct required a couple moments of hum-m-m before the answer. "No."

"Mama, please! It was Mama who called Phil all the other times."

"Such a nice man. We talked, we drank tea."

"Mama, Colonel Roone is here to find out who killed my laying hens."

"Colonel Roone, more tea?"

"No."

"Chief Gruber, such a nice man. Every time I called, he came."

"Can I see where you found the dead chickens?"

"I found them by the back when I was coming back from my walk on the beach. Come, I'll show you."

I followed Anna down the back steps into the shade. "What time was that?"

"One or two o'clock."

That was the time there were the fewest beach strollers. Siesta time . . .

"Always the same?"

"Yes." Anna looked at me. "You want to know why an old lady should be walking on the beach by herself? I saw the look in you. From police, I know!"

"I'm not the police."

"Is the same thing. In France, Italy, during the war. Police—they all chased Jews."

"This is the United States, Mrs. Schneider. Here, even the police can be Jewish. Phil Gruber is Jewish. I'm Jewish."

"I know . . . Phil told me. Come . . ."

Anna led me to two folding chairs still wearing the red Walgreen labels. Plastic and aluminum tubing set up to face the sunset. Mama drew a blue pack of French Gauloises cigarettes from her left pocket, a Zippo lighter from her right.

"Come, we'll sit; soon the sun will set. Sometimes Miriam comes with me, not often. Every evening I sit here and say my prayers. 'Blessed be our God who has brought us to this place and this time.' And I say, 'Anna, here you are an old lady. You have everything you want. A big business, offices in Milan, boutiques in Brussels, Florence, even Harrods in London carries my designs.'

"I was the original Designs by Marina. I named the business after Miriam. We were living in Florence—me a widow with a six-year-old girl and a nine-year-old son. My son Edward runs our factories in Milan. My husband, may he rest in peace, was killed in the French army. A volunteer, no less, in the French Foreign Legion. Jews without citizenship could only serve in the Legion. How we survived is another story. . . . "

Anna smoked deeply, spit the tobacco from her third unfiltered cigarette. She held the cigarette between her forefinger and thumb in the Polish-Russian manner.

"You want to know why I was on the beach. I'll tell you. I can't smoke in the house. I walk on the beach to smoke after breakfast, after lunch, after supper. I can't smoke in my own home. You want to know who killed the chickens?"

"No, I know that, Mrs. Schneider. I don't think there will be any more mysterious deaths in your poultry."

We sat until the sun, copper and russet, no longer reflected from the clouds onto the Gulf. Anna Schneider smoked and I said, "I'll tell Phil Gruber to close the case."

I told Millie the story. "What was I to do? 'Mrs. Schneider, I arrest you for the murder of four Leghorns.' All she wanted was to have chicken soup for Friday night dinner."

"Why didn't she just cook up the chicken and eat it?"

"Marina is a vegetarian. Anna didn't want to offend her, her only daughter."

"So why did she murder chicken two, three and four?"

"Anna was lonely. The Schneiders really don't know anyone on Sanibel. Phil is such a nice man, Anna calls Phil Gruber to report the death of the Leghorns. Phil comes out, they talk, have tea. Maybe Anna would like to see Phil married to Miriam. You know, a Jewish mother never gives up hope—to marry a daughter."

"I didn"t need my mother to catch you."

"I know why Phil called me. He didn't want to fall into the clutches of matrimony!" That with a broad smile and my arms around Millie.

"I don't see you suffering, Colonel Roone."

Proof of Ownership

Aaron Drobner's face was that close to me that I could see his gray hair coming through the cold sore under his right nostril. At almost eighty, Aaron Drobner was still a very big man. Thick neck, shoulders bent forward, he ran towards me. I expected the usual after-morning's-services greeting. A benign handshake and the formalized "good morning." Aaron gave me, "I thought you would be here at services; that's what the Rabbi told me, that you have been coming to the morning service to take your Uncle Al's place, to help out so there would be a minyan for those who have to say Kaddish. That's what we need Benny, young people like you to come back to Rockville."

To which I nodded an agreement, continued to unwrap the thongs of my phylacteries.

"Benny, come into the library with me."

At seven-thirty in the morning the library of Congregation Bethel is the quietest place in Rockville. The light has yet to rise into the one west window. The worshipers have left for their breakfast. We sit, Aaron across the library table from me in a 1950 covert cloth single-breasted suit, white shirt and string tie. It's the same Aaron I left when I went off on a ROTC scholarship to State. Maybe a bit more bent forward but no less verbal.

"You remember my brother, Gerry?"

I say yes, although all I can get out of my cardex is the two Drobners, Gerry, the taller, thinner one and Aaron the shorter, heavier one. Gerry and Aaron the two bachelor brothers. Mrs. Sadie Drobner's unmarried sons. Every Saturday morning at services, Mrs. Drobner, short, square, in a black hat and, veil sitting in the next to last row on the left. Gerry on one side, Aaron on the other. I remembered what my mother had said, "For Sadie Drobner there was no girl good enough for her sons," so they went to college and had big government jobs. Sadie was one mother who wouldn't take the chance of a daughter-in-law.

Aaron whispers, "Benny, can you hear me?"

"Yes, I can hear you."

"My own hearing is not so good."

"So talk louder."

"Someone will hear us."

"We can go outside, go for a walk. That way you get complete security." With this advice I give Aaron my best professional grin.

"I know that you know from these things."

"From what things?"

"From Army things—from security."

To Aaron's confidence, I nod agreement.

"Benny, you know Gerry died four months ago."

"I know."

"I am going through his things. You should see the house. Sixty years of accumulation; letters, papers. . . ."

"If you need help, call the Jewish Federation office."

"I don't need help! I need advice."

"Advice is cheap."

"Benny, you were in the Army." I nod. "You knew things that shouldn't be talked about."

"I had a security clearance."

"I knew I could trust you."

"With what, Aaron?"

"With what Gerry did."

"Whatever he did no longer counts. Gerry is dead."

Aaron gets up from the library table, skates to the door, opens the door, looks right and left, returns to sit beside me. "Benny, you know Gerry was always interested in art. Before he became an architect he had studied art history. When Gerry was in the Army . . . how shall I put it . . . he sent back paintings. These paintings are what worry me."

"What's to worry about paintings?"

"What am I going to do with them?"

"What did Gerry do with them?"

"Gerry do? Gerry had four hanging in his bedroom, one on top of the other. He wouldn't get the room painted. Our house hasn't been painted in thirty years."

"Take down the paintings, paint the room. Gerry won't stop you now."

"Benny, you didn't understand. There are paintings in the attic wrapped in blankets. When Gerry was alive he would go up there, look at them."

"So what is the problem?"

"I want to sell the paintings."

"So what is stopping you?"

"Benny," here Aaron whispers in my ear, "there are no records of what the paintings cost, no records of where they came from. I am the only one who knows."

"Knows what, Aaron?"

"That's why I need your advice, Benny. Gerry sent them home from Europe. I think most came from when he was in Austria after the war."

"What did Gerry do in the war?"

"He was a lieutenant in the field artillery." Aaron takes out an ID photo of a young Gerald B. Drobner, A.U.S. "Gerry sent all the paintings home to Mama. I can't sell the paintings without a proof of ownership. That's what the auction company told me."

"What can I do for you, Aaron?"

"Maybe you could find out, maybe find out who served with Gerry in the same company. Maybe a buddy he trusted; find out how Gerry got the paintings."

"It's possible. There is the Army record center in St. Louis. It may be possible, but that could take months. By the time you find whoever you are looking for, that's months and months more and very costly. There is no assurance they would even remember. Aaron, that is forty-five years ago."

"What am I to do? I want to sell the house."

"You could put the paintings into storage."

"I'm not paying good money for storing Gerry's paintings!"

So I sigh. "I guess I didn't do you any good."

"You did me good, Benny. I have to decide what to do is all. I have to decide what to do with paintings I can't sell."

"You can always give them away. Give them to a museum."

"I tried, but I don't want to spend money for an appraiser, it costs thousands to get an appraisal, the museum won't pay for an appraisal—until they know what they are getting."

"So hire an appraiser. I am sure the director will recommend somebody."

"Sure, from Chicago—he wants expenses. Seventy-five dollars an hour and more if I get a written appraisal. That's just for a look and an opinion of what to do."

"I'll tell you what, Aaron, my Uncle Al knows all about paintings. I'll tell my Uncle Al and one morning after services we'll go home with you."

Aaron writes down his address, 101 Broadway, on the back of my business card, which I drop in the box of accumulated Sotheby's and Christie's art auction catalogs that await the return of my Uncle Al and Aunt Marsha from Sanibel, Florida.

Ten days later, my uncle calls me from Pikestown, Missouri. "Benny, we'll be home tomorrow at three o'clock. Anything new and exciting?"

"Windy, cold and clear."

"That's what I told Marsha. How cold?"

"Twenty-eight."

"That's cold for a poor old arthritic." My uncle is neither old or poor but he is evidently arthritic.

The next afternoon my uncle arrives three minutes late and minus his usual, "So what is new and exciting in downtown Rockville?"

Al walks into his office, reaches for the Tylenol he keeps in the bottom drawer, swallows two without water and sits down very carefully. "Anybody looking for me?"

"Aaron Drobner."

"He wants to rent space?"

"No, he wants . . . " My Uncle Al doesn't let me finish. That's one of Al's impatiences. He finishes sentences.

"What does Aaron want?"

"Aaron wants you to look at some paintings for him. Gerry sent them home when he was in the Army."

"He was in Austria as part of the American occupation forces."

"How do you know?"

"Gerry used to talk art to me. Gerry knew quite a lot about Jewish art and Judaica. More than I did, but I knew more about the Vienna Secession Painters. Although Gerry did learn quite a lot in Vienna."

My uncle considers modesty in regard to his learning and achievement as almost but not quite a false virtue. The only one that my Uncle Al is humble with is his God.

"Hang in there, Benny. I'll take over for you on Monday."

Monday morning I am downtown and my Uncle Al is at services. He comes in. "I promised Aaron we would be at his home tomorrow after services."

"Why me?"

"He values your military expertise."

"With paintings he needs you, not me."

"Benny, Aaron is eighty years old. He is all alone, he needs us."

***

101 Broadway is in the close-to-downtown renewal district. The Victorian mansions had been built as family homes, became three-plexes and now were converting to bed and breakfasts for the tourists attracted to gamble on Rockville's Mississippi Riverboats.

In 1910 when Sam Drobner brought his Sadie to the Queen Anne two-story—four bedrooms and one bath upstairs—101 Broadway was an address of distinction. A tribute to Sam's rise from immigrant boy to downtown merchant. The location was central, ideal, walk to the synagogue, walk to the downtown and only across Seventh Avenue to the grade school. Now the Broadway district has begun to show only meager benefits of City Hall-funded campaigns to fix up, paint up, clean up the "Historic District."

"When decorative outdoor lighting is installed on this block, Aaron's house will go up another eleven percent in value," Al says.

I nod agreement to my uncle's real estate appraisal, which he conveys to me as we go up the three steps onto the porch of 101 Broadway. Aaron has the door open. We enter a hall and living room with ten-foot ceilings, the windows narrow, the wallpaper dingy. The walnut woodwork, the staircase, the wainscoting . . . that's craftsmanship. The red-wool-carpeted stairs don't creak. The leaded glass chandelier and the button electrical switches must be original. Aaron notices my appreciation of the house's qualities. "Benny, wait until you see the furniture my mother had, all original. In the living room, it's all Belter."

Aaron opens Gerry's bedroom door; a brass bed, an oak bureau, under the one window a Mission walnut library table half of which is covered by a 1960 model Halliburton shortwave receiver tuned to Europe. The desk chair is 1990 Herman Miller upholstered in a shade of purple.

"Gerry admired good design." Aaron is the presenter, to which my uncle adds, ". . . and fine art."

My uncle stands at the window, his hands on either side of the glass-covered thin brown frame. "Aaron, this Schiele drawing has to be reframed, rematted. The longer you wait the more it will cost you for conservation, let alone what the drawing will lose in value."

"How much do you think that will cost?"

"Could be three hundred dollars or more to remove the stains." If my uncle is not completely sure, his manner is so overwhelmingly positive that there is hardly a soul left in Rockville who will question him. Certainly it isn't Aaron Drobner.

"Three hundred dollars to fix up a drawing?"

My uncle has his Swiss Army knife out. The frame is face down on the library table, the back is off. "As I thought . . . the acid backing is eating up the drawing"

Aaron looks confused. My Uncle Al looks triumphant. "Look, there is a collection stamp on the drawing . . . an OH in a Star of David." My uncle has drawings number two, three and four on the library table. All have lost their backing.

"All from the same collection. OH, from a Jewish collection or why would there be a Star of David?"

"If you like Aaron, I'll send the drawings off to a fine paper conservator in Chicago."

Aaron snaps his fingers, "Twelve hundred just like that."

My uncle again eases Aaron's hesitation. "Aaron, the drawings could be worth give or take a couple of hundred thousand."

"Each?"

"No, all four."

Aaron doesn't answer.

"Let's get to the paintings in the attic. How many did you say there were?"

"Four."

Up the stairs to the attic. Pink fiber glass insulation had been stapled to the unfinished sloping roof, into the dormers and between the floor slats. On this gray cold March day, the attic is warm and dry. The four paintings dressed in olive drab lean on the walls. My uncle unwraps the World War II blanket from a painting in a gilded frame. He is examining the back of the painting. I lean over, read the label.

"Galerie Oscar Hoffman, Vienna."

My Uncle Al completes with, "Look at the label—that is it, OH, Oscar Hoffman." My uncle turns the picture to the light. I read the label aloud: "'*Portrait of an Old Jew*, by Isador Kaufmann, Vienna.'"

"A very fine example of late Nineteenth Century Realism," my uncle adds.

"Benny, you can read German." Aaron is impressed.

"Why do you think I asked Benny to come?" Uncle Al responds.

"Al, tell me how much do you think it's worth?"

"Sotheby's in New York would know."

"You know, you won't tell me."

"Aaron, Jewish art is not my specialty."

This first admission of any deficiency in my uncle's art expertise does not stop his "Should be more than a hundred thousand dollars."

This disclosure activates Aaron to bring painting number two to my uncle. "Another Kaufmann with the same gallery label." Number three is also Kaufmann's. With number four, my Uncle Al stands and expounds, "Oscar Hoffman knew Jewish art! A Lazar Kristin synagogue scene. Look at the old man's fur hat, his beard, his prayer shawl. The children's side locks. Good, but not as good as Kaufmann."

"How much is it worth, Al? Tell me."

"Less than the Kaufmanns. You know why, because Kristin was Kaufmann's pupil but Kristin was overly influenced by the French impressionists. He lost the purity of color that collectors of Realism desire. The Kristin could bring thirty-five to fifty thousand at an auction. I doubt it would bring a penny more."

Aaron is adding aloud. "A half of a million dollars in paintings in my attic." With the same breath Aaron is talking about letters. "Benny, I have some letters from Oscar Hoffman from Vienna, in German. Can you read them to me? Gerry saved everything."

I sit in Gerry's bedroom in the Herman Miller chair, my back to the one window reading the letters.

"What do they say, Benny?"

"The first one is from Mr. Hoffman's daughter, a Mrs. Dora Hoffman Gershon. She thanks your brother for having bought the four Schieles. For sending her two thousand dollars."

"When was that letter written, Benny?"

"In May of 1950."

"That was just before Gerry was called up for duty in the Korean War. He left in June or July of 1950. That may explain the other, letters that Mrs. Gershon wrote."

"What did she say, Benny?"

"Mrs. Gershon would like to get paid for the three Kaufmanns and the Kristin."

"How much?"

"From what I make of it, Gerry promised to find a buyer, inform the Hoffmans of the best price he could receive, and if they found that acceptable, sell the paintings and send the money to Vienna. Mrs. Gershon definitely wants and needs the money to reopen her father's gallery."

"Huh . . ." is what Aaron hums.

"Mrs. Gershon is very disturbed that Gerry doesn't answer her letters. She wrote once a month from June of 1950 to October of 1951."

I put the envelopes back in their order, 1950-1951, replace the rubber band. My uncle sits on the bed, the four Schieles spread out beside him. Aaron is on the table dangling his feet.

"Thanks, Benny."

My uncle is up. "Aaron, I have to go."

"Thanks, Al. Al, would you call Sotheby's for me? Help me sell the paintings? I think I would like to sell the paintings as soon as possible."

"I don't think so, Aaron. Time to go, Benny."

On the drive back to our office, I sit beside my silent uncle. A state he has maintained since we left Aaron Drobner, a most unnatural condition for him. I try cheerful conversation. "You liked the paintings?"

"Best of their type I have ever seen, but of course I have seen very few. Mostly in auction catalogs."

That was my entry. "Why wouldn't you help Aaron with Sotheby's? You have been doing business with Sotheby's for thirty years."

"I have had enough of Aaron for one day. Not once did Aaron say, 'Let's try to contact Mrs. Gershon,' not once." The delayed answer was, for Al, very precise.

"Maybe Gerry paid for the paintings. Mrs. Gershon quit writing those complaining letters."

"I'll tell you, Benny, I didn't want to hurt Aaron. Gerry was back home by August of 1951 and if he had paid for the paintings, I know Gerry, he would have saved the proof. A letter, a check, something."

"How do you know so much about Gerry Drobner? That was decades ago."

"I was in the same reserve unit."

Then my uncle begins to laugh.

"What's so funny?"

"Without proof of ownership, I'll bet Aaron can't get the paintings sold. He may have to look for Mrs. Gershon yet."

"You know what I don't understand? Al, Gerry appreciated fine art. Why would he have kept such fine paintings wrapped up in the attic?"

"You are the investigator, Benny. Not me."

Benny Roone and the Catalog Raisonné

My Uncle Al, the founder of the Roone Companies, benefactor to the arts, donor of the Roone Art Library, the most complete collection of the Catalogs Raisonné of the Twentieth Century's European graphic artists. Bonnard, Braque, Chagall, Klee, Masereel, Moore, Picasso, Morandi and more.

Why and how my Uncle Al collected German, French and Italian art catalogs is another story.

My father's explanation: "Al's buying, buying! Books! Poring over catalogs—that is a genetically transmitted disease. Your Uncle Al got that from our mother Rebecca. Thank God, I didn't inherit that."

I nod, agree, never dispute. Do not tell my father, "It's more complex than that, Papa. If Uncle Al has the 'Cache Syndrome' or as you call it Goncourt's disease, he would not have donated his collection to the Rockville Library. He would have kept his books with him until he died."

I hear my father's answer. "Benny, the only reason your uncle Al gives away his books is so he can start another collection." Then Dad goes right on "Benny, I bought the finest example of Philippine basketry I have ever seen in a little hole in the wall shop in Brussels."

Collecting is evidently a family disease that I have so far escaped. This success I attribute to the insistence of my wife, Millie.

"Colonel Roone, if you can't pack it in a shoe box, we are not taking it on our next move."

That's how I got my collection of French paratroop beret emblems from Washington, D. C., to Rockville. In a shoe box that fits in my desk drawer.

As soon as we are settled in our home on the Rockville bluff (four bedrooms, two baths, one fireplace in the basement family room), which we bought at one third the price for a comparable colonial brick in Maryland or Virginia suburbs, my Uncle Al and Aunt Marsha go off to Paris, London, leave me to be the property manager for the Roone Companies. My uncle's only instruction:

In property management, Monday mornings are the worst. Tuesday and Wednesday are so-so. On Thursday you will have time to write your "Memoirs of the C.I.C."

The Monday morning calls are the accumulation of our tenants' frustrations of not being able to reach us on Saturday or Sunday.

"The air conditioning is out. In our lease it says . . ."

Then, I recall my Uncle Al's soothing. . . .

"Mr. Abernathy, the air conditioning only goes out in the summer. The heat only goes out in the winter."

Mr. Abernathy's responds, "I know, the roof only leaks when it rains."

"Not to worry, Mr. Abernathy. All will be repaired before you open your store at noon."

"Uncle Al, how can you be so sure, so positive? What if we can't get a new part?"

"Details my boy, details."

With that, my Uncle Al returns to reading his art book sale catalog, *The New Yorker* or *The New York Times*.

It must be my military training, but when I answer the phones, I say, "Yes sir, yes sir, we will do the best we can." The response from the tenants is, "Thank you."

These shorter more efficient conversations result in a time savings that gives me the opportunity to write the Monday morning letter to my uncle in London.

> "Dear Uncle Al - Aunt Marsha,
> Really getting along very well. No new crisis.
> Sincerely (Regards from Millie),
> BR"

The call at nine twelve was not from a tenant. Too hesitant, not irate enough.

"Mr. Roone?"

"Benjamin Roone here."

"Alan Roone, please."

"Mr. Alan Roone is out of the country."

"I spoke to Mr. Roone some three weeks ago about his collection of art books. This is Cyrus Morgan. I am the chief of the Rockville Library."

"Yes."

"As you no doubt know, Mr. Roone retained the rights to borrow the books he so generously donated to our special collection."

"Yes."

"Is there any possibility that Mr. Roone has borrowed a Kirchner catalog and the Vitali Morandi catalog?"

"Not in the past three weeks he hasn't."

"Are you quite sure?"

"He left Rockville twenty-three days ago."

"Huh . . ." Pause. "Then the catalogs are missing."

"Perhaps they were misplaced."

"Not in the special collections room. To be honest with you, Colonel Roone, we have so little on the special collection shelves, the catalogs could not get lost there. For the most part it's your uncle's collection, and I have already searched. I am afraid the most valuable of our catalogs have disappeared, gone."

"When did you first notice the loss?"

"Our librarian Mrs. West is very disturbed."

"When did you discover the books to be missing?"

"About ten minutes ago. I went through all the shelves before I thought of calling you. I really didn't think that your uncle would borrow a book without telling Mrs. West, but then he is getting on, and Mrs. West says, that when your uncle starts reading, he is, shall we say, distracted. Friday afternoon was a particularly busy time at the library, vacations and all. Mrs. West was the only one on duty and when Mrs. West opened the special collections room this morning, she noticed the catalogs were gone from the display. The display honoring your uncle. Calling your uncle was my idea, my last hope. I don't know how I can ever explain this disappearance to your uncle."

"My uncle won't be home for four weeks. Perhaps in that time—"

"What am I going to tell your uncle?"

"I would suggest, the truth."

"There is no way to ever replace those catalogs, even if I could get the twenty-two hundred dollars, I doubt if I could get the replacements here in a month. That's when the official opening reception will be for the Roone Special Collection."

"Does my uncle know of your plans?"

"The invitations haven't gone out yet. Colonel Roone, your uncle told me all about your career in the Counter Intelligence Corps. Would you help me?"

"Monday morning is particularly difficult here. I am all alone. I could come by this afternoon about three, when our secretary comes."

"I would certainly appreciate that."

It's three blocks from the Roone Building to the library, a turn-of-the-century gray brick square, whose classic Greek entry is surrounded by a wheel chair ramp to a self-opening double glass door still guarded by sandstone pillars.

The check in-check out books desk is up a flight of wooden stairs. To the right, the reference desk, to the left the catalogs of the collection. Behind them the shelved fiction.

Mr. Morgan, who until now I had only seen as a flitter—a flitter between the video tapes on the lower floor and the second-floor staff dining room—had left instructions at the reference desk.

"Colonel Roone."

"*Mr.* Roone."

"Mr. Morgan is waiting for you in his office. I'll show you."

Between the fiction shelves and the periodical room, a half-glass opaque door. The reference librarian knocked, walked in.

Jonathan C. Morgan, all thirty years of him, leaned on the glass-topped walnut desk. Morgan, in blue long-sleeved shirt, blue knit tie in place, behind blue jacketed folders between which rolls of blueprints were stacked one above the other.

Morgan rose, offered me the straight-back walnut side chair. "So good of you to come, Colonel Roone."

"Benny will do."

"Mrs. West is waiting for us."

It was down the stairs to the lower level—children and video to the left, special collections to the right.

Mrs. West sat behind a small desk, behind a computer. Mrs. West, a woman of a certain age. A short thin muscular fitness freak, probably road training four times a week for her next month's Senior Olympic medals.

Mrs. West rose, shook my hand so that I could share her vigor.

"If I leave the room, Mr. Morgan comes down. That's how important the security of the Roone collection is to us. I was here all the time the room was open to the public. The minute I found the catalogs missing we closed the collection to the public."

"What are your hours?"

"Ordinarily? Two-thirty to four-thirty, Monday, Wednesday and Friday."

"Are you getting lots of visitors?"

"They sign in."

The daybook was an old looseleaf. Three, four names a day.

"Mostly students from the community college. Our computer and theirs are linked. The Art History teacher at Rockville Community, Mr. Horn, has assigned readings in the catalogs."

"Anyone else coming in here?"

"Only the staff. We have to go through this room to get to our book-packing room."

Through another half-glass door—packing tables, rolls of brown wrapping paper, corrugated cartons, tape—then an outside door into the parking lot.

"Very convenient for us. We take the books to the post office. The special request books that we are returning or lending to other libraries."

"Who does that?"

"The library apprentices. We have two apprentices from the University of Iowa. One is helping us with the Roone collection. The other is into children's lit."

On the tables waiting to be packed, single books, piled books, computerized addressed cards on each. At the end, packed, stacked books ready for the post office, labels affixed. Each hand-stamped on the brown wrapper paper, "Media Mail."

"When does the mail go out?"

"This afternoon about four-thirty. Adria will take the packages over to the post office on her way home."

"Is Adria the apprentice for the Roone collection?"

"Yes."

The packed books, addressed, University of Illinois; Evanston Public Library; University of Chicago; the last under all, University of Iowa Art Library, hold for A. Mackee, personal.

"Adria's last name is Mackee?"

"How did you know?"

"Elementary, Mr. Morgan."

Morgan did not chuckle, nor did he smile.

"May I open the package addressed to the University of Iowa?"

"Of course."

The large blade on my Hoffritz Swiss Army knife cut the wrapping paper, exposed the two thin Kirchner catalogs and the red cover of *L'Opera grafica di Morandi*.

"You have your catalogs back."

"How did you know?"

"To know what to take, you either must know value or have a special need—special need in Rockville—for Kirchner, a German expressionist, and Morandi, an Italian etcher who started as a surrealist. That would be very unlikely. It had to be someone who knew value, rarity and had opportunity. The first thing an art librarian learns is what things cost. Adria was doing your valuation for insurance."

"Colonel Roone, that's incredible. How do you know that?"

"Benny, will do me."

"Mr. Roone, how do you know that?"

"The ARS LIBRI catalog—volumes one and two, Modern Art, lists all the current prices. The catalog is on Mrs. West's desk."

"I hadn't noticed."

"Here, '*E. L. Kirchner Dube-Hevnig Ann Marie dos Graphische Werke Munchen Prestil* Verlag 1967, 2 Volumes' . . . fifteen hundred dollars."

"I hadn't realized you were an authority on art catalogs."

I laughed. "No, I just read my uncle's mail—follow his instruction. My uncle is now buying American prints catalogs. My uncle's parting words: 'Benny, if there is a copy of Peter Morse's catalog of John Sloan prints, call ARS LIBRI—order it.' Sloan comes after Kirchner so I read catalogs."

"Amazing."

I laughed again. "Not amazing—lucky, another hour, the books go out to the post office. You would never have recovered them."

West was perplexed. I could see Morgan was irritated by my laugh.

"What is so funny, Mr. Roone?"

"The library was going to pay for the transportation of stolen property. Such a lovely simple idea. I'll have to tell this one to my old boss, General Brennan."

"Let the drama continue."

"Is that Shakespeare, Mr. Roone?"

"I did agriculture in college."

"Mrs. West, that quote does sound familiar."

"If you like, I'll ask Miss Peters in reference."

"No need." I re-taped the package, replaced the package where it had been, on the bottom. "Let's just sit and wait, it's almost four-thirty."

Adria Mackee was tall, with blond hair to her shoulders, too tight a white T-shirt, jean skirt and Nike walking shoes. Twenty-three or -four, creases beginning around her eyes. I looked up from the table. She had gone into the packing room, shut the door.

"What are you waiting for, Mr. Roone?"

Morgan was not a patient man.

"Waiting for Adria to put the books into the mail bag."

"Now, Mr. Roone."

I followed Morgan into the packing room.

"Please sit down, Miss Mackee."

Mr. Morgan was in charge. He pointed to the only walnut chair in the packing room.

"Sit down, Miss Mackee."

Miss Mackee sat. Mrs. West emptied the mail bag onto the packing table, one package at a time I slit the tape of the rewrapped package, presented the wrapper to Miss Mackee.

Mr. Morgan began, "Adria, you were mailing the books to yourself."

"To the library. I was answering a request for an inter-library loan."

Mrs. West went to the computer. "Adria is quite correct. The request came in Friday morning."

"Is it usual for you to take two catalogs from a display exhibit?"

"I was going to have the catalogs back before the dedication ceremony."

"If you got caught, you had an excuse—and if not, you could erase the computer entries. The catalogs are yours. No way to trace them to you, is there Adria?"

Adria began to sob into her handkerchief. Morgan was silent. I gave the retrieved catalogs to Mrs. West.

"Call me if you need me."

I walked up the stairs, out the door into the western Illinois Mississippi Valley ninety-degree heat and ninety-percent humidity. My uncle was right. No one today built like they did in 1912. Without air conditioning, the Roone building was cool. The light on the telephone blinked red.

"This is Peggy in four eleven. Our air conditioner just went out."

"Peggy, this is Benny Roone. I'll be right there."

"Thank you, Mr. Roone."

Apple Pie and Eva Sundine

Last year to bring the prosperity of tourism to western Illinois, our legislature authorized Illinois cities along the Mississippi to license river boat gambling. Paddle wheelers, showboats, "Ol' Man River," "Summertime," Al Jolson singing "Mammy." Huck Finn theme parks with slots and blackjack. Dinner with banjo pickers, then roulette and slots for dessert. Blues singers on the anchored dinner barges and floating casinos.

> Join the Marcus Brothers on their 35,000-square-foot showboat, *Emerald Lady*.
> Opening Day April First.

If riverboat gambling was going to restore western Illinois' faltering economy was yet to be determined, but as my Uncle Al said when he read that it was the Marcus Brothers who were to receive the gambling permit from the Rockville aldermen, "I'll have to admit the Marcus boys know transportation, but what do they know about entertainment? Harry Marcus can't tell a joke, Paul doesn't know when to laugh."

My uncle refers to the Marcus Brothers as "boys" because he went to Hebrew school with their father, Ben, and caught rides with their grandfather Harry, in his red Mack truck.

> MARCUS TRANSPORTATION COMPANY.
> EVERYDAY SERVICE BETWEEN ROCKVILLE AND CHICAGO.

If you ask me what is remarkable about the Marcus brothers is that they have stayed together, caring for each other, and that's not easy in a family business.

Harry is older than Paul, must be sixty. He is the taller of the two at almost six feet. Both are thin and both dress in sport clothes by Brooks Brothers; soft gray herringbone tweed sport coats, dark gray flannel trousers, blue oxford cloth button-down shirts, silk rep ties with regimental stripes. That country gentleman style fits Paul better than Harry. Harry is stiffer, straighter, who would be more comfortable in a three piece suit by Freeman. Like in *Fortune*, when they full feature deal makers, which is exactly what Harry does. Expansions and acquisitions.

Paul talks very quietly, very sincerely. Paul is the one who is at services every Saturday. Third row on the left is where the Marcuses sit. Paul never stays for after service wine, whiskey, cookies and punch. Uncle Al has explained that to me. Paul has become a borderline diabetic. "All that management stress or maybe it's the diabetes. Anyway Harry tells me Paul forgets to take his pills. Worst of all, when it comes to drinks if Paul starts on one he doesn't stop at two. For Paul it's all or nothing. Moderation seems unattainable for him." That's the kind of man Paul is.

Harry was the one who built the barges and the tugs that carried corn and soybeans down the river and the ore up river. The one who named the tugs after the family. *The Jenny Marcus*, *The Benjamin Marcus*. Thirty or forty tugs, hundreds of barges, the biggest barge line between Rockville and Cairo. From boats the Marcus Brothers know. From their gambling corporation the Marcus Brothers sell a piece to International Novelties out of Las Vegas so now they have partners with gambling expertise.

When I heard of the sale, I stopped Paul as he was leaving services. "Paul, now you be sure that your partners send in some Jewish dealers, pit bosses, skimmers. We need bodies for the morning Minyan." Without a smile he answers, "Skimming is not funny, Benny. Gambling is a regulated business. For skimming we could lose our license." With that, Paul turns and leaves me without even a good Shabus.

As my uncle said, "Paul doesn't understand a joke." Maybe that's why Paul never married.

The Chamber of Commerce is heading up all the preparation for the good times coming with the theme, "Prosperity is on the river – Ready Rockville for a better tomorrow." Bill Turner of Turner Travel organizes a tour, "Visit Alaska Special," with stops in Seattle, Vancouver, Victoria. "See how tourism helped cities grow. Learn now so that you are ready for the tourist influx that riverboat gambling will bring to Rockville. All projections proven with statistics. With two million visitors Rockville will need more motels, restaurants, specialty shops."

My Uncle Al, the eternal optimist, believes in the Chamber's predictions. Why else would he have bought a half-empty sixty-thousand-square-foot building, with retail space for rent, in the best business block of downtown Rockville, only three blocks from the river. All this may come true, but what is true is that since deindustrialization, eleven years since the farm machinery factories shut down and sixteen percent of the work force have left for jobs in the Sun Belt, no one but my uncle has seen business opportunities in downtown properties. This is not all bad because if not for my uncle's most enthusiastic appeals—"Benny, Millie, now that Benny has retired from the C.I.C., come home. Your aunt and I will go to Florida in the winter, travel in the spring and fall. You manage the building. You will have the time to write, play golf, go to concerts, enjoy. Sell your home in Chevy Chase, make a profit and buy the same home in Rockville for half."

That's what we did; return to Rockville, Illinois. After Washington, D.C., Brussels, Paris, it was all incredibly as my uncle had promised. No traffic, no queuing at the golf course, concerts from symphony to Dixieland. The weather . . . the weather was no better than when I had left thirty years ago to join the army Counter Intelligence Corps.

My uncle, who is into long-term planning, enrolls Millie and me in the Alaska tour, leaving Rockville for Seattle on 7 July, on to Anchorage where a motor coach transfers us from our hotel to the Alaska Railroad. Our observation car, "The McKinley Explorer," winds through the spectacular scenery of Alaska en route to Denali National Nature Park.

Our Rockville Chamber of Commerce tour group are all in one coach, in assigned seats. Millie and I are four rows behind Paul Marcus whom I greet with, "So nice to see you, Paul."

"You too, Benny." He doffs his green baseball cap inscribed *Marcus Barge Lines* to Millie and then whispers to me, "Harry tell you to keep an eye on me?" and winks.

Then I see why because Bill Turner has seated Paul Marcus next to Eva Sundine. Gorgeous Eva she was called when she played competitive tennis. Thirty-five years later, Eva is still gorgeous with the help of Clairol and Dr. Lipton, Rockville's own plastic surgeon. Rumor has it that Eva has had two face lifts, but her eyes need help. She can still fit into the size twelve that she sells at *Eva's*, Rockville's only designer boutique.

Turner has put the two singles, Paul and Eva, together. Eva is cheerfully sucking bourbon as I pass to get two tonic waters for Millie and me. I see Paul drinking slowly and smiling

"It's only seltzer, Benny." That is when I get Paul's second wink.

I tell Millie, "Paul Marcus and Eva Sundine . . . that is an odd couple."

"Nothing odd about a widow wanting another man."

That is also true. Eva has been widowed three times. But she always marries older men. The talk around town—in Rockville, everyone knows everything about everyone (at least they talk like they do)—is that Eva got her boutique with the life insurance from the demise of her first husband, and expanded it with the death of the second.

This news about my contemporaries appeared in a weekly letter from my Uncle Al with comments and additions from the clippings of the Rockville *Messenger*. News from the home front to bolster the troops overseas is how Millie described my uncle's letters.

With my news about Paul and Eva faithfully delivered to Millie, I return to reading *The New York Times*. In a few minutes Millie spoke up.

"I do hope Eva isn't contemplating getting herself married to Paul Marcus."

"For Paul she would convert."

"No Rabbi would marry them. Three times a widow, she is not eligible for another chance at matrimony."

"Do you want me to tell her."

"Don't be stupid. You and your sense of humor."

By the time the coach leaves Fairbanks, on our cross country adventure on the famed Alaska Highway, formerly known as the Alcan Highway to Beaver Creek, Yukon Territory, Canada, Eva and Paul are sitting side by side. This in a coach that has fourteen empty seats.

Day nine, the day our tour sails on the Westerdam from Juneau to Vancouver. In these four days that we are experiencing a display of glaciers, mountains, and marine life, Paul and Eva are together in the dining room, in the piano bar, at the movies. Eva even appears behind Paul at the Friday night services. When Millie sees that she whispers to me, "That is one smart cookie, that Eva."

"She made the honor roll in high school." I don't mention that Eva was also the highest-kicking pompon girl at the Friday night basketball games.

As our memorable cruise sailed under the Lions Gate Bridge to anchor in Vancouver, Eva and Paul are walking the deck, her arm in his.

"Eva is making progress," is Millie's report when she sees them debark.

"You don't know Paul Marcus."

"I know women."

The tour broke up in Vancouver. Millie and I went off to Victoria, Paul and Eva back to Rockville. When we returned, a week later, my Uncle Al insisted on a written report, "Roone Realty Prepares for Tomorrow," for the IRS file.

"Benny, now tell me—Benny, Millie, what did you learn about tourism?"

"Tourism is an industry run by the young for the old. All the guides, drivers, all college kids off for the summer, herding around tourists all over sixty-two years of age."

"Millie, what is your impression? What can we do to prepare for tomorrow's good times?"

My Uncle Al believes in the woman's view point because that's where the money is. In the woman's checking account.

Millie tells Al, "We will have to wait and see, if the Marcus Brother' *Lady* becomes a big attraction, if thousands come in to gamble, then we may get some of the fringe benefits. Maybe a boutique in our retail space."

"For this I spend six thousand?"

My Uncle Al throws my "position paper" on the table behind his desk, into the file marked pending.

Then it was back to the day-to-day of August, preparing boilers and roofs for winter.

I didn't think about Paul Marcus until the day after Labor Day, when my uncle called me at eight a.m. "Benny, I didn't want you to hear it on the radio!"

"Hear what?"

"Paul Marcus died last night. Harry is here now, he wants to talk to you, and the Rabbi is here, too. Benny, can you come right over to Paul's place?"

"Sure. I'll be there in half an hour."

The minute I hang up, to give the orders of the day to Ken, our one maintenance employee, the phone rings again.

"This is Eva Sundine."

"Good morning, Eva."

"Not good for me, Benny. Benny, you know about me and Paul. I didn't know who I could tell, you were the only one I could think of. I knew you wouldn't misunderstand. Harry called this morning to tell me."

Eva begins to cry. "I loved that man."

Eva knew that Paul was dead before she called.

"Benny, when can I talk to you?"

"I'll stop by your shop on the way back from Paul's. I was going out the door when you called."

"Thanks, Benny. Benny, knock on the door. I'm closing up until after the funeral."

Paul's place was the penthouse of Westville Towers. The only condominium in Rockville with an outdoor swimming pool and an underground garage. In western Illinois' ice and sleet, the garage was for me more attraction than the pool. I parked in the landscaped turn-around, entered the marble-tiled lobby. The name 'P. Marcus' was the topmost. The entry door was locked. I rang; the voice from the speaker was my Uncle Al.

The buzz allowed my entry into the lobby, all silver wallpaper and "dead red" silk poppies. The hydraulic elevator was slow, quiet. The door opened into a foyer. My uncle, Harry, and the Rabbi were in the living room, seated on the stuffed and flowered sectional that faced the picture windows.

Nice to sit here, smoke a cigar, watch the sunset over the Mississippi. There were no ashtrays on the burled walnut coffee table. On the left, off the foyer, the kitchen ... beyond a study, a library, wall-to-wall ceiling-to-floor books interrupted by two sound speakers, three shelves tall. In the center, a Herman Miller desk, chair, side chair. The desk piled with year-end reports, blue folders, files. On the right, behind the closed doors, two bedrooms and baths.

"Don't stand there, Benny, come in. Benny, you know the Rabbi. Harry?"

Harry spoke first. "Benny, I wouldn't have called you but I got the news during morning services. Your uncle and the Rabbi were there. It was your uncle's idea. He said with your experience in the C.I.C. you would know what to do."

"Do about what?"

"About Paul. I want to know who killed Paul. When I find that son of a bitch I'll have friends in Nevada . . . I'll . . ."

The Rabbi took Harry into the kitchen. My uncle sat me down in overstuffed settee. Behind me, the mirror wall had been covered to make Paul's penthouse a house in mourning.

"Who found Paul?" I asked.

"Mrs. Granger. She works for everyone in the building—Tuesday morning, that's Paul's day. She called Harry. Beverly, Harry's wife, called the synagogue."

"I remember Beverly."

"Harry wants you to look at Paul before we call Hancock's." Hancock's Funeral parlor catered to the Jewish trade. All wooden caskets, burial within twenty-four hours, no embalming, no post-mortem.

"Harry doesn't want to get the police in unless . . . That is why I called you."

The Rabbi and Harry, shoulders drooping, came, Harry, water glass in hand.

"Benny, come. Come into the kitchen. I want to talk to you alone. Rabbi, Al, don't make any more arrangements."

Harry and I sat around the glass top table. Harry had been crying.

"Benny, I wouldn't have called you if I didn't need you. Your Uncle Al suggested . . ."

"It's all right, Harry. Tell me from the beginning. Begin yesterday, Labor Day."

"Labor Day was our biggest day yet. Biggest casino take of the year. Paul and I visited the *Lady*. That was just after five. She docked about five p.m. We went home to my place, had a couple of drinks to celebrate. Beverly grilled some steaks. We talked. Had some apple pie. It was about nine or a little thereafter Paul called Eva, and then he left."

From Harry's to Paul's, on a holiday evening through Rockville's four traffic lights, six miles, fifteen minutes to get home.

"I think Paul—Paul has been getting threatening telephone calls."

"Have you had any calls?"

"No, that's what I don't understand. I'm as much involved in the business as Paul. Why is it only Paul gets the threats? That's why I want you to find out how Paul died."

"What were the threats about, Harry?"

"The usual labor problems. The Las Vegas unions want in. My partners don't want them. It's our partners who run the gambling, reach the decisions. That's why Paul never took the threats seriously. Now Paul is dead. When the threatening calls came into our office, Paul would laugh at them, right on the phone. You know what he told them?"

"No."

"He put on his southern accent, 'Sir, I'm only a barge line operator. I don't hire, I don't fire. That's International's responsibility. They run the gambling operation.' Since Eva, Paul is a changed man. He laughs at threats, he tells jokes."

"Doesn't sound too terrible."

"Maybe he shouldn't have laughed at the unions. Now Paul is dead."

Harry sat with his head in his hands.

"I'm ten years older. I always thought I would go first. That's the way we organized the business. I was to go first. We bought life insurance so that my boys would have the money to pay the estate taxes. Now Paul is dead."

I offered, "Paul had diabetes. He has been sick for a very long time."

"Benny, my mother had diabetes. She lived to be seventy-two. Benny, go in, look at Paul before the Chevrae Kiddushai Burial Society come to wash his body."

Paul's bedroom, the first door on the right. A bedroom between a bathroom and study. A bedroom so small that the king-size bed left only two feet on either side as a passage. Paul's body was the rise under the purple and white bluebells of the Elizabeth Ashley comforter. A floral wreath for a dead hero.

Paul, naked on his back; his blue eyes, now open, matched his death-hued face. The upper body muscular, his legs defined, well-shaped, hairy. Paul had been on the high school swim team. No doubt Paul swam in the outdoor lap pool of Rockville's only luxury condominium.

The pillow above his head had been puffed full. The tan fitted percale sheet and the matching top sheet were unwrinkled. With the sheets aside, there was an odor of perfume from Paul. Not a heavy scent, just a faint residual. "Deneuve" eau de cologne was what I found in the bathroom, between the Walgreen's liquid hand soap dispenser and Walgreen's after shave. I sniffed all three. It wasn't "Deneuve" or after shave.

To the left of the door, a built-in laundry bin, empty.

I went back to the body. On Paul's chest perfumed soap matted, knotted his black and gray hair.

The wet tissue rubbed onto the chest hair confirmed soap, the soap on my finger, on the tissue, the same Walgreen's.

Leave Paul for the ritual body washers. Let them perform their deeds of loving kindness. Paul was cold. The pathologist with his rectal thermometer could determine how long dead.

Paul Marcus had left Rockville on a pleasant mild cloudless September day.

On the river, the barges, behind and beside each other, waited to go east through Rockville's Lock No. 15, where the river flowed from east to west. This year or the next the tug *Paul Marcus* would be waiting at the lock.

"Benny"—it was the Rabbi, his voice, with the fixed smile from his round full face in his black suit for death, calling me. Our teacher, now approaching fifty who in our aging congregation was considered young, a boy to my Uncle Al.

What did our Rabbi do all day? Visit the sick? Comfort the mourners? Last year there had been twenty-eight burials at Hebrew Cemetery.

"Benny, don't forget to wash before you come in. I made tea. We are in the kitchen."

I nodded, recalled the pail of water and towel that appeared at the front door of the house of mourning, waiting for those who had attended the funeral who had been in the presence of death to wash their hands before they entered to comfort the bereaved. Harry, his head down in his hands, his teacup half-empty. The Rabbi beside him, his eyes fixed on Harry.

The Rabbi had come from a congregation in Texas where he had performed weddings and Bar Mitzvahs to western Illinois' only conservative congregation in which the middle-aged Marcus boys were considered youthful and vigorous. I drank my tea. My uncle was silent. The Rabbi had become the spokesman.

"Well, Benny?"

"I'll need a couple of hours."

The Rabbi looked at my uncle. "Al, can you stay?"
Uncle Al nodded, "We will stay with Harry."
"Have you called Hancock's?" It was my uncle to Harry.
"Plenty of time."
Harry had not moved.
"Harry, where is the lady who found Paul?"
"Mrs. Granger is doing the laundry, in the basement."

The elevator opened on to a gray hall. The storage sign pointed to the right, laundry to the left. Straight ahead through a gray metal door was the garage.

Mrs. Granger, an Afro-American woman in her sixties, was folding large white bath towels on an ironing board. Storing them in the plastic laundry basket at her feet. Paul's socks had been paired and rolled. The white boxer shorts were folded beside the V-neck undershirts, another basket was on the ironing board.

"Mrs. Granger?" She turned. "I am Benny Roone. Mr. Marcus's friend."

"Poor Mr. Marcus. He was always so good to me. I did for him, on Tuesday and Thursday ever since he moved in. It will be twenty-two years next June."

I opened a folding chair from a row of stacked chairs, offered one to Mrs. Granger. She slowly sat.

"You found Mr. Marcus?"

"Yes. First things I do on Tuesday is strip the beds. There was Mr. Marcus under the blanket, dead. On Thursday I cook. Mr. Marcus liked simple things, chicken and biscuits . . . country fried steak. He do like southern cooking. Mr. Marcus was in the army in Georgia, right close to where my folks live. He be with the Lord now."

Mrs. Granger had folded the towels; placed one Elizabeth Ashley pillow case in the laundry basket. The other she stretched and folded.

"There were two pillows?"

"Yes, Mr. Roone. Miss Eva, she bought everything new. The old pillows were still good, but Miss Eva, she liked new. The old ones are in the closet in the guest bedroom. Mr. Marcus, he didn't like to throw things out."

"This morning there was only one pillow on Mr. Marcus's bed."

"The other be right here, Mr. Roone. It was in the dryer."

Mrs. Granger pointed to the laundry basket at her feet. "It sure do smell, smell it."

The odor was faintly scented Walgreen's hand soap.

"Miss Eva and Mr. Marcus, they was going to get married. She tell me that last Friday."

"Do you see Mrs. Sundine often?"

"Only when I does for her on Friday."

"Have you been working for Mrs. Sundine long?"

"Only just two weeks. Mr. Marcus, he ask me. If Mr. Marcus asks, I give up my free morning. What's going to happen now? Mr. Marcus, he been so happy. Talk, talk, talk . . . that is all he do when he take me home. . . . I'll be right up, just a few more handkerchiefs to iron."

"Were there sheets to match the pillows?"

"Miss Eva bought all new sets. They be right here." She pointed to the laundry basket. "I found them in the dryer with the pillow cases. They be right here all clean and folded. I never knowed Mr. Marcus to do laundry." She pointed again to the bedding in the basket that wafted Walgreen's scented soap. "All that new, and now Mr. Marcus gone."

Eva must have done the laundry; the cleaning up. She washed Paul's chest, changed the sheets. Tried to mask the odor on the pillow. Why? From what? Vomit? Drunk's vomit? Diabetic's vomit?

The round top of my Mont Blanc roller pen fit between Paul's teeth. The point protruded the other side of his complying jaw. The jaw lowered when I lifted the pen. I wiped his mouth with the wet pink tissue. Brown . . . and the stink of vomit.

A knock on the door.

"Benny?"

"Yes, Uncle Al."

"I thought I heard you come in. We were in the kitchen. Well?"

"Not yet. Tell Harry to wait until I get back from Eva Sundine. She called me as I was going out the door."

"Eva knew?"

"Harry had called her."

"I didn't know Eva and Paul were that close."

"Mrs. Granger just told me they were going to get married."

"Who?"

"Betty Granger. The cleaning lady. The one who found Paul."

"Benny, I think Harry wants to talk to you."

"Tell Harry I'll be back in an hour, and Al, don't let the Rabbi call Hancock's."

It was nine fifteen. The barges had cleared the lock. A freight train was crossing the railroad bridge. Traffic was moving swiftly on to the swing bridge that linked Rockville to Iowa. From Paul's penthouse to Mrs. Sundine's boutique is eight minutes down the bluff road. *Eva's*, in the Historical District, had been built as the proud dream home of a riverboat captain. True to the Italianate style of 1875, it had a front entry guarded by two-story pillars. Inside were two front parlors, walnut staircases, a stained glass front door. A hundred years later the captain and his family laid out forgotten in Memorial Gardens; *Eva's* was a retail shop, a successful tax shelter; rehab; recycle. The 1875 dining room and parlors were now salesrooms. The kitchen a stockroom, the butler's pantry the fitting room. The upstairs bedrooms had become Eva's two-bedroom bath-and-a-half apartment furnished with Victoriana. Corner to corner in front of the windows, carved walnut sofas stood beside matching arm chairs, all upholstered in apple red plush.

Eva and I sat in a room so dim that this morning's September sun could not penetrate the red velvet curtains to fade the rugs. Eva on the sofa—she was Kitty in "Gunsmoke." A little worn, eyes a little wet, dependable but alone. Back straight, she sat across the oval marble top coffee table. She was crying.

"Benny. Benny, I knew you would know what to do."

I was going to ask about what. That wasn't necessary.

"I should have called nine-one-one, but I was right there. I tried. God, I tried. I had Paul in the Heimlich maneuver, clearing his choking. The vomit came out all over the bed. Then Paul just went limp. Took one big gasp like a deep breath. I had my fist tight right below his chest. Nothing came up. I knew he was dead, so I cleaned up and left, came back here. Paul and I were going to get married. He told me he had insurance made out last month. He had a policy and Harry had a policy. Paul passed a physical last month. We were going to get married."

"Why didn't you call Harry from Paul's?"

"I couldn't, Benny. I didn't know whether Harry knew that I spent the night there now and then. Benny, you are the only one that knows I was at Paul's last night."

"My God, Eva, there are no secrets in this town. I'll bet everyone in the building knew about you and Paul. Betty Granger knew. She told me."

Eva began to cry. "I smelled so bad. The vomit was all over me. What was I going to tell Harry? Your brother died in my arms? I tried, but I'm a three time loser, Benny."

Eva rose into the violet light of the Wisteria table lamp. It was then that I could see the basic black dress, the black glass beads, the black hose, the black patent leather pumps. Eva was the grieving widow, ready for the shiva, the week of mourning. It was all wrong. Jewish widows sat on low stools in cotton house dresses and wore house slippers.

"That's why I went home, Benny."

What was I to say? Eva, this is 1990. There has been a sexual revolution. No one cares about consenting adults sleeping together. So, I said nothing. Just listened to Eva.

"We were going to get married." The handkerchief was at her nose.

"Eva, what would you like for me to do?" My tone must have been too harsh. Eva Sundine, mourning widow, began deep, hollow sobs.

"Just tell Harry I tried to save Paul's life, and Benny I want to sit with the family at the funeral!"

"I'll speak to Harry."

"Benny, when will the funeral be?"

"Tomorrow, Eva. Tomorrow."

In Rockville the ten a.m. traffic up Sixteenth Street hill is from none to light. In front of Paul's, on the turn around there was only Harry's Cadillac. In the penthouse, all were as I left them: my uncle, the Rabbi, Harry around the kitchen table. At the sink, Betty Granger was washing the teacups.

"Benny, you're back!"

"Harry, can you come into the study with me?"

I shut the sliding doors to the living room. In the garden, the sunlight reflected off the blue canvas that covered the heated pool. Steam escaped from the edges where the canvas had not been tied down. I sat behind Paul's desk in Paul's chair. Harry in the side chair. Harry had tried to compose himself into the business man in control. Eyes and face back in place. He had failed, he sagged.

"Harry, have you looked at Paul?"

"I couldn't."

"I did."

"Thank you, Benny."

"Nothing to thank me for."

I began my report. There are no visible signs of violence, no blows, no wounds, no bleeding.

I hoped the tone wasn't too abstract, too objective.

"Thank God. You can't blame me, Benny. I was afraid for Paul, wanted him to have a bodyguard. Everyone thinks it's me that's the strong one. It's not. It's Paul." Harry stopped; began again. "Paul wouldn't keep a gun in the house and him a Korean War hero. So what do you think, Benny? What should I do?"

"Harry, let me call Hancock's. I'll talk to Denny Hancock. We went to high school together. Harry, who was Paul's doctor?"

"Ray Morton. You know Ray Morton. Do anything you like, Benny."

"Hold on for a little while, Harry. Do me a favor. Stay here."

"Benny, what killed Paul? Why did Paul die?"

"Give me couple of hours more."

To myself I answered, Paul wasn't tired of living, or afraid of dying. Not Paul Marcus who celebrated his business success with a couple of drinks, apple pie and Eva Sundine.

In high school Denny Hancock talked too much, said too little. He still did. Denny could never just say "yes." He answered my requests with, "For you, Benny, anything. If anyone can, Denny Hancock can. I'll be there in ten minutes. Handle it myself. You can trust me, Benny. Come down in an hour, I'll have everything ready."

My Uncle Al says there are advantages to a small town. You get to know people more intimately especially if you are born and raised here. As a hometown boy, I did know where to find Dr. Ray Morton this Tuesday morning. He was reviewing physicians' payment claims at Coal Companies Insurance.

"Dr. Morton?"

"Yes."

"Ray, this is Benny Roone. Could you break away for a half hour?"

"Yes, Benny."

"I'll meet you in forty minutes at Hancock's. Don't go in. I'll look for you in the parking lot. I need your wisdom."

"What are you selling, Benny?"

"See you in forty minutes."

Harry had listened to my calls.

"Troubles, Benny?"

"No, I just want to be sure."

"You didn't tell Dr. Morton that Paul was dead."

"I will. When I see him."

"Benny, why didn't you have Ray come here. He would have, for Paul he would have."

"Hancock's is better. There may be a few tests that have to be done."

"What tests?"

"Just simple ones."

"No postmortems Benny, not without the Rabbi's permission."

"Harry, I promise. Harry, you want to lie down?"

Harry had loosened his collar. He was white.

"I'll be all right. It should have been me, the oldest is supposed to go first. I'm ten years older. We had insurance, physicals. Ask Dr. Morton."

Insurance could be the key word. Word around town had been that Eva Sundine had benefited from the death of two husbands. Possibly three. Eva had also mentioned insurance.

"Harry, on the insurance who was Paul's beneficiary?"

"Me and the business. No one benefits personally until I die. When I die, my boys get a half a million dollars." Harry began to laugh. "You know who benefits? The citizens of the United States. The IRS. They get the half million dollars as estate taxes because that's the way our business was set up. Everything from the first to die goes to the second. All set up to keep our business going."

"Harry, go eat something. Have Betty make you something. You'll feel better."

My advice in the great tradition of Jewish folk wisdom; when faint and under stress, eat.

"Benny?"

"What?"

"Nothing."

Ray Morton was the only doctor in Rockville who wore softly draped double-breasted Armani suits, read Proust, spoke in the polysyllables of an English professor. A career he abandoned to go to medical school, because as Ray Morton would tell you, "In 1965 there was no incoming enemy fire at the University of Chicago School of Medicine."

Morton was leaning on his green Jaguar.

"What's the crisis?"

"Let's go for a walk."

We walked on Fifth Avenue under the russet leaves of the oak trees. "Paul Marcus died last night." I repeated the sequence with the details confirmed from my pocket notebook.

"What is it you want, Benny?"

"A death certificate and your opinion as to cause of death."

"That will be on the certificate."

"Ray, I'd like to know as much as possible . . . that is without a postmortem."

"Without the coroner?"

"Exactly."

"Let's go. I'll get my bag."

We were alone with Paul on a gurney in Hancock's prep room. Ray wore gloves. He collected a urine specimen, a blood specimen, lifted lips with a tongue depressor, smelled and poked and muttered to himself words I could not hear.

"Okay, Benny. Follow me back to my office."

On the way out, Denny stopped us for instructions. "On hold, Denny, until Dr. Morton calls you. Nothing to the newspapers."

"Got it, Colonel Roone." No one in Rockville had called me colonel in the two years and four months since our homecoming.

In Rockville, the doctor's offices are up and down Seventh Street. Dr. Morton's office is the first on the left side of the street, if you are driving south. In the lab Morton spoke as he worked.

"Paul's urine—too much protein, too much glucose. The blood glucose level too high. That's what happens when . . . what did you say the Marcuses had for dinner?"

"Steak, a couple of drinks and apple pie."

"That damn fool. Sure his swimming helped control his diabetes, but Paul knew his kidneys were going out. I had warned Paul, 'stay on your low-protein, low-sugar diet.' His tests were normal a couple of weeks ago. Benny, I could get a blood alcohol."

Without my answer, Ray continued.

"Did Eva well you how much she and Paul had to drink?"

"A few is what she said."

"A few for Eva was too many for Paul. I tried . . . I tried to frighten Paul. I wanted him to go to the Diabetes Clinic. I told him, 'Paul, your kidneys are going to give out. Paul, you could go blind.' Strange with diabetes, some get retinal hemorrhage, some don't. Paul's retinas were never affected. You know how he answered me?"

Then Ray answered himself. An intelligent man.

"Paul's answer was always the same. 'Ray after what I went through in Korea, I am not going to die of diabetes.' He was right, you know. Diabetes didn't kill him."

"What about the blood sugar tests?"

"They are abnormal, but I don't think high enough to kill Paul. You know what I think? Paul got indigestion, vomited in his sleep, choked to death."

"Why would Eva say that she tried to save him?"

"Who knows? Maybe she wanted points with the family. Maybe she tried and didn't know Paul was already dead."

"What shall I tell Harry?"

"Tell him the truth, the whole truth and nothing but the truth."

I finished, "So help me God."

So I told Harry what was on the death certificate. Told it without my reservations. My doubts, I wrote into my notebook.

    1. Did Eva really help?

Not to her benefit to help if she thought she was the beneficiary of Paul's insurance.

    2. But Paul alive, married or not and well, on a controlled diet would in the long run have been of more value to Eva than Paul dead.

    3. Was Eva interested in controlling Paul's diabetes?

Not if they drank together!

    4. Did Eva understand that as a three-time widow there would have been difficulties gaining rabbinical approval for her marriage to Paul, a most observant congregant of B'nai Jacob? She should have. She has been taking instruction from Rabbi Levy. Everybody in town knew that.

    5. And Harry. Why did Harry make drinks for Paul to celebrate?

    6. If Harry died first, Paul got the money. Without children or a wife, Harry's boys are the heirs. With a wife for Paul, Harry's boys are *still* the heirs. Because careful businessman Harry would insist on a premarital agreement between Paul and Eva, presuming they would marry. Harry's boys remain the heirs either way. So I cross off Harry as a suspect. Instead he becomes the doting older brother who couldn't or wouldn't concern himself with Paul's special diet requirements.

. . . Monday, Labor Day. A holiday, a celebration of a business coup. Riverboat gambling had saved the Rockville economy but had cost Paul his life.

    7. Wait and see. Let it act out.

***

At the private funeral, Hancock's, Wednesday at two p.m.. Donations in memory of Paul Marcus may be made to B'nai Jacob. Eva Sundine sat behind Harry and Beverly Marcus and their two sons out in front of the second cousins and the community dignitaries. The Rabbi's eulogy was his usual from Micah: "'Not only a business man but a man who loved mercy, walked humbly with his God.'"

No mention of service to his country. No American flag on his coffin. I made a note to discuss my funeral arrangements with Millie, if not yet with our Rabbi, a newcomer who had only been at B'nai Jacob for four years.

The service concluded with *Elimole Rochomim.* "God Be Merciful," a dirge in a very minor key. Then the Rabbi's routine announcements. "After internment at the Hebrew Cemetery, the meal of condolence will be served in the multi-purpose room at B'nai Jacob. The family will sit shiva at the home of Harry and Beverly Marcus in Westville."

I did not go to the cemetery. Eva was at the condolence meal but not at the Marcuses' when Millie and I came to visit during the shiva.

It was in early November that the Rabbi called me.

"Benny, can you come into see me. It's about Paul Marcus's death. Harry asked me to speak to you."

We sat in the library, in the quiet of disuse. The Rabbi and I at the corner of the table for fourteen. The view out the window wall was browned frosted lawn. The Rabbi in gray pinstripe, cleared his throat, placed his hands on the table.

"Mr. Roone."

"Call me Benny."

"You have never sent a bill to Mr. Marcus."

"A bill for what?"

"For your investigation and your help. Harry would like to close up Paul's estate. Pay off any debts."

"Harry doesn't owe me."

"There is the possibility that you might be called on by the insurance company."

"Dr. Morton would be better qualified than I."

"But if you were questioned."

"I wouldn't testify."

"I think Harry would still be pleased to pay you."

"If Harry feels so guilty about Paul's death, let him make a contribution to B'nai Jacob."

The Rabbi rose, shook my hand. "I thank you for what you have done for the Marcus family and the congregation."

At my office I shredded the Paul Marcus file. Wrote in my day book:

> "I hardly knew Paul Marcus. I met him only once when my Uncle Al introduced him to me."

Tales from the Prayer House

May His Name Be Blessed Forever and Ever

The minyan are the ten men who by our Judaic laws must be present when we unite for morning, afternoon, and evening prayers. On Monday, Thursday, and Saturday, during the morning *shacharit* prayer a passage will be read to the congregation from the Torah, the first five books of the Bible. Without a minyan the bereaved of our congregation cannot recite the Kaddish, the memorial prayer for our dead: "magnified and sanctified by the great name of God throughout the world which He hath created according to His will," to which the congregants answer, "May His great name be blessed forever and ever." Without a minyan, sons and daughters cannot pray for their deceased parents and grandparents.

To find ten to rise before dawn to appear at the Prayer House at ten to seven is an achievement for our two-hundred-family congregation. Many congregations have given up *shacharit*, the morning prayer. We continue to appear, Monday to Sunday, ten, eleven, but sometimes only eight or nine.

The core of the minyan are the rabbi and cantor. Sadly, the cantor will leave for a St. Louis congregation before January first. This at the time when so many of our minyan who are retired, leave western Illinois' intemperate winter for Florida, California, Texas and Arizona. Now my fear is our minyan will be no more.

The Rabbi is in his place, in the straight, high-backed oak chair to the right of the ark, ready to announce, "Page 1103. All rise."

It is the Rabbi's fifth year in Rockville, his third or fourth pulpit. Iowa City to El Paso to Rockville, Illinois, by way of a congregation in New York, which he never mentions. The Rabbi, of medium height, rounded at the belly, smiles with brown eyes at his congregation from a shaven face. In his rising inflection, he explains today's Torah reading: "Noah was righteous in his generations."

During the past year the quality of the Rabbi's Monday and Thursday Torah expositions and his Saturday sermons, too, have been improving. That is, the subjects the Rabbi deals with are more pertinent to our older to elderly congregation than the book reviews, world political problems, and injunctions against intermarriage that he so diligently informed us about as we dozed or whispered through his first four years in Rockville's only Jewish congregation.

The cantor, a youthful thirty-year-old émigré from suburban New Jersey via Milwaukee, is non-communicative beyond his prescribed congregational duties. His distance from me I attribute to the problems of integration into a congregation of elderly and widows, and possibly to my sinister, menacing appearance, green eyes, black untrimmed eyebrows, and a gray moustache that droops over the corners of my mouth.

My self-appointed position as gabbai, the monitor who collects and provides the ten souls for the next day's minyan, has so far not developed our conversation beyond, "See you tomorrow, Cantor!"

"Please call me Hazzan!"

This morning the cantor is deep in his chair, to the left of the ark, the twin of the Rabbi's. Tan cotton trousers, Reebok walking shoes, plaid sport shirt, wrapped in his prayer shawl, he yawns, wakes, rises, prays, sinks into his chair until the Rabbi's, "Rise for the Silent Devotion on page 146." We rise again to open the Torah ark. I will carry the Torah on my right shoulder around the twenty-foot prayer room. As I pass the congregants, each will place their right hand which holds their prayer shawl on the Torah, then symbolically kiss the shawl where it has touched the Torah.

The Torah is on the lectern. The cantor intones the prayer before the reading. The cantor, his guide sheet with the vowels added in his left hand, is at the ready. Should the cantor's Hebrew falter, there are always the two silent watchers to his right and left, who follow his intonations in the fully annotated Hertz Bible. The silent readers will keep place for each of this morning's three men who will be called to stand beside the cantor, make the blessing over the Torah before and after he has read the day's portions.

The Rabbi will call the congregants by their Hebrew names, "Elijah, son of Aaron," to read the Torah. Before the three are chosen, the chairman of the religious committee has whispered to me, "Harry, you will take portion three." Portion one is traditionally reserved for a "Cohen," a descendent of the priests, of whom we fortunately have one, the butcher in our minyan, and portion two will honor a "Levi," the lower level of the priestly descendants, of whom we have this morning the toy distributor. So, portion three, my portion, is the one allotted to "Kol Yisrael," the common man.

Until I am called, I follow the reading in Hebrew in my Hertz with ample time to read the English translation and the commentaries. There is a more recent English translation than the Hertz of the five books of Moses that make up the Torah, in which the English is more everyday and less stately, but, as the chairman of the religious committee said, "Harry, what would we do with the old Hertzes? And how would we pay for the new?" These congregational problems can be solved with my "Buy a few of the modern text at a time." The committee has not accepted this wisdom. As the non-traditionalist, most recent member of the minyan, my influence is from little to none. A member of this congregation for only forty-one years, how can I gain a hearing from a committee whose forebears have worshipped in Rockville for five generations?

The Torah is unrolled on the lectern. The cantor begins the reading. This morning it is the story of Noah. When the cantor finishes this morning's portion, I shake his hand. "May you be strengthened! You exceeded them all."

"In speed," is the reply I get. My first sign of humor from our cantor who with this last word darts out the side door to . . . where? Where can he go at seven-thirty in the morning? To breakfast. He is hungry. He leaves without a "Goodbye, Harry."

The minyan are retirees—the butcher, the buyer, the mechanical engineer, the accountant, the toy distributor. For me, they each retain the identification of their business careers, until, at sixty, sixty-two, sixty-five, they have joined the minyan. Each morning it is I who announce, "We have ten," and, if not, I call from my list of those who will respond to, "We need you for the minyan."

The morning minyan meets in the prayer house of the Jewish Center. Four rows of oak pews with red wool, foam-padded seats, entered through the double glass doors to the left of the foyer. The only natural light the architect provided is from a window on the east wall to the right of the ark. A view limited to the planted atrium through which we follow the seasons. The stained glass windows, praying hands, Hebrew calligraphy, Davidic stars in gold and red and blue, through which the morning sun came into the Seventeenth Street synagogue are now the backlit south wall of the prayer house. Symbols turned to decor that no longer signal the morning and evening services.

The entry to the Center, a tan brick compound, is under a porte-cochere, onto the slate floor of the grand foyer. The library, gift shop and washrooms are to the right. To the left are the business office and the corridor to the Hebrew School wing. Beyond the corridor, behind the double glass door, the prayer house. Down the corridor the first door on the right is the Rabbi's private office. The foyer advances to the atrium to the sanctuary, ends at the multipurpose room where after services tea and cookies appear.

The sanctuary seats two hundred in upholstered, red wool theater comfort. We sit facing a post-modernist ark designed by that year's finest Jewish synagogue designer from New York. The designer didn't actually come to Rockville. He designed from the plans supplied by the architect from Arkansas, who had made his reputation building Jewish Centers with atria and dining rooms convertible to theaters, lit by sky lights, cooled and heated under the guardianship of twenty thermostats to control six comfort zones. Surrounded by acres of parking and landscaping, the Center cost so much to construct that no reserves remained from the funds that took fifteen years to gather. On the front lawn, to the right of the porte-cochere, a four-by-four-foot white sign, inscribed in red, announces, "bingo Sunday Night."

Two or three of our minyan are the congregants who come for the Memorial Day of their deceased family member. For those dead without descendants in our congregation, for those who are only a name in the Memorial Book of the Jewish Center, I have taken upon myself, with the approval of the chairman of the religious committee, to recite the memorial prayers on their behalf.

As we repeat the silent devotion, "Heal them, O God," the Rabbi reads the names of the hospitalized, then the psalm for the day, the memorial prayer again, then another psalm, the memorial prayer. The service has ended. The minyan dissolves to reassemble for afternoon and evening prayers, which I don't attend.

This November morning I walk home avoiding the gray ash remnants of the oak leaves. I note the steam of my breath, congratulate my foresight to place gloves in the pockets of my blue jean jacket. It's an eight to ten minute walk home into the oak woods of the cul-de-sac, to breakfast with my wife, Ida. She greets me with, "Going to snow today. Look at yourself, wearing cotton trousers."

"Not to worry, Ida. I added the anti-freeze to your car before I went to services."

Breakfast, toasted bagels from Chicago and skim milk, is with the morning TV news.

"Snow in Wisconsin, snow in Minnesota."

"We are going to have a problem assembling next week's minyan."

"Why?"

"The United Synagogue convention. The Rabbi, the religious committee will be in Toronto."

"You could ask me."

Women do count towards our ten. It's Ida at her finest, willing to get up and out by ten minutes to seven.

"Who was there?"

"The usual. Ray Shore is becoming a steady. It's his fourth week. He could become permanent. Ray is a complete puzzle for me. He just appeared one morning, stayed on. He prays and takes notes."

"Notes?"

"Yes. He writes a line or two on a scrap of paper, then puts it back in the prayer book. Read what I found when I was putting back the prayer books."

"The prominence of man over beast is naught.
We give Thee thanks and we declare
Thy praise for all Thy tender care."

Covet Not Thy Neighbor's Boots

Each morning Irving Rudhitsky is wearing western style goatskin boots to the minyan. Rockville, in western Illinois, is not boot country, at least not in our prayer house. From boots I know, as I served in the cavalry in World War II. Irving's are Lucchese boots, handmade, the kind that I have always wished for and Ida has resented. "Harry, you want to play cowboy boots, buy Acme at Famous Footwear. For what Lucchese cost, you can get a new suit at Brooks Brothers." Lucchese are not worn by twenty-year- olds who drink the beer from the sky blue waters in country music bars. Lucchese are worn by Texas wheeler dealers, like the bankers and brokers who stole from their savings and loans in Dallas.

Lucchese boots are not the stiff embossed leather with man-made-material insides that I see on the Saturday night square dancers. These boots are the brand favored by Oklahoma oil company attorneys and Nevada gamblers. These boots are so comfortable that they are never guilty of causing even a transient twinge of discomfort. The uppers of tanned goatskin are unmarred by decoration to maintain their subtle elegance, to make their unobtrusive statement of wealth and social position. The wearer of these boots is immediately recognized as an upholder of traditional style and status. For a man who has chosen not to bring attention to his feet, not for him the exotic leathers, the lizards and crocodiles and gold Rolex watches that scream "Western" or "Western Newly Rich." So, what is Irv, a retired furrier, doing wearing Lucchese goatskin cowboy boots?

Irving Rudhitsky walks in those narrow-toed and high heel boots without swaying. Nor does he go "Western" above his Luccheses. From collar to ankle, Irv's ready-to-wear is Midwestern traditional two-piece conservatively cut gray suits, cotton shirts and striped silk ties. I cannot help but look at the boots when Irv stands to recite the Kaddish for his recently departed mother, Fanny, who died last month at the age of ninety-two—may she rest in peace! The first week I don't say anything. A man is entitled to wear what he likes. But a month without changing footwear? The same boots every time no matter how beautifully crafted and elegantly impressive? It is not usual for a man who wears a different suit and shirt every day to wear the same boots each and every day.

That Thursday morning after the Torah reading, it was about a month after Passover,

Irv is talking to the Rabbi; everyone else has left. I am shutting off the light. We walk out into the parking lot. It is spring; the forsythia is yellow. The lilacs are in full bloom. Our golfers have left for the municipal course to get the seniors' special cart rental rate. It's just Irv and me in the parking lot.

I try concern. "Irv, with your arthritis, isn't it difficult to take your boots on and off each day?" I could have said Irv, with all that extra weight you are carrying around your belly, isn't it difficult for you to take your boots on and off? "From boots I know, because in our Company A, we had Lucchese wearers from the hills of Texas and the deserts of New Mexico."

Irv is about five foot seven, and a bit of a wag, polite but evasive. He smiles at me and says, "I tell you, Harry, with my back trouble, I lost three inches in height. With the boots I gained back an inch and a half. Now I am again taller than Carol."

I don't know whether to believe Irving or not. I try being helpful. "If you need a boot jack, I can lend you my Naughty Nellie. I haven't used it in years." Naughty Nellie is a 1900 iron casting of a naked woman with curly hair at her crotch. Of course, you have to hold the boot jack down with the other foot or there will be slippage. To balance and remove a boot while standing on one leg takes a bit of practice for an amateur. Evidently Irv is not an amateur.

He grins. "I don't need a Naughty Nellie. I have Naughty Carol." Carol is his wife and, like Irv, she is thickening all over. I can just see her: her back to Irv, his boot in her hands and Irv pushing on her broad backside with the other foot to increase Carol's leverage to remove those Lucchese boots while Irv is holding the chair's arm to remain seated.

From Irv's answer, I reach the conclusion that I'm not going to find out why Irving Rudhitsky is wearing boots each and every day.

The disappointment must have shown because Irv put his arms around me, right there in the parking lot. "Harry, promise not to tell if I tell you?" More than confidential, just a whisper in my right ear.

"You can trust me, Irv. Who would I tell?"

"You can't even tell Ida." Irv's grin rises from his mouth to his cheeks.

"I promise."

"I'm working."

"You are retired."

"I am working, making a movie. I'm the pit boss in the new flick the Italians are doing on the *Rockville Queen*."

The Rockville Queen is our Mississippi River casino boat that does breakfast, lunch and dinner cruises between Rockville and Lock and Dam 15. On the Iowa-based boats you cannot lose more than two hundred dollars a day. The Italians are the Amalfi Brothers, a film company from Rome, who found eastern Iowa and western Illinois cheap and scenic and full of tax incentives. The Amalfis have returned to make Rockville the world production headquarters for their as yet unnamed spectacle. The Amalfi Brothers had bought an abandoned Italianate late 1800s mansion on the Iowa bluff, which they have rehabbed, brought in an Italian camera man and make-up woman, hired local musicians and local actors to make this epic. This film is their second boy-meets-girl, boy-loses-girl on the Mississippi. All this I learned from the Rockville *Gazette* Sunday business section, and it explains why Irv is "working."

Then I tried again. "What size are your boots."

Irv must have seen it in my eyes. "Harry, covet not your neighbor's boots. I'll tell you what I'll do. I'll—"

"I wear a ten and a half B, Irv." Then I was so embarrassed by Irv's awareness of my boot envy that I asked, "How is Carol?"

"Carol is doing volunteer work for the Amalfis."

Irv and Carol are our congregation's "actors." Carol has written all the skits for the B'nai B'rith Frolics since . . . for a very long time. So long that most of us have forgotten that she used to be a dancer-choreographer. Now it all comes back.

"Is Carol in the film, too?" I can't resist, "How is the pay?"

"Extras don't get paid. We get lunch."

Which explains why it is so much cheaper to make films in Iowa and western Illinois than in Hollywood and Rome: in Rockville, one can find a cottage cheese salad on a bed of lettuce, served with cinnamon rolls, tea and lemon, for three dollars. This lunch in the eleventh-floor dining room of the Downtown Hotel includes a free view of the barge traffic on the river.

To show my concern, "Irv, you would think you and Carol would at least get minimum wage. You are there day after day." I count the days that Rudhitsky has been in boots; must be close to two months.

"Not to worry, Harry. I am acquiring new skills."

I cannot deny that Irving Rudhitsky needs new skills. There is very little demand for a "retired" master furrier in our de-industrialized, non-consumer-driven economy that includes a very active "Save Our Feathered and Furry Friends" Humane Society chapter whose members each October picket with "Don't buy fur coats!" signs.

Irv and Carol are leading a productive, active life, taking advantage of their early retirement because about three months later I read that Earl Ruden is going to appear at Rockville's Bluffs Dinner Theater in *Guys and Dolls*.

Naturally, Irving Rudhitsky, now Earl Ruden, is Nathan Detroit, the gambler. Whether he does or doesn't get the girl is immaterial because, as Irv tells me, "Harry, if the producer hadn't seen me working in the *Rockville Queen* film, would I be a second lead in *Guys and Dolls*?"

"Is the pay any better at the Bluffs?"

"Not really, but the meals have improved."

The food I hear is appreciably better since the owners have lured a chef away from the Iowa governor's mansion for the dinner theater.

That very Sunday Ida sees in the newspaper a five-color photo of the new chef admiring his flowering violet rutabagas. "Harry, who eats rutabagas?"

"No one, Ida, no one. That's an elegant table setting, like an ice sculpture."

"How come you know so much from rutabagas?"

"Earl Ruden told me."

"Who?"

"Irv Rudhitsky is working at the Bluffs Theater."

"From this he is going to make a living?"

"Not yet, but it's a step."

To which Ida only answers, "Huh," and goes on to her crossword puzzle.

To support Irv, I offer to Ida, "Irving Rudhitsky has a role in the next production."

"What has that got to do with food being served?"

"On the days that Irv's performing, he gets one free meal."

"That cooking will slim Irv down."

Irv gives me two freebies to the Bluffs Theater Sunday matinee. Irv is good, very good, a talented song, dance and patter man. The food is better than it was, but. . . . For free, I don't criticize.

The big difference is what Irv is wearing on his feet to the morning minyan, white Reeboks cross-training shoes. As the gabbai of the minyan, I am concerned about the health and welfare of our congregants.

"Irv, why the Reeboks?"

"It's my feet, Harry. I'm getting too old for song and dance. My feet just ache and ache. But in the next show," he smiles impishly, "I'm a middle-aged lover trying to make out with my best friend's wife. There I get to spend my time off my feet."

By now all the steadies are depending on Irv's presence at the morning minyan. Every morning Irv comes in with a smile, cheerful. He pats Bill Levy on the back. "Your cold better?" He asks Ira Karp, "When is your son coming to see you?" He praises Leonard Zymanski who mumbles and skips when he leads the first portion of the *shacharit*. When Lenny finishes the last Kaddish breathless, Irv shakes Lenny's hand. "Thank you, Lenny, that was beautiful." Even the cantor stays to talk to Irv between the Torah readings. This is the "new" cantor who has silently sat—"Meditating," he says—in his high-backed chair to the left of the Torah ark. Not one of the steadies can resist Irv's smiles and handshakes. Irv is just about ready to join the inner circle of the minyan, the after services breakfast club.

Ira Karp extended the invitation. "Irv, you want to join us for breakfast?" and Irv answers, "I'm sorry. I ate before the service." And, apologetically, "I don't have time to eat afterwards. Our rehearsals start at nine."

I rescue Irv with, "Irv is not fully retired as we are. He has obligations to his career."

Six weeks after *Guys and Dolls* closes, Irv is wearing plain black wingtip leather oxfords. This is the old Irving Rudhitsky I remember as a downtown business man, a leading tenor at the Rotary luncheon meetings. Irv is back to the minyan and nothing more does he mention about his theatrical career, which evidently is "on hold," "between engagements."

Irv has fulfilled our traditions, eleven months of memorial prayers and mourning period, and he is still coming to services. Which delights me, because in our community even one man is difficult to replace. It's about then that Irv is back into his Lucchese boots. This I notice immediately. His second booted day, I ask, "You making another movie?"

"No."

"Why the boots?"

"Those are my lucky boots."

"What's lucky boots?"

"It's true, Harry. It's because of the boots Carol and I are going to Las Vegas."

"What are you going to do in Nevada?"

"The Amalfi film I was in was being shown at a film festival. A casting director sees me standing behind the roulette tables—me as a pit boss. He remembers my boots. He calls, so now I have a small part as a pit boss in another Italian flick."

"Irv, are you going to get paid for this?"

"Equity scale."

"That's not very much."

"It will keep me out of the cold."

So Irv and Carol spend the winter in Nevada. About April—I remember because it's the Passover week—Irv is back at the minyan, and he is still wearing his Lucchese boots. Not a scratch on them. Not a sign of wear, not a new crease.

After services, Irv's congratulating the cantor, "You exceedeth them all."

"Who?" says the cantor.

"The cantor in Las Vegas."

The cantor grins and says, "Thank you."

Irv is waiting for me. "Tell me, Harry, how are you and Ida?"

"Fine."

"Thank God."

"How was it for you and Carol in Nevada?"

"After the shooting finished, we decided to come home. For us, Rockville is home."

"Maybe you'll get another movie contract."

"I got a job right here."

"Here in Rockville?"

"Hired me in Las Vegas to work in Rockville."

"What are you going to do?"

"Do? I'm going to be a pit boss on the *River King*," and Irv begins to sing "Cruising Down the River." Pit boss and tenor.

"You know from pit boss?"

Irv grins. "I'm playing the part twice. I say to myself, 'Irv, you should learn what pit bosses do.' I had all the moves down pat from the movies. So I go to school for a couple of weeks so now I am hired as a pit boss-singer."

A couple of weeks later, Irv comes into the minyan wearing his Reeboks.

"Irv, did you lose your job?"

"No, Harry. On the boat we wear antebellum costumes. Boots are out."

"What size are those boots, Irv?"

"Ten and a half."

"Irv, would you sell them to me?"

"I'll give them to you, Harry. Standing for me, with my back. . . . On one condition, of course."

"Name it."

"You wear the boots to the morning minyan."

"You've got it."

So, I am joyfully wearing the Lucchese boots to our breakfast club at HyVee, and a stranger comes up to me. "Would you like to be an extra in a movie we are making? It's a Western. You would have to wear your boots." He gives me his card. I read, Amalfi Brothers. Rome and Davenport, Iowa. Film makers. "Let me know."

I tell Irv of my opportunity.

"What did you tell the man?"

"I told him no."

"Why did you say no?"

"I saw what those boots did to you, Irv, started your film career, sent you off to Nevada. For me, no thanks."

"You want to stay in Rockville and be a gabbai at the shul. This is a career for a man of your talents and education?"

So I quoted the saying of the Fathers to him: Happy is the man who is happy with his portion. "For me, it's enough."

Who Shall Be Blessed?

When it comes to rebellion, there are those who are rebellious youths, and those on whom rebellion is thrust by destiny. As when the Maccabees raised their flag of rebellion against the Syriac Greeks. Henry Gottwalt began his rebellion at age eighty-two. He put down his traditional morning prayer book, the one without the English translation on the opposite page, the one with the order of laws on arising. The one with the prayers my mother taught me to recite when awakening from sleep in the morning while yet in bed. "I give thanks unto Thee, O King, who liveth and endureth, who has mercifully restored my soul unto me. Great is Thy faithfulness...." Mother said, "Harry, you must on arising wash your hands three times and say, 'The beginning of wisdom is fear of the Lord. His praise endureth forever. Blessed be the name of His glorious kingdom forever and ever.'"

Henry, the only one to use the traditional prayer book, is our most devoted of congregants. Seven days a week before breakfast he is wrapped in his talleth (prayer shawl), his teffilin on his forehead and left arm. Henry will not eat before praying. Henry is a man of modesty and devotion and willingness to perform deeds of loving kindness. He helps with the Torah readings, keeping place for the cantor but will not accept the aliyah honors that he is surely entitled to. After breakfast he takes our widows shopping, visits our sick.

Henry Gottwalt seeks justice, loves mercy, walks humbly with his God.

Now that I review what caused Henry's rebellion, I believe I can ascribe it to what happened at the last two funerals in Rockville. Members of our minyan are not all involved in attending our community's funerals; with twenty-two to thirty funerals a year, and an equal amount of tombstone unveilings, going to funerals is an obligation which the Rabbi and cantor fulfill for us, unless, God forbid, it's our closest and dearest friends—such as a member of our morning minyan. "God, spare our minyan," I pray during the meditation, and he has for the past two and a half years. Illness we have had: a mild stroke, a slight heart attack, but, thank God, the angel of death has not visited our minyan-goers.

The revolt against the religious committee began after the last two deaths. Until then, rebellion against the religious committee was unheard of, certainly had never happened during my fifty years in the congregation. For our committees are the upholders of our traditions.

The Reformed Temple, across the river in Iowa, has always permitted funerals from their sanctuary. Ours, the conservative congregation in Illinois, has never in my memory permitted a dead body to enter our Center. A stop by on the drive to the cemetery, yes, when the door is opened for the soul to have a last view of our tan, red and gold contemporary sanctuary with its red upholstered theater seats. In a minute or less the synagogue's doors are closed. Then the soul must forever return to the body which will be interned at the Hebrew cemetery sixty feet to the east of our Center's parking lot. This practice has been accepted by our community since I joined the congregation; never had this prohibition been challenged. Not until Henry Gottwalt in the softest of tone and the slightest of German accents came to me. "Harry, we must talk."

As the gabbai, I do not have a private office as the Rabbi and the cantor do. I lead Henry into the library with the assurance that at this hour no borrowers will intrude on our privacy. Henry sits at the head of our library table, I on the corner closest to him. Henry has a soft voice and with his accent and lisp (I admit to a slight hearing loss), I must listen most carefully.

"Morris's funeral was from the Temple. Morris was a member here, and the funeral was from the Temple."

"Morris also had a membership at the Temple."

"Huh," says Henry. Then, "Don Rothstein was also buried from the Temple."

"He also had two memberships."

"Huh," is all Henry says for a moment. Then, "Tell me, Harry. You were born and raised here. Why can we not bury from our synagogue?" Henry is a newcomer. He came in 1939, brought here from the German Rhineland by a cousin.

"It's a tradition. For the righteous, we drive by slowly."

"And open the door, but, Harry, why do we have to go to a strange funeral parlor when here we have our own shul not being used?"

This is true. No more than forty attend the Sabbath and holiday service.

"At a funeral hundreds would come, and the Rabbi and cantor wouldn't have to deal with Gentile funeral directors."

This too is true. There are no Jewish funeral homes in Rockville, but Hudson's does have in its basement display room a full line of wooden coffins. The tradition as I understand it can be explained thus: "Henry, if we don't permit, we don't offend. A funeral from the synagogue is permitted for the righteous of our congregation, although, honestly, I don't remember even one. The religious committee never wanted to decide who was righteous and who wasn't. So the committee permitted no one to be buried."

"So, why in Iowa?"

The answer to this argument is simply that the reformed are all righteous. This too is unacceptable because, as it says in the tradition, all the righteous are equal. The righteous Jew, Gentile, or heathen are all equal. Certainly the conservative and reformed Jews are equally righteous. An answer like that would be an abomination to Henry.

I offer, "Henry, go to the religious committee, appeal to them to change the rules. Maury will be back from Texas in a week or two. Begin with Maury. Maury's father and grandfather were all members of the religious committee. If you convince Maury, the others will be easy."

"You would go with me, Harry?"

"First, let me talk to the Rabbi."

The governing process in our congregation is totally democratically traditional. The gabbai makes his proposal to the Rabbi, who proposes to the religious committee, who proposes to the board, who proposes to the executive board, who reach the decisions that affect our ritual lives. The board members are all elected from a panel submitted by the board. These principles of community participation are so accepted by our congregants that no more than forty will appear at the annual meeting to learn of the board's decisions. Nothing has ever helped to increase the percentage of our members involved in our "open selection" process, not even a free roast chicken supper with strudel for dessert. We, Ida and I, are financial supporters of our Center; intellectually, we are dissidents. Dissidents who once, twice and three times attempted to elect board members from the floor, an effort in which we have never succeeded. So, naturally, we are not board members. The Rabbi, of course, is an ex officio board member.

I catch the Rabbi in the parking lot on his way to his Rotary Club lunch. I hold the Rabbi by the sleeve of his gray herringbone tweed sport coat. "Henry asked me to gain your support to permit burial from our synagogue."

"My support is not necessary. Nothing in our tradition prohibits funerals from our sanctuary." With this the Rabbi backs up his red Plymouth and roars off in a sheet of dust, and I make a note: 1.) Tell the house administrator to give the parking lot a spring spray down; 2.) have our janitor vacuum the rug in the prayer house. Ray Shore is complaining about his dust allergy.

"Harry, will the Rabbi go with us to the religious committee? Tell them what he told you?"

"Not on a year his contract renewal is being negotiated."

Henry Gottwalt leans forward. "In Germany I knew. In Germany we were buried from our shul."

"No reason it can't be done here, Henry."

"What should I do?"

"Revolt. We refuse to pay anything above the minimum dues. We refuse to pay for Torah honors. We must attack the establishment in its deficits. In this synagogue we will attack the financial structure. We have a just cause, Henry. We will overcome."

"Overcome what?"

"Overcome the religious committee."

"I will do what we have to."

"First we must prepare a position paper."

"What is a position paper? You know, Harry, I was not a college professor like you."

"Henry, in the Rockville tradition, our righteous do not have the opportunity to make a last payment to the congregation for the privilege of burial. That is what we must prove—that our congregation will benefit financially by permitting funerals to be held in our Center."

"Like the reformed do."

"It's quite simple, Henry. We must prove that we are not compromising our standards by presuming that all in our congregation are righteous and then, of course, all may be buried from here. And we must prove that it will be advantageous to our congregational coffers."

"What?"

"We must prove that funerals are money makers."

"That's what you taught in college?"

"In economics, we must prove a cost-benefit ratio."

"What does that mean, Harry?"

"It means that our revolt must cost our congregation both grief and financial loss. We can begin with a position paper. If our argument is rejected, we will follow with informational picketing, lobbying our board, and last, we will withhold our services. Sort of a rent strike. We will no longer pay and pay for aliyahs"—calls to the reading of the Torah—"for me shabarachs"—special blessings. "For the Hebrew school, for the building fund, for the mortgage fund."

"In Germany, we used to pay the poor to attend the minyan. Harry, we could refuse to go to the minyan."

"It's all possible, Henry."

"You will write this paper, Harry?"

"Not to worry, Henry. Remember, Henry, a majority of one is all we need when our cause is just."

"Such a Hebrew scholar you are, Harry. How come you were never Bar Mitzvah?"

"I had a socialist father who believed in Hebrew study. He was not quite sure enough about religious observances to force me into Bar Mitzvah studies."

I patted Henry on the back. "Our cause is righteous. Fear not." And I sang, "Hope thou in the Lord."

"What did you say, Harry?"

"Nothing, Henry, just something I used to sing in school."

It would be two weeks before Maury would return. Maury would arrive in Rockville the week after Passover. The second day he comes back I will talk to him. The first day I will listen about his son, the broker in Texas, and his daughter in Arizona. On the second day Maury will tell me, "Now that I am back, I will review the Torah honors from December to April." Maury will say after he adds up my billings for the Torah honors, "Only fifty-four dollars?"

"Ray Shore paid for three aliyahs."

"That was in February, Harry. In March you only called Ray Shore to the Torah once. Only eighteen dollars."

"Ray Shore had a bad cold. He wasn't at the minyan."

Recalling the previous years' conversations with Maury, I decided to use the financial instruments. Better with honey than with threats. The position paper would be all honey. Then on to demonstrating the cost-benefit ratio of funerals to the Rockville Jewish Center congregation. "Funerals Can Be Profitable."

Under the cost column I could only ascribe ten dollars for clean-up of the yarmulkes that would be left in the lobby by those attending the funeral eulogy in the sanctuary. It is only suspicion, best not even discussed, but I suspect that the common usage skull caps on the table at the synagogue doors are used again and again, so their replacement I noted as negligible, simply included the cost estimate as another ten dollars under miscellaneous, bringing the total cost for one funeral to twenty dollars.

On the profit side, the Rabbi's and the cantor's saved time (not going to the funeral parlor) which they could devote to instruction of the children, to adult education, public relations, speeches at the noon Optimist Club and personal guidance to prospective converts. Time savings utilization I value at one hundred dollars per funeral. Plus the in-house increase of revenue created by the kitchen rental fees for the use of our kitchen to prepare the consolation meal.

Then the mourners head fee of fifty cents for each mourner entering the sanctuary for the eulogy, not to exceed two hundred dollars even if more than four hundred attend. A one-time-only fifty dollar charge for those funerals that will produce more than four hundred mourners. This fifty dollars would offset the necessary expense of opening the folding doors between the all-purpose room and the sanctuary to permit two hundred additional mourners to hear the Rabbi's eulogy.

All fees would be doubled for those departed who were not members of our congregation but wished to be buried from the Rockville Jewish Center.

As an incentive to join our congregation, a fifty-dollar credit would be issued for the survivors to join us at least during their eleven months of mourning, when our laws demanded the daily Kaddish be recited for the departed.

I did not ascribe any savings to our Gentile funeral directors. They would, of course, have the savings of lesser distance for their hearses to traverse, sixty feet from sanctuary to cemetery. No more stopping, no more door openings, no more leaving engines run on their Cadillac hearses to keep our unembalmed members in constant air-conditioning. Realizing how profitable it would be, the United Undertakers of Rockville would endorse our procedural changes.

Naturally, I did not compute any savings by the undertakers from using the Center rather than a funeral parlor. That would be presumptuous, too much. I had determined the profit to the undertakers but crossed that out as gauche and irrelevant.

Let us assume only a six-hundred-dollar profit to the synagogue per deceased at twenty-six deceased per annum, computed on five years of statistical experience, our gain would be $15,600, plus intangible improvements in our moral condition, because the income from death will decrease our dependency on our Sunday evening bingo parlor.

This projection I presented to Henry, who in his wisdom asked me, "Harry, can we count on your figures to be accurate for the next five years? Otherwise, I don't think the committee will consider our proposal."

"Not to worry, Henry. Based on our demographic study, the death figures are quite conservative and should be met within plus or minus three percent—an acceptable level of error in a statistical study."

"This is what you did in college?"

"This, and more."

"If your figures are accurate, in ten years who will be left in the congregation?" Henry has that precise German education and mind that made him so successful in producing the finest corn whiskey in western Illinois.

"Let's not consider ten years. Let us solve our immediate needs. We have to get buried from the synagogue."

"Harry, aren't you counting too much on the dollar? After all, there is the tradition."

"When in doubt, Henry, count on greed."

"You said that?"

"No, Henry, Balzac said that."

"I thought you were in political science."

"I began in nineteenth century French literature."

"From this you made a living?"

"That's why I took up political science and economics."

"Harry, I think we should gain more support for when we go to the board."

"Who?"

And Henry thought. "Those who are the oldest. Look at what the families could save."

"Everyone should support us because who knows when we will die?"

"You try, Harry. You are the gabbai—with your education, your position . . ."

I tried. I began with the minyan, Karp, Zymanski. Ray Shore was particularly enthusiastic. "A novel crusade, Harry, something that should have been considered years ago."

Twenty-two signatures and a month later, I sit Maury down in the library, face to face. Maury, to his credit, is a listener. First, I prepare him. "Look at it this way, Maury: there are surely newcomers who join the reformed congregation for the burial privileges."

"Their congregation is so much younger than ours. Young people don't think about dying."

Rather than concede to Maury's wisdom, I continue. "Look what we can gain. At least fifteen thousand six hundred every year; in a good year, much more."

"Your figures are impressive, Harry, but—" and I don't let Maury finish with his always "Tradition is our strength."

"Maury, our strength is in the cemetery. We have more members in the cemetery than on the membership rolls. Maury, speak to the Rabbi. There is absolutely no reason that we cannot bury from—"

"Like the reformed," Maury finishes.

"Like we should be doing for our future. You know, 'from dust to dust,' Maury."

"I'll speak to the committee."

"Do you want for Henry and me to come to the meeting?" At that moment I hand Maury the petition with the twenty-two signatures. "I could get more signatures. This endorsement is only from those members who have come to morning prayers during the past month."

Maury puts the petition in his inside suit coat pocket. "I'll get back to you."

Maury is in the great tradition of committees. A month goes by; two months go by. Three months go by.

Henry is restless, anxious to assert our rights, begin our revolt. "Harry, what if we the minyaners withheld the eighteen dollars for the Torah Honors. That will bring an answer by next Monday."

"Patience," and I quoted Job: "For his later days were greater than his former."

"Look at what Job went through before."

"All right. I am going to speak to Maury. I know that Maury won't do things until he speaks to the House committee." The head of the House committee is Abner Harris, the oldest, most revered of our congregants, a sage in his own time, a scion of Abraham Harris of sainted memory—who in 1880 bought the land on which our cemetery and Center were to be built. Abner is frail, residing with his diabetic legs in a wheelchair with an attendant. Abner only appears at services on those Sabbaths when there are Bar Mitzvahs with a full lunch and desert table for the congregation.

Our first Bar Mitzvah this year is scheduled for the second week in May. After the Bar Mitzvah, after Abner has had a prelunch, Jack Daniels straight up and sponge cake, which he follows with bagels and blintzes and Black Forest cake, I sit down beside him. Abner allows himself these transgressions in the name of our tradition of joining in the simcha (the joy) of the Bar Mitzvah boy becoming a responsible thirteen years old. I wait until Abner has licked the corners of his moustache.

"Has Maury spoken you about permitting burial from synagogue?"

"This is the second time this has come up in sixty years."

A revelation to me—that sixty years ago our congregation had faced these same burial problems. "So, what happened then?"

"Nothing."

"Why not?"

"The house committee thought with all the mourners coming into the synagogue, in no time we would have to replace the rugs, the seats, the yarmulkes. We don't have a replacement fund, Harry. You know the bingo only covers our utilities."

At ninety-four Abner still wears the Harris head, a full head of gray hair accentuated by a full gray moustache which encloses a memory of fifty, sixty years ago that is unencumbered by events of our recent past. His son, Jackson, at seventy-two, is still practicing law. His daughter, Emma, seventy-one, teaches modern body movements at Rockville College.

"Harry, why do you and Henry trouble yourselves with burials? Young people like you should be golfing."

"Abner, this is a problem we all face."

"Later is better."

"Can I count on your support?"

"You don't need support, Harry. All you need is a replacement fund."

Thirty thousand invested at seven percent equals twenty-one hundred dollars a year, about what we will need to keep the rugs, skull caps, and seats pristine. That's where our revolt lies today, waiting for thirty thousand dollars.

I will have to tell Henry, "This tradition that we prohibit burials from the Center is based on the fear that our carpets will wear out. I have a way, Henry: All we have to do now is raise thirty thousand dollars. Henry, the committee has accepted the Rabbi's opinion; now it's only the money. I am so pleased. It's because of you, Henry, that we now have a way to bury our dead from the synagogue. All we need is money."

"Harry, is money stronger than tradition? That's the question." I know Henry will ask that. I know how his German mind works. All I need now is an answer to Henry's query: "Which should come first, Harry, money or traditions? A man of your education, Harry, in economics and Judaism. Certainly you can find a better answer than we need thirty thousand dollars. Tell me, Harry."

From Your Mouth to God's Ear

Memorial Day, Monday, was memorable because for once we had twelve for the eight a.m. holiday service. Secondly, it was the first of the Hebrew calendar month with required special prayers. Thirdly, the Rabbi had forgotten to read the names of those of our congregation who had died in service of our country, and fourthly, Henry Gottwalt was using our large letter prayer book.

That was the morning that our Rabbi leads the service, so I gently whisper in his ear, "Seymour Heller is here. I believe he came because his brother died in the war. You remember, naval Lieutenant Heller, the one the Navy names a destroyer after."

"So?"

"You didn't read the names of our war dead."

"Harry, you didn't prepare the list for me."

"Now, Rabbi—"

"Harry, it is your duty." With that the Rabbi threw off his prayer shawl, turns his back to me.

So, now it's my fault that our Rabbi didn't have his computer printout of our war dead. I shake myself in disbelief, say nothing.

The Rabbi rushes out the side door without a wave. Henry had heard our Rabbi's tone and manner. Henry never says anything unkind, ungenerous. Everyone has his own ways. Henry I don't understand. He drives the widows here, drives the widows there, attends all the community meals, but won't take a Torah Honor. It certainly can't be because he doesn't want to donate a few dollars for the blessing, the me shabarach, that follows the Torah Honor. That's one puzzle, a question our old cantor, the one before Silver, the one who served our congregation for forty years, advised me not to pursue. "Harry, don't ask Mr. Gottwalt to read from the Torah. Don't ask me why. He won't do it." So I never have, but that doesn't mean I can't sit down beside Henry and ask him.

"Henry, who are you reading from the large letter prayer book?"

"I have a cataract on my right eye. My son says I should have it operated on." Henry's son is a pathologist in Chicago. "I have no faith in doctors."

"So, pray. During the silent meditation, Henry, pray that the doctor has skillful hands, that all goes well with the surgery, that you be healed."

"Pray to whom?"

"To the God of Israel. As we invoke in Deuteronomy, 'Hear, O Israel, our God is one.'"

The answer I receive is, "Since the Holocaust, ours is a flawed God."

In June we go to Los Angeles. When I inform the Rabbi I'll be gone for a few weeks, he answers, "Travel in good health and return in good health." I answer, "Thank you," leave without shaking his hand. In July there is always the scurry to find the ten; this keeps me very involved. Henry is with us every Monday and Thursday morning; he stands beside the open Torah scroll, at the ready to offer "the connected word" should our Rabbi falter in his reading of that morning's portion.

It was in the first week of August, the Rabbi's month to rekindle his Jewish lights (this year in New York City), I finish the service. Ira whispers, "I think Henry has made up his mind to have the cataract surgery."

To confirm Ira's medical report, I catch Henry in the parking lot. "Ira says you are going to have your cataract out."

"Next Tuesday morning. In and out in one day."

"The most frequently performed surgical procedure. Not to worry." My enthusiasm does not seem to have the fortifying effect I hoped it would.

Henry answers, "Surgery is surgery."

On Tuesday Ira does the service. When he stops the silent meditation, I read, "May God bring a perfect healing of body and soul to Henry Gottwalt." Ira continues. Henry is not at services on Wednesday, which I think nothing of. What is so unusual for a man past eighty to take a day or so off after the stress of cataract extraction? Henry does not appear for an entire week. Not even at Saturday morning services. Each day I intended to call him, but with the Rabbi gone . . . and of course I presumed that if Henry isn't there today he would certainly be there tomorrow. Had I not been so successful in finding our ten, I would have called Henry. Who does live alone, still drives his own car, so independent, so resourceful, but I did not call on Henry, not even on the telephone. From my success in keeping the minyan, I lost the blessing of visiting the sick.

Next Monday Henry is in the second row from the back, on the right aisle, his usual place. Henry holds the prayer book very close to his face. After services, I am beside Henry. We are the last. All have left.

"Tell me, Henry, how did it go—the surgery?"

"Not so good. I have no more vision than I did before."

"You prayed?"

"I prayed, but I didn't believe."

"You are here every morning, reading the Psalms, praising God."

"That, Harry, has nothing to do with praying. A God that didn't save the six million Jews, the Gypsies, the Communists, should notice Henry Gottwalt in Rockville, Illinois? You expect too much, Harry."

"Still you came back, Henry. Here you are, praying with the minyan."

"What has community prayer to do with God helping Henry Gottwalt. Tell me."

I could have given Henry all the traditional answers, but then I was sure Henry had the wisdom of our fathers. All I say is, "Give it a little time, Henry. Maybe in a couple of weeks your vision will improve."

"From your mouth to God's ears."

I shut off the lights, turn off the air-conditioning. It was going to be a rare day in western Illinois, cool, low in humidity. The breath of the Minnesota forests had descended into the Mississippi River valley.

For Righteousness Shall Be Vindicated

At this morning's prayers, we read the psalm for Wednesday. "Happy is the man whom Thou instructest, O Lord, and teachest out of the law, for righteousness shall be vindicated and all the upright in heart shall follow it. Who will rise for me against the evildoers? Who will stand up for me against the workers of iniquity?"

It was Monday; it was Thursday. Then it was the Saturday and Sunday, and it was again Monday. It was a week and then it was a month. Was it May or was it June? It was end of May in the upper Mississippi River valley. Next week, the oats would be ready for cutting, the corn planting would begin. It had been wet, hot and humid, more summer than spring—like the spring of '69. Weather that required the fertilized lawns to be cut every five or six days.

Gray skies, partly cloudy, forty percent chance for rain. Partly sunny, a hot humid morning for eastern Iowa and western Illinois. I hung my sport coat on the hook of the Lincoln Continental, drove east to my downtown office, opened the sliding roof of the Lincoln, put on the air-conditioning, shut the roof. It was no cooler.

"I would sell to Archie if he just wouldn't push me so hard. Just give up what the building is worth, based on the tenants we have in place."

After a year of negotiations, on one thing I agree, Archie Daniels disagrees, wants to pay less. An implacable foe as it says in the prayer book. It was Archie who had started the negotiations slyly, cunningly. Archie had sent his partner, his smiling, pleasant, manicured partner, Pete Morrow, round in front like a bland Buddha. Pete was the smiling face for D and M Realty, the front for Daniels's money.

Pete appeared one late winter afternoon, a few minutes before four, just as I was locking up. Pete smiled, took off his overcoat. Overweight, Pete didn't exercise sufficiently. Rumor in Rockville had it that Pete was beginning to have a drinking problem. "Pete should join A.A."

"Lenny," Pete placed a computer printout, a spreadsheet, on my desk, columns of figures, percentages of gross incomes. Pete unfolded into the side chair beside my desk. "I would like to buy yours and Elsa's building. This is our payment schedule. The more we rent up, the more we pay you. All we have to agree on is the time of the sale and the down payment. We are talking a major out-of-town buyer."

All I heard was the time of sale. Then I heard my wife, Elsa, her monthly plea as she paid the bills. "Lenny, look for a buyer, list the building for sale. Times are changing. The gambling boats on the river are bringing Rockville national attention. The Rockville downtown will be like in the old days, people on the streets. We need that old building like a hole in the head. Lenny, you didn't hear me.

"In 1960, the building was an investment. The stores were rented, dentists, doctors in the offices. Look at it now, Lenny, fifty percent empty."

"It's not costing us."

"This is no way for you to spend your life. We should be traveling, enjoying planning for retirement."

So, I answered, "Could be a sale, Pete. I'll talk to Elsa."

Daniels belonged to the congregation. Daniels's mother spoke to Elsa. Maybe Elsa said, "Zymanski isn't what it used to be," or "The downtown isn't what it used to be," or "Lenny should be doing more for himself. Lenny"'s a fine painter. Lenny has a studio set up on the second floor, but he doesn't find the time to paint. Thank God, Lenny is not going down to the building on the weekends."

Archie didn't have to hear about the Zymanski Building from Elsa. Rockville is a small town. B'nai Jacob is smaller each year. Everyone knows everything, knew that the Zymanskis were no longer the "big givers," no longer belonged to the Country Club, bought only the smallest denomination Israeli Bonds, and Elsa was driving her 1984 Oldsmobile in 1991.

As soon as I came home I told Elsa, "Pete Morrow came by, hinted at buying us out. All very iffy, very dependent on their 'out-of-town' space buyer. Pete doesn't have a thing. I'll bet he doesn't even have his Cadillac paid for."

Elsa nodded in agreement, and added, "Archie has been doing well."

"When things are bad, that's when the Archies come out."

"Archie's is the only offer we have ever had."

"We'll see."

"You pursue it, Lenny."

"I will."

"First thing, you call Pete."

So, I called Pete, who said, "Come on by. We will talk."

I got Archie and Pete. Archie, thirty-two or -three, couldn't be any older, gets his hair styled, plays scratch golf at the Country Club, does deals in the members' bar. D and M Realty has signs on half the commercial buildings in Rockville.

That's what Archie learned at Harvard Business School: How to succeed. It's the times. A young man comes home. He cuts commissions—not really cuts—offers incentives. He pays for golf outings at the Club. He hands out golf balls, golf bags, dinner invitations for the wives. Daniels-Morrow, a full service agency, insurance, commercial real estate sales, appraisals, rentals, management, developing, financing. In an up market D and M Realty builds a shopping center, a small strip center with limited partners, other people's money, of course. D and M gets a development fee, a management fee. D and M, not Pete Morrow. I bet Archie doesn't share anything but a sign with Pete. Archie sells the malls to Providential Insurance for its investment portfolio. Archie buys a condo at Westwood Towers, swims in the lap pool, hosts parties around the Westwood Towers' barbecue pit. Not really parties—more like a gathering for prospective limited partners for D and M Development.

"These are the new ways, Lenny."

"The Zymanskis always used their own credit, their own money."

Pete sat behind Archie, sat slouched. Archie sat straight, face to me, Archie in his Armani double-breasted, softly draped suit accented by a hand-painted tie.

"Lenny, we can't give you quite as much as we thought we could." Archie's disclaimer for Pete's offer.

"In this market—" Elsa was anxious. "It's for your own good. It's time, Lenny. You listen."

"We know your building is paid for," Archie, the good guy, "but we want to be as fair as we can be. You know what the rental market is like."

Archie wouldn't buy unless he had a prospect.

"There is no neglected maintenance, nothing for you to fix, Archie. No other building has twenty thousand square feet available for a user. It's a beautiful building. Old, but beautiful."

"Don't be stupid, Lenny. No way Archie will pay you for the marble wainscoting, the slate floors, the ceramic tile. Not Archie."

"Make me your best offer, Archie."

Another spreadsheet comes across the desk at me. The offer was addressed Mr. and Mrs. Leonard Zymanski.

"It's so much less than you offered before. I don't think . . ."

Archie had gotten up. He stood above me. Then Pete towered over me, and he began that "Lenny, in this market—." Elsa had predicted Archie's "in this market."

"In any market, if only for our bricks and concrete, your offer is nothing. Less than four dollars a square foot. The city is buying property on the next street, tearing it down, and paying twenty dollars."

"Lenny, see what you can do. Don't say no to Archie. Listen."

"Yes, Elsa."

That was when I asked Philip Segal to meet with D and M. No better man than Phil, a respected downtown merchant, city housing commissioner. "For you, Lenny, I'll speak to Archie." He did. He told me word for word. "All Lenny wants is a fair deal, no more than the city is paying. Elsa and Lenny will live with the payment schedule, but they can't accept your price."

Phil returned with a No, but said, "Thank God you don't have to sell to Archie."

"Phil, I would like to please Elsa. She wants us to travel more, get away for the winter."

Phil tried Archie again, even bought him lunch. "Nothing, Lenny. You know Archie: He says he doesn't know how long it will be for the economy to turn around, says his out-of-town buyer won't commit."

"Phil tried to get a fair deal from Archie. I tried to get a fair deal from Archie. Elsa, we are better off not to deal with Archie. Someone else will come along. The city has big plans for a municipal parking garage across the street from us."

"The mayor promised you that in 1975."

"Okay, Elsa, I can't succeed with Archie. I could do business with Pete."

"You could try to get along with Archie. Forget, forgive."

"Forgive a man who bought the Miller Corner from Harry Miller's heirs, and then resold it in ten days to the state Department of Transportation—for four times what he paid the widow? Protect the widows and orphans is what it says in the prayer book."

I considered the deal with Archie dead, gone, kaput, until that morning, when Archie appears at morning prayers just as the silent devotion was beginning, Archie with a woman. Both stood in the last row on the right. So, I say to myself, Maybe Archie has come to recite the Kaddish, the prayer for the dead which we recite at the end of the service, once before the daily psalm and once after the psalm. But there is no Daniels on the memorial list of this week's dead, nor a Gould, either. Archie's mother was a Gould. Archie had no need to recite the Kaddish. It was the woman who wished to be at services. If she was observing the eleven months of mourning, she would return for tomorrow morning's prayers, and if Archie was escorting her, driving her in his Mercedes-Benz with the cellular telephone, she was from out of town.

Then I spot Archie and the woman driving down Fifth Avenue. There is his Mercedes parked in front of the bank, in the loading zone across the alley from our building. So, I drink my morning tea and look out the window. Half an hour later, the woman and Archie leave Marie's Paris Café.

The woman was in mourning, was observant. She did not eat before the *shacharit*, the morning prayer that blesses God for his goodness.

Tomorrow, on Thursday, the Torah will be read. As a visitor, a stranger, the Rabbi or the hazzan will give the woman the honor of reading one of three Torah portions. She will come the Bimah in which the Torah scroll is spread. She will stand facing me while her portion is read by the hazzan.

On Thursday, there is Archie and the visitor. She recited the blessings in a Sephardi French accent. Afterwards she made an unusually large donation to B'nai Jacob, "Fifty dollars in memory of my husband, David, son of Benjamin."

Over her navy blue sack dress she wore a Hermes scarf. Her face long, her hair gray, her eyes blue, her body square. A woman of a certain age who uses perfume in the morning, who speaks Litvak-accented Yiddish to the sexton.

Captain Leonard Zymanski, Polish Army in Exile, speaks French, German, understands Hebrew. Captain Zymanski, who spent the war in England attached to the Polish Government in Exile. Captain Zymanski, who came to the United States as a displaced person, married Elsa Kline, war widow, whose brother owned a downtown office building, became a big landlord, a big success.

It was only yesterday. It was a lifetime. It was more than forty years ago.

After the Torah reading, the woman left without shaking the hands of the hazzan, the Rabbi or the prompters. After the Kaddish she and Archie were out the door. The woman stopped to read the notice board that is in the entry. I spoke to her when Archie had to go to the can.

"Shalom. *Bienvenue*. Welcome to B'nai Jacob. I do hope you will join my wife and me for the Sabbath. We would be most pleased for you to have dinner with us on Friday night. My name is Leonard Zymanski."

"Shalom, good morning," she answered. "Miriam Pollack." She smiled. "I will try. It is possible, but not for sure."

"*Nous espérons*." We hope.

"You speak French?"

"It has been a long time since I have had the opportunity."

"You knew I was French-speaking. Archie told you."

"Archie did not tell me. I heard the accents."

"You have been to France?"

"After the war. Several times since."

"We must talk again."

"*À demain*." Until tomorrow.

I drove downtown.

I look out the window of my office. There is Archie, opening the car door for Miriam Pollack. Miriam stops, looks up at our building, and gets into the Mercedes.

I call home. "Elsa, I spoke to her. Her name is Miriam Pollack. If you would, call the Blackhawk Hotel, invite Mrs. Pollack for Friday night."

"I don't like it, Lenny. You may have an implied contract to sell to Archie. If you make a deal with Mrs. Pollack, Archie could sue you for his realty agent's commission and more. You know Archie." Elsa's Stanford University Business School education is showing. Elsa worries about the weather, the children, the business. Not like her father, but a throwback to her grandfather, a Hebrew teacher. In business there are risks. The Klines, the Zymanskis made their way by taking risks. Elsa has never approved of risks.

"Archie's offer is not a contract in any way. We did not accept. We rejected."

"Don't be so sure, Leonard."

"Elsa, please call Mrs. Pollack at the Blackhawk Hotel. Elsa, you understand the invitation is only for Mrs. Pollack."

"Lenny, promise me, no business on Shabbus."

I laugh. "I'll talk business until you light the candles. Then peace, Elsa. Ask Mrs. Pollack if she would like to light the Sabbath candles with us."

Elsa put out the embroidered linen table cloth, the Lenox china, the silver, the St. Louis crystal, the chalah, the wine. Mrs. Pollack had flowers for Elsa, two pink roses and stems of bronze chrysanthemums. "In Paris I would know the florists. Here . . ." It was not an apology to Elsa, more an explanation. "It was most kind of you to pick me up."

"My pleasure. A stranger in Rockville should not be alone for the Sabbath."

"I did not expect—" Mrs. Pollack pointed at the prints that hung on the dining room wall. "A Matisse lithograph. A Villon etching."

"Yes."

"Lenny was in Europe after the war."

"Those were not easy times."

"We know."

"Dinner isn't ready yet. Let's sit down."

Mrs. Pollack chose the Herman Miller chair. Elsa and I sat on the sofa separated from Miriam Pollack by the coffee table. Elsa had warned, No business. I didn't say a word until Mrs. Pollack said, "The Eames chairs are very well designed. I know from design."

"You are a designer?"

"Yes." Miriam laughed. "For the full figure. I am Marina, not yet a household name in the United States, but we intend to be. America will be a fabulous market for Marina Boutiques."

It was Elsa who asked, "What brings you to Rockville?"

"My nephew was in Rockville." She hesitated. "It is almost two years ago. He gave a concert in Rockville. Francois Baumann, the cellist."

"We heard him."

"My sister's son. He was treated so well. He found things so reasonable here. He told my sister. My sister is in our company. My son, too, my daughter-in-law. My husband wrote to the Chamber of Commerce. We were to come together, but. . . . It was his heart. It will be a year in July."

"I am sorry."

"You would have liked David. Everybody did. David made up his mind faster than I do. I have been in correspondence with Mr. Daniels for months." She counted her fingers. "Almost a year. He does not like the building I like." She smiled. "It's your building, but Mr. Daniels says you a very difficult man."

"Not my Lenny, not with women. Lenny is very charming. Lenny likes women."

"So I have noticed."

It was Elsa who asked, "What brought you to Archie Daniels?"

"The Chamber of Commerce recommended him."

Elsa smiled. "I told you, Lenny, not to give up your Chamber membership."

Elsa was scoring points. "Lenny, you don't listen to me. Lenny, you don't advertise. Lenny, your marketing is lousy. You don't know a damned thing about marketing. Haven't you noticed, Lenny, times have changed? It's not 1960."

"What are your space needs, Mrs. Pollack?" That's me, direct, open.

"About twenty thousand square feet, about what Mr. Daniels tells me you have between your second and third floors."

"We have freight elevators to both floors."

"And you have a willing owner, Mrs. Pollack." Elsa again. "We can talk?"

"It's not Sabbath yet."

"I meant confidentially, as friends."

"Of course."

"Rockville is a very central location."

"We knew that before we, I, came."

"Dinner," said Elsa.

"Sunday we will talk business."

"I can pick you up," offered Elsa.

"That would be very nice, Mrs. Zymanski. Here I am sorry I never learned to drive. In Paris there is a car and chauffeur. Mr. Daniels has been so kind."

"There is no need to bother Mr. Daniels on a Sunday. It's his golf day."

"So he explained to me."

"We go on a picnic on Sunday, a drive along the Mississippi to Savannah, then lunch. Chicken, white wine on the Palisades above the river." Elsa is helping.

All day Sunday there was no talk about the sale of the building until Mrs. Pollack was at the door of the Blackhawk Hotel.

"Lenny, Elsa, may I impose upon you? Could we go through your building? Sunday is such a good day for that. The offices empty, no one to disturb."

"Of course."

We showed Miriam the fifth floor, mostly leased, to the fourth, half leased, to the second and third, mostly empty. Mrs. Pollack smiled and nodded. "We will need to do a few things, but not too much. The tax credits will more than offset our costs."

That encourages Elsa. "There has been a Kline in this building since it was built in 1912."

"From tradition I know, Mrs. Zymanski."

"I would like to keep my offices here. Five-oh-one is my second home."

"For you, no rent."

"For that, I will give you all the maintenance equipment and a fine staff."

"Thank you for a lovely day."

"I have always liked the Midwest, so much opportunity."

Even after hearing Miriam, Elsa wasn't convinced. "Don't be so sure, Lenny. Miriam Pollack didn't really say she would buy."

"Not to worry, Elsa. *Pas de problems*. No problems. The worst that could happen is that she will ask for a lower price or better terms."

"Would you give them to her?"

"If it doesn't hurt us, why not?"

"You could have sold to Archie months ago."

"Not for four dollars a square foot."

"You didn't try. He would have come up if only you had come down."

"It's worth thirty."

"Only in your head, Lenny."

"I know the market."

"There is no market, Lenny."

On Monday Miriam appeared in my office with Archie Daniels. She came in, closed the door to the hall, took off her green raincoat, pointed Archie into the chair beside her. "Mr. Zymanski—"

Now she was Marina, wearing her originals for the mature figure, a gray sack dress accessorized with a Hermes scarf worn around the neck and down the left shoulder. The both—six hundred dollars; with the Gucci sports pump nine hundred fifty dollars, seven hundred thirty Euros.

"I am sorry, Mr. Zymanski. I regret I missed this morning's service. I was touring, visiting other locations with Mr. Daniels. Mr. Daniels showed to me space in suburban shopping centers. No charm, no design. No tax credits. Not like your building." Marina extended her hand. "Mr. Zymanski, please tell Mr. Daniels your price."

"Twenty dollars a square foot."

Marina smiled. "As I told you, Mr. Daniels, I save when I buy from Mr. Zymanski."

Archie was the surprise. He did not protest and did not call me until three-thirty. "Lenny, you owe me a commission. I figure ninety-eight thousand. I sold your building for you."

"Now, now, Archie. Mrs. Pollack bought our building, but you didn't sell it. Mrs. Pollack told me everything. Actually, I got a statement to that effect from her yesterday. Mrs. Pollack noticed the building when you took her to breakfast at the Paris Café. She spoke to Marie, in French, 'Who owns the building? Can it be bought?' Marie told her our name. Miriam liked the building because of the design. Until Sunday afternoon, she had never been in the building, only admired the outside."

"Mrs. Pollack received my professional advice. You'll have to pay for that. I advised her on the probable price. I described your available spaces to her."

"Thank you, Archie."

"I would have gotten thirty for you, Lenny. That is how much your building is worth."

"I am sure you would have."

As I was about to hang up, Archie began again. "I introduced your building. I'll sue."

I told it exactly as it was to Elsa. "Miriam bought the building. Archie wanted ninety-eight thousand in commissions, and I told Archie, 'Sorry, no fee.'"

"Don't be so cocky, Lenny. Archie will sue. You know Archie. He isn't going to pass up a chance for ninety-eight thousand."

"Smile and enjoy, Elsa."

"Enjoy a lawsuit between you and Archie?"

"He won't sue, not after I give one hundred thousand to B'nai Jacob to honor Archie Daniels. We get a charitable deduction to offset the profit from the sale. Archie gets his name on a bronze plaque in front of the sanctuary with all the other big givers. Archie is a big giver, revered forever."

"I never thought you would sell the building to Mrs. Pollack."

"I did, didn't I?"

"Archie could still sue."

"You worry too much, Elsa."

"Lenny, you don't worry enough."

"For now, let's enjoy."

Elsa did not answer me.

And If by the Grace of God He Gives Me the Years...

"Harry, does Milton think he is too big a man to come with us to HyVee?" Ira asks me.

I say, "Milton has his business obligations."

"Milton tells me his son-in-law runs the business."

"Milton still goes to market to buy the piece goods. That's why he won't go with us for coffee. He has to be in Chicago by eleven."

Ira is not satisfied. "Harry, you ask him to come with us. Maybe if you ask him, he'll come. So he gets to Chicago a half hour later."

"I'll ask him the next time he comes to services. What is so important for you to talk to Milton?"

"It's important, Harry, believe me."

Next Monday Milton Krouse is back to the minyan. Ira pulls my sleeve. "Now, Harry, you ask."

Milton has just about folded his prayer shawl into the velvet carry sack with the gold embroidered Star of David when I come over to him. "Milton, Ira would like for you to join us at HyVee for a cup of coffee."

"I'm going home to make my own coffee. Look at me. I can't go to HyVee." Milton points to his ankles. He is without socks. Milton has on tan trousers, a white golf shirt, a blue blazer and Reebok walking shoes. Milton has been a widower for thirty years, isn't about to allow anyone to direct his choice of clothes, cars or next spring's ladies ready-to-wear for his six stores. But now he reconsiders. "Okay, Harry. Ten minutes. But I don't stay if Bill Levy is there."

"No, just you and me and Ira."

"Good."

"Tell me, what's with you and Bill Levy?"

"You are the only one I'll tell, Harry. Bill is the tightest man in Rockville. I ask him to buy a ticket for the Epilepsy Golf outing, only fifty dollars. 'Bill, dinner, a cart, prizes, all for a good cause. A loving fifty dollars.'"

"Maybe he isn't into epilepsy."

Milton parks his new Cadillac beside my ten-year-old Olds. I admire his taste, his choice of colors, his wisdom about automobiles. "Nice shade of blue you have there, Milton."

"Harry, it's a new world. Now it's cheaper to lease."

To which I nod and approve. "Frees up thirty thousand you can use in your stores."

"Harry, you learned all that in college?"

"Out of books on marketing, Milton."

"For merchandising, you need hands-on experience. It's a feel, Harry. David—fifteen years in the stores, all he knows is from bookkeeping. Who is going to go to market to buy when I am gone?"

I don't answer that. I switch to compliments for the Krouse family. "David is doing good things with the Center's books. First time in years everything is up to date. David's put us into the computer age."

"When my Becca married David, I never thought it would last. Now look at them, two fine children."

"Milton, that's what life is all about. You have to think positive about the future."

Ira and his coffee cup are seated at the darkest, farthest corner from the glass bubble through which the June sun is warming the Medicare recipients and their breakfasts. Milton pours a half cup of coffee from the Silex brewer, throws his quarter into the plastic box, sits down across from Ira. I sit beside him. I wave at Shirley and Paul Farber, who do seven a.m. power walking instead of the minyan; they wave back. I made a note: Call Paul Farber—"You could come to the minyan in your jogging clothes."

Our corner is definitely discrete, as isolated as can be achieved in a Rockville supermarket that has a full service post office, an aggressive lottery sales program and offers the best fresh fruit at the best prices. This morning the loudspeaker specials are cherries, blueberries, watermelon.

Ira is at ready. He goes, "Milton, we have to think about tomorrow. You have two beautiful grandchildren, bless them, in the Hebrew school."

I nod. Milton takes a taste of his coffee. "You call this coffee— water! I make better coffee than this from instant."

Ira is back with, "Milton, we need you—" but Milton doesn't let Ira finish. He sings, "Everybody needs somebody . . ."

This only delays Ira for a moment. He takes a sip of coffee which increases his vigor. "Milton, I need from you a hundred thousand dollars."

Milton grins. "It's a good round number. You going to tell me why?"

"To pay off the congregational mortgage."

I add, "That's good business, Milton. We save the ten percent interest."

"You are right, Harry. It takes money to make money."

Ira reaches across the table, reaches for Milton's hand. "What do you say, Milton?"

"Not so fast, Ira. Not so fast. So I give a hundred thousand, you need seven hundred thousand more."

"I have prospects. Fred Weiss, the Kramers."

Milton gets up, shakes Ira's hand. "You get Bill Levy to give you a hundred thousand, you got mine."

Then Milton is gone. Ira gets up, refills his cup, drops a dime into the plastic collection box, returns and sinks onto the bench seat of the booth. "That, Harry, was a lot easier than I thought it would be."

"Ira, Milton didn't say yes."

"He didn't say no. For Milton, that is a yes." Ira grins. "All I have to tell Bill Levy is Milton gave. So then Bill will give. You know Bill—just as tight as Milton, but Bill isn't going to let Milton get his name on the bronze plaque without his right beside it."

I nod. "There is a long way to go. Ira, that's only two hundred."

"I have Fred Weiss on a conditional."

"What does Fred want?"

"He gives, we give up bingo."

"I didn't know Dr. Weiss was on an anti-gambling crusade."

Ira laughs. "It's not the gambling. It's the cigarette smoke. Fred is allergic. Every Monday morning he comes to service, he coughs."

"So, you have a possible third."

"And Ray Shore makes four."
"He won't give another nickel."
"He gave plenty until—"
"Ray Shore joined the Temple because the board said no burials from the Center."
"For a hundred thousand, the board will change its mind."
"Ira, you are an optimist."
"From little acorns big oaks grow."
"That takes forty years."
"That's the trouble, Harry. Rush, rush, hurry, hurry, and still I don't have enough time." Ira gets up.
"Where are you rushing, Ira?"
"I have an appointment over at Kramer Brothers. I get two, three hundred from him and Edna, then Haskel Roth. I am getting there, Harry, I am getting there if only the Lord will give me time."

A Rabbi Is a Leader

When Rabbi Cohen invites me into his office, that is something. "Harry, I wanted to tell you what I said to the hazzan Silver. I said, 'Jordan Silver, you were made for bigger things than being a cantor in Rockville, western Illinois.' Those were my words to our young hazzan as he drove his red Camry south to the joys of suburban Judaism in Meadowlark Lakes, Missouri. You know, Harry, all Jordan wanted was a word of recognition; one word now and then from the religious committee would have done him fine or at least kept him mollified. Praise from the minyan-goers was not enough for young Jordan Silver. Last Monday morning after he led the service, Dr. Gross shakes Jordan's hand. 'When you read the Torah and when you did the second part of the service, that was truly melodic, very nice.'

"Does Jordan say thank you? No. Jordan says, 'I'm not an early morning person. Why don't you come to the Saturday services. I'm even better then.'

"Before Silver, for forty years we had a cantor, a Brooklyn-born, Williamsburg-raised cantor, not one of your college-educated hazzans. He retires to Florida; we get a 'Please call me Hazzan.' A hazzan is a cantor in a Sephardi synagogue, synagogues of the Eastern tradition in which the members are from Turkey, North Africa, Iran, with traditions from fifteenth century Spain. In Rockville, the hymns, the order of prayer, the traditions is Ashkenaz, the western tradition, and Jordan Silver wants to be called hazzan.

"Our Rockville congregation was formed in 1882 by European Jews from Poland, Russia, Austria, Germany. Our synagogue's music is from that tradition. At their most daring, our melodies are improvisations on themes that are centuries old. Even the introduction of the great Cantor Salomon Sulzer's variations which he sang in the last part of the nineteenth century at the Vienna Temple would today in Rockville be considered as too radical a departure from tradition to be acceptable to our religious committee 'mavens,' the know-it-alls. This is one hundred years after Salomon Sulzer is dead, buried, accepted and idolized. Sulzer's variations sound like Mendelssohn, sometimes like Schubert, but many times his variations are on our more ancient liturgy. The nineteenth century traditional Sulzer melodies would not be considered for Rockville's services because Sulzer wrote for a four-part choir, a cantor and an organ. In Rockville, an organ is no, never. A choir we have only on the Holy Days and a cantor . . . a cantor shouldn't turn his pulpit into a stage.

"We still have those who say, 'Who needs a cantor anyway? The Rabbi can do it.' To which I always answer, 'We need a cantor. The congregation may not need a cantor, but I, Rabbi H. K. Cohen, need a cantor. Because I am not going to teach our twice-a-week Bar Mitzvah class, do the twice-a-month lunch-and-learn and the evening adult education. Our President Katz tried that on me just once.' As soon as Sandra arranged for Jordan's 'outplacement,' Sandra comes in my office without knocking. The door was only open a crack. She sits down, puts her briefcase on my open copy of *Commentary*. 'Rabbi, next semester I doubt if we will have a cantor.' To which I nod.

"'The committee thought that you should do adult education only two nights a week for four weeks, maybe six weeks. Tuesday and Thursday. Members of our congregation have been complaining that they have to go over to the Temple for adult education.'

"I don't answer. Tuesday night I finish my Sunday *New York Times*. Thursday night I watch *Mystery*. Sandra says, 'Tell me, Rabbi, what subjects you would like to teach. I'll have it put in the bulletin, right on the front page.' There is only one way to handle President Katz's constant demands.

"'As you know, Sandy, a Rabbi has to study. Tuesday and Thursday are my study nights.' Sandy does have a dubious virtue, a grating persistence which she demonstrates with a cough and a rise in inflection. 'The temple has adult education. We are going to have adult education.' Compromise and moderation are my virtues, not direct confrontations a la Jordan Silver. Although with a lifetime contract, I do have choices, privileges Jordan did not have. 'Sandy, if you get ten to sign up, I'll teach.'

"That puts an end to that request forever. Sandy can offer adult education, an opportunity to grow in Judaism for the next four weeks. Ten we have never had in the classroom. Then President Sandra must prepare for the annual Board meeting, which will leave her no time to direct this Rabbi. No more 'Rabbi, may I bring something to your; attention. . . . Here is a list of courses we could offer to our Jewish community.'" After the morning *shacharit* service Jordan could have come in; we could have talked. I could have taught him, 'To get along, you have to say "Yes sir, boss," take two steps backward and bow.' With my advice, Jordan would still be here. At any rate, he would have made it until August.

"Today, who really wants the Rabbi's advice? In the old days—read Isaac Bashevis Singer—the Rabbi's wisdom was sought out to settle business disputes, domestic quarrels, community decisions. Now rabbis do family counseling, drug counseling, social services. Here am I, trained in law, accounting, financial planning, management: I didn't need all that Columbia Business School education. The Rabbi's business is ten dollars here, fifty or a hundred there for a wedding, for reciting special prayers for the ill or Kaddish for the dead. Those monies are so insignificant the I.R.S. doesn't even contest them. The executive board has never come to me saying, 'Rabbi, how would you handle our mortgage problems?'

"All Sandra Katz had to do is make an appointment. 'Tuesday morning at 8:30 would be good,' and I would explain to her, 'My dear Sandra . . . My dear Sandra, your eight hundred thousand deficit is really not an insurmountable problem, not at all. When I was at Columbia Business School, we had a similar case. The solution is quite elementary, actually there are two or three avenues we can explore for your congregation.

"'First, I suggest we review the facilities we have and hardly use. As you know, Mrs. Katz, we have a mikveh, a ritual cleansing bath that is not used more than once or twice a year. Christians who believe and follow total immersion would be very pleased to pay a generous fee for the use of our mikveh. The mikveh is adjacent to the multipurpose room. We can rent the multipurpose room to the mikveh users. The kitchen adjoins the multipurpose room. You can have separate fees for the use of the baptismal font (the mikveh), the multipurpose room and the kitchen. Of course the kitchen will be under a volunteer monitor to insure that only kosher food is used. Please note that renting to religious organizations will not threaten your tax-free status, but please do not rent your facilities for weddings, class reunions and hospital fundraisers. You may allow for-profit organizations the use of your Center, but do not accept a fee or you will pay real estate taxes.

"'Now, for the second solution to the deficit, here I want to deliver a homily. The trouble with our members is quite simple. They don't know the past. Look at the morning minyan-goers. Levy, Karp, Stern, Gottwalt, Gross. Not a one of them knows Jewish history. Not a one has studied Talmud or Zohar. I would venture they haven't even read *The Sayings of the Fathers*. So they pray to the dead like Egyptians who prayed to Isis. Now, if you don't know the East. Our father, Abraham, came from the East. Our financial salvation can come from the East. From India, from the Hindu Indian doctors who have migrated to Rockville, who live in the best bluff homes that overlook the Rock River. Hindus, Sandra. Hindus do not have a particular day set aside for prayer. There is the opportunity. Rent a niche to a Hindu god. We have so many hours when no one uses our synagogue, the Center. Rent Sunday afternoons to the Baptists, Monday through Thursday the Hindus. Friday we will reserve for the Jewish meal site—we don't want to lose our Federal grant. Saturday is for the Sabbath service. Sunday morning for Sunday school. Sunday night is bingo. Mrs. Katz, we are already heating and cooling six thousand square feet. The increase in costs will be negligible. In ten years, though the magic of rental fees, no more mortgage. Then, Mrs. Katz, build reserves. That's where it's at, reserves. I have seen the same problem as yours. No money left to retire a mortgage. Such a beautiful building, but so much debt. Reserves, Mrs. Katz, like Joseph built in Egypt.'

"When Columbia University adopts my Masters in Synagogue Management curriculum then perhaps the Executive Board will come to me. But, as my uncle always said, 'A prophet is not heeded in his own community.'

"Only once did Jordan come in to talk to me. What does he want to talk about? Synagogue music. I told him that when Robert Schumann was in Vienna and he made it a point to go to hear Sulzer. 'That doesn't mean that you, Jordan Silver, are going to introduce Sulzer's variations into the Rockville Synagogue service. Here in Rockville, no one comes to hear the cantor. Here they come to say prayers for the dead. Jordan. You don't need an organ. You aren't going to get an organ. Our limited resources will not be used for music education, only for mortgage reduction.'

"Jordan began his bluzing, his pouting, like a little gray pigeon. His tenor's chest actually doubled, but he didn't say a word. He didn't say a word until his chest goes down. Then he says, 'Thanks for the advice,' and starts to leave. Then he turns again.

"'Rabbi?'

"'What, cantor?'

"'Please call me hazzan.'

"So I told him, 'Hazzan, remember a fool and his congregation are soon parted.'

"'Now you are quoting Benjamin Franklin to me?'

"'No, I'm quoting H. K. Cohen,' and I sang to him, 'A wandering rabbi I had been. . . .'

"'That is Gilbert and Sullivan.'

"'That is correct.'

"What can you expect from the young? What do they learn in college. Rockville was Jordan's and Harriet's second position—really his first as cantor, Talmud Torah teacher, morning prayer leader, adult education instructor, tenor solo chosen over the Greek Orthodox bass chanter for our ecumenical Thanksgiving service at St. Aloysius Catholic Church.

"The one thing that our hazzan never grasped is that Rockville is a congregation driven by its need to service an eight-hundred-thousand variable rate mortgage. The greatest communal religious experience in Rockville is the Hallelujah that follows 'This year we paid off forty thousand dollars. . . . This year we received ten thousand dollars from Ray Shore, thirty thousand from the raffle and gala. And let us thank God that interest rates are falling.'

"'Hallelujah!'

"Jordan did add song to the morning service. It was Jordan who insisted we chant the last verses of the Sixth Psalm. 'O Guardian of Israel, preserve the remnant of Israel. Let them not perish, Thy people Israel. . . .'

"Why I didn't think of singing the psalm, I don't know, but most mornings Jordan just sat in his red velvet chair to the left of the bimah, silent, meditative, arms folded observer of our minyan. After services Jordan rushed out the door, where to I don't know. Jordan didn't have a thing to do until three o'clock when the Talmud Torah classes begin. Then nothing until the six o'clock evening prayers. Those are only a half hour. It's only twice a week that he has to come back to the Center for the seven-thirty to nine evening classes.

"After the morning services, Jordan and I could have sat down, had a cup of coffee, a bagel with cream cheese, schmoozed. He could have learned from me about Rockville, gained from my eight years in western Illinois' only synagogue. I could have explained why the big givers are either dead, moved to Florida, or gone over to the Reformed Temple in Davenport. Beware of congregations run by accountants. Accountants know only from numbers, Jordan. Judaism in Rockville is not numbers. It is nostalgia.

"I had told Sandra, 'I don't eat out.'

"She says, 'Mr. Karp arranged for a kosher caterer. Rabbi, we lost thousands. Thousands!'

"'I wasn't hired to do fundraising,' I say.

"That stopped Sandy right there. You can't really allow the president, the board, the religious committee to tell me, the rabbi, what and when. The rabbi has to have his own agenda. I have the management curriculum to work on, the weekly Rotary luncheon, the twice-a-month Churches United meetings, and the burials. Twenty-eight last year.

"Tell me, Harry, should I have sat Jordan down and told him, 'Jordan, if you want I'll go to the religious committee with you. Maybe we can work something out for you to stay on in Rockville. Jordan, I need you. I need your help. Jordan, we need each other.' Why didn't I say that, Harry?"

I put my arms round our Rabbi. "There always will be another hazzan."
"I'm not so sure."
"Let us hope."

Send Us, O God, Speedy and Complete Healing

Monday morning, the stink of Sunday evening cigarettes from the multipurpose room, from the bingo, pervades the prayer room. Dr. Weiss begins to cough. The doctor has a history of asthma. My allergies started from the hog dander when I was vaccinating hogs. "Harry, please ask Ronald to put on the air-conditioning as soon as he comes.

I wrote, "Ron, A/C on in prayer house at 7:00 a.m."

The air-conditioning was on. Fred sneezes once, twice, four times during the silent devotion, as the Rabbi begins "May it be Thy will, Lord our God and God of our fathers, to send from heaven to Herman Bernstein and others of Israel who are ill speedy and complete healing that shall be a healing of soul and healing of body." Herman was in the hospice. How long would it be before uremia and coma. Herman had chosen no dialysis. Prayer. Why not prayer? There were miracles in our time. The Ethiopians had been freed in our time. Freed to emigrate to Israel. Thousands of Jews were leaving Russia, an exodus like when we were slaves in Egypt.

My notes for the day are on the back of the business card that goes in my shirt pocket. Visit Herman Bernstein. Call Rabbi Cohen re Russian family coming to Rockville.

The service over, I walk slowly through the synagogue parking lot, stopped to pick up a gum wrapper, a styrofoam Hardee's sandwich container. The day lilies are open in the entry door border, the tricolored New Guinea impatiens are doing well, getting a bit too much morning sun but will recover when I water them after the evening prayers.

The hospice was across Union Hospital's sky walk from the Oncology Center, Radiation (burn out the bad, save the good), conveniently adjacent to Therapy. Learn the way to the hospice . . . a gradual introduction, a day at a time . . . to acceptance.

The hospice was of the 1950s, cozy, single bedrooms, a home away from home, with hospital beds and wheelchairs, velour upholstered arm chairs that had once been cheerful and now were dull greens, blues and browns. There a television on a cart, in the corner a small brown refrigerator, a microwave: A house is not a home. A hospice is a hospital with bright wallpaper and nurses in pastel polyester pants suits.

"Mr. Bernstein? Two-one-two."

"Herman, how are you?"

"Call me Ralph."

Lieutenant Ralph Bernstein, Herman's brother, killed in action in 1944, crashed in his Dakota troop carrier onto a plowed potato field in Holland. Two years older than Herman, he had completed pilot training in 1943, flew paratroop drops until that night that he overran the runway. The right engine caught fire. Lieutenant Ralph Bernstein became a gold star on the bronze plaque in the Rock County Court House.

"Okay, Ralph, how are you feeling?"

"How should I be feeling?"

"You would feel better if you would get on dialysis."

"Not yet. I haven't made up my mind."

"If you haven't made up your mind, why did you go into the hospice?"

Herman grinned. "Wanted to be close to the hospital in case I changed my mind."

"Lenny sends his regards."

"He give up on me?"

"He sent in the first team to visit you."

"Remember 'Nearer My God to Thee,' that old hymn from high school? Jew boys singing Christian hymns."

"Didn't do us any harm."

"You are right, Harry, it's a Christian world. We might just as well get used to it."

"I have known that for a long time."

"You are looking good, Harry. I like your seersucker jacket. The blue goes well with your suntan trousers."

"You don't look so bad yourself, Herman."

"Ralph. Please call me Ralph."

"Do you want me to take you anywhere?"

"Where would I go?"

"To dialysis. I am going to say it straight out, Herman: Dialysis is a lot better than dying."

"I'll tell you what I'll do with you, Harry. I'll make you a win-win proposition. If I get any worse and the doctor says, 'Ralph, this is your last chance,' I'll call you to pray for me, and I'll go on dialysis. But I don't think it's going to come to that. Not since I changed my name."

"Anything you say, Ralph."

"You don't understand, Harry. One night I woke up—it was almost one-thirty in the morning. Sweats, the chills. I knew the angel of death had been here. Had been here and gone away confused, put off because I was Ralph. I heard those old wives tales from my grandmother, from my mother. It's a *bubbe meise*, a grandmother's story: Change your name and the angel of death can't find you. Believe me, Harry."

"Herman, I do."

"Ralph. Please call me Ralph. I knew you would understand. Harry, I assure you the angel of death was here."

"Tell me. Tell me how you know."

"Like during the war. It's a cold puff of air behind me. I had felt it before in our company aid tent, around some of our wounded. Not all. Just some. I never knew who the angle of death would come and carry off. Sometimes I was sure that one was going to die, both feet gone, guts hanging out. That one lived. One kid got a grenade thrown at him. He lost a leg, almost bled out—he lived. Another kid, a couple of pieces of shrapnel—dead."

"No one knows who lives and who dies."

"The angel of death knows. Thanks for coming, Harry. Tell Lenny not to worry. Tell him the food is better here, almost Kosher. Individualized low cholesterol, low protein, microwaveable snacks. Anything I want I order for the next day. The hospice is like it was in the evac tent. When the time comes, no one wants to die, no matter how much pain, how far into the valley. Look at me, Harry." Bernstein rolls up his sleeve, points to the surgical patch on his right arm. "All ready for dialysis."

"I'm pleased, Herman." I laugh, take Herman's hand. "I am sorry. Ralph."

"That's why I got ready."

"What?"

"You come in, call me Herman. Lenny comes in, calls me Herman. The angel is here two, three times a week. He is just rushing through, just a routine surveillance, in the hall looking for room two-sixteen, two-nineteen. He hears, 'Herman.' He puts that into his computer: Herman Bernstein, two-one-two, Union Hospice, Rockville, Illinois. Next time the angel knows where to find me. That's why I'm going to start on dialysis. I'm going to get out of here, not leave a forwarding address."

"Good idea, Herman. I'll stop by next week."

"I won't be here."

"I'll find you."

"How?"

"I'll check with the dialysis lab, see when you are scheduled to come in."

"Not if I am registered as Ralph Bernstein."

"See you, Ralph."

"Thanks, Harry. Say hello to Lenny."

What Does God Require of Thee? Seek Justice, Love Mercy

The July heat and humidity grew the corn tall, filled out the soybeans, ripened the tomatoes, turned the green grass tan. Those were the weeks that our congregants visited their children in Colorado or toured from Maine to Nova Scotia. I didn't think that it was that unusual that Ray Shore was not at the services. I call and receive only a taped "Please leave your message." I ask Ira, who knows everything, "Where are the Shores?"

"Went up to Minnesota."

This is the week that Ray drives up to Minneapolis. I remember last year's Shore Report on contemporary art at the Walker Museum, what is playing at the Guthrie and how well it is played, and how beautiful the River Road that hugs the west shore of the Mississippi is in its full summer foliage.

Sure enough, in a week Ray Shore walks in as usual, just one minute before the announcement, "Page one-oh-three." Why Ray can't come in two minutes or three minutes before services begin, I don't understand. By the time I complete the personal blessing, "Praise God that you made me an Israelite," Ray has his prayer shawl on. With ten in the prayer house, we continue to "Mourners' Kaddish," the prayer for our dead. Ray Shore stands, recites the Kaddish.

At the Kaddish for our rabbis, Ray again stands and joins the mourners. He rises for the Kaddish that completes our service. Ray stays for the Monday post-service psalm reading, which allows him to recite yet a fourth Kaddish. It is the inclusion of this additional Kaddish into our morning service that so provoked Hazzan Jordan Silver that he never takes part in it. Jordan mutters, "Harry, I'll do the Torah readings, you do the prayers. Just don't expect me to stay for the after-the-service Kaddish." As I see it, if we have three or four in our minyan who are mourners, the Kaddish is what they come for. An extra Kaddish is an incentive. Each Kaddish sends the departed one step closer to heaven. Where I heard that, I don't know. Certainly not from my father, not even my grandfather. Our family tradition is Polish liberal socialist, with more emphasis on Jewishness or peoplehood, less on heaven. That step to heaven I must have heard from my mother's sister, Rachel, the only one of our family who prayed every morning. She, of course, prayed at home, as fifty years ago women did not come to weekday services.

Deaths in the families of our congregation are announced at the morning prayers, so those who wish may attend the funeral, where the family will be sitting Shiva, the seven days of mourning that does not include Saturday—when the mourning is set aside to celebrate the Sabbath. There has been no death announcement from the Shores or the Golds, Mrs. Shore's family.

"Ray, from whom are you saying Kaddish?" I ask.

"For my second cousin, Annie. Annie was the daughter of my grandmother's sister. That's a second cousin, or is that a cousin twice removed?"

"Whatever she was, you don't have to say Kaddish for so distant a relative. The law only requires it for parents, children, and, God forbid, a sister if she has no children."

What harm is there in an extra Kaddish-sayer? For the next eleven months, Ray will be faithful to the minyan, a benefit to our community. Ray is a generous giver. He will donate eighteen dollars for each Torah honor. Two Torah honors a month is thirty six dollars. Let's assume ten month: That is almost four hundred dollars towards the mortgage relief fund. In eleven months, Ira may even have his hundred thousand dollar pledge. That will depend on the religious committee's decision to allow burial from the synagogue. The only thing dependable about the religious committee is that historically they reach the wrong decisions. That's what happens when a committee retains and safeguards yesterday and has no concept of today and no vision of tomorrow.

"Sorry about your cousin, Ray."

"Annie was ninety-four."

"May she rest in peace."

"Thank you, Harry. Harry, sit down." Ray takes out a check book, writes a check for one hundred dollars to B'nai Jacob Memorial Fund, in memory of Annie Lavine Margolies. "Now, on the anniversary of her death, Annie's name will be read from our pulpit forever and ever."

"From generation to generation."

"I realized that." Ray sighs, makes no effort to leave, which is most unusual, as he is always going, going. "When we came back from the funeral, at the consolation meal, here I am: Ray Shore, seventy years old. Now I am a patriarch, the only link between the generations. I was the only one left that knew Annie's mother, the only one who knew her daughters, grandchildren. From Annie's mother to Annie is one generation; from Annie to her daughter is two. From her daughter to her grandchildren. That's all girls—five generations of girls."

"It's the females who transmit our traditions."

"I know, Harry, 'from generation to generation.'"

"How was your trip?"

"Wonderful, Harry, wonderful. We stopped in Red Wing. Red Wing is all prosperity and discount stores. You know, where the pottery factory used to be. That's all antiques, ice cream and souvenir stories. Forty years ago Red Wing was a shopping center, a manufacturing center. Then it all died, and now it's a tourist attraction as prosperous and busy as it was."

"Things change."

"Sometimes for the better, Harry, sometimes not."

This is not Ray's usually optimistic "Invest in Rockville, for Rockville's future." "Invest in the arts." "Make Rockville a more attractive location for new industry." The Shore Companies offer lower rents as incentive to start-up businesses. So, I ask Ray, "How are things downtown?" That's a general question which should get for me a complete economic profile for the second half of this year, a projection for the next eight years in the office rental market, and the two to five years for the construction of good, affordable housing.

"You really want to know, Harry?"

I nod.

"I'll tell you more than you ever wanted to know."

"I taught economics."

"There is no real market out there. City Hall gives incentives, gives an out-of-town developer three and a half million to build an office building, to buy out existent leaseholds, to move tenants from one location in Rockville to a new office building across the street from my 1912 office building. The incentives lower rent, but there are no newcomers in Rockville, only relocations. So rents stay depressed, but the rents have been depressed for twelve years."

Ray Shore is a man of faith, faith in God, faith in America, faith in our free enterprise system. If Ray is pessimistic, why does he keep building, rehabbing?

"Ray, if things look so grim to you, why are you building single-family houses?"

"I guess that's what I do. That's what I told my banker, but you, I'll tell the real reason. Remember, Harry, there is a reason, and always a real reason."

I nod.

"We own the land. The land I can't sell. For twelve years I am paying taxes; no one buys a lot. So, if I put a house on the lot, make no profit on the house, maybe someone will come along, realize what a bargain the house is, and buy it."

I don't answer that. It's getting late. The impatiens have to be watered. We had one adequate rain in the middle of June, and although each morning we pray for the summer rain, the impatiens demand watering.

"Harry, that's what I like about you."

"What did you say?" Compliments are rare, to be savored, amplified.

"Each year you plant the impatiens to make borders of red flowers. It's a pleasure to walk from the parking lot to the prayer house."

"Thank you. You are the first to ever mention, to notice."

"I am sure others notice. Maybe they are too busy to mention. What you do, Harry, does not go unnoticed. Don't worry, Harry. 'It will be all right already'. For forty years Cantor Citron said that to us every morning."

Ray laughs. "Remember, Harry, when we come back from the war? Did you know

Citron fought in the Philippines? A cantor from Brooklyn who had been an infantryman in the Second Marine Division. That, Harry, is the miracle of America. You can be anything you want to be."

"If you are white and educated and motivated."

"As usual, Harry, you see more than I do. You are right. You and my wife. If I listened to her, I would have never bought a piece of ground to use next year, never built a home, the years after never planted a tree."

"I didn't mean anything by that, Ray."

"That I know. I have to go." Ray gets up. He is wearing his high top farm boots with the cleated soles.

Ray looks at his Baume and Mercier watch. "Going to meet the forester. Time to cut some of our oaks down. You know, Harry, like it says in Ecclesiastes, 'There is a time to sow and a time to reap.'"

"The price of timber is not very good."

Ray laughs. "The price of lumber has gone up ten percent since this spring."

"That's not fair, Ray."

"That's opportunity pricing, Harry. You know that. You taught economics."

That's what I admire about Ray. All the little things that so many of us put off, he does. Many years ago I asked him, "Ray, you polish your boots before go to out to your construction sites. The boots get dirty. You have to polish them again.'"

"Harry, that's what life is all about, duty."

"Duty to polish shoes?"

"Duty to keep going the best you can."

"Where did you learn that?"

"Right here in the prayer book." Then there was a long pause. Ray laughed. "And in the Army."

"Where are you going?"

Of all our minyaners, Ray laughs the most easily. I mentioned that one time to Ira, one time only. "Ray Shore is always in such good humor."

"That's a coverup. Ray learned that. That's a survival technique, like meditation. You ought to try it, Harry."

I write in my pocket notebook, "Ask Ray Shore, How can you laugh?—you with business headaches with your arthritis with Mrs. Shore's health problems."

I did. He answered, "Not to laugh, not to smile, not to be pleasant with the people you meet, the ones you do business with, that would be worse. After all, it's not their fault that you have sorrows."

Then you know what Ray did? He sang to me!

"All God's children got trouble. . . . You have no idea the troubles I have seen."

"For me, Ray, all that cheerfulness is difficult."

"What's difficult, Harry, is trying to do the right thing in business every day. That's the toughest of all."

To the Golden Country

On the first Thursday in August, we were too few, only eight at the morning minyan. William Levy had scheduled a hernia repair; Ray Shore was at the University of Iowa spinal clinic, only a checkup. The Rabbi announced, "We will read the Torah tomorrow."

Then he asked me, "Where are you running to, Harry?"

"A Senior's Day at the golf course. Going to play golf with Sy Rosen."

"Don't forget, you have to go to the Federation meeting for me."

"I'll be there."

The Federation office on the second floor of the Rockville Bank Building has a fast copy machine; Jane, the meal site administrator; a slow volunteer; Anne, a part time secretary and Molly, the executive. The office space had been made available to the Federation of Jewish Charities by Sylvan Gould. That was when Sylvan Gould was the majority stock holder of the Rockville State Bank, before his son-in-law, John, the bigshot from Chicago, had taken him into the valley strip mall the very year the farm machinery factories shut down. The mall never rented up. The son-in-law lost the mall to the mortgage holder. Sylvan had to sell his bank shares to pay off John's operational losses. All this in a continued down market. John left Sylvan's daughter, Kim, for a younger woman of twenty-six. Kim moved back to Chicago and married a widower of fifty with a Standard and Poor's rating of A-minus on a credit line of two million six hundred thousand.

Sylvan thought it would be best to take early retirement and invade his pension plan. The Rockville State Bank was merged into Illinois Banks, with headquarters in Peoria. Illinois Banks remodeled the Rockville Bank Building, raised the rent from free to affordable. The Federation office stayed on in its two-room-and-alcove suite, a memorial to the generosity of Sylvan Gould, who in forty years had compounded his father's three grocery stores, Gould's Golden Groceries, into a major regional chain, which he then sold to a national chain, bought the majority interest in the Rockville State Bank, pledged his shares to build the Rock Valley Mall, lost the mall to become Sylvan Gould, retiree, living on his fixed assets annuity, Sylvan Gould, the largest contributor to the Federation, living in a two-bedroom, two-bath condo in Arizona.

The Federation budget, supported by only twenty-five percent of the Jewish community, needed eight thousand dollars for the Emergency fund and the Russian Refugee fund, and didn't know where to find it. That's what kept the Temple and the Center together, deeds of loving kindness for the living and the dead, the Federation budget and the congregational cemeteries. As the rabbis had taught, "Deeds of loving kindness are superior to charity, because charity can be accomplished only with money. Deeds of loving kindness can be accomplished through personal involvement as well as money. Charity can be given only to the poor; deeds of loving kindness can be done for both rich and poor."

The Federation meeting began at seven o'clock. Attending were Harry Stern, for the conservative congregation; Rabbi Kaplan of the Reformed Temple; Molly, the executive who had insisted "Thursday at four"; and James Markowitz, attorney, president of the Temple.

The whispers were that the day Molly's husband, Elroy, had retired, Molly had scheduled a year of breakfast meetings, luncheon speaking engagements, and Monday, Tuesday and Wednesday evenings committee meetings—Russian Refugees on Monday, Holocaust Memorial, cultural events and meal site on Tuesday, and the coordinated Reform Temple and Conservative Center school board on Wednesday. Thursday night was out with the Toastmistresses. Molly had her hair and nails done Friday, the day the Federation closed at noon. Saturday was the Sabbath, and no one had ever worked in the Jewish Federation office on Sunday.

The conference table was between Molly's desk and the copy machine.

Harry Stern spoke first. "Rabbi Cohen couldn't come."

"Wouldn't, because he knew Rabbi Kaplan was coming," muttered Molly. Molly was the chairperson. Manny Silverberg, the president of the Federation, wasn't there either: the ex-officio chairman of all the committees was selling mattresses in his furniture store. "I got the call two weeks ago," Molly said. "We need eight thousand dollars in ten days. The regional office wants our help to resettle a Russian family. A mother, father, a boy of ten, the mother's parents."

"With or without funds from regional?" Questions of funding came from James Markowitz, who now did tax law, had been an accountant. Once an accountant, always an accountant.

"If we take the funding, we have to take an unfunded family, too."

"One family at a time. We haven't got enough volunteers for two families, to drive them to the doctor, take them shopping, teach them English. As soon as you get them set up, they leave."

"Russians like to be with Russians."

"So, why do they want to come to Rockville?"

Rabbi Kaplan, telling, retelling his own experiences: a not so successful year with the first Russian family, who, as soon as they learned "American," picked themselves up—without a subsidy, thank God—and moved to Des Moines, to better themselves.

"The regional director tells me, 'Molly, Rockford is taking three families. Des Moines is taking three families. Certainly Rockville can handle one family.'"

"So, what did you say?"

"Harry, I said I'll send you eight thousand dollars to give to the family that's going to Rockford. It's the best deal I could make."

"What about this Litvak family?"

Rabbi Kaplan looked at the agenda that was before him. "Nothing we can do about the Litvak family. They are coming on their own."

"When?"

"Next week. Wednesday. They want to get settled over the summer. Esther Litvak was here last Wednesday."

"How much?" That was Markowitz again.

"Nothing. She has a job at Brewer Paper. She is a computer person."

"Will her salary support the family?"

"Esther Litvak said it would be cheaper for them to live here than in Albany."

"Did she get the job on her own?"

"All by herself."

"What does her husband do?"

"Power plant engineer."

"That's going to be tough."
"Esther knows that."
"What do they look like?"
"Old, Harry, old. Esther is thirty-five, looks close to fifty."
"Molly, where are we going to get eight thousand dollars?"
"We either send the money to regional for Rockford or take a family."
"I'll get the eight thousand for you."
"Harry, don't make promises."
"It's not a promise, but I think I can."
"Where are you going to get eight thousand in a week?"
"From the morning minyan."
"Not from the Rabbi, you won't."

Grant Perfect Rest to Our Loved Ones Who Have Entered Eternity

From Monday to Saturday Bill Levy rose in the dark to the light of the red-eyed digital mantel clock, out to the prayer house so early that the sun had lit only the undersides of the night clouds.

Sunday, a day when the minyan was at eight a.m., was the day that Bill Levy did not attend *shacharit*, the morning prayer. On Sunday he unfolded rather than arose. From Monday to Saturday Bill was out of his bed, barefoot into the bathroom with his hands full of underwear, shoes, socks, belt, in a swift silent motion that would not disturb Lilly. Barefoot because his scuffs on the wooden floor would awake her. This Sunday morning he heard Lilly groan, moan. He stretched, arched his back, turned on his right side, put his left arm around Lilly, kissed her neck. Her face to his she answered, "I couldn't sleep. I have been up since two."

"I know, I heard you. Try to sleep. Nothing you have to do."

Lilly rose, dressed immediately, began to sort the laundry. Bill cut the grapefruit in half and then cut it again into sections. Lilly's half he put on a plate, placed that in the refrigerator. His half he ate bent over the sink, spit the pits into the insinkerator, leaving the skins in the sink. The laundry started, the Levys ate their Sunday breakfast, bagels and skim milk.

"Do you want coffee, Bill?"

"We'll have time after."

At ten the Levys joined Rabbi Cohen and six others at Mt. Nebo. Four of the six they knew well enough to nod to. Two were strangers or newcomers or returnees, a younger couple, early forties-late thirties, he tall, full-shouldered, with a red British guardsman's moustache and blue eyes that gave no recognition to the Levys, she younger, shorter, much thinner, wrapped in a tan cotton raincoat for which there was no need on this warmed, sunny green Iowa knoll. The couple stood side by side at the outside of the circle that had formed around Rabbi Cohen and his box of new blue Union Prayer Books.

Brother and sister collecting their third generation roots. Visiting the graves of their grandparents; no, a married couple who have lost a child, God forbid. Bill Levy searched the children's section of Mt. Nebo. No freshly overturned sod. No new small white granite headstone. No memory of a death announcement in the Federation newspaper that joined the reformed and conservative congregations. A brother and sister at their mother's or father's grave, a brother and sister from Clinton or Maquoketa, cities without Jewish cemeteries.

The Rabbi began. "Page five-four-six, 'The Memorial Service.'" He read the Hebrew of the Twenty-third Psalm. The assembled read the English. I shall fear no evil. The Rabbi continued.

"We are like a breath, our days just a passing shadow. We come and go like grass which in the morning shoots up, renewed, and in the evening fades and withers. You cause us to revert to dust." Then the Yizkor, and the el malah rachomim. "O God, full of compassion, Eternal Spirit of the universe, grant perfect rest under the wings of Your presence to our loved ones who have entered eternity. Master of mercy, let them find refuge forever in the shadow of your wings. Amen." The final prayers were as in the conservative ritual.

Lilly and Bill Levy shook the Rabbi's hand, replaced the prayer books. "Thank you, Rabbi. It's the first time we have used the new Union Prayer Book. It's very poetic."

"Yes, it is."

All had left the hill, drifted down to the gravel circle road where their cars had been parked.

"I should have introduced ourselves to the young couple, made them feel at home."

"I am sure the Rabbi knows who they are."

Alone, the Levys looked up the hill to their family plot, turned, walked down to their car. William Levy pictured those who would perform the deed of loving kindness, prepare him to be buried, wash him, dress him in his shroud, wrap his woolen prayer shawl around him. He dispelled those thoughts, took Lily's hand. "It was a nice service."

"Very similar to ours."

"My dad meant well."

"It's just that I feel so strange up here. I really don't know all that many up here."

Bill laughed. "We'll have a long time to get acquainted. There are other dead here from our congregation."

"Who?"

"The Shores' son, Alan."

What Was Will Never Be Again

Bill Levy and Leonard Zymanski left HyVee at the same time, Leonard east, to visit Elsie and Herman, congregants now confined to the St. Anne's nursing home wing.

Elsie, tied by a strap into a wheelchair, did not know Leonard nor anyone else. Herman knew Leonard and knew too well that Leonard would soon be visiting him in the hospice and then the final visit, the B'nai Jacob Cemetery.

The nursing home had been created from the oldest wing of the Catholic hospital built eighty years ago. The rooms, mostly singles, were small, with one window, one bed, one chair. When the nurses' aides came to make the beds, pick up the laundry, rinse the floors of the bathroom, the residents had to be wheeled into the dimly lit hall.

Herman Bernstein, his stump covered by a cotton blanket, sat in his wheelchair reading *The Wall Street Journal*. On his once- or twice-a-week visit, Leonard Zymanski brought news of the congregation B'nai Jacob. International and financial news Herman could read by himself. Leonard, with "How are you today, Herman?" for which he did not wait for an answer, wheeled Herman to the end of the hall to the dayroom where the artificial bamboo plant occupied the corner and the *Sunday Messenger* sat on the one end table beside the only seating, a pumpkin-colored loveseat on which Leonard sat with his back to the window that opened on the parking lot. Herman, facing him, put the newspaper behind his back.

"So, Lenny, what is new in beautiful downtown Rockville?" A reference to Leonard's career as a downtown property owner. Herman's retail career had been in a Westville liquor store, a fine location when Iowa had been dry. Herman's Liquor had been at the foot of the toll free Iowa bridge across the Mississippi, the first exit off to the right. Western Illinois liquor stores, open seven days a week but not until noon on Sunday, had done well, but that was a long time ago.

"Today it's all price, Herman. Service is nothing. On price alone, how can a little man compete against Walgreens?"

"That I know, Lenny. That I knew twenty years ago."

"Paul Schneider had a heart attack, only a little one."

Herman smiled. "How can you have a little heart attack?"

"That's what the Rabbi said."

"The Rabbi now is a medical authority?"

"He must have spoken to the family. What did your doctor say? Any good news, Herman?"

"Without kidneys?"

"You could try the dialysis."

"Not for me, Lenny. Not yet."

"When is your daughter coming?"

"Elana will be here for New Year's."

"We are praying for you. The Rabbi is reading your name every day."

"It won't hurt." Herman laughed. "It's all in the genes, Lenny. I just got bad genes for diabetes. Thank God Elana hasn't become a diabetic."

"All we can do is pray, Herman."

Herman chuckled. "I'll tell you a story. Our casualty collecting company had just crossed over into Germany. A barrage started. I was returning a soldier to his infantry unit. I grabbed him, pulled him into a slit trench. I was on top of him. I was the one in danger. He starts to pray. I started to cuss the Germans up and down, really good. He turns to me, 'Sergeant, you should pray, not cuss.'"

"So, what happened?"

"After the barrage we had to send the infantryman back to psychiatric."

"And what happened to you?"

"Nothing. The barrage lifted. We moved forward, pushed the Germans back through the hedgerows. Then I was lucky—fourteen months of combat, not a scratch."

"Were you fighting German troops?"

"All Germans."

"On the eastern front we had Rumanians, Hungarians, Ukrainians, all fighting with the Germans."

"I guess they had reason."

"Who knows, Herman, who knows?"

"You were in the Polish Army, weren't you, Lenny?"

"Polish cavalry." Leonard took from his wallet a full length photo. "I was twenty." He wore a long military overcoat, square hat with bill, cavalry saber, point into the floor of the studio. Both hands over the hilt.

"Looks like you."

"I was thinner. Younger, too."

"Weren't we all?"

"What did you say, Herman?"

"I said, 'Thank you for stopping by.'"

"The Rabbi come by to see you?"

"Usually on Thursday afternoon."

"How is Elana?"

"With two little ones, a job, a husband, now she has a sick father to worry about."

"It's not your fault, Herman. You couldn't stay home all alone."

"I could have stayed if someone had come in."

"To cook, to clean, to shop, to give you your injections."

"It's not like in the old times."

"What did you say, Herman?"

"It's not like old times in Rockville when families were together, like when I was a kid. I had aunts, uncles—they all helped. My mother got sick, we ate at my aunt's."

"What was will never be again, Herman. You recognize that? It's from a Yiddish song, 'Vas is geven is geven is nicht da.'"

"How is the minyan, Lenny?"

"Harry had a stroke, you know that. Only a mild one. Thank God he is getting better, but he hasn't returned yet. His nephew, Alan, who used to come with him, can't come because Harry is taking it easy, and now Alan has to open the store. So we lost two."

"Where did you get replacements?"

"We got Shirley Brill and Tessie Kramer, that is if they remember to come. I have to call them the night before to remind them."

"So, now you are counting women."

"Times are changing, Herman."

"Not in here. Same old thing. Nothing but death and bingo."

"The sisters been around?"

"Every morning. 'How are you, Mr. Bernstein?' 'Fine, Sister Agatha.' 'Anything I can do to make you more comfortable, Mr. Bernstein?' Yesterday Sister Agatha asked about Elana's children. Sister Agatha used to come into the store. Think of it: an Italian girl from a Pennsylvania mining town running a nursing home in Rockville, Illinois, for Jewish patients."

"Somebody has to do it."

"I wish we had our own nursing home like in Des Moines."

"We had our chance. Herman, all that government money was available."

"Our community was too small. I can't get used to the pork on my plate. You know, since the army I haven't eaten pork."

"You could tell Sister Agatha. I am sure she would see that you get something else."

"I don't like to complain."

"Mr. Bernstein, your room is ready. How are you feeling this morning?"

"Fine, Nancy. Just fine."

"Physiotherapy at nine, Mr. Bernstein."

"I can take Mr. Bernstein back to his room."

"I'm not going to run off with Leonard. Don't you worry, Nancy, I'll be here."

Minus a leg. Herman's joke. Herman looked at his watch. "Busy, busy, busy, all day long. I don't know where the days go. Okay, Nancy, back to my chamber." Herman grinned. "That's our code, Lenny. I have to go potty," he whispered.

"See you, Herman."

"Thanks for coming, Lenny."

The nurse's aide wheeled Herman down the dim hallway. Leonard drove back to the Jewish Center. The Rabbi had not returned. Vera Newcomb, the office manager, was in. Leonard, elbows on the counter, looked down at Miss Newcomb seated in front of her computer. Why does Vera want to look middle-aged? She'll be old soon enough. If she wore make-up . . . She shouldn't draw her brown hair back into a too tight bun that overexposed her forehead . . .

Office help was hard to get and Miss Newcomb had worked in the registrar's office of the Bible College. She was a silent girl who did give the Rabbi his telephone messages. That was more than April Lovett had done. What had been April's constant comment? "Mr. Bernstein, you tell the religious committee there is too much here for one person to do." Vera didn't complain. The synagogue bulletins were out on time.

"Time to do the bulletin, Vera." Vera rose from her command module, notepad in hand. She faced Leonard without a smile.

He said, "First, the dates of the Rosh Hashanah, 20 and 21."

"In my calendar it says *erev* Rosh Hashanah the nineteenth."

"*Erev* simply means the evening before the New Year. *Erev* Rosh Hashanah is not the name of the holiday."

"Yes, Mr. Zymanski."

"Vera—?"

"Yes, Mr. Zymanski?"

"Selihot is on Saturday night at 11:30."

"Yes, Mr. Zymanski. Anything more, Mr. Zymanski."

"Just the usual meetings, Sisterhood, Men's Club."

"I have the list, Mr. Zymanski."

"Thank you, Vera."

"Do you know when the Rabbi is coming back?"

"He is at the *Dispatch* explaining the holidays to the religious editor."

High Holy Days is what Leonard Zymanski said to himself. There was nothing to hope for. The Jewish Center hadn't had a Jewish secretary since Sarah had retired to Florida.

Leonard counted: that would be almost nine years. Riverboat gambling on the Mississippi was coming to Rockville, Illinois. Gambling would be here next April. Surely among the dealers, gaming bosses coming from Atlantic City or Los Vegas to set up the casinos there would be a nice Jewish girl who knew Hebrew. She would volunteer to help Vera with the bulletin, help her with the Hebrew words, with the correct names of the Holy Days: Rosh Hashanah, Shabbat Shuvah, Kol Nidre, Yizkor.

To Visit the Graves of Our Fathers

On the eleventh morning before Rosh Hashanah, the New Year, William K. Levy counted the minyan: thirteen. That is, if the two women were counted; if they were not, then there would still be eleven men, one more than was necessary to recite the memorial Kaddish prayer, to read the Torah and to sound the ram's horn, trooey, trooey, trooey.

William K. Levy, Bill Levy, son of Mordecai, grandson of Ariah Levy, was first into the prayer house to occupy the first seat on the right, a position from which he was closest to the ark that held the three Torahs. A seat from which he watched the sun descend into the atrium through the only window provided by the Christian architect from Arkansas, a cost-saving designer of synagogues with multipurpose rooms and gyms without showers. The prayer house had been one of his economies, a room only twenty by sixteen. "The prayer house will be large enough to fulfill your congregation's needs." The demographic study had fulfilled the architect's prophecy. "The entry to the prayer house will be the first door on the left off the grand foyer with the gray slate floor. The building code requires an exit door on the other side of the ark."

"To permit the Rabbi to duck out without facing the congregation," said Bill Levy when the Rabbi began escaping through the exit after the morning service.

"So the Rabbi doesn't have to explain why it was permissible to count the Torah as a member of the minyan," said Henry Gottwalt. "If you count the Torah as one, the next time we have only eight we will count two Torahs to have ten."

Ira Karp heard the comment, although it had not been addressed to him. Ira, who sat beside Henry, a man as orthodox as Henry but who said little, nodded his approval twice to "The Torah should not be counted," and added, "Next we will have Dr. Schwartz pray in English." This to Bruce Schwartz in the row behind Ira and Henry. Dr. Schwartz, who wore only a prayer shawl, said, "Don't worry, Ira. When I will lead the prayers I will put on my phylacteries."

"You have phylacteries, why don't you bring them? I'll show you how to put them on."

"Only if you let me do the prayers in English."

The Rabbi announced, "Page one-oh-three." Ira rose to lead the prayers. Henry turned to his orthodox prayer book with its limited English translations. Dr. Schwartz read the prayers in English as he followed Ira's Hebrew incantations for the Week Day.

Prayer Book, conservative edition. It was Monday, a day the Torah was to be read. The Rabbi rose to give the preamble to the Torah portion. "When the nefarious plot was hatched by his ten brothers to sell Joseph into slavery, Reuben withdrew. The plotters then called on God, as a witness, to make God a co-conspirator who bound the brothers together in their vow of silence. Thus we have an example of evil committed in the name of God. Many evils have been committed in the name of God."

After the service Bill Levy, who couldn't correlate invoking God in evil with invoking God as a member of the minyan, an act of loving kindness, in no way evil, was puzzled; he had framed the question carefully, "Please, Rabbi, explain to me, how can we equate invoking God in evil with counting a Torah for the minyan?"

As Bill Levy rose for the last prayer for the dead, the Kaddish, the Rabbi removed his prayer shawl, replaced his phylacteries in their red nylon pouch, darted out the door of the Jewish Center into his car, accelerating so quickly that Fred Weiss had to take two steps back onto the curb wheelchair ramp to get out of the way of the Rabbi's Bing Cherry red Plymouth.

Bill Levy put his prayer shawl in its velvet case and then into the imprinted white plastic bag with the drawstring. Rockville Illinois Country Club--Your pro shop for all your golf needs. He walked slowly to his sports coupe, drove right then left to the HyVee supermarket for our everyday self-service breakfast special, $1.99: eggs, toast and coffee.

In the Levy tradition, Bill ate his breakfast after morning prayer, because Bill's grandfather, Ariah, had never eaten before morning prayers. Maybe a little orange juice with his morning vasodilating pill to control his high blood pressure. Or if his arthritis was flaring, when Ariah needed a little something in the morning because he felt tired and weak, a bowl of shredded wheat and skim milk. Coffee, hot food, scrambled eggs—that was for after the morning prayers that praised God, because it is written, "Blessed art thou our O Lord, our God, King of the universe, who givest bread from the earth."

Bill Levy was tired, his legs ached, his back spasmed. He had slept poorly. He had risen in the dark to be first at the 6:50 morning prayers. Last week on Monday, Wednesday, and Friday he had carried the monitor's sign, "Quiet Please," for the full eighteen holes of the Pro golf tournament. He had rested on the Sabbath and did little on Sunday. Cutting the grass was all. Volunteering for the week of the million-dollar golf tournament had exacerbated his degenerative arthritis.

But if I am only for myself, what am I? The monies from the tournament supported the Rockville Hospital. The least a retired purchasing agent with good health, thank God, could do was donate one week a year to the community charity golf tournament.

At the HyVee deli, Bill Levy took his tray with the breakfast special to the booth that already held Henry Gottwalt and Leonard Zymanski, other members of the minyan. Levy, still slim, eased himself in beside Henry to face Leonard. Leonard, thinner, shorter, and older than Bill, had only coffee. Ten cents a cup for members of the HyVee Coffee Club.

"Lenny, the sweet rolls are on sale today. They'll heat them up for you."

"I ate at home."

"Before *shacharit*?" It was Henry's question. "In Germany we did not eat before prayers." With this statement, Henry Gottwalt answered his own question. At eighty-two, the senior member, Henry spoke with the authority of German Jewish experience he could trace back six hundred years.

Bill Levy sipped his coffee. "In Rockville, my grandfather Ariah, may he rest in peace, said. 'Billy, it's all right to eat, but it has to be cold, a cold fruit, cold cereal, but not hot.' So all I have before prayers is cold Raisin Bran with a little skim milk."

"How can you ask for God's blessing to provide bread from the earth if you have already eaten?" Henry pursued very softly.

Leonard Zymanski spoke softly, his rising inflection holding traces of his Polish Yiddish, his first language learned at mother's knee. "In Poland, in Czestowa, we had thirty thousand Jews, all kind—from Hassids to Germans. My father was a Hassid, a most holy man. Every two weeks he spent the Sabbath with his Rabbi. He took the train to Belz on Friday morning, rode the hundred and twenty miles to be with his rabbi for the Sabbath. My father ate both hot and cold before *shacharit*. Every morning he had hot tea."

Bill Levy rose, returned with a coffee refill and a steaming Long John. "Leonard, that was in Europe fifty years ago. In Rockville fifty years ago we had three minyans. At seven for the peddlers and the junkmen—they had to get up early. At eight for the storekeepers. At nine for the retirees. At each minyan there was a bottle of whiskey, but no one took a drink until after the morning prayers. Old Man Horowitz stayed for three minyans. By ten o'clock he was so drunk I had to take him home."

"In Germany we did not drink." Henry's statement as he edged out of the booth was not challenged.

"Where are you rushing to?"

"Have to take Zelda shopping. She is waiting."

"Henry is off to do his good deeds, taking the widows shopping. A different widow each day." That from Leonard.

"What else should a widower do but look at the widows?"

"At his age?"

"Never too old, Leonard, never too old."

From HyVee Bill Levy drove over the Arsenal bridge to Davenport, continued north on Brady, right on Eastern, then turned left over the single railroad track. Mount Nebo. The sign, Mount Nebo, was a small slab of gray granite with an arrow left. Bill Levy then went right at the three-way intersection and up to the Levy family burial plot. He parked, took the ladder, the brush saw and the pruning clippers from car's trunk. He trimmed the lowest branches of the pin oak, then carefully mounted the ladder to reach other branches. The twenty-year-old oak resisted. Bill stopped from time to time, gathered the pruned limbs, threw them over the chain fence into the ravine. Finished, he replaced the tools, washed the headstone face, the footstone's.

> Leah Levy, Mother (1901-1968)
> Robert Levy (1945-1970), Son
> Mordecai Levy (1901-1970), Father

He washed the quote from Micah: "What does the Lord require of thee? To seek justice, love mercy, and walk humbly with thy Lord."

The black granite cleansed, he found a chestnut shell, placed it on the tombstone. His wife, Lilly, did that when she visited alone, so he would know she had been. If Lilly and Bill Levy came together, Lilly always said, "Bobby loved the squirrels. Do you remember when he was sick that winter? He would lie on the floor on his chest, look out the sliding door, look at the squirrels play in the snow."

Levy returned to the car, took a notebook from the pocket behind the driver's seat, wrote, "Call monument company. Lettering needs to be renewed."

***

Lilly came out the side door of the two-story postmodern house as Bill Levy came up the drive. "Where have you been. I was worried about you."

"I went up to the cemetery."

William Levy returned the tools to their hooks on the garage wall, came into the house, sat down.

Lilly had been swimming. Maybe her arthritis wouldn't be as painful today. Maybe Lilly would sleep through the night. Swimming helped; the anti-inflammatory pills did little to alleviate her pain. "Myofibrositis, Mrs. Levy. The pills are only fifteen percent effective." With the University of Iowa Medical School rheumatologist, the internist, it was always the same, "Keep moving, Mrs. Levy."

Lilly had finished *The New York Times* crossword puzzle, a success with which to start her day. Monday and Tuesday were the easy crosswords, Wednesday less so. Thursday more difficult, Sunday impossible.

"You look tired, Bill."

"Getting old, Lilly."

"Who isn't?"

Lilly never complained. During the night Lilly groaned, moaned, tossed, awoke, left their bed to read, eat unsalted pretzels.

"You did good on the crossword."

"It was easy."

"You should be pleased."

"I am. Bill, did you speak to the Rabbi about holding services at Mount Nebo?"

"Yes."

"What did he say?"

"Let Rabbi Cohen do it. Rabbi Cohen is holding services at Mt. Nebo on Sunday at ten. It's not the same service as ours. . . ."

"You can't blame yourself for that. You can't blame your dad for buying a family plot from a reform congregation."

"You're right, Lilly. Dad meant well. B'nai Jacob didn't have family plots then, so."

"Your dad wanted—"

'I know, my father wanted us all to be together. I told Rabbi Cohen we would be there."

In a Plain, Wooden Casket

Sy Rosen laughed and laughed. That wasn't the response Herman Krause had hoped for, not from a friend, not from a golfing companion. Sy hadn't taken his request as it was intended, a serious effort to solve his need. That Monday morning, after the *shacharit* service, Herman had stopped at Sy's wood shop, parked behind Sy's van, walked down the two steps onto the slippery soft sawdust that made him afraid he would slip and fall and have to have a hip prosthesis. Then it would be ten days at the University of Iowa hospitals and six weeks in the nursing home and three months before he could drive and six months before he could walk without a cane. The surgery and recovery and after-care would make it very difficult for Ethel, his wife of almost fifty years, because Ethel had her own problems. This year it was this and that and it was all becoming a bit more than Ethel could handle.

Sy was standing under the single bulb, a wood mallet in his right hand, a chisel in his left hand, fitting the bottom channel of a head board with each blow.

"You had your coffee yet, Sy?"

"No."

"Let's go."

They walked across the alley to the donut factory with the out- front retail space. Six formica tables, twenty-four tubular chairs beside the steamed display window that obscured the view of the street. Signs on the window glass proclaimed, "Donuts by the dozen!" and "Yesterday's donuts at special prices!" At the counter they sat on the two stools closest to the drip coffee pot. Two retirees, both more than sixty-five, Sy in his suntan work clothes, Herman in gray suit, rep tie, striped shirt, on his way to "managing," "leasing" his property. The waitress came from behind the swinging doors, dried her hands on her pink apron, poured the two cups of coffee. Sy ordered one plain donut; it was delivered on a square of glazed paper. Sy pulled the donut apart, offered to Herman. "One bite won't hurt you."

"I had breakfast before I went to services."

"One bite."

Herman broke off a bite, ate it too quickly. "Chocolate donuts are better. Two months of good eating in Florida and I have to breath in to button my trousers. At our age, weight on is easy; weight off is almost impossible."

"I wanted to talk to you, Sy, about a coffin. I want you to make me a coffin. A simple wooden coffin."

Sy laughed, laughed again. "Any coffin I could make would be like a mummy box in a horror movie—six feet high, two feet wide, a foot and half deep. I could engrave your picture on the lid. You would look like a mummy. You don't want me to make you a coffin. If I made it, who would I get to line it in satin so you don't roll around in it?"

"I don't need it lined. Sy, I want you to pick out the wood. I'll pay for the wood now; when it's finished, then you'll help me put it into my garage. I'm going to use it as a bookcase until Ethel needs it for me."

"Herman, why are you bothering me?"

"I'm bothering you so Ethel doesn't have to go down to Hudson's and pick out a coffin."

The waitress returned, poured more coffee into the two cups.

Sy offered two dollars. The waitress left the change, thirty-five cents. The conversation stopped. The waitress left through the swinging doors, returned to loading dozens of today's donuts in flat gray boxes, wholesale to the trade "out the back door."

"Herman, we'll go to Hudson's. I'll help you pick out a box at Hudson's. I'll go down with you. Hudson's will store it for you until you need it."

"I want one out of oak. I want you to make it a simple box, a couple of handles. No metal screws."

"Herman, if I made it from oak, nobody could lift it."

"With the handles. I'll get help. We'll get the coffin into the garage. Then, after that, let the chevrai keduska worry. There are four of them in the burial society, so make four handles."

Sy shook his head. "My box would look awful. I don't have the kind of turning machinery you need to fit the ends together."

"So, use screws. Wooden screws—no brass screws. Just wood so it will all rot away. 'Dust to dust,' like it says in the Bible."

"So, why all this talk about a box? Why now? You contemplating suicide?" And Sy laughed again. Sy laughed at death. Sy had laughed at death from North Africa to Anzio, through Germany: an infantry man who laughed at death.

"Don't make fun of me."

"I didn't know how observant you have become, running to the minyan every morning."

"I go when I can."

"You'd better be careful, Herman. You blow your brains out, the Rabbi won't bury you in your wooden coffin in Hebrew Cemetery."

"How do you know I had a gun?"

"A nine-millimeter Beretta—you told me when you bought it."

"I have had thoughts. Who hasn't? But I'm not going to make Ethel a happy widow."

"Getting even with Ethel."

"No, because it's against our tradition."

"Herman, religion is getting you deranged. Go out, enjoy. Go see your grandchildren. Let someone else plan your funeral."

"I was only trying to make it easier for Ethel. Sort of tidying up things."

"In contemplation of death, Herman, you are a young man. Look at yourself all dressed up. You look good. Go downtown, go rent some space. I've got work to do."

Herman drove his American luxury car to his downtown property, parked his car in the space reserved for H. R. Krause, rode the elevator to his private office, pulled the file marked Insurance from its rack on his Scandinavian desk, wrote on the cover, "Call Sy, make appointment to go to Hudson's." He called his home.

"Ethel, what did the doctor say?"

"It could be worse."

"What did he say?"

"I'll tell you tonight."

"Tell me."

"It's like I told you the doctor would say. I start the chemotherapy tomorrow."

"You Okay, Ethel?"

"I'm fine. You come home early. I'm making chicken fried steak."

Happy Is the Man Who Is Happy With His Portion

From our children who left Rockville, there are so many success stories. Their success can be attributed to that these, our wisest and brightest and certainly the most motivated, are not willing to spend their lives in western Illinois. Not after they have been to Stanford or Harvard or even the University of Illinois in Champaign.

The Newman boy is in New York, a vice president of Okura Financial Services, a thirty-year-old buying and selling millions of dollars every day. That's how the Japanese have benefitted, by selecting our best. To hear Lizzie Newman tell it, $600,000-a-year salary for a vice president who trades Treasuries is somewhere between only adequate and exploitive because her son makes millions for Okura every day. I am sure he does, because if he didn't, Jeff Newman would be looking for a job instead of going back to Japan to meet with Okura's top management. You have to admit the Newman boy is doing well, and so is Jerry Baker's youngest girl, Shelly, in Chicago, who is also in financial instruments—single-family mortgages. The way Jerry explains Shelly's success at our morning services is, "Shelly groups little mortgages into big mortgages and sells them to banks."

Banks. When Henry Gottwalt hears that, he walks away in disgust and mutters, "Gottwalts made whiskey, good, honest corn and rye whiskey. We sold to the finest liquor stores. Good whiskey is like medicine . . . better than medicine."

Did the oldest Gottwalt son stay in the whiskey business? No. He is a pathologist in Chicago. Henry had to sell his distillery to a Canadian company. However, there is one family, the Kramers, that has been fortunate to have their children return to Rockville. All Joe Kramer could talk about was when his son, Edward, would come back from Harvard, when his Eddie would come back with a degree from the business school, when his Eddie would get his degree from the law school. Joe is waiting for Eddie to come home to the Kramer Companies. This is the holding company that runs Kramer Transportation, tugboats that push grain barges downriver and oil barges upriver; Kramer Sand and Gravel, with cement trucks that pave eastern Iowa; and the smallest, newest Kramer company, Midwest Recycling and Refining, all up to date, ready and waiting for used aluminum cans and corrugated boxes.

I have known the Kramers for three generations. The Golds, too—that's Eddie's mother's family, all good, honest, decent and hard-working. Take Joe Kramer, Ed's father: He got a degree in accounting from the University of Iowa. Phi Beta Kappa, too. By now he could have been a professor of accounting. Joe had all sorts of golden opportunities. Did he go off to New York, Chicago, to look for a Fortune 500 company? Not Joe. He comes back to Rockville, and he works with his father, Charlie. That is, Old Charlie, may he rest in peace.

You ask how Old Charlie Kramer got into riverboat transportation? It was Fred's great-grandfather who started it all, with a coal wagon and two horses, not even a matched team, a gray mare and a bay horse. The old gray was blind in her right eye.

Whenever I tell this story, my wife, Helen, says, "Fred, how can you remember all that? You were no more than five—maybe four."

I answer, "Veterinarians remember things like that. That old mare had iridocyclitis."

That stops Helen, but only for a minute. "I know your grandfather had the best matched team in town, the best mannered team, and what did your grandfather do with all the money he made in transportation?"

That's an unkind reference to my grandfather's bank, the Drover's State Bank having gone under during the Depression. There is no sense explaining to Helen that it was my grandfather's partners, the lawyers from Chicago, who stole. Stole may be a bit harsh. After all, I was only twelve when it happened. My mother told me time and again, "If your grandfather had been less trusting, you wouldn't have had to work your way through veterinary school."

Edward Kramer came back from Cambridge. I would visit him at the Y while he was pumping iron (nothing heavy—a hundred forty- five pounds) from a bench, ten, twelve reps is all, or when he was dressing. His is the locker around the corner from mine, a half locker, some way from the shower, not in as desirable a location as we older members enjoy.

"How are things at the Kramer Companies?"

"Better than ever, Fred."

"Enjoying it?"

"Putting things together. I had no idea how much coordination between our companies will have to be done." With that, Ed is off to the showers. Ed is like all the Kramers, big shoulders, big chest, and two thin legs. I think the legs came from the Golds. Before the war Marty Gold, Ed's uncle, was a world class quarter miler at the University of Iowa. Ed is into the Y five days a week building his upper body and jogging three, four miles a day on the inside track. That gives me lots of opportunities to talk to Ed in the Jacuzzi or in the showers. I always inquire, "How is your dad?"

"As well as can be expected." Which means that Joe has a little heart trouble, enough to limit his work to mornings only.

Ed doesn't miss a day at the Y, fortifying his cardiac output. "How is Dad doing?"

"Holding his own. He is starting on a cardiac regimen."

Now Joe shows up at the Y. That gives me the opportunity to keep my eye on two generations of Kramers. While Joe is riding the airodyne bicycle and watching the Financial News Network market reports, I am giving him advice. "Try massage for relaxation, Joe. Maybe you shouldn't be watching the markets."

"I have been watching the markets for thirty years."

"That's what I mean, Joe. It's time for you to let Ed do it."

Which is exactly what happens. Joe loses weight, loses his paunch, stays on his diet. The angina goes away. And so do Mr. and Mrs. Joe Kramer, to a penthouse in Sarasota, Florida, overlooking the Gulf of Mexico. Ed is now the chief operating officer of Kramer Companies; his picture in the business section is on board the tug boat *Franny Kramer*, one of those staged "taking over the helm" pictures that appears once a week, on Sunday.

I don't see Ed for about a week, which is most unusual. Edward at twenty-eight is a man of very regular habits and sober clothes, dark blue and gray suits, black wingtip shoes, white shirts and rep ties. One Monday at noon, an Indian summer day in November, Ed comes in wearing jeans, T-shirt and crew neck sweater, boat shoes and singing—not actually singing, more like humming to himself.

I can't place the tune. It may be "Cruising Down the River," or it may not be; for a Kramer to be singing is unusual enough. In three generations never has a Kramer been heard to sing, not even in our synagogue choir, which has absolutely no musical standards. Before Ed begins his workout, he comes over to my locker, draws up a stool, sits down.

"Fred, you ever been on the river?"

"Yes, last month. Took a two-day excursion up to Chestnut Mountain. Up one day, back the next, on the *Julie Swain*, the paddle boat."

"Wonderful, isn't it. Our offices are right on the river, and until last week I had never spent a day on the river, or a night, or any time at all. Fred, do you know how many tug boats we own?"

"No."

"Forty-six, and work boats and barges. Now we are building a new terminal."

"Sounds like business is good."

"So good, Fred, I haven't been on the river. Fred, what was it like being a veterinarian? What was it like to practice for forty years?"

Perhaps my answer was too brief. I told Ed, "I had the joy of caring and preventing disease and treating the sick. The dogs—some got to love you. Some sort of cringed when they came in. Years ago there were lots of hogs. The hog industry wouldn't be where it is today if hog cholera hadn't been stamped out."

"Sounds like you were happy in your work."

"Not always, Ed. But most of the time."

I didn't tell Ed of the pain in the cows' eyes during difficult calving, nor of the crying screams of six-week-old pigs when they are held by their front legs to be vaccinated in their armpits.

"Fred, how would you like to go out on the river with me?"

"Anytime, Ed."

I thought that was one of those "we'll do lunch" or "I'll call you whenever" things. Next Friday afternoon we are on the deck of the *Fanny Kramer*. I am introduced to the captain. "Dr. Fred Weiss, an old friend of the family."

Ed has a pair of binoculars; even the white bread mallards in the Rockville lagoon excite Ed. "Look at the green on their heads."

When Ed sees the two white ducks with the red wattles, he turns to me. "What kind are those?"

"Peking. Like Chinese," I explain.

"All God's creatures," he mutters. "Creatures great and small," Ed goes on, which makes me think Ed has been watching too much TV. Too many episodes out of Herriot's reminiscences.

That middle of November Friday was unusually mild, sunny, in the fifties. Towards sunset, about 4:30, the *Fanny Kramer* is headed west, into the wind, back to the terminal. I stop in the galley to reach for a cup of hot coffee. Ed is at the door. "Fred, come out here. Look at that sunset. Have you ever seen anything like that?" It was our usual prairie sunset, a russet sun glowing, radiating in the cloud-free, gray sky.

Hadn't Ed every driven west with the setting autumn sun in his eyes, the copper to red afterglow on the horizon and then the sudden dark until the moon rises to light the fields of stubble where the corn and soybeans had grown? "There'll be a harvest moon tonight, Ed. Go out, go look at the sky." When I was four, my grandpa had a cutter. When the snows came we rode in the sleigh on the country roads. There wasn't a paved road along the river then.

"Fred, what do you miss the most?"

I didn't answer. I was reviewing.

Ed, again, "Fred, what do you miss the most about not practicing?"

I still did not answer, and Ed didn't insist. I haven't given that much thought. Looking backwards is not my thing, never has been, but no one has ever asked. Not Helen, not my daughter.

On the river, twilight had turned into night. The searchlight from the pilot house lit the channel buoys, the green, the red. The *Fanny Kramer*'s searchlight caught the terminal. The captain turned east, upriver, to dock.

I finally answered Ed when he again asked, "You miss practicing?"

"What I miss most is driving the river road at night with the window open to keep awake. The only car on the snow-covered roads. It's quite bright on the moonlit nights. The yard lights marking the farms . . . the farmer waiting at the barn door . . . the smell of the cows . . ."

"You are a romantic, Fred."

"I don't know, Ed. I haven't delved much into myself." I have never thought of myself as a belly button contemplator. I think I was more the type to get in, get out, get on to the next job. "I never thought about such things, Ed. I never thought I had the time for the philosophy of living."

"You didn't need philosophy, Fred. You lived it."

"Did the best I could with what my wife and I had."

"That's what my dad says."

"Ever talked to your dad, Ed?"

"You mean, about the old days?"

"Just about how you feel about things."

"Not much. I will, Fred. First chance I get."

That conversation was a year ago. Ed has not asked me out on the river again. Next spring riverboat gambling begins on the Mississippi. Ed has ordered a four-deck, 35,000-square-foot boat with dining rooms for three hundred, the biggest casino afloat, complete with a dance floor and music. Ed is back in business suits. He is not quite so regular at the Y. When he does come in, he mostly rushes right by our aisle where the retirees are slowing dressing, sitting, visiting. Last week I did speak to Ed in the Jacuzzi, first time in about a month. Tuesday or Wednesday it was.

"Been busy, Ed?"

"Too busy."

"Been out on the river?"

"Haven't had time."

"How's Dad?"

"He says he feels better in Florida."

"You going down to see the folks?"

"Hoping to as soon as I can get away. You know, Fred—?"

"What?"

"I always wanted to be a veterinarian ever since I was in high school, ever since that one day I rode with you. We drove all over the county along the river. You pulled a calf. Then you floated a horse's teeth."

"I don't remember, Ed. I'm sorry."

"I can't forget that day. I can't forget."

The Rich Have Their Problems, Too

Now I know why Haskel Roth waited for me to shut the prayer house lights, put the prayer shawls back on the racks. "Harry, I want to talk to you."

"Why me? Haskel, go to the Rabbi."

I am only the gabbai, the keeper of the ritual. The Rabbi is the learned one. But Rabbi Cohen is as elusive as Red Grange, the Galloping Ghost of Illinois. Haskel waits patiently, sits in the library. Haskel knows I am getting slower. He knows I no longer rush from one Volunteer of the Year job to another. He knows that after the services I go into the library and read existentialist literature. Which has nothing to do with Haskel Roth, because for one, Haskel only reads art catalogs and *The New York Times*.

It was October. It had to have been on a Monday, because I was putting away the Soncino edition of the Hertz Torah text. Haskel is sitting across from me. Haskel looks good—for his age he looks great. No paunch, just a little gray that even wearing his hair short can't hide. Haskel is semi-retired. That is, he goes into his warehouses, leaves whenever he likes. Haskel continues to dress for business, white laundered cotton shirts, silk ties, a different one each morning to match his suit of the day and season. When Haskel started coming to the minyan, Henry Gottwalt, who was trying to cheer Haskel up, used to ask, "Haskel, today you have a meeting? With your banker? Is that why you are dressed up," to which Haskel, with a thoughtful face, always answered, "When the banks need money, they come to Haskel Roth. God forbid I should move my checking account. The First River Bank will have to borrow from the Federal Reserve."

Ida always says, "The only stupid thing Haskel and his brother, Larry, ever did was to be too good to their mother. It's because of her that her boys never got married. No one was ever good enough to be another Mrs. Roth." Sarah Roth told that to everyone before Haskel and Larry got to be "big business" in warehousing, from Davenport, Iowa, to Cairo, Illinois. Ida has always had more insight into people than I do; at least she always told me, "Harry, you stay with construction. When it comes to knowing whom to trust, you leave that to me. Harry, you would trust everyone."

At eight-thirty in the morning, there is no one in the Jewish Center library to overhear Haskel.

"Tell me, Harry, you and Ida—you have been married forty-seven years."

I nod.

"Could you ever think of living without Ida?"

"To tell you the truth, Haskel, when I think of it—being alone—I get sick. I get weak in the feet; my head begins to throb. I get nauseous. Since I came home from the Army, Ida and I have never been apart for more than a week or two at a time."

"That's why I asked you. I remember when you and Ida were married."

"It was only yesterday."

"I met someone. . . . You saw her at services last Saturday. Judy Schreiber's sister, Edith."

"Good-looking girls. Bella Shapiro had three good-looking daughters, though for me Judy is too thin."

"Still looking at the girls, Harry."

"Still contributing to the connubial bliss."

"You better not let Ida hear you bragging."

"Not bragging, Haskel."

"That's what I wanted to ask you about, Harry. If my sexual performance is . . . how shall I say . . . not brilliant, only adequate, do you think a woman—" and I filled in, "Edith," and Haskel didn't interrupt or say no, "Edith would be unhappy? After all, Edith is eight years younger than I am."

"Maybe you had better ask Ida. For what women expect, you can talk to Ida."

"I don't think I could. I value your opinions, Harry, or I wouldn't ask you."

"Ida says I have no insight."

"Nonsense, Harry. Without good judgment, you wouldn't have been that successful."

"Everybody is successful in an up market."

"Don't be modest. I remember from where you and Ida started."

"Haskel, you can talk to Edith, ask her what she wants to do with the rest of her life. I would bet she doesn't mention sex once."

"We have been talking."

"When you walk along the river."

"In this town everybody knows everything."

"It's a small town, Haskel."

In October was my first talk with Haskel. Of course, in Rockville with only one Jewish congregation—with everyone related if not by blood by marriages or by business—and with Haskel coming to the minyan, we are not surprised that in January or February when Bill Levy is gone, and Leonard Zymanski gone to California for a month, Edith Shapiro starts coming to the minyan. I tell that to Ida. "Every morning Edith comes to the minyan. Each morning she is in a different jogging outfit. With Reeboks to match."

"She stand next to Haskel?"

"No. Haskel in on the right by the wall. Edith is on the left by the clock."

"Very discrete."

"What discrete? They are of age."

"They don't want people to know."

"If they don't want everyone in Rockville to know, so why do they go to the symphony together?"

"Who told you?"

"Ira Karp."

"He is an old lady."

"What's the big secret? Two consenting adults—they could be sleeping together for all I care. Edith isn't going to have an illegitimate child, not at her age."

"It's not nice."

"What's not nice, Ida?"

"Two people that age carrying on in public."

"What were they doing?"

"Pauline Karp told me they were holding hands."

"From this you don't get AIDS."

"Since when are you so sexually liberated, Harry? If a girl wants to get married, she has to save herself."

"Who said that, your bubbe, your grandmother?"

"No. My mother."

"Now I know why I had to marry you."

"You sorry, Harry?"

"You are my everything, Ida."

"You only tell me that because I cook for you, sew for you, bore your children, slaved in your office."

"You are an equal partner, Ida."

"I don't wash cars."

"Or do yard work."

"That's men's work."

So I kiss Ida on the neck while she is preparing the frozen spaghetti for the microwave. "You only kiss me when I am busy," Ida says. "I don't think anything will come of this Edith-Haskel romance. Edith has it too good. A condo of her own, a fine pension. What does she need with a man?"

"Why did you get married?"

"I was young. I didn't know any better."

I don't dare ask Ida, "Would you do it again?" Ida is not right; I do have that much insight.

In April Edith was still coming to the minyan; the steadies were all back from Texas and Florida and California. Some mornings we had twelve. Edith is now a regular, taking Aliyah's reading—the prayers before the Torah—reading Hebrew without hesitation. Edith is no dummy; she doesn't talk to anyone, doesn't ask too many questions. She takes her Torah honors, donates to the synagogue. Then that Thursday the Rabbi—no, it was the new cantor—asks her, "Do you want a me shabarach?"—a special blessing—and Edith says, "Yes, for Haskel, son of Mordechai."

So, Edith donates fifty dollars, Haskel gets the Rabbi's blessing, and Edith gets the thank you. Then they go out together. Leonard Zymanski tells me he sees them at HyVee, drinking coffee in the delicatessen. With those full length windows into the parking lot that every passer-by can see into, that is putting yourself on display. You would think that if the two are going out to breakfast together five, six mornings a week, you would think they might just as well be living together.

At first a few of the widows would call Ida, "Haskel and Edith . . ." "Edith and Haskel . . ."

"But that's only because they are jealous," is how Ida explained it all to me.

"This day and age, no one really cares."

The path to love and marriage is never smooth. I read that somewhere, years ago. That is true because here we are again, just the two of us, Haskel and I, in the library.

"Harry, I think it would be good . . ." Haskel is speaking so slowly, I finish, "For you and Edith to get married."

"How did you know?"

"The whole town knows you are going together."

"Just to concerts."

"To concerts, to HyVee for breakfast after the minyan."

"Edith won't eat before the service."

"She could go alone to HyVee."

"That wouldn't be polite. Edith asked me to go with her."

"She asks you every day."

"It has become a habit."

To that I only nod my head.

"Tell me, Harry, what is love? What do your French philosophers say? You read, Harry. No one I know reads as much as you do. You know from everything."

"Haskel, you have read *The New York Times* every day for the last twenty years."

"That doesn't give me an answer to what is life and love."

"The newspaper sure as hell tells you what love isn't, with the murders for hire, murderers in the streets, police brutality."

"That's why I am sitting here with you. Edith wanted to come with me. I said no. I made an excuse. I told Edith, 'I have to talk to Harry about business.'"

"I'll tell you one thing love isn't. Haskel, it isn't business, although I read in today's paper Mrs. Trump got fourteen million dollars for a divorce settlement."

"That's what I am afraid of, Harry, a divorce. Love becoming a business."

I laugh. "You can't get a divorce unless you get married."

"You are right, Harry. So, tell me, Harry, what is love?"

"Love is faith."

"Who said that?"

"Me. Harry M. Stern, B.A., University of Illinois."

"Nothing to be afraid of, Haskel. If you fail, you try again. You fail better."

"Who said that?"

"Beckett."

"I knew you could help me."

"I didn't do anything."

"You restored my faith. You destroyed my fear."

"Haskel, you are beginning to talk like the prayer book."

"That's not all bad, Harry." Haskel picks himself up, turning to go, then turns toward me. "You know what I was afraid of? I was afraid that after all those years of living alone, what if Edith didn't like my music, my habits, my paintings. I eat sandwiches for supper. Now I don't care if we fail. We will try again."

I went home and told Ida of our conversation. "I think I have helped Haskel to make up his mind about getting married."

"Men can be such idiots." Ida has used the Yiddish pronunciation, stress on the d plus the rising inflection. This form of idiot I consider almost an endearment.

"You with your Beckett. You quoted Beckett and Haskel is going to propose to Edith and they live happily ever after."

"Ida, tell me, why are Haskel and Edith going to be married?"

"They will marry because Edith decided she wanted to get married. It's the women who choose. It has always been so."

"I didn't know that."

"How do you think I got you? First time I saw you, I said to myself, 'Ida, that's the man for you.'"

"What did your mother say?"

"She said you would never earn a living. Only mistake my mother ever made, being wrong about you."

"I never knew that."

"I told you a long time ago. Harry, you are wasting your time reading all those European philosophers. Read Ludlum, enjoy."

"It keeps me busy."

"That's one thing you are right about, Harry."

Charity Given Without Being Asked Is Golden

From the synagogue to my downtown office was only eight minutes in the early morning Rockville traffic. Ken, my maintenance man, came in as I was making my first cup of Lipton's. Usually Ken waited with "what happened last night" until I took the teabag from the styrofoam cup. That day he didn't. "Damn vandals. Did you see? I can't get the stains out—that brown yellow crud all up and down the marble ate right into it."

"Tried acetone?"

"I tried all our paint removers. Nothing, Mr. Shore, nothing."

"I'll call the cut stone company, have a marble man sent out."

"I'm sorry, Ray."

"Not your fault, Ken; you can't be everywhere."

"The vandalism wasn't there when I left at five."

"Maybe the marble company can get it cleaned up."

"Damn vandals got to every panel, every bit of marble wainscoting, ruined. "That's pretty sick, Mr. Shore, just destroying. I'm sorry."

That day got no better. I remember my accountant, Doug Holcomb, called. "I'm sorry, Ray. I can't budge the I.R.S. The file went up to Chicago, now it's back here. Simcox thinks you overvalued your gift."

That gift saved HUD millions. It kept the mortgage intact. We could have abandoned the housing rather than donating to the charity.

"Ray, the charity sold the housing in thirty days."

"Explain it to Simcox, Doug. Tell him charities can't run subsidized housing. They sold it to a housing company who promised to keep the housing in the section eight subsidized program for fifteen years. That's low-income housing."

"I know, you know, Ray. Simcox doesn't like your value."

"It's not my value; it's the appraiser's. What does Simcox want?"

"He hasn't said yet."

"It's almost three years—isn't there something we can do to end it?"

"He has until December next year. Ray, there is nothing I can do. In my professional opinion it's the I.R.S.s' move."

"I know, Doug, a special category. So much you can do nothing about."

"It's not that bad, Ray. If Simcox doesn't come to a decision in sixteen months, you can refuse to sign the extension. Then we can go to tax court. At least we'll get our story heard."

"I'll talk to Betty when the time comes. You know Betty doesn't like the publicity of a trial."

"Shouldn't be any, Ray. We are still negotiating."

"Doug, I did the right thing by gifting."

Doug didn't answer. He had hung up the phone.

At 11:30, when I left the Shore Building, the sun shone through the open roof into my American luxury car. I drove east and then south to the Family Y. My hour reserved for the steam room, the Jacuzzi, the breast stroke, the crawl, the backstroke, then the massage table.

"Deep breaths, Ray, relax." That's my massage therapist, both hands smoothing my shoulders, back, warming, patting, readying me for his thumbs on the pressure points. Craig's both thumbs descend into the pressure points of my spinal column. I breathed deeply, dozed, woke when Craig began the deep massage of my left wrist.

"I'll help you turn over, Ray."

"My damn back never quits hurting."

"Those steroid injections do any good?"

"Not much. The massage helped; swimming helped, thank God."

This was my day until 3:30 p.m. I called home. "What's new on the hot line?" I asked, a reference to Betty's telephone support network.

"Cele Gross is worried."

"Who wouldn't be? You read this morning's headlines. The United States wants the UN to censure Israel."

"Cele got hold of me. Ray, it's Herschel. He is writing letters to the editor of the *Dispatch*."

"So what? The 'Speak Out' column is full of letters."

"Ray, in 'Speak Out' the writers' names aren't published. Herschel wrote a letter to the editor that he signed. Hold on, I'll read it to you.

> "'Dear Editor:
>
> "'In these trying times when we need more integrity than ever to face the problems of environmental health there are those in our community who are willing to sacrifice the health of their coworkers in the name of equal employment opportunity. The attorneys who represent these causes no doubt feel that their cause is just, but let them not forget that if the Illinois Appellate Court decides that equal employment opportunity is more important than protecting women of child-bearing age from industrial hazards in their work place, then the courts, the feminists, and their attorneys have done their sisters an everlasting injustice by initiating the lawsuit against Illinois Eclipse Manufacturing.
>
> "'H. Gross, M.D.'

"What do you make of that, Ray?"

"The last sentence is too long. I would have changed it to three shorter ones without ifs, ands and buts."

"Ray, I'm serious."

"Hershel is upset about lead. Who isn't upset about something today? You want to hear about my day, from vandalism to I.R.S.?"

"You are a business man; you know how to handle those things."

"I don't handle them, Betty; they handle me." I sighed. "Okay, we'll eat lunch with Herschel and Cele after the Rosh Hashanah service. You can do your counseling then."

Leave the Corners of the Fields for the Poor

Advice on how to live you can get anywhere, everywhere. From friends, from your barber, from the fellow sitting next to you on your last winter's flight to Florida. For the last month I have been getting my life wisdom, advice from my forebears, from the morning prayer book one or two lines at a time. In this Monday morning's reading: "These are the commandments for which no fixed measure is imposed, leaving the corner of the field for the poor."

I tried that on Rick Harbert who farms for us. "Rick, when you pick the corn, leave a little. That way, if there are any needy, they could pick it."

"Ray, you leave that corn, the only ones that will come and get it are the rats. And you know what Ed McDonald, the health inspector, will say then."

Consider Harbert's statement. His is the ultimate truth. Our cornfield is in the north end of town on the county line road. Since the sewer line was brought through, two homes border our cornfield. We paid for our share of the sewer line, the cost rationalized as a public good. One day more homes will be built; then I'll donate an acre or two for a park where the young and old will play baseball, because surely there is enough corn in Iowa without my six acres. Increased corn production decreases prices. The greatest good would be to give up farming.

Thus our concept of leaving corn in the corner of the fields for the poor was abandoned, because rats, mice would invade the neighboring single-family homes, and if not invade, would be seen by the householders who in fright would call the city administrative health officer, Ed McDonald. "Mr. McDonald, we are getting an invasion of vermin. It's all due to Ray Shore's leaving his corn unpicked in his field next to my backyard. That is where I tie my dog. And next door to me there is a three-year-old. . . ." etc., etc.

So I listen to Rick Harbert but must still believe in the fulfillment of the morning prayer injunction, Leave for the poor.

I come home to Betty to tell my story of abject failure, disappointment in my effort to do good.

"Ray, you are naive, you are not living in biblical times. Now there are food stamps, ADC."

"But Betty," I plead, "with ADC and food stamps there is no opportunity for the recipient to influence and improve his condition."

"But, Betty," is as far as I get.

"Ray, sometimes . . ." and this time Betty does not finish.

I know what Betty had wished to say. "Ray, you don't understand. That was a truly stupid idea."

I cannot accept my failure to provide corn for the needy. In the early hours before I rise to morning prayers, I tell myself, "Ray, there has to be some way to use your cornfield to help the needy of Will's Crossing." I even ask Betty for ideas. Betty has been serving on charity boards for years and years. "Ray, what are you bothering with Will's Crossing for? Just because you own six acres in Will's Crossing doesn't mean you have to improve their world."

"Betty, landowners have their responsibilities."

"It's only six acres, Ray. You are not the lord of the manor. This is not the nineteenth century. Today the government takes care of the needy. Remember, since Roosevelt, the New Deal, Social Security, Medicare."

Betty hadn't realized it, but she had given me the answer, the clue: the United States Department of Agriculture. The Farmers Home Administration will lend me money to build needed housing. I call Will's Crossing, speak to Ed McDonald. Ed is twenty-two, twenty-three, an honor graduate of the Iowa State University Municipal Administrators Program, a young man who knows and understands every word of the Will's Crossing's two-hundred-page Municipal Codes, from Parking to Zoning, from electric to plumbing, from building to burning (leaves, refuse—prohibited except on designated days). Ed is not only respectful but helpful.

"Mr. Shore, we could use housing for the needy elderly, not many. Maybe twenty-four two-bedroom units."

"Anything else Will's Crossing needs?"

"Maybe a park with a baseball diamond."

"You got it, Ed."

"Not so fast, Mr. Shore. First, you have to have rezoning. Without rezoning, the Farmers Home Administration won't lend you the money."

The fee for the Will's Crossing zoning appeal is $75. Our architect designs twenty-four handsome single-story attached two-bedroom units that integrate, complement the prairie green spaces. All is ready for my appearance before the zoning board. Ed McDonald sits at his table behind the zoning board, who surround the oak conference table, large enough to seat the middle-age chairperson between four plump public-spirited gentlemen who are on the zoning board, and John Swanson, city attorney, a thirty-year-old with a long face who wears a brown herringbone three-piece suit. Swanson resembles the minister in a black-and-white Bergman Swedish movie, a minister who lusts in his heart and only smiles on Sunday when he beats his children. The rezoning hearing begins; the chairperson asks, "Are there any who are against Mr. Shore's proposal to build housing for the elderly?"

Fourteen, tall and thin, short and squat, young and old, raise their hands. A teenage nursing mother, whose breasts raise her sleeveless white cotton top inscribed "Hard Rock Café" to reveal her abdomen jumps to her feet. "My neighbors and I don't want those kind of people living next door to us."

The neighbors sit in two rows, on straight-back cane bottom chairs to the right of the zoning commission. Fourteen neighbors rise with one voice, repeat, "No, no, never. No housing for the elderly."

I plead, I explain, "But these homes are for your neighbors. Your own elderly . . . only twenty-four."

"There will be traffic, congestion, danger to our youngsters from all those children coming to visit their aging parents. Ambulances coming all hours of the day and night."

The board votes unanimously, "No."

City Attorney John Swanson intones, "The board, having duly examined the eighteen points as outlined in the city ordinance that must be reviewed with each rezoning petition, denies Mr. Ray Shore's application for multi-family zoning."

Through the early fall darkness, the sunroof open to the harvest moon light, I drive east across the Iowa prairie, cross the Mississippi on the 280 bridge, come home to Betty. "Unanimous. All against housing for the elderly. Betty, is it me?"

"You know how it is in small towns. They don't like big city ideas, don't like people from the outside coming in telling them what to do."

"I wasn't telling them, Betty, I was asking."

"Well, they told you. Forget it, Ray, sit down. We'll have some ice cream. Chocolate, light, low cholesterol, low sodium, full flavor. A man of your means and at your age, Ray, you don't need the stress of going to zoning meetings."

"Betty, it says in the prayer book—I read it every morning, 'These are the commandments, the fruits of which a man enjoys in this life while the principal endures for him, for all eternity ,performing deeds of loving kindness: making peace between man and fellow.'"

"You have done enough for one day, Ray."

"I tried but I failed. Is that enough?"

"I don't know. I don't know."

Ed McDonald called the next morning.

"I surely understand your position, Mr. Shore. You have every right to do anything you wish with your land. You can appeal to the city council."

"What are the neighbors afraid of? Me?"

Ed didn't answer. He is a job-dependent young man who sees both sides of every issue, who rents his three-bedroom, two-bath apartment and had to live in Will's Crossing until his next job, in a town larger than 2,500, away from the Midwest prairie. Ours is a negative population area mostly inhabited by the older and the elderly. The university-educated young move to the Sunbelt, to the financial centers, Chicago, New York, San Francisco, move to large cities to capitalize on their education, experience and insight gained in the small towns of Iowa and western Illinois.

The zoning appeal before the Will's Crossing City Council went as Betty said it would. The council followed the recommendations of the zoning board. "Mr. Shore's petition to rezone six acres to multifamily unanimously denied."

The architect had tried, prepared the plea. "There will be no more traffic than if the land is developed for single family. The tax base will be increased one-hundredfold. The property across the street is already multifamily. Gentlemen of the City Council, we face an unusual problem. Without rezoning we cannot apply for a Farmers Home Administration loan to build housing for the elderly."

"Mr. Shore, there is no need for housing for the elderly in Will's Crossing."

"Gentlemen, the need will be established by survey. The F.H.A will not lend unless we can prove a need. The city of Will's Crossing thus has a safeguard against our failure."

Zoning denied.

Thirty minutes after the council's refusal, the architect and I stand in the dark of the October evening in front of the pseudo-colonial red brick and white pillared city hall built in 1938 with a grant from the federally sponsored W.P.A.

"Ray, I don't think you will ever build elderly housing in Will's Crossing."

"Why? Tell me why?"

"You are a stranger, Ray."

We were strangers in Egypt, slaves. God set us free.

"Thanks for coming to the council meeting. I like your design. Really fine land use." I shake the architect's hand. He drives north to Cedar Rapids, I drive east to Rockville. I don't have to tell Betty the results.

"You really didn't think the council would rezone for you."

"Betty, it's only twenty-four units. What are they afraid of?"

"Ray, you don't need the stress. Let it go."

"I'll let it go until spring, then . . ."

"You'll sue the city of Will's Crossing in the Federal Court. Three more years of stress. Ray, you don't need the stress."

"You are right, Betty."

"I'm always right, but you don't hear me."

It Is Forbidden To Consult Soothsayers

I'm putting away the prayer books on Monday morning. That was on the Monday after our successful Friday night community dinner. Ira Karp comes over to me. "Harry, I have to talk to someone whose judgment I trust, a man of wisdom." He takes me by the hand into the still, dim library, sits me down. "I have to tell you."

I get up to turn on the lights.

"I can talk in the dark." So, Ira, who I thought never had a care, begins his tale. This is what he tells me.

"In the beginning my dreams were occasional, intermittent, bothersome, but not invading my day. My first visions were of a room, of a gallery designed to exhibit our collection of American modernist paintings, a room with off-white walls, teak floors, track lighting to accentuate the Avery, the Dove, the Guy Pène du Bois, a room in which the light was always dim and where the humidity was controlled to protect the paintings. In the early dreams the walls were stark, reflective white, the entry foyer gray, shadow-filled, impenetrable. The walls were bare of the paintings, all were gone: the Demuth water-color of the tulips, the Nordfeldt spring bouquet, the Walkowitz landscape with the grazing cows, all gone. When I arose from this dream I was not disturbed by the loss of my paintings because with the daylight came the assurance that all were still in my home.

"The appraisals for the modernist American painting collection were current, as correct as appraisals for insurance purposes could ever be. The Sotheby's appraiser had complimented me. 'Mr. Karp, you have done a remarkable job of keeping your values current.' With the cachet of Sotheby's approval, I knew that should claims for losses occur, they would be substantiated and paid. In thirty years I had never filed an insurance claim. That was why the insurance premiums were so low in Rockville, that and because there was a fire alarm, a motion detector and an entry alarm that went on when we left our post-modernist home with its upstairs gallery. In my dream the room was still, no alarms, no claxons, no bells, no lights flashing, no phones ringing as there would have been had an invader removed the paintings. I knew there was no need to be concerned with a loss of the paintings. But what was disturbing was that in the dream there was not a nail in any of the walls. Therefore, the time in the dream was before the paintings were hung.

"I was determined that in the next dream I would examine the walls carefully. Not one painting was hanging. For the record, I wrote this observation on the pad at my bedside. I dismissed the dream as of no significance, nonsense, a throwback to when we were building the house. That was twenty-six years ago. Why had my art collection begun to disturb me now? Why were the dreams about the paintings in our home? There were drawings, watercolors, in our downtown offices. I have never dreamt about the paintings disappearing from the office walls. I was so perplexed by the return of the dream, which was reappearing once a week, usually on Sunday night, that after the Monday morning service I decided to talk to Rabbi Cohen, seek his opinion, his counsel, his Talmudic wisdom.

"'For you, Ira,' he says, 'I always have time.' We sat in the Rabbi's private office, face to face across his glass-topped mahogany desk piled with religious and social texts, the Rabbi's round face fixed in a smile of anticipation.

"'Rabbi—'

"'Yes?'

"'Rabbi, in the tradition, Joseph was an interpreter of dreams.'

"'That is true.'

"'I have been having these dreams. One in particular that reoccurs.' I drew out my notebook from my pocket, reported my dream. 'The room was bare, not a nail in the wall.' The Rabbi said nothing. 'I would have come in to see you, but yesterday I had another dream I can't forget. Only once, but disturbing. My wife was dressed in a fashionable two-piece suit, her skirt just below the knee, matching dark brown silk blouse. Hilda was wearing very high heels. Hilda never wears high heels. She is all alone, not a soul around her, on a broad outdoor stair like in an Italian plaza or like the stairs you climb at Mayan temples. Hilda turns towards me—I am above her. She falls backward, is gone, no scream, no cry of pain. Rabbi, what I am asking is . . .'

"The Rabbi rose from behind the desk, pulled the second side chair close to me. 'Dreams can be disturbing. Scientifically, many believe that dreams are safety valves, a place for our primitive fears to be expelled so they don't invade our daily lives.'

"'This I understand. But, Rabbi, what I really wanted to ask you is what significance can you see for me, Ira Karp?'

"'Dreams are only dreams, Ira. We have a tradition against consulting soothsayers.'

"'I wasn't looking for your insights into the future, Rabbi. I wanted to talk to you, ask if you saw the same message, the same meaning in both dreams. Rabbi, I am beginning to believe that whatever these dreams are about, they are about the same thing.'

"The Rabbi gets up and starts out the door, turns and says to me, 'Ira, they are only dreams. Go, enjoy. When are you and Hilda leaving for Florida?'

"'Not until after Christmas, Rabbi.'

"That night, it was the first week in December, it turned cold, and rather than get up to get another blanket (and I didn't want to close the bedroom window), I turned over to sleep in Hilda's arms. In this dream I was entwined by two or three round roseate Renoir women, the exact number I could not determine. I could feel their softness and warmth. But then I left their arms, their legs, their breasts, and went down a stairwell from which I could find no exit. When I went back up the stairs, all was gone, the women, the bed. This dream I could understand, explain to myself. Full-bodied Hilda was the accented-in-reds Renoir model. Hilda always left our bed before I did. Hilda had taken her warmth with her.

"But that noon I was disturbed again. As I was swimming in the Y pool, the empty room appeared in the sun swirls that arose off the pool's ceramic tile floor. This continued appearance of the empty room was invading my daily routines, invading the calm I had always found in my noonday swim. I described the apparitions in my day journals, my explorations and cautious conclusions preserved for the next generation of Karps, and just went on with my business.

"It was the last Saturday in December, the last Saturday before we were to start the drive to Florida, that for no reason that I can remember I decided I needed to attend Sabbath services.

"I came in just at the Torah reading. The Rabbi saw me, called me to the Torah. After the reading, the Rabbi pronounced the me shabarach, a protective prayer for us as we were to go off on our car trip. The silent devotion followed. The congregation rose and read "In Thy great love Thou givest life to the dead, King who send death. . . ." It was at that moment that it came to me: All of the dreams spoke of death. With death the Karp collection of paintings would disappear, sold to pay estate taxes. With death, the comfort I found in Hilda's arms, the joy that came when we returned to our home. . . . All would be gone. God, in whose care we live, protect us, guide us, give us the insight, the opportunities to seek justice, to love mercy, to perform deeds of loving kindness. . . .

"Harry, I know death is in the course of human events, in the hands of our God, but I could save the paintings, keep the collection intact, together, as a gift to the Rockville Museum. The Museum would build a new gallery, the Karp Wing, to house and shelter for time immemorial 'the greatest collection of American Modernist paintings between Chicago and Denver.' When the Avenue of the Saints, from St. Louis to St. Paul, would be built in ten or twenty years, thousands of tourists would descend on Rockville, Illinois, where the Mississippi flows from east to west, to view the Karp Collection. Henry Frick is certainly remembered more for the paintings he gave to his museum in New York than as an industrialist. A hundred years later, wasn't the Ryerson name preserved by their Impressionist paintings at the Chicago Art Institute and not their steel company? Who would have known that Elliott had been an attorney in Cedar Rapids if he hadn't donated his twentieth century European paintings to the University of Iowa?

"After services on that Monday morning, I called Bob Ballard, our attorney. 'This afternoon Hilda and I want to talk to you about our estate, about after we die.'

"'This afternoon is fine, Ira.'

"I prepared Hilda for an afternoon of estate planning by taking her to lunch. 'Are you sure this is what you want, Ira?'

"'Yes.'

"Bob Ballard offered Hilda coffee.

"'Yes, thank you.'

"Bob left the room.

"'Hilda, I'm sorry, but these things have to be discussed. If we don't make the arrangements . . .'

"'I know, Ira. It's just that contemplating our own demise is not my idea of a fun afternoon.'

"Hilda hadn't said death. Is demise less final than death? Did not talking about death make it less inevitable? Less fatal? What had Ballard said when I had called to make the appointment? Death and taxes, two things you can count on. Hilda has always worked with me. We built together; now we will have to dispose together.

"The moment Ballard returned, I went right at it. 'Our children will choose the paintings they wish, and the remainder will become the Ira and Hilda Karp bequest.' At that point Hilda interrupted. 'You need your name on things. I don't. Leave my name off.'

"I tried to placate Hilda.

"'It's your thing, Ira. Do as you like.'

"Ballard tore the first page off the legal pad, crumbled it. 'When are you leaving for Florida?'

"'After Christmas. We wanted to talk to you before we left.'

"'Planning takes time. It shouldn't be rushed into.'

"'We wanted to talk to you about our paintings, what would happen to them.'

"'First thing that happens, Ira, is there is an appraisal and, of course, the value is added to your estate. The estate will pay the taxes.'

"'Up to fifty-five percent,' I added.

"'Ira, let Bob talk. Ira never lets anyone talk.'

"'Hilda, I always let you talk!'

"'Sure, when I insist.'

"Hilda, an equal partner in Karp Distributing, was insistent. 'Bob, I don't want my name on the gift. I don't need the honors. Ira does! Let him have it.'

"'You'll be doing a great thing for the community.'

"'And saving estate taxes.'

"'Ira, let Bob talk.' Harry, you know Hilda doesn't mean anything when she talks to me that way. So, I tell her, 'I'll talk to the college. I'm sure they will be delighted.'

"'The college will have to provide the space and the security. That means an addition to the art department.'

"'No space, no gift.'

"Bob was confident. 'I can't imagine, given the notification of your gift, that by the time of the transfer the physical conditions won't be met.'

"'Bob, you call me in Florida after you speak to the college.' Again I tried to please Hilda. 'The gift could be anonymous. Would you like that?'

"'You know how I feel about our name on things.'

"'Okay, Bob, all settled. The gift is anonymous.'

"Bob laughed and nodded and patted my back. 'Anonymous is better than from a "From a gentleman's estate." I'll do as you like, Ira, but in Rockville, everyone will know whose paintings they are.'

"'And in the next generation, they won't remember anyway.' Thus Hilda finished Ballard's sentence.

"On the way home, I tried once more with Hilda. 'When we were putting the collection together—when we were buying American modernists—no one else was. What harm is there in recognizing that achievement?'

"'I don't want it. Ira, I don't need it.'

"'If that's important to you, Hilda, that's how it will be.'

"'You know, Ira, Goncourt could have been correct. Those French are cynical, but he may have had the better answer. You know he wrote in his will, "My paintings are to be

sold at public auction so that others may have the same joy of collecting them as I had."'
Hilda studied art history.

"'It's not too late yet. We can always change our minds. Bob is only doing a preliminary exploration. We will have years to make our final decision.'

"'You are right. Ira, you wouldn't be disappointed?'

"'Disappointed about what?'

"'About not having your name on the new wing of the Rockville College Art Museum. You know selling the paintings at auction will get the children more money.'

"'But then the paintings would leave Rockville,' is the last I said.

"'Do as you like, Ira. Do as you like.'

"Not reaching a decision is also a decision. That's what I tell myself. What is a man to do, Harry, please his wife, sell the paintings, gift to the college? Harry, what is a man to do?"

I waited to answer.

"Harry, tell me, what would you do?"

"'A gift by a man who gives when he is not asked to give, that is like gold.'"

"Who said that?"

"Maimonides. But . . ." I say.

"What kind of but?"

"Have you asked your children, David and Jill, and you have grandchildren—maybe they would like a painting."

"They have never said."

"Have you asked, Ira?"

"I will, Harry, I will. Harry, thank you. Hilda said you would know."

"Tell me, Ira, why didn't you ask the Rabbi straight out, like you asked me?"

"Rabbis. What do young rabbis know from?" Ira got up, went off muttering to himself, "Huh, rabbis . . ."

This Too Is for the Best

There isn't a colleague of mine, not one classmate at Hebrew Union College, the Cantors Institute of the Jewish Theological Seminary, that would believe my "Rockville Experience." Fortunately, I will soon be able to turn this one and only year at western Illinois' only conservative congregation into a faded memory.

Rockville is what the small Jewish community will become in the twenty-first century. That is my wife's, Harriet's, forecast. Harriet has a B.S. in Social Science with a major in The Family. If Harriet and I had known what Jewish life in Rockville would be, I would have stayed in Milwaukee on half pay waiting for Cantorial positions available in August, which is when most cantors' career changes occur, before the High Holy Days.

We left Milwaukee for Rockville in April of last year, right after Passover. The why was that I stood with the "Give our Rabbi a second chance committee." So, when the Rabbi was forced to leave, I was asked to depart. "Do try to get another position, Mr. Silver."

This Solomonic decision our president achieved after five months of Monday meetings with our committee, and Thursday meetings with the Executive Board. That's how long it took the president of the congregation, a psychiatrist, to decide, "We don't want a rabbi with homosexual tendencies to be with our children." It was I, of course, who taught the children in the Talmud Torah, not the Rabbi. He was too busy with ecumenical meetings, visitations and future planning. The Rabbi had assured me, "Jordan, I swear it, believe me, this was my one and only time," and I did. For this pursuit of his male sexuality, for this leap into discovery of self, our Rabbi chooses a public park renowned as a homosexual rendezvous. Why he couldn't pick a quiet, dark bar is beyond me. No doubt it's because rabbis have more time for sex in the daytime than in the evenings. The police raid at the insistence of the P.T.A. was another first in the history of Milwaukee, because, as the Chief said to the judge, "Consenting adults—that's not really any of our business."

So, it's all circumstances beyond my control. An explorer rabbi with a starved-for-sex wife which must be a recent condition, because there are two children. A police chief who, in response to the Parent-Teacher Association, chose that Thursday afternoon at two o'clock for a raid that captured a rabbi, a pediatrician, a florist, a well-known downtown merchant. For this feat of daring, the Chief got early retirement to Florida, because the florist turned out to be the county treasurer of the Republican party and a cousin to the City Attorney. In thirty days the rabbi gets another position, with a larger home and a better car allowance in Sioux Falls, South Dakota. That is why I responded to "Cantor needed in Rockville, western Illinois. Oldest Conservative congregation. Write or call Sandra Katz, President. 309-788-6666."

Female presidents, female rabbis, female cantors. That is no longer unusual. There is little doubt that President Katz is the chief operating officer. "Mr. Silver, your entire benefit package is well above what congregations affiliated with United Synagogues of America are offering. For this we are expecting you to attend the morning minyan. Our congregation insists that there be a morning minyan so that the bereaved may say Kaddish for the departed. We do have members for whom the *shacharit* service is a way of life. Services are at seven thirty a.m., Monday to Friday, nine on Saturday and eight on Sunday." This way of life brings five regulars to the prayer house, Harry Stern, the organizer; Henry Gottwalt, our one truly observant congregant; Leonard Zymanski, who married money and is now after selling the Kline block pursuing deeds of loving kindness to offset his capital gains; Ray Shore, who writes notes on index cards which he places in his shirt pocket. Rumor has it Ray Shore is writing an expose of commingled funds in the Rockville congregation. This effort will sell no better than his Benny Roone stories—which the Rabbi tells me sell from little to nothing. This is not difficult to understand. Who wants to read two hundred and twelve pages about a retired Jewish C.I.C. agent who solves his cases without even one sexual experience? *Echet mir* a hero? And, always, faithful Bill Levy. Three generations of Levys have all been community oriented. On the mornings of the Charity Golf Classic, the ecumenical breakfasts, Bill gets his cousin, Burton, to stand in for him. Add the Rabbi and myself, we are seven who appear at the morning prayers—which means that we are short three for the ten needed to recite the Kaddish, read the Torah.

There has been little to no problem to produce three more for the minyan. The reasons are apparent. In Rockville there are more than twenty burials a year that must be memorialized. That our average congregant is beyond three score and ten also helps, for this is when prayers of praise to our Eternal become a serious pursuit. Most of the time, and so it has been for years, as Sandra Katz told me, three or four do appear, and the prescribed prayers are recited, but this winter there are many—too many—gray mornings when Harry Stern shakes his head, looks at his list. "I called last night. Fred promised to come to say the Kaddish for his mother."

"Call him this morning."

"Hazzan, by the time Fred gets dressed, drives here, it will be too late."

"Too late for what? Everybody that comes to the minyan are retired."

"Retirees are busy people, Hazzan."

That Sunday afternoon Harriet and I are riding our mountain bikes up and down the bluffs at Andalusia County Park. We sit, overlook the Andalusia Islands in the backwaters of the Mississippi, watch the bald eagle fish in the pool. I say to Harriet, "It can't be that difficult to get four or five men or women to come to the morning services. There are more than two hundred family members."

"The sisterhood can't get more than eight for a free bagel and lox breakfast."

"I don't understand."

"Enjoy, Jordan," is what Harriet answers. "In the spring we will take our canoe, paddle through the islands, relax."

"Harriet, the services are being performed. It would be so nice to have just a few more bodies. What better way to begin the day than to praise God," and I sing to Harriet "Our Father, our King, be gracious unto us, answer us. . . ."

"Jordan, you don't understand. In the winter, half of the congregation have gone south. It's too cold in Rockville for old folks. In the summer half are visiting their children. Jordan, it's too hot for older folks in Rockville." That is Harriet's theory. "In the aging population, climate controls the practice of Judaism."

It's unfair to be overly harsh about our congregants' shortfalls. Philip Segal, Haskel Roth, Ira Karp will come with only a hint. "We may need you."

How did it happen that in November I was again sending out resumes, Jordan Silver, Hazzan, at liberty . . . Jordan Silver . . . have musical education, reads the Torah, qualified to teach in your Talmud Torah. It happened because Jordan Silver is an advocate of change to meet your changing community needs.

First off, Henry Gottwalt wanted the religious committee to permit burial from the sanctuary. The Rabbi in his wisdom told me, "The religious committee has rejected Gottwalt's plea. Do not take upon yourself a task at which you cannot hope to succeed. Jordan, you are a young man."

"Without a mortgage and a working wife," I quipped.

"This is no joking matter, Mr. Silver. You are putting your future in Rockville in jeopardy."

"I have a contract."

"Contract, contract. Believe me, Jordan, you go against the religious committee, you are at liberty." The Rabbi's wisdom is based on his eight careful years of avoiding causes; for this he has achieved a life contract.

"But, Rabbi, there is nothing in tradition that prevents burial from the synagogue." One lost cause deserves another effort. That one was not the one that brought my outplacement, but it was my effort to help Dr. Gross. Philip Segal started the campaign to which Haskel Roth gave a nod, and Burton Levy and I are a delegation of two to meet with Sandra Katz. Wednesday night we are sitting in the library.

"Mrs. Katz—"

"Call me Sandra."

"Dr. Gross was at services Monday morning. He has been a regular for a month at Monday morning services. Dr. Gross has been very generous. He accepts the Torah Aliyahs, pays for the me shabarachs."

"So, Jordan." Sandra is only five, six years older than I am. Why she can't call me Hazzan Silver I do not understand; everyone else does.

"Dr. Gross hears all the coughing in the congregation. We are quite in agreement with him."

"About what, Jordan? Spit it out. I don't have all day."

"It's the cigarette smoke, the stink, Mrs. Katz. From the Sunday night bingo game. It's in the prayer house. The smoke is in the seats, in the air. It's un-breathable. That's why the coughing. Dr. Gross says—"

Sandra Katz doesn't let me finish my prepared presentation. "I don't care what Hershel Gross says. Without bingo, we couldn't pay your salary."

"And if I quit, will you stop the bingo?" That statement I had not prepared. I had not even discussed it with Harriet.

"Jordan, the finances of this congregation are none of your affair. There is no way I am taking this to the religious committee." With this Sandra shuts her genuine leather portfolio that holds her daybook and appointment schedule, gets up. "Jordan, had I known this is what you wanted, I would not have arranged this special meeting." The folder into her leather briefcase, President Katz is out into the coat room, wraps herself in her Burberry and, boom, is gone. Burton shakes my hand. "We tried."

"That's all I can do."

"Sorry, Hazzan, I have to run. We are leaving for Florida the day after Thanksgiving."

The Rabbi says I did it to myself with all my causes. That is how I got fired, but I was invited by the religious committee to offer "How cantors can increase synagogue attendance during the High Holy Days." It seems that Dora Newcomb, our Gentile secretary, who sits in the foyer, pencil in hand, a duty only a non-Jew can perform on the Holy Days, has reported that this year attendance is less than last year's. Harry Stern confirmed that this loss was reflected in a downturn in the sale of aliyahs honors for the Holy Days. Opening or closing the Ark is fifty dollars; reading a section of the psalms in English is one hundred dollars. The sale of these "honors" is discretely solicited by the religious committee with three pre-holiday direct-to-your-home mailings. "There has been some resistance to the sale of the honors." This from Harry.

"We need the income." This from President Katz. "Jordan, what do you think?"

"I think that if there were more members to sing in the choir, the service could be enhanced by a greater variety of choral presentations."

"Jordan, I am talking about how to increase attendance."

"The choir is a plus."

"There were fewer at the First Day of Rosh Hashanah than last year, and on the second day, the fewest we have ever had."

"The Reformed congregation solved the second day problems." This from Haskel Roth. "They don't have a second day service."

"Haskel, we are a Conservative congregation. We celebrate two days. Next item of business. Jordan, what do you say?"

"I would like to make a suggestion. We could try it for a year or two. It may work, and it may not. I would like for us not to charge for visitors, at least for those visitors who are paid up members of other congregations."

"Then we lose the guest fees." Mrs. Katz is a C.P.A., a senior partner of D.D.B.

"But we increase attendance, Mrs. Katz. That's what this meeting is about. I have never been with a congregation that charges admission to visitors."

"Here it is a tradition, Mr. Silver."

"There are traditions that I am not following, and from that the congregation has benefitted."

"Okay, Jordan, tell me."

"I am no longer sending out birthday greetings like the former cantor did. Greetings that brought donations to him personally and not to the congregation."

"For this I thank you, Mr. Silver."

On the way out, in the coat room, Harry Stern helped me on with my parka. "Jordan, my son, no, never. . . . No one talks about the hazzam's 'business.' Not if you want your contract renewed."

The letter from Sandra Katz came after the Chanukah service.

> "Dear Jordan,
> There are very few synagogue events that will be scheduled between now and Passover. Should you wish to make out of town trips to explore other positions, the board will arrange the necessary time off for you.
> Sincerely,
> S. Katz, President"

As it says in the Hebrew tradition, Gum zu le tova. This too is for the best. Thank God. In January we will be in Meadowlark Lakes, Missouri, a suburb of St. Louis. Harriet is delighted with the opportunities at the St. Louis Art Museum. She is entertaining the possibility of writing her doctorate on the social significance of the later paintings of Max Beckmann. For myself, I have enrolled in the Music Education program at Washington University. You can't be too well educated or overly documented. If the Hazzan business goes there is also public or private education. There is always the possibility of my teaching in the St. Louis Hebrew day school. This is a congregation of mostly professional suburbanites who will send their children to a Hebrew day school where our Boys Choir will sing "Etz Hayim" and "Kaper Chatoeinu Walken" by Joseph Drechsler, who knew Beethoven and was Kapellmeister of St. Stephens Cathedral in Vienna and who wasn't Jewish.

Oh, yes, the compensation package is less than in Rockville. The cost of housing is appreciably more. There is no morning minyan, no *shacharit* service for the Kaddish sayers, but there are compensations. I am free Monday to Friday mornings; Harriet and I have the time to ride our mountain bikes up and down the Mississippi River bluffs. The canoeing in the spring should be very pleasant. Oh, yes, the congregation does have a choir. Next year I have a promise that I can rent an organ. Just as a trial, of course.

Once a Jew Boy, Now an Old Grad

The first of the letters from the Kansas State University appeared in February. "Plan to attend your forty-fifth class reunion. Join your classmates. . . ." It was signed Chuck Turner, a classmate who had returned to join the faculty.

In several weeks another, more personalized letter arrived, a revelation of a list: those of your classmates who have already made reservations at the Holiday Inn, and then the disclosure: "Plans have been completed for a class breakfast at which the Dean will disclose 'The Next Ten Years at this great state university.'" Again it was signed by Chuck Turner, with the post script, "Don't forget to make your reservations now!"

Hilda opens the mail, reads this latest from the alumni office out loud to me while I am listening to *The News Hour*, an interruption that denotes the urgency of the message. "Ira, Ira!" is Hilda's attention-getting voice.

"This requires an answer greater than 'Huh.' Ira!"

"Yes?"

"Ira, you haven't returned your biography questionnaire. You haven't made the hotel reservations."

"We have until April."

"Ira, it's February third."

"So it is."

"Ira?"

I try alternatives. "Hilda, wouldn't you rather go to Europe? April in Paris, chestnuts in blossom, spring at the Musée d'Orsay. We would take the train down to the Cote d'Azur. We haven't seen the Matisse Museum. On the way back, we'll stop in London."

"Ira, your classmates are looking forward to seeing you."

"Who said?"

"Don't you remember the fortieth reunion?"

"I see the ones I want to without going back to Kansas."

Hilda returned the hotel reservation, insisted I do a biography which she reviewed and then, before mailing it, wanted improved. "Ira, why didn't you note that you were chosen Illinois Distributor of the Year in 1990?"

"No one I went to Ag School with cares how much frozen fish we sell."

"Do you think they are more interested that you planted three thousand eight hundred and eighty oaks on your thirty acres of hobby woodland?"

"That's all the space there was on the form."

Hilda gave up on me until April 2.

"Ira, you won't forget we're going to Kansas on the twelfth."

"I have everything arranged."

This doesn't mean that I tell Hilda what I have planned after the reunion at Manhattan, Kansas. I don't disclose my plans for after the reunion until we are sixty miles west of Rockville, just as we are leaving the Liz Claiborne shop at the Williamsburg, Iowa, outlet mall on Interstate 80, where Hilda has successfully purchased a size 16 purple cotton sack dress at one third of last year's price. With Hilda beaming at her trophy, I offer, "After Manhattan, Kansas, we can stop in Abilene at the Eisenhower Library, then drive down to Lindsborg and look at the Birger Sandzen paintings. We spend the night in Bartlesville and then the next day visit the museums in Tulsa. On the way home we can stop at the Will Rogers Memorial, look at the saddles. We should be home—"

This Hilda finishes with, "We can't be home before Sunday evening. I am not missing Carol's party on Sunday. Since when are you so interested in Western art? I changed my hair appointment with Julius to Saturday morning. Ira, we are going to be home by Saturday morning."

Julius is Rockville's equivalent of Sassoon of London; only for Hilda would Julius change an appointment. "Saturday it is, Hilda. No problem."

Hilda nods and goes back to her crossword puzzle.

At Lincoln, Nebraska, I turn south, stop fifteen minutes for a walk through the University of Nebraska Art Museum, which brings forth Hilda's comment, "The building is more significant than the exhibition."

"That's only because you don't appreciate photography."

"I wish they would hang their American collection."

"You saw that the last time."

"That was five years ago."

Marysville is still Marysville. J. C. Penney is on the main street, Sunshine Donuts across the street. The unwashed pickups with their muddied tires are parked at angles in front of the tan brick bank. The corner café has Eats in the window and the tin sign above the door, a hand holding a cold, dripping Coca Cola. In the window are hanging greens, trailing greens, and the black calligraphic warning on a white board, Tea Room.

Hilda is first at the door. "Let's go in."

Inside the café, the slate menu behind the counter advises alfalfa sprouts, vegetable quiche and organically grown fruits and vegetables. Hilda turns to me. "Ira, let's eat donuts."

This choice, I tell you, is both love and understanding of my prejudices, which Hilda consistently explains to her bridge club. "Ira still eats beef. Not as often as we used to, only three times a week. This is Ira's compromise between eating less fat and supporting the American beef industry which is suffering a continued decrease in demand. Ira always says, 'If farmers won't eat beef, who will?'"

"Ira is a tree farmer."

"Yes, but our friends and classmates are still raising beef."

From Marysville to Manhattan is through the rolling flint hills, a land of thin top soil that cannot cover the outcroppings of limestone.

"Not as many cattle as there used to be. Even sheep prices have gone to hell."

To this wisdom and observation, Hilda nods and continues with her crossword.

Just north of Manhattan, as we are passing the flood control lake, Hilda puts aside her *New York Times* puzzle book. "Ira, promise me that you won't call Curtis a shithead. A man of your education can find better words, more appropriate words."

"He called me a Jew boy."

"Then he invited you to his cocktail party."

"That's because he knows I don't drink."

"You drink. Don't give me that."

"I'll try, Hilda, I'll really try."

"That's what you said the last time, and the time before and the time before that. For a man nearly seventy . . ."

"I use young, vigorous language."

"Inappropriate, Ira. Inappropriate for a man of your stature."

This I don't answer.

The Holiday Inn has our reservation. We swim, we greet, we hug, dress up for the 5:30 class dinner at the country club. The Manhattan shade trees are in full leaf. The golf course is in full greenery. The cocktails are served in the glass-walled dining room that overlooks the first hole, four hundred and twenty yards of watered fairway that gently glides into a swale, guarded by a sand trap which this evening is still wet from the spring rains. Hilda has found Alice Parker, with whom she peeled cucumbers in the college tea room. They are deeply into trips to Alaska.

My backache is only a little spasm with leg pain that requires sitting after twenty minutes of cocktail talk. As I start for the chairs that surround the tables for eight, Curtis appears. Curtis doesn't look a bit older. Still straight, almost six feet tall, with that constant smirk that inheriting two thousand acres of the best bottom land in the Illinois River valley has fixed on his face. "Been too long, Ira, considering it's only ninety miles to our place. Why haven't you and Hilda stopped by to see us?"

The best I can offer is, "It's only ninety miles to Rockville."

"You're right, Ira. You are right."

"Five years goes very quickly."

"It does at our age."

I sit down. Curtis draws up a chair. "I see you are drinking."

"It's only ginger ale."

"You and Hilda been traveling? I called you once or twice, got no answer."

"We try to get away for a day or two each month."

"You still working?"

"Every day."

"You and me, Ira, still working. We must be the last. Ira, you ever meet my son, Craig?"

"I heard good things about him. I read in the alumni bulletin he received a Ph.D. in Arabic literature from the University of Chicago."

"In Islamic studies. First in our family."

"That's not all bad."

"Craig is the first boy in three generations who didn't want to farm."

"Tenants need opportunities, too."

"Joyce and I just came back from Saudi Arabia. Craig is teaching there."

"That's one trip Hilda and I are not going to make."

"Very pleasant place."

"No Jews allowed, Curtis. That is, no Jews allowed unless they are wearing a United States Army uniform."

"I didn't know that. Ira, I didn't know a Jew until I transferred into our class."

"When was that?"

"May of forty-three. You made me welcome."

"There was a war to be won . . . to be won."

"Your singing stinks."

"My voice hasn't improved any."

"Ira, my son . . . my son . . . we went to Saudi Arabia to our son's wedding."

"Congratulations."

"Craig married a black woman."

"We are all God's children."

"That's easy for you, Ira. I could get used to that, too, but, Ira, Craig is married to a black Muslim. Craig converted to Mohammadism."

"Is he happy?"

"You sound like Joyce. Think of their children. Half black Muslims."

"They won't be living in eastern Kansas."

"Craig does have tenure at the University."

"They'll come to visit you and Joyce."

"You are the only one I could talk to, Ira. I knew you would understand. You coming to our cocktail party? I bought some Kosher wine."

"You didn't have to do that. I would have come anyway."

"See you tonight, Jew boy." Curtis grinned and shook my hand. "Thanks for listening, Ira. When I heard your son died, I wanted to write to you. I'm sorry I didn't."

"It's been a long time, Curtis. A long time."

Seek Justice, Love Mercy, Walk Humbly With Your God

It happened in August. My fear was that it would be in January or February—when ten percent of our congregation goes to Florida to pray in Reformed temples and six percent goes to Arizona to play golf. February would have been understandable, explainable. After a hard Illinois January, before the thaw, with icy roads and slippery walks. On the telephone hot line: Lenny fell, broke his hip. Then there would be too few for the morning minyan, for the *shacharit* service of praise. On Monday and Thursday we would not have the ten necessary to read the memorial Torah and say the memorial prayers.

In August it was insidious. Maybe it crept in with the heat, with the vacations. First it was this, and then it was that, and then it became impossible to maintain the minyan.

My assessment may seem a bit harsh, but certainly no harsher than our loss. During that first week in August it did not seem like a problem that would not be solved. Like family members who quarrel and then get together, all forgotten, for the next holiday dinner. Perhaps an apology from Ira Karp would have rectified it all, but Ira said, "Harry, I have nothing to apologize for."

"Ira, please, you are older."

"The dinner was in the Silvers' honor, to welcome them to the congregation."

"Ira, they have been here two months."

"She knew about the dinner—it was in the bulletin. Anyway, we need a librarian at the Jewish Center."

It began when Ira wouldn't lead the first part of the service, not if the hazzan did the second part. That the hazzan insisted we sing hymns in the second part didn't help either.

"Ira, you are eighty-two years old. Don't give up your honors; you have earned them."

"Harry, I will not pray with the minyan. There is no law that says I cannot pray at home."

What could I say? Please? I did. And Ira said, "He's a hazzan. We need a hazzan."

The Rabbi, a man who told each congregant what he wanted to hear, had told Henry and me, "I am for permitting burial from the Center. I am supporting you before the Board."

The annual Board meeting was the first Tuesday in July. Henry presented his petition. "Twenty-two paid up members support burial from the sanctuary." Sandra Katz, the president, reads the petition. Sandra is dumpy, frumpy, round-faced, round-bodied, forty years old, a third generation Rockville native, a protector, guardian of the Center's institutions.

"Mr. Gottwalt," her voice is flat, assured Midwestern, "the matter you are presenting was considered by our executive committee. On the advice of our Rabbi, there will be no change in our traditional policy. Thank you, Mr. Gottwalt. The answer is no."

"Mrs. Katz, the Rabbi told us—"

Sandra hears Henry's Germanic lisp. "On to new business."

Henry does not appear on Wednesday morning. I presume Zelda or one of the widows has an early doctor's appointment. Henry does not appear on Thursday morning. On Friday morning, Henry appears.

"Explain it to me, Harry."

"What's to explain. The Rabbi wants a life contract. A life contract you only get by not offending."

"It's an offense to change his position."

"You tell him."

"I tried."

"So?"

"He wouldn't stand still, walked by me, wouldn't listen to me."

On Monday Lenny Zymanski told me, "Henry went to Chicago to be with his son."

"For how long?"

"He didn't say."

Next I hear that Henry has put his house up for sale. Surprise of surprises, in our down economy the house sells and Henry is praying at the Gates of Heaven, the most Orthodox shul in Skokie. So, now I have lost Henry and Ira.

In August is the Rabbi's fermature. Like all of France, he closes down. "I am a fragile vessel, Harry, I need restoration. You can handle all the religious questions."

For Bill Levy, August is his golf thing. He walks up and down the Bluff Golf Course hills on the twelve percent grades with a sign, "Silence." Bill is exhausted. It has been a hot, humid August, and Bill is no spring chicken, seven-four or -five. "I'm going to Colorado, Harry, going to play golf in Estes Park."

There is a list of minyan standbys that I use for emergencies, deaths, funerals, unveilings: Sy Rosen, Hershel Gross, Sanford Kramer, who has just retired from the State's Attorney's office. The Sunday *Bugle's* "This Week's Retirees" is a good source of prospects, although I do believe the Jewish Federation's telephone circle is weeks ahead in circulating the news.

The Rabbi goes off. "To Chautauqua," says the Rabbi.

"Rabbi is going to Las Vegas to gamble," says Fred Weiss.

"He can gamble on the riverboats."

"He has been."

"How do you know?"

"I know."

Fred Weiss, who has been regular—seven twenty-six every morning—goes off on a car trip; his wife wants to go to a wedding in Connecticut. Fred wants to visit a second cousin in Grand Rapids. Mrs. Weiss loves theater. "Why not stop at Stratford?" Fred has a ninety-year-old cousin in New Jersey and a classmate in Massachusetts. "I'll be gone for all of August. I'm sorry, Harry, I couldn't get a substitute. I called Sy Rosen. Sy is moving to Minnesota. I tried to stop him. 'Sy, you are going to be the only Jew for a hundred miles around. God forbid something should happen to you.' 'God is everywhere,' is what Sy answers."

I can't dispute that. "What is Sy going to do in Minnesota?"

"Rehab a cottage."

"Plenty of old homes in Rockville. The mayor will sell him a Victorian two-story for a dollar."

"He wants to live by a lake, fish for walleye."

"Only goyim do that."

"You tell him."

I couldn't because Sy is married to Wilma who, although not of our faith, is a righteous lady. As all the righteous are equal, Sy and Wilma have a right to fish for walleyes.

I did talk to Betty at the Federation. "It's getting harder and harder to get a minyan. Doesn't look good for August."

"That's what you said last August. I have the utmost faith in you, Harry. You'll think of something."

"Betty, is Sanford Kramer in town?"

"Don't you read the papers? Sanford is under indictment."

"For sure?"

"Don't you read the *Bugle*?"

"The front page and the TV schedule, and the obits."

"On page two, yesterday." Betty brings out a clipping: "Sanford Kramer, retired Rockville State's Attorney, is under Federal indictment, accused of S.E.C violations. . . ." I cross out Sanford Kramer. I am sure Sanford will not be interested in our after-services conversation.

I called Hershel Gross's office. "Dr. Gross is attending the AIDS conference in Europe." Hershel and Cele are going to tour Scandinavia, availing themselves of a Mercedes Benz on the drive-and-buy plan.

Then that same week Leonard Zymanski comes into the *shacharit* service, speaking only in Polish. There isn't a soul in our minyan who understands a word of Polish. That's not exactly correct—Fred Weiss understand four words. He left Poland at the age of five. He knows *grubas*—fatty; *Svanta-Maria*—St. Mary; *kustul*—church; *strajnik*—policeman. With these four words he cannot carry on a conversation, but he does learn that Lenny has had a reversion, a throw back. Lenny thinks he is a sixteen-year-old in Poland.

Our steadiest congregants gone, the minyan needing replacements was not unusual. It had happened before.

There were always the ladies willing to put on their sweat suits, their Nikes, and assert their Torah rights. That offended Henry, but Henry was gone. I could recruit the president of the Sisterhood, the president of B'nai Brith women, of Hadassah. It's a simple routine: On Monday we will honor Hadassah, on Tuesday the Sisterhood, on Wednesday Pioneer Women, on Thursday B'nai Brith women, on Friday the Men's Club. That's all there is to that: Each president appoints the delegates to our minyan. We are functional. Ida, of course, is not enthusiastic. "You did that two years ago."

"It worked then."

"Harry, times have changed. More women are working."

"Doing what in this economy?"

"Working on the riverboats. Haven't you heard of riverboats, of gambling?"

"At seven-thirty in the morning?"

"Shirley Krouse and Tybe Marcus are on breakfast cruises. It won't be easy."

It should have worked, distributing the minyan honors and the responsibilities to our Jewish service clubs. After all, the Kiwanis have pancake breakfasts. The Exchange Club mans a beer tent during the Riverboat Days. I expected it all to work, but it didn't.

As my Uncle Al used to say, "Harry, if someone has made up his mind, don't argue."

For August, there were no weekday morning minyans, not once. As Ray Shore said to me, "Harry, you did the best you could."

"The clubs should have—"

"Even then we would still need someone to lead us in prayer."

"Fred Weiss could do it."

"In English?"

"I'll bet Sandra Katz could lead us."

"Harry, she is an accountant, not a spiritual leader."

"How about you, Ray? You could do the first part, I'll do the second part."

"We still need ten."

I tried. I called. All I got was advice. "The Reformed don't have a morning minyan. They have been a congregation for one hundred and thirty-three years."

"Why worry, Harry? We will say Kaddish on Saturday. Quit worrying, Harry, come out, play golf with me."

Even Ida tried to help. "The trouble with you, Harry—" That is Ida's preamble that I defer to her wisdom.

"How would you do it? Tell me."

"Call the religious committee. Call Sandra. She is the president. The minyan is everybody's concern."

"I could not have said that better myself."

"When are you going to make an appointment to see Sandra?"

"Tomorrow."

"Tomorrow, Harry," says Sandra, "I have the kids to pick up at day camp. My mother has to go to the dentist. I have to pick up Jeff at the airport."

"Wednesday would be possible. How about lunch?"

"The Village Inn on First Street, at two. Harry, I have a client at two-thirty. Harry, half an hour do you?"

"Do me fine."

Sandra wears these Elizabeth Ashley little girl print dresses three-quarters long to hide her legs, with a bow above her chest to hide her zaftig bosom. From the overall blue field of her cotton print that is overrun with pink rosebuds, I make out Sandra and her briefcase. We sit in the functioning air-conditioning of the pancake house, at a table for two in the non-smoking area. Sandra is sweating. "Harry, I have to lose weight."

This I never answer. No is a lie. Yes is no better.

Sandra opens her briefcase, sets out a yellow legal pad, a pink pack of Kleenex, a bottle of pills. I look at the pills. "The doctor says as soon as I lose weight, my blood pressure will go down."

I nod.

"It's bad, Harry, bad."

"What's bad?"

"Our bingo earnings--down in half. First it's riverboat gambling, then the Tama Indians are stealing our clientele. The Indians are sending buses to pick up our players. Free food and pop on the trip to Tama."

"That's not Kosher hot dogs, corned beef and pastrami."

Sandra does not smile. "I project thirty thousand dollars decrease in our bingo earnings. Here it is." Sandra has produced a double entry ledger. To date six months, income down eight thousand dollars.

Sandra looks at her Swatch watch. "Lousy service."

"Summer replacement help. Kids working their way through college."

When the waitress finally comes, "What would you like?"

Sandra: "The French toast with the strawberry sauce, and coffee."

"I'll have a salad and tea with lemon."

"No wonder you stay so slim."

"I swim."

"I wish I had the time, Harry. Okay, Harry, what is it this time?"

No apology, no explanation for turning down burial from the Center. Women Sandra's age don't have time for polite talk. They are into today. Tomorrow is still too far away for them.

Sandra looks at her watch. "Harry, I have a two-thirty with a client."

"It's the minyan, Sandra." I tell Sandra all. "Tomorrow is Thursday. I don't believe we will have a minyan—if the hazzan takes off."

"Jordan Silver leaving was the best thing that could happen. I didn't know how I was going to tell him that we couldn't afford to renew his contract."

"Sandra, we have had a minyan since—"

"Harry, that's the trouble with you old timers. You don't understand times are changing. When I was a girl we had two hundred and fifty in the Hebrew school. Today we have forty, and the budget demands are greater. How can I raise more money from fewer members?"

"Prayers are—"

"Make a choice, Harry. That's what I do all day, make choices. Thank God the cantor left. Not paying his salary will offset the losses from the bingo."

The waitress comes with the bill, six dollars and eight-eight cents. "I'll take that, Sandra."

"Thanks, Harry."

I look at my watch. "One thing more."

Sandra looks at her watch, begins to reassemble the table top materials into her briefcase.

"Sandra, Ray Shore has joined the Temple."

"He hasn't dropped his Center membership."

"Don't you know why?"

"Okay, why?"

"Because he wants to be buried from a synagogue."

"I can't stop him."

"We don't have to lose members over things we can change."

"Speak to the Rabbi."

"I did."

"What did he say?"

"Said he was all for it."

"You know the Rabbi: All things to all people."

"What are you going to do next year when I bring up the burial issue at the general meeting?"

"It's your privilege, Harry." Sandra has risen, was ready to leave. "I'll tell you what I'll do for you, Harry. I'll arrange for a life contract for the Rabbi. Then maybe we'll have the benefit of his true wisdom."

"Thanks, Sandra." Her avuncular tone didn't please me.

My report to Ida was short. "No cantor. No minyan."

"Harry, have you done all you can?"

"Yes. For now."

"There is always tomorrow, Harry."

"Tell me."

"Riverboat gambling is turning the economy around. We are going to get a discount mall. Ray Shore says he has rented three suites, one to the F.B.I."

"You expecting a Jewish F.B.I. agent who can do the liturgy?"

"No, but I bet we'll get new families that will join the Center."

"Who?"

"Like the Litvaks, the Russians. Like in 1904, when my folks came from Poland."

"From your mouth into God's ears."

In Yiddish, that's folk wisdom.

About the Author

Alex B. Stone was born in 1922 in a small town in Poland and came to the United States when he was seven. He married Martha Ringler in 1943, in Brooklyn, N.Y. He settled in the Midwest, practiced veterinary medicine, became active in business, cultural and Jewish affairs, and began writing fiction in middle age. He died in September 2015.

Among his books are *A Sabbath Walk*, *Going Home*, *If I Could Sleep*, *Summer: Two Novellas*, *Benny Roone Detects*, *Shades of Benny Roone*, *Country Boy*, *Sunrise at 7:12*, and *Tales from the Prayer House*.

Made in the USA
Monee, IL
24 August 2023